THE

# SKELETON CREW;

OR,

# WILDFIRE NED.

## ILLUSTRATED WITH NUMEROUS ENGRAVINGS.

LONDON:

NEWSAGENTS' PUBLISHING COMPANY, 147, FLEET STREET.

—

1867.

# THE
# SKELETON CREW
OR,
## WILDFIRE NED.

LOOK! LOOK! 'TIS THE CAPTAIN OF THE SKELETON CREW.

## CHAPTER 1.

THE MERRY PARTY AT THE "BLACK BULL"—
THE STRANGE HORSEMAN AND RAMBLING BOB.

THE incidents of this strange and exciting story occurred more than a hundred years ago.

\*       \*       \*       \*       \*

It was in the month of December, and all the country was covered with snow to the depth of more than a foot.

The moon shone brightly over the pure white landscape, and, as far as the eye could range, nought was to be seen but leafless trees, which bowed and shook in a stiff north-west breeze, and their melancholy flutterings seemed to be like gentle moans and sighings at the white death-like pall which covered nature far and wide.

The pretty and picturesque village of Darlington was near the sea, and not more than fifty or sixty miles from London, and was situated in a pleasant valley on the main road, through which mail coaches were wont to pass both night and day.

The inhabitants had been long a-bed, for the chimes of the village church had tolled the solemn hour of midnight, and not a light could be seen anywhere save at the "Black Bull," for on that memorable night some few of the villagers were celebrating the Christmas holidays at the comfortable inn with a merry country dance among themselves.

The sounds of fiddles and a flute, and the skipping of feet, could be heard, both in the parlours and tap-room.

Merry laughter and boisterous jollity resounded on all sides, and the light-hearted shouts of both men and maidens were caught up and echoed by the passing breeze.

The night, though clear and bright, was bitter, bitter cold, and every door and window of the "Black Bull" was firmly closed, and many fires were crackling within.

On a bench outside the tavern, and in part concealed by the deep shadows of its old, overhanging thatch-covered eaves, sat a powerful-looking youth with stick and bundle.

He sat there listening to the music inside, and more than once heaved a deep sigh.

It was almost impossible to see his features, but what little could be discerned showed that he was a handsome-looking and powerfully built rustic youth of about eighteen years of age.

He seemed desirous of remaining concealed in the deep shadows of the house, for he crouched close under the shadow of the overhanging roof.

If any one had been close enough to observe him they would have perceived that this country-looking youth not only frequently sighed but that more than once he hastily, and in an angry manner, dashed away from his eye a stray tell-tale tear-drop that trickled down his sun-burnt cheek.

He listened to the merriment within, and more than once a faint sickly smile lit up his handsome features.

The noise of loud laughter continued within, but all at once a labourer's voice was heard, who shouted out, in stentorian tones—

"Come, lads and lasses, I'll give ye all a toast! Fill up yer glasses to the brim, and do justice to it."

"Hear! hear!"

"What is it, Mr. Chairman?" said one and another.

"Let's have it, Hodge."

"Well," said Hodge, rising in his chair, glass in hand, whose shadow the young stranger could see

reflected on the parlour blind; "well, lads and lasses all, here's long life and good luck to our good, kind old master, Farmer Bertram! his health with three times three."

The toast was responded to with a boisterous "three times three," which shook the glasses on the table till they jingled, and made the windows tremble again.

The young man, when he heard this toast proposed, rose from his seat, and, picking up his bundle and stick, walked hastily away, with down-cast head.

He had not gone far along the beaten snow track in the middle of the road ere he turned his head, and saw the figure of a single horseman approaching at a hard gallop!

The horseman rode a splendid coal-black mare, which seemed to fly over the ground with wonderful grace and ease.

The rider, himself, was elegantly dressed, and muffled up to the chin in a stylish great-coat, while his three-cornered hat was drawn over his eyes, and shaded his features so much that no one could scarce see his face distinctly.

When he approached the "Black Bull," he stopped for a minute, as if undecided whether he would dismount or not.

After a time, however, he put spurs to his horse once more, and soon overtook the youth with his stick and bundle, who was slowly and thoughtfully walking along.

"Bitter cold night, friend," said the horseman, checking his steed into a slow walk.

"Yes, it is," was the sullen answer of the youth.

"Why are you not at the 'Black Bull' to-night" said the rider, with a hoarse laugh. "Some of the lads seem to be enjoying themselves there in fine style. What made you leave so early?"

"Wasn't there at all, if you *must* know."

"Not invited, I suppose?"

"No; nor didn't want to be."

"Why not? Are you not fond of singing and dancing?"

"Yes; as much as any one; but still I wouldn't go there to-night for any money."

"Why not?"

"Because they're keeping up Farmer Bertram's birth-day."

"Oh, indeed," said the strange, young-looking horseman. "You don't like Farmer Bertram, then, I suppose?"

"Yes I do. But he hates me though, I do believe," said the youth, with a sigh.

"He discharged you from the farm, I suppose. What was it for? getting drunk, or poaching?"

"Neither. I wasn't discharged at all. I left on my own account. If I wanted to work about these parts, I could get plenty to do from Sir Richard Warbeck, at Darlington Hall, that white house yonder on the hill, among that cluster of old oak trees."

"You know Sir Richard Warbeck, then?"

"Aye, and have done this many a year; his adopted sons, too—Charley, as is now in London, and Wildfire Ned, as we call the brave lad, as lives up the Hall. I know 'em both, well."

"You seem to know all about the people living around Darlington, I perceive."

"I do. Who should know 'em better than *me*?"

"Who are you, then, my friend?" said the horseman, with a quick glance.

"They call me Rambling Bob, but Bob Bertram is my real name."

"Bob Bertram?" said the stranger, with a glittering eye. "What, the only son of Farmer Bertram of Four Ash Farm?"

"Right, sir. Do ye know him?"

"Me? Bless the man, no!" said the horseman. "I don't know any one hereabouts. I am on my way to a neighbouring village on urgent business."

"More's the pity then," said Bob. "You might travel a long way afore you'd find a nicer or kinder old gentleman than Sir Richard Warbeck, at Darlington Hall."

"So I've heard; and he's very rich also, I am told."

"There's no mistake about that, sir. He's a magistrate in the city of London, and is director of one of the best banks there. He adopted two orphan boys, and brought 'em up as his own sons. One's in the London bank; but young Wildfire Ned, as we call him, won't do nothing but go to sea. If they only mind themselves they are sure to fall into all Sir Richard's money. If they don't, though, and should go astray, they will have the door slammed in their face, as I had to-day."

"You? by your father, Farmer Bertram?"

"Yes; and all because some time ago I picked up with a poor village lass as I loved as dearly as I love my life, and promised for to marry."

"And did your father turn you out of house and home on that account?"

"He didn't turn me out 'zactly," said Bob. "I left, and went to sea for a few months. I was wrecked on the coast here a week back, without money or anything 'cept what I stand up in, and these leggings were given me this very day by Sir Richard's gamekeeper as knows me, so I should go up to the farm and see the old man decent like."

"And what did Farmer Bertram say to you?"

"Why, cause I had made up my mind to marry the lass I loved best, and father the child sleeping at her breast, he slammed the door in my face, and refused to give me a shilling."

"That's rather hard for a father to do," said the horseman, with a cunning glance. "And what do you intend to do with yourself to-night? You can't sleep in the open air, it would freeze you alive. Why don't you try to get a situation of some kind?"

"That's what I want to do; but my clothes are so shabby I don't like to call on any one I knows. I shall creep into the old man's house, and sleep there to-night, somehow, when all is quiet; but for an hour or two I shall stay in yonder old barn beside the road."

"Oh! it's a very hard case," said the stranger; "particularly when you are the only son, and the old man is rich."

"Ha, stranger; but better times are coming, I hope."

"I'm glad you think so. Well, good night. Here's a piece of silver to help you along," said the horseman, offering money to the seedy and needy farmer's son.

"No thank you," said Rambling Bob, with a look of offended pride. "I'm not come to begging yet. I am strong enough to work for my daily bread without charity from strangers."

"What! so poor, and refuse money? Ha! ha! quite a stoic, I perceive. Well, Mr. Bertram, if you will not take money, I've another offer to make. I have taken a fancy to that heavy, knobby stick you carry. Will you sell it?"

"I don't mind that," said Bob.

A bargain was soon concluded; the bludgeon changed hands for a guinea, and the stranger went his way.

That pleasant-speaking young horseman, muffled up to the eyes, was *a deep, designing villain!*

He knew well all about Farmer Bertram's affairs, and his son's also.

Had Rambling Bob only known him at the moment, and fathomed his deep, dark designs, he would have been spared much misery in after life, and others also.

But of this young stranger we shall quickly hear more.

Let us follow him.

He rode direct to see Farmer Bertram at Four Ash Farm.

As he approached the old farm-house, standing some distance from the road, he stepped under a cluster of trees.

In a very mysterious manner he pulled out of his belt a pair of pistols and examined them.

"They are all right," he said, with a bitter smile. "It is best to be prepared, I may want to use them."

Having done this, he rode up a lane and in a few moments stood rapping at the farm-house door with his riding-whip.

"House ho!" he shouted, in a hoarse and unnatural voice.

In a second the door was opened by an aged woman.

The horseman dismounted, and entered the house.

As he did so, the watch dogs began to howl in a most horrible and hideous manner!

The stranger heard it.

His face turned to an ashy paleness, as he thought——

"That dismal howling, I have been told, is always looked upon by superstitious country people as an omen of death!"

It *was* an omen of death!

## CHAPTER II.

### FARMER BERTRAM RECEIVES A VISIT FROM BOLTON—BOLTON'S TREACHERY.

FARMER BERTRAM was in bed when the stranger entered, having had a fall from his horse while hunting.

The horseman said his business was of such pressing importance that he must see the farmer at once.

Bertram recognized the name, and directed his old servant to admit the stranger to his chamber at once.

"From Mr. Redgill, I believe?" said the farmer, "Are you his son? Excuse me not rising to receive you, but I am unwell. I intended to go to London in a day or two, and settle with Mr. Redgill at once, for I have collected all my rents, and sold my crops to advantage, so that I have got a good bit of ready money by me, much more than will pay off the last instalment of the mortgage he holds against me. Let me see," said the farmer, opening a writing-desk near his bedside, "Let me see, here are the receipts; yes, one signed for £300, a second for £200, and a third for £1,000, and now I owe him £2,000 more. What a striking likeness there is between you and Mr. Redgill, though; now I come to look at you in a clear light, I would have sworn that you were his son."

"Indeed!" laughed the young stranger, in an uneasy manner. "You have detected a likeness; most people say the same; but I am *not* his son, and, what is more, no relation either. You have heard of young Bolton, Mr. Redgill's travelling and collecting clerk? Well, *I* am he."

"And is Redgill in such a hurry for his money that he has sent you to collect it? Why, he expressly told me to use my own time, and call myself with it whenever I liked. I'm sure I have always been punctual with him."

"I do *not* come for the money by any means," said Bolton; "Mr. Redgill would not so insult you as to distrust your well-known honesty."

"Because, if even you *did* call for the money, I should not have given it to you," said the old man, smiling, "£2,000 can't be trusted in everybody's hands, you know, and although you may be as you say, Mr. Bolton, Redgill's travelling and collecting clerk, *I* am not to know that; *I* have never seen you before, as I know of."

"True," said the stranger, smiling blandly; "I commend your prudence, Farmer Bertram; but the truth is, I was travelling to Portsmouth on business for Mr. Redgill, and stopped to bait my horse at the 'Black Bull,' and found some of your labourers enjoying themselves."

"Yes, I gave them a treat to-night as it's my birthday. I would have gone among them myself, only I felt very much upset by the wild behaviour of my only son Robert."

"Exactly, and it's about *him* that I have come so far out of my way, in order to inform you of him, and to *warn* you."

"*Warn* me!" said the farmer, suddenly changing colour, and with looks of distrust at the stranger's uneasiness of voice and manner.

"You have had a quarrel with him to-day, and slammed the door in his face."

"I did. Who told you?" the old man asked. "No one but him and I were present."

"I overheard him say as much to another in a whispered conversation."

"Indeed!"

"Yes; he knows that you have a large sum of money in the house, and is determined to rob you of it, and then run off with the slut he calls his sweetheart."

"Rob me! his own father!"

"It is as true as gospel. That I am correct is plain, or how could I have learned so much of his and your affairs unless I overheard him?"

"Mr. Bolton, I'm sure you are right, and very kind to come here and warn me!"

"Oh, no thanks; it is a duty we owe one to another as men and Christians," said Bolton, with a very pious air. "I was well armed myself, and though I am much pressed for time, I thought I would call and see you; fore-warned is fore-armed."

"True, sir, true; and what would you have me do?"

"Do? that depends. Have you any servants about you that you can arm?"

"Not one, save an old woman I keep as housekeeper, more out of charity than anything else; all the rest are at the 'Black Bull,' having a dance and supper."

"I see, I see," said Bolton, biting his lip. "Well, you don't want your son's guilt exposed before the whole village, do you?"

"No! true, sir, true; he is my son, and, with all his faults, I don't want to heap more shame on his head and mine."

"Then I'll tell you what to do."

"What?"

"Send your old servant down to the two village constables with a private message, telling them all about the intended robbery; they will then come up and remain with you all night, and all will be well."

"But the village is two miles or more by the road, and the old servant would take an hour or two to go and return. Bob might come in the meantime, find me all alone, and rob me of every penny I have in the world."

"But he doesn't know where you keep it, surely?" said Bolton, with a dry, cunning smile.

"Yes, he does; he knows I always keep my gold in that chest yonder by the window; but no one, save my friend Redgill, has any idea where I keep my bank notes," said the farmer, with a sickly smile.

The stranger did.

He had heard Mr. Redgill speak of it as a capital joke that Farmer Bertram always concealed his bank notes in the inner lining of his boots!

But of this he said not a word.

"Ah! it's a sad case," said Bolton. "I am very sorry I cannot remain with you until the constables come, but business of pressing importance calls me away."

Betty, the old servant, was instantly summoned, and toddled off to the village in all haste, much amazed at the message she had to tell to the constables.

Despite all the old farmer's entreaties Mr. Bolton would not stay, but left at the same moment old Betsy did.

Both of them went down the lane together.

When they reached the high road Bolton said to the servant,

"If the constables should ask who gave this information, you know my name, old woman?"

"No, I don't, kind gentleman," was the croaking reply.

"You do not think I am Bob Bertram, then?" said the stranger.

"That I cannot say," answered the old woman, "for you keep your hat so far over your face."

"Well, tell them one Mr. Smith, of Portsmouth, called and told Farmer Bertram all about it."

"I will, kind gentleman."

"Make haste. Good night."

Betsy went towards the village, and Bolton turned his horse's head in a contrary direction and galloped away.

He had not gone more than a quarter of a mile when a bend in the road hid him from Betsy's view.

Instead of riding onward, however, he spurred his horse, and leaped hedge after hedge, until he returned to the farm again in less than ten minutes.

He tied his horse to a tree in the orchard, and quietly approached the back door of the farm-house again.

All was darkness save a ray of light which issued from the farmer's chamber.

Not a sound was heard except the mournful sighing of keen December night winds among the leafless trees.

Now and then, 'tis true, watch dogs shook their chains, and howled most dolefully and dismally, in tones unnatural, ominous and death-like.

Silently and softly did Bolton approach the house.

"He is alone," he thought, "and too weak to leave his chamber. Now is my time, while all are away. His treasure must be mine!"

He tried the back door.

It was locked!

"It was not locked when I left," the villain thought.

He tried it again.

The door chain rattled!

A window above was suddenly and violently slammed too, as if by the wind.

This startled Bolton.

He crawled round to the parlour window.

It was open!

He got in, and pulled off his boots.

He softly opened the door, and found himself in the large, dark entrance hall.

The slow and solemn ticking of the old hall clock seemed to strike his heart with pangs of remorse and horror.

He held his breath, and cold sweat oozed from his brow.

He could distinctly hear the loud pulsation and wild, excited beatings of his own vile heart as there he stood with wild eyes peering up the broad dark staircase.

"All is still," he said, and prepared to ascend to the sick man's room.

Each step was taken cautiously, and with cat-like softness.

But the stairs were old, and creaked with a warning sound.

He had reached the first landing, and stood in a dark recess to recover his breath.

Onward he went.

He could see the light streaming through the keyhole of the old man's bed-room.

There remained now but one more flight of stairs.

The first step he took was arrested by an ominous click, which sounded like the cocking of a gun!

Bolton's eyes now glared like two burning coals in the darkness around him.

His hand upon the bannister trembled, and a cold sweat flowed from every pore.

A sense of deadly horror seized him, but he knew not why.

He felt as if some unnatural and hideous being was watching him, and dogging his noiseless footsteps.

What could it be?

He knew not.

Some dreadful fear compelled him to crouch down low upon the landing from sheer exhaustion.

Bang! bang! suddenly burst out upon his astonished ears, and awoke loud echoes in the old farm-house.

A double-barrelled gun had been discharged at him, loaded with buck-shot, and by some one concealed at the head of the stairs.

A loud groan followed the flashes and report.

## CHAPTER III.

THE MURDER OF FARMER BERTRAM—THE LEG-LESS BODY—SUDDEN APPEARANCE OF THE SKELETON CREW.

"BLACK-HEARTED scoundrel!" said a voice, not far off. "Black-hearted scoundrel! I knew by the wicked twinkle of his eye that he meant me ill. Cunning as he was I have outwitted him. He is dead! He came here to rob and murder me! I will go and get a light, and view the body. Heaven knows, I did it in self-defence. What could an old man like I do with such a villain as that lying dead on the stairs, if he had once got into my chamber and found me in bed? Oh! Bolton, you lie a cold and bloody helpless carcase now, and you deserved it. The story of my son was a cruel trick, but you have paid dearly for it. I will go and get a light; I saw him in the orchard, and watched him."

So saying, the old man walked across the landing into a chamber near his own where the lamp was.

At that instant Bolton rose quickly and bolt upright.

He was untouched!

The shot had in both instances missed him, for he had lain flat on the staircase.

He had groaned, it is true.

But this was in order to deceive old Bertram.

In a second he ascended the stairs, looked to his pistols, and, with Bob's bludgeon in hand, stood beside the farmer's chamber door.

He peeped in.

Bertram stood with his back towards the door trimming a lamp.

Bolton creeped up behind him.

In a moment the heavy bludgeon was raised, and descended with frightful force on the old man's head!

A fearful crash it was.

In a second afterwards Farmer Bertram lay groaning on the floor.

"Murderer! my footsteps shall follow you wherever you go. When least you expect me I will appear to you! on land or sea; in your gay moments, in your sad moments; when alone, or when surrounded by friends; sleeping or waking, I, Bertram, your murdered victim, will stand by your side in the most horrid form, and follow you wherever you go!"

While thus cursing, Bertram rose, and, in his death grasp, took hold of Bolton's throat, but Bolton, with a loud shriek, dashed the murdered man from him, and hurried into the next chamber to search for his gold.

He found several bags of money in an old oak chest.

The sight of the glittering coin ravished his eyes, dancing as they were with fiendish triumph.

"'Tis well," said Bolton, "the old man is richer than I thought. Now for the notes; he has them concealed in the lining of his boots.

Emptying the gold into his many large capacious pockets he unsheathed his dirk.

"I will cut his boots open, and secure the notes," said he.

Lantern in hand, he re-entered the room where the lifeless body lay.

His eyes almost darted from their sockets at the sight he then saw.

Each hair on his head stood on end; he trembled in every limb.

His very marrow was frozen at the awful spectacle before him.

The body was legless!

Each leg had been disjointed just above the knee!

The limbs were gone!

"How could this happen?" mused the guilty man, trembling from head to foot.

Just at that moment he heard loud laughter outside in the garden—laughter not like that of men, but of demons.

He rushed to the window, and saw below the hideous forms of a dozen skeleton men, dancing and shouting in wild delight.

"Some of the Skeleton Crew!" he gasped, placing his hands before his face to shut out the horrid sight.

On the instant they vanished in the darkness, with loud shouts of mockery, like things of air!

Almost struck dumb with astonishment, he stood there, as if transfixed to the spot.

A gust of wind blew out his lamp.

In the dreadful darkness he heard the heavy footfalls of a man descending the stairs with slow and solemn step, while a voice, exactly like Farmer

Bertram's, was heard repeating in sepulchral tones in the hall below—

"My footsteps shall follow you, Phillip Redgill, for ever!"

"Phillip Redgill," gasped the murderer, "that is my name! Oh, God! it is the farmer's voice, and yet he is here, lifeless and legless! Hark, what steps are those I hear? who could have limbed him thus?"

While Bolton (or Phillip Redgill, as the spirit voice now properly called him) stood trembling thus, the ghostly voice said loudly again—

"Phillip Redgill, beware! my footsteps shall follow you for ever!"

Dropping the blood-stained bludgeon beside the body, Phillip Redgill rushed from the room, dashed down stairs, opened the back door, and ran towards the orchard.

He mounted his horse, and was about to start off at a furious gallop, when he gave a sharp, horror-stricken shout at something he saw.

The gory legs of the farmer stood bolt upright in the snow beside him!

"Phillip Redgill, I follow you."

The murderer plunged spurs into his steed, and dashed from the spot with the swiftness of the wind.

He perceived Bob Bertram at some distance, who was approaching his father's house.

It was as much as he could do to controul his feelings; but he said to Bob,

"I have soon returned, you see."

"Yes, ye haven't been long."

"No, and I have been so successful that I wish to be generous to all I meet to-night, and, if you are not too proud, I'll begin with you."

"How so, sir?" said Bob.

"You complained when last we spoke that you wanted good clothes in order to make a respectable appearance?"

"I did. What of that?"

"Why, I am a rich man and you poor. I'll exchange clothes with you, and give you a purse full of money to start you a-fresh in life. What say you? I have taken a particular fancy to you, and like you."

"I have not any objections," said Bob, much amused at the horseman's strange freak. "But where can we change?"

"Oh, this old barn will do, but we must be quick," said the stranger, dismounting.

Bob soon exchanged clothes with the horseman; but he couldn't help but remark that his companion had a very large amount of gold coin about him.

The stranger told him he had been out collecting for a very large London firm.

"There," said Phillip, surveying Bob, "those clothes will make a man of you."

"Mine alter your looks very much," said Bob, laughing.

"Never mind that, my boy. I can afford to play such queer pranks, for I am rich. It will take my father quite by surprise to see me dressed in this manner."

"And so it will mine when I go again."

"Why not go to-night? Come, cheer up; put this purse in your pocket, and have a pull at my brandy flask; it will cheer you up. Go to him at once; he can't be always angry with you."

The stranger's words were so kind and encouraging that, after he had galloped off, Bob determined to go boldly to his father's house, and demand a lodging for the night.

The stranger's brandy had aroused him, and made him feel rather flattered with his altered and gentlemanly appearance.

Thinking thus, he walked across the fields towards Four Ash Farm; but as he approached the dwelling he felt a sense of deep depression from some unknown cause—a feeling of chilliness and fear took possession of him.

He walked boldly up to the back door, however, and found it wide open.

Instead of the dogs joyfully yelping when he approached them, they rushed at him to the full length of their chains, howling most dismally.

He entered the house.

All was unearthly quiet.

"I will not disturb any one," thought the prodigal son, "but creep into the parlour, and sleep on the sofa until morning."

This he did on tiptoe, for fear of being heard, and was soon fast asleep.

In less than half-an-hour Betty returned, and with her two village constables.

They went upstairs to the farmer's bed-room, conducted by old Betty.

She knocked at her master's bed-room door three times.

There was no answer.

No light was burning.

She opened the door, and peeped in.

No one was there.

She next looked into Master Robert's old bed-room.

Next moment she screamed aloud, and fell staggering to the floor.

"Murdered! murdered!" she cried.

The two officers went in, and turned deadly pale, as they beheld the lifeless body lying ghastly and gory before them.

"Murdered! murdered!" screamed the servant, again and again, in piercing tones.

The dreadful sounds aroused Robert.

He leaped from the sofa, and rushed upstairs.

"Oh, here is Mr. Bolton; kind good gentleman; oh, tell us who did this?" said Betty, weeping.

"It is not Mr. Bolton," said one of the officers; "it is Bob Bertram."

"What means this?" gasped Bob, pushing by the officers into his own old bed-room. "What means all this screaming when my father lies sick in bed?"

"It means murder, Bob," said one of the men.

"What! murder?"

"Yes; and you did it," said the other, "if I'm not much mistaken."

"Me?"

"Aye you, Bob; look at your fine clothes stained with blood!"

And so they were. They had been wiped, but the stains were there upon them still.

"Oh! heavens! have mercy on me!" said Bob, turning white as a sheet, and fell into an arm chair, stricken to the heart with surprise and sorrow.

"We did not think you would do such a horrid thing as this is, Bob," said the officers; "but we were warned of your threats, and your coming here to rob your father, and came to prevent it."

"Me? Rob my father? Come here to murder? Warned of it beforehand?" gasped Bob, with staring eyes. "What means this? Is it all a terrible, horrible dream, or what?"

"No; it is an awful reality, and we must take you in custody, on the charge of murder."

In an instant the two officers handcuffed him.

He did not utter a word or move a muscle.

He was pale, and looked wildly about him as if in a dream.

"Poor Nance!" he sighed, thinking of his pretty persecuted sweetheart and intended wife. "Poor Nance, this news will break thy young heart!"

Bob hung his head.

The constables were sorrowful and silent.

Betty looked like a crazy woman, as she sat on the floor, sobbing.

Not a word was spoken.

All was still.

The silence was at last broken by the slow, measured tread of some one coming upstairs.

The footsteps crossed the landing.

All turned anxiously towards the door.

Judge of their looks and shouts of fright and horror !

The bodiless legs walked slowly into the room !

## CHAPTER IV.

### SIR RICHARD WARBECK AND WILDFIRE NED— THE ONE-LEGGED SAILOR'S NARRATIVE.

DARLINGTON HALL, the country residence of Sir Richard Warbeck, was an immense old building, high, strongly built, containing many galleries, vaults, and mysterious ins and outs, with numerous towers, effigies of men in armour on landings, corridors, and rooms, the old baronial edifice covered with ivy for the most part, and stood in a spacious, well-wooded park, not many miles from the sea.

The knight, from some unknown cause, though immensely wealthy, had never married, but consoled himself with adopting two friendless orphan youths, Charles and Edward, or Wildfire Ned, who, in his honour, took the name of Warbeck.

Charles, the elder of the two, was in London.

"Wildfire Ned," as he had been christened by the country people, on account of his mad freaks, loved to live at the Hall, so that he might have ample opportunities for indulging in shooting, fishing, hunting, swimming, and particularly sailing in a small bay near by, a sport of which he was so passionately fond that old salts always called him " Ned, the Sailor Boy."

His adopted uncle loved Ned, perhaps more so than Charles, for he was a handsome, brave, and adventurous youth of about fifteen years old, the ladies' pet, and the envy of all young men for miles around.

The old knight had long tried to curb his roving and seafaring propensities, but all to no purpose.

On the cold December night on which the story opens—the night after old Bertram's murder—the knight sat by a huge log fire in his library, reading.

Ned was pouring over some favourite " tale of the sea," and sighing for a chance to distinguish himself against the many bloodthirsty pirates and buccanneers that then infested the neigbouring seas.

" Oh! isn't that jolly ?" said Ned, striking the table with his fist. " Oh! I wish I had been there."

" Where ?" said the knight, looking up in surprise.

" Why, in the ship I'm reading about. Didn't they give the pirates and smugglers something, that's all ? Why, uncle, a small English sloop of war with six guns, fought a whole fleet of buccaneers. Wasn't that jolly, eh ?"

" Still thinking of the sea, eh, Ned ?"

" Yes, uncle (for both he and Charles always so called him), and why not ? Our sailors are the bravest and finest fellows in the world. Wouldn't I like to be a middy in the king's navy, that's all ? I'd lay my life I should be an admiral before I was twenty."

Sir Richard did not reply; but walked to the window thoughtfully, and looked out upon the cold, snow-covered landscape, and as the winds sighed mournfully down the chimney, he tapped Ned affectionately on the head, as he said,

" Ah, my lad, your brother Charles will make the best man of the two yet; see, he is not much older than you are, and yet he stands well in the East Indian house, and will be a rich man one of these days if he's industrious and behaves himself."

" Perhaps so," said Ned, biting his lip ; " but I never did like pen and ink and figures; that sort of work is too slow for me."

" I know it. You would rather go hunting and boating ; but, believe me, there are more hardships at sea than boys like you ever dreamed of, Ned."

" I shouldn't mind 'em."

" And danger, too."

" That's just what I should like," said curly-headed Ned, laughing. " I wouldn't give a dump for an English boy without he liked adventures and danger, and could well beat any foreigner he came across."

While he spoke the lodge bell rang.

" Who is that ?" asked the knight of a footman who entered.

" Tim, the groom boy, sir, as he rode home, picked up a poor one-legged sailor, for he was afraid, he said, to pass the gibbets on the wild heath alone."

" Who, the sailor or Tim ?"

" The groom, sir."

" I thought it wasn't the sailor," said Ned. " An English sailor without legs at all is more than a match for any foreigner with two, and as to being afraid to pass the gibbets, ha! ha! British tars ain't afraid of men dangling in chains."

" Silence, Ned. What of this poor sailor ?"

" Tim said, sir, as how Master Edward were fond of sailors."

" So I am ; Tim was right."

" He brought him to the Hall to pass the night."

" Good boy, Tim," said Ned. " I owe him a shilling for that. Won't we pump all the yarns out of him before he goes to-morrow, that's all ?"

" Where is this cripple, then ?"

" Tim is stuffing him in the kitchen, sir."

" Well, when he has done eating, show him up here. Stir up the fire ; put more logs on ; that will do. And now, Edward, since you are so fond of reading trash about the sea, we will hear what this poor cripple has got to say. I have no doubt when you hear his story of real life, it will help to cure you of your wild and foolish notions about the navy. If you want to go to sea for a time, take a trip in a merchant ship."

" That is not like the king's navy, no more than a militia-man at home is like one of the royal guard who has fought against the French, uncle."

" If you wished to take a trip, my old friend Redgill has half a dozen ships, and will be glad to oblige me."

" I don't like the name of Redgill, or his ships either," said Ned, with a scornful curl of his lip.

" What is that you say, sir ?"

" I can't help it, uncle ; I don't like any of the Redgills ; as to Phillip, I hate him."

" Remember, Edward, they are relations of mine, which you are not."

" I know it, uncle," said Ned, with a sigh " Charley and I depend upon you for everything We are poor, friendless orphans."

" And perhaps may remain friendless and moneyless, too, if you do not do my bidding, young sir ; remember that."

"I know it, uncle; but I hope to gain my own living ere many months have passed over my head. But whether I am rich or poor, I shall hate Phil Redgill all the same."

'Why, sir?"

"He is a rank coward. I despise him."

"Coward!—despise him! What mean you? Do you know he may one day inherit my fortune?"

"I do. I don't hate him for that; but he is a coward and a cunning knave into the bargain. He is much older than I am; but I could thrash the very life out of him in ten minutes, if he'd only stand up like a man. I have told him that more than once, uncle, and have shoved my fist in his face often and often; he is a sly thief and a liar, uncle," said Wildfire Ned, getting red and very passionate. "Tim and I know what he has done before now. Charley and he are very thick, I hear, in London; but, if brother took *my* advice, he would shun Phil Redgill like a snake in the grass. If he don't come to the gallows in time, why, then, he must have more lives than a cat, that's all."

The knight was astounded at this; but while he stood staring at Ned, the door opened, and in walked the footman and Tim the boy groom, leading in the one-legged sailor.

Timothy, the groom, or Tiny Tim, as he was called, on account of his small stature, looked pale and frightened.

His staring eyes, and hair standing on end, told plainly that he had been frightened by something or somebody on the road from Portsmouth.

"What's the matter, Tim?" Ned asked, laughing. "Why, you look as if you had seen a dozen ghosts on the road."

"So I have, Master Edward, more than a dozen."

"More than a dozen ghosts, lad?" asked the knight, laughing. "Did you bring the letters safe?"

"Yes, sir," answered Tim; "here they are, sir; but I had to ride for my dear life like the devil."

"What does the lad mean?" the knight asked. "Surely he is not crazy? Sit down and compose yourself."

"Well, sir," said Tim, "directly I got the letters I started back home again; but as I was trotting along I saw a man on horseback waiting for me; he looked like a highway robber, so I turns my horse down another road to get out of his way."

"Well, what then?"

"I hadn't gone far, sir, and was just passing the Red Man's gibbet, as they calls it, at the cross roads, when the wind began to howl and cry like so many living voices."

"You were not afraid of all that, I hope?"

"No, sir, but the vultures were flying about the gibbet, and their eyes sparkled in the moonlight like so many coals of fire."

"Well?"

"I didn't care much about that, but when I got fairly under the gibbet, and was about to pass by, I looked up, and I saw the Red Man's eyes glaring on me, and he seemed to shake himself, for his chains rattled awfully."

"Nonsense! he has been dead this many a-year; it was all fancy, Tim," said Wildfire Ned, chuckling.

"No, it wasn't, sir, all due respect to you, sir; he was alive."

"Alive?"

"Aye, gentlemen, alive; I could swear it as sure as I live."

"You were timorous, that is all, and fancied so."

"No, Sir Richard, I never was so brave in all my life, although I felt my blood run cold. *It spoke to me.*"

"Spoke to you?"

"Yes sir."

"What did it say?"

"'Halt!' it shouted, and on the instant my horse stopped, and would not budge an inch. 'Halt!' it said, in awful tones, glaring down on me with its fiery eyes. 'I am one of the Skeleton Crew,' it said; 'go, tell your master that Farmer Bertram is murdered!'"

"Dead?" "Murdered?" said several in surprise.

"When did this foul deed take place?" asked the old knight.

"'Murdered last night,' said the Red Man from the gibbet, 'as the Darlington village clock tolled the hour of one! Ha! ha! the Skeleton Crew still lives, and rules the seas, and will long defy the power of man. Fly from this spot, or become one of the dead!'"

"This is a most horrible revelation," said the old knight.

"I did not stop to hear more, for I shouted with fright, and galloped madly away, feeling as if frozen to the very marrow, for *I had spoken with the dead!*"

Tiny Tim looked exhausted, and shivered in every limb.

He could not proceed with his story very quickly, for his teeth chattered again.

"Give the lad a stiff glass of brandy, Ned," said the kind-hearted knight.

Ned did so; a *very* "stiff" one indeed, it was, which made the groom's eyes twinkle again.

The one-legged sailor was treated in like manner, when Tim continued—

"I galloped along till I reached the edge of the wild and barren heath, but then I felt faint, for I perceived another horrid sight in the distance! I was compelled to cross the heath, for it was my only way here to the Hall. Unable to guide my horse, I sat still shivering in the cold, knowing not what to do, when all of a sudden the one-legged sailor seemed to spring out of the earth close beside me.

"The next moment I found him sitting on the horse beside me!

"He took the reins, and the mare dashed onwards like lightning, as if neither of us were heavier than two straws.

"All I remember is that as we galloped along we came up to three fires on the roadside which burned with a dark blue flame, and around them were, shrieking and dancing—the Skeleton Crew!

"I fainted. When I came to my senses again we were at the Lodge gate."

Sir Richard, Ned, the footman, and other members of the household, who had now gathered around, listened to Tim's story with bated breath.

The footman looked terror-stricken, and trembled so, that, during the groom's story, his pigtail (the fashion in those days) gradually rose, until at last it stood stiff and erect above his head, a powdered pillar of horror.

"Is the lad dreaming, or is he turned crazy?" said Sir Richard.

"No; the lad is right, sir," said the one-legged sailor, making bold to speak. "My name is Ralph Spray, your honour, late of the king's navy; and, if so be as how I'm not intruding, I well tell you all about it. This 'ere good-natur'd lad, the groom, is almost turned grey wi' only havin' a peep at some on 'em, but how must it be wi' me, who has fought with the Skeleton Crew?"

"Is it true, then, that there *is* such a crew?" asked the knight, in surprise.

"Aye, true, sir, as I sits here, for I lost my other leg among 'em. I ought not to forget 'em, for they

WILDFIRE NED VISITS THE RED MAN ON THE HEATH.—See No. 3.

have given me plenty o' reason to remember 'em by."

"Do you say, then, that you believe there *is* such a thing as a Skeleton Crew?" asked the knight, very slowly, and looking very hard at Ned's interested face.

"Do I? why, in course I do," said the one-legged stranger, in a huffish manner, "for I'm one on 'em my——"

"What!" gasped every one, rising to their feet.

"I'm one on 'em myself—as suffered by 'em.

"O-h-h-h!" said one and all, very much relieved,

for they thought that the cripple was going to say that *he* was one of the Skeleton Crew.

"Well, as I were about to say, gentlemen," Ralph Spray continued, "I served as an able seaman on board His Majesty's sloop of war 'Dolphin,' and we lay in the Sound. We hadn't been there long afore the news reached us about the wild doings of the Skeleton Crew. At first we didn't believe any o' the strange tales, but at last we were ordered off to cruise after the Phantom Ship and Skeleton Crew."

"And did you ever overhaul them?" asked Ned, impatiently.

"Lor' bless yer simple heart ! overhaul them ? No, not us ; but they *very soon overhauled us*, my lad !"

"Is it possible ?  Overhaul one of the king's ships ?"

"Ha, my God ; and massacred every soul on board, save one !"

"And who was he ? "

"I myself ; Ralph Spray."

"You ?"

"Yes, I."

"Why, how can that be ?  You must have had at least 150 men on board the 'Dolphin,'" said the knight.

"'Zactly ; and the Skeleton Crew couldn't muster half as many, I suppose you mean ? "

"Just so."

"Aye, sir, but we on board the 'Dolphin' were men."

"Brave men, too, no doubt."

"Yes ; but them on board the Phantom Ship weren't men at all."

"What, then, in heaven's name ?"

"Why, devils !"

The footman, hay, every one of Ralph's audience, were listening open-mouthed and with staring eyes.

"Devils ?" asked Ned.

"Yes, devils, young man."

A pause took place, and every one took a long breath, and creeped closer to the fire as Ralph continued—

"We caught sight of the Phantom Ship once.  It was painted red.  We gave chase, and came within two miles of it, when it changed its colour to blue !  We wasn't going to be taken in, so we fired a broadside right into her, and——"

"Sunk her," asked Ned.

"Not a bit on it, it vanished into *mist*."

Several of the servants and members of the household whom the kind knight had allowed to listen to the cripple's tale, now wished themselves in their bed-rooms, or in the servants' hall.

They were unable to leave their seats, however, for they felt fastened down to them, and in some manner fascinated by the charmed eye of the speaker.

The footman's pig-tail worked to and fro like the pendulum of a clock, and, at certain passages, stood bolt upright as its owner inwardly and sometimes audibly groaned at what he heard.

"Vanished into mist, eh ?  How extraordinary !" said the knight.  "Then it must be a charmed ship, and a charmed crew."

"'Zactly, sir, and I'll tell yer how I proves it. The 'Dolphin' often gave chase to this Phantom Ship, but could never catch it, although sometimes *we* caught more than we liked."

"Indeed ! what was that then ?"

"Why, a well-aimed broadside."

"From the Phantom Ship ?"

"'Zactly, and a devil of a mess they left us in more nor once, and we were glad to sheer off."

"Extraordinary ! it sounds like a dream."

"But it ain't, though, for one foggy night, when the 'Dolphin' lay anchored in the Sound, me and Tom Robinson were keeping watch on deck, and never thinking of any harm, for all the crew were snug in their hammocks, when it almost turned me grey to see three score of the Skeleton Crew clamber over the ship's side like shadows, and begin to cut and hack us about awful.  The deck was cleared in a second."

"Did you not alarm the ship, and beat to quarters ?"

"What was the use ?  I rushed to go below, but only put one leg down the hatchway ladder when it was cut off clean as a whistle."

"Didn't the crew rush up to assist you ?"

"How could they, they were all dead !"

"Dead ?"

"Yes, dead as door nails.  The only ones to rush up was a gang o' the Skeleton Crew who had been below quietly murdering the men in their hammocks."

"Horrible !"

"Astounding !"

"But there's worse to come," said Ralph.

The footman, with his pig-tail standing on end, made a move towards the door.

The old housekeeper was almost fainting.

Tim's hair was like the quills of a porcupine as he listened with open mouth and distended eyes.

"Well, as soon as they got possession of the 'Dolphin' these skeleton devils weighed anchor in a jiffey and made sail away.

"They pitched the dead overboard, every mother's son of the crew, mind ye ; but, as well as I could, I bound up my leg tight to keep it from bleeding, and crawled into an old cask.

"There I stayed for two days and two nights as quiet as a mouse a watching of these skeleton devils, and I heard and saw as much as would have killed any ordinary man."

"Learn any of their secrets, do you mean ?"

"Yes, sir."

"What were they ?"

"Why, I learned that they never would and never could be conquered by all the king's navy, for every one on 'em, ships and all, had charmed lives ; but, as far as I could understand, they all trembled when they heard the name of a boy who had been born to destroy 'em."

"A boy born to conquer and destroy that horrible band ?"

"Aye, just so, sir ; for they admitted among themselves that he was charmed more than they were, and would be sent to scourge them from the sea."

"Wonderful !"

"I wish *I* were that boy," said Ned, with a flushed cheek.

"Do you ?" said the cripple.

"Yes, I do," said Wildfire Ned, proudly.  "I don't believe in charms or spells, but I do believe if I had a good crew I should soon annihilate the whole of them."

"Perhaps you are boasting, young man ?"

"No, I'm not."

"Do you say, then, you could, and that you would, face the whole Skeleton Crew single-handed ?"

"Yes ; and trust to heaven for strength to destroy them."

"You never have seen any of them yet ?"

"No ; but I much desire to do so."

"Then behold !" said the one-legged sailor, stamping his foot on the floor, and pointing towards the window.

In an instant a crash of glass was heard.

Every one, save Ned, screamed aloud at the ghastly sight before them.

There, with his head and half of his body visible at the window and protruding through it, stood a horrible form !

It was one of the Skeleton Crew !

In an instant Wildfire Ned pulled out a pistol and fired.

The ghastly form moved not !
He thought he heard the ball rattle among the bones of the Skeleton.

He fired again.

With a loud laugh of derision and triumph the Skeleton waved his plumed hat and vanished.

When Ned turned towards the crippled sailor—
He had disappeared !

---

## CHAPTER V.

### CONSTERNATION AT DARLINGTON HALL.

THE consternation that ensued among all assembled at this unlooked-for conclusion of the mariner's tale was evidently great.

The old knight jumped to his feet in amazement, and with trembling limbs.

He tried to speak, but could not.

Tim's eyes rolled in wild excitement, while the footman fell upon his knees, and began to mumble out his prayers in a very rapid manner, for he had come to the humble conclusion, in his own mind, that for once in his life he had been in company with some demon of darkness.

He groaned aloud, and pulled very comical faces, while others made a sudden rush towards the door !

Among them all there was one who looked on the matter with lightness and good humour.

That one was Wildfire Ned.

Pistol in hand he dashed towards the window as bold and fearless as a young lion.

"If ye be mortal, die !" he said, firing his weapon after the retiring skeleton figure.

With the agility of a cat he jumped on to the window-sill, and looked out into the darkness.

The ghastly apparition had vanished !
Whither or how had it gone ?

"Strange," muttered Ned, angrily, as he returned to his seat. "Where's the cripple ?"

All looked around.
He also had vanished.

"There is some strange horrible mystery in all this," said Ned, "and I will perish before I give up the search without unravelling it."

"It all seems to me like a dream," the knight said at last, with a great effort. "Some strange and horrible nightmare."

"I wasn't frightened, sir," said Tim, plucking up his courage. "Nothing could frighten me now, seeing as how I rode home with one on 'em."

"It's all a trick, I know," said the footman. "Some of the villagers have got it up for a lark, seeing as how it's Christmas time."

"Perhaps so, Roger," the knight replied, with a smile ; "but I noticed you soon fell on your knees, and began to say your prayers."

"And so did Tim," Ned laughed ; "but now it's all over, you may retire," he said to the servants who were there, "you may retire. Uncle and I wish to be alone."

Tim was the first to go to the door, and he opened it with a shaking hand.

In order to reach the servants' hall, they had to traverse several long dark galleries, and descend the main staircase.

Tim wanted his fellow servants to look upon him as a very bold youth, but he took great care not to be the first to go out into the dark gallery.

In this way, also, the chief footman thought, but didn't like to say so.

"Why don't you go on ? " said he to Tim.
"Why don't *you* ? "
"You were the first at the door."
"Suppose I was, that don't matter."
"You're afraid ?"
"No I ain't."
"Yes you are, Tim."

"If you think so, then follow me," said the young groom, plucking up all his spare courage, and flourishing his riding-whip.

The domestics left the room, and proceeded cautiously and slowly down the stairs towards the servants' hall, creeping along, one after the other, in the dark.

They had all got as far as the large, old oak baronial dining-room, on the ground floor, and were creeping along through the spacious entrance hall, towards the head of the kitchen stairs, when every one stopped.

For a moment they stood in the darkness, breathing very hard, when their ears were startled by the sudden clanking of chains !

The sound proceeded from the baronial hall, where for centuries had stood wooden figures, clothed in armour !

The clanking noise sounded so horrible, that they all rushed down the kitchen stairs, one on top of another, in wild confusion.

Roger, the footman, was the first to make the descent, which he did six stairs at a time.

But directly he and the rest got to the bottom in breathless haste, they were still more horrified at the sight that confronted them.

For there stood at the foot of the stairs a skeleton form, sword in hand !

"Ha ! ha !" he gruffly laughed, as he flourished his weapon.

The footman shouted in terror, and turned on his heel to flee upstairs again.

The rest followed him, bellowing and screaming at the top of their voices.

Upstairs they flew in wild dismay, tearing their clothes, and knocking each other about in the darkness, making all haste to leave far behind them the dreadful form they had seen below.

No man, or woman either, ever mounted flights of stairs with such expedition as did the servants on this memorable occasion.

Coat tails were torn off, wigs were lost, trousers were torn behind in very unpleasant and uncomfortable places, and more than one received hard thumps in the ribs from some one they knew not.

But this was nothing, so that they could escape with their lives.

Once in the entrance hall again they ran towards the great drawing-room.

The door was unexpectedly and very hastily opened for them by a skeleton !

With a cry of agony and surprise they turned towards the baronial hall as a place of safety.

They reached the doorway almost fainting with fatigue and fright.

A man in armour strode forth to meet them, lance in hand !

More than one fainted on the spot.

Roger, the footman, like a brave man, trusted to his legs once more, followed by as many of his fellow servants as had any strength left in them; he vanished up the great staircase at lightning speed.

It seemed to be a race for life or death with all of them.

Round and round the staircase they manfully ascended, never casting a single look behind.

They had gained the long, wide corridor which led to Sir Richard's library, and all felt safe.

Roger, as may be imagined, was first, and opened the door.

His foot caught in the carpet on the threshold, and down he went on his face, swelling his nose to the size of a cucumber.

The others, in wild confusion, rushed after him and tumbled, men and women, head over heels on the prostrate footman, nearly smothering him with their combined weight.

"What mean all this uproar and fright?" said the old knight, rising in great anger. "Are ye all turned mad, ye noisy, raving knaves? Explain, I say, explain!"

But none of the servants could explain anything, for they were all out of breath, and as pale as death.

After a time, when Roger was dragged out with his nose bleeding, he looked about him with a wild and frightened gaze, as he stammered out,

"O-h-h-h, s-i-r! we-e-'ve s-e-e-n him!"

"Seen him! Seen who, knave? Speak quickly! or, by my honour, I'll whip my sword through your trembling carcase!" said old Sir Richard, getting red in the face. "Speak, some of you!" he continued, looking daggers at his alarmed domestics.

"Oh! m-e-r-cy! master, m-e-r-cy!" croaked out Roger, falling on his knees.

"Speak, rascal! Who have ye seen?"

"The skeleton! ghastly, ghostly, all bones, and sword in hand, grinning like an angry demon."

"A skeleton!"

"Aye, sir; two on 'em."

"Two, do you say?"

"Yes, Sir Richard; one at the bottom of the kitchen stairs, and t'other opened the drawing-room door! H-o-o! ask 'em all if it ain't true, good master!" continued the footman, rolling his eyes and moaning.

"And another grim rascal in armour rushed at us lance in hand at the dining-hall door?" whined Tim, the valiant groom. "Oh, lor, the whole place is full on 'em, I do believe."

For some moments Sir Richard did not know what to do.

All around him knelt his frightened domestics, groaning and shaking.

"Why, but just now, knave, you said it was all a lark, perhaps, got up by some of the silly villagers to frighten us. Ghosts and living skeletons indeed! There, go down and get your suppers at once, and let's have no more of such silly nonsense."

"Nay, good master, we dare not."

"Stuff and nonsense," said Ned, laughing; "how can you be geese enough to believe in such old women's tales. Get up off your knees at once, I say, and don't stick there shivering like leaves. I have lived in the Hall this many a year, and have never seen anything of the kind. I only wish I could come across the rascals who are playing such

tricks, that's all; I'd soon find out whether they were ghosts or not."

"Would you? Ha! ha!" said suddenly a voice.

"What was that? Who spoke?" said Ned, colouring with anger.

"Would you? Ha! ha! then you shall soon have a chance, bold youth," said the voice again.

"Who or what is that?" said old Sir Richard, starting.

"That's him, master; that's him! the ghosts! ho-o-o!" said Roger, with chattering teeth.

"This is strange," thought Wildfire Ned, "there cannot be any doubt but that there is some mystery hanging about the old Hall. I have long been persuaded of it, but it will not do to let my uncle or his people know what I think of this mystery."

"What is that you are saying, Edward?" asked Sir Richard.

"Nothing, uncle," he replied. "I was only smiling at the foolish fears of these tremblers here."

"Come, rouse up all of you," said old Sir Richard, "and follow me!"

"That's just what I was about to propose, uncle," said Ned. "We'll soon get to the bottom of this strange affair."

Arming himself with a sword, Wildfire Ned led the way, lamp in hand. "I'll lead the way," said he; "follow me! Uncle you can remain behind; there is nothing to fear. I care not for a hundred skeletons, or ghosts either; follow me."

---

## CHAPTER VI.

THE SKELETON CREW AT DARLINGTON HALL—THE CONFLICT BETWEEN THE SERVANTS—DEFEAT OF THE SKELETON CREW BY WILDFIRE NED.

EVERY one knew what a brave, bold, adventurous boy Wildfire Ned was, and directly he said "follow me," each one regained his courage, and prepared to follow him.

They were all unarmed save Ned; but Roger, very cunning, stole a short poker from the fire-grate without being perceived, and stuffed it under his coat.

"I don't so much fear now," he thought. "I've got the poker, and if any of 'em come near me I'll try and smash their ugly skulls in quick time; that is, if they will let me."

Bold as a lion, and with an eye like a night hawk, young Wildfire Ned led the way, followed by the male servants.

They searched in every place that could be imagined, but neither ghosts nor skeletons could be found.

The rest of the servants were summoned and closely questioned by Wildfire Ned.

No such thing as ghost or skeleton had been seen in other parts of the old Hall, and the bare mention of the armed man in armour, who rushed out upon them, caused great merriment among the majority of the servants, who laughed outright, and called Roger and Tim "two old women."

So there was every prospect of a quarrel among the servants on this great question.

Roger was very indignant, and when he pulled out the short poker from under his clothes, he flourished it about in great wrath, threatening to massacre the coachman, butler, and every one, indeed, who did not believe him.

Order, however, was soon restored among them, and when the supper bell rang all repaired in great haste to the servants' hall to hear the various odds and ends of the footman's strange adventure.

They were all seated round the table, playing sad havoc with rounds of beef and good old ale, when all at once the lamps went out !

Roger would have fled on the instant, but he was afraid of being afterwards branded as a coward, and, therefore, remained in his seat, but felt very uneasy.

The French cook, at the head of the table, left his chair to go for other lamps.

At the moment that lights reappeared the whole assembly were struck dumb at what they then saw.

Behind the chair of each there stood one of the Skeleton Crew !

They would have shouted out loudly, but one of the Skeletons, who appeared to be chief of the party, said, sternly, and in a sepulchral tone, to a gigantic Skeleton,

"The first one that stirs—the first one that speaks above his breath, despatch him !"

Roger groaned inwardly, and felt more dead than alive.

Tim wriggled on his chair like a half-skinned eel.

The chief cook's eyes were wildly dancing, and his long working cap rose up to a prodigious height, while, with open mouth, he stood shivering and shaking.

The others were in a state of collapse, and almost slipped off their seats, while they looked about in trembling fear.

The chief of the Skeleton Crew made a sign to some of his grim attendants to listen to all he had to say.

Turning to the chief cook, butler, and pantryman he said, in a sharp, hissing tone,

"Wine—the best—quick !"

Roger and Tim rose from their seats like a shot, but were each slapped on the head by a hard bony hand, which made their jaws rattle again.

Three grim skeleton guards followed the cook, butler, and pantryman, to see that their captain's orders were carefully obeyed.

The wine was soon produced.

"Where are the silver goblets ?" the chief asked, sternly.

These were soon found.

Each skeleton filled his goblet to the brim, and raised it aloft.

"Here's to the Skeleton Crew of the Phantom Ship !" he said ; "confusion to our enemies."

In a moment the wine was quaffed.

The terrified servants did not know what was coming next, and looked on gasping like so many stranded fish.

"Remove the table," said the chief ; "let us have plenty of room, we have much business to do."

"They are going to murder every mother's son of us," groaned Roger.

Tim began to think seriously of saying some short prayer.

But they had to swallow their own feelings and fears, nor did any of them dare speak, for behind each stood a skeleton, dagger in hand.

The table was removed to one corner of the inner servants' hall.

The domestics were now sitting in a circle, face to face.

"The rope," said the Skeleton Chief, hoarsely.

In an instant each of his crew produced a long stout rope, about two inches round, and flourished it before the eyes of their captain with a savage grin.

"I thought so," groaned Roger. "Oh, dear ! oh, dear !"

"All U.P. now," Tim groaned.

"They wouldn't believe me," said the footman.

"Good-bye everybody," said Tim.

Roger and Tim had another sound thwack on the jaws from their skeleton guardians, which shook every tooth in their heads.

"Sling your ropes," said the grim Skeleton Chief, quaffing more wine.

In a moment each threw one end of his rope up in the air over the numerous beams and rafters of the servants' hall.

"Make each his noose ; mind they fit their necks nicely."

"Oh, the cold-blooded rascals !"

"The merciless villains !"

"Mercy !"

"Have pity on us," gasped the servants, as the Skeletons were making the noose in each rope.

"If they speak again despatch them with your daggers," said the chief.

"Hanging is better than that," sighed Roger, "so I'll keep quiet. I hope my turn will come last, though," he piously prayed.

"Give the rascals five minutes to say their prayers," said the chief, with a gruff laugh.

"It won't do them any good, great chief," said one of the Skeletons ; "they are sure to go to the devil."

"Yes, oh, yes," gasped Roger, "five minutes—say ten, only make it ten, or a quarter of an hour, and it will do us a world of——h-o-o! ha! ho-oh !"

A knife glittered before the footman's eyes ere he had finished his sentence, and he sank upon his knees very humbly and meekly.

If any lot of poor wretches ever prayed fervently they did so on this occasion.

Roger, who seldom had said a prayer in all his life before, fired away very rapidly.

Each one was endeavouring to pray more than the other, and the most wicked among them were loudest.

"Be quick," said the chief, sternly, "be quick with your praying ; the hanging must commence at once. We will begin with the men."

Many of the servants called down more hearty curses on the Skeleton Band than they did blessings on their own heads during their prayers ; but it was useless to offer resistance, for each was in the power of a grim, gaunt enemy.

"Rise !" said the Skeleton Chief.

All the servants did so, except Roger.

"Rise," said the Skeleton. "Don't you know we are in a hurry ?"

"I haven't finished my prayers yet," piously gasped the suddenly converted footman.

"How long does it take you ?" asked one of the Skeletons, chuckling.

"All night sometimes," said Roger, with a sigh.

"Oh, then, you are pious ?"

"Yes, I always was."

"Then as you are so much the better prepared than the rest, we'll hang you first."

Roger groaned and rose up like a shot.

"You have heard of the Skeleton Crew, I know," said the chief aloud, "and that they neither fear man nor devil ?"

"We have," said several ; "quite true."

"I wish the devil had *him*, though," groaned poor Tim.

"And," continued he, "you have heard that the chief is cruel, and has no mercy to his enemies."

"I wish I only had the luck to be one of his best friends at this particular moment," sighed Roger, trembling.

"But you see," said the chief, "I am *not* cruel, or I would have hanged you all without giving a moment's warning.

"Cursed perlite !" said Tim, under his breath.

"And, to show you that I am not as bad as people say I am, I'll give you all a chance as to who dies first, provided——"

"What ?" gasped several, eagerly.

"You will answer me one question."

"What is it, oh, most mighty and merciful skeleton ?" sighed Roger. "What is it ?"

"Who considers himself to be the greatest rogue among you all ?" asked the chief. "Be careful how you answer."

A long, solemn and awful pause followed this ominous and all-important question.

The grim chief need not have warned them to be careful.

They were *very* careful indeed, and took a long, long time to consider.

"It won't do for *me* to answer," thought the trembling servants, "for they will be sure to commence hanging the biggest rogues first."

"So there is no rogue at all among you, I find, eh ? Ha ! ha ! Well, then, who thinks himself the most pious among you ? Tell me that."

Roger was about to reply, but the words stuck fast in his throat, as he thought,

"If *I* answer, they will do for me first as the best prepared to die ; no, no, he don't entrap *me* with his puzzling questions."

So thought the rest.

"No goodness among ye all, then, eh ?" said the chief. "Why, a moment ago ye were all praying like so many saints. Come, answer me this, the third time, then I'll give some of you another chance. Who considers himself to be brave among you, and don't fear death ? Answer me !"

No one did so, however.

"How artful this blood-thirsty monster is !" each thought ; "for those who don't fear death are sure to be hung first !"

"Well, no one answers, I find," said the chief, laughing. "I'll give you a last chance, poor devils ; mark me, the only one you'll have. Who is the greatest coward among you, and fears most to die ?"

"I do."

"I am."

"That's me."

"Oh, spare us !"

Such were the unanimous answers of all, and in one breath.

"Ha ! ha ! you have answered at last, eh ? Well, then, since there are no good nor brave men, but plenty of cowards, we'll hang you altogether, for none of you deserve to live."

Groans were now heard on all sides, and many repented not having answered before.

"If there had been only a few brave men among you I would have spared——"

"I'm brave ! I'm brave !"

"I'll do any mortal thing."

"A lion's courage is nothing to mine !"

"Only just try me—a tiger is nothing compared to me !"

"I'd face the devil, *I* would !"

Thus gasped out many when they found that brave men only were to be spared.

"Oh, that's it, eh ?" said the Skeleton Chief. "I now find that all of you are brave."

"I'm the bravest," said Roger, very meekly ; "on my word, I am !"

"You are, eh ?"

"No, he isn't," said the coachman ; "*I* am."

"Oh, you are ; then this footman must be a liar."

"So he is," said the coachman, "an awful liar ; the biggest as ever lived !"

"Then we will begin with you two first, and give you a trial," said the chief. "How do you best like to fight, with swords, or what ? Daggers are the quickest to do the work with !"

"I'd prefer fists," said the burly coachman.

"And what do *you* prefer my brave fellow ?" asked the chief of Roger.

Roger much preferred to escape out of the mess altogether, but it could not be.

"Strip," said the chief, "you've got a fair chance to settle ; the one who gives in first shall be hung, and the conqueror shall have the choice of poison or a bullet if he refuses to join my crew. We only have well-tried men alive or dead on board the Phantom Ship."

Neither Roger nor the coachman saw any very great choice in the terms offered, but ere many minutes they were pounding each other's ribs in gallant style till the sounds of their own blows reached through the immense hall.

Both combatants fought for ten minutes fiercely and fast, and went at it like two blacksmiths.

At last, however, Roger began to blow like a grampus, and with a well-directed smack on the nose the burly coachman knocked him down.

"I give in," gasped Roger.

"Bring the rope," said the chief, calmly.

"No, I don't ; stop a bit," said the footman. "D—n it ! I'll have a few more rounds ; anything's better than being scragged like a cat."

At it they went again hammer and tongs, pounding each other, and puffing at a great rate.

But while this was going on several other "brave" individuals were engaged, with swords, proving their valour, one against the other.

The doors were all locked, the windows were closed, and the servants' hall being so far away from the knight's apartments the noise was not heard.

Curses, not loud but deep, were heard on every side, and the Skeleton Crew looked on with delight, as they saw the blood flowing an all sides, while their chief sat on a high seat, quaffing wine, and delighted with the bloodthirsty, fiendish work going on around him.

It was a terrible feast of blood!

The Skeleton Band hideously grinned and chuckled at the sight of blood around them.

Shouts of pain and death groans were like music in their demon ears; the writhings of several victims, as they hung from the beams above, thrilled them with joy, as, with bony hands, they pointed to them twisting and dangling in the air.

This horrible carnival had lasted long.

The best looking of the females were then carried off by several of the Skeleton Band to some rendezvous near by, with limbs bound and their mouths gagged; but those left behind were hung to the rafters quickly, and without mercy.

\* \* \* \* \*

This was an annual gory banquet, which the chief of the Skeleton Crew kept up to celebrate his career as the famous Scourge of the Sea!

He and most of his crew had come with the firm resolve to massacre every one in Darlington Hall.

This was but the commencement of their horrible sport.

Well might the Skeleton Crew and their charmed Phantom Ship have long been the terror and fright of all the coasts and seas around.

Many a family had been slaughtered in cold blood on shore, and many a good ship's company mangled and their vessels plundered and sunk by these aptly termed Demons of the Deep.

But they had not come to Darlington Hall solely to satisfy their thirst for blood.

It was the villain and murderer, Redgill, they assisted.

He hated Wildfire Ned with bitter animosity because he could not supplant the brave youth in the affections of young Alice, the wealthy daughter of Countess Bluefield, sister to Sir Richard, whose estates were hard by.

But hitherto Redgill had been successful in his knavery.

Alice had suddenly disappeared.

She had been kidnapped from her home.

And while from home her parents had been slaughtered and the mansion sacked by the Skeleton Crew.

It was now the aim of these fiends to murder all in Darlington Hall, and for Redgill to forge a will in his own favour, and to claim the estate.

But the cleverest villains are caught in traps of their own making, as will be seen in succeeding chapters of this story.

Suffice it to say that on this occasion the Skeleton Crew were carrying out their plans to murder all the servants first and the owners afterwards.

\* \* \* \* \*

For an hour or more did these demons revel in this horrid spectacle of cruelty and blood.

Those who did not kill each other were ruthlessly murdered by the Skeleton Crew, so that the servants' hall presented a sickly and revolting sight, with the dead and dying lying around in all directions.

While the barbarous chief and his demon band were rejoicing at this human slaughter they drank deep of wine, and were roused up to a fiery pitch with the bloody work around them.

"Hurrah for the Skeleton Crew! the Scourge of the Seas!" said the chief, tossing off more wine. "In another hour old Sir Richard, and his braggart lad, Wildfire Ned, as he is called, will be no more. The old hag at the gibbet says the boy has a charmed life, but we shall quickly see. Ha! ha! there is no charm against cold steel, my lads!"

While thus he drank and laughed aloud in mocking tones he suddenly rose to his feet in alarm.

He drew his ponderous sword, and with fiery eyes listened!

A loud noise was now heard without.

The heavy doors were forced open with a crash!

With a loud and ringing cheer, there dashed in upon them fifty bold British tars, pistol and sword in hand, led on by Lieutenant Garnet and Wildfire Ned!

Death-wing (for such the Skeleton Chief was called), with a sudden bound, leaped from his high seat, sword in hand.

"Treachery!" he cried, and dashed upon Wildfire Ned, with bitter curses on his lips.

The conflict on all sides was dreadful.

Lieut. Garnet and his men did all that men could do, and performed prodigies of valour.

But their weapons did not seem to make any impression upon the Skeleton Crew.

Guns and pistols were fired at them, but all in vain.

The clash of swords and the gleam of daggers was heard and seen on every hand.

More than one of the gallant sailors was struck down by their ghostly foes.

"Death to them all, and spare not!" shouted Death-wing, the Skeleton Chief, with a loud laugh of triumph.

His ponderous sword swept through the air like a lightning flash.

On all sides he cut with unerring aim; but though he assailed Wildfire Ned with the fury of a demon, he could not slay him.

In rage and disappointment he growled, "This brat must have a charmed life; on to him, men, on to him, cut him limb from limb!"

With a shout of defiance Wildfire Ned met the onslaught of more of the Skeleton Crew.

But he handled his sword with such quickness and precision that he gallantly beat them back.

The tide of battle ebbed and flowed.

Success for a moment attended the Skeleton Crew, and they drove the sailors to the wall.

In an intant, however, and as if by magic, Wildfire Ned dashed again to the front.

"They are beaten!" he cried; "they give ground! Down with the demons! scatter their ghastly bones! Follow me!"

It was quite true.

The Skeleton Band did give way.

They had never met with such a fierce resistance before in all their lives.

They retreated in dumb terror before Wildfire Ned.

That brave youth rushed here, there and everywhere among his bloodthirsty foes, as if he courted death itself.

But no harm came to him.

His life was charmed, but he knew it not.

As if he had the strength of a young lion he fought his way to where Death-wing was, hand to hand with Garnet.

The lieutenant was struck to the ground, and in a moment would have been despatched.

Ned rushed to the rescue.

He stood over the body of the fallen sailor.

He confronted Death-wing face to face.

The Skeleton Chief retreated a step or two in fear from Wildfire Ned.

"I have tried to avoid you, but cannot," he gasped; "wherever I go you are in my way. Retire, boy, or I'll cleave ye in twain."

"From you! Never!" said Ned, "never, while I have health left in my body or strength to wield a sword!"

With these words he rushed at the grim chief, and again their weapons clashed in deadly conflict.

Sparks flew from their flashing blades.

Ned was getting weaker and weaker.

His legs trembled violently.

He made a last blow at his fierce antagonist and fell prostrate over Garnet.

Death-wing, with a laugh of triumph, raised his sword high in the air on the point of cutting Ned in two, when, with a wild shout, he rushed from the spot!

His sword was knocked from his firm grip!

He and his band looked with terror at the sight which then appeared.

A man in armour, glittering from head to foot in polished steel, rose out of the stone flooring as if by magic.

With shield and sword he was ready for the fray!

Sir Richard and the sailors were struck dumb at the strange apparition, and fell back in awe.

Death-wing and his Skeleton Crew hastened from the spot like shadows.

Before Sir Richard and his friends could recover from their astonishment the spectre of the armed knight in dazzling armour had vanished.

They were now alone.

With wondering eyes they looked at one another in mute astonishment.

"Is this all a dream?" gasped Sir Richard, breathing with great difficulty.

No one replied.

At that instant, however, all could hear the heavy tread of a mailed warrior as he clanked across the stone floor.

They looked about in surprise, for now all was darkness.

Their torches had been lost and extinguished in the heat and fury of battle.

Again they heard the heavy clanking footsteps, and the jingle of spurs cross the stone floor, but could see nothing.

They turned towards the door, through which they had found their way.

There stood the spectre knight glittering in steel, and with vizor down.

A long blue plume waved from his helmet.

His shield was of dazzling brightness.

Over his armour he wore a white tunic with a large red cross on his breast.

He raised his gauntlet-covered hand on high, and pointed to the adjacent stone corridor, as he said,

"Cut the victims down! Succour the wounded! Bury the dead!"

And vanished!

But long after these solemn words were uttered, and before any one could recover from surprise, they heard the heavy, distant foot-falls of the Spectre Knight.

Darlington Hall was haunted!

Cold perspiration oozed from their brows.

They trembled with awe, as, turning to the window, they saw a strange-like Will-o'-the-Wisp light dancing in the distant gloom.

Another moment, and the casement was dashed open.

Then a sound as of the clanking of chains and bones was heard, and a hollow voice saying,

"Behold, I am *the Red Man of the gibbet!*"

The Will-o'-the-Wisp light still danced round about, and in the centre stood the skeleton of the Red Man.

"What art thou?" said Sir Richard, fear, like an electric shot, passing through his frame.

The figure remained silent.

"Speak," said Wildfire Ned, "or my sword shall find out if you are man or devil!"

Saying so, Ned advanced towards the horrid shape at the casement.

"Back!" said the Skeleton form, stretching out his finger at Ned. "Your time has not yet come; but know, boy, I am your fate. Yes. Ha! ha! your fate!"

Ned, for a moment, felt slightly awed at the strange words spoken by the mysterious figure, who, with the light still playing about his head, stood regarding all with a terrible look.

"You lie!" replied Ned. "My fate is not in your hands, and I defy you. The Skeleton Crew shall find I have not gained my name of Wildfire Ned without being able to keep it."

"The Red Man," said the voice, "in the name of the Skeleton Crew, accept your challenge, and I now throw down my gage in token of defiance."

So saying, the figure threw down a hard substance on the floor.

Wildfire Ned picked it up.

It was a glove, and inside a SKELETON HAND!

"Ha! ha! now follow me if you dare!" shouted the Red Man, clanking his chains.

"I do dare, and will," said Ned, breaking from his uncle's hold, and dashing through the window after the Skeleton.

"Follow, follow quickly!" cried Sir Richard.

At the same moment they all fell back in fear as a shriek of mortal agony was borne along the wind and resounded throughout the old building.

"Oh, God!" cried the old man, "I fear the brave boy is slain."

---

## NOTICE TO OUR READERS.

REMEMBER!—A most valuable present is in preparation, and will be presented to all our regular Subscribers with an early Number. Full particulars will be announced in Number 6.

# THE SKELETON CREW; OR, WILDFIRE NED.

"THE MIDNIGHT DANCE OF THE SKELETON CREW."

Sword in hand Wildfire Ned dashed after the dreadful apparition, and well nigh overtook him as he ran along with wild fantastic leaps towards a densely-wooded copse.

It was at this moment, when, finding himself pursued, that the Red Man of the Gibbet gave that wild cry which so much alarmed Sir Richard Warbeck and his servants.

It was a terrible shriek, truly; more like that of a fiend than anything else.

What now followed was more horrible still, and caused Wildfire Ned to pause from sheer astonishment.

As the shriek came from the skeleton there sud-

denly sprang forward more than a dozen forms, and dashed in between the Red Man of the Gibbet and his pursuer.

With wild shrieks and yells the Skeleton Crew formed a circle round the Red Man, and in a second seemed to vanish into air!

Astounded at what he had seen, Wildfire Ned stood gazing like one just recovering from a trance, and observed not the approach of Sir Richard and his friends, who now rushed upon the scene, fearful for Ned's fate.

"Return, lad, return!" said Sir Richard, with a tremulous voice. "This night has been one of horrors; I fear for your safety. Whether they be men or devils, it matters not ; but of this rest assured, they are bent on your destruction."

A grim smile played upon Ned's features as he was reluctantly led back to the hall by Sir Richard and a large troop of friends.

When left alone to his own thoughts, and in the silence of his chamber, Wildfire Ned began to ponder on all that he had seen and heard.

"This is a terrible state of things ; but I will not sleep this night until I learn more of this strange horrible mystery, if it costs me my life."

When all was silent in the Hall, Ned buckled on his sword, and slowly left his chamber.

He traversed the lonely galleries of the Hall like a spirit, with noiseless step.

He quietly went towards the stables to saddle his favourite horse.

As he approached the stable door he was confronted by Tim, who looked more dead than alive.

"I could not sleep, master," said the groom, "the horrid sights as I have seen this ere night is enough to turn one grey."

"Nonsense," said Ned, with a light laugh, "nonsense, lad, you see it hasn't turned *me* grey."

"No, sir, truly ; but then you ain't made like common folks ; they say Wildfire Ned is all cast iron."

"Nonsense, Tim ; it's all a delusion to think that this Red Man of the Gibbet could leave his chains and go prowling about when he likes."

"No it ain't, sir, all respect to you, sir. I've heard people say that at some seasons of the year he does leave his chains. If he could talk to me, as I rode home, he can do anything ; that's *my* humble opinion."

"It can't be true," said Ned. "And, to prove it, I'll wager a hundred gold pieces that if we ride over to the Lonely Heath this very night we shall find the gibbet tenanted as it always is."

"Ride over to the gibbet, master ?" said Tim, in horror. "Surely, you can't think of doing anything so rash, and to night, too, when we know that all the country around is alive with that demon gang called the Skeleton Crew ?"

"Yes ; but I do though, Tim. I shall mount my brave mare, Starlight, and go at once."

"Oh ! master, pray don't," pleaded Tim ; "I'm sure that some harm will befal you."

"And I'm equally sure none will. Prepare Starlight at once. Saddle the brown cob also."

"The brown cob, sir ? You surely don't want two horses ?"

"Yes I do, Tim."

"What, the brown cob for the Red Man of the Gibbet," said Tim, aghast. "You surely ain't going to take a moonlight ride with such a horrible devil as he is."

"True, Tim, I am not," said Ned, laughing ; "the brown cob is for yourself."

"For me ?" said Tim, rolling his eyes.

"Yes, you. Come, be quick. Let us start off at once."

With many groans, Tim prepared the horses, and ere many minutes had elapsed, both master and servant were on their way to the heath.

Tim sadly tried to lag behind, but Wildfire Ned would not allow him to do so.

"Here, Tim," said Ned, producing a brandy-flask ; "take a good suck at this ; it will drive all the blue-devils out of you. Have courage, lad, no harm can possibly befal you."

Tim liked the brandy, but did not much relish his young master's stubborn resolution.

Nevertheless he had not got far upon the journey when his spirits began to rise rapidly, and his head became light and giddy.

He pulled out his sword in a very valorous manner, and made vicious cuts and slashes at the trees as he passed them, like a man valiantly fighting imaginary foes.

Ned perceived the effects the brandy had upon his servant, and gave him some more.

This had the desired effect of fortifying Master Tim with false courage.

Ere long he began to curse and swear at the Skeleton Crew and the Red Man of the Gibbet, in very loud tones.

After some time they approached the edge of the heath.

As they did so, the gibbet gradually came into view.

Tim's courage now began to ooze out of his toes, and he rode very close to his brave young master, but somewhat behind him.

"There it is, Tim," said Ned, pointing to the gibbet in the distance. "Can't you hear the creaking sound of its rusty iron as it sways to and fro ?"

"Y-e-e-s," answered Tim, and his teeth began to chatter. "Y-e-e-s, young master, I do ; but if you haven't any objection, I'll stay where I am until you return."

"But I *have* objections, Tim, and very grave ones. Haven't you promised to go to sea with me, and brave all the dangers and perils of the ocean ?"

"True, sir ; but I didn't bargain to go and confront living devils though," groaned Tim.

"Very well, then, it is in order to make you accustomed to strange sights and strengthen your nerves, that I brought you with me to-night."

"Very kind of you, sir," said Tim ; "very indeed ; but I thinks as how I've seen enough of strange sights to-night to strengthen my nerves for ever, if it's all the same to you, sir."

It was all to no purpose, Ned would not allow Tim to remain behind on any consideration, but smiled, as he cast a sidelong glance at his servant's long, pale face.

They had now approached within a few yards of the gibbet, and stopped to gaze at it.

"I told you how it was," said Ned, laughing. "It must have been all a trick, or delusion. Why here is the Red Man safe and sound in his iron gibbet ; he couldn't be in two places at once."

For some time the two horsemen remained motionless, intently gazing at the horrid gibbet, as it creaked and swayed in the moonlight.

The skeleton's bones were of unearthly whiteness and stood erect in their iron cage.

The winds sighed mournfully through the trees.

A feeling of awe took possession of the horsemen as they stood and gazed at the ghastly object.

Their steeds even trembled with excitement, and snorted and shied at the gallows and the shadow of its skeleton tenant.

"What are you trembling about ?" said Ned. "Be more of a man, Tim ; *I* don't see anything very strange."

"No, sir ; but *I* do. Look ! look ! see the red eyes are rolling about. I told you it were alive. See ! see ! Oh, horrors !" said Tim, shivering.

He would have backed his horse away, but Ned seized Tim's rein with his right hand firmly.

True enough, however, the skeleton in the gibbet *did* move.

Its eyes, which before were invisible in their deep-sunk sockets, now turned a deep, dark, fiery red colour, and rolled about most alarmingly.

Ned's horse reared and danced about, and he sat

looking on in mute astonishment, but with bold, firm-set features.

"It is alive ! it is alive, master! Let us get away ! it is—it *must* be the devil himself !"

"Hold thy peace," said Ned, in a petulant whisper.

And, then aloud, he addressed the ghastly, hideous form.

"Be ye devil or mortal, speak !" said Ned, fiercely. "Who and what art thou?"

The Red Man raised his skeleton arm, and suddenly thrust it through the grating of his prison-house, as he pointed his long, lean fingers, and said,

"Edward Warbeck, I am thine enemy ! Beware !"*

"Mine enemy ?" said Ned, with a grim smile.

"Aye, the same you saw this very night. At certain times and seasons I walk the earth ; beware, I say, of the Red Man of the Gibbet and the Skeleton Crew. I am thy fate ! When we meet again thou wilt tremble at my presence. Until we meet again, adieu !"

The long arm descended again by his grim, bony sides.

His red eyes lost their fiery lustre.

His marrowless bones shook in their iron cage.

All was still, quiet and solitary as the grave.

Nought was heard—nothing was seen but a stray vulture as it circled in the air near by and pounced on the gibbet.

Wildfire Ned was astonished, but not dismayed.

He laughed aloud in wild derision, as he said,

"Tremble at thy presence ? Never !"

The Red Man echoed the laugh in sepulchral tones.

Ned turned his head to look around.

Tim had left him, and was then madly galloping away.

Ned was alone at that awful spot !

---

## CHAPTER VII.

### PHILIP REDGILL'S ENCOUNTER WITH WILDFIRE NED.

IT was a lucky moment for some of the servants that old Sir Richard and his party of sailors did so suddenly burst upon the scene, and thus put an end to the bloody ordeal that was then taking place.

They had hung several to the beam, and some of the maid servants had been carried off.

Roger and the coachman lay upon the floor, thoroughly exhausted, bleeding from all parts of the body.

Tim, the groom, like a lively monkey, managed to climb up the rafters unseen, and hid himself behind a great beam.

But the sudden inroad of Wildfire Ned so exasperated the Skeleton Crew, that they gave no heed to the domestics, but turned all their attention to Lieut. Garnet and his sailors.

In the meantime the unfortunate servants stopped the deadly duels among themselves, and crawled out of the way of further harm.

Tim, however, directly Wildfire Ned appeared upon the scene, gave a wild shout, which almost cost him his life.

One of the Skeleton Crew perceived that he had got out of the way among the beams and rafters of the ceiling, and fired at him.

The bullet just grazed his cheek.

An inch more and he would have tumbled down dead.

As it was he merely screened himself safely again.

When he saw a good chance he whipped out his knife, and cut several of the ropes with which some of the servants had been hung.

They fell to the ground heavily.

But the shock seemed to revive the almost extinct life of several.

Tim then slipped down from his lofty perch, picked up a sword, and rushed to the side of Wildfire Ned, and capered about, and was such a thin, wiry young rascal, that the Skeletons always missed their aim.

Tim seemed to them to be made of india-rubber.

They couldn't touch him, do what they might, for, although his clothes were tattered, he escaped with a whole skin, much to his delight.

*     *     *     *     *

Several days after the stirring events we have just narrated, the wounded men were all provided for, and the dead buried.

This strange visit of the Skeleton Crew to Darlington, and the frightful scenes in the old immense servants' hall was the talk of the country far and wide.

It filled every one with amazement, and people began to think that, perhaps, after all, the mysterious murder of Farmer Bertram might be traced to the same source, particularly since poor Bob, the farmer's son, protested his innocence so loudly and boldly.

But appearances were strongly against the farmer's son.

His own thick walking-stick was found beside the murdered man.

The old farmer's purse, one he had but a week before bought in the village, was found in the pocket of his accused son.

These evidences of guilt were too strong to allow of any doubt but that the unhappy son had, in a moment of anger and revenge, murdered his own father.

There was one, however, who *did* believe in poor Bob's innocence.

That was Wildfire Ned.

He visited Bob in prison, and spent several hours with him.

When he came away he told old Sir Richard that the prisoner was an innocent man, and was sure he had been duped by some cunning villain.

"Bob must not suffer," said Ned ; "he *shall* not suffer, while I've got a hand to help him."

"*Shall* not!" said Sir Richard, in amazement ; "Who's to prevent it, if he's found guilty?"

"Who ? why, *I* will," said Wildfire Ned, colouring to the temples.

"You ?"

"Yes, *me*, uncle. No rope shall ever go round Bob's neck while there is a sword in the village to prevent it."

"Silly boy," said the knight, with a smile, "I know that you are brave, no one can doubt that ; but what could *you* do against so many ?"

"Let them dare attempt to hang him in Darlington, and you would soon see what Wildfire Ned would do."

"But they will not hang him here in the village. Most likely they will take him to the nearest large town, perhaps to London, for all I know."

"I wish they *would* take him to London," said Ned, with a smile.

"Indeed ! And what then, pray ?"

"Why, I would arm and lead on a party of gallant youths. We would soon beat back the soldiers."

While they were speaking thus, a servant announced that a stranger had arrived at the Hall.

"His name?"

"Mr. Philip Redgill, sir."

"Show him up; *he* is no stranger; he is a relation. Show him up."

The knight seemed pleased at the unexpected coming of his nephew.

Phillip soon entered.

He was most elegantly attired, and carried a sword.

His face was rather handsome, but he had a dark, wicked-looking eye.

There was an uneasy twitch about his mouth, and when he smiled he showed a set of large teeth.

When he entered the room, he cast a quick, vicious look towards Ned.

Immediately after, however, he wore a forced smile, and shook Sir George very cordially with his ungloved hand.

He turned towards Wildfire Ned, and extended his hand towards him also, in a cold, formal way.

"It is not necessary," said Ned, with a proud toss of his head; "your hand is cold and clammy; it gives me the shivers; its feel is fishy, Phillip Redgill."

Saying this, he left the room with a flashing eye and proud step.

"Queer youth that, Sir George," said Phillip, with a bitter smile.

"At the same time," he thought, "I'd give a thousand pounds to know he was dead; he seems thrown in my path to thwart me."

"But he is a brave youth," said Sir George, in flattering tones.

"Is he," laughed Redgill; "I have often thought he was a very rash one."

"His best friends say the same; but it will all wear off with age and experience."

"Perhaps so, Sir Richard; but it strikes me very forcibly he will never live to be any very great age," said Redgill, very slowly and with great emphasis.

"Why not?" said the old knight, quickly.

"He is too passionate. Had it not been for my own good temper, and the respect I have for you, I should have publicly horsewhipped him for his rudeness to me on more than one occasion."

"But you are older than he is, Phillip," sternly said Sir Richard; "you must remember that."

"True; but no more of that. I have come from London expressly to inform you that my father, through his influence with the king's government, has managed to get a midshipman's commission for Ned, this great favourite of yours. If you like to consent, he can join his ship at once; it lies at Portsmouth, ready to sail."

"It was very kind of your father, truly; but I have not made up my mind about it."

"Not made up your mind? Why, when last I was down here, you said it would be the very best thing that could be done for him."

"True; but I have altered my mind since then. I should be very sorry to part with young Ned, and if any harm were to happen to him, I think it would kill me, for the more I see of him the more I like the lad."

"Ha, ha!" laughed Phillip; "there is no fear of that; the ship he would join will never sail more than ten miles out of port, so there's no fear that your intended heir to the Darlington estates will come to harm."

"The intended heir to my estates, Phillip Red-

gill!" said the old man. "Ned and his brother are poor orphans, and have no real claim on me."

At this moment Ned entered the room quietly and heard all that had been said.

"I was only joking," Phillip replied, with a dry laugh.

When his eye caught sight of Ned he changed countenance on the instant.

Ned gazed at him fixedly with a look of proud contempt.

"Phillip Redgill," said Ned, defiantly, "I have by mere accident overheard all you have said."

"What! an eavesdropper in the hall!" said Redgill, with a sneer.

"If you say so, you lie!" said Ned, fiercely; "and, to show you how little I think of you, how much I despise you, take that!" he said, slapping Redgill in the face, "and, if you dare, resent it."

In an instant the colour rose to Redgill's face.

He drew his sword and darted towards Wildfire Ned.

"Come on," said Ned, whipping up the old knight's sword that lay on the table.

"Put down your swords," the old man cried, getting between them. "What is the meaning of all this?"

Redgill looked for a second at the firm, handsome features of Wildfire Ned, and the eagle-like glance of the brave lad cowed his own craven heart.

He could not look him in the face.

"Come on," said Ned. "Nay, turn not so deadly pale, coward."

"Put up your weapons, I say," the old man said, sternly.

Redgill did so, and bit his lips until they became bloodless and white.

"Why carry a sword if afraid to use it?" said Ned, scornfully turning on his heel.

After a pause Wildfire Ned said, calmly and slowly—

"Redgill, you are not a man; you are a coward, a snake in the grass; you leave a poisonous slime wherever you go. Bloody deeds follow in your wake wherever you tread! There is no love lost between us, 'tis true; but you are a mischief-maker; a deceiver; I could say more perhaps."

"Say on," said Redgill, turning pale.

"Murderer is marked on your face, Phillip Redgill," said Ned, sternly. "Nay, do not tremble, for I know nought of what you have done; but I suspect and despise you, leaving it in the hands of heaven one day to disclose what you are. You need not fear that *I* shall stand in your path to wealth or fame. Trust me, I have too much heart and spirit to eat the bread of charity longer at Sir Richard's table; but, ere I leave, remember these my words. Redgill," he said, after a solemn pause, "you will one day grace a gibbet; rogue, vagabond, and murderer is deeply written on your countenance. You cannot, you dare not look an honest lad openly in the face. Your own cowardly heart tells you I speak the truth; and, were it not for the disgrace to good Sir Richard, I could slay you as you sit, and think, aye, know that I had done right in the sight of man and heaven. Sir Richard, I now leave the Hall, my everlasting love is yours. Upon the wide world I go to seek my fortune; but beware of that man's evil eye. Sir Richard, shun him like a snake. Phillip Redgill, we shall meet again."

"We will," was the bitter answer.

In an instant Wildfire Ned left the room.

The village clock tolled the hour of midnight.

He left Darlington Hall, and perhaps for ever!

## CHAPTER VIII.

RELEASE OF BOB—CAPTAIN JACK'S BAND—THE UNEXPECTED ARRIVAL — THE QUARREL — THIRTEEN DEATH WARRANTS—FLIGHT OF THE THIEF-TAKERS.

BOB the outcast, as we have seen, was thrown into prison, and safely guarded by the village authorities.

As may be supposed, poor Bob was almost turned crazy by the terrible event, and walked up and down his prison cell looking pale, thoughtful, and miserable.

He protested his innocence on all occasions.

Many believed that the murderers or murderer would in time be traced to the far-famed Skeleton Crew, who prowled around the neighbouring coasts.

The keeper of the village prison was a timid old man, and much feared that the red-hot zeal on the part of some of Bob's sympathisers might lead them on to attack the gaol, perhaps attempt a rescue.

This so weighed upon the chief constable's mind that he wrote off to London, begging of the authorities there to take the case in hand.

In accordance with the wishes of the village authorities a party of men were sent down to Darlington for the purpose of conducting Rambling Bob to London.

The party consisted of seven mounted men, all armed to the teeth, who arrived in the village one evening, several days after the commission of the murder.

They pulled up their horses, and alighted at the "Red Lion" public-house.

With many loud words, a great deal of bombastic talk and swearing, they clattered about the inn yard, shouting to the ostlers and servants in such a grand style that old Hornblower, the publican, began to think that perhaps his visitors were none other than royal personages, or nobles, at least.

Old Horn (the "blower" always being left out in common discourse) was very much mistaken; the new arrivals were none other than six thief-takers, and as big rogues and rascals as ever strad-dled horses, or swaggered about with swords at their heels.

They were dressed in their best, however, and seemed very flush of money; how they got it will be seen hereafter.

They rang the bells loudly, shouted and swore right and left until old Horn and his servants were almost driven mad.

"Who be they?" asked the ostler.

"Don't know, lad; but suppose they're very great folks."

"They ride good nags, anyhow."

"And kick up a darned big fuss, too. Can't ye hear 'em?"

"They be Londoners," said the housemaid; "I can tell by their talk, and they allers do make a noise when they goes in the country."

"What do they want down here, I wonder?"

"Can't tell; but they ask for the best beds in the inn, and the best wine in the cellar, so they mun have plenty of money."

While the servants were thus talking among themselves the old landlord and his kitchen domestics were busy in providing supper for the hungry travellers.

"Boots" was nearly run off his legs, and didn't know what to do first.

He became confused, and forgot half of what he was told.

"Here, lad," said one, "bring me some brandy. Quick. Hot, mind!"

"Brandy, sir, yes, sir. Hot sir? With or without? Just so, sir. Brandy hot without, sir? Thank'ee, sir."

And off he shot.

But before he had fairly closed the door,

"Here! hi! waiter! quick!" said another. "Mulled port for me. Quick, for your life! I'm almost frozen to death!"

"Port, sir? Yes, sir. Mulled, sir? Thank'ee, sir."

Off he went; but the bell was rung violently again.

"Here! hi! waiter!"

"Come here, lad!"

"I want you, do you hear?"

"Serve me first."

"No; I gave my order first."

"No you didn't."

"Spiced ale."

"Bring me a chop in less than five minutes, or I'll cut your head off!"

"My brandy and water, you idiot!"

"If my hot spiced ale doesn't appear in three minutes by the clock, I'll blow the rascal's brains out."

"Will you never let me have my brandy and water, you villain?"

"Cut the rascal's ear off."

"How's my horse getting on?"

"Let my bed be warmed."

"Not mine, stupid; his, mind."

"Where's the landlord?"

"Brandy!" "Ale!" "Rum!" "Bottle of wine! "Beefsteaks!" "A chop for me!" "Clean my boots!" "See to my horse!" "Long pipes!" "Stir up this fire!" "Put more coals on!" "How long's supper going to be?"

These and such-like orders rung in the bewildered ears of Nat the boots.

He rushed hither and thither like a wild man all of a sweat.

He forgot half his orders, and so mixed up the others that he was kicked and cuffed about like a foot-ball by the noisy and by no means polite strangers.

Take them altogether this half-dozen were as ugly and as villanous-looking a lot as could be well met with anywhere.

They all had the marks of rogues and cut-throats engraven on their countenances.

Some were decorated with black patches across the forehead, over the eye, or on their high cheek bones.

One or two were minus an eye.

One individual's nose was almost level with his face.

Several had part of their front teeth knocked out; but each had big thick fists, with which from time to time they struck the table until they made the glasses dance and ring again.

Loud and coarse was their laughter, and when they smiled at any passing joke or observation, their countenances were more like those of hyenas just about feeding time than human beings.

The recognised leader of this desperate half-dozen was called Captain Jack, an individual of great strength, who delighted in much swearing and obscene conversation. Jack what, no one knew for certain, not even those who employed him.

When at last supper was provided for this very select and genteel party they set to work vigorously with knives and forks, and soon demolished a huge amount of meat and vegetables, more than would have sufficed for any ordinary supper party of twenty individuals.

They feasted, and swore, and laughed, and bolted their food in a heathenish style, as if all of them had been fasting for a month.

Long, copious draughts of various beverages washed the prog down their capacious throats, and they occasionally enlivened the proceedings by throwing potatoes at Nat the waiter, and hitting him in the eye, on the nose, &c., until "Boots's" face was bumped and swollen.

When the repast was over these six elegant individuals and their captain stretched themselves on chairs, and puffed clouds from long pipes, as if they were the first gentlemen in the land instead of the greatest rascals unhung.

"As I was saying, lads," Capt. Jack observed, after drinking some brandy and water, "as I was saying I shouldn't have taken this pretty job in hand, you know, only it gave us all a chance to do a little business on the road on our private account."

"True," growled Tom Bates, an oldish, ugly-looking person, with one eye and a broken nose, "true, captain, and when yer did want anybody, in course you knowed where to find 'em. Ah! we've had some r-a-r-e old times together, haven't we, cap'n?" said Bates, with a long-drawn sigh, which he further suppressed with a flood of spiced ale down his throat.

"True, Tom; but the idea of the 'Baker's Dozen,' as we are called, was yours."

"In course it were," said Bates. "But I arn't at all proud; it were only a lucky thought. When you got your fust job from the justices what could a-been a neater idea than to have a company o' twelve or thirteen good trusty lads about ye, when times were busy, all sworn to secrecy and fair shares o' booty?"

[It must be here explained, for the reader's information, that Captain Jack had been such a noted thief and rascal in his time that he had often been, and was now regularly, employed as thief-taker.

But this position only gave him opportunities of becoming a still greater scoundrel. With this view, he and Tom Bates formed the idea of having a band of twelve or thirteen men, who should act under the captain's orders, and, under cover of being the thief-taker's occasional assistants, would thus have an ample chance of "turning a dishonest penny to their own account."

This was agreed upon, and the band formed; the name under which they were known was the "Baker's Dozen."

Each man had a particular talent, one for house-breaking, a second for counterfeiting, a third for horse-stealing, and so on.

The authorities never dreamed that such a banded company existed, and placed all faith in Captain Jack, although he was the greatest rogue in England, as will be seen in this exciting narrative.]

"We've often heard the whole story before, Tom," said Faulkner, another of the company, "so cut it for the present; it's been many a good year in existence, and I warrant ye hadn't as many grog blossoms on your nose afore it started as ye have now."

"Stow that, Faulkey," said Bates. "I've got corns as well as grog blossoms, mind, and you wouldn't a-been one o' the dozen at all 'cept for me—no, that yer wouldn't; but I know what yer would a been."

"What?"

"Why, meat for wultures and night carrion birds, as pay their respects to the gibbets."

This remark made all laugh, for it was well-known among them that Faulkner would have

been hung on the charge of robbery had not Bates induced Captain Jack to swear that he was innocent.

"Well, enough of charf," said Captain Jack; "let's to business. Is that door shut?"

"Yes."

"Well, let one of ye go and stand outside to give the office if any one comes in."

This was done.

They all clustered round the table, and dived their hands down into their capacious pockets.

One produced a purse, another some finger and ear-rings; two others had a bundle of bank-notes, watches, snuff-boxes, the diamond hilts of broken swords, jewelled shoe and dress buckles; and other things of value were displayed.

"You haven't been idle on the road, I see," said Captain Jack, with a grin. "This makes up for our unpleasant journey down here for that silly bumpkin."

While they were dividing the booty Captain Jack was deep in figures, and so was Tom Bates, that the entire swag might be apportioned so as to give themselves the greatest share.

While thus engaged, Bates raised his eyes towards the parlour window.

"Dam'me if there ain't some one peeping through the round hole in the shutter!" he stammered.

In an instant he pulled out his pistol, and fired!

The ball smashed the glass, and went right through the hole.

Some one was heard to fall outside.

Tom Bates rushed to the window, and flung the shutter open.

No one was there!

"Well, if I didn't hit him, I must have shaved him closely," said Bates, and closed the window again.

The moment Captain Jack had divided the spoil, a horseman was heard to halt at the inn door.

"A traveller, and at this late hour. Who can it be?" said the select party in the parlour. "Who can it be?"

"Here, waiter" said one and another, "don't let the place be over-crowded, there are seven of our party here already; you can't accommodate any more."

"I swear I'll have no half bed to-night."

"Nor I either."

"Tell him to seek lodgings elsewhere in the village, landlord!"

"He shan't sleep with me," growled Bates, "whoever he is."

"You needn't put yourself out of temper, friend," said the stranger, entering in a free and easy manner. "You needn't put yourself into any flurry, for I wouldn't have such an ugly-looking bed-fellow for all the gold in England."

As he said this he cut Bates across the shoulders with his riding-whip.

"Hillo, what means this?" said Bates, spluttering with rage. "I say, my fine, dandy gentleman, do you know who you're cutting about the shoulders with your riding-whip? Take no such liberties, young man, or you may repent of it."

"Tut, tut, man, you don't know how to stand a joke."

"That's no joke, as you'll quickly find, if you're not very civil," growled Bates, puffing his pipe.

"This parlour is engaged," said Captain Jack.

"I see it is," the stranger said, coolly.

"The beds are all engaged."

"You had better go elsewhere."

"We don't wish to be disturbed; we are all friends here."

"So I perceive," said the stranger, coolly; "and I'm the last man in the wide world to make you enemies."

He was cloaked, and wore his hat over his eyes. A strongly-built, elegant-looking gentleman he was, with pale face, fine eyes, and a dashing moustache.

His hands were remarkably white, but he seemed to have the strength of a vice in them.

He took a chair, and drew up to the fire.

"That chair belongs to one of our party, sir," said Faulkner.

"Then let him get another," said the new arrival, very coolly. "Waiter, bring me a bottle of wine, and call the landlord. I wish to speak to him."

Nat brought the wine.

The stranger sipped it, threw a sovereign to the waiter in a careless manner, saying—

"Keep the change. Here, landlord, I want my horse looked after, give him the best stall in the stable."

"There is not a stall vacant, sir."

"Then turn some horse out, and put mine in. I want a bed also, the best bed in the inn."

"All my beds are occupied."

"It matters not; do as I tell you, or you'll repent it."

"You are a werry rude bragadocia fellow to speak thus in the presence of gentlemen," said Tom Bates to the stranger.

"What do you say, old bilberry nose? Mind your own business."

"I say, sir, that in the presence of gentlemen—"

"Gentlemen, ha! ha!—that's good, hang me if it isn't—you look very much like a gentleman, certainly; if that large wart was off the tip of your nose it would much improve your appearance."

"Sir-r-r!" growled Bates, rising in anger. "What do you mean? Do you know who I am?" said he, slapping his sword hilt.

"Oh, sit down and take it coolly," the stranger replied, laughing. "Don't stand there gaping like a half-stuck pig. Know you, of course I know you."

"Then, sir, if you do, you know me to be a gentleman—an administrator of justice."

"I know you to be a d—d old thief, the biggest liar, and, at a pinch, the biggest coward in all London," the stranger replied.

"Thief! liar! coward!" gasped Bates, whipping out his sword. "If you are a man, defend yourself."

"If you are not a fool, sit down; you can't frighten me. I'm too old a bird for that."

This quarrel had now thoroughly aroused Captain Jack's party, who were noisy and boisterous; but they did not interfere, for they imagined that Bates was more than a match for the stranger.

"Draw, I say!" growled Bates, "or I'll slay ye like a dog! Clear the way, there, comrades; leave this impudent rascal to me."

"Sit down, or I'll knock your head off!" was the cool reply.

Bates, all furious and maddened at the stranger's calmness, made a fierce lunge at him.

The instant he did so, however, the stranger fired a pistol, and knocked the large wart from the tip of Bates's nose, and next instant gave him such a smack on the jaw as laid that hero sprawling on the floor.

Tom Bates was thunder-struck, and sat upon the floor looking at the stranger with eyes of wonderment.

His friends were equally astonished, and for a moment it looked as if the whole party were intent on slaying the new comer.

"Stand back," said he, waving them off; "put up your sword. I fear ye not, vagabonds, but listen to me; if one dare approach nearer I'll scalp him."

There was so much of determination, and an air of superiority about him, that all stood still and looked at him as if transfixed to the spot.

"Listen to me, knaves," said he, eyeing every one of them with a keen look. "How many chief high roads are there leading out of London?"

"Thirteen," Captain Jack answered, after a moment's thought. "But what has that got to do with us?"

"Much more than you imagine. Since you left London, a new gibbet has been erected on each of those thirteen highways, just where they branch off at the cross roads."

"Well!" said all in a breath, "and what of that? I don't understand what all of this means."

"But I do! It means this: those gibbets have been raised at the sole expense of a particular friend of yours."

"For whom?"

"For each of you."

"And who is this very particular, very dear, friend of ourn?" growled Faulkner.

"I am he!" said the stranger.

The rascals were tongue-tied at the stranger's boldness as he went on.

"You came to conduct Bob Bertram to London?"

"We did! who could have told you?"

"Who told me that each of you went plundering on the way, and divided the booty just now?"

"Ha!" said Captain Jack; "watched, betrayed!"

"Silence," said the stranger; "if you do not wish to be gibbeted before your time, This youth is accused of murder, but he did it not. He is not in Darlington gaol."

"Not in gaol?"

"No; he has escaped."

"How know you this?"

"I just came from the village. All is in an uproar. Wildfire Ned, Sir Richard Warbeck's adopted nephew, is the hero who released him."

The thievish thief-takers were amazed at what they heard.

"And now," said the stranger; "since your mission here is ended, return to town; do you hear me? Return this very hour and carry this strange news to the proper authorities. And mark me, Captain Jack, every one of you remember that if you do not track and discover the real murderer of Farmer Bertram in less than two months, I'll report you to the king; your death-warrants are now in my pocket. See them," said the stranger, exhibiting a bundle of printed forms. "Here is one for Captain Jack, another for this red-nosed ass on the floor—Bates, I mean—a third for Faulkner there; in fine, I have been kind enough to provide each of you with a passport into the other world. As you may observe, they only require my signature."

"And who the devil are you!" gasped out one and all.

"I'll let you see—but I had better write it on one of these death-warrants, say yours, Captain Jack, it will save me trouble afterwards. Landlord, pen and ink."

"Do you know that name?" said the stranger, after writing it.

All the rascals looked at it in astonishment.

"The devil!" said Captain Jack.

"Not the devil, exactly," said the stranger.

coolly; "but your very humble servant, *Colonel Blood!* a gentleman, I can assure you, who will feel great pleasure in introducing each of you to the common hangman, unless you produce in two months the real murderer of Farmer Bertram, and serve me at all times."

The stranger was in truth no other than Colonel Blood, but what brought him so far from London was a mystery which we shall have to clear up shortly.

## CHAPTER IX.

THE MILLER'S DAUGHTER—COLONEL BLOOD FALLS INTO ROUGH HANDS—THE MURDER ON THE BRIDGE.

THE reason that Colonel Blood was so far from London is easily explained by what took place in Darlington the second night of his visit.

The miller of the village, Hugh Harmer, had a very pretty daughter named Ellen, who was the pride and the toast of the surrounding country.

Like a hawk poised in the air, gazing on his intended prey below, did Colonel Blood hover around Hugh Harmer's house close by the bubbling and splashing mill-stream.

He had espied Ellen by chance, and in her saw not the virtuous village maiden, but a beautiful object for his master, the Merry Monarch, who, Blood knew, would pay any price to gratify his beastial passions.

Captain Jack and his rough party had left the inn but half-an-hour, when a card was brought to Blood by some one old Horn had never seen before.

"Admit the stranger, landlord," said Blood.

A sorrowful-looking fellow walked in, hat in hand. He was very wet from head to foot, and his clothes were in rags around him.

"Have you seen her?"

"Her answer is here," said the stranger, producing a small note out of his breast pocket.

Blood tore it open, and read it.

His eye sparkled with fire, and his handsome features twitched as he perused its contents, which ran as follows:—

"SIR,—Our first meeting, I fear, has caused much uneasiness and unhappiness to both.

"But, notwithstanding your constant letters and frequent visits to Darlington, I fear that your intentions cannot be so disinterested towards me as your eloquent notes would have me believe.

"This thought has often occurred to my mind since I first imprudently met you, and is more and more confirmed by the fact that you impress upon me the necessity of keeping our correspondence a secret from my dear old father, which no person, having honourable intentions, would ever propose to a simple country girl.

"As a last favour I beg that you will no more insult me with your proposals of eloping from my father's roof, or ever again presume to throw yourself purposely in my path to pour poisonous councils into my ears.

"In fine, sir, I fear I have too long been the dupe of your designs, and until, as a virtuous girl, I can sign my name on the marriage register of the village church, I will never leave my father's home, even should I love the man ever so much who bade me act otherwise.

"Your humble servant,
"ELLEN HARMER."

"Clever as she's pretty; but quick and sharp as a needle," thought Blood. "So much the better for King Charles."

"Did you miss the old man as usual?" asked Blood.

"No, sir; for once he caught me," said the servant, with a very rueful face.

"Then you had an adventure. What said he to you?"

"'Oh! it's you, is it? Here again, eh, and always when I'm out,' says he, flourishing his walking-stick, and then he shouted to the dogs, 'On to him Rover! give it him, Spot! hold tight, Jip!' and all the while he was laying on to me with his thick stick without mercy.

"Quite a pleasant affair," said Blood, with a smile.

"Yes, sir, to think about; but not very agreeable if you have to go through it."

"Well, well, I don't wonder why old Harmer takes so much care of her, for she's one of the daintiest little maidens that ever trod the earth," said Blood. "No matter, if he had her locked up in a castle it would be all the same, she must be the king's. To-night is the last time she'll sleep under her father's roof. Come, Jonas," for such was his shivering servant's name; "go change your clothes, and have a stiff glass of brandy, I shall want you about midnight to go to the miller's house with me."

"Again to-night, sir?" gasped Jonas. "Why, only you look here," and as he turned round he exhibited to his master the seat of his trousers, his cloak, and other parts of his attire all in ribands.

"Never mind, Jonas, you always had a reputation for courage; here's a guinea for you. Go, prepare yourself."

Midnight was passed, and at an appointed time Jonas met his master, and both proceeded towards the miller's.

Colonel Blood sauntered along in the silence of the night towards Harmer's house, as handsome, bold, and cool-handed a knave as ever lived.

He had just reached the narrow mill bridge, when he perceived the dark figure of a young man leaning over the hand-rail, and gazing in the shining water. Directly he heard the approach of footsteps, he turned, and his eyes sparkled with fierce delight.

"'Tis he!" said the young man, "I cannot be mistaken. I have long desired this meeting. I came to bury myself beneath these shining waters, but ere I do, let me crush the skull of this villain, who has ruined me and blasted all my happiness; for, before his accursed shadow darkened our village, I was happy: but now, alas! Ellen Harmer's heart is another's."

Colonel Blood approached, and had reached the centre of the bridge, when the youth suddenly confronted him with boldness and flashing eyes.

"What, Andrew Gamble!" said Blood, starting back a step or two in surprise.

"Aye!" said Andrew, with a quivering lip. "Does that name startle your wicked heart?"

"Startle *me*, knave!" said Blood, with an air of great contempt. "Make way, there! why do you cross my path again?"

"Because you've crossed mine, and shall die," said Andrew, advancing.

"Make way, there, I say!" said Blood, drawing his sword. "Let me pass, I like not your looks—there is murder in your eyes. Make way, I tell ye, before I cleave ye to the ground."

## NOTICE TO OUR READERS.

# THE SKELETON CREW; OR, WILDFIRE NED.

THE FIGHT BETWEEN WILDFIRE NED AND THE SKELETON CREW.

"Ha! ha!" laughed Andrew, "you can flourish your toasting-fork, I see, just as cleverly as I can my father's flail; but you don't frighten me, for all that, fine gentleman as you are."

"Once, for all, make, way fellow! or I'll cleave No. 4.

your skull," said Blood. "I cannot afford to waste valuable time in parleying with a country clown."

He had scarcely spoken the word, when Andrew Gamble rushed suddenly upon his enemy and disarmed him in an instant.

Colonel Blood was thunder-struck.

The action had been so sudden, and the weapon so cleverly wrenched from his grasp, that he stood gaping in surprise.

"Make way there," said Andrew, flourishing the sword in a malicious manner, much as a rustic would a stout oak cudgel.

Colonel Blood retired a pace or two in evident fear of his brawny antagonist.

"Villain! you quail," said Andrew, with a savage laugh; "you quail and turn pale before the very man you just now threatened; but fear not, I will not, as you would have done, raise my weapon against a defenceless man. I could take thy life; for, until the unlucky day your shadow darkened our village, I was happy. Happy! aye, as happy as a king. I loved, and was loved in return, but your hellish schemes and flattery have torn her from me; you have poured poison into my loved one's ear, you have taught her to despise the one who would willingly have laid down his life for her. Listen, villain, your rascality has long been known to me, but chance has never thrown me in your way until now, and here upon the mill bridge, in the stillness of the night, let me tell you that one or both of us must *die!*"

These words were uttered by Andrew Gamble with a great effort.

His manly breast heaved, and his voice became tremulous as, in a few words, he disclosed the secret, and the cause of his enmity to the stranger.

"*Die!*" said Blood, calmly, but with a trembling lip.

He seemed charmed and fixed to the spot by the fierce brilliancy of Andrew's eyes.

"*Die!*" he muttered again, half aloud.

"Yes, *die!*" said young Gamble, with a fiery pride. "Think you I care to live and see Ellen Harmer given to another? Could I, can I live, now that the only charm life had for me is snatched away?"

"I never harmed you," said Blood, coolly and collectedly.

"'Tis false, villain!" the youth replied. "Have you not had spies around her? have you not dazzled her with your dishonest words and manner? have you not written dozens of letters to her inviting her to run from her father's home, and become a lady in London? Why not show your face at her father's house like any honest man? Why traduce me? Am I not as good as you? If you are a man so am I; we are equal; the tinsel and ribbons of your court-cut coat makes you no better gentleman than Andrew Gamble, the farmer's son. Nay, curl not your lip, but hear me. This meeting: it is our first and last. You see this sword," said Andrew, passionately; "there is but one between us, we will divide it."

So saying, he placed the weapon across his knee, and snapped it in twain.

"Choose," said Andrew, "the hilt or point, whiche'er you will."

"You are bent upon bloodshed," said the colonel; "you are rash, wild, and know not what you do; neither do you know me, if you did you would tremble at such an encounter. I am the best swordsman in all England."

"And I the worst," said Andrew: "it matters not, come on."

Colonel Blood took the point half of the broken sword and wrapped his handkerchief round the thick end for a handle.

Andrew had the thick half.

The two blades met.

Blood was as cool as ice.

There was upon his handsome face a smile of confidence and contempt for his rustic rival.

Andrew, on the contrary, was all on fire, and trembled with haste and excitement.

In an encounter between two such swordsmen the result could not for a moment be doubtful.

Andrew made a lunge that was prettily stopped by Colonel Blood.

His next attempt, however, was more successful.

Andrew rushed to closer distance, and pricked the arm, from which blood flowed copiously.

"Damnation!" swore the infuriated swordsman. "To be beaten by this country clown is a lasting disgrace; nevertheless, he shan't live to boast of it!"

He gathered himself together for a final stroke, which would have proved fatal to the brave rustic, but Andrew turned the colonel's point.

A desperate struggle now ensued on the narrow bridge.

They seized each other by the throat.

Their weapons were in dead lock.

A single moment would decide all.

The strength of each was about equal, and giant-like were their struggles.

But a trick saved Blood.

He quickly placed one foot behind Andrew's leg and back-heeled him.

This was fatal to Andrew.

He fell.

In the act of falling Colonel Blood stabbed him.

The brave rustic threw up his hands with a sharp cry of pain, and rolled into the shining river.

"Fool!" said Colonel Blood, with a contemptuous oath, as he looked into the bright waters beneath him, rippling and eddying in the moonlight. "Fool! How dare the village dolt to cross my path; so be it with all who dare cross the path of Colonel Blood."

He threw the red blade into the small narrow river stream, and bound up his arm with his handkerchief.

"Now for the pretty wench," said he. "If I succeed in carrying her forth, my fortune is made. Stop! what was that sound?"

He stood and listened.

"Help! help!" cried a distant voice. "Murder! Help! help!"

---

## CHAPTER X.

### JONAS MEETS WITH A STRANGE ADVENTURE.

WHEN Jonas left his master to go to their rendezvous he little dreamt of what was in store for him.

The horses and carriage were drawn up at the appointed spot, and Jonas, thinking of the large reward which the colonel had often promised him, was on the bright look out for the pre-arranged signal.

Now, as we have seen, Miller Harmer had been informed of this mysterious stranger in Darlington, and had watched him and his servant, and even heard the pre-arranged signal.

He had long sighed for an opportunity of confronting the bold stranger, who so slyly had crept into the good graces of his daughter, but whose name, rank, and intentions he knew not.

The first thing to do was to procure assistance.

He went straightway to the lock-up, and informed the authorities of his suspicions.

"It may be one of them chaps as came in masks t'other night and rescued Bob Bertram," said a burly officer, indignant at the idea of the disgrace which had thus been cast upon them.

For it must be explained here that Wildfire Ned and his groom had effected Bob's rescue in the manner described about one o'clock in the morning, when all the village was wrapped in sleep, and the two constables on guard were half tipsy.

"If it only be one o' *them* chaps," said the chief officer, "I'd give a hundred gold pieces, that I would, for I shall never rest content till I have cracked one o' their skulls; the mean devils, to come when no one expected on 'em, and fight their way in and out of the lock-up."

This thought was alike echoed by all.

They felt great annoyance that two youths should have possessed the nerve and courage to fall upon the lock-up guard, and thrash them as Wildfire Ned and Tim the groom had done.

If Ned had sent warning that he was coming to rescue Bob, the constables, of course, would have been there a dozen strong to oppose him, and this they considered would have been "fair play."

But now that Miller Harmer brought information that there was more than one suspicious stranger in the village, the constable made sure that they were the identical two they so much desired to capture.

From the bustle and preparations made by the half dozen constables one would suppose that the valiant guardians of the public peace were bent upon storming some castle or stronghold.

With lanterns and staves and clubs they sallied forth.

"Lead on, Mr. Miller," said the chief, buttoning up his doublet. "Lead on, sir, we'll give the two rascals such a dressing as they never had before in all their lives."

Old Harmer conducted the constables to his mill.

He unlocked the huge doors and admitted them.

They hid themselves behind a lowering pile of corn and flour sacks, and darkened their lanterns.

"Stand firm, my merry men," said the chief of the party. "Stand firm; and when the signal is given arrest the rascal as he enters."

Miller Harmer now went to the half-opened door.

He gave three shrill whistles, each after an interval of about half a minute.

"Here the villain comes," said Harmer, hiding himself.

Jonas at that moment was observed approaching in a stealthy, cat-like manner, crawling along under the shadow of the trees and cottages of the village.

He was seen to stop once or twice, and look furtively around him.

He did not know why, but a feeling of suspicion assured him that in some way his master's scheme for abducting Ellen Harmer would involve heavy blows, if not broken sconces.

He had armed himself, therefore, with a stout, short club of oak, which he concealed under his cloak.

As he approached the mill door he was half-inclined to run away again."

"Courage, Jonas, courage," said he to himself, half aloud. "Remember the rich reward in store for you. The colonel, my master, is a bold, brave devil, and I must be so likewise. So I am," said Jonas, slapping his chest. "Who knows but what I may be a gentleman one of these fine days, if all goes on well? Won't that be grand? Courage, then, Jonas; none but the brave deserve the fair. Onward! rewards and honour await you! That whistle, though, didn't much sound like master's," he thought, "and yet it must be. There it is again. All is right; the girl is secured. Onward, Jonas;

teach these rustic villagers what brave stuff Londoners are made of."

He crept towards the mill slowly and very carefully, and it must be confessed that his legs trembled violently under him, and his teeth chattered.

"He comes," said the miller, in a half-whisper. "Make ready to receive him."

Jonas crawled up to the half-opened mill-door, and peered into the darkness before him.

"That you, master?" he whispered.

"Y-e-e s," was the soft answer.

"Have you got the maiden safe and sound?"

"Y-e-e-s."

"Won't the old miller be surprised in the morning when he finds she's gone, ha! ha!" chuckled Jonas.

He passed the threshold, and was much astonished to see the door shut behind him.

Before he had time to breathe freely a long staff was aimed at his head.

The stroke was well intended, and a powerful one also; but it missed the right object, and fell with a hard crack on the head of a constable by mistake in the darkness.

A loud groan and a curse followed the fall of the oaken staff.

In an instant Jonas comprehended all.

He was entrapped, and escape impossible.

"Oh! the bloodthirsty scoundrels!" he groaned. "That blow was meant for me."

He produced his own small cudgel, and laid about him right and left in the darkness.

He then fell upon his hands and knees, and crawled from the midst of his enemies.

Total darkness prevented the officers from seeing what they were doing or ought to do.

But they hit right and left among themselves, and some of them were tripped up by Jonas.

"I've got him! I've got him!" roared the chief constable. "He tried to crawl through my legs, but couldn't."

"Give it to him, then!" said another.

And sure enough the chief constable *did* give it to him.

But he had the wrong man between his legs, and was pounding away on the back of an unlucky prostrate comrade, like as if he were thumping a big drum.

Shouts, oaths, and groans were now heard on all sides.

Jonas, as nimble as a monkey, climbed on to the sacks of flour piled up right and left.

His own weight toppled them over.

They fell among the combatants, and knocked several of them over.

Old Harmer, surprised at the change in the state of things, and, fearful that Jonas should escape, rushed to a long rope, and pulled the mill bell, which hung in an old tower.

He tugged away, and alarmed the whole village.

In less than five minutes the male portion of the villagers rushed forth from their houses, half dressed.

Dogs barked, men shouted, women screamed, and children cried.

All was now a scene of great excitement and confusion.

Some armed with pokers, tongs, old rusty swords, pitchforks, and oaken clubs, rushed along the village green.

"To the mill! To the mill!" roared some.

"'Tis the Skeleton Crew!" shrieked others.

"They have murdered the miller, and run off with Ellen!"

"The constables are half murdered!"

"On, lads, on !"

These and similar shouts were now heard on every hand.

The rustics looked pale and startled at the bare mention of the Skeleton Crew, for they had long known what a savage, remorseless band they were.

Many, at the bare mention of the Skeleton Crew, ran into their cottages again, and barred their doors.

Not a few fell on their knees, and began to mumble out their prayers in a very rapid manner.

Some dozen or more stout-hearted, broad-backed fellows, however, boldly ran towards the mill, and dashed in.

They asked no questions, but commenced to hit right and left in the darkness, and it was some time ere they discovered their mistake.

When they did, however, they began to swear at each other in a very violent manner ; nor did they heed the sighs and groans of the chief constable and his unlucky followers, who were half smothered under the sacks of flour.

They searched the mill in every direction, but, for full half-an-hour, were unable to discover Master Jonas.

That worthy youth had clambered over the sacks, and made his way up to the third story of the mill.

He looked in every direction for some means to escape, but found none.

The infuriated rustics, led on by old Harmer himself, now ascended the stairs in single file, and instituted a vigorous search.

They brought with them several dogs to assist in the affair.

One of these, more diligent in his search than others, scented out Master Jonas, who was concealed behind a flour-bin.

He might have long remained there, unknown to the searchers, but the miller's dog gave Jonas such a quiet nip in the leg, as made that worthy howl aloud with pain.

"He's here !"

"We've got him !"

"No you haven't," said Jonas.

With a sudden bound he rushed from his hiding place, and dashed towards the two trap-doors through which the sacks were raised from below.

They stood open ; and in front of him dangled a long rope almost to the ground.

This he seized, and began to slide down with the skill of an acrobat.

But an accident happened to him that he least expected.

The crane was pushed out from the wall, and, to Jonas's horror, he found himself dangling right over the mill-dam !

"Oh, the murdering villains !  What must I do now ?" thought the luckless servant.  "They have shoved out the crane, and here am I dancing between the sky and a deep mill-dam."

"Cut the rope ! cut the rope !"

"Drown the rascal !"

"He can't escape !"

"Lower the rope !"

"No, cut it—cut it !" roared old Harmer.  "D—n the rope, so we capture the villain."

With right good-will, several began to cut and hack the rope.

Jonas felt the rope's vibration, and shut his eyes.

"It's all over, now," he said.  "D—n the colonel, and all Darlington put together.  I wish I was safe in London again.  If this is the grand reward the colonel promised me, confusion to him."

Jonas had a passing desire to say his prayers, but he was such a thoughtless knave that he had forgotten them long ago.

"That's it, that's it," cried many voices.

"Help ! murder ! thieves ! cut-throats ! help— help !" shouted a dozen voices.

This was the confusion and noise which Colonel Blood had heard when he took the last glance at Andrew Gamble, who was carried away by the stream.

But he never for a moment dreamed that all this distant hubbub was occasioned by the tight rope performance of his man, Jonas !

With a vigorous cut, the rope was at last severed !

Amid the shouts and cheers of the bystanders, Jonas fell from a height of twenty feet right into the deep mill-dam, with a loud splash !

"Fish him out, fish him out, lads ; we musn't let the rogue escape us now.  He is one of those who rescued Bob Bertram."

Poor Jonas rose to the surface, and in desperate despair clung to the branch of an overhanging tree, some distance from the edge of the dam.

In a moment the villagers were very busy with pitch-forks, rakes, and the like, "fishing him out."

One fellow, with more vigour than judgment, took aim with his long fork, but missed his distance, and gave Jonas a painful thrust in his seat of honour, instead of hooking his clothes, as intended.

"Five gold pieces to any one who secures the villain," roared the chief constable, who now rushed upon the scene, puffing and blowing.

The promised reward caused a very great deal of excitement in those present.

A rope was now procured.

With great dexterity some one present made a noose in it, and very cleverly threw it over Jonas's head.

"Pull away, lads," said the rope-thrower.  "Now, then, all together !"

"You'll choke the varlet," some one said.

"Small odds," said the rope-thrower, "small odds, so we get him dead or alive."

"Now, then," said another, "altogether ; a strong pull, and a long pull, mind."

So vigorously did they haul away at the rope that in less than a minute Jonas was dragged to the bank, half-strangled and half-drowned.

"Light ho ! lights here !" cried a dozen voices, and lamps were immediately brought to the spot.

"That's him ! that's one on 'em !" said the chief constable.  "I could tell him out of a hundred ; that's him as has been prowling about Darlington, and rescued Bob Bertram."

"He looks a villain every inch of him," said old Harmer.  "I'm sorry we haven't got t'other ; he's the worst of the two ; and the rascals ain't satisfied with what they've already done, but must concoct a scheme for running off with my daughter Ellen."

"Horrible !"

"Aw-ful !" chimed in one and another.

"Undo the rope," said the chief constable, "at least, loosen it a bit ; we don't want to hang him yet."

"No ; that fun has to come," said another, with a loud laugh.

"Bring him along, lads ; I'll lead the way with the light !" said the chief constable.

And poor Jonas was dragged forth to prison with a long halter around his neck.

He was dripping wet, and soaked to the marrow.

His thighs were bruised and wounded by cuffs, the fork-prongs, and dog-bites.

His legs trembled from under him.

Dogs barked at him, men jeered, and women clapped their hands.

He was cast into gaol by the chief constable with looks of professional pride and triumph.

"Got one of the scoundrels, any how!" said he.

Wet and exhausted as he was, and presenting a very sorry sight, Master Jonas was thrust into a cell.

The villagers crowded around him and gazed through the prison bars, with gaping mouths, as if they were looking at some strange, half-tamed animal in a travelling menagerie.

But what has become of his master, Colonel Blood?

The next chapter will show.

---

## CHAPTER XI.

THE ABDUCTION—THE SKELETON DANCE—THE PURSUIT—HORRIBLE DOINGS IN THE VILLAGE.

THE sounds which Colonel Blood had heard for a moment aroused his bold spirit, and as he crossed the mill bridge, slowly and calmly, he resolved upon arriving at some explanation concerning it.

But the very hubbub and confusion which reigned were of infinite use to him in regard to his projected scheme with the pretty Ellen Harmer.

Her father, the miller, and the whole of the villagers, as we have seen, were thoroughly aroused and greatly incensed at the behaviour of Jonas.

Some began to talk of hanging the unlucky servant on the morrow, and, dark as it was, they gathered together in groups, discussing the subject with great animation and many angry gestures.

But this very confusion assisted the bold, conscienceless colonel.

He walked up to the miller's house, and found it deserted.

Not a soul was in the dwelling, save Ellen herself.

Half stupefied with the strange stories she had heard, Ellen remained in her own chamber, trembling that the Skeleton Crew were in the village.

A single lamp burned dimly in the miller's parlour.

Colonel Blood, as he crept towards the house, felt satisfied that she was alone.

"Now is my time," said he; "none but the brave deserve the fair; now or never."

He walked boldly into the house, opened the parlour door hastily, and entered the apartment.

Ellen had been on her knees praying, and her face was deadly pale.

She started suddenly as she saw the handsome stranger enter.

"Fly! fly for your life, fair maid," said Blood, in accents of alarm.

"What means this intrusion, sir?" said Ellen, drawing herself up to her full height, and with a proud look. "What means this strange intrusion?"

"It means this, Miss Harmer, that the village has been set upon by that desperate gang called the Skeleton Crew, and that they are intent upon murdering all who oppose them. Fly! I beg of you, do not delay a single instant, or all may be lost!"

"Sir!" cried Ellen, half aloud, distrustful of her own senses, and yet knowing not whether to believe or disbelieve the colonel's words.

"Nay, stop not to parley, dear Ellen," said Blood, taking her by the hand; "there is not a single moment to be lost in explanation. Feel satisfied that what I say is true. Your father has sent me; he begged of me to conduct you to a place of safety until such times as the horrible Skeleton Band should have departed again."

"Sir, all this may be true, but how am I to know it for a certainty?"

"Nay; do not hesitate. Your very life may depend upon it."

"And my honour also, sir," said Ellen, with a proud look. "Honour to me is dearer than life."

"Great Patience!" said Blood, in a petulant manner. "Would you not save your father's life?"

"My father's life?" said Ellen, suddenly changing colour. "Is he in danger, then?"

"He is. He is now in the power of the Skeleton Crew, and if you are found here five minutes longer you will surely be dragged off a captive by Death-wing, their chief."

"Whither, then, would you lead me?"

"To Darlington Hall. Sir Richard and his servants are out and armed against this famous band. It is by old Sir Richard's desire, coupled with your father's, that I now come here."

"Then you are known to Sir Richard?"

"Yes, fair one. I am a nephew of his. I have used deception with you up to the present; but the time is now past for all that. I am Sir Richard's nephew. Come, fly with me to the Hall, 'tis the only place of safety. Remember the dreadful scenes which have been enacted round the coast by this horrible band, and flee on the instant."

Ellen seemed stupefied by all she heard, and mechanically threw a light wrapper round her shoulders.

In a few moments she left her father's house, misled and deceived by the oily tongue of as great and fearless a scoundrel as ever lived.

"This way!—this way!" said Blood, blandly. "Haste, fair one, haste!"

He placed a rough, strong arm round the maiden's waist, and helped her along.

"This way is the nearest," he said, with a grim smile of satisfaction, as they both hurriedly approached the mill bridge.

When they were about to cross, several of the planks being old, loose, and rotten, began to creak ominously, and the winds sighed dolefully.

Ellen stopped for a moment.

Her eyes enlarged to twice their ordinary size.

She saw something on the bridge that startled her.

"What is that?" she said, half-gasping, pointing to something on the planks which looked red.

"Oh! nothing, nothing, fair one," said Blood, grimly smiling.

"But it is something," said Ellen, turning pale, and gazing intently. "Look! I see here—and here—and here—they are large clots of gore!"

"Impossible!" said Blood, coolly.

"Yes, they are; and here," she said, "is part of a broken sword. How came all this? Nay, do not hurry me onward. I tremble—my feet refuse to walk, for I fear something horrible may obstruct my path."

"Nonsense! nonsense, fair creature!" said Blood. "If anything has happened it is all the doings of that horrible band of Skeletons. Nothing more. If you wish to escape yourself, follow my advice at once."

"I will, I will," said Ellen Harmer, trembling in every limb.

She and the colonel had crossed half of the bridge when both suddenly stopped.

"What was that?" said the miller's daughter, looking pale as death. "What voice was that?"

"Oh, nothing, nothing, fair one; 'twas only the murmuring of the wind among the oziers on the river bank, or perhaps the babbling waters. Come, quickly, I say!"

"Oh, help! murder!" sighed a voice near by among the ozier bushes.

"D—nation!" growled Blood, half to himself. "that lout is still alive! Would for a thousand crowns he were dead! Come, lassie, think no more of it; it was your imagination only, nothing else, I assure you."

"Oh, help!" sighed the voice again, faintly. "Ellen Harmer, I am dying! Beware of the courtly villain! Help!"

"'Tis *my* name that he calls," said Ellen, turning red. "Unhand me, sir; and if you are a man help me to discover who and what this poor creature is!"

"Help!" faintly sighed the voice from among the trees.

"'Tis the voice of Andrew," said Ellen. "Some foul villany has been here at work; this blood upon the planks is his!"

"Help!"

"'Tis Andrew Gamble's voice."

"D—nation!" growled Blood, and, then, in a persuasive voice, "Come, fair one, come; 'tis all imagination, believe me! Hark! do you hear the loud shouts of the villagers? Come, let's haste away; the Skeleton Crew are butchering all they fall across. Come, haste!"

Blood put his strong arm round Ellen's waist, and half by persuasion, half by force, bore her away, pale, trembling, and more dead than alive.

"Egad! 'twas well I used mild force with the pretty wench," said he, "or she would have discovered all. I must return, if possible, and give that rustic a finishing touch; it will never do to let him recover and go babbling over the village, or we may be traced to London, and then all fun would end. 'Twas lucky she didn't look in the right direction as I did, or she would have seen Master Andrew washed by the river among the bull-rushes on the bank. I just caught sight of his face in the fitful moonlight; how white and horrible it looked!"

He was so impatient to bear off Ellen Harmer to his carriage that he actually took her up in his arms.

This he explained to the struggling maid by saying that they were pursued.

Faint, weak, pale, and unresisting as she was, Ellen Harmer was so terrified at all she had heard, that it took but little to convince her that what all Blood had said was true.

With the soft tongue of a deceiver, then, he consoled her; while, with the strength of a young ox, he tore off his fair prize with the greatest ease.

"This is a good night's work," thought he, as he hurried forward; "his majesty will amply reward me for all this trouble, and, who knows, may raise me to the peerage, for many a man has had that reward for doing less than I have."

Thus he mused as he went on his way.

Ere long he approached the spot where Jonas had agreed to place his carriage and horses.

His own saddle horse was there, truly, but not the carriage.

"How is this?" growled Blood. "Surely that fool, Jonas, could not have misunderstood me? I told him near this spot."

He was now approaching the church, and resolved to wait near an old archway close beside the village green, with its May-pole, until such time as Jonas should appear with the carriage.

He remained close under the shadow of the old archway, but all was still.

The village green, with its May-pole, was deserted.

Not a soul was visible.

He threw his cloak around the miller's daughter, and tried to comort her.

All at once, he was astonished at the sight he saw.

His own carriage dashed up, and passed him at a furious rate.

The driver was a skeleton!

Behind the carriage stood, in grim outlines, two skeleton footmen, cocked-hats and all.

Inside, Colonel Blood could see four or five skeletons, who grinned and laughed hideously as they looked out of the window and shook their bony hands in triumph.

In the midst of the inside passengers, Colonel Blood saw two prisoners.

One was the Colonel's coachman, the other was the fellow-footman of poor Jonas!

This unearthly and ghastly apparition was not seen by Ellen Harmer, for Blood's cloak had been adroitly thrown over her head and face the moment the strange and horrible coachman appeared in sight.

It must be confessed that this coach-load of grim skeletons filled the colonel with wonder, if not with fear.

"I should never have believed it had I not seen it," mused the bold colonel.

At that moment his horror even increased tenfold, as was that of the fair Ellen.

Loud laughter was heard proceeding from the village green.

It sounded not like that of mortal.

He hastily turned his head, as also did Ellen.

They both looked through the old archway towards the May-pole.

The sight they then beheld was appaling.

Round the May-pole danced a circle of skeletons!

On top of it there sat perched a grim-looking skeleton, playing ear-piercing, diabolical music from some sort of flute made out of human bones.

One of the dancers had a tambarine, with jingling bells.

As they danced and capered about in most fantastic styles, they shook their bony hands in a dismal manner, which made Colonel Blood's flesh to creep again.

Directly Ellen Harmer caught sight of this dreadful exhibition, she fell back into Blood's arms.

She now fully believed all that the colonel had told her, and relied upon his protection as a man of honour.

She was too much frightened to speak, and trembled violently as the colonel supported her.

But Blood seemed fastened to the spot.

He looked, and looked again at the terrible dance of the skeletons.

He had never dreamed of ever seeing anything so hideous or horrible.

"Who and what are they?" said Blood, half aloud; "are they men or devils?"

"Devils!" said a chorus of unseen voices. "Who stabbed Andrew Gamble? Ha, ha! Who wants to run away with the pretty daughter of Harmer the miller, eh? Go, tell your master what you have seen—go, tell him; he may one day expect us. Away, Colonel Blood, away!"

These words were uttered in such fierce tones, and with such a hissing sound, that they grated on Blood's ears.

"I fear not man nor devil," he growled savagely in return.

But the continual sight of the strange, wild, skeleton dance seemed to discompose him.

He seized Ellen Harmer round the waist, and with the greatest ease vaulted into his saddle.

"These devils have seized my carriage and servants," said he, "but 'tis lucky they did not discover my horse here under the gateway, or all would have been lost."

While in the act of mounting his splendid animal, the colonel did not perceive that the skeleton dancers had approached him.

When he looked to the right and left he found himself surrounded by the grim disciples of Death-wing, the grim skeleton chief.

With a shout, and an oath of surprise and annoyance, he raised his riding-whip and cut his way from the midst of those around him.

He put spurs to his horse, and plunged forward on the road towards London, with Ellen Harmer on the saddle before him.

He had not gone two miles when he turned round to ascertain the cause of a distant rumbling noise.

Not far behind him, he could perceive his own carriage, driven by a skeleton coachman, in full pursuit!

Skeleton heads were protruding from windows on each side of the coach, who waved their long arms and shook them in gestures of savage revenge.

"Pursued!" thought Blood; "and by this terrible band."

He dug his spurs deeply into the flanks of his gallant steed, and fled like the wind.

But the Skeleton Band was slowly and surely gaining on him.

It was now a race for life or death!

---

## CHAPTER XII.

WILDFIRE NED, TIM, AND RAMBLING BOB SET OUT UPON THEIR TRAVELS—STRANGE AND EXCITING ADVENTURES.

THE first thing which Wildfire Ned did, when he 'eft his uncle's presence, and had publicly insulted Redgill, was to proceed to the stables, and saddle his own gallant mare "Starlight."

"What, off again, Master Ned?" said Tim, rubbing his eyes. "Why, surely you ain't going anywhere this time of night?"

"Yes, I am, Tim. I am going to leave Darlington altogether."

"Leave it altogether, sir! Why, you must be joking."

"No I'm not, Tim. Come, saddle my mare at once. I must leave this place within half-an-hour. Will you come with me?"

"Why in course I will," said Tim. "But it did appear to me all so very strange like. I can't understand it. What! you leave the Hall, and all for nothing?" said Tim, in great surprise.

"Never mind being surprised at all about it," said Wildfire Ned, biting his lips. "I'm going to leave, so that's quite sufficient explanation. I've got a good sum of money of my own in my pocket, so have resolved to go to sea, and chase those Skeleton Pirates we have heard so much of. Will you come, Tim?"

"Yes, young master, in course I will. I'd go to the devil with you, thee knows. (But, for all that, thought Tim, I don't much care about facing them terrible skeletons led on by that awful wretch called Death-wing.)"

Few words were passed by Ned. He mounted his famous mare "Starlight," and, followed by Tim, galloped away towards the village of Darlington.

"Tim, are you brave?" said Wildfire Ned, grinning, as they rode along side by side.

"Brave, master Ned, why of course I am. I'd face the very devil if I had any one to back me. I always feel safe when I'm with you."

"Well, do you know what I'm going to do?"

"No, master."

"You know Bob Bertram?"

"The old farmer's son, sir? Yes, sir; and a fine good-hearted young fellow he is as ever was born."

"I'm glad to hear you say so, Tim; and glad also, to think you like him so much, for he, also, is coming with us."

"Him, master?" said Tim, in surprise. "Why, how can that be? He's in the round-house, and accused of murdering his old father. But he didn't do it, I'll swear," said Tim to himself. "He couldn't do it. Bob Bertram's heart is too good for any such bloody work as that, or else I'm no judge of human nature."

"Right, Tim; you are right, my lad," said Ned, who had overheard his servant mumbling to himself. "And I feel proud to think your opinion about that murder is the same as mine; but, then, you know, he'll never suffer; he's going to escape to-night."

"Escape, master! Why, I have heard that he's guarded night and day. It were even whispered that some officers of the crown were coming down to take him down to London."

"I have heard all that, also," said Ned, laughing; "but when they do come, the bird will have flown. Do you see these, Tim?" said Ned, displaying a pair of pistols, "Do you see these?"

"Yes, master."

"Well, we call these things 'barking irons,' and if the two officers won't behave themselves, and act civilly towards us when we call, why then you must blow the brains out of one, while I do the same to the other."

Ned said this very coolly, but Tim's eyes rolled in fright at the bare idea of bloodshed.

He did not give utterance to his fears, however, but jogged along by his young master's side.

Ere long they approached the village, and Wildfire Ned leaped from his mare.

Tim did likewise, and both nags were tethered to a road-side post.

"Come along, Tim, we must do the rest on foot. You know the 'Red Lion?' Well, go there, and tell the landlord I want a horse for a few hours; when you come back I shall be here at this post waiting for you. Be quick, mind, and see that he lends you a good steed, for we have a long way to gallop."

Tim went off on foot towards the "Red Lion."

Wildfire Ned walked rapidly towards that part of the village where the lock-up or round-house was situated.

All was darkness and profound quietness in the village.

"This is just the time to do the trick," thought Wildfire Ned.

Saying this, he put on a black velvet mask, and walked up to the prison door.

It was open.

He walked in quietly.

Two officers lay on benches before the fire, snoring loudly.

They did not hear his footsteps.

Ned looked around quickly to ascertain in which of the several cells Bob Bertram was confined.

He knew not which.

Presently, however, he saw two eyes peering between the iron bars, and from the hard breathing of the prisoner he felt sure it was Bob.

Ned made a sign which Bob understood, and then approached the prisoner.

"Those are the keys hanging up behind the door," said Bob, in a soft whisper; "but be careful, Ned, or you will awake them."

On tiptoe Wildfire Ned took down the keys, and approached Bob's cell.

He passed them through to Bob, and while he was turning the bolt of the lock Wildfire Ned stood over the two sleeping officers, pistol in hand.

"If they should wake up while Bob is getting out, these two little bulldogs will keep them quiet," thought Ned.

He had not thus stood guard over the two slumberers many minutes ere Bob Bertram was free.

"Fly," said Ned, "towards the Hall; you'll find the horses waiting for us on the road-side near the finger posts."

Young Bertram had scarcely quitted the prison ere the two officers awoke.

They opened their eyes very slowly, but when they discovered the young man in the mask standing over them, pistol in hand, they rolled their eyes, and gaped in astonishment and wonder.

"Oh, lors!"

"Who are you?"

"Put down them pistols."

"What do you want?"

"Did you not expect some officers from London?"

"We did; but, for the lor's sake, don't put the muzzle of that pistol so near my head, it might go off."

"I am one of them," said Ned, scarcely able to keep from laughing, "and have a very disagreeable duty to perform."

"What is it?"

"My comrades called here, and found you asleep. We took the prisoner in our own charge, and my duty here is to lock both of you up."

"Lock *us* up?"

"Yes, both of you, and to feed you on bread and water for a month, for not attending to your duty."

"It warn't *my* fault; it were *his* watch," said one.

"No quarrelling," said Ned, grinning under his mask; "rise, both of you; Bob Bertram's cell is now open and empty; go into it, both of ye, and this instant, knaves, or I'll drive holes into each of you."

Ned's manner was so firm, cool, and determined, that the two astonished officers were compelled to obey him.

Reluctantly they rose, and hobbled after each other into the cell.

Ned turned the key upon them, and there left them alone in their glory.

"If either of you make any noise for the n xt half-hour I'll clip your ears off," said Ned, as he walked coolly away.

He had not gone many yards ere both of the officers began to bawl at the top of their voices.

Ned returned to them, and just placed the muzzle of his pistol between the bars, when the two officers fell upon their knees and sued for mercy in a very humble manner.

"I only asked you to remain quiet for half-an-hour before," said he, "but now listen to me; if either of you make the slightest noise for the next twelve hours I will blow your brains out. Remember, and rest assured if you do not obey me this time both of you are dead men."

Ned left them a second time, but did not forget to bolt and bar and lock every door, so that it was a matter almost of impossibility for either of them to escape or even be heard by any one passing outside.

In less than half-an-hour Wildfire Ned, Bob Bertram and Tim were on their way to the sea-coast.

But ere they reached their journey's end a strange adventure happened to Wildfire Ned.

Each of them were well mounted, and they galloped along the road at a merry pace.

Bob Bertram was in ecstacies at his unlooked-for liberation, and swore eternal friendship and fidelity to Wildfire Ned.

He told Ned all, or at least as much as he knew, about his father's murder, and what had happened to him on that eventful night.

He also described the stranger who had exchanged clothes with him so minutely that Ned could not, or at least did not, for a moment hesitate to say that Redgill was the man, for he knew that from the garments Bob was then wearing.

He did not say much to Bob concerning it, however, but bit his lip, and vowed to have revenge on Redgill the first opportunity that offered.

The three riders stopped at a roadside inn, and knocked up the landlord.

The old man opened his door with a trembling hand, and in the course of conversation informed his guests that they must beware of the Skeleton Crew, for a party of that terrible band had called there that very night, ransacked and robbed the place of all it had, and were well-nigh murdering everybody.

"Was Death-wing, their chief, along with them?" asked Ned.

"He was," said the old publican, shaking; "but oh! young man, don't smile, for if you had been as close to, and seen as much on 'em as I have to-night, you would tremble in your shoes."

"*I*?" said Wildfire Ned, laughing boisterously. "Not I, landlord, you are much mistaken. Nothing in the world would give me greater pleasure than to meet this same Death-wing to-night."

"You?" said the publican, aghast. "Rash youth, beware!"

"Nay; you need have no fears for me. It is my resolve to beard the lion in his very den this very night. Think you they are on the heath?"

"Without doubt, young master, they are; but take an old man's advice, do not go near them. When you catch but a glimpse of their horrid forms, flee for your lives."

"Never mind, friend, never mind this Skeleton Crew. Bring us a bottle or two of your best wine," said Ned. "If I do not unearth the hobgoblin devils to-night, my name is not Ned Warbeck."

"Warbeck?" said the old man, in surprise, "Warbeck?"

"Yes, Warbeck. What makes you look so surprised?"

"They were speaking of you," said the old man, turning pale.

"Well, what of that?"

"They drank to your death."

"To my death?" said Ned. "What else, old man?"

---

## NOTICE TO OUR READERS.

THE ENCOUNTER BETWEEN WILDFIRE NED AND THE SKELETON CREW.—SEE PAGE 40.

"They vowed to hunt you down and slay you."

"Ah !" said Ned, "and why ? What have I done more than any one else to deserve such kind consideration ?"

"I know not, young man. All I heard them say was, that, at the moment of your birth, some infernal power told them that you were sent to be their deadliest enemy on land and sea."

"So be it, then," said Ned. "If I have any strength or power or will, I will use it all against these demons, and never rest until I have exterminated every one of them."

While Ned spoke thus, the old landlord, who was about to leave the room, hastily returned.

"What makes you so pale, old man ?" asked Ned.

No. 5.

The publican did not reply. He seemed struck dumb with astonishment.

At the door stood two of the Skeleton Crew. They walked slowly into the room, and looked at Wildfire Ned with a long, stedfast gaze.

Ned jumped to his feet, and, quick as thought, fired both pistols at them.

The balls could be heard rattling through their bones.

But they stirred not.

With a laugh, loud and mocking, they seized Tim by his arms, and would have borne him away.

Tim, almost in a jelly with fear, wriggled and writhed like an eel.

The skeletons swung Tim to and fro for a second

or two, and then threw him with great violence into a corner near the coal cellar, and there he lay very humbly and meekly, and did not dare stir an inch.

"Are such the men, young Warbeck," said the two skeletons, "you would gather round ye to slaughter the Death-wing's band?"

"No, foul fiends," said Ned, rising and brandishing his sword, "such are not the men ; but here are two. I and young Bertram here defy all your power."

"Foolish boy!" said one, in tones of mock compassion. "I would not harm ye. Yet, when you have arrived at man's estate, I might meet you on equal terms."

"Nay, let not that be your vain excuse," said Ned ; "old or young I defy you, and in token of my eternal hatred take that," said he, at the same moment throwing his glove at the skeleton face.

"Impudent varlet !" was the angry rejoinder. "It seems as if your footsteps were purposely directed across my path. I know, I feel, that eternal, unquenchable hatred exists between us, and yet not now would I cross swords with ye. But think not, bold youth, that I reject your gauge of battle. No, I accept it. Beneath the old oak, on the moor, meet me in an hour."

"I will ; and with greater pleasure than e'er I did aught in all my life."

"Until the hour, then, adieu ! You will, of course, come alone?"

"I will."

These few angry words were quickly spoken, and before any one could well realize the fact, the two grim skeletons disappeared.

They mounted two horses that stood outside the inn door, and vanished like the wind.

"Thank heavens, they are gone !" the publican gasped.

"Amen !" groaned Tim.

"But you surely will not keep your promise with the grim rascals ?" said Bob.

"I most surely shall," said Ned.

"But they mean you mischief," said the publican, "you will never return alive."

"You need not fear."

"But, brave youth, I *do* fear; you know not so much of these awful creatures as I do."

"Perhaps not, but I shall very shortly," said Ned, laughing.

"Why, that old oak tree on the heath is the favourite spot of Death-wing, their chief."

"So much the better, the sooner I shall make his acquaintance, then ; that's all."

"But there are, at least, a dozen dead men hanging on the leafless branches ; all have fallen victims to Death-wing's sword, and now hang rotting in the sun."

"So I have heard! will you be kind enough to show me the way thither, landlord ?" asked Ned, smiling.

"*Me !* lord bless the lad, I would'nt go near that tree for all the gold in England ; no one ever comes back alive from that spot."

"Then I will go alone."

"Nay, stay !"

"You must not go, Ned," said Bob. "Why throw yourself in the way of those bloodthirsty scoundrels ? If you do go, I must accompany you, and so will your groom, eh Tim ?"

"Y-e-e-s !" groaned Tim, who was rubbing his sore bones with a very rueful face. "I don't mind if I go to the devil, for I'm going there very fast it seems to me."

With a face flushed with excitement, and eyes sparkling with delight at the prospect of encountering some one of the Skeleton Crew in mortal combat, Wildfire Ned rose from his seat and paced the room.

Before he was perceived Ned left the apartment in a free and easy manner, as if merely going into the back yard.

Bob Bertram never imagined that Ned had any intentions of going forth alone.

The old landlord saw him mount his horse, and turned pale as he thought of the great danger into which the bold, rash youth was about to plunge.

"For heaven's sake !" said old Boniface, approaching Ned, "for heaven's sake, give up this wild freak. How can you, a mere lad, think of conquering any one of that desperate gang when so many valiant men have fallen in the attempt ? Take *my* advice, Ned Warbeck, steer clear of that murdering crew."

"Look here, landlord," said Ned, gaily, "there is one favour I have to ask of you, and that is, keep a still tongue in your head. I shall only be absent an hour or two at most. Do not tell my comrades which way I have gone should they ask, but say you think I have gone towards the Hall for something I have left behind. Do this, and I shall well repay you in times to come."

So speaking, Wildfire Ned dashed away into a neighbouring thicket, and was soon lost to view.

In a few moments he emerged again into the open country.

Over bridge and ditch he gaily rode, humming a tune. The moon came out, and shone with unusual splendour.

Ere long he approached the borders of the lonely heath, which, like a white expanse of silvered scenery, lay open before him.

His brave mare Starlight had carried him nobly, but from pure instinct began to snort and slacken her pace as she approached the wilderness-like plain.

In the far distance Wildfire Ned saw ravenous night birds circling in the sky, and alighting on a huge oak tree.

As he approached still nearer his mare stood still, and cocked her ears.

Ned now had a full view of the famous old oak tree, and on its wide spreading branches he distinctly saw dark rows of dead men hanging against the bright sky.

The sight filled him with horror, but not with fear.

"What inhuman scoundrels !" he sighed. "They must be fiends ever to act in this manner."

Nothing daunted, he dismounted from his mare, and tied her to a stump.

As he did so he heard a voice, which said, slowly and solemnly—

"Edward Warbeck, beware ! Retrace your steps ; no one approaches the blasted oak and lives !"

"Lying fiends !" said Wildfire Ned, "lying fiends ! wherever you be, I fear not your crazy croakings !"

As he spoke fire flashed from his eyes, and he boldly advanced.

Dry leaves rustled in the wind, the breezes sighed, and as he looked up at that fearful gibbet with its many human forms dangling in the air a sudden tremor thrilled his whole frame.

The face of each hapless victim was turned downwards towards him, and they seemed to smile grimly and savagely at his upturned face.

Beyond this, however, nothing was visible.

"The sight is indeed horrible," said Ned, half aloud ; "but where is the much-vaunted Skeleton

Crew? Where are these savages hidden? and whence came that voice of warning?"

Wildfire Ned's position, as must be confessed, was a critical one.

Here was a bold youth, alone and single handed, gazing on the dead, and standing, as it were, on enchanted ground.

"Come forth, grim demons of the land and deep," said Ned, with a ringing defiant tone. "Death-wing, come forth and encounter me!"

He turned his head suddenly.

There stood before him a gaunt, ghastly member of the Skeleton Band, sword in hand.

"Who calls so bravely on the Skeleton Crew, and defies them?" said a sepulchral voice, in mocking tones. "Is Death-wing's band to be laughed and scoffed at by a babbling boy?'

"Boy!" said Ned, indignantly.

"Yes, brat, if that will suit your pride the better; get you gone from this awful place."

"I came by appointment. Death-wing and I are to try conclusions to a deadly issue here," said Ned, bravely.

"You face Death-wing?" said the skeleton guard, with a mocking laugh. "He who has braved the land and sea this many a year, ha! ha! Look above ye, and see there dangling the lifeless bodies of more than a dozen who have dared intrude upon this deadly spot.

"Bombastic liar!" said Ned, in tones of scorn. "Death-wing fears me. But, at all events, I will not be disappointed; these rows of bodies shall no longer grace these oak branches as tokens of your prowess. Have at ye! man or fiend, my good battle-axe shall prove to all what ye are."

With a desperate rush Wildfire Ned dashed to the fray.

The skeleton guardian of the gibbet, however, was not taken unawares.

He also was armed, and parried Ned's desperate blows.

The combat was a fearful one.

Sparks flew from their weapons.

Wildfire Ned, with the courage and endurance of a dozen men, stood his ground.

His blows fell thick and fast upon his grim opponent, and the clash of marrowless bones resounded upon the night air.

For a moment Wildfire Ned paused in the combat and looked upon his opponent with wonder.

"He must be a devil," thought Ned, "or my last blow would have cleaved him to the earth.

"Ha! ha! growled the skeleton, as he rushed at his enemy again, "one more victim for our gibbet!"

"Never!" said Ned, aloud, and with an angry oath.

The fight was again renewed, and now with still greater bitterness and fury.

Ned was getting weaker and weaker.

His rival, however, danced around him as nimbly as ever, and every limb seemed to be acting on springs.

He struck at Ned repeatedly, but could not do more than draw blood.

It seemed impossible to hit Ned Warbeck in any vital part, for he was so well guarded with his weapon.

He bled, however, as we have said, and the sight of gore seemed to act like electricity on the skeleton guard, who shrieked aloud with joy.

He made a terrific dash, a last and final attempt upon Ned, and shouted aloud,

"Edward Warbeck, die! Down, down! die!"

"Never!" said Ned, as with a well-aimed and powerful blow he struck his opponent fair on the head, and felled him to the earth.

"Conquered, conquered!" shouted Ned, aloud, in wild triumph.

He turned to look for his smitten foe.

He was nowhere to be seen!

Astonished as he was at this strange occurrence he was much more astounded at what he then heard.

While looking about in search of some trace of his grim, gaunt opponent, the sounds of pistol shots and loud shouts reached his ears!

He listened.

Again and again he could distinctly discern quick, successive reports of fire-arms.

"Help! help!" faintly sighed the breeze.

"What is all this? What new wonder is to happen on this eventful night?" thought Ned.

At that moment his good mare Starlight neighed and became restive.

"Hillo! what means this? The mare would not neigh without cause. There is some one in danger; the mare recognizes some old stable companion. I will away, and quickly return."

"Help! help!" was borne upon the breeze.

In a moment Wildfire Ned vaulted into the saddle and dashed forward to the scene of strife and danger.

The report of fire-arms to Wildfire Ned was like the sounds of most delightful music.

His heart leaped within him as he mounted his brave mare, Starlight.

"Heaven grant it may turn out to be some more of these skeleton devils," he said, with a merry laugh.

Over hedge and ditch he galloped in the clear moonlight, and soon reached the high road.

In the far distance he could perceive a carriage and four, which had been stopped by a party of roadsmen.

"Egad!" said Ned, "this is another adventure to-night. I must not let poor travellers be waylaid and robbed by rascally highwayman if I can help it."

He rode straight towards the crowd, and as he approached, perceived the carriage to be that of his uncle.

Old Sir Richard Warbeck, it would seem, had started out after Wildfire Ned, in hopes of bringing him back to Darlington Hall.

Phillip Redgill, who had professed much friendship "for the wayward lad, Ned," volunteered to accompany Sir Richard to town. But they had not progressed far when the carriage was attacked by Captain Jack's party of horsemen, who had resolved not to leave the neighbourhood of Darlington without spoil of some kind.

Hence, when they sneaked off from the inn in which Colonel Blood was, they were so enraged at being thus made fools of, that they determined to have revenge on some of the landed gentry thereabout.

The first person to fall across them was Sir Richard Warbeck and Phillip Redgill.

Captain Jack's men masked themselves, and counted upon an easy conquest.

But they were much mistaken.

Old Sir Richard, the moment he was attacked by the ruffians, fired his pistols through the coach windows, and wounded one or two of the rascals, old Bates among the number.

Jumping out of the coach, sword in hand, he kept his assailants at bay, manfully and bravely.

Phillip Redgill, however, slipped out of the

coach by the opposite door, and soon made his escape unharmed.

As he was fleeing, Captain Jack overtook him.

"A thousand gold guineas if you slay the alderman," said Redgill, in a confidential whisper.

"Done!" said Captain Jack.

Redgill gave the robber chief a large purse, and promised the rest at a certain time and place in London.

In a few moments Redgill mounted one of the robbers' horses, and galloped away unperceived by old Sir Richard, who thought Phillip had been killed or desperately wounded.

"No quarter, lads; no quarter," said Captain Jack; "the old baronet fights like a fiend. He has wounded several already. No quarter, lads; no quarter."

It was at this moment, when surrounded by Captain Jack's desperate men, and each moment in expectation of being killed, that Wildfire Ned darted upon the spot full speed.

Bang! bang! went his pistols right and left as he approached.

Whipping out his sword, he spurred Starlight into a maddening gallop, and actually rode down all before him.

Captain Jack was unhorsed in an instant, and rolled into the ditch with a loud curse.

Old Sir Richard was astonished at the dash and valour of the youth before him; but from the mask which Ned wore it was impossible for him to detect his nephew.

Wildfire Ned was too busy with those around him to pass any compliments or exchange recognition.

The fight now was between the highwaymen on the one side, and Sir Richard and Wildfire Ned on the other.

Sir Richard, however, was on foot, and could not do so much as Ned, who pranced and danced around on Starlight, cutting and slashing in gallant style.

Perceiving that several of the highwaymen were disabled, and had left the spot, the coachman and footman emerged from their hiding-place under the hedge, whither they had at first fled.

With thick clubs in hand, they now joined the fight, and laid about them with such right good-will, so that Captain Jack and his party were only too glad to escape with their lives.

As soon as the fight was over, and Sir Richard could gain sufficient strength, he tottered up to Wildfire Ned, and said—

"Gallant youth, whoever you are, how can I sufficiently thank you for your timely aid? I had a fellow traveller with me, a noble young man of unstained honour, but I fear he has fallen a victim to these scoundrels who attacked me. Your name, I beg, young man; your name, that I may recount your noble deeds this night to the king."

"Sir Richard Warbeck," Ned replied, with a forced utterance and a feigned voice, "no thanks are needed, I have simply done my duty. My name you cannot—must not—at the present know, for I have not made a name for fame as yet. When I have done so, however, you will hear of me at Darlington Hall."

With a low bow to Sir Richard, Wildfire Ned galloped from the spot, in pursuit of the fleeing highwaymen.

"Lor' a mercy me, master," gasped the coachman, "didn't thee know 'un? I do."

"Ah! Sir Richard, it be Wildfire Ned," said the footman. "He were disguised, but I could swear to it when I seed him ride."

"There's not another lad in all England as can straddle a saddle like Ned, Sir Richard," the coachman remarked.

"What! am I blind?" Sir Richard said. "Could that brave lad have been no other than my own Ned? Am I dreaming? and yet all along through the fight my heart told me so. Brave boy!" he sighed.

And as he spoke true tears trickled down the old man's cheeks, for he dearly loved Ned.

"Harness the horses quick," he said. "If that be Ned, I must overtake him. Quick, I say, and harness the horses. Drive for your very lives. I must, I will, overtake the gallant youth!"

## CHAPTER XIII.

CAPTAIN JACK AND REDGILL MISCALCULATE THEIR FORCES — THE RECOGNITION — THE RESCUE—BOB BERTRAM'S ESCAPE.

CAPTAIN JACK and his half-dozen companions were so thoroughly disappointed and disgusted with their ill-success in and around Darlington, that they made up their minds to depart for London forthwith, and seek no other adventures.

Their disabled companion shared the horse of Faulkner, and as they journeyed slowly along to the nearest public-house, the whole party were loud in cursing their late bad luck.

"Who the devil could have been that youngster who assailed us so furiously?" said Captain Jack, with an angry oath. "I tried to wing him several times, but always missed."

"Yes, hang him, but he took d—d good care he didn't miss me," old Bates growled; "he knocked the pistol out of my hand as clean as a whistle, and just at the moment, too, when I was going to pop at him."

"As to handling a sword," said Captain Jack, "he seems the very devil at that game."

"I thought that I could do a little in that line," said Faulkner, "but, lor' bless yer, he gave me an awful dig in the left arm, and if it hadn't been for a stroke of good luck I should have been killed, for he was just on the point of having a full cut at me, when I ducked my head, and—"

"Yes, and that stroke cut down a thick branch much tougher than your head or neck," said Bates. "I saw it, so cut it, for I had enough on it."

While thus speaking of their inglorious exploit, Jack's party arrived at the roadside inn, where, it will be remembered, Wildfire Ned had left Bob Bertram and Tim.

Believing what the landlord had said to them, namely, that Ned Warbeck had only ridden back to the Hall for something he had forgotten, Bob and Tim waited patiently for his return.

When least they expected it, however, and greatly to the surprise of both, Captain Jack and his rough companions entered the inn, and, with their old style, swaggered about and talked and cursed very loudly.

Tim, by instinct, knew who they were, and trembled.

He slunk into the dark corner still farther, so as not to be perceived, but Bob Bertram remained cool and collected.

Captain Jack called for various refreshments, and, together with a companion or two, were very busy in binding up the cuts and wounds of those who were hurt.

"You seem to have fallen into rough hands, gentlemen," said Bob, civilly.

"Well, and what if we have," Bates growled; "is that anything to do wi' you? Who are you?"

"Keep your temper, Bates," said Captain Jack; "let's have no more quarrelling to-night. The young man didn't mean any harm."

"Quite true, gentlemen, quite true; we are two of the civilest fellows as ever was," Tim began.

"And who asked *you* to speak?" Bates growled, in such a wicked manner as made Tim stop on the instant.

"Misfortune follows misfortune," sighed Tim to himself; "it is out of the frying-pan into the fire. When will all these strange ups and downs cease?"

"The truth is, young man," said Captain Jack to Bob Bertram, after he had bandaged his comrades' wounds, "the truth is as you say, we *have* fallen into rough hands to-night—very rough hands indeed. Did you ever hear of a person hereabouts called Bob Bertram?"

"Yes, I think I have," said Bob, coolly. "What of that?"

"Well, its all through him that we've got all these cuts and wounds."

"Indeed!"

"Yes," said Captain Jack, inventing lies as he went on; "we are officers of the crown, and were sent to escort this Bob Bertram to London, but he escaped just in time. We got scent of where he was hiding, and overtook the carriage in which he was escaping. Like brave men and good officers, we attacked it, but just as we were on the point of securing the rascal, out pounces a score of villians upon us from a wood. After a desperate encounter we killed and wounded a great many, but were at last compelled to fly, for the whole village was at our heels."

"Indeed!" said Bob, in wonder; "but are you sure that the person in the carriage really *was* Bob Bertram?"

"Not a doubt of it!" said Captain Jack, pleased with his well-told string of lies.

During this conversation, and while Jack was dilating at great length upon the bravery of himself and comrades, a stranger entered the room and took a seat on the dark side of the fire-place.

Bob and Tim exchanged quick looks at one another on the stranger's entrance.

It was not Wildfire Ned.

Who, then, could it be?

It was Phillip Redgill.

The place where he sat was shaded from the fire-light so completely that he had a good view of each person's countenance, but yet no one saw his own.

"You are mistaken, my friend," said Redgill, at the conclusion of Captain Jack's remarks, "you are mistaken; the murderer, Bob Bertram, was not in the carriage at all."

"No!"

"Who dare dispute our word?"

"Who told you so?" said Bates, Faulkner, and Captain Jack in a breath, and in tones of annoyance.

"*I* did!" said Redgill, rising, "the murderer was not near the spot."

"Not near the place?"

"No! he was sitting quietly in the parlour of a road-side inn during the whole of the fight."

"Prove it."

"Do you want to make us all out liars, then?"

"I *can* prove it!" said Redgill, all the time speaking in a forced voice, quite unnatural to him; "and if you put me to the test, I can tell you where the murderer is now at this present moment."

"Ha!"

"Where?"

"There's a good reward offered, tell us at once," said Captain Jack and others.

"You have not to look far for him," said Redgill, with a triumphant laugh.

Bob Bertram's blood now ran cold.

"I am betrayed," he thought, "and must fight my way out of this."

"And who told you?" said Bates.

"A youth called Ned Warbeck. I met him on the road: he has been to this inn once to-night, has he not landlord?"

"I believe he has," was the innkeeper's answer.

"But where is this Bob Bertram, then?" said Captain Jack impatiently.

"*There!*" said Redgill, pointing to where Bob Bertram sat. "I know him, so does the landlord, and so does that thin-legged groom in the corner."

But they held their peace.

"Scoundrel!" said Bob Bertram, rising instantly. "Scoundrel!" he said, and fired at the informer.

Redgill anticipated something of this sort, and dodged so cleverly that the shot missed its aim.

In a second, Bob Bertram was surrounded by Captain Jack's party.

He fought most manfully to get loose from his assailants, but they were too numerous for him.

Besides that, his confinement and anxiety for the past few days had weakened him very much, so that he did not at the moment possess one-third of his ordinary strength.

Old Bates was the first who dared to assail Bob, but a well-directed blow, clean from the shoulder, knocked the red-nosed rascal off his legs.

Right manfully did Bob fight, but it was all to no purpose.

He was bound with cords; resistance was hopeless and useless.

He cast a look at Redgill—a glance that was filled with venom and scorn.

"Villain!" he said. "We have met before, blood-thirsty scoundrel! Do you remember the night of my father's murder, red-handed knave? You shall not always triumph; *my* day will come."

"What does the rogue say?" Redgill remarked, coolly.

"Oh, never mind *him*, sir," said Captain Jack, recognizing in Redgill the young man who had escaped from the carriage and given him the purse of gold, "never mind him, *sir*; he's only raving. All your great criminals rave and rant when officers lay their hands upon 'em; it's quite natural, just like pigs when they're going to be killed—they always squeal most then. Lor, bless yer, sir, we've had lots of criminals in hand in our time, ain't we, Bates?"

"I believe yer," said that worthy.

Turning to Bob, who was bound now with cords he said, "What d'yer mean by calling this 'ere gentleman names for, eh? Why, we knows him well," said Bates, in allusion to Redgill.

"If you do," said Bob, "take care of him; *he* is the man who murdered my father, not me; his name is Bolton."

"Quite mistaken," said Captain Jack; "his name ain't nothing of the sort—it is Mr. Phillip Redgill."

"Quite true," said Phillip, with a smile of contempt. "And, now that I have assisted you in re-capturing this vile murderer, I will mount and journey to London."

"Quite right."

"Many thanks, my noble captain."

"A pleasant journey."

"Don't forget our appointment," said Redgill to Jack. "I suppose he is——"

"Dead as a herring," whispered Captain Jack. "I shot the old 'un through the head, but we couldn't do much with the young 'un, though, so had to hook it."

"Young 'un?" said Redgill, in surprise. "What young 'un do you allude to?"

"Why, that young Wildfire devil as came galloping and pistolling and slashing among us single-handed."

"Who could it have been?" said Redgill. "Was he near my size?"

"No, less than you; not near so strong; but, lor bless yer, he's as active as a cat, and rode a splendid mare he called Starlight."

"Starlight?" said Redgill. "There is but one mare of that name around Darlington, and that one belongs to——"

"Wildfire Ned," said young Warbeck, entering at the moment.

Redgill turned pale as death, and averted his face.

Tim and Bob Bertram were overjoyed at this un-looked for arrival.

Captain Jack and his party were thunderstruck.

"The devil!"

"'Tis he!"

"The very one I spoke of."

"Edward Warbeck, gentlemen, at your service," said Wildfire Ned, bowing.

"Cut the brat in two!" (said old Bates, with his eyes glaring in anger like two live coals. "Cut the brat in two."

"Blow out his brains—the bastard!" said Philip Redgill, feeling safe among so many friends. "Blow out the bastard's brains!" he said, in a hissing tone.

"Down with him!"

"Spare him not!"

"H-o-l-d!" said Wildfire Ned, in a loud tone, and waving his hand in command. "H-o-l-d! I say! The first man that stirs shall fall by my sword."

These words were said in such a clear, ringing tone, and with an air of such cool defiance that Captain Jack and his followers were astounded.

Without a word of apology, Wildfire Ned cut the rope that bound Bob Bertram, and then said to Captain Jack—

"You are the leader of this party?"

"I am," was the gruff reply. "How dare you interfere with our prisoner, then? We are officers of justice."

"Injustice, you should have said," Ned coolly replied, laughing, "and if you are not all hung within a week you owe it to my clemency."

"To you?" said Bates, with a curling lip.

"Yes, to me, old man; nay, don't growl so. I fear you not, you cannot bite any one. Think yourself very lucky that I do not punish your insolence on the spot."

Ned's manner was so firm, cool, and brave, that it seemed to act like a spell on all present, for no one moved from where they stood or sat, but looked on with surprise and curiosity at what then took place.

Walking up to Redgill, Ned said, calmly, but in tones which all could hear—

"We have met again."

"We have," was the hoarse response of the dark villain, as he curled his lip in demon-like scorn.

"You called me bastard," said Wildfire Ned, in a tone of fiery anger, "this is my answer!"

So speaking, he slapped Redgill in the face, and then spat upon him.

"Hollo! what's all this?"

"He's struck our friend."

"Knock the brat down," said one and another.

"Keep your places," said Ned, with a look of scorn; "the first man of you that dare interfere in this quarrel shall in less than a minute lie at my feet a bleeding corpse!"

Throwing off his cloak, he stood before Phillip Redgill, sword in hand.

"Come on!" said he, "I told you we should meet again; draw, I tell you, draw villain, or I will slay you where you stand, Phillip Redgill!"

"He shall not fight!" said Captain Jack; "but, if you will kick up a shindy, and insist upon blood-letting, why, then, I will accommodate you."

"Yes, and I!"

"And I!"

"Wait, then," said Ned. "Trust me, you shall all have your turn, but I will commence with this one first. Phillip Redgill, draw!"

He did so, but with an air of great reluctance.

Ned stood upon his guard.

On the instant, however, and before he was aware of any treachery, Redgill fired at him.

The ball grazed Ned's cheek.

"Cowardly hound!" he cried, and rushed on his foe with the fury of a fiend.

In an instant, the whole place was in an uproar.

Bob Bertram, Tim, and the landlord were surrounded by Captain Jack's followers, and a deadly encounter took place.

The clash of swords, the report of fire-arms, and the shouts and cries of all in the house, awoke wild echoes in the silent night.

To add to the confusion all the lights were overturned and extinguished.

At the first opportunity Master Tim crept under the table out of harm's way.

But Bob, the publican, and Wildfire Ned, pushed their antagonists so fiercely that in less than ten minutes Phillip Redgill was carried out into the yard bleeding and pale.

Captain Jack and his men were thoroughly beaten, but they continued the fight outside the house, on the spacious green in front of the door-way.

Here in the moonlight was seen the flash of swords, and heard the deep guttural curses of the antagonists.

"We must get out of this at all cost," said Captain Jack to Faulkner; "all our chaps are wounded; we must beat a retreat at once. Get our horses, Faulkner."

Captain Jack vaulted upon one animal, Faulkner did so upon another.

Just when about to start off, they were surprised to see a horseman approaching at a terrific gallop.

In his arms he held a lovely female, whose snow-white garments were streaming in the wind.

It was Colonel Blood with Ellen Harmer!

In about five minutes Captain Jack and Faulkner were seized with horror at what they then saw.

Colonel Blood's carriage, with its skeleton coachman and footman, and with weird-wild skeleton forms inside, dashed past the inn door in pursuit, waving their bony arms and shrieking most hideously.

This strange, unearthly spectacle seemed to fill all with horror.

Even Wildfire Ned desisted from the combat and gazed steadfastly upon the grim cortége as it passed the inn.

Suddenly a piercing and uncommon cry was uttered by Phillip Redgill as he turned his eyes towards the vehicle.

The coach stopped.

In an instant the skeleton descended from the box.

Those inside alighted with great expedition, and, weapon in hand, advanced towards the inn door.

Wildfire Ned was astonished, but not dismayed.

He bit his lip, and his eyes flashed fire.

Without a word of warning the Skeleton rushed upon him.

Captain Jack and Faulkner spurred their horses away from the spot as speedily as possible.

They did not stay a single moment longer to witness what took place.

They only thought of their own safety, and galloped off as if they had suddenly confronted so many devils.

One of the Skeleton Crew secured Redgill as he lay bleeding under a tree in the garden, and conveyed him to the coach.

Tim did not much relish any fresh encounter whatever.

Inspired with curiosity, and a keen desire to lay hands upon anything which the coach contained, he went up to the door, and peeped in.

The suppliant cries of those inside affected Tim's heart, and he loosed them from their bondage by cutting the cords with which they had been bound.

This he did, but only on condition of their promising to help his master, which the liberated coachman and footman swore most solemnly to do.

When they stepped out of the carriage, however, they breathed very hard for a moment or two, and, seeing the fight going on all around them, took to their heels like lamplighters, nor even turned their heads.

Up the road they ran, as nimbly as rabbits, until, breathless, and almost on the point of bursting a blood-vessel, they fell headlong into a marshy pool, and lay there without attempting to move.

Wildfire Ned, Bob Bertram, and the plucky innkeeper, however, had, up to this time, been busily engaged with their grim opponents.

The publican had closed with one of them, and, in fast embrace, were then wrestling on the ground.

Bob Bertram used his sword with both hands, and, much to his delight, cut off the arm of one and leg of another.

Judge of his astonishment and horror, however, when each of those grim worthies picked up his severed limb, and hobbled off towards the coach, perhaps there to reset them, for all he knew, since they never returned to the combat again.

Ned, however, with his back to a tree, contended with two at once.

With his good sword he hit right and left, first at one and then at another.

But it seemed as if to no pupose, for as often as they were cleaved to the earth, they rose again, as nimbly as if they were made of india-rubber and springs combined.

"There's only one vulnerable part with these devils, I'm told," said Ned to himself, "and that is to fairly pierce them between the eyes and nose."

With well-directed thrusts Wildfire Ned attempted this feat repeatedly, but failed, and his efforts were rewarded by loud derisive laughter by his enemies.

At last he succeeded.

With a wild, ear-piercing shriek, a grim monster fell to the earth, and his marrowless bones crashed together with an unearthly sound.

"That's one of them," said Ned, in high glee, but, before he could utter another word, he saw approaching, right and left, a whole company of skeletons marching in great haste to the spot.

"We shall all be massacred," said the innkeeper, in horror; "the whole band are out to-night."

"Fall back, lads; fall back," said Wildfire Ned; "get into the house again, and let us bar the doors."

This was quickly done, and greatly to Master Tim's annoyance, for he was now shut out.

With the nimbleness of a cat he climbed up the water pipe into a chamber window.

He could not get in very well, and hung outside for some moments, dangling just above the heads of the Skeleton Crew below.

Ned pulled him in, however, and warded off several vicious blows aimed at Tim, which, had they struck him, must have killed him on the spot.

"We are safe now for a time," said the innkeeper, bravely; "but I fear they will burn us out. We shall be roasted alive."

Tim heard this remark, and was seized with a wild frenzy.

He threw chairs and crockery out upon the heads of those below, who, now very numerous, were clamouring at and endeavouring to burst in the door.

"Set fire to the house," said Death-wing, who had now arrived. "Set fire to the house at once; they will soon cry for quarter, but give them none; as they rush out, kill them on the spot. We'll soon make them surrender."

"Never," said Wildfire Ned, at an open window. "Never!"

In a few moments, however, the house and stables were set fire to, and the Skeleton Crew, sure of consuming their foes, danced round and round in wild, unearthly joy.

"Oh! heaven protect us!" the innkeeper gasped. "We shall all be blown up."

"What!" said Ned, never for a moment loosing either coolness or courage.

"Blown up, Mr. Warbeck," said the host. "I have a hundred pounds of powder in a cellar which is situated a few yards before the front door."

"One hundred pounds of powder?" said Bob.

"Yes."

"How came it here?"

"Lieutenant Garnet and a party of sailors found it on the beach not many weeks ago. It was destined for the Skeleton Crew, but Lieutenant Garnet placed it here, saying he would call and remove it soon."

"That's just the thing we want," said Ned, in high glee.

In a few moments, Bob and Wildfire Ned descended into the cellar described, and, after putting a slow match to the barrel, firmly closed the cellar-door, and returned again to the room above.

Ned threw a rope out of window as if about to escape.

This was noticed by those below, who hailed Ned's appearance at the window with derisive cheers as they brandished their weapons, and sung about their long white arms in a ghostly dance.

"The fire is doing its work," said Death-wing, in high glee. "We'll have revenge on the publican, he has always been an enemy of our crew, and a friend to Garnet. Look out, they will be burnt out like rats in less than five minutes. Stand by, every one of you, ready to receive them as they jump out of the window. Let them fall on the points of your sword."

When least they expected it, however, the powder exploded!

The earth about ten yards in front of the main doorway suddenly upheaved.

An awful rush of fire succeeded.

Many of the skeletons were blown into the air.

This concussion was very great, and for a moment the house trembled as if it would crumble into dust.

It did not, however.

All in the house who had not laid themselves down on their faces were thrown off their legs.

The windows were smashed.

The doors flew open as if by magic.

"Now's our time," said Ned, and, followed by the innkeeper, Bob Bertram, and Tim, rushed out sword in hand.

By the light of the burning dwelling and stables the fight was continued, and now more desperately than ever.

Tim, in his hurry to rush out and get away, stumbled into the deep hole made by the explosion.

He had scarcely reached the bottom, however, when one of Death-wing's band seized him, and almost squeezed him to death.

Tim was now bound to fight or die, and as he much preferred the former condition of the two, he kicked and bit and fought like a tiger, each one of them rolling over one another by turns, and almost burying themselves in the loose earth.

Wildfire Ned sought out Death-wing, but not where could that remorseless chief be found.

He called upon him to stand forth and engage in deadly combat, but there was no response to this bold challenge.

When least expected, however, and when in the fulness of his vigorous onslaught upon the grim gang, he, Wildfire Ned, was seized by some one from behind !

A thrill of horror ran through his whole frame.

Death-wing, with a loud shout of triumph, cried out,—

"Victory ! victory !  Ned Warbeck is our prisoner!"

"Liar !" Ned growled, and with a mighty effort released himself from Death-wing's grasp.

They now stood face to face.

That moment to each was momentous in the extreme.

Each one was nerving himself up for the final struggle.

Loud shouts now burst out upon Ned's delighted ears.

With an irresistible rush, cutlass in hand, Lieutenant Garnet, with a brave band of blue jackets, dashed upon the scene.

With a wild, joyous shout, such as British tars alone know how to give, Garnet's men pressed their way into the thickest of the fight.

The combat now was a grand sight indeed.

The night had turned to inky darkness.

Not a star was visible.

In the foreground was the mixed assemblage of fierce combatants.

Blue jackets of the sailors mixed with the white, skeleton forms which danced hither and thither like ghosts in the darkness.

All the background was brilliantly lighted up by the blazing tavern, and conflagration of numerous stables.

Wildfire Ned and Bob Bertram each took command of a party of sailors, and attacked Death-wing's gang in every direction.

Death-wing mounted his coal black charger, and endeavoured to arouse his followers to greater efforts and more desperate acts of daring.

Ned and Bob Bertram followed the example.

Once on the back of Starlight, Ned felt more at home.

Everywhere he sought to confront Death-wing.

All his efforts were in vain.

The skeleton chief seemed to be ubiquitous.

Wherever he was seen at one moment he disappeared on the next.

Beaten back at all points, Death-wing and his followers gave way.

They gradually retreated towards a dangerous morass, and thence into a dense wood, whither it was deemed inadvisable to follow them.

Indeed, it seemed impossible to follow them, for they disappeared like myths, or Will-o'-the-Wisps, in the marshy bog.

When Lieutenant Garnet and his men were collected, it was found that many of them had been very dangerously wounded by the gang.

It must be confessed that on this occasion Death-wing had used all his generalship and courage.

But nothing could withstand Wildfire Ned, Garnet, Bob Bertram, and the innkeeper.

Of Tim it behoves us to speak a little.

He got very roughly handled by his grim opponent, in the deep pit, but that was all.  He extricated himself out of the hole.

He then mounted a tree, and, there perched, had an excellent view of the battle by the light of burning buildings.

He would shout out occasionally, "That's it, Master Ned !"—"Give it to 'em, Bob !"—"Smash the rascals, my brave sailor boys !"—"Hurrah for Lieutenant Garnet !"—"Bravo, Wildfire Ned !"

But Tim became so noisy during the combat that he attracted the attention of Death-wing.

"Bring that fool down," said Death-wing to one of his men, as he rode past the spot.  "Bring that noisy fool out of the tree, and pitch him into the burning tavern !"

"What a civil devil," thought Master Tim, and clambered up the tree still higher.

Death-wing's orders, however, were obeyed.

A skeleton, with a long dagger between his teeth, clambered up the tree.

# THE SKELETON CREW; OR, WILDFIRE NED.

"THE BODILESS LEGS WALKED SLOWLY ACROSS THE PATH."

With a thick bough, which Tim had torn from the tree, he took deliberate aim, and dealt his enemy a tremendous thwack on the skull, when half-way up the tree, and knocked him down again.

This trick Master Tim had played several times with great success; but ere long two skeletons essayed to climb up after him.

For a few moments they amused themselves with firing at Tim with their pistols.

This was very pleasant sport for them, but quite the contrary to Tim, who jumped about as nimbly as a squirrel, and after many attempts successfully hid himself in the upper part of the trunk!

"I'm safe now." thought he; but to his horror

No. 6.

he heard his grim pursuers climbing up and probing the rotten trunk with their swords every yard as they ascended.

One of their sword-blades grazed Tim's shin, and he quickly fell from his perch right to the bottom of the trunk, and some three feet below the surface of the earth.

For be it remarked the tree was an immense old cypress, which in all cases have hollow trunks.

The two skeletons searched and searched in vain.

They cut, and hacked the soft bark, and, wherever they found a knot-hole, plunged their long sword-blades into it, in hopes of transfixing the unlucky, and timorous groom.

But with a long-drawn sigh, Tim thanked his

stars that he was now safe, and, as he turned his eyes upwards, he plainly saw the two skeletons looking down upon him.

But they did not perceive him.

They gave up the search, thinking that their intended victim had escaped by crawling out on to a large branch, and then dropping to the ground among the combatants on every side.

They left the tree; and Tim, all alone in his momentary glory, had serious misgivings as to how he should escape.

He could *not* get up again, for his own weight in his descent had forced him down, with a little squeezing, but it could not force him up again!

"I'm doomed!" groaned Tim, in his dismal incarceration; "and shall be stifled, or die of hunger here."

His position, it must be confessed, was an unenviable one.

" I'm in a living tomb," he groaned, and as the rats, mice, insects and other creeping things now began to nibble him in every part of the body, and with great industry, he shouted out with horror and positive pain.

Crouched up as he was, and sitting almost like a tailor upon his curled-up legs, he had no power to move.

Wherever he thrust forth his hand it came in contact with some slimy, creeping thing, which made the blood curdle in his veins.

To add to his misery, he now heard the voices of Wildfire Ned, Bob Bertram and Lieutenant Garnet shouting to their followers in tones of triumph.

Next followed a rousing cheer from the lusty sailors as they left the spot in pursuit of their grim and stubborn enemies.

Tim shouted again and again with his utmost power.

But his voice died away, and was not heard in the noise and confusion which reigned on every side.

"I'm lost! I'm lost!" he cried, and gave way to despair.

All was now quiet around the old cypress tree.

Save the crackling of the burning dwellings and the sharp cries of many who were wounded, poor Tim heard nothing.

He resigned himself meekly and humbly to die.

" If I had only acted bravely," he thought, " this misfortune wouldn't have happened to me. But how could I help it? Wildfire Ned is a perfect devil, and don't care any more for a sword-cut than I would for a flea-bite. This all comes of being a coward," he groaned. " Curse the Skeleton rascals! D—n this tree which offered me protection! If I could only get out of this stifling hole, I'd give——"

" What! what would you give?" asked a solemn voice near to him.

Tim began to shiver in every limb.

" Was that a voice I heard?" he sighed. " No, it cannot be; it must have been all im——"

" Reality!" interrupted the voice.

For a moment the frightened prisoner dared not move.

" 'Tis the devil," he muttered.

Before he could utter another word Tim felt the earth moving from under him.

With a groan he endeavoured to cling to the inside of the tree.

The effort was vain.

When least expected he felt himself gradually going.

At last he suddenly fell into a cave some twenty feet below!

## CHAPTER XIV.

### THE BRIDAL BALL—UNEXPECTED VISITORS—THE DREAD ALARM—THE MUFFLED PEAL OF BELLS.

WILDFIRE NED, Bob Bertram, Lieut. Garnet, and the brave old innkeeper, followed the Skeleton Band as far as they possibly could, but, as we have said, soon lost sight of their grim and bloodthirsty enemies.

The sailors, meanwhile, acting under Garnet's orders, now returned to the burning tavern and exerted themselves with great courage and labour to extinguish the flames.

This they succeeded in doing to some great extent, and soon were joined by crowds from the village of Darlington, who had been attracted to the spot by the lurid glare in the sky.

The spirit-room of the tavern was saved, and all it contained, but little else.

Old Nettles, the landlord—for such was his right name—was too much overjoyed at vanquishing the Skeleton Crew to think much of his loss, particularly as Lieutenant Garnet had informed him that he would be recompensed by the king himself for all he had lost, and much more given to him besides, for so bravely fighting in the cause of law and order against Death-wing's friends.

Full of joy, and not caring a button for his wounds, he helped to gather up all the stock which had been saved, and, amid loud applause, distributed ales, wines, and spirits in abundance to all comers.

The sailors were in their glory, and drank health and long life to Nettles, landlord of the " Grapes," in many a flowing tankard, and many a brimming glass sparkling with good old Jamaica rum, as they merrily squatted on the green grass smoking their pipes.

Among others who had hurried to the scene of conflict, with his servants well armed (but who by accident arrived too late), was young Lord Walton, from the Abbey, some five miles away.

The old marquis, his father, had a large party of lords and ladies assembled at the Abbey that night to celebrate the marriage of his only daughter, Lady Julia.

Lord Walton, the son, however, did not remain a moment in the ball-room when it was whispered to him that the Skeleton Crew were abroad.

Unknown to any one, he gathered together a band of trusty servants and hurried forth to lend his aid.

But if he arrived too late, he greatly admired the courage and daring of those who had so long contended with the Crew; and in token of his admiration invited Lieutenant Garnet, Wildfire Ned, and Bob Bertram to pass the rest of the night at the Abbey, and partake of the hospitality there, and join in the merry marriage dance.

This just suited the three heroes, and with little pressing they accepted the invitation, particularly as this was the last night which Wildfire Ned intended to pass on shore.

He was to join Lieutenant Garnet's ship on the morrow, for on the spot the brave sailor offered Ned a commission as midshipman, which he readily accepted.

Away then they sped across the country and soon reached Walton Abbey, when the soft crash of music, and the gliding of graceful figures past the many windows, proclaimed that the marriage festivity was at its height.

When the truth was told about Wildfire Ned and the others, and of their gallantry in dispersing the Skeleton Crew, every one was amazed, and fair dames smiled on Ned as he gaily whirled in the dreamy mazes of the dance.

But soon a change came o'er the festive scene.

The bells of the village church, with muffled peals, suddenly broke forth upon the night with a discordant funereal clang.

The dance was stopped.

All looked amazed.

Young Lord Walton entreated all to be calm, and meanwhile with an old and trusty servant went to the entrance hall to ascertain the cause of a sudden noise heard there.

The doors were flung open.

There stood before him a grim sight.

Death-wing, among his mounted band, with torch and link in hand, all in a blaze of lured light, in a hoarse voice, demanded admittance to the ball.

For a moment the young lord remained motionless.

He could scarcely believe the evidence of his own eyesight.

He had often heard of the Skeleton Crew before, but had never seen anything of them.

Until that night he looked upon that band as a myth, believed in only by the dull and ignorant rustics around him.

Had not the story come from the lips of young Warbeck and Lieutenant Garnet, who had more than once encountered those grim creatures, he would have still believed that they were all imaginary creatures.

But here was proof positive of their existence.

The hair of the old servant who accompanied the young lord to the hall door stood up with fright as he looked out upon the ghastly gang before him, and his knees began to tremble.

"Who and what are ye?" asked the young lord, in firm and determined tones.

"Death-Wing and his crew," was the hoarse response.

"What want ye here, at this hour of the night?"

"Open wide the door," said a chorus of Skeletons.

"Stand back," said young Walton, as he drew his sword, and flourished it; "the first of ye that stirs shall perish!"

A coarse laugh was the only response.

In a second Death-Wing, with a heavy blow, knocked young Walton senseless to the floor.

The old butler fell flat upon his face with horror in the entrance hall.

Before they entered the Skeleton Crew threw their torches in a heap upon the ground, and walked boldly into the hall.

Some few of them remained behind to mind the horses.

All was now darkness.

On the first landing Death-Wing halted, and directed his men to enter the rooms to the right and left.

One of these rooms was at that moment being prepared for the bridal supper, and many servants were engaged in laying out the tables with costly plate.

Two or three Skeletons entered.

The servants gave a loud shout of terror, and vanished through an opposite door.

They made their way at a terrific pace towards the ball-room.

"What means all this commotion?" said the marquis.

"Where is my son?" demanded the marchioness.

"My brother, has aught happened to him?" said the trembling bride.

Before any explanation could be given one of the doors opened, and in rushed several of the Skeleton Crew.

On the instant they were confronted by Wildfire Ned, Lieutenant Garnet, and Bob, and most of the gentlemen present, who whipped out their swords, and darted at the grim intruders.

Some of the ladies fainted.

One or two old gentlemen jumped on the window-sills out of danger.

Others tried to escape.

But, as they rushed in one direction out of harm's way, other doors opened and different parties of the Skeleton Crew came into view.

All was a scene of terror and confusion.

It seemed to the affrighted assembly as if the dead had risen from their graves.

The combat was fierce and fiery.

The bridegroom was one of the first to fall in the melee.

Lady Julia ran forward to assist him.

On the instant, however, and unperceived by the many, Death-Wing advanced with hasty strides, seized the bride, and carried her from the room.

This was the sole object of Death-wing in making his visit.

When it was accomplished he darted down stairs, with the fair one fainting in his arms, and mounted his horse.

A shrill cry he gave, which was recognised by all his followers, as he mounted his strong horse, and galloped away.

His band understood the manœuvre, and as quickly as they could, fought their way towards the entrance-hall, leaped upon their horses, and flew away like the wind, with wild shouts of triumph.

"Pursue! pursue!" shouted Ned, fierce with anger.

His advice was followed on the instant.

Horses were called for; but the terrified servants were loth to come forth from their hiding-places to answer the summons.

They had madly rushed to all manner of places for concealment.

Some had made their way to the top of the mansion, and there concealed themselves behind chimney-pots, and even in the deep rain gutters.

One or two had actually climbed up chimneys, and were almost smothered in soot.

"Anywhere! anywhere!" was the cry among them.

Somewhere or anywhere to hide, so as to be out of sight and reach of Death-wing's awful band.

More than one had locked themselves into pantries, among the plates, dishes, and so forth, and great was the crash of valuable earthenware.

No one among the whole household seemed to care what they did or what they broke, so that they could get out of the way.

A fat footman who had rushed to the coal cupboard, found it occupied by another corpulent servant, who had managed to squeeze himself in there.

Dirty as he was, he darted into the beautiful bridal chamber, turned down the bed-clothes, and tumbled in boots and all!

With this state of confusion reigning, therefore it was impossible for Wildfire Ned, Garnet, or any one else, to get their horses quick enough to pursue the villains with any chance of success.

Bob Bertram was foremost at the stables.

There were more than twenty horses there besides his own, and those of his friends.

He ran hither and thither, busy with hands and voice, and ere long a party of gentlemen started in hot pursuit, led on by Wildfire Ned, who, with loud shouts, dashed spurs into Starlight, and was foremost of them all.

———

## CHAPTER XV.

### IN WHICH SOME OF THE VILLAGERS ARE MADE SANDWICHES OF.

THE village of Walton, near to the abbey, never forgot that memorable night on which Lady Julia, a newly-made bride, was carried off by the chief of the Skeleton Crew, and her young husband cruelly killed.

It was an event which shocked the most hardened.

During the day, the whole village, and its surroundings had been making holiday in honor of Lady Julia's nuptials, and everything had passed off with the greatest satisfaction to every one.

But few persons were astir, and these consisted of the village clerk, the butcher, the druggist, the post-master, and a few other notabilities, who were warming their legs round the tavern fire, and indulging in all manner of stories, both wild and strange, until long after the church clock had struck the hour of twelve.

The parson's clerk was just in the middle of a ghost-story; his hearers, with open mouths, and staring eyes, listened in wrapt attention.

The wind sighed down the chimney most dolefully, and the clerk began to look very nervous and shaky.

He had just got to that part of his tale where the ghost appears upon the scene, when the village bells in a discordant peal clanged out upon the silent night.

Every one in the parlor of the " Black Bull " was startled.

For a moment they looked at each other, and then towards the door, as if expecting that the ghost so often mentioned in the story would really step in among them.

They listened again and breathed very hard.

Still they heard the dismal clanging of the village bells.

" Who is that ?"

" What can that mean ?"

" How comes this ?" said one and all.

" Don't thee hear it ?"

" Why, in course we do."

" What can it mean ?"

" Oh, it's some o' the drunken ringers as have got into the steeple, and want to frighten us," said the courageous butcher.

" Then, let us go and stop 'em," said the clerk. " Who'll go wi' me ?"

" I will."

" And so will I," several replied at once.

They left the cosy parlour, and, lanterns in hand, proceeded through the village, armed with thick, stout cudgels, bent on giving the drunken bell-ringers a sound thrashing for thus disturbing the silence of the night.

It would have been bad enough, the worthies thought, if the ringers had pealed out merrily; but, instead of that, as we have said, it was a muffled funeral peal which issued from the old tower.

Besides the clerk and his friends, there were numerous others, who left their warm beds intent upon finding out the cause of all this strange and startling disturbance.

Straightway this valiant band of villagers proceeded towards the church, and could plainly see lights in the belfry, and the reflection of persons against the windows and through the lattice-work.

Mr. Clerk led the way up the narrow winding stairs of stone, and, if it must be confessed, swearing the while most lustily against the " impudent varlets " who thus disturbed the peace.

He had not gone far up the stairs when the ringing ceased.

All lights were suddenly extinguished in the belfry.

This was a good sign, the clerk thought, and grasped his thick stick with vigour.

With a loud shout, he and the others rushed into the ringers' room, lanterns in hand.

At that moment the bells, this time unmuffled, gave out a most horrible, clanging sound.

The clerk started back in fright towards the door, and hastily turned on his light.

He and the rest groaned most dolefully, for, there, standing before them, were eight Skeletons, each with a rope in his hand, and, while pulling away most vigorously, grinned most diabolically at the intruders.

The clerk and his friends would have given all the money in Walton to have been a mile or more away.

But there they were, unable to stir, riggling and writhing, and knowing not which way to retreat, or what to do.

" Oh ! mercy on us," said the clerk, almost distilled to a jelly. Why, it's some of the Skeleton Crew; they have changed from a funeral to a joy peal."

" What can all this horrid thing mean ?" said another.

" Mean ? Ha ! ha !" gruffly laughed one of the skeletons, in a voice that made the entrapped villagers quake again. " Mean, eh ? Why, it means that we are so glad to see you, that's all. We wanted some amusement."

" What can these monsters mean or intend to do ?" sighed the clerk, who much wished to get away if he could.

" Mean ? intend ?" repeated the horrible voice again. " Why, it means that we intend to celebrate Lady Julia's marriage with our great chief, Death-wing, and will do honour to the event by hanging every mother's son of you !"

Dismal groans were now heard on all sides.

Some began to gasp from fear.

Others fell to praying.

But the Skeleton Bell-ringers were as good as their word, as we shall see.

They stopped pealing the bells, and glared most hideously at their intended victims.

" So you came here with stout cudgels in your hands, did you, and intended to give us all a good sound thrashing, I dare say ?"

" Not me."

" Nor me."

" I hadn't the remotest idea of any such thing, most august and ghostly strangers," chimed in the terrified clerk, as his legs almost gave way from under him.

" As we know you are lying, parson's man as you are, why, you might as well come forward first. We intend to make an example of."

The poor clerk was dragged out from among his fellows.

Two of the skeletons pulled down the heaviest bell, and much of its slack rope was coiled on the floor.

They held it down.

" That bell is too heavy to swing up one," said

the chief. "Take the apothecary, and make a 'sandwich' of him and the lying clerk."

Much to the astonishment of all present, the clerk and the apothecary were placed back to back.

The slack rope of the great bell was twisted and tied round their bodies, and fastened into a knot.

At a given signal the two skeletons who held down the great bell let go the rope.

Up went the two unfortunate devils, shouting at the top of their voices, and dangling in mid-air, like a couple of spiders on a single thread of web.

In like manner all the rest were " sandwiched," as it was called.

Each rope was wound round the bodies of two at least.

And there they hung, to the infinite amusement of their tormentors, writhing and groaning, their own weight drawing down the bells from time to time, and making the most horrible and discordant noises.

Satisfied with this pleasant handiwork, the Skeleton Bell-ringers left the belfry; and the worthy villagers, fighting like cats tied on a clothes line, pulling each other about, and dancing a most painful hornpipe between the ceiling and floor to the inharmónious jangling of the bells, were left all alone in their glory.

———

## CHAPTER XVI.

### PHILLIP REDGILL IS FOUND TO BE NOT SO CLEVER AS HE CONSIDERED HIMSELF.

PHILLIP REDGILL next appears on the scene of our story in his father's offices.

His father was very rich, and had extensive dealings with ships and valuable merchandize in the City of London.

He was a widower of nearly sixty summers, and had no child but Phillip.

This youth had been well educated, and was allowed an ample income to live on.

But he looked upon commerce as something degrading, and felt ashamed to own among the gay gallants of the town that he was anything less than a person of noble blood.

His propensities for gambling had well nigh ruined his father more than once.

But the fond old parent had overlooked his son's misdemeanours very frequently.

At last it was discovered that Phillip had so far forgotten himself as to forge his father's name to certain heavy bills, and squandered the money on gay persons of the town.

From that time forth a great coldness existed between father and son, and Phillip was told for the last time that he *must* make his annual allowance suffice for his pleasures, and that should he again so disgrace the time-honoured name of Redgill, he would take the consequences, for the law should be enforced, which in those days was "death for forgery."

Phillip, however, had become so accustomed to high life about town, that he looked upon his father's conduct as something very cruel, and resolved to rob him all he could rather than be lowered in the estimation of his "lordly" acquaintances.

A libertine soon brings many a good and rich parent to ruin.

But old Redgill was a man of firm purpose; when he once had made up his mind to anything, and although he did not tell any one of his intentions,

he frequently informed Phillip privately that his conduct was bringing sorrows and misery on his old age, and that if he did not reform he would disinherit him.

All this Phillip Redgill looked upon as a good joke, and set his wits to work to get money as best he could by hook or by crook, so as to still keep up the reputation he had already gained among the gayest of the gay, as " Reckless Redgill."

One of the first things which Phillip did when he found it no longer possible to "screw" money out of his rich old parent, was to form the acquaintance of the notorious Death-wing, chief of the Skeleton Crew.

Old Redgill had two ships on their way from the Indies, laden with gold, spices, and silks.

In consideration of receiving half of the cargo, Death-wing and his infamous crew resolved to waylay these two ships and attack them when about fifty miles from the Land's End.

This was done.

The crew of both ships were murdered in cold blood.

The vessels were run into a snug inlet on the West coast of England, near to where Death-wing's caves and store-houses were situated.

Phillip received but one-fifth of the spoil, instead of one-half.

But he was much too wise to say anything about his disappointment and annoyance.

This system of villany was repeated more than once, but as his father's ships did not arrive in port except at intervals of many months, Phillip often found his money running short, and without any visible means of replenishing his exhausted purse.

In his father's offices he had often heard of old Farmer Bertram's indebtedness, and of how much money was still due on the mortgages at Four Ash Farm.

Mr. Harry Bolton, he also knew, was his father's travelling collector, and was about to start on his usual journey.

As we have seen, Phillip forestalled Bolton's visit to Four Ash farm, and by impersonating Bolton, obtained an interview with old Bertram and murdered him.

Young Redgill was a cool-handed villain, and knew not what remorse was.

Bloodshed to him was quite a usual thing.

He was not a brave young man by any means, as Wildfire Ned often proved.

But it was whispered by those who knew him best that when returning from wine parties he would have no scruple in picking a quarrel with any inoffensive citizen he might fall across, and feel no regret at drawing his sword and wounding any one who was unarmed.

Many a simple shopkeeper and unsuspecting night watchman had been " pinked " by " Reckless Redgill," and no one was any the wiser.

But, like all great rogues and rascals, Phillip was very careful, very careful indeed, in picking quarrels, or drawing his " toasting fork," upon any one who was at all likely or able to resent it blow for blow.

He had up to the present time run along in his career of crime undetected and unsuspected.

But all things have an end.

And so it was with Phillip.

From petty thefts in his father's offices he gradually and swiftly descended to greater villanies, until at last, as we have seen, even coolly-planned murder did not shock or retard him in his life of crime.

Like an apple, he was only getting sufficiently

ripe to fall into the hands of justice, and, as will be seen in due course of time, he met with his proper deserts.

Weak and pale, Phillip sat in his father's counting-house, in which were busily engaged dozens of industrious clerks.

He had sauntered through the offices with a supercilious air, and to those who politely bade him "good morrow" he only returned a contemptuous look, as if they were so much dirt, and beneath his notice.

As usual, he was elegantly dressed, and a servant assisted him into his father's private office, where he lounged in a capacious chair, and toyed with a pet spaniel.

Old Redgill had been informed of his son's wound, but up to the present time knew nothing as to what had occasioned it, for Phillip did not, in truth, in his own words, "he would not condescend" to live in his father's house, but kept up a small but elegant "establishment" of his own, where wine parties, card playing, and magnificent suppers were the order of the night.

After a time old Redgill, the famous East India merchant, entered, and the father and son spoke of many things.

"But you have never told me how you got that sword thrust, Phillip," said the father, in a very anxious tone. "I suppose you and some gay spark fell out on the road and had a pass or two at some roadside inn? I know your proud spirit, my son, and your headstrong valour."

Phillip smiled faintly in a patronizing way, as if "a pass or two" with gay sparks was an every-day occurrence, although his own heart told him that he was one of the greatest cowards and villains unhung.

"No, sir," was the calm reply, "the whole affair occurred in this manner. When I left Darlington Hall with old Sir Richard Warbeck, our carriage was attacked by a band of highwaymen."

"I see, I see," said the fond father, in great glee, "and in beating them off you got wounded?"

"Not that exactly; let *me* tell the story. Old Sir Richard escaped through the assistance of some gallant gentleman unknown to him or myself, and he travelled on alone, for after fighting with the vagabonds, and after I had wounded several of them, they took me prisoner."

"Took you prisoner, eh? What a mercy you escaped at all! You surprise me."

"It will surprise you more to hear what I've got to tell. These ruffians conducted me to a roadside den, some house of call of theirs, and who should I discover but Ned Warbeck among them."

"Ned Warbeck? Impossible!"

"No, it is a fact seeing him there; and knowing what a young rascal he is I accused him of having set on the villains to rob and murder his uncle so as to fall heir to part of the estate."

"Oh, the young scoundrel! And so you think he did so?"

"Think!" said Phillip, with a curling lip. "I am *sure* of it, for who but he could have known of his uncle's intended journey?"

"I see, I see,—go on: this adventure is intensely exciting. And what happened?"

"He knew that I was in the power of his friends, and the young villain became very defiant. He drew his sword, and would have rushed upon me unarmed as I was."

"Cowardly, cowardly boy!" said the father.

"But, when least expected, I whipped a weapon out of the scabbard of one present, and went at him."

"Good! excellent! What then?"

"At the first thrust I disarmed him, and the young villain cried for mercy. I granted it, but when least expected, the whole gang dashed at me, furious that their young chief—"

"Chief! you do not mean, then, that Ned Warbeck has joined a band of robbers, and been made their captain?"

"I do, though, just as you say. They rushed at me with savage oaths. I retreated to the door, fighting as I went, and reached my horse. Just as I was about to escape, young Warbeck dashed out upon me, and gave me a sly thrust."

"Oh, the young imp of the devil!" groaned old Redgill, "just to think of his cunning and roguery: to leave his uncle's home to be captain of a band of highwaymen! Why, the young varlet will shortly grace a gibbet."

"Not a doubt of it, and I shall never rest content until I see it come to pass."

While father and son were thus conversing, one of the clerks entered and announced a stranger.

"Who, and what kind of person is he?"

"An officer of the Crown, sir; a tall man with a black patch over his eye."

"An officer of the Crown," thought Phillip, and his face turned crimson.

"What can he want here?" the old merchant asked.

"I know not, sir; but he is a swaggering kind of person, and is now walking up and down the stone passage entrance-hall, clanking his sword in a very fierce and valiant manner."

"Did he give any name?" Phillip asked, in an uneasy manner.

"No, Mr. Phillip."

"Admit him," said the old man, impatiently. "What can any officer of the Crown want with us, I wonder?"

"I know not," his son answered; "but, as it may be a matter of secresy, I will retire."

"Nay, do not, my son; stay with me."

Phillip, however, rose from his chair with difficulty, and proceeded towards the door.

At that moment it was opened.

Captain Jack stalked in.

For a moment he was staggered at seeing Phillip Redgill, and opened his eyes very wide.

Phillip put his finger to his lips slyly.

Captain Jack coughed significantly, and said not a word.

Phillip now altered his mind, and sat in a chair.

"Your business, sir!" said the old merchant, impatiently.

"My name first, and business afterwards, is the style, I think!" said Captain Jack, doffing his hat, and stroking his chin.

Without invitation he squatted down in a chair, and stretched out his immense long legs to the utmost.

Seeing a decanter of wine on the table, he helped himself to a large tumbler-full, and tossed it off, saying,

"Ah! who wouldn't be an East India merchant to have such sack as that? Ah! d—nd fine stuff for a dusty day."

"Your name, sir?" the old merchant inquired impatiently.

"My name! eh? Ah! just so," he replied indifferently, and with much composure pouring out another glass of wine. "My name, sir, is Captain Jack, and yours is Mr. Redgill, I think; here's health to you, old boy!"

"And your business, here?" said the merchant, amazed at the coolness of his vulgar visitor.

"My business ! eh ? Well, if you want to know, I'm one of the most active, zealous, and valiant officers the Crown can boast ; and as to catching rogues, vagabonds, and cut-throats, there isn't my equal in all the kingdom. I've only got one fault, and that is, I love the bottle."

"All this has nothing to do with me, sir !" said the old merchant, getting red in the face with anger. "Your business here, I demand again ?"

"Don't get frothy, my old friend !" said Captain Jack, "I'm coming to that now."

"And what is it, pray ?"

"I'll just tell you," said Captain Jack, "but as we don't want any intruders, I may as well lock the door."

He rose and did so, and put the key in his pocket.

Phillip was now apprehensive of danger, and turned deadly pale.

His father began to stutter out something, but could not speak plainly.

"I have come here on a very important bit of business," said Captain Jack, "and like an honest man, as I am, don't want to hurt the tender feelings of any one."

"I don't understand you," said the old merchant.

"Well, there has been *murder* committed, that's all," said Captain Jack, with a low chuckle.

"Murder !" gasped the old merchant, retreating a step or two in surprise and horror.

"Murder !" echoed Phillip, with a well-feigned look of astonishment.

"Yes, murder, gentlemen, that's all."

"And what have *I* to do with such a foul charge ?" asked the merchant, indignantly.

"*You* haven't ; but—there—are—certain—parties —not —a — very — great—way— from— here—as —*have*," said Captain Jack, very slowly, and looking carelessly in the direction where Phillip sat.

Young Redgill felt the blood run coldly to his heart as he heard these words.

But he spoke not.

"Some one in *this* house ?" asked the merchant, astonished.

"Yes, in this very house, and no other. Not only murder, mind you, but robbery," said Captain Jack, very coolly. "And a pretty good haul the chap made of it, so I hear. He bagged lots of gold coin. Do you know old Bertram, of Four Ash Farm ?"

"I do ; he is my creditor to a large amount, and has to pay me heavy arrears on a mortgage I hold of him. I expect him in town every day."

"You may expect a long time, then, for he's the chap which was robbed and murdered."

"Impossible !" said the old merchant, turning white. "What a horrid affair ! And have they found out who did it ?"

"Not exactly," said Captain Jack ; "but—I—think — I — can — find — out — afore—long," he answered, slowly and ominously. "I'm coming to that point now. Have you a travelling collector in your house of the name of Bolton ?"

"Bolton ? Yes."

"Of course you have, father," said Phillip, eagerly. "Surely *he* couldn't have been such a wretch as to——"

"Steady, my friends, steady," said Captain Jack, coolly. "Don't be in any flurry, either of ye, but answer me. Did he call at old Bertram's ? Did you order him to call there, and collect your debt ?"

"Yes you did, father. I heard you tell him to do so in my hearing, when last I saw you."

"I know I did, my son ; but when you had gone

I altered my mind, and sent Bolton in quite a different direction. He was not within fifty miles of Four Ash Farm, I'll swear ; that is, unless he went there unknown to me, and contrary to my orders."

A heavy sigh escaped from Phillip's lips, and he felt a cold sweat upon his guilty brow, as he said,

"I know you told him ; but if you countermanded the order, of course that's a different thing. It's an awful charge to be accused of is murder."

"Yes, ain't it !" said Captain Jack, with a wicked grin playing around his large mouth. "And robbery, too. Have neither of ye heard of it afore ? Not a syllable ?"

"Never dreamed of such an abominable affair," said Phillip.

"Lor ! how strange ! and just to think as how this job has been in my hands more than a fortnight, and all the country knows it ; but is this Mr. Bolton in your offices now ?"

"He is."

"Then let us have a squint at him. Order him in here, for I've got an exact description of the party who called at the farm-house ; he was disguised."

The door was unlocked, and in a few moments young Mr. Bolton appeared.

As he crossed the threshold, with a light step and pleasant smile, he suddenly caught the serious gaze of his master and young Redgill.

"You sent for me, sir," he began ; but turned all manner of colours when he confronted his old master's black looks.

"What is all this ?" he asked.

"I am sorry to say, Mr. Bolton," Philip Redgill began, "that you are suspected of a most foul——"

"Not so fast," said Captain Jack, interrupting. "I understand my own business best and want no assistance from any one."

"Look you here, young man," he began, addressing Mr. Bolton, "one of your master's customers and old friends have been murdered, and you are one of the suspected parties."

"I ?"

"Yes, you ; and all I've got to say is that I have got a warrant for your apprehension as being concerned in it, and you must come with me."

"Arrested on the charge of murder ?" Bolton gasped, and he staggered towards the door, past Phillip Redgill, whose countenance wore a malicious smile of triumph.

The news stunned the young man, and he would have rushed away from the spot.

At that moment, however, Mr. Faulkner and another unprepossessing, ugly-looking member of the "Bakers' dozen" appeared at the door, and politely collared the astonished youth.

He was borne away to prison more dead than alive.

But before Captain Jack left the private office he helped himself to another glass of wine, and, as he went out, whispered to Phillip,

"Can't I see you some time to-night ?"

"Where ?" answered Phillip, in a faint voice.

"At the 'Cat and Bagpipes' over the water."

"What time ?"

"At twelve."

"I'll be there."

"*Mind you do*," said Captain Jack, with an ominous wink, and stalked out of the office in a swaggering manner.

"What did the officer say to you, Phillip ?" the anxious father asked.

" He simply said that the case, as it at present stands, looks very awkward for Mr. Bolton."

" Oh, is that all? Yet, methinks he is an unmannerly officer. Did you notice how he winked and blinked at you while he spoke?"

" No; did he?"

" Yes; and had I not known you well, I should have supposed you knew and had dealings with him at some time."

Phillip attempted to smile, as he said,

" Oh, that is nothing; winking their eyes and stroking their noses is only a habit these officers have got. But," he sighed to himself, " I am in their clutches! but will soon rid myself of the bloodhounds. He must visit *me* to-night. I cannot if I would go there to his den of thieves. I know the place well, and would not trust myself among the ragamuffins who meet there, no, not for a thousand pieces of gold. Curse the hour I ever met them. I am tracked and dogged. These fellows shall be removed from my path—they *must* be."

## CHAPTER XVII..

### THE NUBIAN SLAVE AND ELLEN HARMER.

It must be confessed that no man living ever felt less remorse for crime of any kind than did Colonel Blood.

He had been in several wars, and was a rough-handed, cold-hearted villain.

But with all his knavery, he possessed a sort of gentlemanly bearing that admitted him into almost any society of the loose-living period in which he lived, namely, that of the lascivious Charles the Second, whom people are wont to call " the merry monarch."

John Blood had ridden some twenty miles or more; he hired a light and fast four-wheeled vehicle, in order to reach London all the sooner.

Ellen Harmer, almost distracted at thus being forcibly borne away from her father's home, wept and bewailed her cruel fate.

But, had she shed tears of gore, they would have had no effect upon the mind or conscience of her rude, rough-handed captor.

In order to quiet the beautiful Ellen, he administered to her a glass of wine, in which he had placed a noxious drug.

This had the effect of producing sound sleep; nor was she aware of whither the fast-going vehicle was going.

All she knew was, that when she awoke on the following morning, she found herself in a sumptuously-decorated chamber.

Around her were furniture and articles of beautiful design, and evidently of great price.

She rushed out of bed towards the window in great surprise.

It was barred.

But she could see below her splendid gardens, with fountains playing.

Fruit trees and flowers met her astonished gaze on every hand.

All was silent.

" Am I dreaming?" she thought. " Has all that I have passed through been nought but a cruel excruciating nightmare?"

Beside a splendid mirror, in which she could see herself from head to foot, she perceived a massive bell-pull, with fine bullion tassel.

This she mechanically touched.

A soft, sweet sound responded to her touch, like the harmonious tinkling of a silver bell.

The more she looked about her the more she was astonished and confounded at the brilliance, beauty and elegance of all things.

She heard no one approach, but turning suddenly beheld a tall servant, splendidly attired, but his face and bare arms were as black as ebony.

Ellen started.

The servant bowed lowly and smiled.

" Where am I?" the startled girl inquired, with a flushed face and flashing eyes. " Who has brought me hither, and for what?"

The tall Nubian smiled again.

He bowed more lowly than ever, but spoke not.

He motioned to her that he was both deaf and dumb.

" Set me at liberty!" gasped the captive girl, for the first time realizing her true position, " set me free; I cannot breath the atmosphere of this gilded prison. Oh! let me once more flee to my poor old father, or my heart will break!"

So speaking, she sank on her knees before the tall Nubian, and burst into tears.

For a moment the black gazed at the beautiful young creature, and his eyes rolled in wild delight.

He lifted her up from her prostrate position on the floor, and kissed her snowy hand with every token of affection.

This act surprised and startled Ellen more than ever, for the strange intruder was a fierce, tall man, and one who seemed to possess, when he willed it, both the strength of a lion, or the gentleness of a lamb.

# THE SKELETON CREW; OR, WILDFIRE NED.

THE MYSTERIOUS BARBER.

But with all his ferocious exterior there was a something in his smile both tender and re-assuring.

He placed a finger on his lips, and led her gently towards the window.

He next, and with great air of mystery and caution, pulled out of his silk doublet a small ivory tablet.

He partly wrote upon it these words :—

"You are a stranger to me, and, rough as I look, I love you, love you dearly."

Ellen's eyes darted fiery anger at him as she shunned the smiling black.

He took no notice of her seeming repugnance, but smiled, and in the act showed his rows of shining teeth.

No. 7.

He rubbed out the words he had written, and quickly pencilled these others :—

"Do you wish me to be a friend or foe, fair one ?"

"A friend," said Ellen, trembling.

He placed before her the tablet again, and she read—

"I *will* be a friend to you, and a true one, on a single condition."

The girl's blood almost curdled in her veins as she read what he had hastily scribbled, for she now trembled for her honour and chastity.

"Name your condition," she gasped.

"Can you, *will* you keep a secret ?" he wrote.

"I *will*," she answered.

"On your life and honour?" he wrote again.

"Yes, on my life and honour," she answered, firmly, for a moment feeling re-assured by his change of manner.

He now wrote on the tablet.

"I am the slave of Colonel Blood ; they call me Sinbad, and am supposed even by my master to be both deaf and dumb ; but I am not."

"Not deaf and dumb?" she answered. "Then you knew the sounds of the bell I rang?"

"I heard it," he whispered, "and knew its meaning."

"My meaning?" she asked.

"Yes; and my master's also, for he left word with his confidential valet that directly you rang he should be summoned."

"For what purpose?"

"That I will afterwards explain. I knew that you had been abducted, and that when you had fully recovered from the drugs administered to you last night on the way hither you would ring the chamber bell.

"This bell I watched," said the Nubian, "and muffled it in order that I might know when you had awoke from slumber, and forewarn you of all that is to happen to you this day."

"Happen?" said Ellen.

"Yes, maiden ; look not surprised, you are not the first fair victim who has fallen into the treacherous fangs of my master, Colonel Blood."

"For what purpose, then, was I brought hither? I have never harmed any one. What crime am I guilty of?"

"Your beauty is your only crime," the Nubian whispered. "He has brought you hither as a fair one who may be dishonoured, and, thereafter, for a time pander to the lusts of the king, his master."

"Impossible !" Ellen gasped.

"Nay, 'tis true ; but, remember, I have fore-warned you, and if you do but keep your promise I will be your friend ; in helping you I seek my own revenge. I cannot tell you the horrid in-dignity which I have suffered at my master's hands, but you may perhaps at some time learn it. In case you should need it, take this dagger ; con-ceal it in your fair bosom. But, hark ! I hear some one approaching !"

As quick as thought the Nubian crawled beneath the bed and listened.

'Twas Colonel Blood who stood at the door !

———

## CHAPTER XVIII.

### IN WHICH CAPTAIN JACK MAKES AN UNEX-PECTED CALL AT MIDNIGHT.

PHILLIP REDGILL was by far too weak from his recent wound to keep his appointment with Captain Jack at the "Cat and Bagpipes" over the water, and therefore remained at home in his own snug apartments, surrounded as he was by every luxury and convenience.

Richly attired gentlemen of gallant appearance called during the day to inquire after his health and condition.

At night also many of them dropped in to have a chat, and crack a bottle of wine with the invalid.

Masque balls, marriages, elopements, and the latest court scandal were the topics of conversation with Redgill and his friends.

The rattle of the dice-box, and shuffling of cards were the order of the evening among these gay revellers.

Gayest of the gay, and loudest among them all, was Phillip Redgill, who, propped up with pillows on a luxurious sofa, joined the gamblers, and puffed a cigar with as much coolness as if nothing were the matter with him.

The hours flew by, and Phillip neglected his appointment with Captain Jack.

When he occasionally thought of his promise, he only smiled as he reflected,

"That long-legged devil recognised me. Well, chance makes us acquainted with queer people sometimes ; that comes of getting into scrapes upon the road. I suppose he wants to borrow some money of me, that's all. Well, well, he's an ugly-looking rascal, though, and I like not his looks. I'll give that worthy a call to-morrow ; I can't meet him to night ; if I were to take a sedan chair all that distance it would re-open this cursed wound that Wildfire Ned gave me ; d—m him !"

During the night, other arrivals were announced, both lords and ladies of doubtful standing in society, brilliant in silks and paint.

Music, light laughter, jokes, wit, and repartee, echoed through Phillip's pleasant suite of rooms.

Languishing smiles, whispered words, eloquent winks, nods, and pressure of the hand, passed and repassed from one to another.

Some sang, others danced ; here was a boisterous wine party, and there a gossiping set.

The hours flew by, nor did any one give heed to thought or care.

Midnight chimed from the church towers.

The half hour tolled.

But the merry makers took no notice of the flight of time.

One o'clock struck.

A loud knock was heard at the door.

A servant opened it.

Captain Jack stood there, accompanied by several friends.

They were comparatively well-dressed ; but slightly the worse for liquor.

"Who are you, gentlemen?" the servant asked.

"We are——" Captain Jack began.

"No we ain't," replied Faulkner.

"Yes we are,'" said the captain, hiccupping.

"What, sirs ?" asked the servant again.

"Why, gentlemen, to be sure," said Captain Jack, leaning against the door-post.

"I perceive that," the servant replied ; "but I fear me, sirs, you are somewhat the worse for liquor, and have missed your way, and called at the wrong mansion."

"No, dam'me, if I have !" said Captain Jack. "How dare you say that I am the worse for liquor, knave ?"

"I had better shut the door, gentlemen," the servant said.

"And if you do, I'll brain you," said Faulkner, with an oath.

"Go and inform your master that I am here," said Captain Jack. "If he can't keep *his* appointment, why, then, I'll keep *mine*, for I have made up my mind long ago to visit him."

"Yes, and tell him that *we* are here," said Faulkner, and "desire to see him."

"Who shall I say, sir?" the puzzled servant answered.

"Oh, say anything."

"Tell him that my Lord Smash and friends have called," said Captain Jack, laughing. "That's as good a name as any."

"Just so," another replied. "Do you hear, varlet, announce Lord Smash and friends immediately."

Before the astonished servant could recover his breath, Captain Jack and party pushed their way into the hall, and almost terrified out of his life, he bawled out, the parlor door in hand,

"Ladies and gentlemen — Lord Smash and friends."

---

## CHAPTER XIX.

### MASTER TIM GETS INTO THE HANDS OF SMUGGLERS.

THE position of poor Tim, it must be confessed, was anything but pleasant.

He had fallen into the depths below, but how, he could not tell.

All he recollected, when he recovered consciousness, was, that he had fallen into a miserably dark and loathsome place, and not knowing how or which way to move.

"Oh, lor!" he sighed. "Here's a fix to be in. I'd give a thousand gold pieces if I were only out of it."

"Would you?" said a distant voice. "Ha! ha! but, then, you see, you *ain't* going to get out of it, my lad."

"Who are you?" said Tim, trying to pluck up all the courage he possibly could. "Don't you know I've got a dagger left?"

"Yes, I dare say you have," the voice replied. "But, if you had a dozen daggers, or a whole arsenal at your back, they would do you no good here."

At the same moment Tim felt a heavy hand laid upon his shoulder, and his limbs began to tremble.

"What's your name, you shivering hound?" said the gruff voice, with a chuckle.

"Tim, sir, if you please."

"Tim what?"

"Tim Anything—Tim Nothing. I never had but one name; 'tis only rich folks as can afford to have two."

"Come, come, no larking with me," said the gruff voice. "Speak honestly, or I'll brain you."

"You're very kind and obliging, I dare say," said Tim, with chattering jaws. "But, upon my word, I have only one name, and that is Tim."

"You're much different, then, to a young chap as we lately collared, and is now in our custody, for he boasts of four names."

"You don't say so?"

"But, I do, though; you shall make his acquaintance shortly—you'll make excellent comrades. Our hanging days are only once a month now, so you may as well make up your mind to 'swing' when he does."

"Thank'ee," said Tim, gloomily; "you are very kind—very kind, indeed. But, if it's all the same to you, sir, whoever are you? I'd rather be swung up the next month after him with the four names."

The unknown laughed gruffly until he made the cavern echo again with his boisterous merriment.

"When were you born?" he asked.

"I wasn't born at all," said Tim, innocently.

"Not born at all? Why, the rascal is making fun of me."

"'Pon my word I ain't," said Tim. "I wasn't born at all; leastways, not as I knows on, for old Sir Richard Warbeck found me in his stables one morning bright and early, and in them there stables I've been all my life since."

"Sir Richard Warbeck, eh?"

"Yes. Do you know him?"

"I should think I do," said the unknown; "and a nice old fellow he is, too. He has two adopted nephews, hasn't he?"

"Yes, young Wildfire Ned, and Charley Warbeck, who's in the East India House in London."

"Just so."

"And what brought you up that cypress tree?"

"Why, you see, Master Ned and I attacked the Skeleton Crew, and, as they were too many for us, I hooked it up the tree out of the way, and fell through the hollow trunk, and——"

"Found yourself here, eh? Just so. But who told you there was any secret way into this cavern through that tree?"

"No one."

"You lie, knave!"

"On my word, no living soul told me."

"Not old Nettles, the landlord of the public-house?"

"No, he never breathed a word; but fought with the Skeleton Crew like a warrior."

"That's just what *you* should have done, and then I wouldn't have made up my mind to hang you, as I may do yet. Are you sure that old Nettles never said a word?"

"I'm positive, and will swear it!"

"'Tis well, for if he had done so I should be under the necessity of cutting his throat to-night so as to stop his mouth."

"What a blood-thirsty villain!" thought Tim.

"As you will, perhaps, be a dead man shortly, and as dead men don't tell any tales, I don't mind letting you know a thing or two as to who and what old Nettles is."

"What is he?"

"Why, a tavern-keeper; and something more at times," said the unknown. "You have taken notice, of course, what a fine stock of wines, spirits, tobacco, and other things he has?"

"Yes," said Tim, "it has been the talk of the whole country wide, as long as I can remember."

"Quite true; but he owes all his prosperity to *me*, young man," said the gruff voice. "I could have blown him and his house up into the air many a time if I had thought proper. If he had divulged anything about our secret I would do so even now."

Tim groaned.

"This place where you are now in is a cave," said the voice; "a smuggler's cave, mind you."

"Oh, lors!"

"And I am chief of the gang. From this spot there is a long, dry passage, which runs out into the beach at low tide."

"Is the mouth of the cavern filled with water, then, at high tide?"

"Yes, nearly so; but there is sufficient room for an eight-oared boat to float in if the rowers duck their heads."

"How jolly convenient," said Tim, who now began to like the chattiness of his unknown captor.

"At night time we go out of the cavern in our long boats, and meet ships which are creeping close to shore; sometimes they are friends who come from France or Spain with smuggled goods, and sometimes they are strange craft. If they be friends we unload the vessel, and run up our boats into the cave again, then the vessel stands off shore until the next night, and so on until we have emptied her; but if she is *not* a friendly craft we act according to circumstances. Sometimes we seize her goods, if we are very short, and the articles are of any value; they can never find us out."

"But did you never fall across any of the king's cruisers?" said Tim.

"Yes, many a time; but, lor' bless yer simple heart, we don't mind them, you know."

"Don't you, though?"

"No, not in the least."

"But they carry long guns, and might——"

"Exactly; but that ain't nothing when you are used to it."

"No, I suppose not," said Tim, with a sigh. "A ten pound cannon shot playing nine pins with your legs ain't nothing when you get used to it; but getting used to it is the thing," said Tim, very slowly and solemnly; "but I shouldn't—never."

"Yes you would."

"No, I shouldn't."

"Lor, man! a broken arm, or a leg or two knocked off, don't make much difference to any of our gang."

"Nor a broken head either, I should think," Tim said to himself, doubtingly.

"We've got a famous cook, a bit of a tailor, a good doctor, a gunsmith, and other chaps in our band, so we manage to make a pleasant life of it."

"I shouldn't like it."

"Why not?"

"Because you might fall foul of such a man as Lieut. Garnet and *his* crew some day; and if you did ——"

"And if we did, what then? We should have to fight hard, that's all."

"That's all, eh?" thought Tim; "but that's a little more than *I* should care about."

"Why, a fight once in a while is the life and soul of a bold smuggler. You have no notion how it gives one an appetite."

"I should think that a ten-pound cannon shot in one's stomach would be a trifle more than even a smuggler could digest," said Tim; "but, as you very wisely remarked once before, there's no telling when one gets used to it."

"Just so, my brave lad," said the smuggler chief, laughing. "I like to hear you talk in that light-hearted way, for it convinces me that, after all, you've got some good stuff in you, and that your heart is of old British oak. Our boats are going out to night; we expect a schooner off the shore from France about midnight, just after the moon sets. I'll take you with me; and, to try you—unless you wish to be hung as a useless knave among us—I'll give you the honour of mounting the stranger's decks first."

"First!" gasped Tim. "The first man to board the stranger's decks! Why, she might be a revenue cruiser or a well-armed stranger."

"That's what she really is, a well-armed stranger, nothing else. She must come within gun-shot of us, for she's obliged to round the headland in order to get into port."

"In that case, sir," said Tim, "if it's all the same to you, I wouldn't dare to have the impudence to take the place of honour, and be first to scale the stranger's sides—it's too much honour to confer on such a poor good-for-nothing as I am. I would much prefer to be *last*, if anything."

The smuggler chief laughed out loudly, saying, "You're a droll devil, Tim, and no fool, I can very well see; but come this way, I will introduce you to my comrades."

So speaking, he tumbled over head, and fastened the trap through which Tim had fallen into the cave.

"See, Tim," said the smuggler chief, as he entered a second cave in which dimly burned a horn lantern, "do you see this?" he said, pointing to a trap-door in the ceiling.

"Yes, I do," said Tim, scrutinizing for the first time his tall, gaunt, rough-handed companion, and not much liking the looks of his black eyes, shaggy hair and beard, clothed, as he was, in red flannel and an immense pair of water-boots that reached above the knees, at the same time not forgetting to cast his eyes on two pistols and a cutlass that hung in his broad black belt.

"Well," said the chief, "that trap-door leads into the old tavern. Nettle sells all our goods for us, and a pretty penny he gets by it. He's very rich, but a good-hearted old cock as ever lived. He's got a very pretty daughter, too, they call Katie; and if you join us, and prove yourself a brave fellow, as I know you are, why I'll introduce you; and when you're tired of smuggling, you can settle down, like many an old sinner does after he's made heaps of money, and lead a quiet respectable life."

"You're very kind," said Tim, with his head bewildered with all the chieftain said.

From one cavern they passed to another, some of which were artfully ventilated and lighted by holes in the rocks over head.

At last they reached a very large apartment, which had been formed ages ago by the action of the sea, and cut just as cleverly as if done with a chisel.

Round a long table sat smoking and drinking twenty or more rough, hardy-looking fellows, who were card-playing, throwing dice, sleeping, snoring, and the like.

All of them hastily rose as the chief entered, and Tim was introduced to the company in words which conveyed the idea that the stranger would become a valuable member of the band.

Smoking and drinking continued, and soon Master Tim found himself the centre of attraction, and as he was, of course, expected to be a very brave fellow, he favoured the company with a long string of lies, in which he narrated his several encounters with the Skeleton Crew, and against whom he had displayed prodigies of valour.

The chief, however, left the company, and wended his way through the dark caverns towards his own particular abode.

He found standing at his door a special messenger.

"That you, Dolphin?" said the chief. "So soon returned?"

"Yes, worthy Sea-hawk." was the reply. "And I bring most important news."

"From whom?"

"The Skeleton Crew and Wildfire Ned—it needs instant attention."

"It shall be attended to at once. Come this way."

The Smuggler Chief and his trusty messenger entered the apartment together.

---

## CHAPTER XX.

### CAPTAIN JACK PLAYS A TRUMP CARD—THE GAY COMPANY SURPRISED.

As we have narrated in a previous chapter, Captain Jack and his friends insisted upon thrusting themselves uninvited upon the gay and fashionable company assembled in Phillip Redgill's elegantly furnished suite of rooms.

"Lord Smash and friends," said the astonished domestic, announcing the stranger in a loud voice.

"Lord who?" said Philip, in astonishment, as he turned his eyes, and beheld Captain Jack before him.

For a moment he knew not what to do or say.

The thought struck him that they had actually

found out all about old Bertram's murder, and were come to arrest him.

Cold sweat poured from his brow.

His heart felt chilly, and his sight grew dim.

But when Captain Jack, with a broad smile on his ugly face, shook Phillip by the hand, and said, "All serene, old fellow," Redgill felt great relief, as he said to the company with a forced smile,

"Ladies and gentlemen, allow me to introduce to your notice an eccentric friend of mine, who rejoices in the extraordinary title of Lord Smash. These gentlemen, also his companions, are friends of mine, every one; at least, they have proved themselves such, for I owe my life to their bravery and valour."

"Indeed!" said all, in surprise. "Men who would risk their own lives for the sake of another must be friends indeed."

"I quite agree with you there, ladies and gentlemen. I invited them to call upon me at their pleasure, and although they have come at an unlooked-for moment, I am none the less pleased."

"Certainly not," chorused many, "certainly not; but how did the affair happen?"

"This, then, accounts for your painful wound, Redgill?" several gallants said.

"Just so," said Phillip, glad at the happy turn the whole affair had now taken, and particularly pleased that the true character of the intruders had not leaked out.

Upon the instant, and with ready invention, Phillip Redgill concocted an imaginary story, in which he did not fail to laud his own valour, and that of the new arrivals, all of which was agreed to in side-winks by Captain Jack and Faulkner, who, from time to time, drank heartily, and swore roundly that all the company heard was strictly true.

"But now I come to look at your eccentric friend more closely," said a gallant, tapping his snuff-box, and speaking in a whisper, "the more he reminds me of one of the crown officers, called Captain Jack."

This he said with a knowing wink to Phillip, who frowned.

Captain Jack heard the observation, and approached the speaker, and whispered in his ear,

"And now I come to look at *you*, my friend, the more I find you exactly correspond to a young gentleman as Captain Jack has been on the look-out for on the charge of forgery."

The gallant blushed deeply, took a pinch of snuff, and bowed himself away.

"Not so fast, my friend," said Captain Jack to him, as he whispered again. "You are in very snug quarters at present, and I don't wish to disturb you; but if you know how to keep a still tongue in your head, while here in the company, so do I. You understand; is it a bargain?"

"I fear, my eccentric friend, that you have made a slight mistake," said the elegantly-attired young gentleman, with a curling lip. "I know you not."

"I have made no mistake," was the whispered answer; "I can, you know, when I like, swear black's white. But let me ask, do you know a certain person in the India House, a gay young spark about town, named Charles Warbeck?" said Captain Jack, winking.

The stranger tried to smile, but could not.

It was Ned Warbeck's elder brother!

He turned deadly pale, cast a quick glance at Phillip Redgill, and joined the card-players again.

But, though he attempted to be merry and careless, care sat upon his brow, and he sighed to himself.

"I am innocent, but still suspicion is strong against me. Whoever it was that forged Sir Richard's signature to that bill was no friend of mine."

And he could not help thinking, as he sat in that gay and merry throng,

"It was an unlucky day I ever made the acquaintance of you, Phillip Redgill. Still, the end is not yet."

Captain Jack's companions made themselves very much at home, in a rough, off-handed manner.

They were adepts at dice and cards, and, although they began to gamble on no capital whatever, they none of them were long ere they had won large sums from those present.

This happened not so much through fair as foul play, and downright roguery.

However, as long as their cheating tricks were not discovered, or even suspected, they continued the play, and, together with fine wines, spirits, cigars, and the like, they seemed to be enjoying themselves very much, nor did they for a moment know the true reason why Captain Jack had called there that night.

This, however, was soon explained.

The first opportunity that offered, Captain Jack sought Phillip Redgill's side, and began a whispered conversation,

"You did not call at the 'Cat and Bagpipes' as you promised."

"No," said Redgill, "I was too unwell."

"Perhaps the company didn't suit you?"

"True; I must confess it wouldn't look well for a person of my standing to be seen in the company of thieves, vagabonds, and the like."

"Of course not; I forgot all about that."

"Besides, my wound is painful at present."

"Of course it is; it was on account of that I came here myself, in order to save you a long journey."

"Why did you bring all those fellows with you?"

"In case I might need them," said Captain Jack, grinning.

"Need them? I do not understand you," said Redgill, turning red.

"But you may do so after a time."

"Indeed! and what may be your business here, I should like to know? I do not allow persons of your standing to intrude upon me," said Phillip, with a curling lip.

"Indeed! Lor how amazingly proud you're getting," Captain Jack answered, with a sneer, and tossing off a glass of wine. "I thought we should meet as friends."

"Sir, I do not understand you," said Phillip, trying to shake off his rough companion, much like a sparrow frets and struggles when in the talons of a hawk. "In truth, your room is much better than your company."

"I dare say; that's what a good many say. But, then, you see, the Crown can't get along without such as me and my friends."

"The Crown, sir? And what have I to do with you or the Crown, I should like to know? You wish to insinuate something; but, as a man about town, I know too much of you fellows."

"Ha! ha! how clever you are. Lor, who'd a thought it?"

"Thought it? Thought what?"

"Why, that young Bolton is in prison," said Captain Jack, with a smile.

"Serve him right, then, if he is guilty of that foul deed of which you accuse him."

"Yes, now you come to think on it, it *was* a foul and bloody affair, wasn't it?"

"Most horrible."

"And, just to think as how the old man didn't offend even a mouse, and to be cruelly butchered for the sake of a few hundred pounds, and his son clapped in gaol as an accomplice in the deed! He must have been an artful chap as planned that affair."

"Yes, truly, he must, and an heartless villain also," said Phillip. "But why do you stare at *me* so?"

"Nothing. I was only going to ask you a question," said Captain Jack, stroking his chin in deep thought.

"What is it?"

"Your father is very rich?"

"Yes; what of that?"

"And has many ships?"

"Yes."

"And sometimes he insures cargoes?"

"And lives also for those who wish."

"Exactly," said Jack. "And if you were going abroad, how much would you insure *your* life for?"

"That depends. Are you going abroad?"

"Perhaps so."

"I should insure myself even for the benefit of my friends, if nothing else, in that case, and I should take good care it was for a good round sum also."

"That shows your wisdom, Mr. Redgill. But how much do you consider yourself worth?"

"Well, you and *I* are different persons entirely," said Phillip, with a careless sneer. "But *I* should insure myself for at least £5,000."

"A very nice sum, indeed. Well, the *other* question I was going to ask is this: Will you make me a present of that sum?"

"Me make you a present of £5,000? Why, the man is mad."

"Not quite; just the contrary," said Jack, smiling.

"What do you mean?"

"Mean?" said Jack. "Listen; in a whisper, mind; would you rather swing on a gibbet, or give the sum I name?"

Phillip turned deadly pale, as he stuttered,

"What *can* you mean?"

"Oh, only this; we have been looking after that murder case of old Bertram, and if you give us that sum, why, we won't find out the right party, that's all. You understand?" said Captain Jack, with a knowing wink.

"Has it come to this?" said Phillip, after a pause, and, as he thought, unheard.

"Nothing shorter, my lad; it were a clever job, you know, and by mere accident we found out all about it."

"You want that sum from me, say you?"

"Yes, and nothing less."

"Do your band know of this?"

"Not a word."

"On your oath?"

"Yes."

"And will Bolton suffer?"

"Why not? suspicion is against him. He had better swing than you; besides, we *must* have somebody to hang over the job or the judges will think us worthless and useless. For the honour of our craft we must hang or transport somebody, you know, innocent or guilty, it matters little."

Phillip felt as if a serpent were gnawing at his heart, as he listened to Captain Jack's words.

For some moments neither Phillip nor Captain Jack spoke.

"There cannot be a doubt now but that this knave has discovered all about old Bertram's murder; and yet for a price he will screen the guilty, and have the innocent to suffer. What a scoundrel this fellow is! Yes, 'tis true: from little things, thieves and rogues take to greater ones, until, at last, the gallows is their fate. I little thought it would come to this."

For some time he shaded his face with his snow-white hand, in deep thought.

But at last he aroused himself, and even attempted to be gay, as he said,

"You wish to borrow that sum for a short time, eh?"

"Yes," said the captain, smiling; "I wish to borrow it, if you like to call it so, and will return it," he added, very ominously, "whenever you like to demand it. You understand?"

"But I have not such a sum at command. You do not want it all at once, I suppose?"

"No; a few hundreds to commence with, and the other by instalments will suit me; I'm not very particular with friends."

"But how am I to get this large amount together?" said Phillip. "If my father is rich *I* am not."

"Oh, you can get it easily enough. I dare say you have written your father's signature before now."

"What!" said Phillip, reddening.

"Nothing. I was only thinking," said the captain, carelessly.

"Would that I could give the rascal a bullet through the heart on the quiet," said Phillip, as he bit his lip until it became white again; "but I'll be even with him yet."

The arrangement was agreed to between them; but Captain Jack could see *revenge* sparkling in the young man's eyes, as he handed over a large sum of money to the knave.

In a short time Captain Jack and his friends retired, and shortly afterwards it was discovered that they had been not only remarkably successful in dice and cards, but that several snuff-boxes and watches were missing.

"Who shall I victimise to get this large sum?" thought Phillip. "This fellow will not be joked with."

And as he pondered long and silently he whispered to himself—

"It is a matter of life or death with me; it must be attended to, and at once; but who shall be my dupe? From whom can I get the money, by fair means or foul? It is no use trying to get a farthing from my father beyond the yearly allowance I am entitled to, and I have forged his name once too often to think of doing so again, for the last time I did so he threatened to disinherit me. Besides, if such a transaction were to reach the ears of old Sir Richard Warbeck, I doubt not he would scratch my name out of his will, and not leave me a farthing."

"But stay," he mused. "That good-natured simpleton, Charley Warbeck, will answer my purpose; he often goes out and collects large sums. Suppose I were to steal the amount I want from him. Aye, that's it; it shall be done. I will kill two birds with one stone. I hate these two Warbecks, both Charley and Ned. I detest the very name of Ned," said he, writhing with his wound. "I know how it shall be done; I will get Charley disgraced, and then old Sir Richard will disown him. Aye, that's it."

Thus the villain thought; and yet, as he bade Charley good-night, Redgill smiled, and shook him by the hand as cordially as if he were the truest and best friend in the world.

"How innocent he is," thought Phillip, when left alone, "and how handsome, too! Well, never mind; I care not who suffers so I do not. I might as well be hung for a sheep as a lamb."

And, as he thought of his intended plans against Charley, he grinned like a hyena.

"To-morrow shall decide it," he said, and smiled at the thought of the pit he would dig into which young Warbeck should fall.

## CHAPTER XXI.

### THE WOLF AND THE LAMB—A SCOUNDREL OF THE FIRST WATER.

UNLUCKILY for himself, it was an evil day when Charley Warbeck first made the acquaintance of Phillip Redgill.

Phillip, as all knew, was a great don about town, and maintained a handsome suite of rooms, to which the gayest of the gay resorted.

His father was a very wealthy man, so all the world said; a great ship owner, and "a merchant prince of the good city of London."

To be patronized by the son of such a person poor Charley considered "a very fine thing."

"Wasn't Phillip Redgill one of the sparks of fashion? Did not fair dames (of doubtful virtue, perhaps) smile bewitchingly upon him? Was he not nodded to by this lord and that one? Could he not handle a sword with almost any man?" said Charley, and many others. "And was it not a 'great thing,' therefore, to be known to, and to be hand and glove with such a person when I am only a chief clerk in the India House, and nought to depend upon but my own advancement and old Sir Richard's generosity?"

Yes, this was all true; but Charley Warbeck little dreamed of what a cool, conscienceless villain Phillip was, and how he gained the money he sported with so lavishly "about town," as it was called.

It was true that Sir Richard Warbeck's signature had been forged to a valuable bill, but how it was done no one could tell.

Suspicion had fallen upon Charley, and, in truth, *he did* sign his uncle's name to the bill in question, but was unconscious of having done so, and was guiltless.

This singular affair, the first link in Charley's after misery, but not the first in Phillip's chain of crimes by any means, occurred in this manner.

After Charley had been some time intimate (as they should be, Phillip said, on the score of relationship) young Redgill gave a party at his lodgings, to which Charley was invited.

During the evening Phillip wrote a note to Sir Richard Warbeck, and folded it in a neat wrapper, after the manner of those days when envelopes were unknown.

"Here, Charley," said he, "direct this for me."

Charley, who had been drugged by Phillip, directed the note to Sir Richard Warbeck, and nothing more.

"That will do," said Phillip, and he took up the note in a careless manner, while Charley dropped off to sleep. "That will do excellently. If old Sir Richard had written the direction himself it couldn't have been a better fac simile of his own handwriting, for there are not any two persons under the sun who write so much alike as the old knight and Charley. Bravo! it was a clever trick of mine; an excellent thought, by Jove!"

As he said this, chuckling, he took off the cover-ing of the letter, which proved to be nothing else than a promissory note for a thousand pounds!

"All I wanted was this signature," said Phillip, in high glee. "How neatly I got it, too! I'll get it discounted among the Jews to-morrow; it can never be traced to me again."

The bill was passed among the Jews, and Phillip got the money.

In time it became due, when the trick was dis-covered, and Sir Richard refused to pay.

Officers had the case in hand.

It came to Charley's ears, and although Sir Richard never breathed a suspicion of what he thought, Captain Jack long suspected him, but could not obtain any positive proof to convict him, unless, as he often did, enter the witness-box and complete his chain of evidence by deliberate false swearing.

Though many persons laughed at the loss which the Jews suffered in the transaction, the final bill-holder, a long-bearded English Israelite, Moss, by name, swore solemnly never to let the matter rest; nor did Captain Jack ever lose sight of Charles Warbeck, despite his respectable position and the powerful Sir Richard.

\* \* \* \*

The very next day after Captain Jack's visit to Phillip's apartments, Charles Warbeck was sent out to collect various large sums on account of the India House, of which old Sir Richard was one of the managing directors.

He was watched and dogged throughout the whole of the day by a spy employed by Phillip, and the news was brought to him that Charles had then in his possession a large sum, which, as usual, he was to account for that same evening.

But on his way back to the India House, Phillip Redgill met him, and, in a careless manner, said he was very short of cash, and begged of Charley to loan him fifty pounds, until the end of the week, as he was going to a masque ball that night.

Charley had not any such sum, but promised to see what he could do by borrowing, and would see Phillip that night.

This was agreed to.

But ere they parted, wine was called for, and the hours flew by rapidly.

Quicker than he imagined the time passed at which he was expected at the India House, and, after cursing his bad luck, he drank again and again with Redgill, until at last he became very much the worse for liquor, and had to be carried to his lodgings by two chairmen, yet all the while, and through all his drunkenness, taking great care of the bundle of notes, which he had secreted in his breast, next to his skin, for fear of theft or accident.

It was now nine o'clock at night, and the two chairmen, being paid, left the young man at his own door.

With all his ingenuity he was unable to use his night-key, and stood fumbling at the door a con-siderable time, and swearing not a little.

Charles was in a fog. The keyhole seemed to be removed from its accustomed place, for he could not find it from the unsteady motion of his hand; the latch-key dropped many, many times, and it was doubtful how long he might have remained there, shivering in the cold, had not the oft apos-trophized and obstinate key fallen into the area, and raised his anger to the highest pitch.

"I'll bring *some* one down to the door," said he, and commenced knocking at it with great vigour and noise.

In a few moments Dame Worthington, the good

old gentlewoman his landlady, appeared at the door attired in undress, and could scarcely recognise her lodger ere that unsteady gentleman, who, swaying to and fro, but holding the area railings, stumbled into the passage and tumbled over the astonished housekeeper, who, gasping and groaning, could scarcely be extricated by a female servant, who, candle in hand, rushed to the rescue, and bore off her mistress to the back parlour bed-room.

Charley tumbled upstairs as noisily as a young elephant might be expected to do, knocking down the flowers and flower-stand on the landing, the globe of gold fish on the window-sill, and raised the whole house by his laughter, swearing, and heavy tread.

"Just to think of that young man serving me so!" said Dame Worthington, when sufficiently recovered from her state of collapse to articulate coherently. "Just to think of him who's been more than a mother, to knock over my flowers and the gold fish, to tumble over me in the passage and go to sleep lying in my room, without word of apology, in a state of senselessness; laughing with the lodgers on the stairs, and to go to bed with Mistress Haylark in a delicate state of health on the landing! Oh, Mary, Mary! that I should have lived to see him with my own eyes in bed in the parlour, laughing, making fun, and tumbling over me before you and Mistress Haylark's daughter, which is old enough to be his mother! Deary me, Mary, my dear, deary me! Such is the way, my dear, that the black bottle in the cupboard which lodgers marked 'pison' operates at the dead of night upon a poor defenceless housekeeper and widow who's been quiet and kind to him in the passage, but not old enough or forgetful enough to disremember the young man in her night-clothes named Warbeck, who has lost her lawful consoler, which smells, on the top shelf behind the pickles, for ten long years, like gin!"

It is difficult to imagine, perhaps, the dreadful state of feeling in which the garrulous dame found herself after the consolations of her lawful consoler which smells—on the top shelf behind the pickles, for ten long years—like gin; but of this we are fully assured, that when Charles Warbeck had had a pleasant nap in his cosy room, and concluded a long consultation with the water-pitcher, he discovered, unmistakably, that several hundred fairies, or demons rather, were busily engaged at wood-chopping under the canopy of his cranium, and threatening every moment to split his invaluable head into halves.

Pale, penitent, and full of pious intentions for the future, Charley Warbeck lay on the sofa before his fire, buried in thought.

The church clock struck the hour of eleven, and, as he heard it, he sighed,

"What a fool I have been to-day in not taking that packet of notes to the India House. I shake like a leaf, and I know not why; and haunted by every imaginable terror. I cannot gaze firmly at any one; the sound of every voice seems like a demon bawling in my ears, and every step that approaches appears to be that of some officer ready to tap me on the shoulder, and march me off to prison. I'd give anything in the world to have had this cursed money delivered to-day, and should not have dreamed of such a thing as to absent myself, but for Redgill. He has continually bored me to lend him money and lend him money, until my own poverty almost tempted me to steal. D—n the money!" said Warbeck, in a rage, slamming the packet of notes upon the table, and tossing about in his chair. "It burns my very pocket, and my brain even seems on fire since I've had that wine."

For some time young Warbeck sat looking at the notes, and would willingly have gone to the India House then, but it was too late.

While thus reflecting the door noiselessly opened, and Redgill entered the chamber!

Approaching the table he was much surprised at Charley's absence of mind in not awaking from his reverie, but was pleased to see the bank package lying on the table.

Pretending not to have observed anything of the sort, he slapped his friend familiarly on the back, who, awaking to his senses, seized the package in much haste and confusion, and placed it, as he supposed, unseen, beneath the cushions of the sofa.

Redgill, cold as ice, perfectly collected, and fully resolved in purpose, observed his friend's perturbation and confusion, but smiled good-humouredly, and conversed with animation.

"Any money on hand to-night, Charley, my boy, eh? You promised, you know. I thought I'd call, and see if you had got the £50."

"Money!" said Charley, with affected surprise, gazing with much earnestness at his friend smoking; "money? No! How should I have any? I never have any, you know; I'm not like you fellows with rich daddies, who can give 'em a check occasionally. I wish I had, my boy, but I haven't got a penny. Sorry I disappointed you, Phillip; I imagined I could borrow it for you, but couldn't."

Conversation was continued between the friends, but on the part of young Warbeck with much difficulty, for his unnatural excitement almost choked utterance.

During a pause in their conversation a single knock was heard at his door!

# THE SKELETON CREW; OR, WILDFIRE NED.

THE ATTACK ON THE CASTLE.

Full of wild imaginings, Charley opened it, and old Sir Richard, one of the directors of the India House, walked across the room, and without ceremony took a seat on the sofa beside the fire, but without speaking a word.

Pulling off his gloves very slowly and solemnly, he bowed to Phillip, and said, with a frown—

"Would you be kind enough, Phillip, to allow me a few moments' private conversation with Charles, on very important business, indeed, I can assure you—very—on India House matters, Mr. Redgill, which admits of no delay. Thank you."

Finding he was out of place at that moment, Phillip bowed in a hurried manner, looked for his handkerchief and gloves, which were thrown about

No. 8.

the sofa pillows, and left the room with a flush face.

"Charles," at length Sir Richard began, looki the young man sternly in the face, "what am I understand by your unaccountable conduct?"

A solemn pause.

"Good heavens!" mentally ejaculated Charle "I am discovered, disgraced, and punished, and so soon!"

Overcome with emotion, he hung his head shame and perspired unnaturally at every pore.

"What am I to think of you, sir? Is this reward of all my labour, anxiety, money, and solic tude? Have I not educated you, taken you by th hand, and lifted you up step by step to what y are, eh? And do you now, when I expect to see all my labours rewarded, turn round upon me, and disgrace me?"

"Spare me! Sir Richard! spare me, for heaven's sake! My heart is bursting, and my brain is all on fire," said Charles, mournfully, averting his head from the old man's gaze.

"There are very few things which occur *in* the India House or out of it which do not quickly reach *my* ears, Charles. I only heard of it just now, sir, and must confess I felt shocked. Good Dame Worthington told me."

"Dame Worthington?" said Charley, astonished. "How could she have known it?"

"Yes, Dame Worthington knew it? Why, of course she does, and every one in the house! Isn't it the talk of the whole neighbourhood?"

The young man's agony was painful, and his face became more haggard in a few moments from mental suffering than age could have effected during a course of years.

"What do you think they will do with me, Sir Richard? I shall plead guilty, and save unnecessary trouble and expense."

"Guilty? Yes, I think so, when so many were witness to it; and your sentence will be to reform, keep early hours, leave wine parties alone and gambling, and beg the old dame's pardon for swearing at her to-night."

Had he been shot Charley could not have been more suddenly startled.

Starting to his feet, and looking wildly about him, he comprehended all—Sir Richard knew nothing of his having the bills; and, with a heavy sigh, which then escaped him, there was lifted an insupportable weight of doubt and pain from his soul, and he breathed more freely and rapidly as one who has been running fast, or carrying a heavy load.

Infinitely relieved, the young man even attempted to smile at the unexpected and fortunate turn his imaginings had taken, and, with as much self-command as he could bring to bear upon the conversation, laughed, and begged Sir Richard's pardon for his wild life of late, and inebriety that night, when the kind old dame was knocked over in the passage, and his own nose had come into violent contact with the stairs.

When Sir Richard had departed, in good humour with the repentant youth, Charley drew the sofa nearer to the fire, and began to congratulate himself upon escaping an anticipated suspicion.

"I was *sure* he knew all about it," thought Charles; "and felt as if I was suspended between heaven and earth! Oh! what a relief it was. It is the *first*, and I will take care it shall be the *last* time I ever act so carelessly again, as sure as I live! If professional thieves suffer only half what I have done since evening, and for no crime whatever, I am sure they would never follow their trade very long. Let me see—I placed the package under the sofa mattress; if either had seen it lying on my table, I should have blown my brains out! But where is it? Gone!" said he, in astonishment, as he examined in every place, "gone! Who could have taken it? No one knew it to be there. Gone it is, undoubtedly. I have searched everywhere, but it can't be found. Good Heavens! What shall I do? Which of them could have taken it? No, no, *neither* of them could have seen or felt it; it *must* be here!"

Charles searched in every imaginable nook and corner, but could not discover the missing roll of bills.

He had placed it under the sofa mattress, he was confident, and unknown to either of his visitors.

Whither or how it had disappeared was a marvel.

Distracted with countless thoughts and emotions, he put on his cloak, and, late as it then was, left the apartment, walking aimlessly up and down first one street and then another, until he found himself opposite the theatre, with its blazing links, oil-lamps, and variously-coloured lanterns.

More from habit than design, Charles passed its portals, and soon found himself among a crowd of gay acquaintances.

"Seen Redgill?" asked he of one and another, until, tired with waiting, he was about to depart, when both met at the door!

"Did you see a small paper packet lying about my room, near the sofa, to-night?" asked Charles, carelessly.

"A small paper packet? No. Why, have you lost one? What was it like?"

"Well, it didn't look like anything particularly, but it was, you know, very much like one of our bank packets. It was a packet of long envelopes and other papers."

"Bank packets, eh? No, my boy, I didn't see it; I was too much taken up with thinking of money matters. If you remember, you said you hadn't a penny, and I was racking my brain to devise means for borrowing some, for there is a grand bal masque on here to-night. Is it very valuable? You look vexed—perplexed. What's the matter, Charley, my boy? If I can help you out of the scrape command me, you know——"

"Well, the fact is, Phillip, the package I speak of, which so much resembles a bank package, contained something very valuable, more valuable than my life, in fact. Without I recover it my existence is henceforth a blank and worthless. I am *dishonoured!*"

"Don't say 'dishonoured,' my boy; that is impossible; *you* could never do anything which would reflect dishonour on yourself or your many acquaintance. Cheer up; you may find it to-morrow. If it is a hundred or two you want, you can have it in a day or two from me even."

Charles went home almost mad.

"Lucky thing I called at Warbeck's apartments to-night," said Redgill, to himself, as soon as Charles had left him. "What brought that money on *his* table? Methinks I smell a very large-sized mouse," said he, with a fiendish smile, drinking wine at a small wine-shop near the theatre. "I managed to abstract it rather neatly, I must confess; his head wasn't turned more than a minute—and it contains £2,000. What care *I* if the fool *is* ruined? I only wish it were Ned Warbeck instead; how my heart would leap with joy—the young viper!"

---

## CHAPTER XXII.

### FEARFUL ENCOUNTER BETWEEN THE SKELETON CREW AND THE SMUGGLERS.

"WELL, Dolphin, and what news of this new wonder, Wildfire Ned?" asked the Smuggler Chief. "He has joined Lieutenant Garnet, say you?"

"He has."

"And what does he intend to do?"

"He swears to exterminate the Skeleton Crew."

"So much the better for us, then," laughed the Smuggler Chief. "If young Ned Warbeck can only rid the seas of such monsters as they are, then there may be some chance of honest folks, like ourselves, getting along a bit farther than we have done of late," said the Chief, with a dry grin.

" Just so, Sea-hawk," the Dolphin replied ; " if he can manage to rid us of such grim devils as they are, all well and good ; for, you see, we don't stand much of a chance with them, for they have played the very devil with us smugglers of late years, And as to Death-wing, I don't think there is any hope of getting him out of the way, for he seems to be made of cast iron."

" I only hope this young dare-devil, Ned Warbeck, will only let *us* alone, though," said the Chief, " because you know he might turn his attention this way after doing the first job."

" That's just what he *is* going to do."

" You don't mean that ?"

" I do, though. I found out all his plans, as well as his instructions."

" Indeed !—how ?"

" You remember what I said about the marriage at Walton Abbey, and of Death-wing running away with the young bride ?"

" Yes."

" Well, Garnet and Wildfire Ned, accompanied by Bob Bertram, and others, started in pursuit."

" Did they overtake the Crew ?"

" That you will quickly hear."

" For some time, Wildfire Ned and Garnet continued the chase over hedge and ditch ; but they went at such a terrific pace, that in less than half an hour they had distanced all who followed them, save Bob Bertram.

" But still they could not make out or trace the route taken by Death-wing.

" In about an hour, however, they perceived some of the band in the distance.

" With swords drawn, they shouted in defiance, and made at them.

" But the Skeleton rascals declined the combat.

" The chase then continued.

" But, as before, they lost sight of them, for the last trick was only a ride to gain time in order that Death-wing and his fair captive might get off clear."

" Clever, artful devils," said the Chief, with a gruff laugh ; " and *did* they get off clear ?" he asked.

" They did. Wildfire Ned rode like a madman in every direction after them. But it was all to no purpose. They escaped, and Death-wing and his crew made their way to the sea-shore, and got safely on board their Phantom ship before Garnet or Wildfire Ned could overtake them."

" Well, and what next ?"

" Wildfire Ned and Bob Bertram made the best of their way to Garnet's ship, the ' Diamond,' and went on board. The ship set sail immediately in search of the Skeleton Crew, and every man on board swore to be revenged."

" If they fall in with Death-wing, then, we may expect to hear of some stirring news," said the chief. " If they conquer Death-wing, or he conquer them, it's all the same to us, you know, Dolphin."

" True," replied the messenger ; " but I would much rather hear they had made short work of the Skeleton Crew, for we *can* generally manage to escape the revenue cruisers, but it would puzzle the very devil to get out of the way of these grim and ghastly wretches," said the Dolphin.

" So far we agree," said the grim Chief. " But now to business. Have you found out anything more about that vessel you wrote to me about ?"

" What, that ship which we have long expected from the East Indies ?"

" Yes."

" Of course I have ; she is now in the offing ; and,

if the wind rises, we may expect her abreast of this place by midnight."

" Good. Did you hear how many men she carries ?"

" Only fifteen."

" That ain't too many ; so far, so good ; but about her guns, Dolphin, *that's* the question ; I heard she had four."

" But I know better ; she hasn't got a single one."

" Not one ?"

" No ; not even a pop-gun on board."

" What's her name, say you ?"

" The ' Sea Spray.' "

" Then she will prove an easy prize ?"

" No doubt of it."

" What's her cargo ?"

" Silks, spices, and gold dust."

" Hem," said Sea-hawk, " then we must prepare for her. Tell the night-watch to have a bright look-out, and get all the boats ready. How is the weather ?"

" It looks as if we should have a dense fog to-night."

" So much the better, then," said the Smuggler Chief. " There's nothing half so nice as a thick fog when one wants to come up to a craft unseen. Get all the boats ready, and let them be moored outside the cave for instant service."

These orders were obeyed.

During the day great preparations were made to board and capture the long-expected East Indiaman, and a look-out man was perched high upon the rocks outside, with telescope in hand, watching the distant movements of the " Sea Spray " as she lay becalmed in the far distance, her sails lazily flapping in the foggy atmosphere.

As night approached the wind freshened, and all was wild excitement and merriment among the smugglers, who looked forward to the capture of the vessel with impatient joy.

Master Tim saw all the warlike preparations going on, and felt very uneasy.

The sight of pistols and knives, cutlasses, boarding pikes, and the like, struck terror to his soul.

But he dared not show it, or express any thought about the danger all were about to encounter.

He even tried to smile and look merry.

But it was all sham.

Poor Tim could be as brave as any one as far as words went, but when it came to blows and hard knocks he wished himself a thousand miles away.

Some of the smugglers provided Tim with plenty of arms.

" As I *must* go," thought Tim, " and as there is no getting away from these villanous, black-looking band of smugglers, I might as well arm myself to the teeth ; the more weapons I have the greater chance I have for my life."

With this thought uppermost in his mind, Master Tim put on an immense pair of water-boots that reached above the knee ; and although he could scarcely walk in them, on account of their weight and clumsiness, he never said a word.

" For," thought Tim, " it won't do to let these devils think I am afraid, after all the hard lies I have told 'em to-day ; besides, if they thought I wanted to get away, they'd scrag me on the instant."

Next he put on an immense waist-belt, and stuck into it half-a-dozen pistols, all double-shotted.

Besides these, he thrust into his belt a heavy cutlass, a dagger, and a long knife.

Not satisfied with all these warlike preparations,

he seized a heavy blunderbuss, and filled up to the muzzle with powder and shot.

This he slung on his back, and walked up and down the cave, thinking—

"It's very nasty, dangerous work, attacking ships ; if this one Sea-hawk is going to capture to-night had been well-armed and manned by a stout crew, I shouldn't a' thought of rigging myself this way ; I should a' fallen on to their decks, like a dead man, and let the smugglers fight it out their own way, and then joined the victors ; but if the ship is unarmed, and there is much gold on board, I want to throw dust into Sea-hawk's eyes, and get as much as possible for my share ; and then, when I *have* got the gold-dust, I shall hook it, for I know the way now into old Nettle's place up through that trap-door."

Tim tried to look very fierce, and smoked a pipe to keep down his fearful feelings.

But he looked like a walking arsenal more than anything else, and could scarcely move with the immense weight girt about him.

From time to time as night closed in, word was passed from the watchers outside that the "Sea Spray" was gradually approaching.

When first he heard this report, Tim pretended to be overjoyed, and very anxious to encounter the stranger and show the smuggler band what a courageous fellow he was.

But when Sea-hawk at last gave the order for all his men to make ready to start out on the expedition, Tim's heart began to flutter and to beat very loudly.

He took a good draught of rum, however, and, as well as he could, got into the boat.

When all had assembled at the mouth of the cave, Sea-hawk called the six boats' crew together and gave them his final instructions.

Three of the boats with muffled oars, under the Dolphin's command, was to go on some little distance ahead, and creep through the dense fog unseen, so as to attack the stranger on the windward side.

Sea-hawk, with the other three boats, would follow, and at the same time assail the "Sea Spray" on the leeward side.

At a given signal the boats put off towards the doomed ship, which had been suddenly becalmed opposite the smugglers' cave.

It could just be seen through the thick fog, and Sea-hawk was delighted with the prospect of its speedy capture.

"We'll make short work of it," said the chief to Tim, in a jolly tone.

"I believe you," Tim replied, in a soft voice, with a ghastly attempt at a smile.

Onwards the boats' crews rowed in dead silence.

In a short time they came within full view of the dark sides of the vessel, as, like an ominous object, it loomed out through the dense mists.

The first three boats had got round to the other side of the vessel, and were waiting for Sea-hawk's signal.

This was soon given.

With a loud shout the smugglers' boats pulled towards the vessel.

"Let one man remain with each boat," said the chief, "while all the rest board the craft."

"I'll do that," said Tim, eagerly.

"No you won't," said the chief ; "you are to be the first man to board the ship. Here we are ; up you go," said Sea-hawk, shoving Tim up the ship's side with so much violence that Tim fell over the bulwarks.

Tim was awfully scared, for he expected to be shot or stabbed the instant he reached the deck.

Judge of his happiness, then, when he discovered there was not a single soul on deck.

Perceiving this, and before any of his comrades could clamber up, he began cutting, and slashing, and swearing at imaginary foes, stamping his feet, and hacking at old empty barrels, with such a vengeance and so much noise as to make every one believe that he was at the moment performing prodigies of valour.

"Die ! down ! surrender, villains !" he roared.

And the more he shouted, the more he cut and hacked right and left, without meeting with a foe, except a cow and a few sheep on board, which he slaughtered unmercifully in a few seconds.

When the smugglers leaped upon the deck, they were astonished at not meeting with or finding any opposition.

Tim was puffing and blowing, as if wearied and exhausted with his terrific efforts, and pointed to the hatchway, shouting,

"I have beaten the villains ten to one ; they are down the hatchway ; down after them, my bold boys, down after them !"

Perceiving blood on his sword, the smugglers believed what he said, and therefore rushed down into the hold of the ship, sword in hand, bent on slaughter.

Tim was immensely tickled that he had earned the reputation for valour so cheaply, and thanked his stars Sea-hawk believed him.

While Tim was alone on the deck, however, he suddenly heard unearthly shouts, screams, oaths, and the like, proceed from the hold of the ship.

"What's all that ?" thought Tim, trembling in every limb. "I wonder if they have found out any one. I didn't see any of the crew."

He was not left long in suspense.

There issued from the hold, the cabin, and the forecastle of the ship a band of skeletons, sword in hand.

Tim, at the first sight of them, fell on his knees, and then slipped into an empty water-barrel that was near by.

From this place he could perceive all that passed.

The Smuggler Chief had been deceived ; and so had Dolphin.

But how and by whom neither of them could tell.

Instead of boarding the East Indiaman, they found themselves on the decks of the Phantom Ship !

The confusion, uproar, and clanging of arms that now ensued were dreadful.

Sea-hawk, Dolphin, and the rest of the bold smugglers, fought like demons.

"To the boats ! to the boats !" shouted Sea-hawk above the din of battle.

All his men endeavoured to fight their way back again to the boats as directed by the chief.

But their retreat was cut off.

The Skeleton Crew, infuriated against their old enemies, the smugglers, fought with desperation.

Pistol-shots scattered about the decks like hailstones, and Tim, unfortunate as ever, had the misery to find that more than one stray bullet struck the cask in which he was hiding, and grazed his body and legs ; but beyond a few scratches he escaped unhurt.

Sea-Hawk, as brave as a lion, fought long and desperately with the grim crew ; but many of his men were dying and wounded around him.

"To the boats ! to the boats !" he again shouted.

Many of his followers did not need this second

warning; but leaped over the sides of the vessel, and plunged into the sea in wild despair.

On every part of the ship did the Skeleton Crew swarm like bees.

Up the rigging they climbed like monkeys, making the most hideous noises.

Death-wing, with his black banner on high, and with an immense cutlass in hand, seemed to mow down Sea-hawk's men; and in less than fifteen minutes from the time the action commenced, the Phantom Ship was cleared of all its intruders save the dead and dying.

The smugglers, entrapped as they had been, fought like bears; but nothing could withstand Death-wing and his grissly band.

And ere Sea-hawk and his boats pushed off from the vessel, two cannons, loaded up to the muzzle with grape and canister shot, were fired after them, and the missiles of death swept the waters around the Phantom Ship with a hissing and fatal sound.

---

## CHAPTER XXIII.

### NED'S FIRST BATTLE—THE SHIP ON FIRE.

AFTER the action, the first thing the Skeleton Crew did was to examine the bodies of the dead and dying.

Some were cast overboard immediately; but those whose wounds gave some hope of recovery, were, for the moment, more mercifully dealt with.

For they were reserved for after tortures!

Tim was in an unfortunate position.

He was neither dead nor wounded.

But from the passing remarks of the Skeleton Crew, he almost wished that he had been dead, for he trembled to think what tortures and unearthly agony they intended to make all such as he was, undergo.

"What an unlucky devil I am," sighed Tim. "I no sooner get out of one trouble than I fall into another; it's out of the frying pan into the fire with me always. I wonder what star I was born under, for there's no good fortune ever befalls me. Heigho! just hear those grim monsters talking. Why, the smugglers were gentlemen, compared to such fiendish devils as these."

Tim crouched still more closely in his hiding-place.

"How many dead men have the smugglers left behind?" asked Death-wing, when they had all been counted and thrown overboard.

"Over a dozen," was the reply.

"Good," said Death-wing, with a chuckle.

"Just hear him," groaned Tim. "I do believe, if there had only been three dozen he'd jump for joy. Oh! horrors upon horrors accumulate."

"How many wounded?"

"We have found six."

"Only half a dozen, that is not a great number," said Death-wing; "there ought to be three or four dozen, at least."

"Yes, so there would have been, Death-wing; but those who were slightly wounded jumped into the water, or into their boats, at the hazard of drowning or breaking their necks, rather than remain in our hands."

"Ha!" said the grim chief. "They know us of old."

"Hark! how the villain sighs," said poor Tim. "I shouldn't wonder if he hasn't got tears in his eyes over it because they wouldn't stay behind to be skinned alive, poor devils."

"I wish we had but one sound man among the six prisoners," said Death-Wing. "I should like to make an example of him on the spot."

"Oh-h!" groaned Tim, "I'm in for it this time; they'll cut me limb from limb; but it's better to die here like a rat in this barrel than to get into their hands."

Tim, up to the present, moment had not dared to poke his long nose out of his hiding-place, yet, out of curiosity, he now did, so as to see what they were about to do with their wounded prisoners.

The moment his head appeared, one of the crew with a loud shout of joy jumped towards him and seized him by the scurf of the neck.

In a second the poor fellow was dragged out of the hogshead, and pulled along the deck towards where Death-wing stood.

"What, another of 'em," said the grim chief, with a loud laugh of mockery, "and armed to the teeth, I perceive! This must be one of the head leaders, I think; disarm him."

In the twinkling of an eye, Tim's blunderbuss, pistols, dagger, knife and cutlass were taken from him, and he knelt before the chief, trembling and quaking.

Around him danced several dozen skeletons in wild joy, snapping their fingers and making the most horrible noises.

"I think I have seen this rascal's face before," said Death-wing, with an oath.

"So do I."

"Yes, that's him."

"Are you not one of my worst enemy's followers. —Wildfire Ned?"

"Me? lor' bless you, no," said Tim, "I never heard of his name afore in all my life."

"Liar!" said one, giving him a slap that made his jaws ache again.

"Liar!" another one remarked, kicking him vigorously from behind; "didn't we get up a tree after you, and you escaped?"

"Yet now I come to look at the rogue more closely, the more I am convinced he is one of young Warbeck's followers," said Death-wing, "and as such, he must —"

"Die!" said all, in a solemn chorus.

When the verdict was made known, the whole of the Skeleton Crew commenced dancing around him in a wild unearthly fashion, and as each came near him, they gave the luckless fellow a kick or a blow, until he was black and blue.

"Bind him hand and foot," said the grim chief; "this rascal has many secrets to reveal about Wildfire Ned, and Sea-hawk's gang; we must extract them all from him, or cut him joint from joint."

"Bind him hand and foot, and tie him to the main-mast!"

This was done.

All the crew, save one, all the while stood round the victim, while Death-wing began to question him.

So silent were the crew upon extracting from him every item about Wildfire Ned, that they took but little notice of the intense fog which now enveloped the ship, or where it was drifting to.

"The first question I shall ask you," Death-wing began, "is, do you know where Wildfire Ned is? if you do not confess, your arms shall be —"

At that instant, a loud booming noise was heard, and not far off either.

Every one rose to his feet.

In a second after an eighteen-pound cannon shot came crushing through the bulwarks!

"Treachery!" Death-wing cried.

Bang! crash! were the sounds repeated.

"Every one to his post!"

Whiz—bang! came another shot, and almost frightened off all the hair from Tim's head, as he stood tied to the mast, and unable to move.

"Who are they? Can you make them out?" shouted out Death-wing to his crew.

"A frigate is bearing down to windward of us."

"Steer the 'Phantom' in towards the shore! Double shot your guns! 'Tis the 'Diamond'—I can make her out through the fog. Fire away! Never surrender! Up with the black flag!"

The fight now became hot and desperate.

Cannons flashed and roared, but still the frigate did not approach any nearer.

In truth, she could not do so.

They were too near land, and the "Phantom" was of a much lighter draught, and could draw less water.

Hence it was that Death-wing had the advantage of his enemy, for he now neared the land, and seemed bent upon stranding his vessel and escaping rather than surrender.

But he was much mistaken.

Although it was the "Diamond" frigate he was fighting, he little dreamt what was in store for his crew.

Although now the shots of the frigate took but little effect from the increasing distance, Death-wing was surrounded with dangers.

Lieutenant Garnet with one boat, Wildfire Ned with another, were pulling through the fog at a desperate rate towards the "Phantom" to cut it out from grounding, and were followed by Bob Bertram in a third, all of which were crowded with brave blue-jackets.

When least expected, Death-wing heard the gallant shouts of his fearless foes.

"Let every one arm to the teeth!" he said.

"Stand ready to resist boarders!"

Another loud shout was given by the blue-jackets as they pulled towards the vessel.

"Pour broadsides of grape into them!" said Death-wing.

In a second the boats bumped against the ship's sides and were made fast.

"They are upon us!" said Death-wing, brandishing his sword.

In a second the gallant tars swarmed on to the ship's decks.

The first to spring among the Skeleton Crew was Wildfire Ned.

With a loud shout he dashed at Death-wing and cleaved him to the deck!

Wildfire Ned was quickly followed by Lieutenant Garnet, who, at the head of his brave boat's crew, cut their way up on to the decks.

And close at his heels followed Bob Bertram, supported by a strong body.

The fighting was now dreadful on all sides.

Wherever Wildfire Ned dashed he left behind him dozens of victims.

Tim was in great danger, both from friend and foe.

Glancing shots, and accidental strokes from swords and cutlasses came very near him.

By continual shouting he attracted the attention of Bob Bertram, who immediately cut the ropes and set him free.

Tim took advantage of his liberty to conceal himself as best he could under the bulwarks.

But he amused himself very greatly by pounding on the skull of one of Death-wing's band, who had been literally smashed to atoms by Wildfire Ned's blows.

The Skeleton Crew, finding that their vessel must now be stranded, and no hope remained of saving her, determined to blow her up.

"Fire the magazine!" roared Death-wing, high above the din of battle. "Blow Wildfire Ned and his followers to atoms!"

"Ha! ha! so *you* are getting something for yourself this time, eh?" said Tim, as he recognized Death-wing's voice; "but you don't catch *me* staying here if there's anything of that sort going to take place."

So saying, Master Tim crawled over the vessel's side, and got into one of the boats, and lay there very snugly out of harm's way.

Wildfire Ned, however, had a terrible task before him.

He wanted to find the missing bride.

He searched through the cabin.

But no trace of her could be found.

Not to be foiled he looked everywhere.

"Blow up the magazine!" roared Death-wing again.

As he spoke, a terrible thought crossed Ned's mind,

"Perhaps the fiends have placed the young bride there!"

The thought was almost too horrible.

With desperation and vengeance in his face, Wildfire Ned leaped into the hold below, sword in hand.

Led by instinct, but why he knew not, Ned rushed madly to the stern of the vessel.

In the lower hold he perceived a long fusee burning.

There remained but two or three inches of it.

In a few seconds it would reach the powder.

"'Tis for life or death," said Ned.

With a fearful leap he descended into the lower hold

All was pitch-darkness around him.

Save the bright red fusee spluttering and burning not a glimmer of light could be seen.

He groped his way along the bottom of the ship.

But when least he expected it, he was grasped by a skeleton hand!

With an oath, Wildfire Ned drew his dirk.

A terrible conflict ensued.

One minute more, and the magazine would explode.

"We shall die together, young Warbeck!" said the skeleton.

And now began a duel which never had equal before.

In that dark hold they struggled for mastery.

It was a terrific struggle.

At last, with a mighty effort, Wildfire Ned snatched up a small hatchet which his foe had let fall.

With one fearful blow he crushed in the skull of his grim enemy.

With a loud shout and laugh of triumph Wildfire Ned ran towards the deadly fusee.

The sparks were even then spluttering near to some waste powder.

In a second more all would be lost.

He fell upon the fusee!

He quenched its flame carefully in his hand.

Next instant, with a mighty blow of the axe, he smashed in the magazine door.

With a cry of joy, Ned saw before him the stolen bride !

She was tied unto several powder barrels !

This was Death-wing's especial order !

Ned cut the cords which bound her, and let in a torrent of sea-water into the powder and swamped the magazine.

The bride was insensible.

He took her in his arms and hurried to the hatchway.

Then a fearful cry was heard from above.

" I defy you !" roared the terrible voice of Death-wing. " In one moment more the ship will be blown in the air. Ha ! ha ! the powder magazine is open! the fusee is burning. Away, my men, away to your rendezvous on shore ! One moment more and Lord Walton's sister will be a black and charred mass—vengeance against Wildfire Ned ! eternal enmity is between us !"

" The ship is on fire !" Ned heard Garnet shouting. " Where is young Warbeck?—the ship is on fire in two places !"

" Help ! help !" cried Ned, from the bottom of the lower hold.

His voice was heard from above.

" Help ! help !"

In a moment, Garnet and Bob Bertram, with a few others, threw down the end of a long rope to Ned.

Young Warbeck tied it round his body.

Clasping the unconscious maiden in his arms, he was being drawn out of the hold, when the flames burst out all around him.

" Quick ! quick ! or we shall perish," said Ned. " Those Skeleton fiends have fired their vessel in several places."

" Pull away, lads, pull away !" shouted Garnet.

The flames increased every second.

And yet with all the efforts of the seamen, Ned could not get higher than the lower hold.

The rope had caught in some bolt or block below !

Here was a perilous position.

The flames were now almost all around him.

He hung suspended between life and death.

In a second more the forked flames would catch the maiden's dress.

Bob Bertram, without a word, slipped down the rope, and disentangled it.

A loud shout from above rewarded his valor and daring.

" Quick ! quick !" faintly cried Ned, now almost suffocated with smoke. " Quick, quick ! I am choking ! Quick, Bob, or all is lost !"

With the energy of despair the sailors pulled away at the rope.

Yet all the time they had to fight against the vile Skeleton Crew, who every moment were trying to cut the rope.

Some were up the rigging, firing down on the brave men.

Others plunged overboard, and swam away towards the shore.

All was a scene of intense excitement.

Yet, with a tremendous effort, Wildfire Ned kept himself alive amid the dense smoke and flames around him.

With a ringing cheer he reached the deck.

" Saved ! saved !" said Ned, and almost fell from sheer weakness !

But at that moment a low, rumbling noise like distant thunder caught the ears of all !

It was the sound of a mighty torrent of water rushing into the ship's hold.

" The ship is scuttled ! Away ! away !" cried many voices.

In a moment more the ship trembled from stem to stern.

In a second she broke into halves !

## CHAPTER XXIV.

IN WHICH PHILLIP REDGILL IS FORCED TO RAISE THE WIND TO PAY HIS DEBTS TO CAPT. JACK, AND IN WHICH THE READER BEHOLDS THE PHANTOM LEGS, AND IS INTRODUCED TO THE SKELETON BARBER.

NOTWITHSTANDING his robbery of Charley Warbeck, Phillip Redgill had not near enough of money wherewith to pay the heavy debt Capt. Jack had against him.

Which way to turn he knew not.

" I must do 'something,' or I shall swing on a gibbet in less than a month's time.

" Oh, there's no earthly hope of raising the wind 'out of him,'" thought Phillip, in regard to his father, " and I know not how to manage the matter. Let me see !" and he went on with his calculations very rapidly. " How strange it is that those who borrow will seldom lend in return ! Among all my acquaintance I know of none who at all seem inclined to accommodate me. They entertain no doubt of my honesty, so they say ; but as to lending a fellow a thousand or two, that is out of the question. Well, I must either post up the money or swing and loose the four hundred already gained. I have three clear days yet. I'll have a glass of brandy and think awhile."

The brandy and a good French dinner wonderfully enlightened Mr. Phillip's faculties, for he had but just pulled off his coat for a comfortable snooze ere a bright thought flashed across his mind.

" Why didn't I think of it before ? Why, there's old Sir Andrew, the money-lender and insurance broker ! Just the man, by Jupiter ! If he fails, why then I'm done. I'll go to him at once."

Old Sir Andrew was one of those " very smart" men, an insurance office president, who had sprung from nothing, but had become possessed of very large means, acquired rapidly, and none could imagine how.

A constant church attendant, and economical in his donations to " charities," he was generally considered to be one of the pillars of his church, and a particular strong man on 'Change, whenever he deigned to visit that extensive gambling salon.

From the number of persons who had constantly visited his offices in times past, it was shrewdly imagined he had done a considerable amount of very close " shaving" in bill discounting, and, perhaps, was not over scrupulous, or troubled with many qualms of conscience in financial transactions.

This was the individual to whom Phillip applied in his emergency.

"Again?" asked Sir Andrew, when he recognized his visitor ; "come again, so soon? Why, dear me, Phillip, what can the matter be? Take a seat. Oh, *that's* it, eh? want £3,000 for a week! Phew! young man, you talk as if pounds could be picked up in the street. Why, bless you, I haven't got such a sum by me ; besides, you owe me £10,000 already, for which you have given nothing but promissory notes, with interest, on the death of your father, and *that* event looks as distant as ever, judging by his ruddy countenance and activity on 'Change the other day. Your father is speculating very extensively of late ; but no one knows, in these squally times, *how* speculations may turn out. Things are not what they used to be, Mr. Phillip ; every man with two or three hundreds in his pocket, gambles in stock now, and, if things continue as they have been going on for the past six months, I shouldn't be at all surprised to hear of our banks closing, and to go 'popping' off all round us like fire crackers. It can't be done, sir ; I have been unwise in lending you money at all, perhaps, on such precarious terms ; and really, if I were to speak the truth, Mr. Phillip, a little less of horse-racing, wine parties, 'ladies' in satin, and so forth, would greatly improve you, both morally and physically. But young men *will* be young men, you know," added old Sir Andrew, with a peculiar look which gave the lie to all his affected modesty and sanctity. "Why not try the Jews? Your worthy father's name is good, you know," added the money-lender, with a grin ; "but I suppose you have written his name instead of your own sufficiently often, perhaps, eh? Ha! ha! Well, well, don't fret and bite your nails. You wish he was in *heaven*, you meant to say. Well, I hope we shall *all* get there one of these days, but it is very tight times on 'Change, I can assure you. Why, a young man like you should have ingenuity enough, I think, to raise such an amount as *that*, without much trouble! There are *plenty* of men who would jump at the chance of obliging *you*, Phillip ; particularly as you will be very rich one of these days. Ha! ha!"

Despite the utmost importunity, old Sir Andrew was inexorable, and smiled at the disappointment, rage, and revenge, which evidently flashed from the young man's eyes ; for, although he begged for favours which were not granted, and loathed the very person from whom he had expected to receive them, yet he dared not give vent to his almost suffocating fury, for old Sir Andrew, mild-spoken, and perfectly at ease, held forged papers in his possession, which hung over Phillip's head as the sword of Damocles.

"I wish I could poison the old miser," muttered the youth, walking back towards his apartments in high dudgeon. "I'll make a 'smash' *somewhere* before the week is out, if I *swing* for it."

He *must* have cash from somewhere, he thought, so determined to do that which many "very smart" men had the reputation for having done during life—namely, to get money by any adroit means that should escape detection and proof, or, at most, only injure his "name"—for your greatest rogues, after all, he thought, are usually the greatest "sticklers" for so-called "honour" and "reputation."

"What's the difference *if you are not found out?*" he muttered. "Who can point out to *one* honest man? The true secret of success is to get all you can, and keep all you get. How many can say the foundation of their prosperity was laid in undisputed honesty?

"How would the best of us fare if justice was fairly meted out to all?

"'*Go as close to the gaol as you please ; but don't go in!*' is the maxim in our times. Rich men's knavery consigns them to the ease and luxurance of a palace. Poor men, for the same, may rot in dungeons. 'Do whatever you please, but don't get found out,' is the practical philosophy of the day. Those who succeed, retire upon large fortunes, and are austere bigots and pillars of hypocrisy ; those who fail, are cuffed and kicked, and never stop rolling until they roll into the grave."

Thus mused Mr. Philip Redgill, bent on fresh crime.

THE INTERVIEW.—*See No.* 10.

## CHAPTER XXV.

PHILLIP REDGILL CONTINUES TO PLAY HIS GAME OF
VILLANY—HE DETERMINES TO MARRY AN HEIRESS
—THE DISCOVERY OF FALSE NOTES IN THE
MONEY-SAFE AT THE INDIA HOUSE—CHARLEY'S
REMORSE AND CONFESSION—"LET NOT THE IN-
NOCENT SUFFER FOR THE GUILTY."

ONE would have thought that such ill success in
his system of villany in thus becoming the slave of
Captain Jack would have been a very practical, as
it certainly was a very expensive lesson to young
Redgill, seeing that he had agreed to pay the great
thief-taker five thousand pounds for his silence.
Yet, instead of cooling, it only seemed to irritate
Phillip, and to such a degree, that he was not sober
one day for a whole week after his interview with
the renowned thief-taker; but, nevertheless, bore up
under his losses with the airs of an honest millionaire.

His father was rich, every one said, and had ships
at sea, which, laden with teas and silks, were on
their way from China.

"The old man won't be nice to a thousand or two

when they arrive. Why, old Sir Andrew's office
has insured them for five hundred thousand pounds,
so their cargoes *must* be worth a tr fle! Go a-head,
father! make all the cash you can—*I'll* manage to
spend it for you when you drop off the hooks."

It was certainly true that Mr. Redgill, senior,
had extensive dealings on 'Change, for in the single
item of two ships homeward bound he held insurance policies for not less, as we have said, than
five hundred thousand pounds.

"What a good thing it would be if young Redgill
could manage to marry my only daughter, Fanny!
I'd see if it *can't* be done," thought the miserly old
Sir Andrew. "It would be a capital match! But
I see a great many fond parents have the same idea
in regard to *their* daughters, judging from the endless invitations to balls, &c, Phillip is continually
receiving. He'll be a fine 'catch' for some one.
I'll see what can be done in that matter, and consult
with 'my lady.'"

Old Sir Andrew's consultation with "his lady"
was so far successful that Phillip and Fanny were
soon on most excellent terms; but as she was "anything but a beauty," even when assisted by paints,

flowers, silks, and false hair, many gallants about town, of inquisitive turn of mind, were unable to imagine the reasons which had determined so good-looking a young man as Phillip Redgill to pay such strict court to her.

The truth was that Phillip wanted "money," and was greatly embarrassed.

He even desired the match, hoping thus to draw heavily both on *her* father and *his own!*

But, although he pressed his suit with much ardour, the intended marriage was always postponed at Redgill, senior's, request.

But if Mr. Phil'ip Redgill could withstand his losses and disappointments in his career of crime with so much equanimity of temper, and even propose to himself matrimony as a solace for all his losses, it was not so with Charley Warbeck.

When that young gentleman, full of repentance, had calmly reflected upon his perilous situation, he was filled with alarm, and trembled for the fate which must surely overtake him.

He attended the India House as usual, but day by day he became more deathly pale.

His limbs seemed to have lost all strength, and he moved to and fro with unsteady gait and aching heart.

As often as he approached the huge iron safe where, in a moment of madness, he had cleverly placed a packet of false notes in lieu of those he had lost, in order to lull suspicion for a time, he became dizzy from excitement, and could scarcely stand.

Remorse and shame were punishing him more fearfully than actual imprisonment could have done.

When the day arrived upon which the India House usually issued a statement of their affairs, he was in a high fever, and, despite all remonstrance from his good old landlady, Dame Worthington, and old Sir Richard Warbeck, he persisted in going to the India House as usual, and even counterfeited gaiety.

The accounts soon showed a large deficit, and a buzz of astonishment was heard among all the clerks.

The directors of the India House seemed undisturbed, nor did they betray any token of great concern.

They smiled as blandly as before, and even joked with the terrified clerks, who were unable to speak, for all of them were implicated in suspicion, and none could imagine on whose head should rightly fall the actual guilt.

Each was distrustful of the other.

Towards the close of business hours Charley became really ill, but as he had been unwell for several days previous, no remark was passed upon his going home earlier than usual.

Excitement caused fever, and the latter superinduced lightness and flightiness of the mind.

In truth he was not now sane.

When he entered the house, Dame Worthington gazed upon him for a few moments, and then burst into tears.

He was unable to walk upstairs, hence the good old dame led him into the snug parlor, and put him to bed there upon the couch, and sent for medical assistance.

The whole house was astonished at the sudden and dangerous change in the young man, and when Clara Haylark heard of it, she rushed downstairs in great haste, and proffered her services in any way in which they might prove useful—for Clara had a lurking suspicion that her curls and captivating ways might have had a little something to do with Charley's sudden indisposition.

At least she intimated as much to her mother, in answer to a query ; for she solemnly sighed, turned up her eyes with eloquent meaning, and said, " Poor Charles ! I'm sure he cannot blame me, mother dear ! " and covered her face—the little hypocrite—with a lace-edged handkerchief !

For several days Charles remained half demented and in high fever.

Dame Worthington, for reasons to be hereafter made known—and good ones, too—was crazed with care, and scarcely left him for one moment, either by night or day, but carefully watched his bedside with more than maternal care.

Mistress Haylark, the fair Clara's mother, also was loud in her advice, and concocted various little palatable dishes and drinks, which Clara, in her curls, and with a serio-comic voice and gesture, administered to the patient with great grace of manner and captivating attitude.

She would read to him, and tell him stories, Dame Worthington always being present, sitting in her chair at a distance, in the shadows of the room, rocking herself in thought, and gazing with a look of care and anxiety upon her " poor, sick boy," and when Charles was able to move about again, Clara would invariably go to the harp and play a few soft, plaintive airs, which soothed her patient, and won his affection more deeply than the index of his eyes had ever before betrayed to the gay and light-hearted Clara.

At the close of an afternoon spent in this manner, and his courage being greatly stimulated by a glass of brandy prescribed by the doctor, Charley said, " Oblige me, Clara, by singing that beautiful air again."

His accents seemed so earnest that, as Clara complied, her voice and fingers trembled with unusual excitement.

At the close of the piece, no one being nigh, Charles approached her, and without a gesture of warning, kissed her !

She rose as if shot, looked at him inquiringly for a moment, burst into tears, and left the room !

No one could imagine why Clara absented herself from the parlour for several days following, and not even her mother — although, from the soft and mysterious conversations held by Mistress Haylark and Dame Worthington upon the landings, and in the passages, on several occasions, it was apparent that womanly sagacity had intuitively suggested the real facts to their minds, although they only smiled and nodded and winked in that peculiar manner known to mothers and very elderly persons.

Sir Richard Warbeck, it may be taken for granted, was not remiss in visiting his protegé, but evinced the greatest anxiety for his health and speedy recovery.

His visits were daily, and he always brought some trifle which might be grateful to a sick palate ; but Mistress Haylark—that aged thermometer of passing events—always noticed that Dame Worthington always was in unusual spirits upon his coming, but suddenly depressed whenever he departed.

There was " something mysterious " between them, Mistress Haylark thought, but what it was it seemed impossible to divine.

As Clara seemed to be constantly in high spirits,

and delighted always in company with the good-looking Charley, Mistress Haylark began to assume airs of great matronly dignity, and, if the truth must be told, confessed that she began to feel older and older every day, and that "her sole thought was concerning the future happiness of her darling beautiful daughter."

Mesdames Haylark and Worthington became almost inseparable and extremely confidential, and on one occasion, when Mistress Haylark complained of a pain in her stomach and would have gone upstairs for "a thimbleful" of ginger wine, Dame Worthington vehemently protested, and forthwith introduced her old family specific from "the top shelf, behind the pickles," forty drops of which, slightly diluted with water, effectually relieved all pain, and threw them both into such high spirits, that they continued discussing family and household affairs and secrets, until long after the church clocks had chimed the hour of midnight.

But while Charley is recovering, under the combined effects of love, philosophy, and kind treatment, the Directors of the India House have been assiduous in their endeavours to trace out the true depositor of the packet of counterfeit bank notes.

They went to work very quietly and coolly, but despite their own, and the hawk-eyed exertions of clever detectives—Captain Jack among the rest—they were wholly unable to fasten solid suspicion upon any one of their employeés.

An anonymous note, evidently written in a counterfeit hand, and signed "R," startled them.

Charley was the person pointed at by the unknown correspondent; but Sir Richard Warbeck and others who were consulted would not believe the insinuation, and the matter seemed to drop indefinitely.

Charley, being fully recovered in body, returned to the India House as usual, and was received with tokens of much respect by all the directors.

He attempted to appear gay; but all his endeavours were vain.

He was not the same person he had been, and could not look any one fairly in the face without evident effort.

There was a worm at his heart gnawing deeply, daily and hourly.

From being a gay, light-hearted youth, of fresh colour and dashing manner, as he had always been before he knew Phillip Redgill, he now appeared like a person of age, on whose shoulders a heavy weight was pressing.

Some thought it might arise from an unfortunate disappointment in love affairs; but these hints he parried with a faint smile, and attempted to joke in his old manner.

One morning a young, bright-faced clerk was called into the Directors' Council Room, and returned therefrom looking very pale, and with large tears standing in his eyes.

"Good day, Charley," said he to Warbeck, with much emotion. "I'm going; they don't want me any longer. I've done nothing wrong, you know; they lay no charge against me, yet I feel certain that they have formed wrong suspicions against me, on account of the unfortunate packet of counterfeit notes that was substituted for good ones in the safe a month or two ago. Good day, my boy; *this* will break my poor old mother's heart. She has no one to depend upon but me. I am lost, ruined, disgraced!"

The youth leaned upon the counter, shading his face, and tears flowed from him fast and hot.

His breast heaved convulsively, and he would have fallen from weakness but that Charles placed him in a chair, and gazed upon his guileless face long and intently.

Charley's features wore a ghastly smile.

His lips became bloodless and blue, and quivered with emotion as he attempted to speak.

He could *not* speak, however, for his voice faltered, and the words stuck in his throat.

Loosening his cravat to avoid a sense of strangulation, to which of late he had become sometimes subject, he seized the youth by the arm with an iron grip, and striding towards the Directors' Council Room.

"Come with *me*," he exclaimed, in a hoarse, hollow-toned voice, "come with *me!* You shall not suffer for the deeds of *others!* Gentlemen," he began when he had shut the door and stood before the Board of Directors, "gentlemen, I wish to say a few words before this young man leaves the India House. I wish to inform you——"

He caught the eye of old Sir Richard Warbeck gazing intently at him, and his courage failed him.

Summoning all his energy, with a great effort he approached to lean upon the council-table, and, casting his eyes upon the ground, continued, amid a solemn silence,

"I wish to inform you that *I* alone am answerable for the charge brought against, or supposed to exist, against this young man. *I* lost the money, and replaced the amount with a packet of false notes—no one else. I acknowledge it was my intention to have confessed it all on the following day. I have never had or spent a single penny of the amount, but lost it all by some unaccountable means the same evening on which I neglected to return to the India House. Prosecute me, and I will suffer cheerfully; anything is better than the hellish remorse which I have already suffered. But do not—do not, I beg of you, harbour suspicions against this sinless youth, on whose labour and reputation a poor widowed mother depends for bread!"

Charley Warbeck sank into a chair, and wept like a child.

The Board of Directors were astonished at such an unexpected disclosure from one of their favourite and much-trusted clerks, and sat for many minutes in mute surprise and profound reflection.

---

## CHAPTER XXVI.

THE PHANTOM LEGS—PHILLIP REDGILL CONTINUES HIS CAREER OF VILLANY—HIS FRIEND CAPTAIN JACK—YOUNG REDGILL'S MOTIVES FOR MARRYING—THE SUDDEN DEATH OF HIS FATHER—WHO CAUSED IT?—CHARLEY WARBECK IN PRISON—HE IS VISITED BY HIS FALSE FRIEND PHILLIP.

THE sudden disclosure so much appalled Sir Richard Warbeck that he hung his head, and was unconscious when Charles was led away by two burly, rough-looking men.

His first impulse was to rush to Dame Worthington's, and seek for him t'ere; but on arriving, of course, found him not at home.

His agitation and tears filled the poor, fond old woman with alarm, for, from what she could gather she imagined that Charles had been taken violently ill, or, what was far worse, perhaps had died!

When Sir Richard had explained everything to her, she screamed, and sank into a fit; and Mistress Haylark, dashing into the apartment, stood almost petrified to find him supporting her in his arms, and addressing her with words of endearment.

Clara was the next one to appear upon the scene, and, in her curl-papers, struck several melo-dramatic attitudes, and gracefully sank into the arm-chair, where she gave vent to a volley of ejaculations, and relieved her young feelings in a genuine flood of tears.

\*     \*     \*     \*     \*

Phillip Redgill, when informed of the affair, was consulting his intended father-in-law regarding his prospective marriage with Fanny, and heard the news with indifference, or at most with a great display of affected surprise.

"Don't say so! Charley, eh? Ah! he always *was* fond of fast living! That's what comes of going beyond one's means. *I* have learned *that* long ago. P. or fellow! confessed it, eh? Well, he *was* an ass and no mistake. *His* prospects are gone. and no mistake. Not half-a-dozen Sir Richard Warbecks will ever re-instate *him* again. But about *our* business, Sir Andrew. As I was saying, I am devilish short, upon my word; I aven't a coin in the world, and the 'old man' refuses to come up; I have asked him. I shall be rich, as you know, one of these days. Now these two young Warbecks are out of the way, old Sir Richard is sure to make me his heir."

"Ah, it is a great pity! So much comes of living beyond one's means. What would *you* have done, Phillip, if I were to have let those prettily executed pieces of paper signed by you in your father's name have gone floating about, eh?" said old Sir Andrew, grinning.

"Oh, never mind all *that*, you know. I am an altered man *now*, you see. I am going to marry and settle shortly. I have sown all my wild oats, and shall prove an exemplary member of society, you know—a member of parliament, or something of that sort, see if I don't. But how about the ships *Eclipse* and *Racehorse*? Didn't my father insure them in your office? I thought so—for £500,000, I believe. Lord! they tell me they have splendid cargoes of silks and teas on board. The last we heard of them they were sailing in company and had put into Pernambuco for water and supplies. The 'old man' will make a pretty penny by that 'spec.,' see if he don't, and then I may expect him to sign my marriage contract. But, in the meantime, good Sir Andrew, let me have a thousand or two—say £5,000; that ain't much, you know. I want it for a special purpose. Come, open your heart for once, old fellow, you'll be my father-in-law soon, I hope."

Sir Andrew, the old usurer, *did* open his heart, and in view of the expected marriage between Phillip and Fanny, his only daughter, let the intended husband have the amount he required.

Phillip passed a few moments with his "intended," in the garden, but left the house suddenly. But why did he leave his intended bride so hurriedly?

The reason was this:

While with one arm round Fanny's waist he was poring soft nothings in the ear of his intended bride, and forgetful for the moment of all the villany and ruin he had committed in the world, the startled maiden screamed aloud in horror.

Phillip, drawing his sword, and, while supporting the fainting maid, turned suddenly, and, to his amazement, beheld within a few feet of him the "Phantom legs."

The blood was frozen in his heart as he heard the ominous words,

"Phillip Redgill, I follow you for ever." (See cut in No. 6).

With superhuman exertion he conducted Sir Andrew's daughter in a fainting state to the mansion again, and assured the affrighted maiden that what she had seen was all imagination. But, meanwhile, filled with terror at the memory of old Bertram's murder, he left the house, trembling and pale, intent upon drowning his feelings in wine.

His steps were directed to a flash gambling-house where he lost considerably at cards; and, if the truth must be confessed, he spent the rest of the night at a house of bad repute, in company of Captain Jack and others, indulging in expensive wines and general debauchery.

Having spent most of his money, except what he had paid to Captain Jack, he visited Charles Warbeck in prison, and condoled with him in an off-handed manner, and at the same time mentally chuckling at his own superior tact, and cursing Charley's simplicity, or, as he termed it, his "stupidity."

"Why couldn't he have kept it to himself; he could never be found out, the fool? Conscience be hanged! Whoever heard of such a thing in these days? Well, *I'm* all right, *that's* all *I* care about, let every one look after themselves; a rogue is honest till found out. If a man betrays himself, so much the bigger fool he is, say I."

Phillip's visit of consolation was of short duration, and as he departed from the prison walls he mused,

"So my father refuses to sanction this marriage, for some time, and for 'special reasons,' does he? What can be his 'special reasons?' He says he's 'considerably involved, and wishes to see his way clear first;' the same old tune! Fathers are *always* the same; he never *did* coincide with any ideas of mine, the old brute! Well, never mind, he can't last long, *that's* certain; and *I don't think it would take much trouble to put him out of the way*, if all comes to all! Lord! what a fine time I should have then, eh? *I* don't care about old Sir Andrew's daughter, not a particle; she's *rich* and *that's* the main point now-a-days."

With these thoughts Phillip visited his grey-haired father, whom he found sitting before his office fire, gazing at the glowing embers, and buried in deep thought.

"How the wind blows to-night, Phillip! how fearfully it blows! I wonder how the sea is to-night? Is it rough weather, think you? How is it, stormy say you? Does the telegraph say so? The 'Racehorse' and 'Eclipse' must be fairly in the channel, or near it by this time, what think you? I hope they'll get through safely, Phillip; if *they* were to go——!"

"What then?" asked Phillip, laughingly; "your prospects are not centred solely in them, surely?"

"Ah, my son, you know nothing of business yet, I see. All my prospects *are* in those ships, and if anything befalls them, I am ru——!"

"Oh, the old story," thought Phillip, and was so

disgusted that he made his visit of very short duration, and, taking up his hat, left his father's offices in profound disgust.

"These old fogies never will learn wisdom," thought he. "As if the ships aren't fully insured—what stuff! It the old driveller don't come up to taw, I'll soon put him out of the way, and no mistake. His tune has always been the same for the past five years—*always* on the point of bankruptcy, and yet always making no end of money! Well, well, I'm tired of it—he shan't keep me like a beggar *much* longer, *I* know!" And he paced up and down the street for some time in profound reflection.

*     *     *     *     *

Mr. Redgill, senior, went to his offices on the following morning as hale and hearty as ever, and appeared on 'Change the same as he had already done for many years before.

Telegrams from different parts of the coast, both north and south, confirmed previous rumours that the severe gale of the past few days had been unusually destructive, and that many vessels were reported wrecked or stranded. Several fast-sailing ships, which arrived the same morning, reported having passed the "Racehorse" and "Eclipse" off the Irish coast. "all well."

This news cheered the old man up so much that he consented to dine and go out with Phillip for an evening drive.

On the following morning newspapers detailed "the sad and unexpected death of the famous merchant, Mr. Redgill, who was thrown from his vehicle and drowned the previous evening, while riding with his only son, Phillip, the pair of horses having taken fright and ran away."

The account added that "Mr. Redgill, jun., had a miraculous escape," but, with wonderful agility, he leaped from the conveyance and saved himself, the horses and carriage, with his father, having tumbled into the Thames, and were drowned!"

---

## CHAPTER XXVII.

### OLD NETTLES IS SHAVED BY TWO OF THE SKELETON CREW.

A BARBER'S has been often, and very wisely, called a "gossiping shop."

If this is true of tonsorial establishments in town, it is particularly of such places in a village.

In a hamlet, or small town, the barber knows all the news, the latest joke, and the newest scandal.

There is nothing that he does not know, in fact.

No item ever escapes the "professor" who cuts your hair, or shaves you.

Thus thought old Nettles, the tavern-keeper, a few days after the eventful and dreadful conflict between Wildfire Ned and the Skeleton Crew, on the ocean.

For many miles around there were wild rumours of the ferocious battle which had taken place.

But no two persons had the same tale to tell,

Some said that Death-wing had killed young Ned Warbeck.

Others swore that Death-wing and most of his crew had been drowned.

But old Nettles knew differently.

Yes; but how?

Through the agency of Sea-Hawk and his smuggler band.

For when Sea-Hawk and his party had been decoyed on to, and afterwards beaten away from the Phantom Ship, they rowed rapidly to their cave again.

Later in the night, however, the sounds of distant fire-arms, and the booming of cannon over the ocean aroused their curiosity.

They took to their boats again, and sallied forth.

At a respectful distance from the scene of conflict, the Smuggler Chief had witnessed all, and was not slow to inform his old companion, Nettles, of the particulars.

When, therefore, Nettles went into the village-barber's shop to get shaved, the tonsorial professor was very loquacious, and, at great length, told him all he had heard about the conflict.

"Don't be such an ass, Mr. Barber," said Nettles, waiting for his turn. "Don't be such an ass as to tell such idle tales. I tell thee that Ned Warbeck or Wildfire Ned was not killed, nor brave Lieutenant Garnet either, for Ned rescued Lord Walton's sister from the 'sinking ship, and she is now safe and sound at the abbey again."

"Thee doesna' mean that 'ere, Maister Nettles, does thee?" said the astonished barber.

"Yes; but I do though, and more nor that I did hear that the king has raised Wildfire Ned to the rank of a lieutenant in the navy, and has given him the command of a rakish, fast-sailing, ten-gun sloop of war, and that at this very moment he is cruising about on the bright look-out for this Skeleton Crew, what remains of 'em, and a pretty overhauling they'll get, too, if Wildfire Ned should fall foul on 'em."

"But they do say these skeletons are invincible, Maister Nettles," the barber remarked, "and can't be hurt by anything."

"All stuff," said Nettles, contemptuously. "I dare say they don't like hard knocks no more than common folk, if the truth was known. I don't fear none on 'em, if they did set fire to my tavern."

"They say they be all charmed, maister?"

"So I've hearn; but don't believe it. The Red Man of the Gibbet is worse than all on 'em."

"How so?"

"Why he were one o' the founders on 'em, and the story goes that he gets out of his gibbet at certain times, and plies his trade."

"His trade! Why what does thee mean, Maister Nettles?"

"Mean! Why, didn't thee hear; the Red Man o' the Gibbet had been—once on a time—a barber."

"A barber! Lor' bless the man! thee can't mean that."

"I do, though. He were once a barber, and cut the throat of a nobleman for his money."

"Awful!"

"Yes, and afore they caught him he joined the Skeleton Crew, but was afterwards gibbeted; but that didn't seem to concarn him much, for they say he can get out at certain times and seasons, and goes on the spree."

"On the spree! What! a sperit goo on the spree, Maister Nettles?"

"So they say; but I can never believe it, nor will I until I sees it with my own eyes."

The conversation of Nettles with the village barber so much interested the open-mouthed villagers, that many lounged into the little shop to hear it.

This arose from the fact that all felt greatly interested in listening to his narrative of the brave and heroic exploits of young Warbeck on sea and land, and especially interesting at the present time, since it was whispered that old Sir Richard Warbeck at the Hall was in deep grief through the sad disgrace which Charley, Ned's elder brother, had fallen into lately in London.

The sudden disappearance of the miller's daughter, the horrible murder of her rustic lover, the escape of Bob Bertram from prison, and the half strangulation of the sexton, parish clerk, and others in the belfry by the Skeleton Crew, all tended to heighten the interest of any remarks old Nettles might make.

This was more so when it was well known that the old tavern-keeper had actually fought a battle with the terrible Death-wing and his gang.

With staring eyes and open mouths, they listened to Nettles, who gratified his audience with most alarming stories of the Skeleton Crew, so much so as to make many of them tremble in their shoes.

It was now Nettles' "turn" to be shaved.

He sat in the chair, and a small boy placed a napkin under his chin.

Yet all the while he was laughing at the villagers about their childish hobgoblin notions regarding the Skeleton Crew.

They in turn began to laugh also, until the shop re-echoed with their boisterous merriment.

When the barber's boy, lather-box and brush in hand, had half "soaped" Mr. Nettles, he gave a sudden shout of alarm and dropped his utensils on the floor.

His hair stood on end with fright, and he trembled violently in every limb.

And well he might.

He cried for help.

But the barber and his audience rushed out of the shop yelling like lunatics at the sight they saw, leaving Nettles and the boy alone.

How it happened no one could imagine.

But while the valiant Nettles was discoursing about and jeering the many stories about Death-wing's gang——

A skeleton appeared, razor in hand, and seized Nettles by the hair of his head !

Beside him, and grinning most horribly, stood the black spectre of the Red Man of the Gibbet, sharpening a razor on a strop attached to the wall (see Engraving in No. 7), and preparing to shave his enemy, old Nettles, the terrified tavern keeper.

More dead than alive, Nettles shook in every limb.

The barber's boy collapsed all of a heap upon the floor, and was howling like a mad dog.

"Shave him !" said the black spectre, in sepulchral tones.

Nettles was almost melted into a jelly.

He was in the hands of his worst enemies.

What became of him we shall shortly see.

## CHAPTER XVIII.

PHILLIP REDGILL'S UNEXPECTED FORTUNE — HE IS ALONE IN THE WORLD—THE CORONER'S INQUEST OVER HIS FATHER—THE VERDICT — THE VILLAIN PURSUES HIS CAREER OF CRIME — SIR ANDREW'S DAUGHTER FANNY, AND WHAT SHE DID — THE PRANKS OF A KNAVE.

THIS event of his father's death filled Phillip, apparently, with unbounded grief. He was so much afflicted that, at the coroner's inquest, the body having been dragged for and recovered, he could scarcely articulate a word.

He averted his face from the corpse, and simply explained that "the mournful accident had happened by his father driving too close to the edge of the bridge ; and the first intimation he had of danger was the sudden tilting of the vehicle and the falling of the horses, with his father, into the river."

The verdict rendered by the coroner's jury was "accidental drowning."

The funeral of the much-respected deceased was attended by numbers of well-known merchants and brokers on 'Change, who condoled with Phillip upon his unexpected bereavement.

Old Sir Andrew appeared seated in the first coach as one of the chief mourners, and if the size of a white handkerchief was any index of the extent of his grief, Sir Andrew's sorrow must have been of very extensive dimensions ; for he held the said handkerchief to his face all the way to the cemetery and back, and sighed very often and emphatically.

He did not fail to preach a sermon on the way to Phillip, on the vanity of earthly things—the old hypocrite !—but that youth simply sighed hypocritically, and, if the truth must be told, felt extremely glad that his parent was laid in the grave.

"I know what old Sir Andrew's about !" mused Phillip, as they rode home from the funeral ; "he can't fool me ! he wants me to marry his daughter, eh ? What an idea ! I'm not fool enough to think of such a thing now—of course not ! Marry her ?— Such a weazened-faced old maid as she is ? Not I, indeed ! All the governor's property is mine, now ! I have no more use for old Sir Andrew and his money-grubbing lot. I'm rich enough without him, and will marry some dashing belle when my father's affairs are arranged, and fool Sir Andrew—he'll see if I don't !"

The truth is that Phillip had all along desired a marriage with Sir Andrew's daughter for the sake of money only ; but now that he was master of his own actions, and inheritor of all his father's wealth, he instantly conceived different ideas.

When young Redgill had returned from the funeral, he discovered that Jacob Slowman, Esq., the lawyer, had already arrived to read the will, and, among the uninvited, was old Moss, the Jew.

After light refreshment, the company adjourned to the large parlour, where Mr. Slowman was busily engaged in arranging his papers.

Sir Andrew, and a dozen other gentlemen present, intimate friends and relations of the deceased, were loud in their praises of the defunct, and nothing could be said that was too good in honour of his many inestimable qualities.

He was—

"A model father !"

"An exemplary Christian !"

"An honest and irreproachable merchant !"

"Upright citizen !"

"Ornament to commerce !" &c., first one and then another remarked, until at last, Phillip began to imagine, for the first time in his life, that his father must have been much more than an "ordinary" gentleman.

When the will was read all the relations were much surprised to discover that nothing had been left them, and that everything had been bequeathed unreservedly to his only son, "after the payment of all just and honest debts."

Sir Andrew, although not related, appeared much disappointed, yet, concealing his chagrin at receiving no token of his profound friendship for deceased, gave vent to his feelings by giving long and fatherly advice to the heir.

In truth, Mr. Slowman had scarcely finished reading the will, ere every one found they had important business elsewhere which required their instant attention, and did not stay one moment longer than necessary, to pay any more compliments to the memory of the "exemplary Christian" and "model father," whom they had so loudly praised before the last will and testament had been read.

For several weeks Phillip visited but little, and many observed that his grief must be "really genuine," or he would have appeared in company long before.

Many members of polite society called at his residence and left their cards, and among them not a few intriguing ambitious mothers, who had rather suddenly discovered the vast importance of Mr. Phillip Redgill, and of the unbounded friendship which they had "always" entertained for that "interesting, good-looking" young man.

Sir Andrew, it must be confessed, was not behind any of the "polite" circle in frequently calling upon "his young friend," and giving him fatherly advice.

Yet he could not help grimly smiling at the "insiduous attempts," as he termed it, of the many inquisitive, and industrious matrons, who were continually inviting the young man to sojourn with them for a few days, in order to "drive away his deep-seated melancholy," and "make love to their daughters," perhaps might have been added.

At least, Sir Andrew imagined so, and did not fail to inform his wife and daughter, who threw up their hands and eyes in holy horror at the "worldliness and unscrupulousness of certain parties!"

The true reason for Phillip's non-appearance in society arose, not so much from "genuine grief," or "deep-rooted melancholy," at what all termed "the sad and lamentable bereavement," as from anxiety to ascertain the true state of his father's affairs.

In truth, he so much chafed under his confinement in the old house, and seemed so tremulous, that he never visited his father's apartments without a thrill of horrible excitement, and would often jump out of bed at night, as if suddenly alarmed by dreadful apparitions.

He daily imbibed large draughts of brandy, and this resort seemed to cheer him.

But the practice grew upon him hourly, so that the brandy lost much of its customary effect, and he accordingly drank deeply to sustain his drooping spirits.

Not being one of the executors himself, he knew but little of his father's indebtedness; but when he questioned old Moss, the money-lending Jew, on one occasion, regarding that point, the old Israelite said that "he would plainly tell him," and remarked very solemnly—

"When all debts are paid, your father's estates are not worth one penny! He was generally considered to be worth more than he really was. He sustained many losses, and kept afloat on credit! If the 'Racehorse' and 'Eclipse' safely arrive, there will be a little something for you, perhaps, when the cargoes are sold; but if they do not, there will not be a penny to spare. But, worse than all, many of us creditors, Phillip, will have to bite our fingers!"

It is unnecessary to say that this piece of confidential information surprised the young man considerably.

But not so much as might have been expected; for, from a careful study of his father's books, he had arrived at something like the same conclusion himself.

"Well, there's no help for it," thought he, drinking deeply of the brandy, "It will be a month, at least, before lawyer Sloman and the executors can present a balance sheet—I'll marry Sir Andrew's daughter, Fanny!"

Phillip's first visit to Sir Andrew after the funeral was of the most interesting nature.

The mother, "my lady," embraced him as a son.

Sir Andrew shook him cordially by the hand, and heartily welcomed him once more beneath his roof.

But both parents soon vacated the apartment in favor of their daughter, whose rustling silk could plainly be heard approaching upon the stairs.

The meeting between the affianced was solemn and tender.

Fanny struck a captivating attitude upon entering the room, tottered slightly towards the sofa, holding a handkerchief to conceal her tears!

Phillip rushed forward to break her fall, clasped her round the waist, kissed her with great gallantry, and, amid many ejaculations of "Phillip, dear!" and "Fanny, my beloved!" the couple passed several hours in delightful child's play.

Fanny's irresistible toilet, made up as it was for the most part of paints, flowers, false hair, puff combs, hoops, and silk, played so powerfully upon the sensitive and innocent heart of Phillip Redgill, that as he gazed upon her bewitchingly enamelled features—as her fair head leaned lovingly and confidingly upon his manly breast, he determined to allow of little delay in marrying.

And this resolution he whispered fondly into the not unwilling ear of his loved one, who blushed and sighed, and put her lace-worked handkerchief to her eyes, and appeared absorbed in deep emotion and crimson confusion.

When consulted upon this matter that same evening in his library, Sir Andrew sat in his easy chair with much affected state, and played with his watch-chain and keys in a smiling, self-complacent manner.

"I couldn't entertain any such project for the present; at least, not for one year, out of respect to Mr. Redgill, senior's, memory, by which time you will have fully wound up your affairs, and perhaps think more seriously upon the point, Phillip."

The coldness and calculation of old Sir Andrew simply had the effect of redoubling the ardour of the lovers, who sighed and condoled together on the proverbial "cruelty of parents" with much melodramatic tenderness.

Fanny did not confess it to her lover, but told "mamma" in confidence that she thought *three* months would be sufficiently long to postpone the event.

"For, who knows what may happen, mamma dear? I can't get such a chance as dear Phillip every day. He is young, handsome, rich, and much courted. *Who* knows *what* might happen in twelve months?"

Phillip, on the other hand, had his own motives for hastening the marriage, and sought every opportunity to visit and make love to his affianced.

His eloquence and importunities were so impressive that he found the fair Fanny daily yielding to his arguments.

And, knowing that she possessed a great vein of romance in her disposition, he played upon it so effectually that she finally consented to a clandestine marriage.

"We can easily procure a 'licence' and get married a few miles out in the country without the old folks knowing anything about it, and then we can avow the act whenever we see that your cruel father will relent."

In accordance with this plan Phillip procured a marriage licence.

Fanny met him, and, after two hours' ride, they alighted at a small country town, and were privately married.

CAPTAIN JACK COMMITS MURDER.

No one knew them there, so that information could not be sent to town.

Having spent the day very pleasantly together, the young couple returned in the evening, and when she arrived home Miss Fanny informed her anxious and loving parents that "she had been spending a very pleasant day with an old schoolmate."

Phillip called that same evening some time after Fanny's return home, and, hypocrite as he was, assumed all the manners of one who had casually "dropped in" for a customary evening chat.

As usual, the old people retired into the inner drawing-room to allow the lovers to converse with freedom, and Sir Andrew came to the conclusion, in consideration of the unusually late hour at which

No. 10.

Phillip departed home, that "the young couple were getting to like each other daily more and more, and would make a most excellent couple,"

## CHAPTER XIX.

### CHARLEY WARBECK IN PRISON—TRUE AND FALSE FRIENDS.

WHILE Phillip Redgill was congratulating himself upon the gradual completion and success of all his villanous schemes, Charley Warbeck was pining in prison, and totally deserted by all his "fast," and "gallant" friends of olden times.

None of them would ever visit him.

"It was not respectable" to be seen within the shadows of a jail, they said.

Yet, if the truth were known, many of these fine "sparks," and "gallants," deserved to be *in*, rather than *out* of such an institution.

More than one, had justice been cognizant of their "little speculations," would have consigned them to worse apartments than that assigned to the brave-hearted, but foolish, Charley Warbeck.

Of all who knew him in his days of prosperity, gaiety, and unimpeachable character, there was not one who visited him, or made the slightest inquiry regarding his wants or necessities.

He was consigned to oblivion in general estimation, and many of his former acquaintance stoutly denied that they had *ever* known or spoken to him in all their lives.

Old Sir Richard called at the gaol several times, and proffered all the aid in his power : but as Charles had already publicly acknowledged his guilt, and persisted in avowing it, legal assistance was considered to be of little avail.

Dame Worthington was an almost daily visitor, and brought every kind of refreshment for the prisoner, and her tears ever flowed copiously as she embraced "her dear son," as she endearingly called him.

In truth, she frequently transgressed the rules of the prison, and remained much longer in her visits than the regulations allowed.

But her sorrow was so sincere and apparent to all, that the turnkeys, individuals apparently constituted partly of iron, and partly of stone, looked on with much compassion, and always remarked as she departed—

"If that there old lady was his own mother, she couldn't hang around that young man more tenderly and lovingly than she does."

Mistress Haylark and daughter were also frequent visitors to the unhappy youth, and brought him many little trifles which might comfort and console him in his solitude.

Miss Clara, in truth, was rather romantic in her behaviour, for she often passed herself off to the prison authorities as "his sister," and gained ingress thus very frequently.

Charles had already explained to her the true nature of his offence, and the unsophisticated young lady firmly believed every word he uttered.

She forgot all about her curls and curl-papers, and was ever intent upon devising some scheme for his relief or comfort.

In her increasing love for the young man, she even suggested various methods for his "escape," and proposed the exchange of garments for that purpose.

"Speak the word, Charles dear," she would say ; "and *I* will stay in your stead, if there is any prospect of escape."

She related to him all manner of devices for getting out of the dismal walls, and in her enthusiasm spoke of Claude Duval, &c., but Charley listened to her interesting prattle with a smile, and kissed her tenderly for the affection which had prompted her to suggest so many and such romantic schemes.

Clara was "in love," but could not realize it !

Charles was no better, yet smiled philosophically at the gradual, but positive growth of his attachment for the whimsical, romantic girl, with her luxuriant growth of curls, and mentally ejaculated—

"'A friend in need is a friend indeed.' I can't help but *like* her ! There's something about her which *makes* me love her ! I *do* love her, but, alas, I am not worthy of her !"

Several weeks passed away, and trials at the Criminal Court had not yet commenced.

Old Sir Richard was sick from over anxiety for his protege, and his consultation-visits with good old Dame Worthington were long and frequent.

"If all the money I possess in the world could rescue the boy, I would freely give it," was his constant expression.

And, as he sat on the sofa, beside good Dame Worthington, frequently without more light than that of the fire, he would press her hand affectionately, and the old lady would shed tears—yes, tears of bitterness.

"My poor, poor Charles !" the old lady would say.

"The poor lad !" was always the rejoinder.

And thus they sat before the fire, hour after hour, communing with their own thoughts, and recalling again from the vista of the past sunny hours of youth, when love had warmed their hearts, and made them oblivious of consequences.

Clara Haylark was Dame Worthington's chief comfortor, for she was always consulting with the old lady regarding everything that might alleviate the sufferings of "poor Charles," and that would add to his comfort.

On several occasions Clara became so enthusiastic in regard to Charley that, with her head all shaking with curls, and tears in her eyes, she openly avowed her love for the young man, and averred that "she never would marry in her whole life without it was with him."

This so much pleased the old lady that she caressed the young woman, and sat with Clara's head in her lap for more than an hour without uttering a word.

As the Criminal Court trials approached the visits of Sir Richard Warbeck, Dame Worthington and Miss Clara (unknown to her mother) became more frequent.

Yet, despite all their endeavours, Charles persisted in refusing the aid of all legal talent, saying—

"I have avowed my guilt. No one is responsible but myself, and I am willing to suffer the utmost penalty of the law."

When his day of trial came on there was a considerable muster of India House clerks and others in court, who, because he was unfortunate, were loud in their denunciation of the prisoner.

Dame Worthington, Mistress Haylark and Clara were present also, and as Charley, good looking and gallant in bearing, stood in the dock and pleaded "guilty" to the charge preferred, Clara and the old dame gave vent to their tears copiously, and fainted.

As the India House had been reimbursed "by some unknown individual" for the sum lost, the directors refused to prosecute, out of respect to old Sir Richard, who, it was well known, entertained great love for the accused.

Charley's penalty was not so great as many expected.

Previous to his present fault, he had borne an irreproachable character, which tended much to lighten his sentence.

He was condemned to two years' imprisonment with hard labour.

Had it not been through much influence at Court, and the blazing report of Wildfire Ned's glorious deeds, he would have suffered death.

When returned to his cell, he was visited by a few friends, who congratulated him on his escape from a heavier penalty, and among the visitors was Phillip Redgill, Esq.

"I don't like to see you in gaol, my boy," was Phillip's first remark. "I'm supposed to know nothing of your transgression ; but I must acknowledge you *were* a fool, a *big* fool, for confessing it· If you'd only kept your tongue still you would never have been found out. Good-bye, old fellow ; I hope to see you out again one of these days. We must *all* pay for our experience, you know. I jeopardise my position in society by visiting you here, you know, but for old old acquaintance sake I thought I'd call."

"Thank you," was Charley's laconic reply, as Phillip left the prison. "If the truth were only known we might exchange places, perhaps."

## CHAPTER XX.

### PHILLIP PROGRESSES IN LOVE—HIS FURTHER SCHEMING.

WHILE Charley Warbeck is receiving the last visits of a very few friends, prior to his journey from London to the State Prison, Mr. Phillip is in daily consultation with his legal advisers and his father's executors.

From a deep study of his accounts, those interested came to the conclusion that Mr. Redgill deceased, was deeply involved in debt, and far beyond what any one might have expected.

"Who'd a believed it ?" said Mr. Sloman, the lawyer, in surprise, when confidentially informed. "Who'd a thought that such a man as *he* was should be so much involved ? Well, I've had *some* experience in worldly matters, but I never could have believed him to be so much in debt ; no, not if an angel from heaven had warned me. What ! old Redgill to be insolvent ? I *can't* believe it !"

Mr. Moss, who, as we know, was deeply interested, confessed that "his worst fears had been realised."

He always supposed that the old gentlemen had been speculating too extensively.

"He owes me £50,000, with interest, on various notes," said the Jew. "If his ships arrive safely, then I am safe, although there will be a very little margin left for Master Phillip when the other debts are paid. Let us hope, Mr. Sloman, that the ships *will* arrive safe, or else—I don't mind confessing it to you, you know, Mr. Sloman—I am a ruined man."

By some mysterious means old Sir Andrew had obtained an inkling of the true state of affairs, and when Phillip paid his usual evening visit to his fair daughter Fanny, who was always elaborately dressed, and in waiting for her husband-lover, the old gentleman's manner materially changed.

Nor did he smile so benignly and fatherly upon the young man as was his wont.

"You must not give too much encouragement to young Redgill, Fanny," said Sir Andrew, with, much solemnity, on one occasion, while walking the room in a perturbed state of mind, "for it might turn out that he isn't worth one penny."

His daughter only smiled at her father's fears, and when her husband-lover came she received him in the drawing-room with more marked tokens of attachment than ever, with this difference, that the fond parent did not retire so far into the back drawing-room as of yore, but remained within ear-shot of all that transpired between the young people.

"Love laughs at locks," it is said.

And so it happened with Phillip and his young wife.

They spoke in enigmas, and passed an hour or two each evening as happily as if the old folks were miles distant.

In truth, Miss Fanny's evening walks became more frequent since her flying visit with Phillip to the country, so that man and wife often met clandestinely, unknown to her parents, and their invariable success in eluding her natural guardians often caused much merriment and satisfaction between Fanny and Phillip.

On one occasion the footman informed Phillip that Sir Andrew desired to see him in the library.

The old gentleman's demeanour was so solemn and forbidding as he entered the apartment that Phillip imagined his marriage had become known to him.

"Mr. Redgill, is it true what I've heard, sir, that your very worthy parent died insolvent ? Really, sir, I cannot believe it, but such are the rumours, and painful ones they are. Of course, you are aware, sir, that I allowed you to visit my daughter supposing you to be a member of society, who, in the event of marriage—an event, I know, happily, yet far distant, and farthest from the thoughts of both—would be able to keep her in the style to which she has hitherto been used all her life. Of *course*, I could not think for one moment of allowing a *penniless* young man to make any serious advances towards one of mine."

Phillip scouted the idea that his father had died insolvent, and re-assured Sir Andrew.

"For," said he, "if my father really *does* stand insolvent, as his books might seem, and as rumours would have it, you are, of course, aware that his ships, when they arrive, would fully liquidate all claims of his creditors, and leave a very handsome surplus. In fact, you are aware, sir, that commercial communities think so highly of his transactions that even the insurance company, of which you are the president and greatest shareholder, have insured them for not less than £500,000."

This latter argument was potent, and fully re-assured the misgivings of old Sir Andrew, who ordered in wine, and explained many matters to the young man of which he was not before fully aware.

Among the items of information thus gleaned in confidential conversation, after drinking much wine, it appeared that Sir Andrew's insurance company was not so responsible and respectable as its "advertised" capital would lead the reading public to believe; for, in truth, Sir Andrew confessed, that should any serious loss fall upon it he could not honestly meet it, and that it might occasion a sudden collapse of the whole concern.

"Not that *I* should suffer so materially," added Sir Andrew, with a knowing wink, "for I have all my private funds deposited with the 'South Sea Bank' unknown to any one, and in another party's name, so that whatever might befall the insurance company I am all right and safe from personal danger."

A few days subsequent to this conversation the executors returned a balance sheet, illustrative of the deceased Mr. Redgill's affairs.

And it appeared, to the astonishment of every one, except those in the secret, that the late much-respected merchant really was insolvent, and owed his creditors much more than any would ever have anticipated.

If the "Racehorse" and "Eclipse" should arrive all claims could be satisfactorily adjusted ; even if the ships were lost, and the insurance paid, this end might be accomplished ; but without it the liabilities stood £200,000 beyond all assets, the chief debtor being the Jew Moss, for not less a sum than £50,000 !

When the worthy executors had arrived at these unpleasant conclusions, and revealed them confidentially and unofficially to the gay young Phillip, he bit his nails in anger, drank off his brandy very copiously, cursed his father in a volley of bitter oaths, and in his fury burned the picture of the deceased, which hung over the mantle in the library.

Yet, fully alive to the consequences which any such disclosure of affairs might have upon his own worldly prospect, he called " a council of war," and beseeched the worthy executors to make no disclosures for the present.

" Not for my sake, gentlemen," he said, with much warmth and emphasis, " but for the sake of the reputation of my worthy and much-loved father. I have no mother, nor kindred of any kind, except Sir Richard Warbeck, and therefore show my disinterestedness in its true colours. All I desire is to save my father's reputation in the community where he has lived and been respected for at least half a century ; therefore I beg, gentlemen, that you will say nothing of this for the present. When the ships arrive there will be enough, and more than enough, to liquidate every claim, and thus preserve the honour of my family. As to myself, I care not a jot if there is not a penny remaining over and above all his just and honest debts ; all I desire to see is that every creditor may be satisfied, even if I, his only son, go forth on the world penniless and in rags !"

Such sentiments were much applauded by the executors, who thought it might be wise to say nothing until the arrival of these vessels.

By some means, unknown to himself, Phillip discovered that old Sir Andrew had become aware of the true state of things.

But the young man argued so well that the insurance office director was comforted.

" These reports you have heard, Sir Andrew, are untrue," said young Redgill, with much warmth and emphasis, " circulated, doubtless, by some unknown enemy, who, knowing my ardent love for Fanny, has sought this method to poison your mind against me ; not that money could influence you in such an attachment as that which has always existed between myself and your daughter, for you are fully aware how ardent my love is, and how long it has existed, and I am positive you are too high-toned a gentleman to allow mere considerations of money to interpose between your daughter's happiness and mine, for if I knew this moment that Fanny was not possessed of one copper it could never alter my attachment. I love her for herself, and expect nothing with her, and I am certain you would never object to me on any financial consideration."

Old Sir Andrew, in the largeness and generosity of his hypocritical heart, confessed that money— ' mere paltry lucre "—had never entered his thoughts regarding the apportionment of his daughter and her settlement in life.

" For, although I am rich, and beyond all want," said he, " I should not object to my daughter marrying the poorest youth in the country, provided he was honest, sober, industrious, of good family, and talented. No, indeed ! money is farthest from my thoughts ; yet, still, I should, of course, like to see Fanny fairly matched with her intended husband in that regard, and would rather see her marry a rich than a poor man—for money, after all, Mr. Redgill, is not to be despised."

For the third time Phillip had quieted Sir Andrew's misgivings, and he visited Fanny, his wife, as before, regularly every evening ; but, after profound consideration, the young couple decided not to disclose their *true* relationship for a week or two.

The " Racehorse " and " Eclipse " were frequently reported by fast-sailing ships to be on their way, " all well."

In truth, the captains of both vessels had written letters, stating how successfully their voyage had progressed, and what valuable cargoes they were bringing.

The last letters were dated from Land's End, where they had put in on account of wild and dangerous weather, and the captains said that but a few days would elapse ere they would be reported by the telegraph station at Holyhead or Gravesend.

The insurance-office of which Sir Andrew was president was particularly pleased at this information.

Sir Andrew was jubilant and in ecstasies.

" I must manage to get rid of this young Phillip," thought he. " *I* know the state of his father's affairs much better than he supposes. Ha! ha! he can't blindfold *me!* I know a thing or two ! Men on 'Change, as I am daily, hear many very curious things within a few hours.

" When the cargoes of these vessels are sold, and old Redgill's debts are paid, there will not be much to spare, particularly when he pays me the fifteen thousand pounds he already owes me.

" He wants to marry my daughter, does he ?

" What a smart youth he is, to be sure !

" As if *I* didn't see his nice little game !

" No, no, Mr. Phillip—*my* daughter is destined for a *richer* man than you are !

" 'Tis true, she likes him, and all that ; but what's *that* to do with it ?

" Lord ! she'll soon get over all childishness when she learns the true state of things.

" I'm mighty glad, though, that those two vessels are perfectly safe ; if they were lost, it would be a very serious thing for *me*, and no mistake.

" Never mind, I must take care not to take so heavy a risk next time, and then it will save an immense amount of anxiety.

" Heigho ! well, this is a curious world. I will dismiss Phillip, and take Fanny to the continent out of the way. We'll have a gay time there, and she'll soon forget that young schemer, Phillip.

" I wish those vessels were arrived, the cargoes sold, and my money paid in, and then—"

" Letter, sir," said the servant, handing in a note, and retiring.

Being in the daily receipt of letters and messages about ships and the like, old Sir Andrew paid little attention to the present one ; but, observing that " Ship news—immediate," was on the envelope, he opened it, and read:—

To Sir Andrew McTurk,
        President of the London Insurance Company.
    SIR,—The captains and part of the crews of the China ships " Eclipse " and " Racehorse " have just landed at Holyhead, and report the total loss of their respective ships, which were attacked and stranded, robbed and burnt by the famous Skeleton Crew off the Land's End a week since. Nothing could withstand Death-wing and his band. The crew had scarcely time to get to the boats ere the ships struck the rocks, and were instantly smashed into pieces.
        Yours truly,
                CAPTAIN BROWN,
                King's cruiser " Seagull."

If a twenty pound keg of gunpowder had exploded beneath Sir Andrew's easy chair he could not have risen from his seat more suddenly than he did when he read that letter.

He seemed to have jumped into the middle of the floor.

And there he stood gazing at the round table, as if he saw thereon a nest of vipers.

"Gone!" said he, with an affrighted look, pulling his hair about, with eyes distended and open mouth.

"Gone! lost! *Both* of 'em? Captured by those sea-fiends! It *can't* be!"

He read the fatal letter again, word by word, and then sank into his seat with a spasmodic groan.

"Ruined!" he muttered mournfully, and groaned again.

———

## CHAPTER XXI.

### TWO KNAVES QUARREL—THE STARTLING CONFESSION.

SIR ANDREW rose and walked about the room like a maniac.

The unfortunate cat came in his path, and that he kicked through the window, slammed the room door and was about to leave the house!

At that precise moment Phillip Redgill arrived, and there they stood gazing at each other in the hall like two beasts of prey.

"What do *you* want here, sir?" said old Sir Andrew, in a terrific rage. "Get out of my house, you penniless scamp. Get out of my house, you miserable intriguer! I curse the hour I ever saw you!"

"Sir!"

"Sir! Don't 'sir' me, Mr. Redgill; this is no time for compliments, sir, and you know it. I want you to pay me what you owe me, sir, without any delay; the £15,000 which I have loaned you at different times! I want it, sir, paid up immediately, sir, and I'm bound to have it, too, or else——"

"Sir!" continued Phillip, astonished.

"Don't stand there 'siring' me, Mr. Redgill; get out of my house this instant. I loathe the very air you breathe, and wish I'd never laid eyes on you."

"Really, sir, and madam," continued Phillip, addressing husband and wife, for the latter, attracted by the noisy altercation, had arrived upon the scene, "really I cannot understand what all this means. I really——"

"You can't, eh? Well, come here, sir," continued old Sir Andrew, entering the parlour again, and dancing about into every corner of it; "you can't, eh? Then read *that*, sir," said he, throwing down the letter, "read *that*, sir, and then get out of my house as quickly as possible."

"Lost?" gasped Phillip.

"Lost, aye, lost! So are *you*, and so am *I*, and so are *all* of us lost—down to the bottom, among the silks and teas."

"This news, sir, is astounding!" said Phillip, looking very pale, and biting his nails. "The Skeleton Crew did it, eh? This almost unmans me, Sir Andrew."

"*Does* it? Well, then, sir, what must *I* feel, who have to bear nearly all the loss? You'll oblige me, Phillip Redgill, by getting that money of yours together—I'll stand no more delays. And I'd thank you never to set foot in my house again."

"Really, Sir Andrew, your conduct is inexplicable! I came to see your daughter, my——"

"You *did*, did you? Ha, ha! he, he! But let me tell you, sir, that *before* she should be *your* wife, I would rather see her in——."

"Sir Andrew, dear," interrupted Lady McTurk, getting in between the two angry gentlemen. "Husband, dear, be calm, I pray!"

"Go away, wife, I know what I'm saying well enough. And let me tell you, sir, that I do not want the honour of your presence in my premises any longer; I don't allow penniless, good-for-nothing vagabonds to prowl around *my* house! Come to court my daughter, eh? Ha, ha! Whoever heard of such a thing? What *next*, I wonder?"

"I do not come to *court* your daughter, sir; I come to claim her as my——"

"Capital! capital! To claim her as your—— Ah, ah! capital! capital! Who ever heard of such impudence in all their life?" said Sir Andrew, dancing about like a half-crazed monkey. "Get out of my house, sir, I tell you for the last time—get out, or I'll kick you out!"

And acting up to his words, he was about to put his threat into execution, when Fanny, his daughter, rushed upon the scene, blooming in paints, crinoline, and flowers.

"Father, dear, hear me!" she said, falling on her knees between her parent and Phillip. "Hear me, father, dear! Pity me! pardon him if he has offended you! For *my* sake, forgive—pardon my—my—*husband!* Father, dear, I—am—his—*wife!*"

"His *what?*" gasped Sir Andrew, as if shot, looking first at his daughter and then at Phillip. "His what, did you say?"

"His *wife*, father dear. Pardon me, I am his *wife!*"

Sir Andrew looked at Phillip for a moment with an eye full of devilish meaning.

That young gentleman advanced a few steps, and said very coolly,

"Wife! Yes, Sir Andrew, my wife! If you doubt it, read that," he added, throwing down on the table the marriage certificate.

Sir Andrew glanced at it for a second with a quivering lip, then sank upon the sofa, and groaned with the intense weight of agony oppressing him.

Like dutiful children Philip and his wife approached and knelt before the astonished, half-petrified father, while the mother was in hysterics in the back ground.

"You needn't ask any blessing from me," swore Sir Richard, rising, and rudely shoving the couple from him. "Blessing! What next? Daughter! you have made a fool of yourself; and, as for you, Phillip, you have had my blessing already, and will continue to receive it every day of your existence. As, of course, you did not marry for money, and have plenty of your own, I should feel extremely obliged if you'd pay all you owe me, Mr. Redgill, and take yourself and your bride out of my house just as quickly as possible, for another meal neither of you will ever eat under my roof. John, show this gentleman to the door," he added, putting on his hat, and rushing into the street.

———

## CHAPTER XXII.

### IN WHICH SIR ANDREW SUDDENLY TURNS VERY PIOUS—A STORMY MEETING.

THE loss of the well-known vessels, "Racehorse" and "Eclipse," and their destruction by the Skeleton Crew under Death-wing, was a serious blow to several gentlemen in the habit of daily attending on 'Change, and their countenances wore the marks of care and anxiety, for Mr. Redgill, senior, had drawn heavily on his friends in making his grand China speculation in silks and teas.

Old Moss the usurer was like one demented.

He was seen rushing from place to place, making all manner of inquiries regarding the "soundness" of the London Insurance Office, but his fears were dispelled by the universal good opinion which prevailed in commercial circles concerning it.

"Pooh! pooh, man!" was the general expression. "Sir Andrew is all right. Bless you, it is as safe as the bank. Why, that office is worth any amount of money!"

The executors of Mr. Redgill, senior, were not long, of course, in presenting their "policies" for adjustment at the insurance office.

But Sir Andrew was "out of town, and was not expected to return for several days; but upon his return all just claims would be settled," said the clerk.

Mr. Moss, as one of those principally interested, felt comforted, and awaited Sir Andrew's return with recomposed feelings, but hot impatience.

When the affairs of the "London Insurance Company" were examined commercial circles were greatly surprised to find it unable to meet the heavy loss which had unexpectedly fallen upon it by the wreck of the vessels, and that, far from being able to pay £500,000 to the estate of Mr. Redgill, deceased, it was not possessed of more than a fiftieth part of that sum.

In truth, at the time in which these events occurred, the latter part of the merry monarch's reign, the London money market was in a very unsafe, unsettled condition, and commerce was trembling on the brink of ruin from inflated currency, wild speculation, and general distrust.

Leading men had predicted the inevitability of "a general smash" should things thus continue, yet none were, of course, able to divine in which direction the storm might first break out.

When it was known on 'Change, therefore, that Sir Andrew's office was unable to meet its liabilities many raised their hands and eyes in wonder, and exclaimed—

"Who'd a believed it?"

This was poor consolation to old Moss the Jew, and other persons interested in the settlement of Mr. Redgill's affairs.

With a stooping gait, shrivelled face and hands, old Moss journeyed to and fro in an undeniable state of despair, and was in such a rage that he ordered his agent to turn every poor devil out of his numerous tenements who had not paid every farthing of their rents.

Sitting in his lonely, dirty office, without fire, or comfort of any kind, he gathered himself into a heap in a large, old arm-chair, and looked like some wild animal in wait for its prey.

Hour after hour he there sat, thinking of the past, and cursing every one in any way connected with his losses.

He cursed both the living and the dead, with an earnestness and an enthusiasm which greatly relieved his pent-up feelings.

To such an extent had his loss preyed upon him, that his face had become like a livid corpse.

He stalked through his dusty, dingy offices like one possessed by the devil, and when an unfortunate servant poked in her head from the back room, to ask a question, Moss raised a heavy ledger with great energy, and threw it at her.

"So Sir Andrew has returned to town again, has he? Ha, ha! Oh, he's a nice gentleman—the intended father-in-law of that young vagabond, Redgill, eh? I see the scheme! No wonder the insurance office couldn't pay its lawful debts! I know what their plans are. I'll go and see him. I will see him; he can't fool me, old as I am. I'll tell

him what I think of him. I'll have my money, or I'll see why!" cursed old Moss, walking about like a maniac.

The furious old Jew put on his tattered overcoat, buttoned it up to the throat, and with a good thick stick in his hand, trudged off towards Sir Andrew's residence.

The servant said his master was engaged, and could not be seen.

Mr. Moss would take no denial.

He would see him, and without further ceremony flourished his stick at the footman's head, and made his way up-stairs to the library.

As he stood at the door, he heard the sounds of several voices, high in oath and angry altercation.

He entered quietly, took a seat near the door, and, finding the gentlemen to be creditors like himself, soon took part in their grievances, and opened an extra broadside of abuse upon the unfortunate Sir Andrew McTurk.

Sir Andrew, in his easy chair, one leg over the other, played with his watch-chain and seals in the coolest manner imaginable.

This was one of those occasions in life which "try men's souls," and call forth their Christian virtues in bold relief against the revilings of an angry audience.

Sir Andrew's resignation and Christian forbearance was extraordinary.

He even smiled, as one after another of Mr. Redgill's creditors grew red in the face, struck the table, and told what they thought of him.

Old Moss, the Jew, was "sitting on thorns," for he was very uneasy in his chair.

He at last arose, and, approaching the Christian and martyr-like Sir Andrew, he flourished his clenched fist in the face of that meek and smiling gentleman, and said,

"I'll tell you what *I* think about you, Sir Andrew McTurk—you are a d—d rogue, sir! and the whole lot of you are a gang of thieves, and ought to be hung, if there was any justice in the world."

With wonderful forbearance, Sir Andrew listened to all these personal compliments, but at last said, with much mildness,

"Really, gentlemen, I cannot understand all this! I owe you nothing; neither does the late company, of which I, unfortunately, was president. You had better present your claims to the executors of Mr. Redgill's estate. They are the proper persons to whom you should apply. I have nothing to do with all this.

"The London Insurance Company certainly closed their doors very suddenly, but I was out of town at the time, and only heard of it by letter. We have had very extensive losses of late, but, had I any capital, it would have given me infinite pleasure to meet all claims—it would, I assure you!

"In truth, I make the humiliating confession to you, gentlemen, despite your angry and unjust accusations, that I, personally, have not one penny in the world!

"Were it not for some funds, which I cannot legally touch, owned by my wife's sister—"

Mr. Moss groaned very audibly at the words "my wife's sister."

"On deposit at the South Sea Bank, we should not be worth a fraction, and would be all turned out into the streets!

"But, my dear friends, why do you come to me about these affairs? I have nothing to do with them."

All this was said with a faint smile, which was like wormwood to all present.

Mr. Moss, who flounced about the apartment like

a mad morris dancer, flourished his walking-stick, and said,

"The reason I come to see you, you sanctimonious old scoundrel, is to tell you what I think of you!

"Had you paid the insurance on those vessels, like honest men would have done, I and every other creditor would have been satisfied in full; but now we don't get one penny!

"No, not a solitary farthing!

"And do you think I don't know all about your scheme?—eh, you smiling old villain?

"Don't I know that young Redgill is going to be your son-in-law, eh? and that if you had paid the insurance, he wouldn't lawfully come in for one penny?

"Do you think I don't know all about it, you scheming scoundrel?"

Mr. Moss was bursting with rage.

This disclosure only tended to raise the ire of the other creditors, who became so furious and noisy that they crowded round poor Sir Andrew, gesticulating and cursing so that they reminded one of a pack of hungry and furious wolves.

Sir Andrew was placid as a lamb, and said not a word.

He played with his watch keys, and gazed at the fire, until, when his noisy visitors had departed, he smiled, and said,

"Well, let them howl as much as they like. I am all right—so that's all that concerns me! It wasn't a bad idea! They can't touch the money of mine now which my wife placed to the account of her sister, for it is all in the name of a third party, and is taken for her own personalty. Who cares if others do lose? Why, if we had paid the policies, I shouldn't be worth one penny! In fact, we couldn't pay it. By closing doors we have 'done' them all, and saved ourselves! They may say what they please; 'business is business,' but let every one take care of themselves."

## CHAPTER XXIII.

MISERIES ACCUMULATE THICK AND FAST—FEARFUL SITUATION OF SON AND FATHER-IN-LAW.

EVERY one did take care of themselves.

No sooner had the news spread that the insurance office had closed up its business than a whole host of tradesmen sent in their "little bills," and Sir Andrew's residence was besieged with creditors.

In order to escape their annoyance and importunities it was resolved that the much-persecuted gentleman should make a sojourn in the country, by which time "the storm would have blown over."

"How much money did you draw from the bank to-day on your sister's account, wife?" asked old Sir Andrew, of his spouse, as they both sat before the parlour fire, talking of his intended journey.

"Five thousand pounds, my dear," was the reply. "Thinking you would prefer it, and that it would be more safe, I drew it in a single package of notes. I went very early, and escaped much notice. Phillip Redgill is a clerk there, now, I see. The bank messenger brought the packet. It is in the safe."

Evening had now closed in, and the parlour blinds were drawn.

A loud knock was heard at the door, and rudely shoving the servant out of the way, Phillip Redgill somewhat intoxicated, ushered himself without ceremony into the parlour.

"How often must I forbid you my house, Phillip Redgill?" Sir Andrew began, rising in fatherly majesty and wrath. "How often will you compel me to insult you, sir?

"You have been the cause of all my losses and humiliations, and I curse the hour I ever saw you.

"You have robbed me of my only daughter; you have repeatedly dishonoured that miserable old man, your late father; you have lost all honour yourself, and now you dishonour me.

"For the last time I tell you to be gone!

"Leave my house, sir, and never place foot in it again!

"My daughter is now yours——Be calm, my wife, and don't interrupt me——You have clandestinely married her, contrary to my hopes and wishes, and now you must provide for her the best way you can.

"I have disowned her!

"She has married the poor, penniless beggar, forger, and blackleg, as you are, sir, and no longer has any claims on me.

"You are a beggar, yourself, and a blackleg, a scoundrel, I repeat; but don't imagine for one moment you will ever receive a penny of mine—no, not a farthing. Go!"

"Dishonoured you, you old scoundrel!" Phillip began, laughing and grinning, "dishonoured you? Why, it is you who have dishonoured me! Why don't you pay the insurance policies on my father's ships, you old rascal? If you were to do so all the debts would be paid, and to the utmost fraction; but you managed to fail, did you? Well, your turn will come one of these days.

"I do *not* come, sir, to ask from you anything for myself. I would *scorn* to receive a penny from your miserly dishonest hands, but I come to demand from you, in the name of my wife, the £5,000 which you hold that belongs to her, as her aunt's legacy; *this* is my business with you, sir, and I shall not stir until you pay it."

"You won't, eh?" said Sir Andrew, rising. "I suppose you saw my wife drawing from the bank this morning, as you are a clerk there now, and thought it a proper time to come and bully me, eh? No, no," said the old man, opening a small safe and taking the packet of notes therefrom, "no, no, I am penniless. I am a ruined man, and all through *you*, Phillip, I haven't a penny of my own now. I am totally dependent on my wife. I am a beggar, and can pay no one. You needn't trouble yourself by calling again, sir; I shall be out of town for several months. *This*, sir," flourishing the packet of notes, "*this* sum, sir, is all I can now call my own, and part of it is my travelling expenses."

He placed the notes upon the table, saying,

"This miserable sum is all I can now call my own. Tell your be-lov-ed wife, sir, that when my affairs are a little settled, and I can see my way clear, I will, *perhaps*, pay her aunt's legacy; but even, in *that* case, she must call for it *herself*, for I wouldn't trust *you*, Phillip Redgill, with a penny piece."

"You will not pay her then, eh? you old villain," said Phillip, intently eyeing the old man, who was undoing the packet of notes. "Well, then, I'll *take* it," said he.

Rushing towards the table, he nearly succeeded in seizing the packet, but the old man's hold upon it was so firm and tiger-like, that Phillip was unable to do so.

In the scuffle which ensued, the packet fell to the ground, and the notes were strewn about in all directions; but, to the horror of both parties, it was *not* a package of bank notes, but nought else than a package of bank scrip given in mistake!

This sudden discovery startled both father, mother, and son.

They stood looking at the bank scrip as if in a dream !

Sir Andrew sank in his chair, hiding his face with his hands.

"There is roguery and robbery on every side," said he, in a husky voice. "*That* packet came from the South Sea Bank, Mr. Redgill, and should have contained bank notes.

"There is some one about that establishment who is a deep-dyed scoundrel ! *You* have succe ded in getting a situation there lately, I hear," said the old man with fiery eyes, "and perhaps *you* might guess his name, sir, !" he added, rising, and looking Phillip full in the face.

"When the bank opens in the morning, I shall inform the directors of this beautiful little trick, and seek redress. So you have imitated Charley Warbeck's knavery already, eh, sir, I find ? You will live to repent it."

"It will avail you little to tell the bank of your suspicions, old man," Phillip answered, with a triumphant scowling look, "for I beg leave to inform you that the South Sea Bank, of which I am a clerk, suspended payment at three o'clock this afternoon ! Their notes are exactly worth nothing !"

Sir Andrew convulsively clasped his temples ; his limbs trembled under him, and he sank upon the sofa, like an inanimate heap of humanity.

He groaned despairingly, and most furiously gave vent to his Christian feelings in a volley of oaths.

His wife, in tears, was kneeling by his side, and would fain console him.

Phillip Redgill, demon-like, and laughing, stalked forth into the street again, triumphant and beggared, yet a villain to the heart's core !

---

## CHAPTER XXIV.

CHARLEY WARBECK'S FRIENDS—PRISON LIFE— TRUE LOVE—THE SURPRISE AND PARDON.

MR. CHARLES WARBECK had now been in confinement for more than three months, and even had become more or less reconciled to his lot.

His luxuriant head of hair was cropped so closely, according to "regulations," by the prison barber that very little capillary substance was left upon his cranium, which now looked very much like a close-worn blacking-brush.

His highly-prized bit of whisker, upon which he had bestowed so much fondness and care—his moustacheos, also, which, with the aid of unguent, much combing, brushing, and Hungarian paste, had assumed of yore quite a fierce and military twist— were all now sacrificed to the barbarous razor.

And shorn of these hirsute charms, he felt very little sorrow or humiliation when vested and officially enrobed in the zebra-like suit of striped flannel jacket and trousers, which was the apparel of the prison.

Although by no means a rogue, he was herded with a gang of ruffians, murderers, swindlers, pickpockets and the very off-scourings of all the earth.

And such society, it must be confessed, was a much greater punishment to his sensitive feelings than the confinement, remorse, or a thousand inconveniences and annoyances to which he was daily and hourly subjected.

Had he been of pliant nature he might soon have become as utterly depraved as his companions.

But his demeanour was so gentle, his manner so mild, and general deportment so humble and resigned, that the prison authorities soon removed him from the bands of ruffians with whom he had hitherto laboured in the quarries and on the public roads.

He seldom spoke, and although there was a mild resignation in his looks and bearing, his eyes had a light of honest independence about them, and his voice a firmness of tone which told of a guiltless soul suffering from some chance misfortune over which, in a moment of temptation, it had not sufficient control.

The prison keepers and guards were unanimous in pronouncing his conduct "excellent," and so stated it upon their several day-books and weekly reports.

The chaplain, indeed, with whom Charley had as frequent interviews as could be allowed, was loud in his praises of the gentlemanly prisoner, and when Charles had confessed to him, in conversation, the whole story of his misdemeanour, he shook him by the hand, and said,

"I fully understand the whole case ; it was a pity."

"And yet," he added, "although paying the the penalty of what might not be considered actually a theft, since you had fully determined to deliver the packet, this, your present experience, may be of incalculable good to you for your whole life."

Good old Dame Worthington was a frequent visitor to see "her dear boy," and was always provided with a basket of considerable size, containing a plentiful supply of whatever the authorities would permit to prisoners.

Not unfrequently, also, Miss Clara took the same journey, sometimes with Dame Worthington, but more often alone, for the distance was not very great, so that she could go and return very easily in a few hours.

The interviews between Charles and Dame Worthington were of a painful description to both.

Sometimes old Sir Richard was present likewise, by "mere accident," as he said.

They were loud in their hopes of obtaining a pardon from the king.

With the prospect of speedy relief Charley's spirits rose, and his health began to improve so much that he soon acquired a strong, hardy, robust look, from wholesome hard labour, a good appetite, and a pure conscience.

His hair began to grow again, and curl as luxuriantly as ever.

Miss Clara was in raptures at his improved appearance, and seemed so lost in his company that she frequently came very near losing her conveyance, which would have been not only very annoying, but must have disclosed these frequent visits to her mother.

Mistress Haylark, in truth, often checked her daughter's eloquence when discoursing of Charles and reminded her in a whisper that he was a "convict," and that "it would not do to have anything to say, or even to know such a person."

"Besides, my dear, you have good prospects in life, and money to receive when you marry ; but if your ambition doesn't run higher than to love a penniless fellow like him, without character or prospects, why then you are not ' a Haylark,' that's all I can say about it."

# THE SKELETON CREW; OR, WILDFIRE NED.

A MYSTERIOUS VISITOR.

Despite all that could be said by her mother, to the contrary, Clara was constantly thinking and dreaming about Charles.

She had committed a grevious theft, and stole his likeness on ivory from Dame Worthington's back parlour, and having made a case for it, hung it round her neck inside her bosom, and whenever feeling particular sentimental, she would draw it forth, kiss it, put it back again, and then indulge in that inexpensive luxury known to females as "a *good* cry!"

Miss Clara had fully made up her mind to marry Charles when he came forth from prison—that is, if she could get him.

But upon that point she sometimes had very serious misgivings.

For she knew several young ladies in the neighbourhood, who in former times were "setting their caps" at him.

Such disagreeable reflections often threw her into fits of despondency, and on such occasions no one could prevail upon her to sing or play in the parlour, as was her custom of an evening.

And she had been known to flounce out of that apartment in high dudgeon, on one occasion, when some one had mentioned the name of Miss Josephine Smith, who lived next door, and enjoyed a great reputation for a pretty figure, and a graceful dancer—two things in which Clara innocently supposed herself to be greatly deficient.

On a particular afternoon, Miss Clara had been excruciatingly miserable, and knew not the reasons why.

When twilight came she went into the parlour and uncovered the harp, with the intention of playing some pathetic air by way of consolation; but, upon entering the apartment, she perceived Dame Worthington and old Sir Richard Warbeck in earnest conversation in the back parlour, and Charles's name being mentioned, Clara leaned against the half-opened folding doors and listened.

"Well, I *know* that the affectionate little Dolly likes him, as much as any girl ever *could* do, but I don't think he cares so much about *her*, perhaps," said the old dame.

"Say no more about it ; if he makes a judicious match I will assist him in the world; but as to mere 'curls, and 'harp playing,' and all that superficial nonsense, I know he has an ambition above all *that.* The girl *he* carries in his heart has greater qualifications than *these*, or I am much mistaken. *I* know the lady *he* admires most, and she doesn't live *more* than a hundred miles from this house," Sir Richard said.

Clara Haylark could hear no more ; she rushed from the apartment in despair. The die was cast ! Charles was lost for ever !

For several days she kept her rooms, and could not be prevailed upon, despite all importunities, to appear in the parlour after tea.

No one could assign a cause for her absence, and a certain Augustus Fumbleton, Esq., who was hopelessly paying his addresses to her under the secret auspices of her mother, called evening after evening without seeing his idol on the music-stool, and retired to his cold and lonely lodgings in meek resignation, luxuriating in melancholy madness, yet feeling an intense dismal satisfaction that he could truthfully report to his intended mother-in-law that he was daily decreasing in rotundity, and fast falling into a galloping fashionable decline !

\* \* \*

Charles, who, in his legal seclusion, far from all temptation and the frivolities of the world, knew comparatively nothing of what was passing within the sphere of the good old dame's respectable hotel, was much surprised at the altered language in which Miss Clara now addressed him, and could not divine the causes therefore.

Clara's notes, which formerly were full of hope, love, fidelity, and all the tender and most interesting passions, now pictured to him nought but her bleak and blank despair.

She told him she was "lost."

That all she wished for now in this sublunary world was "a quiet grave," where, of course, moss-roses, violets, and forget-me-nots might bloom.

But of aught else she had neither hopes nor expectations.

She told him, moreover, that her heart was broken, and intimated that nought on earth could mend it, or join the dissevered parts anew, &c.

Finally she said his heart was given to another, and that she was left alone to droop and die !

Surprised beyond measure at the change in her style of language, Charley Warbeck chafed exceedingly, and could not understand what had happened to cause a rupture between his "little curly head," as he jocosely termed her, and himself.

Surely no one could have divined the temporary passion which had inflamed him for the old gaoler's daughter, he thought ; and save this slight indiscretion, his heart had not strayed from the affectionate, unsophisticated Clara !

Until now, he knew not how much he had loved her !

Now, indeed, his passion began to flame with tenfold ardour ; and when she no longer visited him in prison as of yore, and sent no word of love or kind ness by the much-expected and long looked-for post, he begun to decline in health, and visibly to pine.

"Some enemy has been at work," thought he.

"I would give untold wealth to have this thing explained ! A more true-hearted girl never breathed the breath of life, and I would give ten thousand kingdoms to call her mine !

"She has been faithful to me in all my adversity.

"She, of all I ever knew, is the only one who does not despise me.

"If I live I will make her my wife, or else have none at all, if I could even exist for a thousand years."

Dame Worthington, and also Sir Richard, visited the prisoner as of yore. They abated nothing of their former kindness—if anything, they loved him all the more—yet Charley's health visibly declined, nor could his friends imagine the cause thereof.

Mental anxiety had laid him upon an hospital bed, and there he lay for many days.

The good doctor had watched his case with more than ordinary anxiety and care.

When making his usual "rounds" to the patients, he came laughingly to Charley's bedside one morning, and jocosely observed, as he passed on, "I will not prescribe for this case to-day," and placed in his patient's hands the King's pardon !

Surprised beyond measure, Charles read the document time after time, as if distrustful of his senses, and then begged permission to leave the prison walls immediately !

The good doctor smiled, and at last permitted it ; and Charles, weak, pale, and subdued in spirit, put on his best clothes, and was soon on his way to Dame Worthington's.

It was past the time for dinner.

He saw by the light in the parlour that some one was there !

The door stood ajar.

He went into the passage, and noiselessly entered the parlour !

At the harp sat Clara, and behind her Augustus Fumbleton, Esq., who was pressing her to sing.

She hesitated much, and begged to be excused.

As there were no other persons present, her beau impudently attempted to kiss the player.

But this was more than Charley could bear.

He quietly advanced, knocked Fumbleton aside, and kissed her himself !

Clara's surprise was great !

She gave a little scream, rose from the music-stool, and embraced Charles unreservedly.

Fumbleton, Esq., perceived at a glance that he was not at all wanted, and considerably "out of place."

Like a wise youth, he vacated the apartment very expeditiously, and was never seen there more !

It was some moments ere Miss Clara was released from the strong arms of Mr. Charles, and even *then* he seemed much loth to part with the mass of curls which had nestled so affectionately and confidingly around his neck.

But her little scream had been heard by Mistress Haylark, who, in maternal anxiety for her fair, accomplished, and only child, quickly arrived upon the scene, puffing and blowing, and, discovering the true state of things, gave a second edition of her daughter's little scream, and sank upon the capacious sofa completely exhausted with her efforts.

Dame Worthington, hearing the rumpus, came into the room.

She looked at the youth for one moment, and would have fainted, but Charley supported her.

After much kissing and hugging, and re-kissing and re-hugging, she fully recovered, and began laughing and crying and bustling about, preparing a substantial meal for " her boy."

And so the time passed, until a messenger having informed old Sir Richard of the course of events, that worthy and much-esteemed gentleman arrived.

He shook Charles cordially by the hand, and retired for a private chat with Dame Worthington in the back parlor, where—as Mistress Haylark often afterwards solemnly affirmed—he was observed through the keyhole to kiss and embrace her as affectionately as if he were a youth of twenty, and she of not more than sixteen summers.

Be that as it may, we only know, through the " Truthful Chronicle," that the evening passed extremly cheerful, and that all those acquainted with the true state of things drank more than one glass of wine to Charley's success ; that Dame Worthington wept and embraced him often and often ; that old Sir Richard shook him repeatedly by the hand, and that Clara Haylark was more than once called out of the room by a whisper from the servant, when Charley way-laid and kissed her so often as to seriously jeopardize the safety of her cherry and seductively pouting lips.

———

## CHAPTER XXV.

WILDFIRE NED AND MASTER TIM FALL INTO A VERY SERIOUS TRAP—THE INNKEEPER'S GREAT GENEROSITY—THE SECRET MINE—THE BULLET-PROOF STRANGER—THE " HAUNTED HOUSE."

THE news of Wildfire Ned's first exploit on sea was soon the talk of the whole country.

So much mischief, and such dreadful depredations, had been committed by Death-wing's ruthless band, that it was considered impossible that any crew, however well manned, could withstand them.

Wildfire Ned, however, had proved how silly this idea was, for during his first battle on the water he had everywhere wished to meet Death-wing, the grim chief, in mortal combat, but as often was he disappointed.

However, the Phantom Ship, one of those which the Skeleton Crew possessed, had quickly succumbed to Ned Warbeck's prowess, and the crew, at least for the present, scattered to the four winds of heaven.

Ned Warbeck and his faithful Tim would have continued to cruise with the brave Lieutenant Garnet, but Ned was ordered to London to report in person to the king and to the board of merchants regarding Death-wing's band.

As he heard also of Phillip Redgill's villainy and of his brother Charley's disgrace and misfortune, this spurred him on all the more to reach London quickly, so that he might inquire into the whole affair himself.

He swore to be revenged on Phillip, and was burning with impatience to reach his journey's end, that he might disclose to Sir Richard Warbeck all he had learned from Bob Bertram about the old farmer's murder.

Through sunshine and shower, therefore, Ned and Tim journeyed from Walton Abbey, on two capital steeds which the grateful marquis and the young lord had placed at their disposal.

Through the rain, sleet, and snow they journeyed, as fast as horseflesh would carry them, and among other eccentricities, in order to surprise and astonish the simple country folk, and in awful dread of again being recognised by any stray member of the Skeleton Crew or Sea Hawk's smugglers, Master Tim blacked his face, and wore semi-theatrical attire, much to Ned Warbeck's amusement.

\* \* \* \* \*

It had just struck eleven by the parish clock when the inmates of an inn in a small town in the south of England were disturbed by a sudden clattering of hoofs on the pavement, and presently after by a loud knocking at the door.

" Who in the world can that be ? " cried the sexton, aroused from a comfortable nap, " the devil a bit would I open the door at this time of night ; for it must be the Old One himself, or Death-wing, chief of the Skeleton Crew, to weather such a storm. Why, the rain falls fast enough to drown a horse, and the wind would blow a millstone to London. I say," addressing himself to the landlord, " don't you open that door upon no account ! We might——"

Here he was interrupted by another forcible appeal to the knocker, which made the glasses and cans rattle on the table.

The sexton, rubbing his eyes, shook with fear, while the host hobbled to the door as fast as his extreme corpulency would allow him.

" Who's there ? " cried he, with a voice which would not have disgraced a sentinel giving the challenge.

" Who's there, and what's your business ? "

" A shelter for the night," was the answer from without.

" That's impossible; all my beds are taken, and my house is full."

" A corner in your hay-loft, or in the stable, will be enough. Open the door, for goodness' sake, and you shall be rewarded for your trouble."

At the word " reward " the landlord unfastened the bolts of the doors and cast a keen glance on his nightly visitor.

" A wet night, this," said he, opening the door wide.

" Ah, so it be, master," answered a third person, whom the landlord had not yet discovered.

" You are not alone, sir traveller, it seems," said the landlord.

" It is only my servant," replied the young gentleman, entering, and shaking a broad-brimmed hat, dripping with wet.

At the same time he bade his servant lead the horse to an adjoining shed, the landlord's stable being fully occupied.

It was none other than Wildfire Ned and Tim, on their way to London.

He then unclasped his cloak, which he threw upon a bench.

He was dressed in the uniform of a lieutenant in the navy.

The sexton, relaxing from his former harshness, invited the young officer to approach the fire, around which were seated five or six persons, whose uninteresting appearance requires but a few words.

The most conspicuous amongst the group was the landlady, a short, fat, buxom dame on the wrong side of forty, who might have been considered considerably handsome but for a small pair of twinkling eyes, disproportionate to the rest of her features.

At her right was seated the sexton.

A jolly, stout fellow, whose fiery face attested his devotedness to old Plymouth rum or nut-brown ale.

Next came the blacksmith of the parish, whose black leathern apron, spread over his knees, served as a screen for the landlady.

Not much could be seen of the others, who were seated in the background.

But they seemed to be pot companions of the blacksmith, with whom they were in earnest conversation.

Such was the party among whom the young officer found himself seated. To all their questions he was mute, or gave a short, evasive answer.

A few moments had elapsed when he received from the landlord a tumbler of hot rum and water, which he had ordered on entering.

To this he joined a few slices of old English beef, with a round or two of the landlady's home-made bread.

Feeling himself more comfortable, both as to his inward and outward man, he was disposed to enter into conversation, which he had hitherto avoided.

"May I ask you," said the landlady, observing him listening to the quaint jokes of the sexton, who was the oracle of the parish, "may I ask you—mean no offence, your honour—what brought you out here in this hurricane?"

"Why, my good woman," replied the young officer, "I will not be deceitful enough to say that I came out on purpose to see you. I went, you must know, to see some friends, but, returning to my uncle's home, the darkness of the night made me lose my way, and here I am, but where I know not."

"Among friends, I hope," cried the sexton, offering him at the same time a drink from the tankard.

He was in the act of putting it to his lips, when the young officer's servant entered by the back-door with his horse-cloth strapped over his head.

"Well, Tim," said his master, "I suppose you are in want of something to warm you? What will you take?"

"You are very kind, Master Ned; I'll take whisky—what you know I always takes when I be cold."

He flung the horse-cloth aside, and discovered to the inmates his grinning countenance, which he had blackened.

"Lawk-a'-mercy 'pon us!" exclaimed the landlady, "is that your servant, sir?—mean no offence, your honour, only he's rather ugly; he may be a good servant for all that, though," said she.

"Yes; and a faithful one, too," replied Ned, his master, laughing and telling a fib. "I brought him over from the West Indies with me about five years ago, and he has never left me since, not even in the midst of danger."

"I believe you," vociferated the murky blacksmith; "black persons are generally faithful."

Ned Warbeck could not repress a smile, and ordered in some refreshment for Tim, who, without any ceremony, seated himself on a three-legged stool by the side of Ned, his master, the others willingly making room for him.

His ivory grinders were soon at work, and the whisky flask in a short time was emptied of its contents.

He had scarcely ended when Ned, feeling weary, requested the landlord to show him to a place of rest for the night.

"Willingly, sir," said the landlord; "but I am hearty sorry I cannot give you a bed, for, d'ye see, we've got several farmers who've been to the fair near by, and they're rum sort of chaps, who wouldn't stir an inch for any one; free and easy, sir.

I will, as you observed, give you a place in the hay-loft, where you must put up for to-night with a truss of hay for your pillow."

"Good enough," replied the young officer; "I've often had a worse bed than that. Come along, Tim, my boy; make ready, and to the right about—march!"

"A thought strikes me," replied the landlord, "but I dare not propose it."

"What is it? Speak out," said Ned.

"Well, sir, I have at some distance from here another house, which I've had to let for these ten years, but nobody will live there, because they say as how it's 'haunted,' though I've been in it several times myself in the day, and I have never seen anything."

"But I have, though," bawled out the sexton. "'Twas but the other night, as I was coming from the veterinary surgeon, and as I passed by your house yonder, I sees a light in your top room, and a large hand stretching out o' the window, that gived the shutter such a slap. I trembles now at the bare idea of it, and if that there young gemman takes my advice he'd better sleep in the hay-loft. Nothing will disturb him there."

"I thank you," said Ned, "for warning me of the dangers I may have to encounter; but I have always been fond of singular adventures, and as this promises to be one of uncommon attraction, if the landlord will lead the way, I am ready to spend the night in the 'haunted mansion.'"

"Amen," said the sexton, "one bird in the hand is worth two in the bush. 'Drink deep, and snore deep,' that's my motto, and for my own part I would rather sleep quietly here than run the risk of being murdered, slaughtered, or Heaven knows what, by ghosts or the Skeleton Crew."

"Not so with me," said the dauntless son of Neptune, dropping at the same time a purse into the landlord's hands, "at all events, if I don't return, 'twill be but a job for you, Mr. Sexton," said he, with an arch look. "My servant Tim may stay here if he likes, and I will take him up, on my way home to-morrow morning, if hobgoblins don't eat me up before."

"I'll not stay here, Master Ned, but go with you. I never saw a ghost, and would very much like to see one," said Tim with a grin.

"Well, my boy, your wish shall be gratified; go and fetch the pistols out of the holsters, which, with another trusty friend I have here (striking at the same time on the hilt of his sword, which was lying on the bench) will give them a warm reception should they wish to annoy us."

Ned and Tim were soon ready.

In the meantime the landlord prepared a bottle of brandy, some pipes and tobacco, which he put in a large bag, and slung over his shoulder.

"We will all go and see you safely in," said the inmates, "but you must excuse us if we don't share the dangers with you. We've had enough of ghosts and skeletons in our time about here."

"Oh, certainly," was Ned's careless answer, "much obliged to you for your kind offer."

All was ready, and Tim had just returned with the pistols, upon which, the whole party having bid good-night to the landlady, sallied forth about half-past twelve.

The rain had not entirely ceased, and the night, to use the sexton's expression, was dark as the parish vaults.

The landlord walked first with a huge lantern, the reflection of which upon the wet stones formed a striking contrast with the surrounding objects.

After him came Ned Warbeck, between the sexton and the blacksmith.

Tim brought up the rear with the rest of the party.

They having arrived at the "haunted house," the landlord soon applied to the door a key of vast dimensions.

It creaked on its hinges, with a harsh noise, as if forboding some calamity.

They all went up a few steps, looking cautiously around them, and came at last to a small apartment on the first floor.

This was to be the scene of action.

The landlord in a moment raised a sparkling flame on the hearth, and placed a table near it, with the refreshments already described upon it.

After having made his guests as comfortable as the place would allow, the host departed with his companions.

The young officer let them out with strict injunctions to the landlord to take great care of his horses; then, shutting the door, he put the key in his pocket, and prepared himself to meet with courage whatever might happen.

Young midshipman (or as he now was Lieutenant) Ned's first step was to search the apartment.

But all his own and Master Tim's endeavours to find an intruder were useless.

Three cupboards were divested of their contents, and the old tapestry, which served as wainscoting, was lifted up.

But all to no purpose.

They then proceeded to the room above, which underwent the same examination.

They looked into every corner likely to conceal a man.

Finally, tired of a fruitless search, they returned to the comforts of their own fireside.

But judge of their astonishment at finding the candle removed from its place, and also extinguished!

After a short pause, however, Ned attributed it to the wind which arose from the opening or shutting of the door.

Ned Warbeck remembered the candle before he left the room again, not wishing, he said, to leave two such irreconcilable enemies near one another in their absence; meaning the brandy-bottle and candle. Satisfied that nothing could now disturb them, Ned took a seat near the fire, and desired Tim to do the same, who, nothing loth, obeyed the mandate.

He drew the cork from the bottle, and loaded his pipe.

His master, for greater safety, examined the primings of the pistols, and, giving them a fresh supply from the powder-horn, laid them on the table by the side of his naked sword.

This done, they both agreed to try and keep awake, for which purpose they each took a draught from the brandy bottle, and trimming their pipes, began smoking at a tremendous rate.

Now and then laying these aside they relapsed into a friendly, humorous chat, till, overcome by the fatigues of the day, Ned at last showed symptoms of drowsiness, which soon communicating to Tim, they eventually sunk in their chairs overpowered by sleep.

They had not been long in this position when Wildfire Ned starting from his slumber, thought he heard a distant rattling of chains!

His first impulse was to seize a pistol, and then to listen more attentively to the sound.

All was silent for a short time, and Ned was induced to think he was labouring under the effects of a dream.

He was half disposed to resume his seat, when he was again startled by the same noise, which this time seemed much nearer.

Surprised but not alarmed, he gave Tim a hearty shake to awake him, and beckoned him to take up the remaining pistol.

He himself seized the sword, which he replaced in the scabbard and girt to his side.

They now distinctly heard footsteps.

A moment after, they saw in a corner of the room the shadow of a tall man!

Tim drew near to Ned Warbeck, his master, and silently pointed to this apparition, which now seemed to have stopped!

They were not left long in this suspense.

The figure advancing, stalked into the room and stood motionless at the further end.

It seemed to be about seven feet in height and was clothed in a loose red robe, which came to its heels and concealed the feet.

The head-dress was composed of a large steel cap which covered the whole face.

A thick chain encircled the body and hung to the ground.

"Advance not an inch further," exclaimed Ned bravely, "or I will kill you dead on the spot."

"I too," said Tim, resolved not to be behind-hand, "we will drive two bullets through your gizzard if you'll not be off," said Tim, bravely.

These threats had not the desired effect.

The figure began to march towards them as if regardless of their presence.

Tim and young Warbeck fired at once.

At the report of the fire-arms, the figure stopped once more, and, by a significant nod of the head, invited Ned to come towards him.

Excited by this extraordinary circumstance, Ned drew his sword, and determined to run all hazards to see where it would end.

He gave the pistols to Tim, with orders to load them, and walked fearlessly up to the figure, which, turning on its heels, took the direction it came in by!

Tim, though fond of his young master, followed reluctantly.

"For," as he was heard to say afterwards, "he was sure it was a skeleton, and bullet proof, as he had never yet missed his aim, and that had he been the devil himself he would have brought him down."

They proceeded for a considerable time through a dark hall, which must have had a secret door that had escaped their observation, since, in their search above mentioned, they had seen nothing of the kind.

Suddenly, at the end of the hall, which gradually became lighter, the figure disappeared, and Ned Warbeck, with his servant, Tim, felt the floor give way under them, and soon perceived they were descending at a rapid rate by the means of some invisible machine!

———

## CHAPTER XXVI.

### MR. PHILLIP'S MARRIED LIFE.

ALL Mr. Redgill's calculations for worldly prosperity had hitherto proved untrue.

Disappointed in his father's affairs, he had married wholly and solely for mere consideration of money.

But the smashing of Sir Andrew's offices, and of the South Sea Bank, in the general monetary "crash" which had suddenly and unexpectedly come upon all the banks, had found him bereft of nearly every friend, with no money, little credit, and a very gaily-inclined wife to support.

Sir Andrew and lady had retired to their little country house to reside, where they expected to be somewhat relieved from the importunities of creditors.

And thus Mr. Redgill was left alone in his glory on the scene of his bygone triumphs.

He knew not in which way to move to gain an income commensurate with his habits and his wants.

An ordinary young man would have sought out and taken his spouse to modest lodgings, the rates and expenses of which he might reasonably expect to meet and readily defray.

Such economical ideas did not coincide with Phillip's practice and proverbial philosophy.

He boldly drove up to a first-class hotel, and, with the air of a millionaire, selected elegant apartments, but without the remotest idea as to when or how he should be able to pay for them.

He dined sumptuously every day, and drank expensive wines.

He smoked the very best cigars.

Found fault almost with everything, bullied and harrassed the servants beyond human endurance.

He strutted or lounged about, picking his teeth, and ogling the ladies with all the airs and manners of an unlimitedly-credited ambassador or Nabob.

By borrowing money from former associates and acquaintance, but more with the manner of one who was conferring a favour rather than begging one, he contrived to meet incidental expenses, and played cards, and attended bear baitings with his former elegant manners, but very adroitly contrived to postpone the adjustment of all bills presented to him.

After two months' residence at the hotel the polite and gentlemanly proprietor presented his bill. and hinted at the desirability of payment.

Phillip Redgill, Esq., towered into a fearful rage, strutted about, spoke of his "honour," credit and family, and left the hotel that same day, telling the proprietor in an indifferent, but tragic manner, to send in his bill to the "St. Charles Hotel," where he intended for the future to reside, intimating in a mildly ferocious style that did he consider the proprietor to be a "gentleman" he should feel no hesitation or compunction of conscience in treating him to an ordeal of fire, ball, and brimstone over in Battersea, or in the secluded Wormwood Scrubbs.

By such method of procedure Mr. Redgill and his "lady" lived for several months during Charley Warbeck's incarceration, and all he did when bills were presented was to find fault, fall into a violent passion, and go elsewhere, or anywhere where his name or appearance would admit or credit him.

Everything has an end, and so had Redgill's braggadocio and credit.

For the sake of past memories few would trouble his own personal effects for debt; but at last he had fallen so low in the social scale that he deserted the hotels, and sought accommodations for himself and wife in private lodgings.

He "hated the noise and bustle of hotels and public thoroughfares," he said.

"Retirement and quiet suited him best."

So that although he frequented card rooms and the like, little altered from his former style of dress and manner, his "whereabouts" were a mystery to all.

Nor could the most urgent importunities make him disclose his lodgings.

How he maintined himself no one was bold enough to inquire.

He was frequently seen in the company of rich young men desirous of seeing and being initiated into the mysteries of the town.

Many said, or rather whispered, that Phillip was nothing better than a card "sharper" and general blackleg.

These, of course, were only very distant rumours.

None were bold enough to publicly retail such reports for fear of Phillip's ungovernable anger, and his frequent allusions to the number of men he had "stabbed" or shot in his brief career upon the town.

Certain it is, Mr. Redgill was more frequently seen handling cards than his prayer book, and a thousand times to one oftener seen in the bear gardens than in church, and, as officers will occasionally talk, Redgill was styled in general terms as "a man about town" "who knew a thing or two," and "could generally in the season average £20 per night" at cards.

Whatever his "averages" might be, it is in point blank evidence that he gave his wife but little— nay, very little.

What with general neglect, harsh words, frequent blows, and general ruffianism, poor Fanny led but an unamiable life, and frequently begged for death as a release from her sufferings

Sir Andrew's visits to the City were few and far between.

Whenever he "ran up" by coach, he passed through the streets in a shadowy manner, without the slightest ambition, apparently, to be recognized by any of his former friends.

He was an "unsuccessful man," and had involved many in losses with that of his own.

Hence, for the sake of peace and quiet, he adopted every little expedient of which he was master to shun his many creditors and acquaintance.

"I have secured my little country-house from the wreck of all my bygone wealth," he sometimes would say; "let me live in peace."

The "retired" gentleman need not have had recourse to any stratagem to avoid those who once had known him.

His present appearance was so altered, he had become so thin and cadaverous, and his attire withal was so "seedy" and out of fashion, that few would ever have recognized in him the spruce and scrupulously-attired Sir Andrew McTurk of former days, who could boast of having taken "risks" for almost fabulous sums.

It was not the welfare of his only daughter Fanny, or of Phillip Redgill, his promising son in-law, which occasioned his visits to town.

He hated both of them so intensely that he could not mention them without plunging himself into a fearful rage and stammering out a volley of oaths.

His real motive was pure infatuation—to see if there was any earthly prospect of beginning business again, in some shape or form.

City life had become so necessary to his existence that he seemed to loath the green fields and meadows, and sighed to be once more in the dusty streets round about the Exchange, or up in offices again, handling paper or counting gold.

Old as he was, and far past the meridian of life, the ruling passion for money was still strong in him.

Little temptation, perhaps, would have been requisite to prompt him again to nefarious deeds should the "chance" present itself.

Phillip's wife had casually heard of these visits of

her father to the City, and sought every opportunity to see him.

She did not desire assistance, but wished to beg his forgiveness for what she had done, and resolved that if he still betrayed any affection for her, she would beg of him to take her to his home, far from the City, and far from the ill-treatment and brutality of Philip her husband, whose daily and increasing unkindness and neglect were killing her.

While in waiting for her father, at the corner of St. Paul's churchyard, Phillip met her.

Being partly intoxicated, he abused her in unmeasured terms, and bade her go home instantly, at the same time irreparably wounding her womanly pride by inhuman epithets and accusations.

In tears she stood in the public street, leaning against a lamp-post for support, when who should pass at the moment but Augustus Fumbleton, Esq., who, in despair at his loss of the captivating Miss Clara, had been consoling himself with a serene contemplation of the numerous tombstones in the churchyard, near the railings of which Mrs. Phillip Redgill stood sobbing.

Fumbleton addressed the afflicted lady in a very respectful manner, and proffered to assist her home.

His gallantry and amiability so won upon Fanny, that she sobbingly consented, and he was generous enough to call a conveyance, and saw her safely to her own door.

A few days subsequent to this incident, Redgill and Charley Warbeck met near the Exchange.

The former waited until the latter had passed into a bye street, when he accosted him.

Phillip's manner was so cordial and hearty, as fully to disarm all suspicions which Charley might have formed of him.

Phillip "was intensely sorry" to hear of his misfortune, and swore roundly that he had been the first to petition the king for his pardon and release, and that "the chief judge had said to him" and "he had said to the chief judge" &c., so that Charles began to imagine Phillip was a very "good fellow" and not so bad as he had imagined.

Phillip knew perfectly well where Charles lived and promised to call, particularly when young Warbeck casually remarked that there were apartments vacant which Dame Worthington desired to let to a man and wife without family.

The interview concluded by Redgill asking Charley to take some brandy, and begging the loan of "five pounds for a day or two," a request which Charley was not foolish enough to grant him.

---

## CHAPTER XXVII.

### THE MATRIMONIAL PROSPECTS OF MISS CLARA.

THE sudden and unexpected return of Charles from prison, and the unmistakable tokens of affection he had shown to Miss Clara since his abrupt appearance in the parlour, and the unceremonious departure of Augustus Fumbleton, Esq., had so weighed upon the tender and susceptible feelings of that young lady, that she was somewhat bewildered and in a maze of delightful torment.

She could scarcely be said to be of sound mind, for her imagination was uncontrolable, and she gave herself away wildly to day dreams.

She was deeply in love but would not confess it, yet, as Charles had never declared his passion, she began to doubt if his apparent fondness was genuine, and whether it might not dwindle away into mere flirtation.

She paid particular attention to her toilet, and

resorted to every means in her power to dispel the sorrow, care, and anxiety which of late had possessed him, and made his face so pale, careworn, and sad.

She played and sang more charmingly than ever, and always selected the most lively airs.

Yet all her gaiety seemed to have no power over him.

She began to imagine that Miss Josephine Smith next door, or some unknown lady, had snatched him from her, and that both Dame Worthington and Sir Richard Warbeck were fully cognizant of the fact.

The result of all her imaginings tended to make Clara languid in manner and much depressed in spirit.

She began to look upon the good old dame with distrust, and seldom spoke to any one.

Her appearance in the parlour was seldom.

She had no taste or inclination for gay society, and sought retirement.

Mistress Haylark had watched every movement of her daughter, and began to imagine that her many lectures regarding discountenancing Charley Warbeck's addresses were beginning to have their anticipated effect.

She congratulated herself that no child of hers would be foolish enough to look so lowly as to encourage a person of suspected character.

She often said she would not have stayed a day in Dame Worthington's house, if public opinion had not considered there were many extenuating circumstances in Charley's guilt.

The true cause of Charley's altered manner could easily be explained.

He was looked upon as a dangerous person, and one that should not be trusted.

Former friends and acquaintances passed him in the streets without the slightest indication of recognition.

He had applied for business engagements in various places.

But his name was more than enough to thwart his prospects.

When he informed gentlemen that his last occupation had been as clerk in the India House they put him off with specious promises, but never employed him.

He sometimes felt upon the verge of distraction, and more than once meditated self-destruction.

But some good angel stood by his side in the moment of temptation and bade him hope.

As often as he saw "little curly-head," as he called Clara, flitting through the house, his heart smote him, and he gazed upon her averted face with fondness and sadness.

And then the angel by his side whispered hope more loudly than ever.

"I could not think of dragging her into my disgrace," thought Charley, sentimentally ; "it is enough that my name is stained without causing her a life of live-long distrust, poverty and reproach.

"No, I will not address her. I love her, but she can never be my wife."

Mr. Charley Warbeck's high-toned ideas of life-long self-sacrifice were very commendable and heroic.

But changes came o'er the spirit of his dream.

"What makes her maintain such provoking privacy, I wonder?" thought he.

"How altered she is of late ; how sad-looking and pale ! I wonder if Fumbleton has anything to do with it ?

"He's a nice-looking fellow enough, well-to-do,

and all that; but I wish he was at the bottom of the sea, and out of the way.

"I hate that fellow.

"I saw him a few evenings since; if I meet him again I'll have a little private chat with him, and *sound* him!

"I shouldn't wonder, though, if he *is* after her.

"I see her go out frequently in the afternoon for a walk; I would lay a wager that she meets him!"

This latter thought stung Charley to the quick, and he sighed very deeply.

As he entered the parlour one bright afternoon, he discovered Clara sitting in the shadows of the window-curtains.

She held something in her hand, and kissed it!

The heart of Charley Warbeck beat very quickly.

She was apparently absorbed in thought, and knew nothing of his presence in the apartment.

He noiselessly approached nearer to her, and observed that she had a note in her lap, and frequently glanced at it.

There was no longer room for doubt, he imagined.

His worst suspicions were realized.

"She loves another," was his conclusion; and he involuntarily sighed aloud.

This awoke Miss Clara from her reverie.

She placed the note and likeness in her bosom, and rose to depart.

Her manner was cold, and tinged with sadness.

As she passed him, she slightly bowed, never raised her eyes, and moved towards the door with a dignified and graceful step.

Charley never felt so sick at heart in his life before, and thought that Clara looked more blooming than ever.

In truth Miss Clara certainly *did* look captivating on this particular afternoon.

She was a brunette, of medium height, and symmetrically developed; her curls waved about her shoulders with every gust of air.

Her dress was of light blue, somewhat low-necked, and over her bust she wore beautiful lace, with sleeves of the same material.

Charley had not intended to speak to her.

But, as she was about to leave the room, he mustered all his firmness, and calmly said—

"Miss Clara, I——"

She turned her face, now slightly flushed, and said—

"Sir?" very coldly.

He placed a chair for her in the deepest shadows of the room, and said—

"Miss Haylark, you will really excuse me being so rude, but your looks are so sad of late, and your manners so altered towards me, that I am perplexed and concerned to know the cause.

"You, Clara, who were my only friend in hours of adversity, surely you will not follow the example of the world, and look upon me with contempt or disdain?

"I am unworthy to address you, it is true, but do—I beg of you to explain what I have done to destroy that friendship which has so long existed between us?

"Tell me why you avert your face, and why your eyes are filled with tears?"

Charley could say no more,

His heart was full.

"Forgive me, Clara, if I have offended you," were the only words he uttered.

And as he stood beside her chair, and saw her weeping, without making any reply, he felt like a child, and could have almost wept himself.

For some time the lovers maintained silence, broken only by a suppressed sob from Clara.

At last Charley took her hand, and with much gallantry, kissing it, said,

"Were I a prince I could not rejoice in anything more precious than your friendship, Clara.

"If I had a throne I would ask you to share it.

"I would ask you to smile upon me, and bestow your hand upon me, for Heaven only knows how much I love you, Clara, and Heaven only is the witness of its sincerity.

"I cannot look up to you with confidence, although I love you heart and soul.

"You are too good, too holy, for one like me to aspire to.

"Yet believe me when I utter these true and honest words, that, disowned as I am by a cold, cold world, and looked upon with suspicion, my soul is as free from guilt as it ever was in the sight of God, and the only tie that keeps me in the world, the only regret I should have in quitting it, is the contemplation of one I adore with all the power of my mind and soul."

Charles kissed her hand again and rose to depart.

"Stay," said Clara, speaking for the first time, slowly, and almost in a whisper; "However unintelligible your character is, or may have been, to others, Mr. Warbeck, I have always looked upon you as a friend, and confess it openly everywhere, Charles.

"Were the world to be ten times as cold as it is towards you, I should never, never change, believe me."

This little outburst of honest feeling was too much for Clara's feelings.

She endeavoured to conceal her tears, but they coursed down her cheeks thick and fast until her breast heaved with emotion, and she audibly sobbed.

She rose in a hasty manner to leave the room.

Charley was fired with love, and caught her to his heart.

And she leaned her little head upon his shoulder confidingly, nor did she struggle or resist the many kisses he rapturously bestowed upon her, but sat on the sofa by his side.

And in a long conversation, carried on in whispers, the only two words which Dame Worthington slyly overheard were,

"*Will* you, Clara?"

"Yes, Charles."

THE REPRIEVE..

## CHAPTER XXVIII.

### MATRIMONY AND HAPPINESS.

DAME WORTHINGTON was delighted—Sir Richard Warbeck was delighted—every one in fact was delighted to hear it whispered that Charley and Clara Haylark were engaged.

Mistress Haylark was indignant!

She would not listen to any such proposition, and moved to and fro with an air of offended majesty!

Dame Worthington tried to console the proud woman, but she would listen to no words of solace.

She had "made up her mind against the match," and the only one living fit to be Clara's husband,

No. 12.

she said, was that nice young man Mr. Augustus Fumbleton.

Since her mother was extremely angry, Clara's life was anything but agreeable to her.

For morning, noon, and night, Madame was harping upon the rumoured match, and spoke against it with inexhaustible eloquence.

Miss Clara, however, took but little notice of her mother's ceaseless prattle about the dignity, grandeur, and importance of "the Haylark's," but quietly bore all with meekness and resignation, and loved Charley more and more for all the railings hourly thrown out against him.

As Sir Richard had been fully informed of the

tr state of things by Dame Worthington, he sought an opportunity of speaking to Clara alone.

The girl's manner was so modest and genuine, and she confessed her attachment for the young man with so much artlessness that old Sir Richard Warlock was strongly prepossessed in her favour, and determined to do all in his power to reconcile Mistress Haylark to the match.

What with presents, great gallantry of manner, and marked deference to all her opinions on ordinary topics, he so far won upon the proud lady that her resolution to maintain the honour of "the Haylarks" melted away like ice before his eloquence and earnestness.

And after holding out for some time, "for the sake of form," and in maintenance of her much self-styled "firmness," she consented to the match, and began to bustle about in making suitable preparations for it.

The intended marriage was kept as secret as possible, yet many female acquaintances soon became aware of the fact by some unknown means.

And rumour had it that when Miss Josephine Smith, next door, heard of the approaching event, through the tattling of servants over the backyard wall, she was seized with a sudden fit of hysterics, and gave vent to her disappointment and chagrin, in all manner of double-meaning phrases, and called Miss Clara everything that was unkind.

Dame Worthington was literally beside herself.

She knew not what to do from day to day.

The nearer the important event approached, the more affectionately she behaved both to Clara and Charley.

She laughed and cried by turns, and said, "She always knew it."

Clara would kiss her, and Charley would joke her.

But, despite all her apparent perturbation and anxiety, she found time to have frequent and long interviews with old Sir Richard, until the young couple, seated lovingly side by side on the parlour sofa, could not understand the nature of them.

Dame Worthington deeply regretted that she could not possibly find accommodation for them in her house, but Sir Richard only smiled benignly and said,

"Leave that matter to me, Harriet, my dear."

The old dame, full of confidence in his wisdom, did leave that matter in his hands, fully assured that he would manage it far better than any one else.

When the day approached, the hurry and bustle in the house increased tenfold, and to such a degree, that the servant confessed to Smith's girl, across the back-yard wall, that "she was almost worried to death," and wished the marriage was over.

On the eve of the wedding, when everything had been prepared, two legal gentlemen unexpectedly arrived and after candles were lit in Dame Worthington's back parlour, they arranged their papers with much apparent satisfaction.

Dame Worthington, the august Mistress Haylark, and the modest old Sir Richard, took their seats.

Charley was summoned into their awful presence, Miss Clara following, feeling as she afterwards confessed it, "all of a tremble."

Old Sir Richard acted as chairman of the imposing committee, and informed the young people that, as they were about to be united in the holy bands of wedlock on the morrow, he wished to say a few words to both.

Mistress Haylark had informed him that Clara was entitled to the sum of five thousand pounds as her marriage portion, and, although this was unknown to Charley, he begged to inform him that twenty thousand pounds had been assigned to him

as his portion, left by some person whom he should know at some future time.

In addition to this, kind Dame Worthington, in good-will and love to both, and in consideration of her lasting admiration of their mutual and disinterested attachment, presented them jointly with two thousand pounds—which she had been hoarding up for many years with this express intention—making a very handsome total, with which modest sum they might commence life very comfortably.

In conclusion, old Sir Richard said,

"As he himself had not contributed anything as yet to them, he would give them one of his houses in town, which was already furnished, and awaiting their marriage."

The lawyers were there, he said, to legally ratify all these things, and, as general speaker for those then present, he wished them joy through many, many happy years.

At the conclusion of his remarks, which, it must be confessed, greatly surprised and pleased the young people, Dame Worthington, Mistress Haylark, and Clara were in tears, and seemed deeply affected.

Wine was produced, which tended to revive the two former ladies considerably.

Mistress Haylark recommended Charley to use smelling salts to her daughter.

But that young gentleman had his own specific for reviving her.

He conducted Clara from the back to the front parlour, where soon the sounds of merry laughter and lively music told plainly that she was fully recovered, and in the best of spirits.

## CHAPTER XXIX.

### SIR ANDREW AND PHILLIP HIS SON-IN-LAW MAKE FRIENDS AND ENEMIES.

THE marriage of Charley and Miss Clara was duly announced in the newspapers, and the style in which it was said to have been conducted so astonished the clerks and employés of the India House and other circles in which he was formerly known, that every one unanimously considered that Charles must have had "a windfall," or "a very sudden rise" in the world.

Sir Andrew, in the retirement of his little country house heard of it.

Mr. Phillip Redgill in the smoky, dingy, card and gambling rooms, also heard of it, and both were very much surprised.

The latter thought he would lose no time in congratulating young Warlock.

"For he's well up now," said Phillip, "and will be a sure card for a hundred or two, if I ask him."

Other persons besides these two notable individuals had heard of the marriage.

Miss Josephine Smith was present during the ceremony, and, in giving an account of the affair, said that the bridegroom looked happy and handsome.

But "as to the bride—ugh! good gracious! she was a perfect fright! All curls, as usual, my dear, and looking like a frost-bitten turnip!"

Augustus Fumbleton, Esq., was also aware of the awful event, and confessed that he had now lost every earthly hope, and was fast falling away in flesh and figure.

But as he seemed to be enjoying himself as usual with an evening drive in the occasional company of a fast-dressing woman, who was said to be already married, his most intimate friends could see but little diminution in the rotundity of his form or the proverbial magnitude of his general appetite.

The "lady," with whom Augustus Fumbleton, Esq., occasionally drove out, was said to bear the name of *Redgill!*

Phillip had gradually fallen in the social scale.

He was not attired so sumptuously or neatly as of yore.

He was said to be extremely "seedy" in habits and appearance, and frequently very short of cash.

He seldom visited his wife, and seemed to care little what she did or with whom she might choose to associate.

He had introduced her to all kinds of persons, and she had formed, perhaps, exceptionable acquaintance.

But of this he cared nothing, so that she troubled him little for money, he was indifferent as to her associates and hours of leaving or returning home.

His wife, it must be confessed, was equally indifferent in her feelings towards her liege lord.

He had inaugurated habits of card and wine parties and very late hours and scenes of debauchery at her house, and as she was thrown into indifferent company—as she was expected and almost compelled to do the honours of the house and table to whomsoever visited her husband—it cannot be expected that the gaily-inclined Fanny was proof against the many temptations to which she was almost continually exposed.

She was, in truth, the gay, gambling wife of a gay, gambling, debauched and conscienceless husband.

\* \* \* \* \*

No matter what others might think, it is recorded in the interesting "Chronicle," that Charley and his young wife were extremely happy, nay, supremely so, and often confessed to each other, when sitting in the portico of their new and elegant house, that Providence had been very good and kind to them, and that their cup of happiness was full to the brim.

With a chip sun-bonnet in her head, and leaning on Charles's arm, Clara would go forth, all happiness, for an evening walk, and as they strolled in the green fields, or gazed upon the numerous snow-white sails moving to and fro on the bright splashing waters of the Thames, Clara would often laughingly recount how she first felt a partiality for the husband she then so highly prized and almost adored.

While Charley, full of humour and nonsense, would joke so wittingly and merrily until Clara become crimson in face, and shook her mass of raven curls with bewitching innocence and coquetry.

When it began to be noised abroad that the newly-married couple were well circumstanced in life, and backed by influential moneyed interests, public opinion began to grow very rapidly favourable in regard to Mr. Charley Warbeck.

So that, when he occasionally promenaded with his pretty, curly-headed bride, there were not a few of his former acquaintance who very suddenly recollected his existence and former footing, and did not fail, indeed, to recognise him in fashionable thoroughfares and places of public business.

Many, both young and old, who but a few months before had passed him in the streets, without a word or look of recognition, now bravely advanced to meet him with—

"Ah, Charley, my boy, how do you do? Allow me to congratulate you." Or,

"Hullo, Charley! how are you?"

Many merchants and very respectable men of trade were not backward in offering him shares in their business.

Tradesmen's cards poured in upon him by the hundred.

And he suddenly found himself surrounded by many who literally bored him with their civilities, and proffered to grant him any favour he desired, even to credit, as they said, "for any amount."

The lesson he had received was not lost upon him.

It had given him a greater insight into human nature than he had ever before possessed.

So that he smiled at this sudden "change in the wind," as he called it, and despised these sycophantic leeches with an honest indignation well-nigh amounting to loathing.

He seemed in no hurry to enter into business.

As the times were even yet unsettled from the recent financial panic, he contented himself, therefore, with looking out for some favorable opening for investing his capital to the best advantage.

And, instead of accepting any of the numberless invitations to balls and parties of which his wife was in constant receipt, the fond young couple contented themselves with boat excursions on the river, or frequent evening visits to good old Dame Worthington, with whom, and the stately Mistress Haylark, they passed many happy hours, and never seemed weary of their company.

Dame Worthington, in truth, was fast failing in health.

Yet, despite all her infirmities, she bustled about as busily and loquacious as of yore.

Nor did the mother-in-law lose an iota of that stateliness and solemnity of behaviour which was supposed to be hereditary with "the Haylarks," and upon which, next to her reputation for "firmness," she greatly prided herself.

In truth, Clara's marriage only seemed to expand the mother's importance.

She patronised flaming colours and the "latest styles" more recklessly than ever.

And in her frequent visits to Clara's house, she was the terror of the servants, from the amount of fuss and bother of which she was always the occasion.

Her lectures on housekeeping were long and frequent, during the delivery of which Charley always wisely lit a cigar, and took a stroll in the garden.

The "best bed" and "the best room" were always reserved for "dear mama," and from her increasing volubility on all topics connected with married life, and from the number of times she left her daughter in tears from scoldings regarding household affairs, Mr. Charley Warbeck thanked his lucky stars that she had not proposed to live with them altogether.

For "if such braggadocio and endless lectures are characteristic of 'the Haylarks'" he thought, "I am very glad little Clara has not inherited any of the hereditary virtues of that illustrious family."

If "mama's" semi-weekly visits always ended in Clara crying, Dame Worthington's had the contrary effect.

For the little wife was supremely happy, and always laughing at the old lady's stories about "dear Charley."

In truth, Dame Worthington seemed to know so much about him, and her memory reached so far back, that Clara thought her husband must have been a very young, and a very small child indeed, when the old lady had first made his acquaintance.

At all events, Clara thought,

"She is very loving, and thoughtful, and kind. She loves *me* very much, and, as for 'dear Charles,' she idolizes *him*, and a mother could not manifest more care and anxiety for his welfare and happiness than *she* does."

Sir Richard frequently visited Dame Worthington as usual, and had a long chat with her in her snug back parlour.

And, upon some occasions, the robust, short-breathing, imposing Mistress Haylark would join the party, and monopolize all the conversation.

And it mattered little what topic was broached, Mistress H. always had a very long oration ready at her finger-tips for the occasion, and backed up all arguments or assertions with an everlasting appeal to "the Haylarks," whether living or defunct.

Sir Richard became used to her loquacity, but frequently dozed in his arm-chair, and, falling fast asleep, ignominiously left the field of debate to herself, or to any one couragous enough to take up the cudgel and defy "the Haylarks," constant and only authority on all subjects.

Dame Worthington's house never flourished so much as it had since the wedding; and the old lady, it must be confessed, was "saving money."

She had always contrived to do *that*, however.

So that now, although "times were hard," and "money very tight," as it always *is*, the old gentlewoman was laying by a considerable sum, and seemed to take much delight in saving or accumulating every spare penny.

\*          \*          \*

But if prosperity had attended all the industrious efforts of the good old lady, and her newly-married "children," as she affectionately termed them, there were other persons who figure in our story who had little of which to boast of in that particular.

Sir Andrew's farming operations in the country were productive of little profit.

And he foresaw that ere long he must seek some other sphere than that of agriculture in which to make sufficient to satisfy his wants and daily growing greed.

One would have imagined that such misfortunes as he had experienced might have allayed his ruling passion for money; yet it did not.

The older he grew the more avaricious he became.

And to such an extent that he stinted his farm-servants so much that every one left him, and his immediate household affairs were conducted on such miserly principles that he even begrudged his wife the common necessaries of life!

His sole and absorbing ambition seemed to be mere "accumulation."

"I am not more dishonest than the rest of people," he would mutter, as he walked along the country roads and lanes. "There are hundreds who have failed beside myself, and are now in a flourishing business. Why cannot *I* be the same?"

Christianity, its virtues, and its responsibilities, hung very lightly on the shoulders of this old man.

He went to church, it is true, and sang and prayed as loudly and lustily as any member of it.

It was a "respectable thing" to belong to the church.

But it must be confessed that his most fervent prayer was in supplication for the framing of some law which prohibited all imprisonment for debt!

Sir Andrew, in his arm-chair, comfortably seated before the fire of his little farm-house, spent hours every evening in devising plans for recommencing business.

He was not particular as to *what* it might be, so that money should result from it.

He thought of the banks, and sighed devoutly at the fearful amounts which some were said to possess.

He ran through his personal reminiscences, and past life, and could point to persons in high stations, and of "unimpeachable respectability" whom he had known in years past, and often thought,

"If so-and-so had his due, he would be half-starving, or in prison, instead of rolling about so grandly with his carriage and greys."

Such thoughts arose, not from honest indignation but from envy and gall.

Old Sir Andrew was thoroughly disgusted with himself and the world.

He was determined, however, to make another attempt at success.

But his son-in-law was like a heavy chain bound to his legs, and he could not move in any direction but he encountered either Fanny or Phillip.

And what a change had come over Fanny, his daughter!

She had separated from her husband.

But why?

The cause was this.

One night Phillip Redgill had a card party at his house.

Among those present, and who lost heavily at play, was Augustus Fumbleton, Esq.

Phillip was maddened with wine.

The memory of his wickedness and crime came over him.

Which ever way he looked he seemed to behold the apparition of his murdered father.

The terrible legs seemed to haunt him wherever he went.

While cards and dice were at their height, and all were merry, some one loudly knocked at the door.

The servant went and opened it.

Again the knocks were repeated.

And again did the servants go to the door.

They opened it, and looked out into the street.

But no one was there.

"This seems strange," said one to another, in a whisper.

"I have seen and heard stranger things than that in this house," was the answer. "I believe the place is haunted."

While thus they conversed together with open door,

The heavy sounds of footsteps were heard entering the hall.

The two servants turned their heads.

It was the gory legs of Farmer Bertrand they saw.

With a loud shout, and looks of horror on their faces, the terrified domestics rushed upstairs in dread alarm.

"What means this?" growled Phillip, as he seized one of them by the throat, and drew his sword. "What means this, knave, eh? Go forth into the passage again, and return with better news, or take the consequences."

The servant did as he was bidden, but had scarcely got into the passage when he rushed back again in increased terror, and upset a card table, money, and all upon the floor.

Every one present were now alarmed.

They heard the distant solemn tramp of heavy footsteps.

When, lo! there entered the room, with horrible stride, the gory limbs.

Phillip Redgill turned deadly pale.

His eyes darted almost from their sockets.

He gasped with terror, and his drawn sword trembled in his nerveless hand.

"Phillip Redgill——" the spectre voice began.

"No, no, no; mercy! 'twas not I!" gasped Phillip. "No, no! I see also the ghost of my father; but I did not do it! Away! away! Avaunt! gory, ghostly, damnable spectacle, avaunt!"

"Phillip Redgill, my footsteps will follow you for ever!" said the voice, which died away in the distance.

"Never! never!" said Phillip, staggering from horror.

"Ever! ever!" repeated the spectre voice.

With his heart bursting in fury Phillip tore his neck-cloth into ribbons.

His breast heaved with remorse and passion.

"Wine, wine," he said, with a fiendish laugh; "wine, wine, I say!"

His wife handed him a goblet brim full.

He gulped it down.

He threw the goblet into a corner of the room, and in fury struck Fanny to the ground.

The gallants present immediately stepped forward to protect the fallen woman.

With bitter curses on their lips for his brutality they drew their swords.

"Ha! ha! my braves!" said Phillip, pale as a ghost, and looking half idiotic and wild; "ha! ha! my braves! I see, my wife hath many ready to defend her. Come on, then, one and all."

"So be it," said Augustus Fumbleton, drawing his "toasting fork," and assailing Phillip.

"The man who lays his hand upon a woman except in kindness, is a scoundrel," he added.

Phillip was more like a maniac than a man.

But just as the husband and the lover were about to engage, Fanny threw herself in between the combatants.

"Hold!" she cried, in a voice of pain, and with blood streaming down her features.

"Hold!" she cried, "Phillip Redgill! husband! murderer! if you *will* spill blood, shed mine!"

"Murderer!" muttered Phillip, with chattering teeth! "murderer?"

"Yes, *murderer!*" gasped Fanny, with a firm, defiant tone; "spirits of the dead haunt you both night and day."

"Liar! witch! sorceress!" exclaimed Phillip; "die with that lie in your throat."

He made a desperate pass at his injured wife.

His sword was knocked up.

Next moment he was the centre of a fierce and deadly conflict.

The clash of swords, the sound of smashed mirrors, vases, windows, and the like, was heard on every hand.

\*　　　\*　　　\*　　　\*　　　\*

When Phillip woke next morning he found his house deserted.

No one was nigh.

He lay upon the floor, with a sword cut across his brow, amid the ruins of chairs, tables, glasses, and a thousand fragments of ornaments and furniture.

"Where am I?" he said.

And he looked round with amazement on the wreck.

All things were in a wild state of confusion.

His brain was all on fire with drink, excitement, and pain.

"Oh, now I remember all," he gasped.

The memory of all which had happened that night flashed before his mind.

While he lay in a state of stupor his eye caught sight of a small dagger sticking in the card table.

It pinned down a note.

It was in Fanny's handwriting.

He tore it open and read—

"Farewell and for ever for the rest of her days.
　　　　　　　"Your worst enemy,
　　　　　　　　　"FANNY."

"My wife absconded! the house ransacked! the servants gone! How is this? What can it mean? Am I dreaming?"

"Dreaming? No, man; you were never more wide awake in all your life," said a distant voice, with a coarse laugh.

Phillip Redgill recognized the voice.

It was that of Captain Jack.

"You here," said Phillip, astonished.

"Yes; and why not? Where would *you* have been if I hadn't?"

"I don't understand."

"I don't suppose you do. A man that was dead drunk and half crazy last night, mixed up with tilt and point among a dozen or more desperate gallants is not supposed to have very clear brains the morning after. 'Twas lucky we came to your assistance or you wouldn't be sprawling on the floor as you now are."

"I don't understand."

"Well, the thing is soon explained. I heard that a party of gambling youngsters were gathered at your house last night, and, knowing them to have more money than brains, I, Faulkner, and several others made up our minds to give you a call, so as to relieve them of a little of their spare cash. As we approached the house we heard you all high in oath.

"I rushed in at the doorway, but was fiercely beaten back by several gallants.

"I gave the word to my men to fall on the enemy without mercy.

"Just at that moment I perceived your wife hurrying downstairs, the way being led by one of her many lovers."

"Many lovers?" said Redgill; "surely you do not mean to insinuate that my wife is a strumpet and——"

"Never mind about wasting more breath about her, Redgill," said Captain Jack; "because if you don't know her character, I do, and have done so long ago."

"What!"

"Nay, nay; get not so hot, but let me continue with my story. Directly I gave the word to my men they each singled out a customer, and we fought desperately with our knives in the entrance-hall; the place was too small for the proper use of our swords, so I am sorry to say," said Captain Jack, with a laugh, "that we had to cut the throats of one or two in the entrance hall (see Cut in No. 10), but it was all fair play. They didn't know us, you see, so it don't much matter. We quickly threw their bodies into the river, and they are food for the fish."

"But my wife?" said Phillip surprised.

"Your wife, eh? she seems to give you much trouble all at once."

"Well, what of her?"

"Why, she has run off with the man who gave you that nasty cut across the forehead."

"And who was he?"

"Why, that elegant young man Fumbleton."

A terrible oath escaped from Phillip, and he rose to his feet, looking like a blood-stained demon.

"I will be revenged," said he, "if it costs me my life!"

"And so you shall," said Captain Jack, "if you only let the matter remain quietly for a short time. Fumbleton is rich, and can bear plucking."

"He has been plucked many times, I hear," said Phillip, "and on one occasion to the tune of £2,000."

"I know he has.  I was the one to do it," said Captain Jack.

"You ?"

"Yes, me."

"How ?"

"Well, that I will tell you as we go along.  You must leave this house at once."

"But the furniture—I am not going to leave that behind ?"

"You might as well, it ain't worth anything."

"Worth nothing—what do you mean ?"

"Mean this, my boy ; I have sold the house, furniture and all."

"You ? why it all belongs to me."

"Perhaps so," said Captain Jack, "but then you see why Fanny ran away with Fumbleton.  I knew you would not remain here long, so while you were snoring I bundled off the servants, and sold everything."

"Very polite of you, certainly."

"Oh, don't mention it—a friend of mine gave me a tempting price for the whole lot, so I took it, of course, being short of money, and as you deserve a trifle on our old account, why of course it's all right."

"But it's all wrong.  Where's the money ?"

"In my pocket," said Captain Jack, very coolly, "where it is likely to remain until I want it."

"And what do you want with me so early in the morning ?" asked Phillip.

"Wash yourself, and get out of the house as soon as possible, and then I'll tell you.  There, that will do ; don't take overmuch pains with yourself—you ain't going far," said Captain Jack, with a sinister smile.

"But where to ?"

"You'll soon see; but as I was about to say, regarding Fumbleton ; he's been after your wife a long time, and you are the one to blame, for if you *would* introduce her to all the worst sparks in town, why of course you can't expect her to respect you much."

"You are very kind with your advice this morning," said Phillip ; "one would almost imagine you had turned parson."

"So I have, when there's been a hanging going on, and no one near to read the service.  But as I was saying about Fumbleton ; he fancies he can play billiards, and so unknown to him I disguised my friend Alick Faulkner, some months ago, and they agreed to make a match for £500 a side.  Now, Faulkner and I played a good deal together, but I always beat him, and as Fumbleton always beat me, because I let him, Alick was thought to be a good "mark" for the elegant young swell.  The number of points in the game was to be 1,000.

Gentlemen amateurs who were supposed to have had 'the straight tip' were freely staking any odds on Fumbleton, which the "knowing ones," with Alick as their champion, were eagerly accepting.

"When play commenced in the evening, there was much interest displayed by professionals to watch the game, and from the superior manner in which the young swell was playing, it was evident he would beat Faulkner his antagonist, with the greatest imaginable ease.

In truth it must be confessed that he threw away many chances where he could have easily "counted."

But Fumbleton had so much of a lead, that he frequently amused himself with making "fancy shots" for his own, and the amusement of professional adepts, who loudly applauded him.

Towards ten o'clock the game was half over, and the miserable style in which Alick played, brought down very stinging remarks from by-standers, so that leaving him more than one hundred points in in the rear, out of seven hundred then played, it was agreed to adjourn for the sake of supper and to finish the game afterwards.

Fumbleton partook freely of wine, and was all impatience to recommence the game.

Alick did not seem at all inclined for more humiliation at the swell's hands, and to all appearance returned to the table very reluctantly.

The state of the game was apparent to all.

Fumbleton was considered to be much too far ahead to be overtaken by Alick, and any odds were freely offered on him and taken.

But the game suddenly changed in its character.

Instead of playing in his former slow and undecided style, Mr. Alick hit rapidly, scientifically, and so often, that he materially altered his score, and and was soon close at the heels of Fumbleton, who opened his eyes widely at this sudden exhibition of his opponent's skill!

"Never mind," said he to his friends, "he can't do it *again*, you know ; it was all luck that time, I shall now go in and win with a rush."

Alick had similar ideas also, and gained on Fumbleton so far, that when but fifty points remained to be played Alick was but five behind.

The chances now began to fluctuate, and Fumbleton's friends, being still confident, freely laid odds, which were now eagerly taken.

In truth the silly swell had made such fine play that but five remained to complete his score, and make him the winner.

The other had twenty-five to get ; but these were gotten with so much rapidity that Alick, in enthusiasm, overran that number, amid the applause of those in the "secret," but apparently to his own dissatisfaction, for he seemed surprised and annoyed, whispering confidentially, as he pitched his cue and the bridge into the corner,

"I've won, but, upon my soul, Mr. Fumbleton, I wasn't aware of it ; I had need to lose !"

This was exceedingly poor consolation to the swell, who sat vacantly looking at the billiard board as one in a trance or dream.

It seemed that he considered it *impossible* to be beaten by such an opponent as Alick !

He was mistaken, however, and the best proof of it was that the money was handed over to Alick that same night, and the swell discovered himself to be minus of not less than five hundred pounds out of the six hundred pounds which he had brought to the billiard room with him.

"Who'd a thought," mused Fumbleton, "that I should have lost in so unaccountable a manner ; I am out of luck to-night, *that's* it ! I can beat *two* such players as he is at *any* time ; but you *can't* play against *luck !*"

To console the young swell, the winning parties declared that he was the paragon of players, and hoped he would soon have *another* game, and for a *larger* stake.

This latter remark seemed to contain a little more irony than Mr. Fumbleton could bear, so that he flamed into a passion on the instant, and high words arose.

Excited with wine, and infuriated to find he had been so egregiously duped, the swell gave vent to his feelings in unmeasured terms, calling Alick and his friends a parcel of scheming "black-legs," until finding words would avail but little, they handled him roughly.

A general fight ensued among the partizans, and the last thing Augustus remembered in his cups was a general row, in which certain persons' boot-toes came in sudden and violent concussion with certain parts of his person, and ejected him into the street, where he found himself on the following morning, without money, jewellery, and all high and dry in the mud.

Captain Jack laughed boisterously over what he had said. It was a capital joke, and served young Fumbleton right, for he had not been long from college, and was brimful of conceit and nonsense.

"I always make it a rule to look out for young collegians," when they are running will 'about town,' as it is called, because they think they know everything. That £500, Alick Faulkner and I won, was the making of us."

"The making of you! How?"

"Why, we were so hard-up, we should have had to go to house-breaking or something of that kind."

"Well?"

"I knew a see'y 'enemy' of mine who had gone to house-breaking about that time. He wanted me to join him in the venture. But he little dreamed how much I hated him. I'll tell you all about it one of these days ; but as time is now short, I shall only say that I 'split' on him, and my respectable appearance in the witness-box got him transported for life. That's how I generally pay off old scores with 'lads' who don't act always on the square. After that I was appointed one of the Crown officers, and have been so ever since. I knew the chap at school, and hated him, and always swore to have him hung if I could ; but let us go in here—here is a wine shop, let's have a bottle together," said Captain Jack, with a wicked smile.

"That reminds me of something that happened to me at school. It was the first 'clever' thing I ever did," said Phillip, drinking a long draught of good wine.

"Indeed," said Captain Jack, laughing. "I didn't think you ever had done anything clever except that affair of old Bertram."

"Hus—s—sh!" said Phillip, turning pale ; "don't mention that."

"You'd have been in a gibbet only for me," said Captain Jack.

"Perhaps ; but I bought your silence."

"Yes, so that's all square. Let's hear your story. I've got half-an-hour to pass in idleness ; but all our gang have to muster to-night ; we've got 'a great thing' on hand. Will you join us?"

"That depends."

"Depends? But you must."

"Must, eh! Well then, if you say so, then must it shall be."

"Go on with your story then."

"You won't blow on me."

"Me? You must be dreaming."

"But you'd never expect to hear what I'm going to tell."

"Perhaps not, but whatever it is, out with it."

So encouraged, and even now half drunk with wine, Phillip began his story ; his first step in crime, as he called it.

And as he went on, Captain Jack eyed him like a hawk, and his eyes glistened with deadly malice towards Phillip, as Redgill began :—

"Tom Templeton was generally admitted to be the greatest Greek scholar in college.

"Plato, Demosthenes and Xenophon were eternally in his hands, and his favourite amusement seemed to be to have a 'quiet half-hour' with Homer or Sophocles.

"How he could muster sufficient patience to pore over those tantalizing authors, seemed a great mystery to all the Juniors, but the 'Nobs,' 'Dons,'

and 'Big-wigs' of the university would complacently smile, take a pinch of snuff, and nod to Tom, who, squatted at his ease upon the grass, would loll for hours under the trees of our extensive grounds and park, and smoke with impunity, in open defiance of every rule and regulation.

"He could leap, run, walk, fence, and, in fact, excel at anything to which he seemed inclined to pay attention, except swim, which he never did.

"And he was such a favourite with all, that none seemed to take notice, or be at all surprised at anything he might attempt or accomplish.

"He had been known to kick a foot-ball over the college buildings, three stories high, and had soundly thrashed three or four town bullies, who were said to 'travel on their muscle' for a living.

"He never appeared to study very hard

"A pipe was always in his mouth, and, strange to say, he had fascinated all the university officials so effectually, that he went in and out of places considered sacred to every one but the president, or his high and mighty assistants

"The private gardens, even, were open to him, with all their much-envied riches of plums and fruits of various kinds.

"And Tompkins had more than once sworn that, when climbing the wall one day to get at some pears, he saw him lying full length on a bench smoking in the vineyards.

"Tom seems to have mesmerized the gardeners, or heavily bribed them, for he was never at a loss for the gate keys.

"And should they be out of the way, he would simply scale the wall, and commence his evening promenade with the inevitable meerschaum in his mouth.

"One evening, two Dons caught him.

"They entered the garden, walked along the avenues of vines, and there stood Mr. Tom, smoking as usual, as large as life, with a novel in his hand!

"'I imagined I smelt something,' one of the old professors said. 'How comes it, sir, that—don't you know——'

"Before he could add another word, Tom opened upon him with a fine passage from Virgil, which being apropos as to time and place, and well recited withal, disarmed the anger of the first doctor, who took a pinch of snuff and passed on.

"The second was red with anger.

"And as he totally eschewed 'the use of the abominable weed in any form," was ready to explode with rage and indignation.

"For being a great epicure, he felt certain that most of the grapes would fall to his share at table, and didn't wish their early growth in any way retarded.

"'Mr. Templeton! I am astounded at you, sir. How dare you imagine that——'

"Tom did not appear to notice his remark, but casting a look of surprise upon the pompous old gentleman in cap and gown, burst forth into a Greek oration from the Iliad.

"And before the astonished professor could recover his surprise at the action and voice of Templeton, who was personating Achilles among his 'black ships banked up on shore,' left the vine walks in a state of triumph.

"Tom had been several years at college, and was deservedly reputed to be the best man ever on the rolls.

"He was light-hearted, gay, generous, a good musician, splendid classic, and passionately fond of dancing.

"He was courted and petted by all the mothers in town—anxious to provide for their daughters.

"The young ladies themselves were oftentimes at loggerheads to see who should advance fastest in his good graces.

"As there were several female seminaries within a few miles of town, intercourse was frequent at the houses of mutual friends or relatives.

"Many young men attending the University had sisters at a magnificent seminary but two miles from town.

"And as the yearly gymnastic exercises of our college were about to commence, evening drill was often patronized by the fair, so that the University grounds presented a gay and animating appearance during the beautiful evenings of May and June.

"Templeton had been elected chief of the gymnasts this year, and in his blue uniform, faced with red and gold, presented a fine appearance ; so that there was more than one pair of eyes among the ladies who watched his movements with interest.

"At the end of gymnastic drill, which had been witnessed and much applauded by the fair, an old gentleman advanced to Templeton, and presented a bouquet.

"This was nothing unusual, for the ladies seemed to take delight in pelting flowers at us as we filed past them. But, as he took the nosegay from the old man, Templeton perceived a young girl laughing and blushing among a knot of her school-mates, who were apparently joking her.

"'I never saw her before ; she is very pretty. I will make her acquaintance if I break my neck over it,' thought Tom.

"Templeton went into town that evening, and returned to his rooms very late.

"He was musing in his chair at the window, gazing at the moon, and puffing out volumes of cigar smoke.

"In a week the gay fellow seemed to have changed his nature.

"He was thoughtful, absent in manner, and seldom touched his books.

"Instead of trespassing upon the privacy of the president's gardens at evening, he was often found strumming a guitar, and singing snatches from various operas.

"Months passed away, and none could account for his change of manner.

"He was thin, pale, thoughtful, soft in voice and manner, and juniors whispered one to another that he was ' heavily in debt ;' ' the uncle refused to come up.'

"Others, rather lazy students themselves, would sigh, and say, ' Just as I told you ; now you see the effect of " Nights with Homer and Demosthenes !" he is in a galloping consumption !'

"The lodge-keeper, that terrible portly official with the clanking keys, who frowned on little boys, and slammed the gates with a triumphant bang of self-importance ; that awful, lace-trimmed gentleman, and bottomless depository of college secrets, said nothing, but sighed heavily, stroked his red nose ominously, and remarked—

"'Some folks is wise, and some isn't. I hasn't been here a matter of more nor forty year without knowing that much ; and if you're well up in your Greek you'll know better nor I can tell yer, *verbum sap.*, as Homer wery nicely remarks.'

"And with that, went into his lodge, closed the door, and smoked his pipe.

"It must be confessed *I did* wish to know what the matter was with Tom,

"He had always befriended me since entering college, and usually informed me of all his affairs.

"But during the past few months his conduct had been so much unlike his former self that I felt offended and annoyed.

"'If you are hard pushed, Tom,' said I, ' and your uncle refuses, why not tell me? I can settle all that without so much melancholy and solitude.'

"I could glean nothing.

"'Phil, my boy,' said he, laying his hand on my shoulder, ' you are gold—true gold, but—there is nothing the matter with me, I can assure you ; I am only studying hard for my degree—examinations come off in another month, and then I leave these old walls for ever.'

"'Templeton has passed !' said all the juniors, as Tom solemnly strode through the crowd towards his rooms.

"'How much for your parchment, Templeton ? '

"'Did they bother you, my boy ? '

"'I hope you floored Old Snuffy,' said one or another of the students.

"But Tom, the subject of all these remarks, congratulations, and the like, bowed politely to his schoolmates, and went up to his rooms.

"'I leave to-morrow, Phil,' said he, as I shook him by the hand ; ' my books are all at your service, my boy ; you'll have to pass through the same unpleasant ordeal yourself next year. If you find any use for them, I give them with much pleasure. There are no "crammers" or "coaches " among them ; I despise all that sort of thing as much as you do.'

"'But why look so sad, Tom ? Confound it, man ! cheer up ! there are scores within the walls this moment, who would willingly give thousands for your prizes and parchments. How delighted your uncle will be !' said I.

"There was no response.

"He relapsed into his customary silence and thoughtfulness, and although we both drank heavily that night, not a word escaped him in his cups.

"Next day, towards evening, we drove together towards the coaching station, and when on the top of a hill about a mile from the University buildings, he stopped the vehicle and looked towards them in silence and with evident emotion.

"'How beautifully the sun sets in the west, and how charming the old grounds look bathed in sunlight. See how the steeple casts its shadows across the grand walks, and how the clock-tower and weather-vane glow again with changing light ! I never loved but once, Phil, and that was once too often for my own peace through life, yet the memories of Alma Mater, with its dingy walls, old towers, and chiming bells, unmans me more than all things else in the world !'

"He whipped up the horses suddenly into a brisk trot, and was silent.

"He pressed his hat over his eyes, and averted his face; for once in years of my remembrance, two tears were glistening in his eyes.

"It must have been a fearful struggle between his pride and secret sorrows, to have allowed them to escape; yet there they were, shining witnesses of human feeling.

"We parted.

"Templeton went into the north, and for six months corresponded with me.

"In answer to enquiries, he stated that he was not at his uncle's, but in York.

"I judged, from the tone of his last note, that he was sick and pressed for means.

"I wrote to him again, but received no answer. A friend of mine was directed to visit him and let him have what money he desired.

"But he had removed his lodgings, and was nowhere to be found.

"There seemed to hang some mystery around Tom Templeton; some thought he 'had been crossed in love' while at college.

"Others said that pecuniary difficulties had involved him.

No. 13.

"Both of these surmises certainly must be incorrect. I thought, for he disclosed all his secrets to me. If Cupid had been in the case, some of us would have known it; as to money matters, all the college said his uncle was immensely wealthy, and intended to leave him everything.

"Mystery there seemed to be of some kind, and I was determined, upon graduating, to sift the matter to the bottom.

"I liked Tom as a brother; his troubles were mine, and, if in difficulty, I was willing to see him through it safely.

"When university dons had granted me my parchment with 'A.M.' engraved thereon, I returned home, and was soon engaged in my father's extensive transactions, doing what people might term a 'roaring' business.

"My thoughts would occasionally revert to my lost friend, and while going homeward one evening at dusk, a poorly dressed stranger hurriedly passed me and glided into a back street, as if ashamed to be seen in lighted and thronged thoroughfares.

"I followed him.

"He strode through the streets at a rapid pace, but, by a side glance I got of him, there could be no doubt but that it was the same Tom Templeton of my school days.

"He had not gone far, when he entered a small, obscure house, and, in less than ten minutes, emerged again, but so differently attired and so gay, I could scarce have recognised him.

"Yet on his countenance was still the same calm, pale, melancholy.

"He actually stopped at the same house I was going to, and was admitted.

"What was his business there, I wondered to know.

"I knew what mine was, namely, to make love to the daughter of a very rich man my father had known for years.

"I did not knock at the door, but let myself in with a latch-key.

"When I quietly advanced towards the parlour door, I perceived Tom Templeton on his knees before the idol of my heart!

"What startled me more, was, the lady fair listened to his fair speeches, and returned his advances.

"For the first time in my life, I felt envy, malice, and revenge.

"I said nothing at the time, but I met my old schoolmate afterwards.

"A violent quarrel ensued.

"I accused him of all manner of misdemeanours, and last of all of ingratitude.

"But all I could do or say would not provoke him into a challenge.

"At last I gave him one myself.

"He accepted it readily, and we met.

"He wished to apologise for all he had done and said.

"I would not accept it.

"I fired.

"He fell down dead.

"I rushed towards him.

"The doctors examined him and tore open his clothes.

"Tom Templeton proved to be a *girl*.

"The astonishment that was now depicted on every countenance was great indeed.

"This girl had passed through college, and was first and most expert in everything, and for years lived undetected."

"But why should a girl have played the part of a lover?" said Captain Jack.

"She did not play the part of a lover, as you will perceive.

"Some time after this, my old flame was addressed by the son of the chief die-sinker at the mint.

"I had suspicion for thinking that Tom Templeton (the girl) had a brother, who personified Miss Templeton.

"This I proved.

"They were used as spies by a band of coiners, and so well could these two children of the chief coiner counterfeit either male or female sex, that for years they carried on their traffic in base coin undetected; for, indeed, my father and many other merchants had often and often given notes for gold, and it was not until the gold was tried at the mint that any deception was discovered; but then it was too late to trace it back through the various merchants' offices to the proper persons.

"The reason Tom and her brother were sent to

ifferent schools was, that, they being so highly educated, they might afterwards prove all the more expert, and less likely to be detected."

"But what revenge had you?" asked Captain Jack.

"I revealed what I had discovered to the chief of the coiners, and my silence was bought."

"And afterwards?"

"Because I did not receive another consideration from them, I informed."

"I know you did. But you were too late; the birds had flown."

"How know you that?" asked Phillip.

"Because I was one of the coiners myself then."

"You?"

"Yes, me."

"I am astonished."

"You will be more so when you hear that the coiners not only now exist in the south of England, but that through them I heard of Farmer Bertram's murder, and tracked you."

"Impossible!"

"No, it isn't. Here is a person who will explain all things," said Captain Jack, rising and bowing to a thick-set, military-looking man, who entered.

"Mr. Phillip Redgill, allow me to introduce you to a friend of mine,"

"What name?" asked Phillip, colouring.

"Colonel Blood!" said Captain Jack, with a demon-like sneer.

"Betrayed!" sighed Phillip.

"Yes; why not, you had no more money?" whispered Captain Jack, "so therefore I have no further use for you. It's quite a common plan with detectives."

Then, addressing Colonel Blood in a different tone, he said,

"I have fulfilled *my* part of the bargain, Colonel, about the thirteen gibbets, and I hope—"

"That I will do mine, eh, Captain Jack? Well, you need not fear; your death warrant shall not be signed yet at all events. But," casting his eyes on Phillip, he said, "we have been a long, long time in tracing out your villanies, young man, for you are very old in crime. Captain Jack," he said, pointing to Phillip, "follow me."

Captain Jack whistled, and, in a moment, three others of his men came in and escorted Phillip to prison.

As he was going out of the tavern door, who should he see standing by, but—

Sir Andrew, who grinned like a fiend, and threw up his hands in Christian horror.

He had not gone far down the street, ere he saw Augustus Fumbleton and Fanny riding out together.

"This is worse than death," he thought, and struggled hard to get free.

But Captain Jack's hand, like the grip of a vice, was upon his throat.

## CHAPTER XXX.

THE COINERS' CAVERN—SUBTERRANEAN ABODES —THE OATH—THE RELEASE—THE PROMISE.

"I DON'T much like this, Master Ned," exclaimed Tim, shivering, "where can we be going to?"

"Hold your tongue, you prating fool," replied Ned, angrily, " your idle words will do more harm than good ; do you hear me say anything ?"

"All right, Master, but I ain't Wildfire Ned, you know ; I ain't made of cast-iron."

Tim would have added something else, but a violent jerking of the machine under his feet convinced him that they had reached the bottom.

Before he had time to recover from the shock, he was seized by two or three powerful men, who bound his arms behind him, and led him away.

They also blindfolded him, in spite of his groans for mercy, and, after dragging him along for about a hundred yards, they stopped, and, loosening the bandage from his eyes, thrust him under a vaulted arch.

He was evidently far under ground, and the soil on which he stood was of a whitish colour, similar to that in a lead mine.

The water was trickling down through the fissures of the rocks, and formed all around a stagnant pool.

But what struck Ned most forcibly was the singular appearance of his assassins, for as such he deemed them now to be.

They were all dressed in coarse baize coats, which reached to their knees, and were fastened in front by a huge clasp.

They wore leather breeches, covered by large top boots, which confined the greatest part of their legs.

Each of them had a couple of double-barrelled pistols stuck in his belt, and a rough beard flowed upon their breasts.

"I say, Nat !" cried one of the ruffians, "what shall we do with this black-looking scoundrel, the servant ?"

"Why, leave him here, to be sure," replied the tallest of the three, "and you shall guard him, it's your turn to be on duty to-night, and you may as well take it here, as stand at the tower; and to keep you from the cold, here's my cloak, which will keep out the shivers, I'll warrant ye."

This said he took the arm of his companion, and left Tim, with his guard, who began to pace up and down, without exchanging a single word with the prisoner.

But to return to Ned.

He shared no better fate than his servant, and before he had time to use his good sword, he was bound, and ordered to march forward.

He was led through the midst of five, and then into a sixth spacious apartment, dug in the earth, and lighted by a dim lamp, hanging in the centre.

He was requested by one of his conductors to sit on a bench.

Two of the band left the room, and the others sat near the entrance, and engaged in a whispering conversation.

Ned was then left to his own reflections, which were not of a tranquillising nature.

Nearly half an hour had elapsed when the two men mentioned above re-appeared bearing lighted torches and an order from the captain to see the prisoner.

Young Ned Warbeck was now fully aware that he was in a cave of robbers, and he made up his mind for the worst, and marched boldly at the summons of one who seemed to be the leader of the band.

They proceeded, at a quick pace, through nume-rous vaulted arches, similar to which Ned had been confined in, and they were soon in the presence of the captain.

He was seated at a table with a bundle of papers in his left hand, and a sword in his right.

His dress was the same as that of his followers.

What distinguished him from the rest was a pair of long moustachios in addition to the beard, and a yellow band round his waist·

His dark glaring eyes were fixed for a moment on the countenance of the young and handsome prisoner, who was leisurely surveying all around him.

"Unloose this young man," said the captain, "and stand aside."

Ned was immediately released from his bonds, and his guards took their places silently behind him.

The captain spent a few minutes in conference with some of his associates.

During this time young Ned had the leisure to perceive that he was mistaken in his conjectures respecting those whom he had taken for robbers ; though not of a very different avocation, they could not literally be entitled to that appellation.

They were (as he plainly saw by the die, which at first had escaped his enquiring eyes, and by the heaps of blanks all ready for impression), a set of men who defraud the revenue by circulating, to the detriment of the Mint, immense quantities of base coin—in fact, they were Coiners.

He knew not whether he had any right to be satisfied with the change ; for, thought he, a robber will take your life rather than be detected, so would a coiner, rather than have his lawless proceedings come to light, have recourse to any means ; but then, would they have forced him, as it were, to be an eye-witness of their crimes for the sole purpose of murdering him in cold blood ?

These were his thoughts, which were diverted by an appeal from the captain—to answer his purposes.

"Who are you ? What are you ? and whence do you come ?" asked the captain.

"My name is Warbeck. I am an officer in the king's navy, and have come from Plymouth."

"Well answered. Now, what brought you here ?"

Ned Warbeck, in a few words, stated the circumstances above mentioned.

"Young man," resumed the captain, "you stand charged with having fired at one of my men ; of this I will keep little or no account, it was, as you might rightly observe, in self-defence. You have proved yourself bold and worthy of your profession. Many others have been driven from the landlord's house by the same means.

"Though under very little fear of detection, as the entrance to our subterranean dwellings is known to no others but to ourselves, we have, nevertheless, thought it advisable to adopt some method of screening ourselves more effectually.

"We resolved to render that house uninhabitable.

"We bought it, but not being known in the neighbourhood, and never going out by night, and that only once a month to buy provisions, we deemed it useless, and therefore concocted the plan which you have witnessed, and which you must own requires as stout a heart as your own to withstand.

"The man whom you fired at, unaccustomed to such resistance, against which, however, he was well provided, having upon him a thick steel armour and fire-arms, thought it necessary to entice you to the trap-door, and bring you among us with your servant you may think his conduct impudent, such is also our opinion of it.

"At the first notice of your arrest, we were both surprised and astounded.

"We took council together; you were at first doomed to perpetual imprisonment in one of the vaults, or to be immediately put to death.

"At length your youth and courage prevailed, and it was resolved that you should be set at liberty, if you agree to the following conditions.

"First, you must swear by what is most sacred to a sailor, your honour, never to mention to any one what you have seen here this night, not even to give the slightest hint about it.

"Second, At your return to the landlord. you must tell him that you were dreadfully frightened and alarmed at the apparition you saw in his house, and engage him to pull it down, and make the best of the materials, as nobody will ever live among spectres who have sworn vengeance to him and his family if the house be inhabited.

"Should you consent to these conditions, you shall be set free, and your servant also.

"But mind, if you ever break the oath that is required of you, on the least danger threatening us, the next day shall not see you alive.

"We have confederates in all parts of the country, who will avenge us, and strike the fatal blow your wild will would have deserved.

"Your servant has seen nothing since he has been among us.

"Should he attempt to speak of being let down a trap, and seeing strange men, contradict him flatly, and treat his speech as the wanderings of an imagination deceived by terror, or the effect of liquor.

"I leave you now to your reflections, and give you an hour to make up your mind."

The captain then rose, and walked to and fro with hurried steps, and then left the vaulted chamber.

Young Warbeck requested pen, ink, and paper, and wrote as follows:—

"Captain, I have had for a few moments a most terrible struggle in my mind.

"Honour and duty have alternately presented themselves to my imagination, but I have at last concluded that I can, by fulfilling what you require of me, keep the one unspotted without departing from the other.

"I will take the oath demanded.

"Your humanity and sense of honour have brought me to this determination, which fear or threats could not have extorted from me."

He awaited with impatience the captain's return, who in about an hour re-entered and took his seat at table.

Ned then handed him the letter he had just written.

The captain cast a rapid glance over the contents, and rising bade Ned Warbeck lift up his hand, and solemnly take the oath.

This done, he stepped towards him, and restored to him his sword, in token of freedom.

He gave him also two guides, who led him quickly for about six or seven hundred yards, under immense arches formed by nature, and brought him out near a torrent bordered by a thicket of brushwood.

Two horses were here in readiness for Ned Warbeck and Tim.

As they mounted to ride away, their conductors said, in solemn, warning tones,

"Remember your oath!"

"I will," said Ned, in an under-tone.

He and Tim rode rapidly away.

## CHAPTER XXXI.

SIR ANDREW APPEARS IN A NEW CHARACTER—HIS DESIGNS ON DAME WORTHINGTON'S PROPERTY—HE CLAIMS RELATIONSHIP — THE POISONED DRAUGHTS—THE OLD DAME'S SAD EXPERIENCE IN THE WORLD—A STRANGER COMES UPON THE SCENE—NEWS FROM NED WARBECK.

THERE was some mystery attached to old Dame Worthington, Sir Richard Warbeck, and his two adopted nephews, Charley and Wildfire Ned.

What this mystery was, no one could find out; but Mistress Haylark swore in her own heart that there must be one, and she would have given her finger-ends to have found it out.

All that we can say at present is that, in her youth and prime, good Dame Worthington must have been a great beauty, for even now she bore traces of it.

All we know for a positive fact is that, when rather over thirty, she condescended to marry a sea captain, who, through Sir Richard Warbeck's influence at the India House, had the command of a brig.

There were no children from the marriage and old Worthington proved a worthless drunken fellow, and, when in his cups, gave way to all manner of extravagances.

His jealous, uproarious disposition was fully manifested upon every possible occasion when ashore.

When drunk he would lie on the sofa and sing uproarious songs all night, to the infinite disgust of fellow lodgers.

When, perhaps, only half inebriated, and tempted as usual by jealousy, he would toss the furniture about and break all the crockery.

So that, everything considered, his absence was far more preferable than his presence.

Hence, when the news arrived that the barque "Columbo" had grounded in a gale, on the Florida Reefs, with the loss of all hands, Dame Worthington gave vent to her feelings in a few sobs and a fainting fit, but more than this she betrayed little of that grief which might have been expected from a loved and cherished wife.

Her only true and fast friend through life was, as he always had been, old Sir Richard Warbeck.

He furnished a private hotel for her, the management of which fully occupied her time and brought in much money.

But now that Charley Warbeck was married and settled, she seemed in part satisfied, and looked even younger than ever.

But still she fretted much for Ned Warbeck, who was at sea, for of the two youths she loved him much the best.

He was younger, bolder, and far more handsome than Charley, but he was always a wild, harum-scarum youth; and, since he had run away to sea the old dame fretted much, wept in secret, and would have given the world to have seen her darling boy once more.

But everybody said that, since he had gone out in search of the Skeleton Crew, he would never return alive.

"Don't believe such idle tales," said Sir Richard, often. "Young Ned has got as many lives as a cat. Put him where you will, he is sure to fall on his feet."

But now a stranger made Dame Worthington's acquaintance.

This was no other than old Sir Andrew!

He had got tired of country life, and determined to start again in the city.

He had heard and knew that old Sir Richard was not only very wealthy and powerful, but that he constantly visited good Dame Worthington.

"She is a silly, soft-hearted woman," thought Sir Andrew. "By going to live there, I shall fall across Sir Richard, and it may be that by-and-bye we may get better acquainted, and he may assist me in re-establishing myself in business."

"If any one wants to get favours out of a man, let him flatter the woman that man most respects," thought Sir Andrew.

He was a "canny Scot," and, like all his nation, had a long, calculating head.

He had not been residing long at Dame Worthington's, therefore—his wife was always in the country—when he and she became remarkably chatty together, and communicative.

Sir Andrew passed himself off as a widower, and told such a pitiful tale how he had been wronged and dishonoured by Phillip and his own daughter, that the good dame listened attentively to all the old hypocrite had to say, and not only sympathised with him, but even went so far as to plead his cause to Sir Richard, who, she thought, from his power and position, might help Sir Andrew on to the path of fortune once more.

The cunning Scot knew that nothing pleases a woman more than flattery, particularly in one who is a "good listener," and can hear out the many long stories which widows always have to tell.

Every one have their trials and troubles, as we have seen in this tale, besides Sir Andrew, hence it need not surprise any one to be informed that good Dame Worthington had a very long list of grievances to complain of in her dealings with the world.

It was her settled conviction that old widows were the most oppressed class in existence, and herself the most deeply wronged of them all.

Butchers, bakers, milkmen, and tax-collectors were her abomination, and she often sighed that boarding houses could not be carried on without them.

"For, my dear," she would say, "one has scarcely got a few pounds in hand, before down come the bills upon you, first for one thing, and then for another, so that we *never* have a penny to call our own. And then, there's our *losses*; ah, my dear, you haven't the *slightest* notion of what I have to suffer; poor folks like me have occasion to be 'smart,' these times, I can assure you, for we see a deal of this wicked world in a very short time.

"Just fancy, my dear; little more than two years ago, a very respectable-looking, genteel young man, calls on me.

"'Good morning, Dame Worthington,' says he.

"'Good morning, sir,' says I, 'and what do you please to want?'

"'I have been in search of hotel accommodation, ma'am,' says he, 'for several days; respectable apartments in a respectable neighbourhood, and hearing yours highly spoken of, I have called.'

"Well, my dear, he was the nicest young man you ever see; so mild and quiet, and honest looking, very much like my brother was before he was killed, and I thought that he certainly must be a very genteel, amiable young man, and I let him have the lodgings.

"After a few nights he got more and more at home with the lodgers, and even played the harp and guitar in the parlour; and Mistress Haylark said, and the other ladies also, that he was the nicest young man, that ever lived in my house.

"He dressed very stylish, my dear, and *would* have his apartments arranged, and swept, and dusted oftener than anybody else, for which he was willing to pay 'extra,' he said, if required.

"The number of wax candles that young man had, and the coals, and odds and ends of different kinds, were considerable, my dear, but he said he had never denied himself in anything, being rich, and, therefore, couldn't do without them.

"The number of things which shopmen sent in, was wonderful; new boots and shoes, new coats and waistcoats, and fine linen, until we all began to think, at one time, he was going to make a runaway match with Mistress Haylark's daughter Fanny.

"For he seemed very sweet in that quarter, and Mistress Haylark was very fond of him also; *too* fond of him, *I* think, between ourselves, considering she's a widow just as old as me almost, except she primps and paints, and wears false back hair.

"Oh, bless you, we all liked him amazing, and he was so nicely dressed and well behaved and had so many ways of entertaining a room full of company, that the first month passed like a single week.

"Although my rule is 'weekly payments,' he was so polite, and offered me so many references that I felt I could trust my whole house in his hands.

"I loaned him several sums on different occasions, as he was out of 'small change.' he said, and after he had been two months in the house—oh! that I'm obliged to confess it—he, one night, suddenly disappeared, trunks and all! without paying any one a single penny, my dear!

"Oh, I was never taken aback so much in my whole life!

"Not that I cared for what he owed *me*, you know, although I *am* a poor lone widow without any natural protector, and earn every penny by the sweat of my brow.

"Oh, it hurt Miss Josephine Smith, next door, very much, my dear; she has never been the same girl since, for she was 'dead on' to him.

"Mistress Haylark was frantic almost; she had loaned him £10, and he walked off with her best diamond ring; think o' that.

"How that diamond ring ('paste,' my dear, between ourselves) should have come into *his* hands is a mystery to me, without she gave it to him, which shows how *some* people can lower themselves when they are manœuvring to marry off a daughter.

"But between you and me, although everybody knows that I am not given to backbiting or detracting, which I consider mean in anybody, but specially in a landlady talking of her own lodgers, who pay regular, and give little trouble, I *must* say, my dear, that I think at that time she was trying to get the young man herself!

"Because, although my eyes are not the best in the world, on account of the troubles I have gone through, and the many briny tears I have shed, I *can* see as far as most folks, and when I hear silk rustling on a dark landing, and hear a scuffling going on, it don't take long for me to guess which way the wind is blowing in certain quarters that I know of, my dear."

"You see there are so many different kinds of people, that it takes great experience and the patience of Job, to keep a respectable boarding house the way it should be.

"Now, there's Mistress Tiffler, my dear, who keeps a house just round the corner—why bless you, I wouldn't have a place like her's for all the world—I can't go by the house without turning up my nose, for really it seems to smell of nothing else but grease and dirt.

"*Nobody* looks clean at that house; and, as to feeding, good gracious! you should only see what half-starved wretches they are. Well, how can it be otherwise, my dear?

"She goes off to market, and buys up all kinds of rubbish, which I wouldn't touch. She boards 'em cheap, and is a regular vixen, my dear; a perfect 'hurricane' as my poor, lost sailor husband used to say.

"But then, of course, there is no comparison between me and such a woman as that. How she gets along with the Germans, and French, and others who live in her place, I can't see.

"They are always having rows there, but no one can even whisper, and say that anything of the kind ever happened to my house, except once, when two of the lodgers, young city clerks, fell out about a servant girl, who was rather good-looking, and knocked each other down stairs.

"You have no notion, my dear, of my troubles.

"If I have mutton as the principal dish some one grumbles; if I have beef another sniffs and says he's dined already.

"Then Mistress this is too lazy to come down to breakfast, and almost pulls the bell down for Sarah to take it up to her.

"Then Miss the other, her daughter, don't like tea nor coffee and must have chocolate and toast; while two or three others eat hot cakes faster than we can make 'em; and then there's more grumbling and threatening to leave, until it worries my very life out almost.

"I don't care much about how the *men* talk, you know, because I can manage *them*.

"If their boots and hot water aren't ready I can plead an excuse of some kind, and even if they *do* 'burst out' like, and tell you what they think, and threaten to go, I don't dislike 'em, because, as my poor husband used to say, 'after the storm there's always a calm,' and then *my* turn comes.

"If they owe anything I talks like a sensible woman to 'em, and 'rides a high horse,' but if they don't I only smiles, and takes no notice.

"Oh, I can get along with the men, my dear, I always could. I would rather have to do with *ten* men than *one* woman; and wouldn't have one in the house at all if I could help it.

"But, then, you see, my dear, men *will* have women in the house; I don't blame 'em a bit, it looks natural like.

"A house don't look right without a woman or two but; heaven keep me from having a houseful of young women and young men!

"I tried it once, but it wouldn't answer, my dear.

"Oh, the sorrow and vexation I had with 'em. I had my hands full, and soon gave it up.

"Young widows in the house are just as bad.

"I abominate widows in the house from my heart, particularly when young and handsome, although I am a widow myself.

"There's always trouble about 'em, and they are always flirting with some one, and getting the men into fusses.

"But what can you do, my dear? You must have *some* one that's attractive to keep the men together, otherwise the place would be as cold and cheerless to 'em as an ice-house.

"But, then, my dear, they talk so much, there's no end to their chatter.

"You can't keep 'em from it, and the older they get the more they have to say about their neighbours.

"Not that *I* care, you know, my dear; they can talk as much as they like for all *me*, so they pays their bills, and don't actually insult me to my face.

"But it is very aggravating, my dear, to see 'em chatting and whispering in each other's rooms, passing unkind remarks behind one's back, and appearing all smiles and friendly like before your face.

"It don't matter what you do for 'em, my dear, they will talk about you; and, although I'm no eaves-dropper, and wouldn't listen at any one's door for all the world, I *do* know certain things of certain parties, which would surprise certain quarters, if it was only whispered in their ear confidentially, my dear.

"But I'm *not* one of that kind; I know my position too well for that, my dear, and wouldn't lower my dignity by peeping into their rooms when they are out, not me! or prying into boxes and drawers, and rummaging about with their work-boxes and private notes. No indeed, nothing of that kind in my house, my dear.

"If they meets me on the landing and says,

"'Dame Worthington, will you come in for a few moments?'

"I always says,

"'Certainly, with pleasure, Mistress Perkins; how do you do this morning ma'am? you are looking very well, I never saw you look so young and captivating, indeed I didn't. Come in! of course I will, for a few minutes, to have a friendly chat, like, about old times.'

"But I always says,

"'Please don't offer me any refreshment, Mistress Perkins,' I says, 'because my stomach is weak, and I can't stand it; a thimbleful of brandy would knock me over, my dear, in a minute.'

"Because a glass of ginger wine don't cost *much*, you know, my dear; and if you accepts *their* little deceitful offers, they always takes advantage of it to wear the very legs off the poor servant girl, and me too, if I'd let 'em.

"But I lets 'em ring away till tired, and takes no notice, until they comes down stairs themselves, and then when they knocks at my door, I seems surprised not to hear the bell, and then they gets what they want.

"Bless you, my dear, if something wasn't done, we should wear the stairs out.

"First there's old Mr. Brown up-stairs, he wants hot water half-a-dozen times a day and can't hear the dinner bell without it is rung outside his door.

"Mistress Perkins is always in want of something, and that wretched pet dog of hers is *always* causing trouble.

"It was only the other day I missed a beefsteak off the kitchen table, and at last I traced it up-stairs to Mistress Perkins,' door, where the dog stood growling and showing his teeth, until in fright I upset the servant maid and her pail of water, and fell headlong down stairs."

The smiling old scoundrel, Sir Andrew, would sit and listen to the good old dame, as she recounted her trials and troubles, and would nod in approval as meekly as a lamb.

But he was a deep designing old villain, as we shall see.

It is true that the old dame had fallen downstairs and seriously hurt herself and was then very ill.

He also had learned that, in some way, she was a very distant relation of his, and the only one then living.

This discovery greatly surprised old Dame Worthington, and Sir Richard Warbeck also; but the cunning scoundrel supported his statement to relationship with so much plausible, but fictitious, evidence that both Sir Richard and Dame Worthington took the cunning Scotchman into their confidence.

Sir Andrew had now "the game in his own hands," he thought, and he also came by the information, that should Sir Richard die first, *all* his property, if Phillip Redgill was proved guilty of the crimes of which Captain Jack accused him, would all go to Charley, Ned Warbeck, and Dame Worthington.

"As she has made her will already," thought Sir Andrew, "and left me a small sum, and the rest to the Warbecks, it would not be very difficult to get the will altered altogether in *my* favour,

"*And poison her !*"

This devilish design he resolved to put into execution.

He was very attentive to old Dame Worthington, and would suffer no one, as a "relation," in the absence of Sir Richard, to administer to her any medicine, however simple.

With these opportunities in his hand, Sir Andrew made good use of his time.

He never allowed a chance to pass him, but, day by day, was gradually poisoning her.

The old dame got weaker and weaker every day.

The doctors could not make it out.

Yet the sole object of her thoughts was the adventurous stray one, Ned Warbeck, "her favourite boy."

While propped up in her chair, one day in the parlour, and surrounded by her friends, she was continually speaking of her "poor sailor boy," Ned, when a gentleman, who was present, said,

"Well, madam, I know not who your young favourite is, but I am a sailor myself and love the profession."

"It is a compliment to me to hear you speak in such glowing terms of our gallant tars.

"And the bravest of them all is Ned Warbeck, I know," said the old dame with a flushed cheek.

"Of course he is," said old Sir Andrew, trying to smile, but at the same time, congratulating himself at the potent power of the secret poison he was daily administering for the sake of the good old dame's money. "Ned Warbeck, of course he is the bravest of the brave," he muttered, "there isn't a lad in all the king's navy like to him."

"Ned Warbeck ?" said the stranger, in astonishment.

"Yes, do you know him ?" asked the good dame, in great curiosity.

The stranger did not answer, but said, "If you will only listen, I'll tell you something that will gratify you."

So saying, he lit his pipe again, and commenced his story round the crackling winter fire.

---

## CHAPTER XXXII.

A LEAP FOR LIFE—THE BRAVERY OF A YOUNG MIDDY—THE TALE STARTLES ALL PRESENT —WHO IS HE ?

"THE last cruise I made in the Channel was in search of the Skeleton Crew, in the 'Diamond' frigate, 'Trumps,' as we sometimes used to call our gallant ship.

"We had been tacking and filling for several weeks on the western coast in search of Deathwing's phantom ship of smugglers, and, during that time, we had had some pretty heavy weather.

"When we reached Flamborough Head, there was a spanking wind blowing from west-south-west ; so we squared away, and without coming to at the Head made straight for old Hull, the general rendezvous and place of refitting for our squadrons in the German Ocean, because smugglers are plentiful there.

"Immediately on arriving there, we warped in alongside the quay, where we stripped ship to a girt line, and gave her a regular-built overhauling from stem to stern.

"Many hands, however, make light work.

"In a very few days all was accomplished.

"The stays and shrouds were set up, and new rattled down ; the yards crossed, the running rigging rose, and sails bent.

"And the old craft, fresh painted and all a-taunto, looked as fine as a midshipman on liberty.

"In place of the storm stumps which had been' stowed away among the booms and other spare spars amidships, we had sent up top-gallant masts and royal poles, with a sheave for sky-sails and houst enough for sky-scrapers among them.

"So you may judge the old frigate looked pretty taunt.

"There was a Dutch line ship in the harbour, but though we carried only thirty to her forty guns, her main-truck would hardly have reached to our royal mast-head.

"When we had got everything ship-shape and man-of-war fashion, we hauled out again, and took berth about half a mile from the quay.

"What little wind we had had in the fore part of the day, died away at noon, and though the first dog-watch was almost out, and the sun was near the horizon, not a breath of air had risen to disturb the deep serenity of the scene.

"Even on board our vessel a degree of stillness unusual for a man-of-war prevailed among the crew.

"It was the hour of the evening meal, and the low hum that came from the gun-deck had an indistinct and buzzing sound.

"On the top of the boom cover, and in the full glare of the sun, lay a tall negro, 'Black Jake' the jig-maker of the ship, and a striking specimen of African peculiarities, in whose single person they were all strongly developed.

"His flat nose was dilated to unusual width, and his ebony cheeks fairly glistened with delight, as he looked up at the gambols of a huge ape, which had been entrusted to our care to take to Plymouth, and which, clinging to the main-stay just above Jake's, the big negro's, woolly head, was chattering and grinning back at the 'Darkie' as if there existed some mutual intelligence between them.

"I was on watch on deck, and standing amusing myself by observing the antics of the black and his congenial playmate the ape, but at length tiring of the rude mirth, had turned towards the taffrail to gaze on the more agreeable features of that scene.

"Just at that moment, a shout and a curse burs upon my ear.

"Looking quickly round to ascertain the cause of the unusual sound on a frigate ship, I was horrified at what I saw.

"The commodore was on board that day with his wife, child and nurse.

"The nurse and child had just come out of the Captain's state cabin, when Jacko the ape, being teazed by the negro, plunged wildly towards the nurse, broke his chain, seized the commodore's infant boy, and with a terrific scream rushed up the rigging with it !

"This was a most horrible predicament, for the ape was only half tamed !

"A single glance to the main-yard explained the occasion of Jake the negro's shout and curse.

"The nurse had been coming up from the cabin when Jacko perceiving her near him, broke his thin chain, dropped suddenly down from the main-mast and running along the boom cover seized the nurse's cap from her head, frightened her into a fit, and seizing the child, immediately darted up the main-topsail sheet, and thence to the bunt of the main-yard, where he now sat grinning and screeching most horribly, tossing the child about and each moment threatening to kill it.

"But one of our young midshipmen, a great favourite on board, who was a sprightly active fellow, and called Ned, though he could not climb so nimbly as an ape, yet had no mind to let the child suffer or be strangled without an effort to regain it, and kill the monster.

"Perhaps he was the more strongly excited to make chase after Jacko and the child, from noticing how much the commodore had praised him for former acts of bravery, and by the loud curses of the nigger Jake, who seemed suddenly horror-stricken at what had happened, because it might have been thought that he had been the main cause of the sad occurrence by teasing Jacko.

"'Ha, you rascal Jacko, hab you no more respect for de commodore den to steal his child ? We bring you to de gangway, you black nigger, and get you a dozen on de bare back for a tief, and afterwards skin you alive.'

"The ape looked down from his perch, as if he understood the threat of the negro, and chattered a sort of defiance, showing his teeth, and each instant seemed as if he would bite the crying infant.

"'Ha, ha ! Massa Ned, he say you must ketch him 'fore you flog him, and it's no so easy for a midshipman in boots to ketch a big ape barefoot.'

"A red spot mounted to the cheeks of Ned, as he cast a glance of offended pride and contempt at Jake, and then sprung across the deck to Jacob's ladder.

"In an instant he was half-way up the rigging, running over the ratlines as lightly as if they were an easy flight of stairs.

"The shrouds scarcely quivered beneath his elastic motion.

"In a second more his hand was on the futtocks.

"'Ma-sa Ned,' cried Jake, who sometimes, from being a favorite, ventured to take liberties with the younger officers.

"'Massa Ned, you best crawl through the 'lubber's hole;' it take a sailor-man to climb de futtock shroud.'

"But he had scarcely time to utter his pretended caution before Ned was in the top.

"The infuriated ape, in the meantime, had awaited the gallant middy's approach, until perceiving he held a glittering dirk between his teeth, he began to chatter and scream, and toss and twirl the screaming infant about, until each moment seemed to be its last.

"The sight was sickening, for no one knew how to catch the ape.

"He might at any moment, in his fury, have dashed the infant's brains out against the mast.

"No one dared to fire, for the same shot might have killed the child.

"Besides, if the ape had been wounded, he would then have surely killed the babe for revenge.

"Gallant Ned had nearly got up the rigging, when the ape clasped the baby more firmly, and, running along the yard to the opposite side of the top, sprang up a rope, and thence to the topmast back-stay.

"Up this it ran to the topmast cross-trees, where it again quietly seated itself and resumed its work of scratching the baby's head, and pulling its clothes to pieces.

"The cries of the child were now ear-piercing and heartrending.

"For several minutes I stood watching the gallant young middy follow Jacko the ape from one piece of rigging to another, the ape all the while seeming only to exert such speed as was necessary to elude its pursuer, and pausing whenever the latter appeared to be weary of the exciting chase.

"All on deck were breathless with excitement.

"At last, by manoeuvring thus, the mischievous animal, which looked now more ferocious than ever, succeeded in enticing the gallant young middy as high as the royal mast-head.

"Springing suddenly from place to place, the chattering ape climbed the sky-sail pole, and, to the horror of every one, was actually tying, and did tie, the child on the main truck, a small circular piece of wood on the loftiest mast, and at a height from the deck so great that it made one dizzy to think of it.

"A shout of horror ran through all the crew.

"The ape had succeeded in tying the child with its own clothes on to the highest point of the tallest mast, and there it was, swaying to and fro, and in danger each second of falling off and being crushed to atoms.

"The cries of the mother were heartrending.

"Having done this amount of mischief, Jacko ran nimbly down to the fore-top gallant mast-head, thence down the rigging to the fore-top, when, leaping on the fore-yard, it ran out to the yard-arm, and there began capering about, chattering, screeching, and making the most hideous noises.

"The young middy was completely tired out with chasing Jacko, to save the child; but, unwilling to return to the deck while the child was in such unearthly danger, he took deliberate aim at the ape, and shot it in the head.

"The infuriated monster was only wounded, but with a scream it rushed at the brave middy, and there, in the rigging, took place one of the most awful fights man ever witnessed !

"The excitement on board was now something awful and intense.

"Every moment it was thought that the gallant lad would be killed or crushed to death by the infuriated monster.

"Men on all sides rushed to his assistance.

"But before they climbed half-way up, the gallant middy stabbed the ape and ran it through and through with his sword.

WILDFIRE NED'S ATTACK ON THE SKELETON CREW.—See Next Number.

No. 14.

" Dark gore stained the snow-white decks.

" The next moment, with a loud scream, Jacko fell a lifeless, mangled mass upon the deck.

" Loud shouts recognised the middy's victory.

" But his most dangerous task was yet before him.

" None of us expected he had the strength to reach the main truck and rescue the child, but while I turned my head in sickened horror, I was suddenly startled by a cry from Black Jake—

" ' Oh ! massa, massa ! Massa Ned, the middy, is on de main truck ! '

" A cold shudder ran through my veins as the words reached me.

" I cast my eyes upwards to the dizzy height.

" It was too true.

" There, up aloft, and looking like a speck, the gallant lad climbed and held on to the main truck.

" There was nothing above nor around him but the empty air.

" But still he climbed.

" One moment more, and he has saved the child !

" A loud cheer greets him as he unties the little thing, and he waves his cap.

" But why doesn't he come down with the baby ?

" He cannot !

" He is too weak to attempt it !

" What must he do ?

" He climbs on to the top of the main truck.

" He sits on the round piece of wood, which, from the deck, looks no bigger than a button.

" Dreadful daring !

" If he should attempt to stoop, he has nothing to take hold on.

" Nothing was within reach beneath him but a long, smooth, naked spar, which even then bent with his weight.

" Any attempt to get down with the child would be almost certain death.

" He would lose his balance and be dashed to pieces !

" Such was the nature of the thoughts of every-one on board, as they gazed at the adventurous youth up aloft.

" The parents of the child were now almost frantic.

" They had to be led into the cabin, for they were well-nigh crazed with fear.

" What was to be done ?

" No one dared to go up after him, for the spar even now bent under his weight.

" I looked up, and half thought I could see the brave lad's limbs tremble and his cheeks all red with excitement.

" Each second I thought would be his last.

" I could not bear to look at him, and yet could not withdraw my gaze.

" I myself had the sensation of one about to fall from a great height.

" Making a strong effort to recover myself, like a dreamer who fancies he is shoved from a precipice, I staggered up against the bulwarks.

" When my eyes turned from the dizzy height to which they had been riveted, sense and conscious-ness came back.

" I looked around : the deck was crowded with every man and boy in the ship.

" All the officers had now heard of the young midshipman, and hurried from their berths below to witness the appalling sight.

" Every one, as he looked up and beheld the peril-ous, hopeless condition of the gallant midshipman child, turned pale.

" Once a lieutenant seized a trumpet, as if to hail the middy up in the clouds, but, he had scarcely raised it to his lips, when his arm dropped again,

and sank beside him, as if from sad consciousness of the perfect uselessness of what he had been going to say.

" Every eye was now turned upward.

" All was dead silence.

" ' What is he doing ?' said one.

" ' He is tying the child firmly on his back.'

" ' He is strapping it tightly with his belt.'

" ' Well done.'

" ' Gallant lad.'

" ' See how he rocks.'

" ' What will he do next ?'

" ' Death is certain for both, or it is a miracle.'

" Thus whispered one to another, as they watched the brave youth now more intently than ever.

" At this moment there was a stir among the crew about the decks.

" Directly after another face was added to those on the quarter-deck, it was that of the infant's father, the appalled commodore.

" He had come from the cabin in great haste, and without having been noticed by a single one of the crew, so intense and universal was the interest that had fastened every gaze upon the spot where the intrepid Ned now stood, trembling on the awful verge of fate !

" The commodore was a dark, austere man ; and it was thought by some of the midshipmen that he entertained but little affection for the gallant Ned.

" However that might have been, it was certain he treated him with precisely the same courtesy and discipline that he would any other of the young officers.

" If there was any difference at all, it was not the least in favour of Ned, for young Warbeck, if any-thing, was ' too fast.'

" Some who studied his character closely, affirmed that he admired young Ned as he might have done his own son, but not too well to spoil him.  For Ned intending himself for the arduous profession in which the commodore had himself risen to fame and eminence, the old sailor thought it would be of ser-vice to him to experience some of its privations and hardships at the very outset.

" The arrival of the commodore upon the scene now changed the direction of several eyes, which now turned on him to trace what emotions the danger of his infant son would occasion.

" But there scrutiny was foiled.

" By no outward sign did he show what passed within.

" Immediately on reaching the deck, he had ordered a marine to hand him a musket.

" With this, stepping aft, and getting on the look-out block, he raised it to his shoulder, and took a deliberate aim at his infant son and Ned, at the same time hailing him without a trumpet, in a voice of thunder.

" ' Ned,' cried he, ' jump ! jump overboard ! or I'll fire at you !'

" The gallant lad did not hear what was said, and seemed to hesitate !

" It was plain that he was tottering from intense weakness, for his arms were thrown out like one scarcely able to retain his balance.

" The old commodore raised his voice again, and, in a quicker and more emphatic tone, cried out,

" ' Jump ! 'tis your only chance for life !'

" The words were scarcely out of his mouth before the gallant boy seemed to leave the truck and spring out into the air !

" A sound between a shriek and a groan burst from many lips.

" The father spoke not—sighed not.

" Indeed he did not seem to breathe.

" With a rush like that of a cannon-ball, the middy and his precious burden descended to the water.

" Before the waves closed over them, twenty stout fellows, among them several officers, had dived from the bulwarks.

" Another short period of bitter suspense ensued.

" He rose.

" He was alive !

" His arms are seen to move !

" He struck out towards the ship !

" And despite of the discipline of a man-of-war three loud huzzas, an outburst of unfeigned and unrestrainable joy from the hearts of our numerous crew, pealed through the air and made the welkin ring.

" Till this moment the old commodore stood un-moved.

" The gallant middy and the child were safe !

" The eyes that, glistening with pleasure, now sought his face, saw that it was ashy pale.

" He attemped to descend the horse-block, but his knees bent under him.

" He seemed to gasp for breath, and put up his hand, as if to tear open his vest, but, before he could accomplish his object, he staggered forward, and would have fallen on deck had he not been caught by old Black Jake.

" He was borne into his cabin, where the surgeon attended him, whose utmost skill was required to restore his mind to its usual equability and self-command, in which he at last happily succeeded.

" As soon as he had recovered from the dreadful shock, he sent for the gallant Ned and had a long confidential chat, but so overpowered was he, that he could only grasp Ned's hand, as he said in a faint voice,

" ' Heaven bless you, my lad ; you have proved yourself a hero, and worthy of the profession you have chosen. I shall write to the Admiralty directly and inform them of your grand feat, and I have no doubt promotion will attend it. At all events, Ned, accept my heartfelt thanks.

" ' You have made an old man happy and young again ' "

 *  *  *  *  *

" A most gallant deed," said the old dame.

" Yes, worthy of the Spartans," chuckled Sir Andrew.

" You said the name of the ship was—"

" The ' Diamond.' "

" Why, that was the vessel in which young Warbeck sailed with Lieutenant Garnet."

" I know it was," said the stranger. " She has had a most successful cruise against the Skeleton Crew and the smugglers, and chief among those who distinguished themselves, both afloat and ashore, was the same gallant young middy I have been speaking to you about."

" He must be an heroic boy, whoever he is, and he is called Ned, too, eh ?"

" We used to call him Wildfire Ned," said the stranger, laughing; " he is a lieutenant now, and on his way to London."

" It *must* be Ned Warbeck, then," said several.

" It was none other," said the stranger, laughing ; " and I commanded the ship ; my name is—

" Captain, late Lieutenant, Garnet."

---

## CHAPTER XXXIII.
### THE DISCOVERY OF FAMILY PAPERS BY WILDFIRE NED.

THE first thing which Ned did, when he arrived in London, was to report himself at the Admiralty, where many old naval officers of great reputation met and congratulated him on the great success which had attended him and Lieutenant Garnet in fighting against the Skeleton Crew.

Honours were showered on him everywhere he went.

Yet he was not happy.

He had neither father nor mother, nor any single relation in the world.

Sir Richard Warbeck he knew, and felt in his heart, was only a friend to him, and not an uncle.

Who was he, then ?

" Am I lowly or highly born ?" he thought.

He felt that he must have sprung from a superior stock.

Yes; but how ?

Was he entitled to any great estates in his own right ?

He felt that there was some dark, deep mystery hanging over him.

He would have given the whole world to unravel it.

But he could not.

Sir Richard's manner had always been very kind, good, and fatherly.

But still with all that it was strange.

His manner, it might be said, was like that of a man who knew some grand secret, and yet would not reveal it !

" When King Charles the First was beheaded," Ned thought, " the Cromwellians drove many rich and powerful nobles from the land, and confiscated all their great estates.

" Suppose that my father was one of these !

" He might have been a noble ! Who knows ?" thought Ned ; and as this conviction flashed across his mind, he resolved to let no chance pass by in order to find it out.

" Who was my father ?" Ned had often asked of Sir Richard.

The old man smiled, but answered not.

The more he repeated this question and was put off, the more he resolved to find out the grand secret.

All he could find out was this:—

" I do not wonder that you and Phillip Redgill can never agree," old Sir Richard would say ; " for your families have always been at daggers' points for centuries."

" Indeed !" Ned would say, " how ?"

" How I cannot explain yet," was the invariable answer. " When you are twenty-one years old, you may know more ; but this much I will tell you, Ned, that old Redgill, Phillip's father, hated your father much worse than you do Phillip."

" How I cannot explain !" repeated Ned often, when in the cosy library at Darlington Hall, conversing with the old knight in long winter evenings.

" How ! Why, tell me all."

" You are too young yet ; one day you will find out all if you live to be old enough !"

" If I only live to be old enough," thought Ned " often and often those words sound ominously; but if I am spared I'll find it out before I am twenty-one years old. I am man enough now for anything, and if any wretch still lives who has acted the traitor towards my father, let him tremble.

" There has always been bad blood between the Redgills and my father's family, eh ! so the old knight says; then my name is not—it cannot be Warbeck !"

Wildfire Ned was almost driven mad at the thought of this grand family secret.

" Why do they conceal my real name ? Who knows, I might be the son of some lord !"

With these thoughts ringing in his head Ned Warbeck directed his footsteps to the town house of the old knight, which was situated in Mayfair.

The servants rejoiced at his return, but Ned was moody.

Sir Richard was out, but where he had gone to no one could tell.

He heard the news about his brother Charley, and of Redgill's villany, and he swore like a true tar thereat.

He paced the library up and down, and cast his eyes first to one old dusty book-shelf and then to another, but he did not care to remain in the place; it was so cold and comfortless.

"I always thought that this old library was haunted," thought Ned, "and I never liked it."

He was about to leave when his foot struck against something in the floor.

To his amazement one of the boards of the flooring sprung up.

He had trod upon a secret spring !

To his still greater astonishment he discovered a small old oak chest.

It was bound with clasps and bolts of brass.

It had six padlocks on it.

"This is some hidden treasure," thought Ned.

He pulled out the small chest, and, after locking himself in, began to prize open the chest.

With much perseverance and labour he succeeded at last in breaking it open.

It contained nothing but a packet of musty, dusty papers.

"What can this mean ?" thought Ned.

He eagerly seized the bundle, and on the outside read,

"Family papers ; not to be opened until the death of Sir Richard Warbeck. They then belong to the heirs of the celebrated Sir Edward Lancaster, who was banished from the kingdom by Cromwell. The enclosed is a short sketch of his rise and fall in the state, and of the origin of the Skeleton Band ; how, and when, and where it was formed. Some of the names mentioned are not the right ones. The key to the proper names can be found elsewhere on the death of Sir Richard Warbeck."

"Strange !" thought Ned ; "why, what mystery is here ? Some grand family secret. It may be useful for Charley and myself to know this.

"Sir Edward Lancaster," sighed Ned ; "I have heard of him. But surely that is not my name ? I wonder if any mystery hung over my father's early career, like my own ?"

In great mental excitement he locked and barred the old library doors, tore open the packet, and read, with a trembling hand,—

A STATE SECRET. THE KING'S BASTARD.

"The evening sun was flashing in the west, shedding streams of many-coloured glory on the forests and plains surrounding one of England's fairest villages, and the red brick walls and tower of a quadrangularly built military college threw a deep black shade on the grassy sward and gigantic trees, through which grand walks and carriage drives intersected and united at the heavy iron gates.

"Equestrians galloping along the dusty roads would wheel and halt, or form their position on the hill, gazing intently towards the quiet college grounds.

"But as the gates were yet closed, they resumed their riding, chatting in twos and threes, seemingly impatient for the evening bell to toll.

"One of the boldest and most fearless of the equestrians turned her head frequently to the silent distant tower, and spurring her noble animal into a sweeping gallop, dashed past the sombre gates at headlong speed, her face aglow with the ruddiness of health, and her auburn tresses flowing in girlish negligence upon her shoulders.

"The porter at the college gates, with grey hair and stooping gait, slowly unlocked the ponderous portals with solemn movement, and as he furtively looked at the fearless girl, with whip on high, galloping through the dust at break-neck speed, he devoutly prayed for her safety.

"Despite the pious porter's fears, Lady Emma Bray rode along the road, turned up the forest carriage drive of an elegant neighbouring hall, and without stopping, leaped the gate, to the great astonishment of several rustics at the plough, and suddenly halted before the door.

"Throwing the reins carelessly over a gate-post, she tucked up her dark-green riding habit, and laughingly tripping along the grassy sward, advanced towards a grey-haired old gentleman, who, with coat unbuttoned and slouched hat on head, sat under a peach tree, with his legs resting against the trunk, reading and puffing a clay pipe.

"'Wake up, colonel !' she said, laughing, lightly touching him across the shoulder with her riding-whip. 'I'm come to see Clare. I want her to go with me to the parade. What say you, uncle ?—will you escort us ?'

"Before he could reply, Lady Emma kissed him, and passed into the house singing ; and going into the parlour, sat down to the harp, and dashed off 'Long live the King,' with great gusto.

"'Where's Clare ?' she asked of a maid—'Gone to church ! Bother ! disappointed again. Why, Clare's always at church. Heigho !'

"She flung the music aside, and sat tapping her boots with the whip, while rocking and rolling in an arm-chair, which was in perfect keeping with the costly and elegant rosewood and blue with which the apartment was furnished.

"Lady Bray was re-adjusting her brown gauntlets, and about to depart, when Colonel Temple sauntered into the room with a hound at his heels, which immediately began to caress the young lady.

"'A penny for your thoughts, lady,' said he, laughing. 'There, don't look so cross, pet, or I shall imagine we are not friends.'

"'I'm not cross, uncle ; but you know it is so provoking to be disappointed.'

"'Well, well, pet, cheer up ! When the college breaks up for the season, we'll have plenty of fishing and hunting, and picnics without end. I didn't know that Clare was out until you inquired—gone visiting some poor folks, I suppose, as usual. At church ! Well, well, what a girl she is. She'll soon be back again.'

"'No, I'm sure she won't, uncle, if she's gone to church, for she's the greatest girl for praying I ever saw.'

"'I know it's all very admirable in one's character,' said young Lady Emma, moving about the apartment, and arranging her disordered hair in the mirror ; 'but I could not kneel so long as Clare does—no, not for all the world. Come, uncle, you mustn't laugh and go away in that manner ; I want you to escort me to the parade this evening. I'm sure you'll not refuse—besides, we shall be sure to meet Clare. I'll go into the cathedral and fetch her, if we don't meet her on the way. I know where to find her ; in a snug little pew, shut out from all observation.'

"As blue-eyed, oval-faced Emma, with her radiant

looks and careless manner, took the old colonel's arm, and proceeded, with laugh and joke, through the forest-path towards the small town lying in the valley, they soon came to the cathedral, and the colonel stopped.

"The great door being slightly ajar, Emma stepped lightly in, and its quiet calm and beauty arrested her hurried, impetuous gait.

"Evening service was over.

"The sinking sun shed its rays through stained-glass windows, and streams of blue, white, orange, purple, and pink fell in varied beauty upon its doric columns and tiled floors.

"The slightest sound was audible, and as the boughs of chestnut trees swayed against the windows, and the birds warbled their even-song, each rustle and note echoed through the edifice.

"Emma slowly closed the creaking door, and, stealthily stealing forwards, discovered Clare, whose pale face and dark eyes were raised in deep meditation.

"A touch and gesture were all that passed, and Clare rose slowly and left the place with noiseless step.

"'Not go to the grand military parade, child?' asked the colonel, when Miss Clare had joined them. 'You used to be amazingly fond of such things a few months ago. Come, Clare, Lady Emma has been waiting for you ever so long.'

"Lady Emma looked inquiringly into Clare's face, as they walked side by side, and seemed grave and vexed.

"'Well, then, cousin, as you are indisposed, the colonel, I know, will excuse you. I shall call about seven, and spend the evening with you.'

"Lady Emma and the colonel walked on in silence, until the latter remarked,

"'She's the only one left to me now. Sons and daughters have gone from home—some are in the clay, others are married. My whole life and soul are centred in her, Lady Emma, and it grieves me to see her looking so thoughtful of late. I wish she was as gay a romp as you.'

"Lady Emma did not speak, but seemed deep in thought until they reached the college parade-grounds, where numbers of gay visitors, broken up into small groups, gave variety and animation to the scene.

"Lady Bray was soon recognised by acquaintances, who laughed and chatted round the white-haired colonel as if they were all his children.

"The bell tolled the hour, and soon there issued from the various wings crowds of military students, tired with the lectures of the day.

"The drums beat, the band assembles, and soon there come upon the ground hundreds of students in gay uniforms, who, with sword and musket, fell in, and immediately go through a series of battalion movements, in quick and double time.

"The precision of step and erect soldierly bearing of the collegians elicited applause; and as platoons filed past and wheeled into line, broke into columns of company, and marched in quick or double time, the glittering of the bayonets, the waving of banners, and harmonious strains of the band, was a spectacle that called forth the applause of all present.

"So that when the whole line advanced, halted, and presented arms to numbers of the fair sex screened under the colonnade of trees, enthusiasm reached its height; and the drill and parade passed off with much éclat.

"As soon as the troops marched out of the quadrangle to the armoury at the rear, the visitors slowly dispersed.

"Many of the students obtained a few hours' leave, so that when all dispersed to their residences in town or in the outskirts, there were but few ladies unaccompanied by relations or friends in uniform.

"Colonel Temple and Lady Bray were the object of much attention; and as the old hero was an especial favorite with all, he insisted upon taking some half dozen or more of the young ladies to his house to supper.

"Each lady was gallanted, so that as the white-headed old soldier went along the forest walk, he looked more like a patriarch leading forth his children's children, than a gay-hearted, brave colonel of dragoons.

"'Here we are, girls,' said the colonel, opening the gate and admitting his young friends, 'here we are, young gentlemen, make the place your own as much as you like, only don't hurt my conservatory, else Clare will never forgive you.'

"'Now, then, Nance,' shouted he, calling to the housemaid.

"'Now, then, Dick, bestir yourselves; tell Miss Clare there's troops of friends come to see her; make supper ready quick as possible; and one of you go down to town and bring up a band to play for us. I know the girls 'll like a dance.'

"While the good old man was thus bustling about, frightening the big cook and the butler with a multitude of orders, pale-faced Clare came forth to welcome her many friends; and from the fondness of caresses bestowed upon her by the females, and the hearty gallant behaviour of the gentlemen, her manner became embarrassed.

"Her hair fell loose from continual hand-shaking, and her face was all radiant with blushes.

"'I'm really glad to see you all; this is *quite* a surprise. Come in Mollie. How do, Lizzie? Ah! Josephine, dear. Come in, gentlemen,' said Clare bustling about. 'I'm so glad you've come.'

"And while she bustled about, giving orders to various servants, Lady Bray helped her to do the honors of the house (for the colonel was a widower), and made every one at home.

"Music was the order of the evening, and ere long, harps, flutes, violins, and voices were good-humoredly engaged in quartetts and chorusses.

"The colonel was in his element.

"He was here, there, and everywhere; ordering this, and arranging that, for the evening dance.

"His anxiety was so great to please the young people, and he seemed so flurried with his preparations, that he was red and perspiring, while two or three 'merry imps' of young girls, were following him about, doing their utmost to confuse or amuse him.

"The large and small drawing-rooms were thrown into one; numberless wax tapers were arranged in groups, with vases of newly plucked flowers, and all bade fair for a pleasant party, in which English youth so much delight.

"Cook, with some half dozen assistants, was squabbling over her numerous pots and pans.

First one dish was upset, and then another, until the whole culinary department seemed in a state of haste, noise, bustle and confusion.

"As soon as it became known that the band was going to Colonel Temple's house half-a-dozen or more couples of both sexes hurried thither uninvited, for the colonel's friends never waited for invitations in those good old times, and kept dropping in until the fine old gentleman sat under the verandah laughing and smoking his pipe in a state of bliss.

"Supper had long been over, and here and there along the garden walks couples strolled, laughing in the moonlight, while the sounds of music were issuing from the drawing-room, at the windows of which, opening on the lawn, stood here and there, one or two, enjoying the cooling breeze of the lovely summer night.

"All was gaiety and pleasure; servants were flying hither and thither with trays, decanters, and every sort of refreshment, and more than one rogue of a servant hid behind some door to pay his respects to a half-emptied bottle of wine.

"Clare, with noiseless step and busy air, was studying the comforts of her friends and companions, while Lady Bray, all animation and gaiety, was the life and soul of the party.

"Clare was beloved by all for her gentleness and exalted virtues, while Lady Bray was admired for dashing manners and beauty of feature.

"The lady guests would cluster round Clare, and kiss and toy with her as if she was their sister, while gentlemen took pleasure in courting the company of Lady Emma, who, perfectly conscious of her charms, was pleasantly teazing them with coquetry and wit.

"There was one other of the party, however, who treated the attentions of all with indifference. She moved hither and thither, pre-occupied in thought, and at last sought the verandah, where her father, Lord Cavendish, was smoking with the colonel and other old people, discussing politics.

"Taking a foot-stool she sat between the colonel and her father, resting her head on the former's knee, looking at the cloudless sky.

Josephine Cavendish was the great favorite of Clare and Lady Emma, but somewhat younger than either.

"She was timid in strange company, and, except when seated at her harp, studying alone, was perfectly out of place. She was, in truth, a child-like contemplative, who blushed at the rustle of her own dress.

"Hour passed hour, and so the party continued, and stragglers dropped in one by one, until, by eleven o'clock, the rooms were filled with dancers, card players, and persons promenading up and down the wide verandahs, vine walks, orchard shades, or the long stone passages of the house.

"It seemed a family gathering.

"Every one knew every one; no introductions were necessary; all were at home, and everything proceeded harmoniously and pleasantly.

"The lights of the village had long flickered and died.

"The college chimes tolled the hour of midnight; the broad landscape of field and forest lay bathed in moonlight, and one by one the visitors dispersed.

"Some on horse, others on foot, and more in broughams and carriages—all had disappeared down the carriage drive into the forest path, and the receding sounds of their gaiety and ringing laughter fell faintly on the ear.

"The household had long retired to rest.

"All was still.

"Clare alone was awake.

"By her open chamber window the pale-faced girl sat, gazing abroad upon the silvery landscape, deep in thought.

"Boughs of lofty chesnut-trees, swaying in the breeze, swept against the house.

"Perfume from gardens and orchards filled the air.

"Time passed slowly on; troubled with thoughts and misgivings that cankered her heart, she wept.

"Rousing from melancholy lethargy, she rose, and in part disrobed, as she gazed in the mirror upon her pale and thoughtful face, half concealed by heavy masses of raven tresses, loose about her shoulders. In dishabille as she was, she sat beside her snow-white bed.

"She rose, and, deep in thought, with dishevelled hair and flowing garments, clasped her hands and moved her lips, as she gazed on the dark and lofty towers of the distant college.

"How long she sat communing thus alone, or the nature of her thoughts, none can know.

"But as the moon was dipping beyond the trees, her door noiselessly opened, and closed again, and there flitted across the floor towards her a figure in white. It was Lady Bray.

"'A thousand pardons, dear Clare!' she said, embracing her. 'I could not sleep—you seem so changed of late, I fear you are unwell, and wish to conceal it from both your father and me! Oh, Clare, if you only knew how much I love you—how your father idolizes, and every one doats upon you—I'm sure you would be more happy.' (No response). 'Come, Clare, my dear, dear cousin, tell me what it is. There is nothing in the world that is too good for you; all that wealth and affection can do is already yours, and yet you, to whom the best and wealthiest have bowed and begged—you, my cousin, who are the idol of all—you who should be the happiest of all—you, dear Clare, seem unhappy—sorrow is gnawing at your heart; make me your confidante, darling, tell me all!'

"Clare spoke not, but smiling at the downcast eyes of her cousin, kissed her on the forehead, and soon retired to rest.

"'Tell me nothing!' thought Lady Emma, when in her own room, pondering; 'yet it *cannot* be; but if it *should* be so—oh, poor, poor Clare! Heaven forgive me. I would not thwart you, my cousin, for all the world.'

"Lady Emma remained long awake, revolving all manner of schemes to enliven her cousin, but the same expression came repeatedly to her lips, 'If it should be! Poor cousin, poor Clare!'

"And even *her* strong nature bent under some secret mental weight, and tear-drops flowed freely upon her weary pillow.

"The dark and lofty college tower visited Clare in dreams.

"She once more strolled through its grand quadrangle, and saw the students march, with band and banner.

"She walked in its vineyards and orchards, amid fruit and flowers.

"And then her footsteps strayed into a grassy court, with fountains rising and falling, and splashing in the quiet of a summer afternoon, and there saw, sitting at his window, a handsome, book-worn youth, with desk and pen, absorbed in study.

"A faint smile for an instant lit up her marble features, and she sighed.

"Her lips murmured inarticulate sounds, and she moved restlessly, unconsciously throwing the spotless covering from her heaving bosom, on which reposed a tiny gem of jet, resting as if set in alabaster.

"But, while thus wrapt in sleep, there was an unhappy and restless one pacing, with measured step, in his lonely college chambers, whose mind was tossed with pain and constant thought.

"He had passed all examinations with honour, and now only awaited his degree to go forth into the world to strive for wealth and fame.

"His room was small, and scantily furnished.

"No signs of luxury were there.

"Books and papers lay scattered about; a small study lamp shed its light upon a worm-eaten desk; an old oak chest stood open in the corner.

"A violin, pistols, belt, and sword hung from a rack in the wall.

"Pipes, and slippers, and papers were everywhere; and even as he paced the room, noiselessly and long, he puffed his pipe, and looked forth into the courtyard beneath, where nought was heard but the cool and mossy spray-splashing fountains, sparkling in the moonlight, and throwing up jets of diamond and ruby-like spray.

"'And now,' he thought, 'the present is the most momentous moment of my life! How I have longed for it through long and tedious years of mental drudgery and toil! And yet, now I go forth to the world fatherless, friendless, and moneyless. I begin the battle of life alone!'"

"Why, that is my case exactly," said Ned, thoughtfully, as he read on. "I wonder who this chap turns out to be? Surely not my father! If so, I have gone through all that sort of thing exactly as he did."

He turned over a leaf of the manuscript, and read on :—

"He thought of the long distant time when, as a boy, he played and rolled on the grass plats, forgetful of books and lessons—of scaling the walls, and rambling in the forests.

"Yet year followed year, and he ripened into youth, and passed the collegiate course, a credit to his tutors and himself.

"Fatherless and motherless he knew he was.

"But who had fed and clothed and educated him, were questions he could not answer.

"He never wanted for aught that a gentleman required, yet he felt a pang of pride to think he might be a 'charity student,' for in answer to all inquiries the grey-haired President always smiled, took his arm, and said,

"'Edward, ask no questions—at least not yet; finish your studies as creditably as you have begun—ask for anything you require—know that you are a gentleman by birth, and *not* a subject of charity, and when you have obtained your degree, put as many questions as you wish. They shall all be fitly answered, and to your satisfaction.'"

"Why, this is my case to a dot," said Ned, as he still read on.

"Commencement day at the college was always a grand affair, and its many attractions were such, that not only parents and friends, but strangers from all parts flocked thither to hear the orations, inspect the prizes, and see the troops reviewed.

"Such were the crowds that always came on that occasion, that hotels were crammed, and the college theatre was far too small, so that the exercises were always held in the open air.

"The whole of the quadrangle was decorated with flags and banners, and tiers of raised seats, sheltered from the sun by awnings, while in the centre arose the stage, formed like a Grecian temple, with columns of imitation marble, on which, in a semi-circle, the faculty sat in solemn state to confer degrees, while round about the cadets formed a guard of honour, with bands and flags, and brilliant uniforms. Graduates, one by one, had delivered their orations amid great applause.

"Gold and silver medals were bestowed for conduct, excellence, and diligence, while richly engrossed diplomas with triple seals were handed to the military graduates amid deafening cheers.

"Then followed a grand review, with its marching, counter-marching, volley-firing, smoke, dust, and noise.

"After which a grand banquet took place in the college theatre, at which two thousand or more assisted.

"With its frescoed walls hung with tapestry and banners, the banquetting scene was imposing; the Faculty, with invited guests, sat at the head of the long tables on a raised dais, while to the right hand and to the left were lords, ladies, divines, officers, lawyers, farmers, and others, who had sons in the college.

"Toast followed toast, and speech succeeded speech, bottles popped, and glasses clinked in good fellowship and humour, while jest and joke and laughter almost drowned the music of the band, which in a side gallery discoursed very sweet music during the repast.

"Lawrence left the table early, and retired to his room to write a letter, and make arrangements for his departure, and as he stood reflectively before the mirror, in a dark blue uniform faced with red and gold, with sword by his side, and French cap jauntily placed, he looked fresh and gay in the prime and vigour of youth.

"He gazed about him at the confusion of his room, and smiled.

"His books and papers and numberless effects were untouched, and Livy, Sophocles, Blair, Danté, works on fortifications, tactics, &c., lay strewn over his desk just as he had flung them days before, when he had emerged triumphant from his final examination amid the shouts of his fellows.

"Nothing had been touched, and as he looked at the dusty aspect of everything, with a cat in the window sill blinking in the sunlight, the silence of the quadrangle was only broken by the distant noise and cheers issuing from the banquet hall.

"A dainty note lay on his desk, which read,—

"'The Willows, July, 4 P.M.

"'EDWARD LAWRENCE, ESQ., M.A.

"'SIR,—Uncle desires the pleasure of your company this evening to meet some mutual friends, and trusts that the fatigues of the day will not prevent you gratifying his wish.

"'Your friend,

"'EMMA BRAY.

"'P.S.—I forgot to add that Cousin Clare is unwell. She went to the 'Commencement' this morning, and heard your oration, and was much pleased, as indeed all of us were. The heat and dust, however, were too much for her, and she was obliged to return home. Call early in the afternoon if you can, for we are all excessively dull and moping.'"

"'Colonel Henry wishes to see you, Mr. Lawrence,' said a messenger, entering the room, 'he is walking on the vine terrace.'

"'Ah, Edward,' said the President, shaking the young man heartily by the hand, 'allow me to congratulate you upon your really excellent graduating speech.

"'But this is not the subject of which I wished to speak; it is of yourself. For the last ten years past, with us within these walls, you have been lectured enough, daily and hourly, hence I shall not inflict an oration upon you to-day, which is the most important of your life.

"'There is much in genius, but there is more in courageous industry.

"'You have done yourself credit while with us, and I doubt not your general conduct through life will be the same as that which has characterised you as a student.

"'Of your worldly prospects I know but little.

"'At twelve years you were placed in our hands by Lord Somers, who claims to be your uncle, with these words, 'This boy; I leave with you to be educated for the King's army; every cost will be defrayed by me. If he acquits himself with honour I will own him, if otherwise he shall never know me

In every instance, let him be taught to depend upon himself; for he has no expectations other than those he may, perhaps, derive from me."

" 'It seems very unnatural that an uncle should never have seen you for so long,' continued the president, 'if he *is* your uncle, but he never let you want for anything, which speaks well. As to his injunction about us teaching you to depend upon yourself, without having dreams of wealth, &c., I fully indorse; for it is my experience that those who look forward to, or are sure of inheriting riches, make very indifferent students. It is the poor lad, who has little or nought to expect, who sheds honour on his college in after life, for, having nothing but his own energy and talent to depend upon, he developes both at school, and the habits of industry and self reliance thus generally attained increase with age, and brings success as its necessary and natural reward.'

"Lawrence, with sword jingling by his side, took a field path to the 'Willows,' and as he gaily strode along, puffing a cigar, soon struck through the woods, and came within sight of the house, *from which a horseman had just then departed by another road.*

"Colonel Temple met him at the door, and heartily shook him by the hand, 'Allow me to congratulate you, my boy; you have got through it at last, with honour, and no one feels more pleasure than myself, for you have striven nobly for it.'

" 'I received your note, colonel, and ——'

" 'My note?'

" 'Yes, uncle,' said Lady Bray, opening the long window, and stepping on to the verandah, laughing, '*your* note, I wrote it; don't you remember? You don't? Well, then, I wrote it on my own responsibility. I knew what a favourite you were with uncle, and as he had no company, I thought I would entice you up to the house to enliven him.'

" 'Oh, you rogue. I ——'

" 'And as you were so naughty, Mr. Lawrence, as not to come and see us the other night when the other graduates came, I thought we must have offended you, and so wished to learn all about it before you left college. We all heard your speech this morning, didn't we, uncle? Oh, such a fine one—long sentences and big words. Oh, I couldn't comprehend it all; and then Clare was unwell, and I was dull, and I didn't know what to do, so as we have known you for years, and you have been such a bad, bad boy as not to come and see us for ever so long, I thought I'd ask you to call in uncle's name, so that's all; and now uncle 'll forgive me, and give me a kiss, I know he will,' and the dashing Lady Emma, merry as ever, threw her arms around the old colonel, and went back to the parlour singing and laughing.

" 'Oh, that's a funny rogue, Lawrence.'

"Lawrence met Clare in the entrance-hall, and although her hand shook perceptibly in his, a blush tinged her cheek as she bade him welcome, and opened the drawing-room door.

" 'Now, sir truant,' began Emma, in mock heroics; 'deliver up your arms. Let me unbuckle your sword, sir knight—that's it. I'm sure you don't want it clanking at your heels while with us. Now, Edward Lawrence, Esq., M.A., you are at our mercy; and if you don't ask pardon for your long absence, and promise to be a better boy for the future, prepare for the block,' she continued, flourishing the sword with both hands. 'Clare shall be the parson, and I the executioner! You will be better, eh? Then this time you are safe.'

" 'I was extremely sorry to hear of your indisposition, Clare,' remarked Lawrence, with the air of one very intimately and long acquainted. 'Even now you look fretted and thoughtful.'

" 'Do I? how complimentary! I will reverse it by saying that you appear remarkably well, Edward, if a ferocious captain of cadets, and a profound Master of Arts will allow me to call him by familiar names.'

" 'Oh, bless you, cousin, we must not be so familiar now, you know. No more blind man's buff, and kiss-in-the-ring, as we used to. He's suddenly become very grand; just consider being created a Master of Arts and a captain, all in one day. Dear me, ain't we very grand!'

" 'Come, come, girls,' remarked the colonel, entering the room and seating himself on the sofa; 'don't badger the captain; two to one is not the thing—fair play! You'll be a graduate yourself next year, and——'

" 'Oh, won't that be fine! In white satin, and crowns of flowers, and all that!—Oh, how I envied Clare last year; she looked so pretty that——'

" 'Cousin, cousin,' broke in Clare, blushing and hanging down her head, 'really I never heard such non——'

" 'I dare say you haven't, but you did look nice, everybody said so, the ladies said so, for I heard 'em, and the gentlemen too; one said 'oh how pale; another 'what a sweet voice' and a third, whose initials are E, L, said 'how modest!'

"While they were engaged in music, Clare retired to superintend some domestic duty, and the colonel falling asleep, Emma and Lawrence were left alone, and proceeding towards the windows looking into the gardens, she stood nervously pulling the curtains and thus began, rather seriously:—

" 'You must not joke Clare to-day, Lawrence. *I* heard you, if I *was* making a noise at the piano. She was not well this morning. She has had unpleasant visitors, and it surprises me she is half so gay as she is. I don't know what it is, but I think it was an old beau that displeased her; he insisted upon escorting her home, and after he went away she seemed very much vexed and annoyed.'

" 'That is easily accounted for: perhaps she is partial to him, and it is but natural she should feel annoyed at his hurried departure.'

" 'Nonsence, Edward; you *know* she has no such liking, or I should have discovered it long ago. It was a Captain Redgill, one of your old students, living now in Birmingham; you must know him well, and judging from his looks at parting, I'm sure his visit could not have proved very satisfactory or pleasant. What makes you look so solemn?'

"Lawrence *did* remember Redgill; he had occasion for never forgetting him, and remembering the past, he blushed scarlet.

" 'Nothing, Lady Bray. I was only thinking of a presentiment that has disturbed me all the morning, and which continually recurs, that *some mischief will befal me ere midnight.*'

# THE SKELETON CREW; OR, WILDFIRE NED.

THE MURDER IN THE WOOD.—*See Number* 17.

"'What mischief *can* befal you here ? Oh ! how silly, Edward ; if I had made such a speech, you'd have laughed at me. Why, even good cousin, with her wonderful ghost stories, would smile at you talking of 'presentiments.'

"'Still, such is the fact, Lady Bray, and, if it must be confessed, I am very much depressed at moments.'

"'Oh, what a fine fellow to be a captain of cadets ! Why, if I were a man, I'd fear nothing. Oh, Clare, do come here ; here's Lawrence discoursing of presentiments, and is certain that something very horrible is about to happen to him !'

"'Well, think as you may, cousin,' said Clare, 'I myself rose with forebodings of coming unpleasantness this morning ; and it has come strictly true.'

"'Forebodings, Clare ! Well, I know that a gentleman called to day. I hope it was *that*. It couldn't have been so very unpleasant, judging from his animated appearance when escorting you home ; but both of you appear to agree so well upon the subject of presentiments, I shall stroll in the garden and allow you to discuss its merits at full.'

"'But, how extraordinary it is,' said Clare, 'that so many great events should have befallen you on one day. To think, that after so many years, you should have discovered your relations ; that on

the same day you should have graduated and resolved to change your residence.'

"'But if I go, I shall still be near all my friends,' replied Lawrence, 'for you always go to France for the winter months.'

"'True, but I can assure you it is greatly against my will ; there is too much gaiety there, and as father has extensive acquaintance and relations, it throws me into much bustle and distraction I would willingly avoid. I love quietness and rusticity.'

"'You were always timid, Clare. I have known you long now, and think you are unnecessarily so ; you are the only one at home now ; your father doats upon you, and, with all due respect, let me add, there are few who are greater favouites with all, or who has had so many in supplication at your feet.'

"'You flatter me. I have never given any one reason to think that I ever encouraged their addresses, but, on the contrary, have ever taken the earliest opportunity to dispossess them of any such idea, when it became apparent. A coquette is abominable ; one cannot have two hearts, and when that is already dedicated, all is staked.'

"Visitors called, and this conversation ceased. Lady Bray was busy in welcoming them. Clare was superintending the household ; and, left to his own thoughts, Lawrence mused long, walking up and down the garden walks thinking of the future.

"Some twenty persons sat down to supper, and during the meal a horse was heard galloping up the drive ; the bell rang, and a note was handed to Miss Clare, which, being read, was passed to her father. It was an invitation from Lord Stoner to a ball for all then present, which each one willingly accepted, as Lord Stoner's mansion was but a short distance away.

"Clare did not go at the moment, and, as Lawrence was to escort her, she preferred the cool of evening and the lonely forest path with its birds and flowers to the heat and dust of the circuitous road.

"Lawrence paced the cool stone entrance hall, and Clare soon tripped lightly down from her room with her hat hanging on her arm. She had changed her customary silk tissue for a dark blue silk, and her mass of jet black hair, looped up by simple white and blush roses, was in striking contrast to her large sparkling eyes and pallid face. Her maid followed with a Cashmere shawl, which Lawrence insisted on placing on her shoulders, which unexpected piece of gallantry and attention brought crimson to her cheeks.

"'Well, then, now I am ready, and sorry for keeping you so long, Edward. Mollie, bring my cloak with you.'

"Arm in arm they sallied forth through the orchard and across the fields, until they reached the wood, and as they walked through its shade, the purfume of flowers and song of birds were consonant with the thoughts and feelings of both.

"'This is a very familiar walk to me, Clare ; I often come hunting here in the winter when you are away in France ; there are plenty of rabbits and pheasants ; the corn-fields abound in partridge ; and, altogether, it affords fine sport.'

"'Yes, I often hear when we are away that you collegians destroy all papa's game ; but he only smiles, and says, "Let 'em blaze away, there's plenty for everybody."'

"From where they stood, they distinctly saw, twinkling in the cloudless twilight, numberless Chinese lanterns hanging in the trees round the house ; rockets of many colours were ascending and bursting in varied showers in the calm, breathless air; while strains of music broke upon the ear in delicious dreamy waltzes, and flags on the housetop lazily flapped with every passing gust.

"'How pretty !' both exclaimed, as they stood on the brook bridge gazing, while the ozier banks were rippling with passing waters.

"'Yes, 'tis pretty and pleasant, Clare ; I shall never forget this day, this pleasant walk; and all I regret is that I have not courage to present myself there this evening,' he added, with difficult articulation; 'you know that Lord Stoner has ever displayed antipathy to me.'

"'Lord Stoner an antipathy to you ? What can be the cause ?' asked Clare.

"I know not, Clare, but I cannot go. You will excuse me ; I shall be here in waiting precisely at twelve o'clock, and I dare say the colonel will take this path homewards.'

"Miss Temple here became unusually animated and colour came and went as her companion occasionally looked in her face with pleasure. A hound, which had followed her footsteps, suddenly darted into the forest and growled.

"But no one was visible, and now they had passed through the wood and were at the edge of the meadow-land which intervened between them and Lord Stoner's estate.

"While gaiety reigned at Lord Stoner's, and all thoughts of care were banished by old and young, a strange scene occurred within gun-shot of the house.

"Lawrence had returned to Colonel Temple's and spent several hours there, and leisurely strolled back to the brook bridge to meet Lady Bray and Clare with her father.

"He stood upon the bridge looking down into the moonlit water gurgling over its moss-covered rocks, heeding the gold-backed perch and trout disporting on the surface, and heard the church tower chime hour after hour.

"The sounds of merriment were clearly audible, the merry laugh and joyful shout fell upon his ear in the natural calmness of the spot.

"The moon in silver streams poured through openings in the forest, and the leaves rustled with every gust.

"He felt depressed and melancholy, and every unpleasant circumstance of his life came full upon him.

"Time passed, and still he pondered and thought of Josephine, who, in the whirling excitement of the dance, was oblivious of his existence.

"While he stood leaning on the hand-rail, gazing on the shiny surface of the deep, broad brook, hasty steps approached. He looked up ; a stranger with shaded face stood gazing on his moon-lit countenance.

"'Edward Lawrence, by my soul !' he said, and after a long pause, hoarsely continued ; 'give place! move from my path, snake ! You have thwarted me for years. Move, I say, or I'll send you into eternity !"

"'Philip Redgill ?' said Lawrence, in amazement, disbelieving his senses, adding in a scarcely audible voice, 'heaven help thee !'

"'Help you, you hypocrite. Out of my way, I say, or I'll slaughter you where you stand. What have you done? why, everything ; you have robbed me of honours, position, place, aye, love. By your pale-faced lies, you have come between me and one that was dearer than life. Yes, yes, don't be puzzled. Not have any pretensions there, you penniless impostor? You know you have. Didn't I see you this very day fawning to her in this wood ? There, don't stand canting, but listen to me ; I always hated you from the moment I first saw you. Lying tutors called you a model of living, now show yourself a model of dying.'

"'Dying ?'

"'Yes, of dying ; I have resolved to rid the world of you. You pale before me, eh ? You will be paler still ere morning. Take that hand from your hilt, or I'll send a bullet whistling through your brain, you bastard.'

"Lawrence listened with nervous philosophic courage to all the enraged man had spoken, and he resolved not to draw arms whatever might befall him.

"But the last word exploded all his good resolutions.

"The slur on his unknown mother's honour maddened him.

"The sabre leaped from its scabbard and flashed in the light.

"But instantly Redgill drew back and fired.

"Lawrence fell upon the bridge covered with blood.

"The stranger gazed for a moment on his prostrate form, and muttered, 'I am satisfied. It was to be ; it is done ! Pale cadet in pretty uniform, you are now food for worms, fitting end for a penniless cur ; no one will ever miss you.'

"And with main strength he flung the body into the deepest part of the brook where the willows grew, and it disappeared beneath the eddying water.

"Carelessly lighting 'a cigar, he examined himself to see that no blood bespattered him, and cooly passed through the meadows and presented himself at Lord Stoner's.

"He was known and welcomed. Josephine was all gaiety and danced with him; but Lady Bray and Clare, by common instinct, avoided his company.

"'You are ever talking of Clare, Mr. Redgill; how many times have I not told you that she is perpetually speaking of young Captain Lawrence.'

"'Is he here?' asked Redgill, with a smile.

"'No? I dare say he *cannot* come,' he added with emphasis.

"'In truth, I'm glad he has not; I'm sure *I* didn't wish his company, however much some people may desire and seem to prize it. Oh, there's Clare passing into the grounds looking for her father, the colonel.'

"Redgill followed instantly, and overtook her on the lawn.

"'Mr. Redgill!' she said, in surprise.

"'Yes, Miss Clare; pray be seated.'

"'You will excuse me, Mr. Redgill; I was looking for my father, it is time for us to go.'

"'Only for a moment, one second only.'

"'As you desire it, certainly.'

"'Clare, listen. I am going away, I know not whither; I have known you long, and I have only known you to love you.'

"'Mr. Redgill, do not cause me to give you humiliation; twice before I have told you that your feelings are not reciprocated; they can never be. You will bear witness that I never gave the slightest cause for you to suppose that I liked you other than as a friend. No, I can assure you there have been none to counsel me; I follow the dictates of my heart; your worldly station is fit for any lady, but it is not that. I cannot explain the cause; but, to speak frankly and for the *last* time, I am sorry if I have caused you an uneasy moment, it has been foreign to my thoughts, and I now say unreservedly that I do *not* and never *can* look upon you with feelings other than those of acquaintanceship. My heart is no longer mine; you can never share it, and I feel certain you are too honourable to ever trouble yourself or me again by referring to so distasteful a subject; good evening.'

"Shaking hands she left him.

"'My heart is no longer mine, eh? Oh, if the hound had fifty lives, one less would not have satisfied my revenge. Pass on, proud Clare; if love freezes into hate, you will have cause to remember and regret this hour.'

"Moodily sauntering into the hall, he bowed to the host and hostess and departed.

"While this conversation was transpiring under the lamp-lit trees, the moon was bright and cloudless, and the ozier-banked stream looked innocent and pure.

"It flowed on as usual with gurgling sound, but eddied near the willows.

"No signs of violence were visible, and ere long a man was heard approaching, whistling and carrying a lantern. Presently he shouted to some one still behind him in the wood, and both lingered on the bridge while a hound descended to the brink and began to drink.

"'This is the place for trout, Ike,' said he with the lamp. 'The colonel often says to me, Jack, says he, go and catch a few trouts. Miss Clare allers has fish on Friday.'

"'Hello, what's that, Jack? What is the dog howling about?'

"'Pink, Pink, come here.'

"'What's that?' said both, simultaneously, as they heard a faint moan, and rolled their eyes in the moonlight.

"'Pink, Pink, Pink, come here!' shouted Jack; but still the hound stood in the broad light, howling at something in the shade; and when a second moan, louder than the first, caught the rustic's ear, 'By golly, Jack!' said he, it's nothing but a ghost! this youth is off, sure!' and he hustled away from the bridge in a hurry.

"Ike, however, more courageous than his companion, went down to the brook side and discovered a student lying almost submerged, with his head saved from sinking by a cluster of willow stumps.

"Horrified at the discovery, he knew not what to do, but shouting at the top of his voice, induced his companion to return.

"After much difficulty, they dragged the inanimate form from among the willows; but mud had so disfigured him that they knew not who it was.

"Blood flowed freely from the left breast.

"One of them staunched the wound with a handkerchief, and both rustics carried the body towards the house in front, Pink having the lantern suspended from his neck.

"Had a thunderbolt crashed through the roof, it could not have caused a more sudden cessation of festivities than did the arrival of Lawrence, borne as he was in the arms of the servants.

"The news spread rapidly.

"The company were electrified.

"Every one was anxious to learn the particulars.

"But all was wrapt in mystery, which only heightened curiosity still more.

"The collegians rushed from the ball-room, and taking up the body, swiftly conveyed it to the house.

"'This way, gentlemen,' said Lord Stoner, as he and Colonel Temple led the way upstairs.

"'Enter the first room you come to—there, that's it; never mind (to his wife) if it is your daughter's room; there's no time to stand upon trifles; place him upon the bed—that's it.'

"And the wet and muddy youth was carefully laid on the spotless counterpane, and the doctor immediately began to ply his art.

"'Ike,' said he, 'fetch my instruments, and galop instantly into town and bring Dr. Newman with you; tell him there mustn't be a moment's delay.'

"'It is a desperate case, gentlemen,' said he, addressing a few who were allowed to remain in the room; ''tis naught but life or death; every moment is invaluable. Gentlemen, you will excuse me, I know, when I say it is necessary that you all retire.'

"And the door closed on Lord Stoner, Colonel Temple, Harry Ashton, a collegian, and Susy, the chambermaid.

"The sudden calamity had stunned all present, and one by one the visitors departed.

"Clare and Belle had heard the news.

"But neither spoke.

"They sat apart in silence, waiting for the colonel, who at last appeared, and the carriage drove off to the 'Willows.'

"'Don't ask me any questions, girls,' said the old man, as they rode home. 'I am full of passion, and might say things to offend your ear; but let me tell you, this is a dastardly outrage; it was not a fight, but deliberate assassination, and old as I am, I would walk a hundred miles for the pleasure of putting a bullet into the precious scoundrel who did it.

"'No, we can find no clue to the affair. The

collegians have been down to the bridge, but there are no traces of the struggle, and the poor lad himself is insensible.

"'I don't know how the case stands, but it looks an ugly wound, very, and the doctor shakes his head ominously. I would give ten thousand pounds on the spot to " string up " the rascal who did it.

"' Here we are, girls, home at last. I know you must be fatigued, both of you ;' and as he handed them from the carriage, he kissed them affectionately, and they immediately retired to their room.

"' Jack,' said the colonel to a servant, seating himself on the moonlit verandah, and lighting his pipe, 'bring me a cup of wine—that's it. You acted well to-night, and I shan't forget it. It was "Pink," you say, who first discovered him, eh ? Lucky it was so, or he would have sunk for a certainty. Well, look here, Jack, you and Ike sit up to-night. I'm going to Lord Stoner's again, and if Miss Clare wants to see me in the morning, tell her I shall be back by breakfast.'

"Calling the hound, 'Pink,' the old man shouldered his double barrel shot gun, and went to Lord Stoner's by the forest path, lingering by the bridge for some time in deep thought.

"The breeze of early morning began to blow, and early cocks crew salutations that echoed far and near on the quiet landscape.

"Hour followed hour, and neither Clare nor Lady Bray could sleep.

"Clare had prayed longer than usual, and courted sleep, but it came not.

"Lady Bray, on the contrary, had sat in an arm chair, thinking of all manner of things, and pacing her room to and fro.

"At last she went to Clare's door, and tapped and entered.

"'Oh, Clare,' she said, seating herself on the bedside, 'I feel so miserable ! I cannot tell why it is ; but that poor youth is always before my eyes ! Oh ! I am glad you did not see the sight (Clare had done so), it was awful ! All his clothes were wet and dirty and bloody, and his face like marble. Oh ! what a horrible crime it was ! I cannot sleep for thinking of it ! Let me lie with you, Clare.'

"And both cousins lay side by side.

"'What is the matter, Clare ?' said Lady Bray, who felt tear-drops falling on her hand. ' You are weeping !'

"Clare, who had not spoken, was struggling desperately to conceal her emotion ; but nature was strong, and she burst out passionately in sobs.

"'Oh ! cousin, forgive me ! I cannot be a hypocrite longer ! You, who tells me everything, would not guess how or what I have concealed. Oh ! had it been Heaven's will I would died rather than this should have happened to him !'

"Lady Bray passed her arm round the sobbing girl, and drew still closer to her, listening breathlessly to all that flowed from her as she went on passionately and rapidly,

"'I never knew till now how much I could feel ; but it is too much. I have concealed my thoughts from all. I have worn a mask, but now it falls from my face in an unexpected and unlooked-for moment.'

"Lady Bray rose on her elbow, and looked at the tear-moistened face of her pale. sobbing cousin, and after some time asked, with unnatural calmness,

"'Do you——'

"'Oh ! cousin, do not torture me !'

"And, then, in a paroxysm of grief, added,

"'I—have—for—years !'

"Lady Bray's breast heaved with strong emotions.

"She conquered them after a quiet struggle, and, smiling with compassion on her cousin, drew her quivering form still closer to her, until poor childlike Clare, wearied with weeping, rested her head on her cousin's breast, and went to sleep.

"Lady Bray lay awake hour after hour thinking, and could not sleep.

"She prayed for it, but it came not.

"Racked with conflicting thoughts she lived part of her life over again, and resolved to forget all about it.

"'I thought so,' she mused. 'Clare could not disguise it from me. I saw it long ago ; but it can never be. No ! it can never be, even if he lives !

"'What pain she must have suffered to-night ! How strong is the heart beating in that pale, fragile frame ?

"'No, no, Clare. Sleep on, sweet cousin ; but heaven guide your heart aright, and prepare it for disappointments and trials, for they will surely come.'

"And so passed the night until the sun began to gild the eastern clouds, and even then Lady Bray lay awake, watching the curtains moving in the breeze.

"The night had been an anxious one at Lord Stoner's. All had retired as usual, and, save the lights in his daughter's room, with moving figures reflected on the blinds, all was still.

"Dr. Newman had arrived long ago, and after consulting, both medical gentlemen began operating on the scarcely breathing, inanimate student.

"After difficulty and much effusion of blood the bullet was extracted, and the wound bandaged.

"Everything had been made as comfortable as possible, and the doctors had retired, leaving Ashton, the student, and Susan, the servant, to attend till morning.

"'How is he getting on, Ashton ?' asked old Temple, noiselessly entering the room, and whispering.

"'They didn't say anything of importance ; I only caught two or three words at parting.

"'Desperate !' said one.

"'Yes ; but not mortal, I think,' added the other. 'He is very young, tough, and strong, and will recover, I think.'

"'Good news,' responded Temple. 'Let's have a look at him.'

"And he took the candle and looked at the sleeper, who seemed to breathe freely, with his long hair thrown from his forehead, which was as pale as snow.

"'Look you here, Ashton,' went on the colonel, drawing his chair very close, and speaking in whispers, 'this was a foul piece of work, and there must have been some reason for it. You are his friend ; you and he have associated for years. Can you guess the person or the cause of all this ?'

"'It is a difficult matter to say. I have very good reasons to suppose it was premeditated; but by whom I cannot imagine.'

"'You seem to speak mysteriously. Why not talk plainly ?'

"'Well, then, colonel, to speak plainly, I cannot, and must not, if I would. My great surprise is that I was not also a victim.'

"'You a victim ? Why, you speak strangely, as if there existed some conspiracy. I cannot understand it.'

"'No, I dare say not—at present. perhaps ; but you will, ere many years,' said Ashton, smiling.

"'Well, you may talk in riddles as much as you like; but, if I knew the scamp who did this, he should have to pay dearly for it.'

" ' I feel certain of that. You may rest assured he will never die a natural death, if he lives a hundred years.'

" Ashton spoke in parables to the old man, who did not comprehend; but there was so much earnestness and solemnity in his few words, that Colonel Temple was curious to divine his meaning, but could not.

" ' I do not understand you yet, sir,' said the old colonel, with a red face. ' I know that there is a strong party growing up in the land against King Charles; but surely Captain Lawrence can have nothing to do with it ? He is too young yet to be mixed up deeply in politics.'

" ' No, colonel, he is not; but, on the contrary, is one of the finest writers of the day, and has aided the king's cause not a little.'

" ' Indeed.'

" ' Yes. Do you know much of this Redgill, who was at Lord Stoner's ball to-night ?'

" ' Redgill—yes. He is one of the loud-mouthed party who cry against the king, and that, for one reason, makes them enemies. But you do not mean to say, surely, that Redgill did this horrid deed ?'

" ' All I mean to say, colonel, is this,' said Ashton—' there is a deadly hatred between them, for I believe Redgill has offered his hand to your daughter Clare, and been refused.'

" ' Why, I'd rather have the devil for a son-in-law than him. But what makes your lip tremble, Ashton ?'

" ' Because I hold a great secret regarding Lawrence !'

" ' Indeed !'

" ' Yes ; but before I tell it to you let me ask you one question.'

" ' Name it.'

" ' Would you ever object to Clare marrying the man of her choice ?'

" ' Marrying the man of her choice ?' said the old colonel, in surprise. ' Why, of course not ; if he was a fit and proper person, you know.'

" ' Well, if Lawrence here were to propose for your daughter, I mean.'

" ' I should not ; but still I can scarcely understand you, for, if he lives, I think he will aspire to one of rank and station. But if he did propose for Clare I should have no objection in the world. Bu you must understand, Ashton, that I speak thus in all confidence, for I fancy he would never do so, for, until very lately, Clare has been most distant towards him, and why it is that she shows so much liking for his company now is a puzzle to me.'

" ' Well, then, colonel,' said Ashton, 'as you have been so open-minded to me in this matter I will act likewise, and tell you all I know. Do you see any likeness in Lawrence to any great living personage ?' asked Ashton, in a serious mood.

" A likeness to any living personage ?' said the colonel, with an uncertain look. ' Why, now I come to gaze on him the more, I think I do.'

" And whom does he resemble, think you ?'

" ' Why, he is as much like what King Charles used to be when a young man as two peas in a pod,' said the colonel. ' I have often heard it remarked before.'

" ' Yes, he is like the king,' said Ashton, ' and I have remarked it also, but never named it to him ; but certain circumstances have transpired to-day which make me think that there is more than a likeness between them.'

" ' Indeed ! how ?' said the colonel, astonished and interested.

" ' At the review there were many distinguished people present, nobles among the number.'

" ' I know it.'

" ' But you do not know that the king was there ?'

" ' You are surely joking ?'

" ' I am not, colonel, for after the review was all over, the king, disguised as an ordinary gentleman, went boldly up to the principal of the academy, and had a long conversation with him about Lawrence. They did not perceive me, for I was sitting at my window reading, yet, as they walked to and fro, I could hear much of what they said.'

" ' And what did they say ?'

" ' The king's disguise was discovered by the president, and the monarch did not deny it, but in the course of conversation confessed that he had always felt great interest in Lawrence's progress, for he was his own son."

" ' His own son !' said the astonished colonel.

" ' Yes, his own son—illegitimate, it is true, but nevertheless, his own true offspring.'

" ' And who was the mother ?'

" ' That I did not then learn ; but when Lawrence first came among us as a mere boy to the academy he wore a locket round his neck which was unmistakably the portrait on ivory of the young and fascinating Duchess of Buckingham. (See Cut in No. 13). From this I gather that she must have been his mother.'

" ' I am astonished,' said the colonel. ' And has not the king, then, provided for his after welfare ?'

" ' Without a doubt. I heard him say that some grand and vast estates in France had been passed over to him, and that a large sum in money would be his when he married ?'

" ' Then Lawrence is a false name—he is the king's bastard ?' said the colonel.

" ' He is,' said Ashton.

" ' Then he shall never marry my daughter,' said Colonel Temple. " No bastard shall ever enter my family !'

" And so speaking he left the apartment, with a flushed face, and Ashton remained alone by the bedside of his wounded comrade, who was sighing in his troubled dreams and moaning.

" Memories of years past flitted through his troubled brain, and the image of his adored one, Clare Temple, held supreme possession of all his faculties.

" He had seen and known her when but a child.

" She used to pass the college gardens on her way to school, with books and slate and dimity sun-bonnet trimmed with blue.

" Years had passed.

" She grew into girlhood, and short frocks and sun-bonnet gave place to a seminary uniform of blue-gauze and white chip quaker scoop, and her light and airy manner changed to that of a studious seminarianne in her teens.

" He had spoken to her, but met with no response.

" He had anonymously written poems and tales in her honour.

" But all had passed unnoticed.

" She treated him with cold respect, and met his timid overtures with blunt rebuffs.

" He had met her on the road and in the woods.

" But she passed him with a distant bow.

" Yet if in the greatest glee his presence chilled her into unusual coldness, and although unconscious of the cause she could neither sing nor play in his presence.

" Lawrence had often confessed that his case was hopeless.

" Many disliked him from some cause ; and, following in their footsteps, Clare, he thought, treated him with marked indifference.

" It must be confessed, however, that although

Clare had hitherto disclosed her secret thoughts to no one, yet, when alone, she often thought,

"'Every one is loved but me! I am not pretty, I know, neither have I many accomplishments. I wish I were like Emma Bray, for everybody loves her.'

"And then she would stealthily draw from her bosom a small gold locket which contained a ruby heart on which was cut a simple love motto.

"She knew not who had sent it.

"It came to her in a bouquet found on the dressing table on her birthday, and was the first present she had ever received from any admirer.

"She mused and pondered, but dared not give utterance to her thoughts; yet as she passed the college gardens, and saw Lawrence walking up and down, her cheeks flushed, and bending her head more lowly than ever, she passed the buildings rapidly, and tried to stay her unnatural palpitations.

"Thus ran the wild fancies of the wounded student about his true love, when a loud knocking and rapping was heard at Lord Stoner's door.

"'Who or what can that be?' thought Ashton.

"But still the knocking continued in the dead of night, and the dogs barked in all directions.

"When the hall porter opened the door, he perceived two white figures on horseback, with long, streaming hair.

"The old hall porter rushed away and hid himself, for he swore that two ghosts had arrived at the hall.

"When the truth was made known, it was discovered that the two arrivals were not ghosts at all.

"They were two handsome females.

"They were none other than Lady Bray and Clare Temple!

"'Where is my father?' asked Clare, in great haste and fright, as she dismounted from her foaming horse.

"'Where is my uncle, the colonel?' gasped Lady Bray.

"'What is the matter, ladies?' asked Lord Stoner, in great alarm. 'Why, heaven help us! the two ladies have scarcely anything on but their night-dresses. What is the matter? Explain, I beg, ladies, explain.'

"'Arm yourself and your household!' gasped Clare. 'Arm them quickly!'

"'What means this?'

"'Arm yourselves, all of you, at once, or you are all dead men!'

"'Explain,' said the colonel to his daughter.

"'You know Redgill, who has proposed for my hand?'

"'Yes.'

"'I refused him thrice.'

"'I know it; what of that?'

"'He has joined a band of ruffians who have assumed the singular and horrible disguise of skeleton men. Emma and I were sitting at our bedroom window, and could not sleep. We espied two men dressed in skeleton garb hiding in the shrubbery. We heard them conversing together, and learnt that they intended to carry Emma and myself away, and to murder all who opposed them. I did not stop an instant, for I and cousin crept from our room, saddled two horses, and galloped hither for protection. But just as we were crossing the hilltop, I espied a large troop of these demon-like horsemen approaching, and could hear them singing a song, in which they praised Redgill, their leader and chief, and swore to have the life's blood of

some one they called the King's Bastard, but what it meant I knew not.'

"'Enough, daughter,' said the old man, drawing his sword. 'Ere these bloodthirsty fiends can arrive, we will fly with the wounded youth.'

"In a short time a carriage and four was provided.

"Lawrence was placed in it.

"With a strong guard of mounted men around, in front, and behind it, the carriage drove off towards the sea coast, Clare and Lady Bray, being inside, acting as nurses to the wounded youth."

Wildfire Ned had read this much of his father's exciting history, when a side door was suddenly opened.

Before he could say a word, Captain Jack stood before him, laughing.

---

## CHAPTER XXXIV.

### CAPTAIN JACK PAYS NED WARBECK AN UNEXPECTED VISIT—THE REVELATION.

"Who the devil are you?" said Ned, rising hastily, and drawing a pistol. "Who the devil are you? What do you want, and where do you come from? Answer instantly, or a bullet shall whistle through your head."

"Put down your pistol, my brave lad," said Captain Jack, smiling. "My name is Captain Jack. I am one of the crown officers; in other words, a detective, and am just come from one of the strongest prisons in the kingdom."

"Indeed! and what has all that to do with me?"

"A great deal, as you will quickly hear."

"And how gained you admittance into this library?"

"By a secret door, as you perceive."

"I never knew that one existed."

"No; but I did," said Captain Jack, smiling. "I know all about this house, as well as I do about the ins and out of Darlington Hall."

"Indeed!"

"Yes; a friend of yours informed me."

"A friend of mine? Nay, he must have been an enemy."

"Well, enemy, then, if you like. I daresay you remember his name."

"I cannot guess."

"Phillip Redgill."

"The wretch!"

"Yes; he's all that, and more; but I think his career of crime is well nigh ended. He is in gaol."

"I need not ask for what, perhaps?"

"Murder, Ned Warbeck—murder is his crime."

"And how came you to ferret out all his villany?"

"I have had my eye on him for a long time. When the fruit was ripe we plucked it. Ha! ha! he is safe enough now."

"And what are the number of charges against him?"

"A dozen or more."

"And how did you manage to capture him at last, for I have heard you were a long time in finding him out?"

"Some months, for he lived from time to time in all sorts of holes and corners, and under all imaginable names. He treated his wife, Fanny, in the most shameful manner, and led her also into vice and crime; but as long as she supplied him with money from time to time, he seldom went home, and did not care how or whence the money came. I heard all the facts from a spy, whom I employed, and who, for the last three days before his capture, followed Phillip Redgill about like a shadow."

"Like an evil genius," said Ned, smiling.

"Just so," said Captain Jack, smoking a cigar. "Being extremely hard pressed for money, Phillip thought he would visit his home—the first time, he had done so, it must be confessed, for several weeks—and see what could be realised there.

"He was not surprised to see much company present, for *that* he knew was of frequent occurrence, and had originated with himself.

"But feeling supremely miserable, he was stung to the quick to see his wife in such exuberant spirits, presiding at a sumptuous supper, which he very well knew she was not able to afford.

"Around the table were seated many young men of gay celebrity, drinking wine and joking.

"Madame was decked out in all the fashions of the season, and when her husband arrived she rose very quietly, handed him a chair, and whispered very lovingly,

"'A few of *your* friends, dear !'

"When the company had dispersed, Redgill, who was now intoxicated with wine and passion, broke forth into one of his habitual fits of furious brutality, and threatened to kill his wife.

"He tossed over the supper table.

"He struck Fanny a severe blow with a decanter, and then fell upon the floor helplessly intoxicated among the ruins of the feast—eatables, drinkables, plate, glass, and costly etceteras.

"When the moon peeped above the houses, and threw a faint light into the apartment, he awoke in a maudling state, and staggered up to bed.

"Everything seemed in confusion ; the drawers and chests were rifled, and their contents strewn about the floor.

"The bed had no occupant, and by the lighted lamp which stood upon the dressing-table, he perceived a note addressed to him, in Fanny's handwriting.

"He opened it, and read its contents, which ran something like this—

"'You have struck me for the last time. Love has long departed from my heart. I, whom you have so cruelly deceived without regrets, bid you farewell.'

"'Oh ! that's it, eh ?' said Phillip, hiccuping. 'Gone !—farewell ! and all that kind of style, eh ? Well, all right, it's just the thing ; it couldn't be better ! I'll sell off all the things, and make some ready money. I'll do it this very day. Just what I wanted.'

"Phillip pulled off his boots with much difficulty, and fell upon the bed, and was soon fast asleep.

"The blinds were not drawn.

"The pale moon shed its holy rays upon the disordered apartment, and as morning dawned, the lamplight flickered and died.

"The moonlight lit his haggard face, as he lay half scowling in his sleep, and with fists tightly clenched, and hair disordered, he ground his teeth in dreams.

"The vision of his life passed before him.

"His mother's face and form appeared as in his childhood, and looked with sadness upon him.

"His schoolboy days and boyish loves caused him to sigh and smile, in unconscious sleep.

"His false and early love for one sinless maiden he had ruined came next in view.

"Following in the train of chiding phantoms wept his injured wife !

"He ground his teeth most horribly, but laughed with demoniacal scorn !

"The moon still lit his features.

"Even in sleep, the spy has told me, his face assumed a look of intense horror and surprise.

"He clutched the clothes convulsively, and shrieked out aloud,

"'My father ! my father !' and jumped from the bed in fright.

"'Where am I ? Tell me. Fanny !—my wife ! No, no ; I didn't do it ! It cannot be !' and he fell, gasping, upon the floor.

"'What a fool I am,' said Phillip, with a laugh, when he had recovered his senses, 'what a fool I am to think of such things—such childish, silly fancies as dreams ! Yet that cursed figure haunts me—yes, everywhere, and I suffer all the torments of the damned. Where's the brandy ? that's the thing !'

"Thus he raved, but he little thought one of my men was concealed in the chamber, and saw and heard all.

"Having found a bottle partly full he readily emptied its contents, and Phillip went from the house to negotiate for the immediate sale of all its effects.

"He was followed by my spy.

"Whither his wife had fled was of little moment to Phillip.

"His whole thoughts were directed to the sale of his goods and chattels.

"He owed money it was true, but this he never intended to pay.

"So that when he had negotiated the sale with a broker, and received a large sum of money therefor, he felt supremely happy, and went to his old haunts, and spent money so grandly and lavishly that many winked, and could not comprehend it.

"The furniture, &c., had scarcely been removed from the premises, together with numberless et cetera, when the landlord arrived upon the scene, but, unfortunately, too late.

"Numerous creditors were advised of the event, and were not slow in preparing very long bills for settlement, but when they reached the house, they simply found the place empty, with several other gentlemen, interested like themselves, standing round the door with long and very serious faces.

"They had been 'sold,' they said, but whether this remark applied to the furniture or themselves is doubtful, although from their very blank countenances it is certain they would not have brought much at public auction.

"When Mr. Phillip Redgill was inquired for, he was found at the Royal Racquet Court, elegantly stretching himself in a new suit of clothes, imbibing brandy and water with much apparent satisfaction.

"There was no compunction of conscience in him, and therefore he deported himself very majestically to the crowd of creditors who surrounded him and lustily demanded the payment of their debts.

"These he laughed at, but in a day or two, when he was 'wanted,' I easily tracked him out, and laid my hands on him for the murder of old farmer Bertram."

"Good heavens ! you don't mean that."

"I do, though."

"I always thought it."

"I always knew it,' said Captain Jack, laughing; "but come with me, I want you, Ned Warbeck, on particular business. Come this way, and you shall know all."

Wildfire Ned and Captain Jack left the library together, and went towards Phillip Redgill's prison.

## CHAPTER XXXV.

IN WHICH SOMETHING IS SAID OF PHILLIP REDGILL, OLD SIR ANDREW, AND IN WHICH ONE OF PHILLIP'S VICTIMS IS MADE A HAPPY MAN AND A FATHER.

UPON the elegant house, and its fashionably dressed inmates, in Minerva Street, of which Phillip had heard many strange rumours, Mr. Redgill never bestowed a single thought, although he had more than crude suspicions of who the much-talked-of "Madame Fannie St. Claire" might be.

Old Sir Andrew had never thought of asking Phillip anything regarding his daughter.

She had separated from her husband he full well knew, but as Phillip never broached the subject, Sir Andrew, for purposes of avarice and greed, refrained from doing so.

"She has made her own nest," he would sometimes say to his old and asthmatic wife, propped up in her arm-chair beside the fire, "therefore let her lie in it.

"I don't know nor care where she is. Don't bother me with your questions and nonsense, woman. I have something else to think about.

"I don't care what has become of her—there. Don't sit there snivelling, you old fool, or I'll leave the place altogether.

"In a few weeks, I hope, I shall be doing business in the City, and not in this miserable hole, with a crabbed old woman coughing all day and night.

"What'll folks think then of old Sir Andy, as they call me, when I appear on 'Change again, and with a large banker's account at my back?

"What'll they say then to the old president of the Phœnix Insurance Company, whom they refuse to speak to, or even recognise now, eh?

"I'll show 'em all what money can do. I'm just as honest as any of 'em; it's all speculation in this world; so long as you've got the cash you needn't care a snap of your finger for any of 'em.

"Don't sit there prating, you old hag! If you open your lips again, I'll squeeze the life out of you, I will, you miserable old thing. I hate the sight of you!"

And, from the number of times that old Sir Andrew raised his chair in anger, it seemed probable that at some time, in moments of fury, he really would send the aged and afflicted woman unexpectedly into eternity.

Augustus Fumbleton, Esq., it must be confessed, was not at all troubled with matrimonial jars or grievances.

He was not a married man, but, as he often expressed it, "soon would be."

"In a month or two, all this business of Phillip's will be over, and then I'll settle down," he thought, "turn over a new leaf, and have his wife for my mistress. What a head old Sir Andrew, her father, has got to be sure.

"He attends church regularly, I hear, and is looked upon out in the country as a perfect 'saint.'

"Ah, church-going folks ain't always the best. There's many a man sits with a prayer book in his hand who's thinking of something else. Never mind, we'll do this little trick and then I'll cry 'quits.'"

If Messrs. Redgill, Sir Andrew and Fumbleton were situated as we have described, Charley Warbeck, Ned's brother, was in the greatest sorrow and concern for the safety of his young wife, and very despondent in spirits.

THE DISCOVERY OF THE VICTIM.—*See Number* 18.

Her health had been very precarious for several weeks, and the anxious young husband was troubled exceedingly for her safety.

For the doctors in attendance in consultation looked very serious and gloomy, and held out but little hope of her recovery.

Dame Worthington and Mistress Haylark were almost in constant attendance both day and night.

But the latter was so much given to long naps in her arm-chair, and so fretful during her occasional attendance, that Dame Worthington thought it advisable to stay up at night herself, now that she had somewhat recovered from the poison Sir Andrew had given her.

Instead of frightening the poor girl with stories and hob-goblin notions regarding her particularly critical position, the good, kind, old lady cheered her with all the funny anecdotes she could remember, and often made her laugh heartily and forget all about her sickness.

Oftentimes when Clara was asleep, this ever-watchful old lady would lean across the bed and kiss her, and then turn away with tears in her eyes.

Night after night she watched beside the poor suffering girl, and her delicate patient could not disturb a single curl upon her pillow without she arose, readjusted the bed-clothes and dampened her fevered brow.

No. 16.

The parting of Charley with his wife every morning ere he went to business, was of the most tender description.

He thought, and with sufficient reason, that perhaps he might never see her alive again; and, it must be confessed, as he leaned over her to say good morning, his eyes were moist as she passionately kissed him.

"Don't weep, Charley dear," poor Clara would say, as she passed her thin, white, delicate arms around his neck in unaffected simplicity and affection.

"There, don't, don't weep, my good, good, boy, or you will make me worse, darling; there, smile. Oh, how different you look, pet; what a shame it is that you look so solemn. There, go away smiling, and it will make me happy all the day," she would laughingly add as he bestowed a parting embrace and departed.

While Charley was full of business, one morning at the office—but, it must be confessed, in a very disturbed state of mind—a messenger arrived, saying,

"He was wanted at home immediately, his wife was dying!"

If a shot had struck him he could not have felt more pain and alarm.

He seized his hat, and ran down to the ferry-boat like a maniac.

He had to wait fifteen minutes before the boat started.

It was unearthly torture to him.

He could plainly see his house, on the south side of the river, which appeared to be no more than a few hundred yards distant.

He sought for a row-boat, but none was at hand.

He felt as if he could have jumped across the river, and paced up and down, like one demented.

Just as the regular boat was about to leave the ferry wharf, old Sir Richard appeared, and in company with one of the best physicians of the city.

He had been informed by the same messenger of the critical nature of the case, had left the India House on the instant, and had forced his old friend, Dr. Stevens, to accompany him.

"Never mind your engagements, doctor—this is a case of life or death.  I would not have her die for thousands!"

Within a few moments the boat started, and the three gentlemen were soon landed on the other side.

Two minutes' walk sufficed to bring them to Charley's residence.

Charley rushed upstairs, and would have entered his wife's apartment.

Mistress Haylark, looking double her ordinary size, stood outside the door, blocking up the door, and denied him entrance.

"Go in there, sir," she said, pointing majestically to a back room with her right hand, holding a basin of gruel in the left.

"Go in there, sir!" she repeated, with awful solemnity of voice and manner, "and stay until you're called, and don't dare come in the room!"

Charley, the young and anxious husband, was stupefied, but mechanically obeyed.

He had not remained long in suspense, when the connecting door between the back and front bedrooms opened, and Dame Worthington, all smiles and tears, appeared with something in her arms, which, rolled up in flannels and shawls, appeared to be an armful of newly-made muffins.

"Look at that, my dear ! look at your own dear boy, and kiss him !"

Old Sir Richard, Charley, and Dr. Stevens gazed upon the tiny face of the babe, who, with its little fists tightly closed, half-opened its eyes and began to cry right lustily.

Dame Worthington gave old Sir Richard a peculiar look, and that respectable old gentleman smiled, shook Charley by the hand, took a pinch of snuff, and turned aside.

Dr. Stevens pronounced it "an extraordinary infant," and said it must have weighed ten pounds.

While Charley, overjoyed to hear of Clara's safety, took his first-born from the good old lady's arms, kissed it, and, going into the front room, placed it beside its mother.

Poor Clara, weak, faint, pale, and suffering, languidly opened her eyes, faintly smiled, and sighed.

Charley kissed her, of course, very fondly, and would have remained by her side, but the merry, laughing old dame, and the august, solemn-spoken mother-in-law bade her daughter dry up her tears, and remember she was "one of the Haylark's," and quickly bustled poor Charley out of the room.

Full of excitement, he knew not what to do.

For the first time in his life, he determined to pay court to Bacchus, and old Sir Richard, apparently appearing nothing loth, they both sat down to a substantial meal, and beguiled the rest of the evening by paying exclusive attention to a box of havannahs and some excellent cognac.

In his merriment and good humour, he kissed everybody ; even his mother-in-law, whom he discovered coming up stairs with medicines and gruel ; but that majestic lady, in her cap well stocked with flaming ribbons, frowned, and said he ought to be ashamed of himself, and should have more "dignity," a quality he would have doubtless possessed in superabundance, only he was unfortunately not one of "the Haylarks."

Mr. Warbeck had no sooner become a father, than he began to look and and act like a much different man.

He was gay and lively as ever, it is true, and, if anything, far more so ; but he began to assume the air and bearing of one upon whose shoulders rested serious "responsibilities."

He went to the office every morning with cheerfulness and alacrity ; and there his chief thought during the day was for the approach of evening, when he might hurry homewards, to enjoy the quiet delights of his own fireside, in the company of his wife and child.

Clara, it must be confessed, soon recovered from her illness, and moved about the house with great grace and amiability, looking more comely and captivating than ever.

With "baby" in her arms, she would walk up and down the parlour singing all manner of pretty ditties to solace the child to sleep, and, it had scarcely closed its little eyes, ere she would commence to kiss and hug it, and to talk to it in baby prattle, and wake it again, and then begin to scold some imaginary being for having disturbed its slumbers.

When the day of christening arrived there was much controversy as to the name it should bear. Charles proposed that it should be named " Charles Warbeck," but to this proposition the mother-in-law made vehement resistance.

It was one of "the Haylarks," she said, and should be so named ; so that to quiet the old lady, and to prevent any more quarrelings, and historical lectures regarding her illustrious relatives, both father and mother agreed it should be named "Charles Edward Worthington Haylark Warbeck.'

---

## CHAPTER XXXVI.

### DIAMOND CUT DIAMOND—CAPTAIN JACK'S ADVENTURES.

WHEN Phillip Redgill found himself safely locked in his prison cell, deep, dark remorse took possession of his wicked heart.

He could not sleep, he could not eat.

All he could do was to walk about the stone chamber, and curse everything and everbody.

He called the gaoler and spoke to him.

"They accuse me of fearful crimes," said Phillip, faintly attempting to smile ; "but mere accusation will not avail much, they must prove all they say."

"There can't be much difficulty about doing that," said the old gaoler, "when such men as Colonel Blood and Captain Jack take the affair in hand, for Captain Jack can prove anything if he likes."

"Yes ; and perhaps can disprove anything also if he thinks proper, eh ?"

"I don't know what you mean," said the turnkey, with a knowing grin.

"Perhaps not," said Phillip, with a sad smile ; "but I dare say you might give a rough guess."

"No one has any right to guess about such things," said the turnkey, "and, besides, you must know he is our superior officer, and I have no right to speak about what he does."

"Well, you need not fall out with me," said Phillip; "I have no friends here, but I think I could make one of you."

"How do you mean?"

"Would you take a note to the post office for me?"

"I dare not."

"Not for a guinea?"

"I must not."

"Not for three guineas?"

"Don't tempt me!"

"Yes, do; give me pen, ink, and paper, and I will give you ten guineas!"

"My life is at stake; I should be implicated as an accomplice."

"Nonsense. Do as I wish, and I will give you twenty guineas."

The turnkey left the cell.

But he soon returned.

"Let me see the colour of your money," said he, "and I will deliver your note."

"Agreed," said Phillip, and as he spoke he drew out of the lining of his coat a twenty guinea note, and gave it to the gaoler.

In less than two minutes Phillip wrote a very hurried note, and gave it to the gaoler to post.

He had scarcely done so, and the frightened gaoler had barely time to put the pen and ink into his pocket when heavy footsteps were heard approaching.

The turnkey turned deadly pale as he whispered to Phillip,

"It is Captain Jack, and half drunk as usual."

"Hillo!" said the captain to the gaoler, "what brings you here?"

"The prisoner wished me to lend him a bible and prayer book, that's all."

"Ha! ha!" laughed Captain Jack. "So Mr. Redgill has turned religious all at once, eh? Very good. Ha! ha! it's time he did something of the kind. Get you gone, and don't let me catch you talking to the prisoner any more. Do you understand me? If you do, you shall be dismissed."

"But, captain, I have done no wrong; no offence was meant. You know I have been gaoler here more than twenty years, and a steadier, a soberer, or a honester man never was than myself, though I say it."

"I dare say," Captain Jack replied, with a grin. "All men are honest till they're found out; I'm a real saint myself. Ha! ha! Then leave us, I wish to speak to the prisoner alone. Get you gone, turnkey!"

The gaoler left.

Captain Jack and Phillip Redgill were now alone.

The captain took a seat on the edge of the table, and looked at Phillip much like a wild beast who has got his prey firmly in its clutches.

Neither spoke for some time.

Phillip's eyes glowed with rage, but he spoke not a syllable for some time.

Captain Jack amused himself with whistling and playing with a pistol.

"May I ask what you want with me?" Phillip began, at length, endeavouring to suppress the rage he felt.

"Me want with you?" said Jack. "Oh! I really beg pardon for intruding—ha! ha! but I thought you might want to see me, that's all."

As he spoke he smiled like a demon.

"You have acted the knave towards me, Captain Jack,"

"Have I, though? How complimentary you are!"

"Yes, you have, Captain Jack; you have acted like a black-hearted scoundrel!"

"Go on, go on, I am listening; you can't hurt anybody with your tongue; you are bound too fast to the stone floor to do much harm."

"Am I?"

"Yes, of course you are but go on—I want to hear all you've got to say."

"Why did you take my money, and then arrest me?"

"Because I wanted the cash; and, in the next place, I wished to save my own neck. Colonel Blood swore to hang one or the other, so I thought you might do better than myself, you perceive."

"But suppose I were to tell Colonel Blood what I have done for you?"

"He wouldn't believe you, that's all."

"I don't know that."

"But I do, though. If I had not thought and known so, I shouldn't have captured you alive."

"What then?"

"Why, would have so arranged it that you would have been a dead man, that's all."

"And did you mean that all along?"

"Of course I did."

For some time neither spoke, but looked at each other occasionally with an expression of fierce brutality in their eyes.

At last, Phillip said:

"Suppose I disprove all your charges and accusations—what then?"

"Oh, but you can't."

"Can't?"

"No—impossible."

"But if I get witnesses to swear to my innocence?"

"Why, then, I'll so manage it as to have two witnesses to your one to swear quite the contrary."

"You are a villain, Captain Jack!"

"Lor' bless you! Didn't you know it before? I'm called that name every day—I'm quite used to it now."

"Tell the truth, Captain Jack—What did you come here for?"

"Have you any money?—answer me that first."

"Not a penny piece."

"Then you will as surely die as eggs are eggs, that's all."

"What do you mean?"

"Couldn't you manage to get some money, by fair means or foul?"

"Why?"

"Oh, nothing; but it's possible you might only be transported if you could raise a thousand pounds to pay lawyers to defend you, and—ah—"

"And what?"

"Why, 'palm' Colonel Blood and myself, that's all. The affidavits are not made out yet. I have only taken you on suspicion, you know."

"I understand."

"But then the suspicion is very strong, you know—very, very strong indeed; it almost amounts to a dead certainty, since we've got the identical suit of clothes 'a certain party' exchanged, on the night of the murder, with young Bob Bertram."

Captain Jack smiled as he said this.

Phillip bit his lip.

"How did you procure the clothes?"

"Ned Warbeck gave the suit to me this very morning, for Bob had kept them by him, and young Warbeck says he could swear they belong to——"

"D—n Ned Warbeck!" said Phillip Redgill, in a terrible rage; "D—n him! he is always crossing my path. I wish he were dead ; yes, buried at the bottom of the ocean he loves so much !"

"Aye, but there's no killing a lad like him," said Captain Jack ; "he's got more lives than a cat, and as to drowning, it's out of the question, for he swims like a duck and can float like a cork."

"Then what do you propose ?"

"I can't propose anything if you can't raise the wind. If you will be hanged, it's your fault, not mine. It would suit me to know you were in a penal settlement quite as well as to know you were buried."

"You are quite disinterested, Captain Jack, and very polite."

"I always was."

"But suppose I do not give you money, that I do not hang or be transported—what then ? "

"Oh, that's impossible ; out of the question entirely ; you must do one thing or the other. Do you refuse to raise the money ?"

"No, I do not."

"Well, then, I have got pens, ink, and paper in my pocket ; write a note, and I will take it to any place you like."

"You are a cunning rascal, Captain Jack."

"No matter ; time is flying—there is no use of wasting compliments. Can you raise the amount by writing for it ?"

"In a case of life or death I think I could."

"Well, that's sensible. Here is the pen."

"But suppose I refuse?"

"Well, then, you are a doomed man, that's all, and there's an end of it. Good-day !"

"Stay ; do not go yet. Upon second thought, I think I will write a note. Will you wait for an answer ?"

"Of course, if the money is likely to be forth-coming."

"But it's contrary to the rules of the prison to write letters unknown to the governor, you know."

"Oh, the governor be d——d ! What matters ? He'll not know a syllable about it. Here you are ; scribble away."

Phillip Redgill took the pen and paper.

"Go out for a minute, Captain Jack, and stretch your legs. By the time you return I shall have the note written."

Captain Jack strolled out of the cell carelessly.

Directly he had gone Phillip Redgill pulled out his pocket knife, and made a small wound in his arm.

The blood gently flowed.

With the liquid he wrote a note in a strange hand, and in a still stranger character, which ran thus,

D——w——g,—By our solemn oath, help me. My former note will explain all. This night decides my fate !
PHILLIP REDGILL.

When Captain Jack returned, the prisoner had finished his note, and directed it with ink to—

CAPTAIN GINGLES,
Blue Boar,
City.

Strictly private and confidential.

"Captain Gingles, eh ? Is that the name of your friend ?"

"Yes."

"It's a queer one, any way," said Captain Jack, taking the note, and balancing it between his fingers in a musing manner. "He's got plenty of cash, I suppose ?"

"Yes, lots of money—that's why he's called Gingles, for he's always got his pockets well filled, and is fond of gingling it about."

"I see, I see ; but what time have I to present it ?"

"Don't go there before twelve o'clock to-night, for he always likes to have his wine undisturbed. You must catch him when he is coming out."

"Very good."

"And when shall I see or hear from you, Captain Jack ?"

"Directly I get the money—to-night, perhaps, or to-morrow morning early."

"That's satisfactory. Give my respects to Gingles, Captain Jack."

"I shan't fail. Keep up your courage ; you will only be transported if we get the coin."

So speaking, he left the prisoner, who, strange to say, now began to smile and look quite elated.

"It is my last card," said Phillip, to himself, " and I have played it. Death-wing will surely not prove a craven to one who has so much and so often befriended him. If all goes well, I may yet escape out of the clutches of this stony-hearted Captain Jack ; and if I do !" he said, clenching his fist, and striking it heavily on the table—"and if I do, I'll have revenge on him first !"

Captain Jack went his way with the note in his pocket, and as he was about to leave the prison he met the turnkey who had been speaking with Phillip.

"Hello ! who gave you liberty to leave the prison, eh ?"

"I only went across the road to have a drop of ale."

"Oh, that's nothing, eh, you rascal ? Don't you know that your prisoner is one of the most determined villains that ever lived ? Keep inside, and mind your duties, and if I catch you having any chat with Redgill, or up to any nonsense with him, such as taking letters and the like, I'll have you publicly horsewhipped, mind ye."

"Letters ?—me take letters, Captain Jack ? I'd never dare to do such a thing."

"I wouldn't trust you further than I could see you," was the reply. "Now go and doubly lock the prisoner's door. If he escapes I will hang you instead, mark me."

With these words Capt. Jack went his way, and he had not gone far when he entered a wine-shop.

"I wonder what this Redgill has said in his note. There's no harm in opening it. I can soon seal it up again."

So thinking he opened the note.

"Hillo, he's written it in red ink ! How the devil did that happen ? My ink was black. No matter, it seems he's cleverer than we thought ; he's got some things concealed on his person yet, I fancy, although we searched him twice. No matter, let's see what he says.

"What does this 'D—w—g' mean ?" thought Capt. Jack, as he puzzled himself over the note.

"There is some mystery here, or why say 'by our solemn oath' ? Perhaps he belongs to some secret band, who knows ? It was well I opened it, or perhaps I might have fallen into a trap !

"'My former note explains all,' does it ? What other note has he written then, I wonder ? How could he write unknown to the prison officers, eh ?

"Ha, ha, Mr. Phillip Redgill, I begin to smell a rat," thought Capt. Jack. "He has made friends with some one in the prison, no doubt ; that cross-eyed turnkey, I shouldn't wonder. Oh, if I catch the rascals up to any kind of tricks to thwart me in my plans, I'll have them all hung, that I will.

"'This night decides my fate,' eh ? Quite right there, Mr. Phillip ; quite correct, and no mistake. 'But I must be careful.' Yes, Capt. Jack, you must be very careful of yourself in dealing with this tricky customer, for it strikes me that this Capt. Gingles may be some powerful friend of his, and an enemy to me.

"What shall I do.

"Shall I take the note myself, or let one of the 'dozen' do it? No, I must take it myself, for if this Gingles gives the money, ten to one my men would bolt off with it."

For several hours Capt. Jack didn't know how to act in the matter.

He didn't want to trust any of his men with such a large sum as £1,000.

For if he had done so, and they for a miracle proved honest, he would have had to divide the spoil with them all.

This was a consideration that Capt. Jack did not at all relish.

"No, no," said he, "I must stick to this little sum myself, and if I get it, why, Phillip Redgill may be assisted to escape without trial at all, and the trial will be sure to fall on the sleepy gaolers, for we *must* hang somebody."

Time was flying, however, and something must be done in the matter.

It was now ten o'clock, and yet he was undecided how to act.

He was sauntering along the dark streets, when he accidentally came across one of his own men.

"Hello, captain! is that you?"

"Why, Ben, my lad, how are you? I've not seen you for three or four days. You seem rather 'mellow.'"

"Yes, captain, 'mellow' is the word. I *am* rather 'mellow, if it comes to that, and I like it."

"So it seems. You seem to be pretty well off for money, Ben."

"Yes, captain, I've made a little this last day or two."

"How was that?"

"Why, seeing that the dozen haven't had anything to do, not a single job on hand for this last month, I thought I'd do a little bit of business for myself on the extreme quiet, for our trade has been as flat as ditch water of late."

"True, Ben; and money is very tight."

"So I thought; but, as I've got a few pounds to spare, you are welcome to them, captain."

"No, thank you, Ben; but where did you pick up the money?"

"At the old 'Bull and Mouth.'"

"Indeed!"

"Yes, the old house is full of people, and there card-playing is going on both night and day. There's one chap there as must have won over a thousand pounds these last few days."

"What's his name?"

"Gingles—Captain Gingles, I think they call him."

"Ah! you don't say so? What sort of a fellow is he?"

"Well, he's rather tall, and strong-looking; but he's got a grey head and long hair, and wears spectacles, and stoops like a very old man."

"Not much good in a quarrel or a fight, I suppose?"

"Him! Bless your heart, no; he's as gentle as a child, and, I warrant me, as weak as a cat."

This description of the person to whom Redgill addressed his note so pleased Captain Jack that he altered his mind again for the hundreth time, and resolved to take and present the note himself, and thus pocket the large sum bargained for.

He soon got rid of Ben, and, with a light heart, bent his steps towards the well-known inn.

He was muffled up to the eyes, and when he had ordered a bottle of wine and other luxuries, he entered the card-room and seated himself in a quiet corner.

He cast a quick glance around him, and instantly perceived old Gingles, who had at his elbow a large sum in gold.

Card playing was now at its height, and so tempting did it appear to Captain Jack, that, after a time, he joined them, and for the first hour won a good stake.

Heated with wine, and flushed with his unexpected success, he made a very heavy bet with old Gingles, and, to the astonishment of all present, *lost* it!

Gingles raked the heap of shining gold into his old hat and put it into his pocket with a wicked grin which almost drove Captain Jack mad.

Captain Jack lost every farthing he had, and was so aggravated that he could have danced around the room with passion, and felt as if he could have shot old Gingles, who, calm, quiet, and unruffled, played on, and still continued to win with astonishing good fortune.

"No matter," thought Captain Jack, "he will have to pay me a thousand pounds for his friend, which will make me all right again. I wish they'd stop playing, I want to present this note, and learn what he'll do in the matter. If he refuses, I'll get one or two of my lads to waylay the old rascal and rob him. I'll have his money, by fair means or by foul!"

Midnight had long chimed, and still the play continued.

The "noble captain" felt very sore about his losses at cards, and chewed the end of his cigar in a terrible temper.

"I should like to get up a game to beat old Gingles," thought he; but ere he had sat long in meditation a great cheer rose from the card-table.

"Gingles won it."

"No, he didn't."

"I say he did."

"I'll swear he didn't."

"You lie, old Gingles!" said the other, who was called Alick, and a notorious card-sharper.

As he spoke, he struck the table violently.

"I tell you I did win the game—the money is mine."

"Lay a hand on that gold, and I'll knock you down, you cheating old scamp!" said Alick, in a terrible rage. "The money is mine."

"It is not. I'll leave it to any gentleman in the room."

"Alick won it fairly," said a chorus of voices.

"No, old Gingles is entitled to the money. He could beat Alick all night."

"Could he?"

"Yes, he could," said several, "and I don't mind wagering a hundred guineas on another game."

"So would I."

"And I."

"Well, then, gentlemen, since there is a dispute about the game, I am willing that we increase the stakes fourfold, and play it again."

"Hear, hear," cried several voices.

"I don't mind," said old Gingles; "but not till I've had some supper, and a walk in the cool air, to freshen me up a bit."

"Well, then, it's decided—put down your money. Gentlemen, in half an hour the game begins again."

"Agreed, agreed!" shouted every one.

The money was put down for the contested game of cards, and great enthusiasm prevailed amongst the audience, all of whom seemed to have plenty of money.

Captain Jack was pleased that old Gingles did not win the last stake, and mixed among the company, who were almost unanimous in their opinion that Alick would be sure to play "his very best," and win, "for," said several, "of all men on earth he hates most, it is old Gingles."

"I am sure to win," said Alick, triumphantly, "and will lay two to one on it."

"Hear, hear!"

"So will I."

"And I."

"And so will I," said Captain Jack, whose brain now began to get muddled with wine and excitement.

"Where's your money?"

"Oh, I shall have some presently," said Jack, "as much as any one in the room."

At that moment he saw old Gingles leave the room.

He followed him.

In a few moments he overtook the old man, and presented Redgill's note.

"In difficulties, eh?" said the old man, eyeing Captain Jack like a hawk; "but he has not stated the amount he wants."

"Oh! he left that to me."

"Indeed! can I trust to your honesty?"

"Oh! honour bright!"

"Then who are you?"

"Well, they call me Captain Jack, and I am one of the Crown officers."

"Oh! yes; I think I have heard your name mentioned before in very flattering terms in your endeavours to suppress or destroy the famous Skeleton Crew."

"Exactly," said Captain Jack, bowing in mock humility.

"And what is the sum you need, my noble captain?"

"Well, I think £1,500 will get him out of trouble."

"Quite a modest sum, certainly."

"But, then, you know, Mr. Gingles, you are very rich, and there are a great number of persons to be paid out of it."

"I see, I see; but how much do you intend to keep for yourself?" asked the old man, fumbling in his pockets.

"Me! my dear sir? I do not intend to keep a farthing. It is out of pure friendship for the poor young man that I do this."

"How very kind of you. Well, captain, all I can say is, that if I give you this amount, I hope you will use it properly; for I must help young Redgill out of this difficulty. I have sworn it on my oath, and my oath must be fulfilled. How much was the sum you named?"

"£2,000."

"Why, just now you said £1,500."

"But I made a great mistake."

"Never mind, never mind; £500 more or less isn't much in a case of life or death."

So saying, the old man pulled a large wallet of bank notes, and paid Captain Jack the large sum demanded.

One would have thought that Captain Jack might have been satisfied with this large amount, and would have gone homewards and fulfilled his engagement with Phillip Redgill.

But he did not.

The more money he had the more he wanted.

Besides this, he had suddenly entertained a deep and deadly hatred against old Gingles for winning his money at cards.

He therefore retraced his steps towards the "Bull and Mouth," and when near the door, who should he espy coming out but Alick, the well-known card-sharp.

"Ah! my noble captain; how are you? I was glad to see you had so much spirit in the card-room as to offer to back me in this game, and as I rather like you, I'll let you into the secret."

"Secret! What is it?" asked Captain Jack, with his ears all cocked ready to receive it.

"Well, you see," said Alick, taking the "noble captain's" arm; "but come away from the doorway first, there may be listeners. You see this old Gingles is very rich, and passionately fond of cards; He has cart loads of money; where he gets it nobody knows; but, at all events, during the past week, he has won enormous sums at the card-table, and how he does it nobody can find out."

"You don't mean that?"

"I do though. There is a secret about it, and I have found it out."

"What is it?"

"All the cards have private marks on the back, which cannot be seen by the naked eye; but his spectacles magnify I have found out, and, therefore, when he looks across the table he can see what cards I hold in my hand."

"Oh! the cunning old devil!"

"Yes; isn't he? But in this game we are going to play to-night I have made a promise that he shan't be allowed to wear his spectacles."

"Then you are certain to win. What a capital idea."

"Yes, isn't it? Those gentlemen brought me there to-night to fleece old Gingles."

"But he won from you all the time."

"Yes, true," said Alick, grinning; "but that was the 'dodge,' in order to give him courage."

"I see it all plainly enough now."

"Very well; and now that I have told you this important secret, will you give me shares in your winnings?"

"Yes, half."

"Agreed. How much have you?"

"Two thousand pounds."

"Well, I will so play that the odds which are on me now shall change on him, and when you think he is winning, do you take up all the odds laid against me."

"I will, and be glad to do it."

"Certainly; why shouldn't you win a thousand or two as well as he?"

"Why not, indeed? and I will, you'll see."

"I know you will if you follow my advice."

"I will to the letter."

"You see through it, don't you? Nice dodge, ain't it, captain?" said he, half reeling with wine. "You'll make a clean four thousand pounds by the job, and hazard nothing, you know; while I win the stake, and make twice as much by outsiders, friends, who, with unlimited cash, will bet on me! Can you see through it, my boy?"

The noble captain saw through it clearly enough, and, although half tipsy, gave Alick an ominous but eloquent wink, and squeezed his hand in token of friendship.

"Come along, my boy," said Alick, taking the captain's arm. "Come along, old boy; don't let's pass a public without a drop or two; they keep the best old wines in the whole kingdom up this street. Come on, now, only one more, captain, and then we'll return. I'm sure to win this match; it is for a large sum, you know. But are you fly to a thing or two? Well, then, listen to me."

Mr. Alick, half laughing and half hiccuping, explained the little game again.

"Old Gingles knows I can beat him now—Lord bless you, I have improved wonderfully of late—but the 'gentlemen' won't believe it, and will back Gingles to any amount. I shall beat him by long odds! I heard him confess it himself; he told me so to-night on the sly, and wouldn't play the game at all, only some gentlemen agreed to stand most of the money for him. Pretty dodge, ain't it? Well, I'll play the match, if I have to pawn the rags off my back. This night's work will supply me with small change, my boy, and then I shall say good-bye to the card table, quit London, begin to lead a new life, and be 'a good boy' for the future."

"Half the world is made up of knaves, Alick, my boy; the other half are fools," said the captain, hiccuping, and with a great air of wisdom.

When Alick returned to the card-room he looked as calm and sober as a judge.

Old Gingles, however, appeared nervous, and unwilling to play.

But the gentlemen present insisted on his doing so; but when Alick demanded that he should play without spectacles the old man got into a terrible rage, and refused to do so.

However, after a stormy discussion, in which it was insinuated that old Gingles had some dishonest motive in wearing them, he threw them upon the floor and smashed the spectacles all to pieces.

The game commenced, and heavy wagers were laid on Alick's winning it.

Old Gingles, however, so turned the odds against Alick that many began to murmur at the extraordinary change in the play.

"Now's your time," said Alick to the noble captain, "the odds are two to one against me; take all you can get at that price. I am sure to win."

The noble captain having received "the tip" from his friend Alick, took all the odds laid against him, until his £2,000 was exhausted.

The game progressed, and was very, nay, intensely exciting.

Now old Gingles was a point or two in advance, but in a few moments Alick was level again, and great applause was the consequence.

The two players now stood game and game.

The third game or the rubber was to decide it.

It began, and was quickly played, but by the merest chance of bad luck Alick lost it by a single point.

"Lost it!" gasped Captain Jack.

"Yes," said Alick; "by the merest chance in the world."

The friends of old Gingles were in ecstacies, and carried him out of the room in triumph, but not before the old man had well-nigh filled his large pockets with his winnings.

Captain Jack was like a madman.

He raved and cursed and swore in the most frightful manner.

He called every one the hardest and the worst names he could think of, and wanted to fight anybody or everybody.

Alick was just as noisy.

He swore that he had been cheated, swindled, robbed, and whatever else his imagination could conjure up.

So noisy and turbulent was he, and "the noble captain," that the gentlemen at last bundled them both out into the street.

There they stood out in the cold with drawn swords, and using the most dreadful language.

"Never mind," said Alick, "we will best old Gingles yet."

"What do you mean?"

"I know where he lives."

"Well?"

"Let us hasten to his house, and, as he returns home, let us set upon him, and fleece him of everything."

"Not a bad idea. I can quickly wake up a dozen lads who will do the trick in no time.

"Never mind calling in assistance, surely two strapping fellows like us can easily 'settle' the old man, and the money will be our own."

"Agreed," said Captain Jack. "I've got a black mask in my pocket."

"So have I."

"Then when we assail him let us wear them, and speak not a word."

This plan was agreed to, and the two intended robbers set out on their journey.

They had a mile or two to go, but by quick walking they soon arrived at the residence of old Gingles.

"It don't look like a gentleman's house," said Captain Jack. "Why, it stands by the river side, like a huge warehouse for goods."

"So it does," said Alick, "and I've often heard it whispered that he is engaged in secret with smugglers, robbers, and the like, or why is he so wealthy?"

"I think as you do from the looks of the place," said Captain Jack. "But I wonder if he has returned yet."

"What time is it?"

"Why, four o'clock," said Captain Jack, who thought for an instant of his engagement with the prisoner, Phillip Redgill.

"Then he must have returned."

"Hang the luck! Who is that, though, whose shadow just now passed across the blinds? There it is again."

"Why, that is the old rascal, for a hundred pounds!" said Alick, in a tone of great disappointment. "What shall we do?"

"Do? Why, we'll knock, and demand admittance in the name of the Crown, and search his premises for stolen goods."

"An excellent idea," said Alick, rubbing his hands, "and as he lives alone, why, we can rob him of every farthing he's got in cash!"

"So we will; but are you sure that he lives alone?"

"I am; there is but one old servant in the whole place, and he is over sixty years of age."

Firmly bent on revenge for what he had lost, and caring not a jot for Phillip Redgill's escape, Captain Jack knocked at the door.

"House, ho! house! Open to officers of the crown!" said Captain Jack, in a very brave tone.

In a moment the window was raised, and old Gingles appeared at it in his night-cap and dressing-gown.

"Who calls so lustily at such an unseemly hour?" asked the old man.

"I do," said Captain Jack, "Open, or I'll break in the door!"

"Call to-morrow."

"Open, I say!"

"Come some other time, madcaps."

"Open, or I'll break it open!"

"Go to the devil!" said the old man, and he slammed down the window again with great violence.

Alick could not but laugh secretly as Captain Jack walked up and down, cursing and swearing.

"Have you any keys?" said Alick.

"Yes; I never thought of that. I've got several skeleton keys in my pocket,"

"Let us stop a little while until the old man goes to bed, and then we can let ourselves in without making any disturbance. The night is dark, no one will perceive us."

After a time, Captain Jack and his friend Alick tried the keys in the door, and were very happy to find that they could open it.

"Now the old rascal must look out for squalls," said Jack; "we have got him at last."

"Won't he be surprised, though!"

"Yes, and no mistake—particularly when he finds out that I am an officer of the crown."

The door was gently opened, and the two intruders entered very quietly.

They crept upstairs.

When they arrived at the top of the landing on the first floor, Captain Jack peeped into the front room.

No one was there.

The room was dimly lighted by a small, solitary light.

Yet, dark as it was, Captain Jack could see that a large dining-table was laid out, as if for the supper of a dozen or more.

"Hullo! what does all this mean?" said the noble captain, in a whisper.

"Rather strange, ain't it?" echoed Alick, in a whisper.

Before they could make any other observation, old Gingles appeared upon the scene, and came from a secret closet so suddenly and noiselessly, that neither of the intruders heard or perceived him until he said, abruptly, in their ear,

"Well, and who are you? What do you want, and where do you come from?"

This was so unexpected by Jack and Alick that the former, for a moment, could not answer, and the latter began to titter in the background.

"Did you come to rob me?" the old man asked, in a determined voice.

"No—that is to say, not that exactly, but—"

"Well, no 'buts' for me—what do you want?" said the old man, advancing towards Captain Jack.

In an instant the nightcap and dressing-gown, the false wig, moustache, and stooping gait disappeared like magic, and, to Captain Jack's horror, he stood before no less a person than the terrible Death-wing.

"Death-wing!" gasped Captain Jack, staggering back.

"Yes—Death-wing—no one else!" repeated a dozen voices behind him.

On turning round Captain Jack perceived that he was surrounded by no less than a dozen of the Skeleton Crew!

Before he could say a word, two of the grim gentlemen took the astonished officer by the scruff of the neck, and held him out at arm's length.

"Where is Alick?" gasped Captain Jack.

"Here I am, you scoundrel," said that worthy, who now re-entered the room, attired like one of the Crew.

"What, was it all a trap, then?"

"It was," said Alick; "it was diamond cut diamond, Captain Jack, and you have lost the game."

**ENTRAPPED BY THE GYPSIES.**—*See Number* 19.

"Do you know that your life is forfeit, fool?" said Death-wing.

"You cannot mean that?"

"I do, though, except on one condition."

"Name it, then, most worthy Death-wing."

"Have you liberated Phillip Redgill with the money I gave you for that purpose, or have you squandered it to-night in card-playing?"

"Oh, no! Upon the honour of a gentleman, I assure you I procured his release."

"Indeed!"

"Yes."

"You did it, say you?"

"I did."

"And how?"

"Well, then, most worthy Death-wing and gentlemen," said Captain Jack, turning to the Crew around him, "I'll unburden my heart, and tell you the truth."

"For once in his life!" said Allick, with a boisterous laugh. "Go on, I am listening."

"In the first place," said Captain Jack, beginning

No. 17.

to invent a string of lies, "in the first place I took the fifteen hundred pounds—"

"Two thousand pounds was the sum I gave you."

"Ahem—beg pardon—so it was—I forgot all about it at the moment. Well, I took the two thousand pounds directly you gave it to me, and mounted my horse, so as to make all the haste I could in order to return and see the famous game between old Gingles—"

"Sir?"

"I beg pardon; I should have said Captain Death-wing and his friend Alick."

"Well?"

"I paid Colonel Blood £1,000 for his share."

"Did he give you a receipt?"

"Why, no, I was in such a hurry I forgot to ask for one."

"And yet you promised to produce receipts for all your expenses."

"So I did, most august Death-wing; but, as I said, I was so much interested in your game of cards, I forgot to take note of my promise."

"Well, go on ; what did you do with the other thousand ?"

"I gave £250 to each of the three gaolers, and——"

"Why, you told me there were but two gaolers."

"Did I ? Ah, I forgot ; I meant to have said three."

"Well, and how did you lay out the other £250 ?"

"I gave it to the prisoner to help him along with in order to escape."

"Very kind of you, indeed," said several.

"Yes, wasn't it ?" said Captain Jack, who was now much pleased with the effect his lies had upon his grim hearers.

"You are sure you did not keep it for yourself ?" asked Death-wing, in a savage tone.

"Keep it for myself ? Impossible ! I could not think of such a thing !"

"Of course not, as an honourable man——"

"As an honourable man, not having the least personal interest in such a matter, I could not think of——"

"Certainly not, certainly not. The noble captain of 'the Baker's dozen' is too high-minded and honest to resort to such a trick."

Captain Jack bowed very humbly to this compliment ; but it must be confessed his knees began to tremble under him from fear.

"And did the prisoner escape ?"

"He did."

"Are you sure ?"

"Positive of it ; I saw him do it."

"And how did it happen, then ?"

"As soon as I gave the money to the jailers, they entered his cell, unfastened his irons, loaned him some of their clothes, and I having procured a horse for the fugitive, he galloped away at full speed. After that I returned to see the match between you and Alick, and I came here with him to tell you all about it."

"Very obliging of you," said Death-wing, "very obliging, certainly ; but it strikes me very forcibly you came here, expecting to find me alone, with the intent of robbing me."

"Robbing you ! Oh ! you cannot think that. I am incapable of conceiving such a thing."

"That may be ; but who have you got to prove all you have said about the prisoner's escape ?"

"I did not think it necessary to bring the jailers with me to witness all I have said ; but it is true, nevertheless, every word."

"That may be ; we shall quickly see."

So speaking, Death-wing stamped his foot thrice heavily upon the floor.

A stranger answered the summons by entering the room.

He walked up towards Captain Jack, and confronted that officer boldly.

He looked pale, haggard, and worn.

It was Phillip Redgill himself.

Captain Jack could have sunk through the floor.

"Do you know this person ?" said Death-wing, speaking to Phillip.

"I do, well ; too well for my own comfort."

"Did you hear his story about your escape ?"

"I did ; every word of it."

"Was it true ?"

"No ; every word he uttered was a lie."

"Did he not bargain not to arrest you for a certain sum ?"

"He did."

"On his promise, as a man of honour and a gentleman, you believed him ?"

"I did."

"You paid the price he demanded ?"

"Yes ; and no sooner did he receive it than he had me arrested."

"Who assisted you to escape ?"

"I know not, or how or when it was, Captain Death-wing. All I know is, that I fell into a deep sleep, and when I awoke to consciousness I was liberated from prison and safe and well here in this house, surrounded by several armed men of the Skeleton Crew."

"Do you hear that, Captain Jack ?" Alick asked, with a sneer.

"I do hear it."

"All this was done," said Death-wing, "while this gentleman here was betting at cards. Instead of paying the sum he spoke of, he lost every note in betting against me. In proof of it, I had every bank note marked, and here they are," said he, presenting before Captain Jack's own eyes the very notes he had lost in bets.

"He is a rogue !" said one.

"An infamous liar !" growled several.

"He is not worthy of life !"

"What shall we do with him ?"

"Kill him ! kill him !"

Captain Jack now felt cold perspiration oozing from every part of his body, and he trembled in every limb.

"You have boasted in your time of having done great things against the Skeleton Crew," said Death-wing, with a grim smile, "but your tales are all lies, for a greater coward than you are never carried a sword, Captain Jack."

"He is not fit to live !"

"I know he is not," said Death-wing, "and he shall die, unless he promises to fulfil all we ask of him."

"Name it—name anything you like, and I will do it," said Captain Jack, trembling.

"In the first place, you received several thousand pounds from Phillip Redgill ?"

"Yes, I did, worse luck."

"Will you return it ?"

"How can I do so ?"

"That remains with yourself to think of. If you do not in less than a week, your life is not worth a farthing !"

"But I have no money."

"Are you not captain of the Baker's Dozen, as your men are called ?"

"I am."

"Well, then, get it how you can, but if you fail in doing so in less than a week, you die ! Do you hear ?"

"I do."

"You will be watched and dogged both night and day, remember. There is not the least chance of your escaping me or my band."

"Well, and what next ?"

"You told Colonel Blood that Phillip Redgill did the murder ?"

"I did."

"And what proof have you ?"

"The clothes which Redgill exchanged with Bob Bertram were given up to me by young Ned Warbeck. The proof is clear against Phillip Redgill."

"You think so ?"

"I know so."

"But you must not 'know so,' if you value your life, Captain Jack !" said Death-wing, with an oath. "Don't be so fast with your tongue, but listen to me."

"I will."

"You know Ned Warbeck ?—Wildfire Ned, as he is called."

"I do, well. He is one of the bravest—"

"Stop!" said Death-wing, with a fierce oath; "would you thus speak of my deadliest enemy?"

"Your enemy?"

"Yes, and that of all the band. I believe the young brat was born to bring disgrace and ruin on the Skeleton Crew, for ever since he was born misfortune has followed us."

Captain Jack listened, but said not a word.

In his heart he loved Ned Warbeck, and hated both Redgill and his grim friends with his bitterest hate.

"Now, I tell you, Captain Jack, that this youth must die, by any means in your power or mine. Could you not, in some manner, fasten Farmer Bertram's murder upon Ned Warbeck?"

"It is possible, but—"

"No 'buts' with us—you must do one thing or the other. You must die here, where you now stand, or take a most solemn oath to arrest Ned Warbeck, and charge him with murder."

"But where are the witnesses to carry out the charge of murder?"

"You can do that easily enough. Once he is in prison, there will be no difficulty in bringing up men to swear to anything we ask of them. Some of your own band, Castain Jack, could do that."

"Yes, if they were well paid for it."

"And so they shall be."

"But where is the money to come from?"

"Oh, you must find that."

"Me?"

"Yes, you. Rob Colonel Blood, or whoever you choose. I care not what you do, so you obey my commands."

"I will do as you wish," said Captain Jack, who was over anxious to get away from such horrible-looking people. "Let me go, and I'll fulfil any commands you like."

"So be it. Remember your oath."

"I will."

"And also remember," said Death-wing, "that every step you take, and every action you do, will be closely watched by some one or other of the Skeleton Crew."

"I will not forget."

"Then, on your bended knees, before all assembled, swear on this sword to fulfil my commands."

"I will."

Captain Jack fell upon his knees, and, then, in the midst of all assembled, swore to apprehend Ned Warbeck on the charge of murder, and to procure witnesses at any cost to support the charge.

In a few moments thereafter, Captain Jack was in the open air again, and free.

He knew not why or wherefore, but directly he got into the streets again, he ran from the house with great fleetness, like a hare which has escaped from a deadly snare.

---

## CHAPTER XXXVII.

### THE OATH—NED WARBECK IS ARRESTED FOR MURDER.

WHEN Captain Jack had run himself out of breath, and had come to a dead standstill from sheer exhaustion, he leaned against a lamp-post, and, puffing and blowing, began to think what he had better do.

"What the devil must I do?" he mused. "I know not which way to go, or what to be up to. If I attempt to rob Colonel Blood to get money, the chances are ten to one I shall get a pistol ball in my head, or a sword through my side. If I do not get the money, why, then, those grim devils will skin me alive. Then I have to arrest Ned Warbeck, not an easy matter, for he has hosts of friends who would fight to the last for him."

"Yet something must be done, and quickly," he thought; "for though I have run away from that cursed house as fast as my legs would let me, I have no doubt that I am watched already, and followed about like a shadow."

While he thus thought, a drunken man knocked against him.

"Hulloa, where are you going to?" said Captain Jack, feeling desirous of drawing his sword, and taking revenge upon somebody for the sad adventures of the night.

"Hulloa, where are you going to?"

"Where are you going to?" was the reply; "don't you know a gentleman when you see one?"

"I do; but you are not one."

"You seem to know me then."

"I do—it's Black Ben."

"Right you are; and you are the noble Captain Jack?"

"I am."

"I thought so; and if it's a fair question, what are you up to so early in the morning?"

"I am on the road to the devil, Ben."

"I don't understand, captain."

"I am on my way to old Sir Richard Warbeck's house."

"What for?"

"You would never guess."

"Perhaps not; what for, then?"

"To arrest young Ned Warbeck on the charge of murder."

"You don't mean that!"

"I do though; he is innocent of the charge it is true, Ben, but still he must suffer for old Bertram's murder."

"Why, you have arrested two on the charge before."

"True; but old Redgill's clerk, Mr. Bolton, is innocent. He is out of prison, and Phillip Redgill has broken jail."

"Broken jail! it's the first I have heard about it."

"That may be; but it is true for all that. I have been in the hands of Death-wing and his band all night, and have sworn on my life to have Ned Warbeck hung, in order to save myself; for old Gingles you spoke ot turned out to be no other than Death-wing. I lost all my money at cards, and was afterwards entrapped into their den, and swore a solemn oath to do this, or would have been killed on the spot."

"But you will not keep your promise now that you are free."

"I must."

"Remember your oath," said a distant voice.

---

## CHAPTER XXXVIII.

### IN WHICH CAPTAIN JACK FINDS ENEMIES AMONG HIS OWN MEN—THE TABLES ARE TURNED.

IT was now very plain, from the progress of our story, that Colonel Blood had fully got Captain Jack and his gang under his thumb, and that their very lives depended on his will and pleasure.

It was also known that he was a great favourite of the king, and that whatever he might say or do was law.

Old Tom Bates—he with the long nose, off which Colonel Blood had not long ago knocked a large pimple—was in exceeding great wrath, and secretly vowed vengeance against Colonel Blood.

If the truth must be told, old Bates had not long before that had a long conference with Captain Jack about this Colonel Know-all, as Bates termed him.

He and Captain Jack met by accident, one evening, and entering a wine-shop, began to drink very heavily.

"I tell yer what it is, captain," said old Bates, tossing off a bumper and winking very cunningly, "I'll tell yer what it is, captain."

"Well, what *is* it ?" said Captain Jack, adjusting the black patch over his eye, and winking with the other.

Well, what I means to say, is this 'ere, Captain Jack. If things in our line don't get a little brisker than they has been o' late, why, I shall leave the Dozen and start on my own individual account."

"Leave the Dozen, Bates ?"

"Aye, why not ?"

"But you can't."

"Aye, but I will, I tell yer, and you nor none on 'em can stop me. What's the good o' having a captain at the head on us who don't do something in the way o' trade ? Why, since that affair of old Bertram's murder, we've had nothing at all to do, and you must recollect, captain, that a man of my mettle can't stand that sort o' game any longer. Give me plenty o' money and little work ; that's my style."

"Well, I'm listening," said Captain Jack, laughing; "go on, I'm all attention."

"You may laugh as much as you've a mind to," said old Bates, in an angry tone ; "but that don't suit me ; I want money, and money I'll have, by fair means or foul.

"Well, then, get it ; it's none o' my business," said Captain Jack, in a surly tone; "I'm just as short as any one."

"And how comes it we are all so hard up, then ?"

"I don't know ; business is dull. I suppose that's it."

"No it ain't," said old Bates, sneeringly. "Business is as good as ever it was, but you are growing as timid as a girl, Captain Jack."

"Me ?"

"Yes, you. You needn't foam, and sweat, and swear, I knows all about it."

"About what ?"

"Why, that affair with you and Colonel Blood ; you are under his thumb, my man."

"Well, suppose I am, what then ? Didn't he threaten to hang every one of the Dozen on the cross-roads if we didn't find out the murderer of old Farmer Bertram ?"

"Well, and so we have. Haven't you got young Redgill in prison for it ?"

"Yes," said Captain Jack, but at the same time he knew he was telling a lie, and tried to whistle.

"Now you've got the right party, what more claim has the colonel got against us ?"

"Young Redgill ain't hung yet ; the bargain holds good, so the colonel says, until that's accomplished."

"Why, that's another condition," said old Bates, with an oath ; "first it was capture him, now it's stop till he's hanged ; there seems to be some mystery about this whole affair, Captain Jack ; there has been some bargain or other between you and this young Redgill.

"Bargain," said Captain Jack indignantly "bargain ! what do you mean ?"

"Why I mean this, Captain Jack, that you've been doing a shuffling business with all of us."

"Do you mean to insult me ?" said Jack, placing his hand upon his sword and looking very ferocious.

"I don't care whether you take it as an insult or not, one man's word is as good as another, and young Redgill told the gaolers that you have had thousands from him one time and another."

"Thousands !" said Captain Jack, indignantly, " why, the fellow must be mad to talk in that way ; why, he never had thousands in all his life."

"Not by fair means, I dare say, Jack ; but there ain't a doubt but what ne has paid *you* well enough."

"Now, look here, Bates," said Captain Jack, "you must be either dreaming or mad ; I only received what he owed me of borrowed money."

"Borrowed money," said Old Bates, laughing out lustily, "borrowed money, eh ? Why, you must take me for a perfect fool, Captain Jack."

"Well and suppose I do ?"

"Why, all I can say, then, you are d—nably mistaken."

"Hullo, Bates, hullo ! what does all this mean, eh ? You get me to crack a bottle of wine with you, and then you turn round and abuse me."

"No I don't, it's you that abuses *me*. Do you think for a moment you could have thousands of pounds to lend to a young rascal like that ? No, no, Captain Jack ; if you *do* think me a fool, I tell you again you are d—nably mistaken, that's all."

"Come, come, old man, let's have no noisy words from *you*, you know you'd have been hung long ago except for me."

"Would I ? and ain't you as thick in the mud as I am in the mire ?  Listen to me."

As he spoke, he leaned across the table and whispered.

"How about that money you lost at cards t'other night ?"

"What do you mean ?" said Jack, reddening.

"I suppose you don't know that Phillip Redgill has escaped from prison, do you ?"

"You are a liar," said Captain Jack, with an oath, trying to look firm and desperate ; "you are a liar, Bates, and if you were not so old, and a faithful pal, I'd——"

"Oh, no, you wouldn't," said Bates.  "I am captain now."

"What's that you say ?"

"Nay, you needn't curse and swear, Jack ; I'm telling you the truth."

"But that ain't the truth."

"Yes it is."

"No it ain't, you old liar."

"Look at this, then," said old Bates, pulling out twelve warrants cancelled, "do you know what these mean ?"

"Why, those are the death warrants that Colonel Blood had when he went down to Darlington !"

"I know it."

"But he had thirteen, not twelve."

"I know he had, but Colonel Blood holds the odd one."

"Indeed, and whose is it ?"

"Why, your's, Jack."

"Mine ?"

"Yes, and no mistake."

"And do you mean to say that Colonel Blood has given the twelve to you and not the odd one also ?"

"I do mean it, and for a special reason."

Old Bates was so triumphant in his manner, that Captain Jack looked staggered and amazed.

"Why, you take all the breath out of my body, Bates," said Jack.

"The breath soon will be taken out of your body, if you don't mind; there's a nice new gibbet waiting for you, so Colonel Bland says,"

"Why, what is all this for?"

"It has come to the colonel's ears that you have been playing false to him, and you know he never forgives an enemy."

"The devil!" said Jack; "do you mean to say, then, that he knows all about Redgill?"

"He does; and since he has escaped, he has made up his mind to have revenge on you."

Old Bates smiled like an old ogre as he pulled out of his capacious pocket a sealed document.

"Do you know what this is?" said Bates.

"It looks like a warrant."

"And so it is—you are not mistaken—it is for your own apprehension."

"You are joking."

"I was never more serious in all my life."

"And do you mean to arrest me?"

"That depends," said Bates. "The Dozen and I have had several meetings, and it was resolved to throw you out of the captaincy, and put me in."

"Well!"

"I begged for your life hard, very hard, Jack, for all the lads swore you had played foully with them, and deserved to die."

"But I haven't, Tom."

"You have, Jack; you have been flashing about town for a long time like a lord, and spending lots of money, which ought to have been divided among us; for we've been as poor for the last few months as church mice."

"What do you propose to do, then?" said Jack, drinking his wine; "what do the lads intend to do? Surely you cannot think I'd let myself be taken by any of my old pals while I carry a sword by my side."

"Your sword would do very little good for you, Jack; for I could call upon the citizens here in this place, and carry you off by fair means or foul, if I liked. Here's my warrant, as you see, 'Arrest him, dead or alive;' those are the colonel's words."

"The colonel is a scoundrel," said Jack, striking the table; "and if I ever come across him I'd—"

"Hush!" said old Bates; "don't talk so loudly; you might be heard by somebody."

"Well, go on, let's hear the very worst. I know you've got me in a very tight corner."

"Yes, Jack, and one from which you cannot possibly escape, if I only say so."

"Well, no matter; a short life and a merry one," said Jack. "Here, landlord, bring me another bottle."

"You have not paid for the last one yet, sir," said the landlord.

"What!" said Jack, indignantly, "not paid? What mean ye, sirrah?"

"I don't mean anything in particular," said the landlord; "but I know your face well."

"What of that?"

"In fact, I know it too well."

"Explain yourself. Do you wish to insult a gentleman like me, eh, knave?"

"Nay, sir, I do not; but the last time you called here you had a party of friends with you; you had the best supper I could provide, and dozens of my best wine, and not a single farthing was paid for anything."

"Zounds, villain, would you insult me?" said Jack, attempting to draw his sword. "Zounds, knave, have I lost all spirit that I must be insulted thus by such a pot cleaner as thou? Out on the man; for a groat I would run thee through and through thy fat carcase."

"Silence, Jack, silence," said Bates; "if you make any disturbance the officers will be called in, and then it will be all up with you. Put up your sword, I say."

Jack thrust his blade back into its scabbard, and growled out a fierce oath of vengeance.

Bates waved off the landlord with a promise to pay all arrears, and then he said to Jack calmly, and in a whisper,

"Never mind the pot-bellied publican's account. I will make that all right. Time is precious; I haven't many minutes to stop here."

"Well, what do you intend to do? Are you going to blow the gaff on an old pal like me?"

"That depends."

"On what?"

"Why this; none of us like Colonel Blood."

"I know that well enough."

"Well, one or t'other must die."

"How do you mean? I or the colonel?"

"Just so; we've come to that agreement. Now it depends upon you which it is."

"Why, then, the colonel, of course," said Jack, laughing, and half drunk, "the colonel, of course, I wouldn't think of having the honour myself yet awhile, you know, Bates."

"That's what all of us thought."

"And the lads were right. I hate Blood; yes, hate him worse than the devil himself."

"And what do you intend to do?"

"Why, waylay him and give him a sly poke in the ribs; for if he's not put out of the way soon all of us will be hung, one by one, when he's served his turn with each."

"That's my idea, and also the opinion of every man in the Dozen."

"Look you here," said Jack, suddenly brightening up, "if the colonel has made up his mind to act in such a rascally manner towards me, I can do towards him."

"What do you mean?" said old Bates, pricking up his ears.

"Why, I mean that there is a secret about him he little dreams I know anything about."

"Ah, indeed! what is it, then?"

"It's worth a great deal of money," said Jack, winking.

"How much?"

"Why, £500."

"I don't understand."

"Of course you don't, but I do."

"Then out with it."

"Secresy and honour," said Jack.

"Yes, of course."

"Well, then, read this," said Jack, pulling out his pocket a printed proclamation, which he placed before the wondering eyes of Tom Bates. "There, read it; there it is."

C.  R.

ATTEMPTED MURDER! £300 REWARD! ATTEMPTED MURDER!

"WHEREAS an atrocious attempt at murder been made upon the accepted suitor of one I Harmer, the daughter of the miller at Darlingt.

"And whereas, by a most miraculous chance body of the unfortunate youth, Andrew, was discovered in the river, and resuscitated.

"Therefore, the above reward of
"£300
"will be paid to any-person or persons who shall give such information as shall lead to the discovery or apprehension of the offender or offenders.

"The unfortunate young man was severely wounded, and the shock has been so great that his reason is for the time being lost to him.

"The village authorities of Darlington, on the night of the attempted murder, noticed the arrival in the neighbourhood of a carriage and four.

"The person suspected had a servant attending him during the three hours he remained in the village. His master, the supposed culprit, was traced to London, and from all accounts bears the following description :—

"About 35 years of age ; 5 feet 8 or 9 inches in height ; thick set and powerfully made ; black moustache ; whiskers (supposed to be false); close cut hair ; wore a cloak, and had the appearance of a military man."

"Why that description," said Bates, looking at Jack in surprise, "corresponds to—"

"Blood !" said Jack, in a hoarse whisper.

"You surprise me."

"Does it ? but wait, I'm not done yet," said Jack, "since he has commenced his games with me, he'll find a tougher fellow to deal with than he expects. Look at this."

"Another proclamation !" said Bates, in wonder.

"Yes, read it, and then you'll find out that I have got my enemy fairly on the hip."

Bates unfolded the printed paper and read :—

C.  R.

ABDUCTION !                    ABDUCTION !

£200 REWARD !

WHEREAS, Ellen Harmer, the daughter of old Harmer, the miller, of Darlington, was forcibly abducted from her father's home by some person or persons unknown, on the night of the attempted murder of young Andrew, her acknowledged suitor ;

And whereas, it has come to the knowledge of Sir Richard Warbeck, the chief magistrate of Darlington, that two suspicious persons, with a carriage in attendance, were seen prowling about the village the night in question ;

"Therefore the above reward will be paid to any one who shall give such information as shall lead to the apprehension of the offender or offenders and enable the young maiden to be restored to the arms of her disconsolate father.

The following particulars regarding the supposed unknown abductor may, perhaps, lead to his apprehension.

'About 35 years of age, 5 feet 8 or 9 inches in height, thick set and powerfully made ; black moustache, whiskers (supposed to be false) close hair, wore a cloak, and had the appearance of a military man."

For a moment or two old Bates could scarcely recover from his astonishment.

At last he gasped out, and in a suppressed tone, "Why, they must relate to one and the same person, Jack."

"I know they do."

"But I never saw these proclamations on the walls about London yet."

"I dare say not, and for a very good reason why."

"What reason ?"

"Why, they were given to me to distribute them, —"

"You didn't I suppose?"

"Yes, I did, but only in such out-of-the-way places where they would do no earthly good."

For some time both men kept silent.

"I understand it all," said Bates, at last, "this person who is unknown you know ?"

"Yes."

"This gentleman none of us can guess at."

"You twig, I perceive."

"Yes, rather. He goes down, half murders the lover, and then throws him in the river ; and, thinking he's dead, runs off with the girl."

"Exactly."

"But she wasn't rich ?"

"No, but she is very handsome; a perfect Venus."

"And what could have been his object ?"

"To gratify the king."

"I see ; just so ; and has he acted a friend to you ?"

"No, not to me in particular ; but as he promised to befriend all of us, I kept the thing secret from the Londoners, for £500 isn't to be sneezed at, you know."

"And do you mean to say that all this is true ?"

"Then he's a villain of the worst sort."

"On my oath, Bates."

"I know he is now ; and more than that I always suspected him, but never expected to find he'd prove such a cool, calculating scoundrel ; but I'll be even with him, trust me."

"And this girl—what of her ?" said Bates ; "we are all pretty hard up at this moment ; two hundred pounds would be a fine windfall for us."

"So it would ; and more than that, I know all about her and where she is."

"The devil !"

"And it would be the easiest thing in the world to rescue her, for she's pining away, and is strictly guarded both night and day by a deaf and dumb Nubian slave—a eunuch, in fact—a fierce, tall, ugly-looking devil."

"Never mind ; if we can only once get into the apartment, we shan't have much difficulty in getting clear off with the girl," said Bates ; "the colonel is not supposed to know that you or I have any hand in this affair. If what you say proves true, Jack, we can easily put the colonel out of the way, and we shall be all right again. What do you say ? Shall we try it to-night ?"

"I'm willing. I'm dying to have revenge on the deceitful rascal."

"Then to-night let it be. Come with me ; the Dozen are assembled in a quiet place, waiting for me. I will settle with the old landlord."

"And so will I," thought Captain Jack to himself, "and sooner than he expects."

"We will have to wear masks," said Bates.

"Yes, and keep dead silence."

"If we meet with any opposition, you know—? "

"Oh, as to that," said Jack, "we won't stand nice on trifles. It's a case of life or death with me."

So speaking, Bates and Captain Jack strolled towards the "quiet place" spoken of, and in less than half an hour Jack, half-drunk, rolled in among the "Dozen," who were already assembled.

They looked daggers at him, and would, perhaps, have resorted to violence, but Bates whispered something to them which cooled their anger.

Captain Jack reeled into a chair, and was soon fast asleep and snoring.

"Keep an eye on him, my men," said Bates, in a whisper ; "I am going out on very important business, which I will explain on my return. Jack's all right. Don't have any rows or quarrels with him ; let him have all the drink he wants, but don't let him go out on any account."

So speaking, Tom Bates buttoned up his coat, looked to his sword and pistols, and went forth alone into the darkness and blinding storm of sleet and rain.

---

## CHAPTER XXXIX.

COLONEL BLOOD MEETS A TARTAR—THE RELEASE OF ELLEN HARMER—THE MURDER IN THE WOOD.

TOM BATES had not gone very far from the rendezvous of the Dozen, and was trudging along through the wind and rain, forming plans for that night's operations, when some one in a dark street laid his hand roughly on his shoulder.

Tom stopped as if by instinct.

"That you, colonel?" he asked.

"That you, Bates?"

"Yes, sir."

"Come this way out of the rain," said he.

And he led the way up a dark, narrow alley, which was lighted by a single lamp.

"Well, and what news, Bates? Have you secured that reprobate Captain Jack yet?"

"No, colonel; it is a more difficult matter than might be supposed."

"Where is he, then?"

"I know not, colonel, but imagine that now we are after him he is hiding away in some of the back slums in or around London."

"But how could he have got any information about my wishes or intentions?"

"That I know not, sir; but certain it is that we have been seeking for him both high and low in every hole and quarter; but I fear me he has left London."

"Left London, and for what, pray?"

"Some two weeks ago, colonel, I heard him say that there were two proclamations out about an attempted murder and a forcible abduction case which took place in the village of Darlington not long since. One and the same person is concerned in both transactions, and altogether a reward of £500 is offered."

"Impossible!" said Colonel Blood, biting his lip. "I have never seen any of these proclamations."

"Perhaps not, sir; but Captain Jack said, the last time I saw him, that he had particular reasons for not having them posted up earlier."

As Bates spoke, Colonel Blood looked straight into his eyes; but so well did Bates play the hypocrite, that Colonel Blood had not the slightest notion that he was aware of the real facts of the case.

"And where are these two proclamations, Bates? Have you one with you?"

"Yes, colonel," said Bates, displaying both at once.

"Strange affair," said Blood, biting his lips in anger, "I never heard of all this before."

Old Bates said not a word; but he could not help but remark how Colonel Blood's eyes flashed with anger, and, in his sleeve, he laughed.

"And so these are the two proclamations you speak of, eh?" said the colonel, unfolding and reading them. "How did you get them?"

"Captain Jack gave them to me."

"Damn Captain Jack!" said Blood, stamping his foot in anger; "and so he has gone down to Darlington to investigate these affairs, eh?"

"Yes, that was his intention. He said he made sure of finding out who it was who not only attempted to murder Andrew, but who abducted the girl also."

"Ha! then he is very clever," said the colonel.

After a pause, he added—

"Important business obliges me to leave town to-night. I must run down to Darlington and arrest this troublesome fellow. Captain Jack is no longer to be trusted; he is not now an officer of the crown, and, therefore, has no business to trouble himself about what does not concern him."

"Leave town to-night, colonel!" said Bates, as if surprised.

"Yes, to-night."

"It is a dangerous journey."

"Oh, as to that I have no fears," said the colonel; "no one will ever dare to attack me."

"But what are we to do in the mean time?" said cunning old Bates. "Are we to give any attention to these two proclamations?"

"No, I think not," said Blood, "at least not at present; not until I return to town again. You could never discover the girl's place of concealment."

"But one of my men says, colonel, that he does already know where she is."

"Indeed!" said Blood, anxiously. "Know where Ellen Harmer is, eh? then he must be a very clever fellow, for I don't."

"Oh, then, colonel," said Bates, bowing, and with a smile, "if you don't know anything about this matter, I'm sure I do not."

"Well, no matter, Bates," said Blood; "I'm glad I've seen you, for Captain Jack must be captured at once, and at all costs, for he is a troublesome, intriguing busy-body. Remain as quiet as you can until my return from Darlington. I have plenty of work in store for you."

"Glad to hear that, colonel."

"Good paying jobs, I mean."

"Better still, sir; but—"

"But what, Bates?" said the colonel.

"Oh! I was only about to remark, colonel, that all the lads, and myself included, are very hard up; if you would so oblige us as to lend us a hundred or two until your return, we should—"

"I understand; well, no wonder you are out of money, seeing how much that scoundrel, Captain Jack, appropriated to his own use. Here," said he, giving Bates a hundred-pound note, "this will serve you until my return."

Colonel Blood left Bates in high glee, and went his way.

"Well, this isn't bad to commence with," said old Bates, putting the note into his pocket; "but I mustn't let any of the lads know I have got so much. I'll have it changed, give 'em £10 to drink with, and the rest I'll stick to as my own perquisites."

Bates changed the note, and when he returned, he found his companions grumbling at his long delay.

The £10, however, revived their drooping spirits.

They called for whatever they liked in eating and drinking, and the time passed very rapidly.

Most of the Dozen had got well nigh tipsy before the hour of midnight, and were very noisy.

However, when they had their fill, old Bates called a council of war.

"Look to your weapons, my merry men," said he; "see that your pistols are well loaded, and that your swords are not blunt—we've got a job on hand to-night."

"A job!" said all, in high glee.

"Yes, and one that will pay us well—get yourselves sober, every one of you."

"What is it?"

"Are the doors closed?" said Bates. "No one listening, I hope?"

"Not a soul," said one and all. "What is the job?"

"Who among you loves Colonel Blood? te'l me that," said old Bates.

The name was received with savage oaths.

"Not one, I perceive," said old Bates; "so much the better. And now I'll tell you what I have on hand."

Solemn silence ensued, as Bates said,

"Blood is going down to Darlington to-night, to arrest Jack, who is here. I have put the colonel off the right scent."

"The devil!—to arrest me?" said Jack, with an oath.

"Silence! Jack," growled several, with threatening looks. "Silence, and listen to Master Bates; he is our captain now—not you."

"Well, and while Blood is away on this wildgoose chase, Jack has proposed to rob his house."

"Capital idea," said all.

"So think I," said Bates; "so come, prepare yourselves. Put masks in your pockets, and bring a rope ladder with you."

"And dark lanterns," said Jack.

"A small crowbar to wrench open the shutters," said Bates, "and in less than an hour we can 'clean out' the whole house. Dead silence must be kept —not a word spoken by any one."

"If we meet with resistance——"

"Well, then, use your weapons fearlessly," said Jack. "The night is dark and stormy—just the right weather to crack such a crib as his."

"Come, then," said Bates, "we'll take a parting glass, and then away."

"Agreed, agreed!"

"We musn't all leave the house together, but go in twos and threes. Just as the clock strikes one, let every man meet at Colonel Blood's house, and hide under the highway."

This plan was agreed to, and the Dozen separated.

\* \* \* \* \*

Colonel Blood's splendid town house was situated in and surrounded by large and beautiful gardens, near the river bank, not far from Whitehall Gardens.

The night in question, instead of becoming clearer, got more cloudy and stormy than ever.

Few persons were to be seen moving about in the streets, for the weather was too boisterous and threatening.

As the neighbouring church clocks chimed a quarter to one, a stranger might have perceived sundry persons cautiously approaching Colonel Blood's house.

Some came by land, but the majority hired a boat, and quietly rowed up the river until they got fairly under the garden walls.

The last two persons who arrived, and they on foot, were Captain Jack and Tom Bates.

As they approached Blood's mansion, they were accosted by two night watchmen, who wanted to know their names and business.

"Name?" said Jack, indignantly.

"Our business?" said Bates, striking an attitude of great importance.

"Yes, name and business, gentlemen, if you please."

"And why so, knaves?" said Captain Jack. "How dare you stop two gentlemen, and ask such impertinent questions?"

"We do but obey our orders, sirs," said the night watchman, civilly. "From your dress and manner, I have no doubt you are a couple of 'sparks' return-ing home, but we have received special orders from Colonel Blood himself this very night, to allow no one to pass near his house, after certain hours, without demanding who and what they are."

"Why, you impudent fellow," said Bates, "Colonel Blood is not in town—he left this evening."

"Ah, sirs, indeed, then you are beforehand with us—who told you?"

"Why, the colonel himself, knaves," said Bates. "How dare you stop me and my companion? We are most intimate friends of the colonel. My name is Captain Bates, an officer of the Crown."

"Captain Bates? really, I beg pardon. I did not recollect you. I'm very sorry."

"Yes, sir, we are very sorry," said the other; "and the name of your tall friend is——"

"Captain! ah, yes, Captain Jenkins," said Jack, on the instant.

"You see, Captain Bates," said one of the watchmen, very politely, "we have especial orders from the colonel himself to allow no one to pass towards his gardens without we know they are strictly honest and respectable."

"And are not we strictly honest and respectable, then, villain?" said Bates, blustering. "Why, for two pins, I'd——"

"Oh, there cannot be a doubt of that, sir," said the trembling night watchman; "you could not be an officer of the crown, else."

"Quite right," said Captain Jack, mollified, and drawing the patch over his eye still lower.

"But you see, Captain Bates, as an officer of the crown, you are fully aware that all sorts of knaves have tried to rob the gallant colonel ere now, and at this time, I fear me he has a greater enemy to contend with than ever before; for I heard to-night, as a very great secret, that Captain Jack is no longer the chief of the crown officers, and has been degraded by the colonel; in truth, we have especial orders to guard the place against him and his gang above all others."

"Captain Jack, eh?" said Bates's long-legged companion. "Ah! now I come to think of it, I heard something like that spoken of to-night, while attending the Countess of Gresham's ball; a great villain that Captain Jack, I hear."

"Oh, monstrous," said the watchmen, in chorus. "Oh, a perfect rogue and vagabond. Instead of doing his duty in arresting rogues and rascals, he has been 'bribed to enormous amounts by them to allow them to remain at large."

"Shocking! monstrous!" said Jack.

"Horrible! he ought to be hanged," said Bates, coughing, "which he will surely be, if the colonel only lays hands on him."

So speaking, and bidding them good night, Jack and Bates went on their way, laughing.

"Fine fellow that Bates," said one of the watchmen.

"Yes; only for his nose; why, it has got a piece clipped out of it, which spoils his beauty."

"He got that in a desperate duel—I once heard him say—but he killed his antagonist, run him through and through the body; fine fellow is Bates. How much did he give you to drink his health with?"

"A gold piece."

"Good luck to him, say I. Let us go into some wine-shop and have a bottle. What say you? Surely the house will be safe for half-an-hour."

So speaking, the two watchmen went into the nearest wine-shop that was open.

Both Bates and Jack had watched them.

"Now's our time, Bates," said Jack.

They both disappeared down the dark carriage-way, which was screened by trees and bushes.

# THE SKELETON CREW; OR, WILDFIRE NED.

A STORMY INTERVIEW.—*See Number* 20.

They both whistled softly, and the signal wa quickly answered.

"All right; the lads are up to their time."

In a moment, where a second before no one had been seen, eight or nine men appeared crouching under the garden wall.

"All right," said one, whispering to Bates.

"Have you taken a good squint all round the house?"

"Yes; all are abed."

"Sure of that?"

"Positive."

"But the dogs?"

"We have poisoned them an hour ago; they are all stiff and cold by this."

"Then let us commence. Where is the rope-ladder?"

"Here it is," said one, unwinding a rope-ladder from around his body, and which had been concealed by a short cloak.

"Let a man watch each side of the house," said Jack. "Bates and I will enter, and pass all the valuables out to you; put them into the boat as fast as possible, and if there should be any alarm, run

No. 18.

towards the river. The boat is large enough to take us all."

"If we only had skeleton keys now," said Bates.

"Hang your skeleton keys," said Jack, in disgust. "Don't I know all about the house? I ought to do, for I've been in it often enough; no skeleton keys in the world would open those doors, they are doubly bolted inside, and cased with iron. Give me the rope-ladder."

With great dexterity, Captain Jack threw one end of the rope-ladder up into the air, and the hooks at the end caught in the iron railings of the balcony.

"Silence!" said Captain Jack, and after trying its strength, he began to ascend.

\* \* \* \* \*

But for a moment let us see what was going on inside the house.

Ellen Harmer was confined therein, and was supposed to be strictly watched both night and day by the deaf and dumb eunuch—the Nubian slave.

The fame of her great beauty had reached the ears of the king; but instead of presenting her to his majesty, Colonel Blood had made up his mind to keep her for himself, after having, as he termed it, "tamed her" into submission.

But this proved a much harder task than the colonel had ever imagined.

Ellen Harmer would *not* "be tamed.'

The colonel had offered her wealth and luxury; but she received all his unmanly proposals with scorn.

"I can afford to wait," thought the hard-hearted colonel. "I can afford to wait, a month or two of confinement and pampering will soon bring down her proud spirit."

In hopes of keeping her away from the king, he had removed her first from one place to another, until at last he imagined that his royal master had given her up for lost.

This, Colonel Blood fondly hoped *was* the case.

But he was very much mistaken.

The king had his spies about as well as the cunning colonel; but it was not until this very day that he had actually discovered the beautiful Ellen's hiding-place.

When he heard of it he was in a terrible passion, and for a moment vowed all manner of things against Blood.

When he heard, however, that the colonel had made a sudden journey to Darlington, he made up his mind to visit Blood's mansion alone, and take her away by force.

He had employed a truculent courtier to be on the spot about three or four in the morning.

"By which time," said the king, "I shall have made an impression on the rustic beauty. If she will not consent to be my mistress, why, then, I will give the signal, Rochfort, and be you ready with a guard and a barge to bear her away by force; but let all things be done in secret so that not a syllable may be known to Blood on his return, for I want to make a fool of him after all his deception with me."

These were the instructions given to Rochfort, and at the moment that Captain Jack was quietly preparing his rope-ladder outside, the king was already secreted in the mansion.

Ellen Harmer, in her sumptuous chamber, was reclining on a sofa.

She could not sleep, and the splendid bed with its satin hangings was uncreased.

The Nubian slave stood watching her, and his dark eyes flashed with admiration as he furtively gazed at the beauty it was his duty to watch and guard.

Ellen tried to read; but she tossed from her indignantly the only books the colonel allowed her to receive—namely, some of the licentious works of the time, which, in our day, would not be tolerated in the lowest of society : but which in the period we speak of, passed off for works of wit and amusement.

"Infamous man," sighed Ellen, "to incarcerate me thus from my poor old father, and endeavour to poison my heart and mind with such beastly reading. Oh, that I were free or dead."

She beckoned to the slave.

He noiselessly approached her, and knelt at her feet.

"You are the only friend I have found," she whispered.

The slave bent low, and kissed her feet.

"Is the house quiet? Have all retired to rest?"

The slave bowed.

"The colonel has left for the country, I have heard."

Again the slave bowed.

"I would escape from this gaudy dungeon," she said.

"It is impossible; the doors are all doubly locked and barred; many fierce dogs are loose in and around the grounds, and would tear you in pieces," he whispered.

"Then I fear all hope is lost."

"Not lost," said the slave. "Hold your breath; make not the slightest noise; I have a secret to impart; all hope is not yet lost; this night is the night of your deliverance."

"What!" gasped Ellen in a sudden, and half-suppressed tremor of joy.

"The king is in the mansion at this moment."

"Impossible, slave."

"'Tis true, fair lady; but, hush, I hear footsteps! hush !"

Ellen did not hear the slightest sound, and seemed to think the slave was mistaken.

But he was not.

He crept to the chamber door on his hands and feet, and listened.

He held up his finger in token of silence.

Ellen Harmer sat rooted to her seat.

She listened, but not a sound was audible.

"It is the king," said the Nubian, in the faintest of whispers. "He came to the house in a good disguise, but I recognised him."

"If it be the king, then," said Ellen, "I will throw myself at his feet, and ask protection from the fiendish designs of your master, Colonel Blood."

"It will be useless," said the slave; "he comes here to take you away to the palace, or some secret place, for the rumours of your amazing beauty have entranced him. You are destined to be his mistress or death awaits you."

"Then welcome death," said Ellen, "ere I submit, and degrade myself to so low a level! Heaven assist me in my sore trial this night!"

While she spoke and wept, the Nubian slave crept back again to the door.

"I hear his footstep again," he whispered, and laid his ear close down to the floor.

At that moment the bed hangings rustled.

With a gasp of horror, Ellen perceived an elegant stranger had effected an entrance into her chamber. It was the King!

The slave had not perceived this, and was still listening, with head averted.

The King, sword in hand, looked at the dusky slave, and breathed a desperate oath.

He raised his sword, and would have killed the dusky but faithful Nubian upon the spot.

In an instant, however, Ellen rose from her seat, and falling on her knees before the King, held up her hands, and with tears in her eyes begged for his life.

The King turned and smiled, and motioning to a corner, the slave rose, and crouched in it.

"Move an inch or utter a word," said he, "and you die."

"He is deaf and dumb," said Ellen; "spare the poor docile, faithful creature. Be merciful, stranger —for pity's sake, harm him not; he is the only friend I have!"

"Ah, I forgot, so he is deaf and dumb," said the King. "I have heard Blood speak of this eunuch before. For your sake, sweet lady, I spare him. But, if deaf, why was he listening?"

"He was praying, sir; that is his usual position when at prayers."

"Ah! so be it, then; I never pray myself—I have forgotten how."

This he said with a sneering smile, and as he turned towards Ellen, he dropped upon one knee, and with the sweetest of smiles whispered,

"Fly, lady—fly with me! I have heard of your

cruel captivity, and have come to release you. All is ready for our flight."

So speaking he rose, and passing his arm round Ellen's waist, bore her, more dead than alive, from the chamber.

He doubly locked the door, and entered an adjoining chamber with his unconscious and fainting victim, in order to await the coming of Rochfort.

\* \* \* \*

Captain Jack's head just peeped above the balcony of Ellen Harmer's chamber at the moment the King had left it.

Noiselessly he opened the lattice, and, disguised as he was, entered, pistol in hand.

"I thought I saw a light here a moment ago," he said; "surely I was not mistaken."

He was not; but the King had taken the wax taper with him, and all was now total darkness.

"Splendid chamber this," thought Jack, as he turned on his lantern and gazed around.

He thought in the far corner he could perceive two dark eyes glistening.

He made a thrust at the spot with his sword.

But the Nubian had perceived him and crept under the bed.

"It must have been a cat, or something," thought Jack, as he began to ransack the drawers and wardrobes.

Watches, jewels, silks, satins, and money he found in abundance.

"Hillo! this will do," he mused, as he filled his pockets in great haste.

But the next thing to be done was to descend the stairs, so as to admit his companions.

He was in his stocking feet, and moved about without making the slightest noise.

After much trouble, he forced back the lock of the chamber door.

Like a cat, he descended the stairs, and withdrew the two huge bolts of the front door.

This was done without the slightest noise, and several of his gang entered and distributed themselves all over the mansion.

In a very short time Jack and his comrades stripped the drawing-rooms, parlours, and other rooms, of all their valuables, and as quickly as possible filled several sacks with gold and silver ware from the plate chest in the pantry.

The butler slept in this pantry, but was almost frightened out of his wits, for one of the band held a pistol at his head while the other tied him hand and foot and gagged him.

They then began to work, and did not leave a single spoon or fork behind them.

These bags of spoil were rapidly passed out to old Bates and the others on watch outside, and conveyed to their boat in the river, moored under the garden wall.

Captain Jack, however, did not trouble himself much about silver spoons, or forks, or gold and silver goblets.

He made his way straight towards Colonel Blood's library.

He closed the door, and then began to ransack every hole and corner of the apartment.

The drawers were broken open, and everything of no value to him was strewn about the floor.

In the colonel's writing-desk, however, he discovered a considerable sum of money in gold and notes.

More than this, his eyes glistened as he clutched a small bundle of paper tied up with red ribbon, and sealed with many seals.

This he put into his breast for greater security,

for his huge pockets were bulging out with valuable odds and ends of all sorts.

Having completely despoiled the library, he retraced his steps upstairs.

"Surely Ellen Harmer must be in the mansion somewhere," he thought.

As he passed rapidly up the winding stairs towards the colonel's own bed-chamber, he stopped and listened.

Two persons were conversing in quick, passionate tones.

The voice of one sounded like that of a female in distresss.

Captain Jack listened attentively to all that passed.

"Nay, let me go, I beg of you, as you are a man and a gentleman," said the female voice, in tones of anguish.

"Nay dearest," was the soft reply, "you cannot fly, except with me. You must—you shall be mine!"

"Rather ten thousand deaths," was the brave, resolute answer of the fair one, "rather ten thousand deaths than consent to my own dishonour! Unhand me, I say, unhand me! I took you for a gentleman—a man—but I am deceived—you are a scoundrel. Let me go—unhand me, I say, once for all, or I'll shame you before all the world—I'll raise the whole mansion with my cries."

"'Tis useless to struggle, angelic being," was the impassioned answer; "your beauty has entranced my very soul. Come, let us fly hence; all wealth, honour, and adulation shall be thine."

"Help, help, help!" was the female's feeble cry.

At that time a struggle was heard going on in the room.

At that moment Captain Jack, lantern and sword in hand, dashed the door open and entered.

Ellen Harmer gave a short, quick cry of joy as she perceived deliverance at hand.

Instinctively she rushed into the arms of Captain Jack for protection.

The king was amazed.

He made a thrust at Jack.

But next moment the weapon was knocked from his hand.

He now stood, unarmed and defenceless, before the bold intruder.

"Who art thou?" said the king, in surprise.

"Thy equal," said Jack, in an assumed voice. "What, is it nothing that you now cringe before me, and yet a moment ago you would for ever have dishonoured this blameless girl? Out upon thee, for a craven!"

"Save me, save me!" sobbed Ellen.

"Peace, lass, thou art safe," said Captain Jack. "And as for thee," said he, turning towards the king with a gesture of disgust, "as for thee, more anon."

"How, knave, wouldst thou dare to stand there prating to your superior, when with one word I could have thee hanged? You know not who nor what I am."

"Nor do I want to know, sirrah; and mark me' do not let thy tongue wag so carelessly, for by my word, be you king or peasant, I'll make a lame duck of ye. Out upon thee, man! would ye, like a cowardly interloper, come poaching on these strange grounds, when you know the master is away?"

"What mean ye, impudent rogue?"

"Mean? why, I mean that you had not courage to try your fortune here while Colonel Blood was at home; but, like a clown, must crawl in when he had gone away."

"You seem to know all this?"

"I do," said Captain Jack, telling a lie. "I know not only all you would have done, but who you are, for all your disguise."

"You do?" said the king; "then, as you know me, stranger, reveal not my name or station."

And as he spoke he placed one finger on his lip in token of silence.

"'Tis the king," said Ellen Harmer, "I was told so to-night."

"No, no——."

"It is not the king," said Jack, again telling a lie, "because if he were he would not give me that signet ring he now wears, as you will see presently."

The king smiled, and, taking off his signet ring, gave it to Captain Jack.

"I told you it was not the king, fair one," said Jack, lightly laughing, "for if it had been he would not have so humbled himself; besides, lassie, the king would never think of insulting a poor defence-less girl."

As he spoke these words, Captain Jack left the room, and as he departed, said to the king,

"Stay you here for at least twenty minutes; if you move I will not be answerable for your life."

He closed the door, and carrying his lovely burden lightly on one arm, made the best of his way into the garden.

As he did so, he heard the alarm given by old Bates and others outside.

Old Bates and his companion watchers whistled very shrilly, and so loud did they become, that Captain Jack and his companions, with their trea-sure, hurried towards the river bank.

In a moment or two, the clash of swords and report of pistols were heard in the garden.

"To the boat! to the boat! my merry men!" shouted old Bates. "We are discovered!"

"On to 'em, men! Cut and thrust! Spare none of them!" was the response of some one who now advanced at the head of a body of men, with links, torches, and the like. "On to 'em, they are all rogues and vagabonds!"

Shouts, and oaths, and cries were now heard on every side.

Captain Jack placed Ellen Harmer in the boat, and, with a furious countenance, he rushed into the thickest of the fray.

Blows were freely exchanged on both sides, and many were wounded.

"Are all the men safe?" said Captain Jack to Bates.

"Yes; they are all near by."

"Then let them stand in a line, and face the enemy."

"What, fight and fall back to the boats?"

"Of course," said Jack. "What else do you mean? Do you think that I or any of the lads would turn their backs to the enemy? You are a pretty fellow to be captain, truly."

As Jack advised, all his companions faced the intruders, and gradually fought their way back to the boat, which was now well laden with spoil.

The fight still continued; but many of the lights became extinguished in the combat, so that the officers and others who had come to arrest the masked strangers began to fight among themselves.

Perceiving the confusion among them, Captain Jack ordered his comrades to jump into the boat.

They did so.

Not one of them was killed.

But several were severely wounded.

As they pushed off from the shore, those in the garden fired a volley after them, and raised a loud shout.

"Pursue the rascals! Get a boat and overtake them!" cried several voices.

But no one dared to follow the bold and daring robbers.

Down the river they swiftly rowed.

And, after some time, landed at a dark, dingy, treacherous-looking wharf.

This was a place used by the Dozen occasionally to store their plunder.

They all got on shore safely.

But while they stood in the darkness, a boat darted past the wharf.

"That's some of our pursuers," said Jack, "we hadn't much time to spare."

"No," said Bates, "it was rather sharp work take it altogether."

"Look! look!" said Jack, "here comes a second boat. By all that's lucky they are going to land at our wharf."

"Boat ahoy!" shouted Bates.

"Ahoy! ahoy!" was the response. "Have you seen any craft shoot past here?"

"What, one with a lady in it?" shouted Jack, in feigned voice.

"Ye-e-s," was the distant answer.

"Just shot down before you. You can't mistake it; row fast. Fire into 'em, it will soon bring the rascals to their senses."

True to this advice the second boat shot after the first at a rapid rate.

Ere long shots were fired in the distance.

"Hang me!" said old Bates, in high glee, "if one boat ain't fighting the other. Why, the fellows are all gone mad!"

"No matter," said Captain Jack; "we have got the lady. Is she safely housed, Bates?"

"Yes, but very pale and weak, poor creature. She couldn't make out who and what we were with those masks on, so I had to tell her we were a party of friends who had leagued together for her de-liverance."

"Very good; but, of course, you didn't tell her that we had leagued together to get four or five sacks full of plunder, eh?"

"Not very likely."

"But what shall we do with her now that we have got her? We don't want any pretty women among our band; the lads would be cutting each other's throats over her."

"No fear of that; she won't stay long in the company of the Dozen. The king would give any price for her."

"Then he shall have her."

"Not so fast," said Captain Jack, leading the way to a small public-house, not more than a hun-dred yards from their storehouse on the river side, "not so fast, Bates, not so fast. She is well provided for the night, you say, and that is sufficient. I must pay a hasty visit to Darlington ere we make up our mind what to do."

They had now reached the public-house, and were conversing in an undertone together when a post-boy rode up and dismounted.

Tired, dirty, and muddy he was, and seemed ready to sink from fatigue.

"Come far to-night?" said Captain Jack.

"Yes, sir, a good many miles, and have ridden faster than ever I did in my whole life."

"Where from?" said Bates, shoving over his bottle to the post-boy.

"From Darlington."

"Darlington?" said Captain Jack, pricking up his ears. "Why, that is the very place I was just speaking about."

"Indeed, sir," said the post-boy; "then, methinks, before four-and-twenty hours more, the name of that place will be in the mouths of every one in all London."

"Why, I do not understand you; explain yourself. Why, I thought of journeying there tomorrow."

"You had better not, sir, for it is a most villainous place."

"Once upon a time," said Bates, "it was one of the quietest little villages in all England."

"Sure, kind sir; but things have changed very much of late."

"How do you mean?"

"Why, old Farmer Bertram was mysteriously murdered there, and it has never been found out yet."

"I know it; there is a royal proclamation about that affair," said Bates.

"And then the beautiful daughter of old Harmer, the miller, was forcibly abducted by some base villain."

"True."

"And she has never been heard of since."

"So I have been told."

"And then her lover, young Andrew, was stabbed, thrown into the river and almost killed; and now, to add to the horrors of the place and its surrounding roads, *another* murder has been committed in the woods near old Sir Richard's mansion."

"Another murder!" said Jack, in surprise

"Aye, sir, you may well be surprised, ; another murder has been committed there, and everything has become so dangerous down there, that I intend to throw up my situation, for I suppose next time I go down there with the mails they'll be for murdering me."

"Oh, nonsense," said Captain Jack.

"You must be mistaken, my lad," said Bates.

"No I'm not, gentlemen; there's no mistake about it, more's the pity. What with the ravages of Death-Wing and his Skeleton Crew, and the increase of murders down in these parts, the village is getting a very bad name; nay, the worst of names in all England."

"And who was murdered this time?"

"I don't know for certain, but I heard it was no less a man than Colonel Blood himself."

"Colonel Blood! impossible," said Jack, snapping his fingers.

"Are you sure it was the colonel, young man?" said old Bates.

"No, gentlemen, I am not quite certain; but old Harmer has seen the body of the murdered man, and he swears it is just like the gentleman who used to come prowling about the mill after Ellen."

"Then what makes you think it *was* Colonel Blood?"

"From cards and notes found in his pockets."

Jack and Bates looked at each other in a very knowing manner.

"How did it all happen?" asked Captain Jack. "Here, sit down, my lad, and let's hear all about it."

"Yes, yes, landlord, give us another bottle; you needn't mind telling *us* the whole truth, you know," said Bates, with an air of much importance, for we are Crown officers, and no harm can befal you."

"Well, you see, gentlemen," the post-boy began, "since Ellen Harmer has been stolen away from her father's house, Andrew, her lover, recovered from his wounds, but is thought to be raving mad at times, and goes raving about in all sorts of holes and corners.

"The people take pity on him, and treat him kindly; but all he thinks of is revenge for the injuries he has received.

"Last night he was sitting in a public-house by the roadside, about two miles this side of Darlington, when who should stop to bait his horse but a person very much like the man who stabbed him on the bridge the night Ellen Harmer was carried away.

"Directly he entered the parlour, poor Andrew began to rave, and the stranger laughed at him.

"Poor Andrew began, as usual, to tell the stranger his troubles, like he does to all who will listen to him; but still the stranger laughed, and began to mock him.

"With eyes glistening like two burning coals, Andrew peered closely into the stranger's face, but made up his mind that, though very much like, he could not be the man who had so cruelly wronged him.

"The stranger pretended to be ignorant of the country he was passing through.

"Yet, at the same time, the landlord says he spoke of Sir Richard Warbeck, and of Wildfire Ned's famous doings, as if he had been acquainted with them for years.

"He knew all about old Bertram's murder, and whatever had happened to Ellen Harmer, who, he said, was safe and sound in London.

"He had plenty of money, and said he was sent down from London on a secret mission to capture one Captain Jack, a famous rogue, who was supposed to be hiding somewhere thereabouts.

"He pulled out rolls of notes and a bag of money, and made such a display of it that the landlord begged him to be very careful, for it might excite the passions of those around.

"'*He* did not care,' he said; '*he* wasn't afraid of all Darlington put together,' he swore more than once.

"While he was talking, Andrew went out of the parlour, and went along the road towards home.

"'You had better take the road through the forest,' said the landlord to him; 'it is much nearer, Andrew, my boy, than by going along the road.'

"Andrew did not make any reply, but went his way.

"In about half an hour the stranger rose, buttoned up his coat, and, with a thick stick in his hand, went forth alone.

"'I'm going to Darlington,' he said.

"'But, you said you were a stranger in these parts,' the old publican remarked, 'and, if that is so, you may miss your way.'

"'Never fear,' said the burly stranger, laughing. 'I heard you say the path through the woods was much nearer than by the road, so I'll take the shortest cut.'

"The landlord begged of him not to go, but go he would and did.

"What happened afterwards I could only learn from his own lips, as he lay weltering in his blood, about half an hour afterwards, for in that time he was brought in by two rustics, with his throat fearfully gashed.

"He could speak, however, and, in reply to questions put to him, he said,

"'I had not gone far along the road, and had just entered the forest path, when I met with two poacher-looking fellows, each with a big stick, and slovenly dressed, with big coats and slouched hats, which almost covered their eyes.

"'They were very civil, and I asked them a great many questions about Darlington.

"'They answered all my questions in a straightforward manner.

"'Have you any strangers living in the village?' said I.

"'How do you mean?' said they.

"'Strangers I, mean, who have plenty of money, and don't seem to do any sort of work for a living.'

"'Oh, yes,' said one; 'there is a flashy-looking chap who stays at the inn, and spends lots of money every night; but what he does none of us know. He says he is a crown officer, but we think he must be a highwayman, or something of that sort, for he has got the cut of one all over.'

"'They described this fellow to me so well, that I made up my mind it must be no other than Captain Jack, a famous rascal I was bent on capturing.

"'I told the rustics this, and they laughed, but promised to go to the village with me, and assist in his capture.

"'We all walked along quietly, chatting together.

"'I gave them a good 'pull' at my brandy flask, and promised them an excellent reward if Captain Jack could be captured.

"'They said they were willing enough if I would pay them before hand.

"'I pulled out my purse to do this, and next moment one of them gave me a sudden blow on the head, and knocked me down.

"'Before I could get my pistols out, the blow was repeated.

"'I struggled hard; but in a second or two one of them pulled out a long knife and jagged my throat, and the blood spurted out all over me. (See cut in No. 15).

"'In a second they robbed me of everything, and darted away into the darkness of the forest.

"'I remained unconscious for some time, but my shouts and cries were heard, and soon afterwards two villagers, who were passing, raised me up and brought me here, and here I am a dying man.'"

"This is what the stranger said, eh?" remarked Captain Jack, picking his teeth, and looking much pleased.

"Yes, that is what he said, every word of it."

"Are you sure?"

"Oh yes, for the landlord wrote it down as he spoke. I have just delivered it to Sir Richard Warbeck, in London here, that he may inquire into the mysterious affair at once."

"But did not the stranger make any other remarks before he died?"

"He did."

"What were they?"

"He said that he could swear that one of the two men was none other than Mad Andrew in disguise."

"Poor devil!"

"And the other one," observed Bates, "had he any idea who he was?"

"He said he thought it must have been Captain Jack himself, in disguise."

"Thunder and lightning! you don't mean that?"

"I do, though; he signed his name as best he could to the dying deposition."

"Oh! it couldn't have been Captain Jack," said Bates; "I'll swear to that."

"And so will I," said Captain Jack; "the thing was impossible."

"Quite so," said Bates; "'tis a very serious charge to make against an innocent man."

"So it is, gentlemen; but then, you see, the character of Captain Jack isn't very good at the best of times, so I hear, and the dead man's oath will be taken before that of any one else."

"Devilish queer affair," said Jack.

"Yes, somebody must swing for it," said the post-boy. "I wouldn't like to be in Captain Jack's shoes for all the money in the kingdom."

"Perhaps you don't know the captain, my lad," said Jack, "or you'd have a different opinion; he is—"

"One of the best men in all London," said Bates, tossing off his wine.

"Honest as the day is long," said Jack.

"People are mistaken about him. As to murdering an innocent man in the woods, and robbing him, too," said Bates, "why, bless you, it is out of the question."

"From what you say about him," said the post-boy, "one would think he wasn't a rascal at all."

"Nor is he," said Jack, fiercely; "I'll stake my life on it."

"And so will I," said Bates, drinking deeply.

"Perhaps you know him, then, gentlemen?"

"No, not exactly; but I've seen him, and actually been in his company once or twice," said Jack.

"So have I," chimed in Bates, "he can sing a capital song."

"And dance a jig."

"And handle a sword."

"Aye! that he can, and fight for an hour with the best gentleman in all England," said Bates, in conclusion.

"And was the dying man's deposition the only reason that made you hurry up to town at such a terrible pace?"

"Not exactly, gentlemen; something more."

"What then?"

"When the dead man's things were searched, we found papers, cards, and documents in his pockets, all bearing the name of Colonel Blood, and the supposition was, that he was that individual."

"And was it?"

"We haven't found out yet, for when I rode up to his mansion, I found the place in great confusion, and the colonel was out of town, so it was supposed."

"I heard he had gone to Darlington," said Bates.

"If he did go there, then he must have been killed," said Jack.

"I knew not that, gentlemen, but heard that his house had been robbed of 1 its plate, jewels, and valuables. Many of the household were killed or wounded in fighting with the robbers, and all was in a dreadful uproar."

"Astonishing," said Jack. "Here, landlord, more wine."

"And have they any notion who committed this audacious robbery, my boy?"

"I heard the butler say he had picked up a sword in the grounds, with the name of 'Tom Bates' upon it.'

"T-h-e devil!" said Jack, who now, for the first time, perceived that Tom had lost his sword in the hurry and scuffle of getting away in the boat.

Old Bates, himself, felt thunderstruck when he heard this, for, until that moment, he had thought nothing about the sword he had lost.

He poured out a goblet of wine, drank it off at a draught to drown his rising anger.

"What else did they discover?" Jack asked.

"There is a tall black slave at the mansion, who, by signs and writing, made known to all assembled that there were several crown officers among the robbers."

"Worse and worse," said Bates.

For a few moments no one spoke.

The post-boy left the house, and in a short time the house closed for the night.

Jack and Bates being good customers, were not turned out when the doors were shut, but remained chatting together.

"This is a bad job," said Bates, "a very bad job for *you*, Jack."

"And so it is for you."

"You will be surely ' scragged ' for this murder."

"And so will you for this robbery, for they will be sure to trace the sword to you."

"Hang the luck," said old Bates. "I wish we had never seen the place."

"What must be done ?"

"I haven't the least idea."

"They won't be long before they are after us you may be sure."

"I don't care what they do, now that Colonel Blood is killed," said Jack ; "he was a deceitful, tricky, devil."

While they thus sat drinking, loud knocks were heard at the door outside.

"Who's there ?" asked the landlord.

"Don't open for them," said Jack, "it's only some thirsty roysterer returning home."

"House, ho !"

"Who are you ?"

"What do you want ?"

"Go home, I tell you ; the house is closed."

"House, ho ! within there ; open, in the name of the king."

"The what ?" said Jack, in alarm.

"In the name of the king," whispered Bates.

"What can it be ?" asked Jack ; "surely not a guard of soldiers, landlord."

"Yes it is, sir; I have just peeped out of window. There is a file of soldiers outside, with an officer at their head."

"House, ho ! within there ! Open, in the name of the king, landlord, or I'll burst in the door."

"What do you want ?"

"Open, I say."

"What are your orders ?"

"To search the house."

"Your name, officer ?"

"It matters not to you ; open."

"I have no one here, I assure you."

"You lie, landlord; you had, if you have not now. Open, I say, once more."

"Your warrant, sir."

"My name is sufficient, old dolt."

"And what is it, I beg you ?"

"*Colonel Blood !*"

Directly Jack and Bates heard this ominous name, they dashed out of the room just as the impatient soldiers were bursting open the heavy, oaken door.

"Fly," said Jack, dashing out into the back yard, "fly for your life, Bates, 'tis the colonel himself ; fly, fly !"

---

## CHAPTER XL.

IN WHICH THE SKELETON CREW ARE VERY BUSY, AND MAKE A RICH HAUL OF PLUNDER, LED ON BY DEATH-WING AND PHILLIP REDGILL.

"WHAT would you have done without me ?" said Death-Wing to Phillip Redgill, when they were once more alone, and in confidential conversation.

"Why, I must have been hung, I suppose," said Phillip, with an attempt at a smile.

"A prospect you much liked, I know."

"Well, it must have been, had not your men rescued me."

"I know it, and yet all through your career of villany you have looked upon me and my band as hardfisted, ungrateful scoundrels — I know you have."

"Not so bad as that, quite."

"Oh, yes, you have. I have heard and know more than you imagine about your doings about town. Had you not taken our oath years ago, not all England could have saved you from gracing a gallows."

"Well, I know it, and am glad I *did* take the oath, but what do you require of me now ?"

"Nay, we do not want you—it is you who need us."

"How do you mean ?"

"Have you forgotten your wife—is there not vengeance in your heart against Fumbleton, who has taken her from you ?"

"There is, and against others besides him."

"Who ?"

"The two young Warbecks."

"And no one else ?"

"Yes, against old Sir Richard himself."

"Do you contemplate killing them ?"

"I do."

"But how ?"

"Through your aid, Death-wing."

"And the price ?"

"Half of all the estates which fall to me—Darlington Hall and all its fair domains."

"But can you get them all at one stroke ?"

"I can, for if these brats, Charley and Ned, are put out of the way, I am the sole heir, as I have said before."

"Then, so be it—it shall be done," said the grim chief, "but not yet."

"Why not ?"

"You must become a member of the Crew first—an active member, I mean—and then we can talk about it."

"I am willing."

"Then to try your courage, I will soon find fitting opportunities. Are you a good shot ?"

"Capital."

"And can handle your sword ?"

"Like any gentleman."

"'Tis well, but—— "

He was about to say more, when two of the Crew entered the room.

"Well," said Death-wing to them, "have you followed him ?"

"Yes, both night and day."

"What news ?"

"He has found favour with the Dozen again, and to-night they have robbed Colonel Blood's house of all its wealth."

"And escaped ?"

"Yes."

"You followed them ?"

"We did, and saw where they deposited their plunder."

"Very good. What else ?"

"They carried off Ellen Harmer with them, and Captain Jack is now in possession of the King's signet ring."

"Impossible !"

"No, Death-wing, it is quite correct."

"How do you know ?"

"I was in Captain Jack's company to-night, and saw the ring upon his red, fat finger."

"Explain yourself."

"I knew the Darlington post-boy, and for a good price learned all the news ; dressed myself up in his clothes, and went into the very public-house where he and Bates were drinking."

"Then he doesn't seem to concern himself about apprehending Ned Warbeck, and casting him into prison ?"

"Not the least, for he is now no longer captain of the Dozen, and Colonel Blood has offered a reward for his head, dead or alive."

"Good news," said Phillip, grinning like a fiend, "excellent news ! I feel happy."

"And who had the commission to capture him ?"

"Bates, the new captain—the very man who helped to rob the colonel's mansion.

"What a couple of tricky villains," said Phillip, biting his lip in rage and disappointment.

"When I found this out," said the spy, "and had deceived them by telling the news I had heard from the true post-boy, I left the public-house."

"And informed Colonel Blood of it all ?"

"Yes ; I wrote a note to the colonel on the instant, and delivered it myself. He had just returned home and found the havoc which had been made of his place. He was in a terrible rage."

"Did he speak to you ?"

"He did. And when—still in the clothes of the post-boy—I told him of the past murder at Darlington, he stormed and raved like a devil."

"What then took place ?"

"I did not remain in his sight long, for I was very anxious to come and tell you all the news, but still I watched all the movements."

"Perfectly right."

"The colonel went to the royal barracks and demanded a file of men to assist him in capturing the bold burglars.

"The officer in command refused.

"Colonel Blood stormed and raved like a madman.

"'Where is the king ?' said he.

"'Dancing in the ball-room.'

"'Take my card to him,' said Blood ; 'it is all-sufficient. He will be sure to see me.'

"'Why not go up into the ball-room yourself ?' said the officer.

"I hid myself under a dark archway and listened to all that passed.

"Blood complained of his dress, and at last a second officer took up the card.

"In a few moments the king descended into the court-yard, apparently in a very bad temper.

"They walked towards the dark archway in which I was concealed.

"I heard all that passed between them.

"'Well, Blood,' said the king, in a cross mood, 'what is the meaning of all this ? You want a file of soldiers, I am told.'

"Colonel Blood explained all about the robbery, and swore in the king's presence like a trooper.

"The king listened, smiled and frowned by turns, and at last said—

"'Blood, what has become of that exquisite lass you abducted from Darlington ? I am dying to see her.'

"The colonel changed colour, and stammered out some excuse.

"'Nay, no apologies, colonel, and all that kind of thing ; I want the girl, I tell you, and *will* have her. Is she safe ?'

"'Well, sire, I think there cannot be a doubt about it.

"'She escaped twice or thrice, it is true ; but I know where she is, I think, and it was more with an object to regain possession of her than anything else I wished to have a file of soldiers. But I want a search-warrant, signed by your majesty, for I fear me she has taken refuge in some noble's house.'

"'I have not got my seal ring to-night, Blood,' said the king, with a bitter laugh. 'No matter, take the soldiers, as many as you need ; break open any house you come across, whether rich or poor, it doesn't matter, so you find the girl and bring her to me.'

"'Your majesty is very kind,' said Blood, bowing.

"'Not so kind as you think, perhaps, colonel.'

"'Sire,' said Blood, in surprise.

"'Listen to me, Blood, kings can be deceived sometimes as well as other people.'

"'I don't understand you, sire.'

"'I will explain myself ; the girl escaped from your custody hence, you say ?'

"'She did.'

"'When had you the maid last ?'

"'Well, not very long ago, sire.'

"'No, I think not, not many hours ago, Blood.'

"'Sire !'

"'Nay, don't stare in surprise. She was in your house this very night.'

"Blood turned pale; his deceit was now discovered, and he could not deny it ; but, he said, with a bold front,

"'Who has so deceived you, sire ?'

"'No one, Blood.'

"'I have enemies who have circulated this report.'

"'But I *know* it to be true.'

"'You, sire ?'

"'Yes, me ; I saw her in your house not three hours ago.'

"'You did, most gracious prince ?'

"'Yes, and spoke to her.'

"The colonel bowed, he could not answer a word.

"'Come,' said the king, 'no more deception, take the file of men you need — bring the wench to me ere sunrise, or you will incur my lasting displeasure.'

"So speaking, the king left the courtyard."

"This is quite an adventure," said Death-wing, "go on; what happened next ?"

"Did they capture Captain Jack ?" asked Phillip, in great impatience. "I hear the colonel shot the villain."

"Listen," said Death-wing, "and don't speak Redgill. What occurred next ? "

"Colonel Blood," continued the spy, "hurried away with the soldiers, and ere long reached the public house.

"I followed them, and as we approached the place I ran forward and listened at the shutters.

"I could hear old Bates and Jack talking together in the parlor.

"There was not any one else in the house, for it was closed.

"I darted away into the darkness and watched.

"Blood did not at first wish to disclose his name, but at last he did so, and, as the publican was so obstinate, he burst in the door.

"The soldiers rushed in at one door, but Jack and Bates escaped the backway.

"I ran to intercept their flight, for I could hear the tilt of swords.

"When I got to the spot, two soldiers were then on the ground weltering in their blood.

"They had been killed by Jack and Bates.

"'Help ! help !'cried Blood's men ; 'up the street ! after them ! they have escaped ! help ! help !'

# THE SKELETON CREW; OR, WILDFIRE NED.

A STARTLING INCIDENT.—*See Number* 21.

## CHAPTER XLI.

THE SKELETON CREW HOLD A MERRY MEETING—
ADVENTURES OF THE GANG—DEATH-WING NAR-
RATES HIS EXPERIENCE IN FRANCE, AND OF HIS
ESCAPE FROM GAOL WHEN UNDER SENTENCE OF
DEATH.

WHEN the spies of the Skeleton Crew had told their
tales, Death-wing much commended them for the
prudence and caution with which they had proceeded in all they had done.

"We will not stir out to-night," said Death-wing,
"there are too many on foot for us to do any business comfortably and quietly ; besides, you know,
comrades, Col. Blood will never be able to discover
the hiding-place of the Dozen. When, therefore,
this little affair has blown over and got cold by to-
morrow night, we will give Captain Jack and his
friends a call at their snug hiding-place, and secure
everything."

"Bravo !" resounded on all sides.

"To-morrow night, then, we will have ample
revenge on the Dozen," said Death-wing, "and
punish the arch-traitor Captain Jack as he deserves
to be."

"What do you propose, Captain Death-wing ?"
asked Phillip Redgill.

No. 19.

"I propose to-night to have a carouse, my lad,
in honour of your joining our band."

"Bravo !"

"Excellent !"

"Bring out the wine, boys, and let us enjoy ourselves to-night, for perhaps in less than twenty-
four hours more than one of us will be laid low."

"No fear of that, captain."

"I don't know about that," said Death-wing,
"something strikes me that it will prove a desperate
fight between us and old Bates's men, for he may
turn tail and get the king's troops to assist him.
Never mind, bring out the wine, and let us enjoy
ourselves."

In a few moments the Skeleton Crew brought out
a great number of bottles and glasses, and, sitting
round the immense dining table, began to enjoy
themselves in great glee.

"Now," said Death-wing, "as our new companion
here, Phillip Redgill, hasn't any clear notion of what
he will have to do among us, let each of you advance
and detail all you have done of late, either by my
orders, or according to your own whims, that will
give our novice a better idea than all the instructions in the world. Advance in order," said Death-
wing, "and stand at my right hand, so that all may
hear and see."

As he spoke one of the crew advanced, and said,
"I threw off my disguise and went to Barnet fair,
where I fell in with two of Captain Jack's band."

"It is against our rules to 'work' with any other
band; but go on, let us hear," said Death-wing.

"We went to a farm-house, and stripped it of
everything, and got clear away without being detected."

"Very good! cleverly done. What then?"

"We were about to divide the spoil, but I drugged
their wine and ran off with all the booty."

"Capital! it serves Captain Jack's men right.
What did the plunder consist of?"

"Silver and gold coin, plate, fine linen, and such
like. I brought it all safe away; it is here, stowed
in the rendezvous."

"Is that all?"

"It is."

"You may sit down. And now for the next,"
said Death-wing, pointing to a huge fellow, who
now advanced to give an account of his doings.
"What have you accomplished?"

"I have had a strange adventure, Captain Death-
wing," was the gruff reply.

"With whom?"

"With a party of noble ladies and gentlemen."

"Indeed, 'tis seldom you trouble them much.
But how did it happen?"

"There was a wedding party down in the country,
and I heard that the father of the bride was going
to give her a large sum of money as a dowry."

"Who was the father?"

"A very wealthy old farmer."

"Well, and how did you manage it?"

"The night before the wedding I took with me
many of the crew in order to make sure of the prize.

"We soon reached the farm, and hid under the
walls of the garden and orchard.

"It was ten o'clock, and the night was cold and
dark.

"As we intended to have a fine feast in the woods
after our little job of robbery, one of my comrades
here got over the wall and crept into the hen-
house, and in less than five minutes he passed over
to us no less than a dozen chickens, lots of eggs,
and, besides all that, strangled two dozen of ducks,
and threw them over also.

"One of our party secured all these things, and
concealed them in a neighbouring wood until such
time as we had performed all we intended to do at
the farm-house.

"One hour passed after another, and still we
remained concealed under and behind the orchard
wall.

"As the village clock struck ten, we clambered
over, and the first thing we did was to approach
the watch dogs as best we could, and kill them on
the spot.

"This difficult little bit of business was accomplished, and all things promised success.

"We next got in at the old parlour window, and
began operations.

"While so engaged, the old farmer awoke, and
came down stairs, gun in hand.

"We heard him approaching, and remained as
silent as mice.

"'Who is there?' he asked.

"We made no answer.

"'Who is there?' he again said, in a determined
tone.

"But we all remained perfectly still, and stirred
not an inch.

"He fired both barrels of his gun.

"But he missed his aim, and the next moment he

found himself gagged and bound both hand and
foot.

"The noise of the report, however, had thoroughly
aroused all his servants, and now began a horrible
scene.

"Any one but members of the Skeleton Crew
would have fled before such impending danger.

"But not so with us.

"In a few moments we prepared for the farmer's
servants, and beat them back.

"Indeed, after a few moments of fighting all was
over with them, for, seeing our skeleton attire, they
fled in the utmost consternation.

"Their shouts and cries were awful.

"We did not lose much time, but ransacked the
house of everything valuable, placed the articles in
a light cart, and drove away."

"Did you get the old man's money?"

"Yes, every farthing. There were five large bags
of gold discovered in an old oak chest, which I have
every reason to believe was intended for his
daughter's dowry.

"But the adventure did not end here."

"What, then, happened?" asked Death-wing.

"We went into the forest, and hid part of our
treasure until such time as we could convey it away
more conveniently.

"We lighted our fires in a deep hollow of the
ground, and cooked the ducks and chickens, which,
together with plenty of wine we had also stolen,
made up a first-rate supper."

"So I should think."

"This is some of the very wine you are now
drinking," said the speaker to his chief.

"Very good stuff it is," said Death-wing, quaffing
off a bumper, and smacking his lips "Very good
stuff it is; but it has one great fault—there is not
enough of it. We must pay the farmer another
visit, I think, shortly. Go on with your story."

"During the night, while we were drinking and
smoking, and enjoying ourselves in the forest, never
thinking that any one had observed us, or knew
anything of what we had done, a gipsy woman
crept up to me, and before I was aware of it,
said,

"'The officers are on your track.'

"'How do you know it?' I answered.

"'I have just come from the farm, and all is in an
uproar. They have got all the county officers there,
and are preparing to 'ollow you.'

"I laughed at this, for I knew they could never
find out where we had got to.

"However, I listened to the gipsy, and gave her
some refreshment, and she became very chatty.

"She seemed to know all about our doings, and
said if she had a mind to do so she could find out
you, Captain Death-wing, any day she liked."

"Indeed; she must be very clever, then."

"At all events that is what she said, and remarked that more than once she has seen rewards
offered for you, but would never divulge who, what,
nor where you were."

"A capital woman, and what was her name?"

"Hannah!"

"I know her," said Death-wing, "but will not
speak of her now. We have had business together
more than once; she is a living repository of
secrets. Go on."

"She told me that the farmer's daughter was
coming from London, and that she possessed presents of immense value which her intended lordly
husband had given her as bridal presents."

"'Is she coming alone?' I asked.

"'No,' was the reply; 'but it is very easy to

attack the escort and secure her ; in fact, I have received orders from Lord Rochfort to do so.'

" ' You ?' I asked.

" ' Yes, me,' she proudly answered ; 'I have a numerous band at my command, and can do anything in that way.' "

" ' And why does Lord Rochfort wish to have her captured ?'

" ' Because her beauty has enslaved his elder brother, whom he does not desire to marry, for if his brother dies without issue Lord Rochfort succeeds to his vast estates.'

" ' But have you told him that you can or will do this ?'

" ' No,' she replied, ' not positively ; she may be escorted by a powerful party of well-mounted, well-armed men.'

" ' No matter,' said I, ' if she is rich in jewels and diamonds, as you say, leave the matter in our hands, and I warrant we will not only secure the girl, but create no noise or bother about it.'

" ' But how ?'

" ' Leave that matter to me,' I replied.

"For some time she would not consent ; but when I had pledged the honour of the crew that no harm should befall the wench she consented, and departed, after telling me the exact time at which the intended bride was expected to pass by that particular part of the road.

"As soon as Hannah had departed I and my comrades started out to have a look at the road.

"Now, not far from the forest wherein we were concealed, there were cross roads with finger posts.

"I hit upon my plan immediately."

"And what was it ?" Death-wing asked.

"Why, to change the finger posts, and thus send them in the wrong direction."

"A capital plan," said Death-wing."

"And did it succeed ?" asked several.

"Yes, as I will explain shortly."

"Early in the morning we got spades and loosened the finger posts, so as to be able to change them in a few moments.

"We waited for hours, but no carriages appeared.

"At last, a long way off, we espied two vehicles approaching.

"But one was about half a mile ahead of the other.

"The first one contained the intended bride, the farmer's beautiful daughter, and a female attendant.

"In the second rode Lord Rochfort's brother, and a few friends.

"Now, I had sent up the road for two of my men, whose business it was in some way to stop or retard the progress of the second coach.

"This they managed to do, and very cleverly indeed."

"How ?" asked many.

"When the bride's coach approached the cross roads we changed the finger boards.

"The driver followed their painted directions, and instead of going by the main road turned short into the forest carriage way.

"Before the mistake could be rectified, I had the gates closed after them, and thus they could not return.

"Meanwhile, however, those whom I had posted up the road had suddenly thrown a lasso round the horses' legs, and down they tumbled carriages and all.

"My comrades then, before the nobleman inside could get out of the half-smashed carriage, jumped into the middle of the road, cut the traces, and vaulting on the backs of the horses galloped away,

leaving the travellers in the mud, cursing and swearing most lustily.

"They dashed down the road and soon joined me, for I was at that moment engaged with the hinder carriage.

"When I ran up to the coachman and threatened to blow his brains out if he stirred, he began to tremble like an ass, much more so, indeed, than the fair one inside, who, all diamond decked, was fair and beautiful.

"Her attendant fainted as I opened the carriage door, but the other one quickly gave up to me all her trinkets and things of value.

"Having secured these, I directed the coachman to drive on along the forest carriage way, for I knew he could not go very far without falling in with Hannah's tribe of gipsies."

"So you secured all her property ?"

"We did ; but did not offer any violence to the trembling one."

"What became of her ?"

"Her coachman slowly drove onwards as I had directed him, and shortly got right into the midst of Hannah's camp."

"Strange to say, among the men there assembled at that moment was Lord Rochfort himself, disguised as a gipsy, and he it was who handed the bridal beauty from the carriage, while old Hannah, with outstretched hands, pointed to the girl, saying,

"Now has my prophecy come true ?" (See cut in No. 17).

"But what prophecy was it ?" Death-wing asked.

"Hannah told Rochfort that for a certain sum she could, by means of her magic art, cause the carriages of the bride to lose its way, and come voluntarily into her power. It was a trick on her part, but Rochfort believed it to be true, for he knew nothing of what we had done in the matter, and remains in ignorance of it up to the present moment."

"So that is your adventure, eh ?"

"It is, Captain Death-wing ; we came back to the Rendezvous much richer than we went forth, and without receiving a single scar."

"Very well done indeed," said Death-wing, quaffing off more wine, and becoming very talkative. "Very well done indeed ; but the thieves or professional gentlemen of the present day are not worth a pinch of snuff compared to what have been in my lifetime."

"You have been in France, then, I heard you say ?" observed Redgill.

"France ! why of course I have ; where is there a place I haven't been to, I should like to know ? I belonged to a gang there when I was young.

"It was made up of both English and French ; English I mean who were obliged to leave their country for their country's good, men who preferred exile to death.

"Well, when I was first introduced to the gang, it was in its full glory.

"We had a great many members in different parts, but the most cruel among them all was one we called the ' Scorcher,' and from him we were always afterwards called ' Scorchers.' "

"This man, hardened as I am now, looked to me like a devil, and through all the years I have lived, I cannot forget the cold-blooded villany of the ' Old Scorcher,' who used to roast the feet of all those who would not confess where their money and valuables were. Now we are more merciful than that," said Death-wing, laughing. "We kill 'em outright, and don't torture ; its much quicker and better, I think. But let me go on with my story.

"'Look you, boys,' said this old rascal one day, at a conference held at a place called Massette, 'you scour the plain, and you work well enough sometimes. You can batter a door in, and garotte a fellow in pretty good style. But this is anybody's work.

"'You don't understand the clean trick—the tender licks.

"'When you have "quieted" a customer, you break open his chests and his cupboards expecting to find the shiners.

"'But the yellow boys are not always kept in such places.

"'Some shabby wretches hide their paltry money where the devil himself could not find it.

"'You get nothing, you only lose your time, and find you have worked merely for the glory of it.

"'That's not the way.'

"'Well, what would you do?' I asked.

"'What would I do, boys, if I had my youth again?

"'This is what I would do?' replied the old rat, becoming quite animated.

"'I would do what I did more times than once when I roamed alone. Now, boys, this is the way.

"'When a wretch will not squeak you must quietly light a wisp of straw between his legs, and if that does not loosen his tongue prick the soles of his feet with a fork, and scorch them.

"'He must be very hardened to endure that without squeaking.

"'If you have to do with a young married couple singe the wife in presence of her husband, or the husband in presence of his wife.

"'It is not always that the singed one speaks first.'

"A less cruel but very important character among us was Baptiste, the surgeon.

"He was amusing, and the Merry Andrew of the gang.

"This Figaro of the treadmill handled the cups and cards as cleverly as he did the lancet and razor.

"This harmless pursuit gained him ready admittance to the farmhouses, where he bled patients for fivepence and a plateful of hashed meat.

"Every branch of industry has its brokers and warehousemen.

"In our gang the brokers were abundant.

"Among them was one Barbe, nicknamed the Cowkeeper, whose occupation was to contrive business or work for us.

"He hired himself as a labourer at farms, where he would only remain long enough to make himself acquainted with the number and character of the inmates, their habits and resources.

"He would then suddenly abscond, and carry to our head-quarters the intelligence he had picked up.

"The warehousemen or storekeepers were the receivers or fences.

"They existed in all the towns and villages within the territories of the gang.

"Some were thieves when opportunity served.

"Others contented themselves with buying stolen property, and robbing the robbers.

"The fences were almost all of them innkeepers or 'knackers.'

"Sometimes the 'knackers' were also innkeepers, a fearful combination for the stomachs of their guests.

"The most notorious among the 'knackers,' of the gang, who had earned the right of bearing the title of his calling as a surname, was 'The Knacker'

—Peter Rosseau, the knacker, of the hamlet of Guendreville.

"In the garden of his house, which stood almost alone, was a subterranean passage, the origin of which was unknown.

"It was, however, supposed to be the secret outlet of some abbey, or feudal castle, long since destroyed.

"Near the edge of a dark, thick wood, intersected by capacious winding paths known only to the inhabitants around, this subterranean passage, a hundred feet in length, and thirty feet wide, solidly vaulted, extended unsuspected under a thick covering of earth.

The door, concealed by brambles, opened to the south, opposite the yard gate, so that it could be perceived only with great difficulty.

"Within it was fastened by a heavy iron bar let into the solid wall, and by a very strong lock, invisible on the outside.

"A staircase of sixteen steps led down into this vault.

"At the bottom was a very large chimney, which would contain a dozen persons, planned so as to facilitate the escape of those who might be surprised in the vault.

"This chimney, furnished with enormous pothooks, was filled with vast boilers on days devoted to great feasts.

"And its flue, large enough to allow a man to climb through, passed up into the mound of earth above, where it was concealed by thickly clustered thorns and bushes.

"Our gang had turned this subterranean vault to very profitable account.

"Here they concealed the spoils plundered from the unfortunate farmers, and their booty taken on fair days.

"Here the cries of their prisoners were drowned in the shouts of drunken madness.

"The clumsy thief, closely pursued to this spot, disappeared as by enchantment.

"It was the asylum and pandemonium of the gang, the common refuge of the weak, the staff-office of the place, and the general workshop of the "Scorchers," as we were generally called.

"The 'little knacker,' Peter, concealed there, or thereabouts, what might be called the 'unattached members' of our gang.

"He had always the barber, surgeon Baptiste, and some tailors in readiness, by whose aid our features and costume could be quickly changed.

"There were storekeepers, also; and a sort of post-office formed part of this establishment, as complete in its organization as any social government could require.

"The two 'fences' at Boisseaux and Remolu, kept by the brothers Thèvenot, were ostensibly storehouses for hides and skins.

"Their tariff never varied.

"For a sheep-skin they gave sevenpence.

"For an ox or cow-hide half-a-crown.

"For a shepherd's dog fifteen pence.

"When they had dealings with any one not belonging to the gang, they made it a rule to pay down half the price agreed upon.

"For the *other* half the poor dupe had to wait for ever.

"However, by way of compensation, these worthies occasionally treated their customers with some highly flavoured dishes.

"They were 'knackers,' and this was a convenient way of disposing of the flesh of cow or horse, cooked in the vast cauldrons in the subterranean passage.

"At numerous other places 'fences' were established under the guise of innkeepers and other legitimate callings.

"Launay of Pithiviers amused his leisure hours by rubbing copper money with quicksilver, to make it pass for silver coin.

"One of the most useful fences to the gang was Peter Mongendre, vine-dresser and apple merchant.

"He bought the horses, oxen, cows, and sheep we stole.

"At Chartres was one Doublet, who kept an inn and eating-house.

"He had a relation in the Government offices, through whose aid he procured passports in difficult cases.

"The gang had also its own 'fences.'

"There was Mother Tiger at Baudreville, whose house, much resorted to by the bandits, was as full of mechanical contrivances as a theatre.

"She possessed a cellar in which as many as fifteen brigands could be concealed if overtaken by the police.

"Mother Renaudin, of Apreux, was a great favourite with the gang.

"Her house was open at all hours, and she always gave the members a kind reception, whether they came with hands empty or full.

"Out of gratitude the brigands nicknamed her Goody Apreux.

"The inn itself had a most miserable, poverty-stricken appearance; but there was a well-furnished cellar, where the brigands regaled themselves jovially and in security.

"Adjoining this was a well-stocked granary, which contained enormous quantities of linen and other articles deposited there by the gang.

"There was also a strong box, employed as a savings'-bank, containing considerable sums in gold and silver, tied up in parcels, with the names of the owners written upon them.

"So far, then, you see," Death-wing continued, "all our arrangements were of the most perfect nature, and we always felt prepared for any enterprize that might present itself.

"After being some time among this band of French and English I resolved to try my own luck, and make a big haul, and so leave the band.

"I took no one into my confidence but Baptiste, the so-called surgeon.

"'Baptiste,' said I, 'you are a trusty fellow, and I have no doubt you are about as tired of these French and half English fellows as I am.'

"'True,' said the surgeon, 'and if you would take my advice you would leave the band, for, although you have been working hard all the time, and are the cleverest among them all, they give you a smaller share of the plunder than any one else.'

"'But it is no use of leaving the band,' said I, 'until I have got a considerable sum of money, for I want to return to England.'

"'Well, that is right enough,' said Baptiste, 'and if you will be guided by me we will do a little business together, and then leave.'

"'Agreed,' said I, 'but whom shall we rob? We must have a rich haul, wherever it comes from.'

"'And so you shall,' said Baptiste, 'if you will only be guided by me.'

"I agreed to his proposal.

"'And now,' said Baptiste, rubbing his hands in high glee, 'I'll tell you who it is I intend to rob; she is immensely wealthy.'

"'Whom?'

"'Why the rich young widow, Donna Evelina.'

"'What! that beautiful young Italian lady?' I said, in surprise.

"'Yes,' he answered.

"'Oh, I couldn't think of being so cruel,' was my reply.

"'Nonsense,' said Baptiste.

"'She is an angel.'

"'Not quite,' said Baptiste, laughing, 'she is my wife.'

"'Your wife,' said I, in great surprise, 'she is rich and noble, while you are——'

"'A robber, you would say.'

"'Quite so,' I replied.

"'That is nothing when you know all,' said Baptiste. 'I was always noted for my "winning ways," as the ladies say, and am not bad-looking when I dress myself and pass off as a noble.'

"'And what name do you go by?' I asked, laughing.

"'Count Ferdinand,' said Baptiste, quite calmly.

"'And do you mean to tell me, seriously, that you are married to the lovely and bewitching Donna Evelina?'

"'I was never more serious in my life.'

"'And how did it happen?'

"'I robbed the house of her father once, and was concealed therein for three days, and could not get out again. During that time I saw a great deal of young Evelina from my hiding place, and fell desperately in love with her.'

"'With her jewels, perhaps,' I remarked.

"'Just so,' he answered, 'and I resolved by fair means or by foul to become possessed of her.'

"'Well, and how did you succeed?' I asked.

"'Unfortunately she got married a week afterwards, and I almost went distracted.'

"'What did you do?'

"'Why, with the money and jewels which I stole I dressed myself up, and often met her husband, Count Felix.

"'He seemed to take a great liking to me, and, as he was rather old and ugly, I began to think it would not take much to make a fool of him.

"'He invited me to dine with him, and I accepted, but after dinner business took him away from the festive board for an hour or so.

"'She sang, and played the guitar divinely, and I got so warm in love that I began to whisper and throw out hints to her that her husband was unfaithful to her, and had at that moment gone forth to meet some strange flame.

"'My words, however, instead of being listened to with pleasure, excited Evelina's anger.

"'I left before the count's return.

"'His wife told him all I had said.

"'He left her with a smile, but with no indications of passion.

"'She did not know or suspect whither he had gone.

"'He sought me down by the river, where the gay world resort for an evening walk.

"'He touched me on the shoulder, and whispered "villain, traducer," in my ears, and touched the hilt of his sword.

"'I knew what that meant, and followed him.

"'We walked a long distance until we came to a small valley surrounded by high hills.

"'No cottage was there, not a soul saw us.

"'The moon alone was the light which gazed upon us.

"'Draw,' said Count Felix, with a quivering lip, 'you or I must die!'

"'I at first refused, and tried to get out of the duel; but he would listen to no excuses.

"'Fight I must, and fight I did, for with all my faults,' said Baptiste, 'I am not a coward!

"'Out came my trusty blade.

" ' We crossed swords.

" ' How long we fought I know not ; but I shall not forget that terrible conflict for a whole lifetime.

" ' We must have been tilting at each other for fully half an hour, until at last, while he was giving a desperate lunge at me, his foot slipped, and I—— I run him through the heart.

" ' He died without a groan.

" ' I took up the body and buried it with my own hands, digging a large hole in the ground as best I could with my own sword.

" ' I went home and washed myself, and walked about as if nothing had happened.

" ' For several days nothing was talked of but the sudden disappearance of Count Felix.

" ' I among the rest seemed greatly surprised, and was often asked my opinion about the matter.

" ' I told every one that my idea was that he had been visiting a strange beauty among the mountains, and very likely had fallen a victim to the revenge of some bold young mountaineer.

" ' After a diligent search for more than a month the remains were discovered by the sagacity of a favourite hound which the count had had for many, many years, who had scented it out, and unearthed the body.

" ' Every one now thought that my idea had proved too true.

" ' Even Evelina changed towards me, and believed my story.

" ' With successful robberies and roguery at dice I managed to keep up my appearance, and was not only always well attired, but had plenty of money.

" ' Through great perseverance I managed to make an impression on Donna Evelina, and often sought her hand in marriage.

" ' I was as often refused.

" ' I know not why it was, but from the first moment I came near her after Count Felix's death, she seemed to take a greater partiality for the count's favourite hound than before.'

" ' The one that scented out the dead body ?' I asked.

" ' Yes,' he said, ' and as often as I came in her presence as often would the beast try to fly at my throat.

" ' Evelina used simply to laugh at this, but she seemed to smile upon me more than ever, and after several months she consented to marry me privately.'

" ' Privately, and why so ?' I asked.

" ' I know not,' said Baptiste ; ' but she promised to become my wife on one condition.'

" ' And what was that ?' I asked.

" ' Why, that I should never divulge the secret, or ask to live with her, or be for even half an hour alone with her until the end of twelve months.'

" ' Singular request ?' said I.

" ' Yes ; but I agreed to it, and have kept my word, for she is immensely rich. But instead of this making me love her more, the conditions she imposed upon me turned my blood, and now I hate her.'

" ' When does the twelve months expire ?' I asked.

" ' This very day.'

" ' Then you will sleep there to-night ?'

" ' Yes.'

" ' But has she never found out your connection with this band ?' I asked.

" ' No, nor even suspects it. Whenever I go there I always dress well, and have plenty of money, and so behave that no one would suspect me to be what I am.'

" ' And do you really intend to rob Donna Evelina, to-night ?' I asked.

" ' Yes, and you must help me. She has great wealth, and I know where it is kept.'

" ' Well, I don't mind,' said I, ' since you don't like the woman, and she has plenty of money. You are her husband, and have a right to some of it.'

" It was agreed on then between us to go to Donna Evelina's that night.

" Baptiste and I left the band, and dressed ourselves out splendidly.

" He went up to her mansion, and knocked grandly at the door.

" It was opened by a servant in livery.

" I also got into the house, through the contrivance of Baptiste, but without any of the servants seeing me.

" Most of Evelina's jewels were kept in a chest in the blue bed-chamber.

" I tried to discover it, but the mansion was so large I could not find it for a long time.

" At last I found it, and was about to search for the chest, when I heard footsteps upon the stairs.

" I hid myself in a closet.

" Two footmen led in Baptiste, who was half drunk.

" He was laughing and hiccupping and singing by turns.

" He threw himself upon the bed, and the servants retired.

" I intended to get out of the closet and wake him, but at that instant I heard a deep growl, and remained where I was.

" Through cracks in the closet I saw the chamber door open.

" There stood Donna Evelina, looking beautiful and grand, but deathly pale, and she was attired from head to foot in black velvet robes.

" In the left hand she held a chamber lamp.

" By the right hand she held a fierce-looking hound firmly by the collar.

" The dog's eyes seemed to be like two balls of fire, as he writhed and tried to get away from her firm hold.

" Still Baptiste snored away loudly.

" With a curl on her lip Donna Evelina said, in a half whisper,

" ' Married, are we, eh ? Yes, a mock marriage it was, by one who, for money, played the part of a priest. No more ! And this is the nuptial night, eh ? Sleeping fool ! ha, ha !'

" These few words were spoken in such terrible tones of quiet anger that I began to fear for poor Baptiste.

" ' Thy marriage-bed shall be thy death-bed also,' said she.

" And she loosed the hound !

" With a bound he darted towards the closet in which I was concealed.

" He growled and sniffed, as if in warning.

" As if by some supernatural instinct, the animal then leaped wildly on the bed.

" A heavy groan was all I heard.

" Baptiste was murdered !

" With one fierce bite the animal had severed his wind-pipe, as clean as if it had been done with a knife !

" The pure white sheets were quickly dyed in blood.

" With a loud laugh of triumph, Donna Evelina left the room, saying,

" ' Count Felix, thou art avenged !'

" I thought of escaping from my place of confinement, but I dared not do so.

" The hound lay before the door, and I could see

his white fangs glistening in the light through his gory jaws, as with fiery eyes he kept watch before the closet.

"In less than half an hour every bell in the house began to ring violently.

The servants began to run to and fro in search of their mistress.

"At last they all rushed into the chamber, lights in hand.

"As they saw the ghastly sight before them they recoiled in horror.

"'Where is the murderer?' they shouted.

"The hound gave a fierce growl, and sniffed at the door.

"'He is here! he is here!'

"'In the closet he is hiding.'

"'Hold the hound while we see,' said many.

"Two powerful men seized the dog, and held him by the throat.

"A third and fourth footman, sword in hand, opened the door.

"I was discovered.

"With a fearful growl, the hound tried to burst away from those who held him, but could not.

"In a second I was seized by several retainers, who with swords pointed at my breast, led me away to prison.

"I was cast into a loathsome dungeon that same night on the charge of murder.

"Heavy irons and manacles weighed me down.

"But I could not sleep.

"The gory ghost of Baptiste was ever crossing before my excited imagination, and a cold sweat oozed out all over me.

"I thought that my last hour was come and that on the morrow I should be hung.

"Judge of my joy, however, when in the middle of the night the governor of the prison entered my cell, and ordered my release.

"He had received a letter from Donna Evelina, who had that same night entered a convent for life, stating the whole truth about what the hound had done.

"I was accordingly released.

"This was a narrow escape for me, and as soon as I got clear of the prison walls, I hired a horse, and left the town.

"I did not have much money to spare, so as I was riding along, I met a merchant.

"I robbed him in a very cool and clever manner, and beside his money, took a pair of pistols and a passport from him.

"I tied him to a tree, and left him alone in his glory.

"My mind was made up to leave France, and accordingly directed my way towards a small town on the sea coast.

"I had not gone far when I was overtaken by two mounted officers, who said it had been discovered that the person just liberated from the castle had turned out to be one of the 'Scorchers,' and they were in search of him.

"I muffled myself up so well, and assumed a strange voice so cleverly, that I threw the officers off the scent.

"I told them, however, that the very man they were looking for had attempted to rob me, but that I had proved more than a match for him, and in punishment had tied him to a tree, by the roadside.

"They believed my story, and hastily galloped back in the direction I had indicated.

"Of course I need not say that I rode off rapidly in the other direction.

"I came to the small town I intended, but it was walled in and had gates.

"I knocked at the gates for a long time, and at last they were opened by a stout sturdy porter.

"He demanded my passport.

"I gave him the one I had stolen from the merchant.

"He eyed me very closely, and said that the passport did not agree with my description, and he should detain me as a rough, dangerous-looking character.

"'Dont be quite so clever,' I said, half annoyed.

"He tried to get hold of my bridle-rein, but I knocked the gate-keeper down with one blow, and started off at a hard gallop.

"'Stop thief! murder! robbers! thieves,' shouted the prostrate official, in stentorian lungs.

"The cry was quickly taken up by the rabble of the town, and I thought it best to gallop right off and gain the open country again.

"'Stop thieves! robbers! murderers! stop him!' shouted the excited mob, in full cry.

"Onward I galloped through the dirty, narrow streets of the straggling town as hard as possible.

"Once or twice my horse slipped, and fell under me.

"I raised him again.

"But from every hand came stones and dirt and rubbish, which was hurled at me on all sides.

"I did not know the right direction of the opposite gate, and so had to guess at it as best I could.

"Far behind me were my pursuers, panting and yelling like so many half-bred hounds, when suddenly my flight was stopped by a high dead wall.

"Escape seemed impossible.

"My pursuers gave a loud shout of triumph as they perceived my progress was arrested, and I had almost given up every hope of escaping, when a sudden thought struck me that the wall might be nothing less than the city wall.

"'I could regain my liberty through a window of one of the houses down the street, and against the city wall,' I thought.

"I saw one with the door open.

"I jumped off my horse, and entered the house with a pistol in each hand.

"My pursuers, however, had seen it, and as I entered one of the rooms I heard them thundering at the street door.

"There was no one save an old woman in the room I entered.

"Seeing a fierce-looking man suddenly enter with a brace of pistols cocked she fainted, and fell on the floor.

"I rushed to the window and looked out.

"Judge of my joy, the fields were beyond.

"I threw out some pillows and the bed into the fields below.

"Next I locked and barred the door.

"After this I strongly barricaded it with the table, chairs, and whatever else I could.

"My next performance was to get up the spacious old chimney, and there I hid myself, waiting impatiently until night should come.

"As I imagined, all my plans proved successful.

"After banging at the door for a long time they broke it open, and rushed in headlong over each other.

"They were staggered when they found I was not there.

"'He has escaped from the window,' said one.

"'Yes, sure; see the bed and pillows lying on the grass yonder.'

"'Oh, the cunning knave,' said a third; 'he threw those things out to soften his fall.'

"They searched the room, and, in fact, all the house; but I was so well concealed up the winding chimney that although they looked up they could not perceive me.

"The old woman and her friends left the room, and there I sat among the soot thinking what should be done next.

"The bed was brought up again, and the old woman tidied her room, and towards night went out, for, as she said, she was afraid to sleep there alone that night.

"She locked the door upon me, and as soon as I heard her do so I crept down, and lay for an hour in her clean sheets.

"When midnight chimed from the church towers I got up and tore the old woman's sheets into strips.

"With these strips I made a sort of rope, and let myself down into the fields below.

"Seeing a black-looking forest not far off I ran towards it, and slept for an hour or two.

"My first business in the morning was to make towards a village to get bread, for I was almost famished with hunger.

"But judge of my surprise when I discovered that in the flight and scuffle of escape I had lost every farthing I had in the world.

"The baker looked very hard and cunningly at me, but I offered to sell him one of my pistols if he would only give me some refreshment.

"The baker agreed to the bargain, and gave me plenty of bread and meat for my weapon.

"But, unfortunately for me, the baker himself had been robbed about a month before that, and he looked upon every rough person as a cut-throat or thief.

"When, therefore, he had got my pistol he told one of his apprentice lads to watch my movements while he went and informed the bailiff.

"The bailiff had exerted himself very much to find out who the persons were who had robbed his particular friend, the pot-bellied baker, so that he felt great pleasure at finding that one of them at least had been discovered at last.

"He fussed about a long time, putting on his sword and pistols, but in the meantime I made the best of my way to the forest again, and began to enjoy myself with the food I so much needed.

"I sat behind a tree smoking after my repast, and then had a gentle dose.

"I was suddenly awakened by four stout athletic fellows armed with clubs, and led on by the pompous bailiff.

"They seized me, hand and foot, tied me with cords, and then carried me through the village in triumph, and put me into prison.

"I protested that I was a runaway German, and wished to fight against Prussia in the French service.

"The French were then engaged in a heavy war, and wanted men; but they did not believe my story, and insisted that I must be one of the famous 'Scorchers' from my ugly looks.

"They treated me awfully in prison, and kicked and cuffed me until I was black and blue, and sore all over.

"As luck would have it, however, after a month's confinement, a party of recruits passed through the village.

"Not being able to prove who or what I was, the bailiff felt very much inclined to give me over to the recruiting officer so as to get rid of me.

"Anything to me was preferable to a prison life, and I gladly volunteered to go into the French army to fight against the pot-bellied, money-grubbing Dutch and Germans.

"As I was a well-made young fellow, the soldier jumped at the chance of having such a fine recruit.

"I joined them, and, after a few days of hard marching, we reached Strasbourg, where I was drilled six times a day until, at last, I began to think they would drill the very life out of me.

"I was all along dreaming of and devising some plan to escape to England, but could not.

"At last an accident occurred which took me out of the army.

"My drill serjeant was more of a German than a Frenchman; in truth he was a naturalized German, and he thought the best way to make recruits learn their drill was to thrash them with a big stick.

"I saw him hit several poor devils about the legs and shoulders.

"Thinks I to myself, 'this won't do for me.'

"Nor did it.

"One day, however, as I couldn't escape, I thought I'd do something, so as to be sent to prison for a day or two, so as to have plenty of time to think over new plans for getting away to England.

"I, among a great many more, were placed under this German drill master, and he began to knock the poor devils about most unmercifully.

"My turn came next.

"I did something wrong, and he was about to strike me with his thick club.

"On the instant I raised my musket, and, with one blow, knocked him down as dead as a herring.

"In an instant I ran away out of the barracks, gun and all.

"They pursued me.

"I turned upon them and shot several.

"Like a hare I ran towards the Rhine, and jumping into a small boat, which I found there, pushed off from shore, and before my pursuers could get near enough I was in the middle of the river, and out of reach.

"Down the river I flew with the wind in my favour, and soon reached the mouth of the river.

"There I hailed a ship which was under full canvas.

"It proved to be an English vessel, and they took me on board.

"For several weeks we were knocking about in very bad weather, and I made myself so useful that one and all took a great liking to me.

"But here again misfortune overtook me.

"After buffetting about for more than a month, we were driven on to the west coast of England, and one night, when least expected, the ship struck on a rock, and was driven violently on shore.

"The night being dark, none of us could form any idea where we were going to, or where we were.

"Next morning, however, explained everything.

"The ship was a total wreck.

"Not a soul among the whole crew was alive but myself.

"I was master of the wreck, and all it contained; but yet I could not get on board very well, for the waves were washing right over it.

"While I sat watching the stranded vessel, and thinking what it might contain, I was startled by what I there saw.

"All around me danced a dozen skeleton men, who seized me by my arms and legs, and bore me away to their rendezvous."

"And who was it?" asked Phillip Redgill.

"The Red Man of the Gibbet. He was the chief of the Skeleton Crew in those days, and that's how I became one of them."

# THE SKELETON CREW; OR, WILDFIRE NED.

A ROUGH RECEPTION.—*See Number* 22.

## CHAPTER XLII.

### THE RED MAN OF THE GIBBET TELLS HIS STORY—WHO FOUNDED THE SKELETON CREW, AND HOW—THE RIVALS.

"WHO speaks of the Red Man of the Gibbet ?" said a sepulchral voice, just as Death-wing had finished his story.

All turned round, and saw entering at the door a most alarming figure.

Whether it was human or otherwise, no one could tell.

Suffice it to say that Redgill sank into his chair again in amazement.

The Skeleton Crew made away for the new-comer, who, advancing to the head of the table, stood and looked fixedly at Death-wing.

The unknown object was clothed in a loose, red cloak.

His face was fleshless, and his grisly hair stood bolt upright, and was grey.

His two eye-sockets emitted a bluish flame, and his hands were long, bony, and fleshless.

"Who speaks of the Red Man of the Gibbet ?" he said.

He turned round and looked contemptuously at the Skeleton Crew, as he said,

"You have listened to Death-wing's story; but he has not told you the origin of the famous Skeleton Crew.

No. 20.

"It dates farther back than to the period of which he has spoken. No one knows it but myself."

"Then, ghastly object, speak !" said Death-wing. "Tell to me and my followers how it came to pass that thou, the tenant of a lonely gibbet, should walk the earth like mortal."

The Red Man grinned in a most ghastly manner as he said, " Peace, and listen."

All were as silent as the grave as the Red Man began :—

"The Skeleton Crew was founded centuries ago.

"Their deadliest enemies have been the Warbecks.

"Their greatest friends have been found in the Redgill family, and since as I know that this night Phillip, the last of the Redgills, has formally joined your band, and will ultimately command it——"

"Command it ?" said Death-wing, with a sudden start.

"Yes, command it ere long—it is but proper that all should know who and what were the founders of the Skeleton Crew, and the cause of its origin."

"Then speak !" said Phillip, looking in amazement at the ghostly, ghastly figure of the Red Man of the Gibbet.

"I will speak, but let each and all listen ; aye, to every word.

"Many, many years, aye, centuries ago," the Red Man began, " there lived an old lord, who had no children nor wife, for they had all died young.

"This noble was named Warbeck, or, as he was called, 'Lord of the Lakes.'

"Unknown to any one, he adopted two male children, and brought them up as his own, just like, at the present day, old Sir Richard Warbeck adopted Charley and Ned.

"Of this, however, no one knew anything; but the children were not of equal age, nor of the same parents, although they always passed as brothers, and bore the family name of Warbeck.

"The elder one was tall, pale, thoughtful, and studious, with black hair, and a martial aspect. His name was Edward.

"The other, who was three or four years younger, was of a different aspect, and not so tall.

"He was fair-haired and rosy-cheeked, with bright blue eyes, and very passionate.

"All went on happily in the family of Lord Warbeck until the children grew up to be men.

"But from the moment that Lord Warbeck adopted these children, an enemy began to work against the welfare of the boys.

"This enemy, Philip," said the Red Man to him, "was your great ancestor, and the next of kin to Lord Warbeck.

"The lads were supposed by every one to be the real sons of Lord Warbeck.

"But Redgill doubted it, although he was unable to prove to the contrary.

"If they had died, therefore, Redgill himself would have come into the possession of the Warbeck estate.

"It was his constant aim and object to kill these two boys, but old Warbeck had them so well guarded, both night and day, that it was impossible to carry out his deep design.

"When they grew up to manhood, this Redgill was about ten years their senior, and went abroad to travel.

"But whither he went, or what he did, nobody knew nor cared to know.

"It was in the month of June, and on the greenest turf beneath an old oak tree there sat three persons.

"Two of the three were the adopted sons, and the third a most lovely maiden, whose parents, when dying, had left her to the care of old Warbeck.

"They were conversing most merrily, when the elder one, who was called Edward, said, playfully,

"'You have twined a chaplet for my brother, dearest Leoline; have you not a flower for me?'

"The beautiful maid blushed deeply, and culling from her flowers the freshest of the roses, began to weave them into a chaplet for him.

"At this moment a servant came up to them, saying that my lord desired to see Leoline immediately.

"The maiden rose, and hastened to the old lord, her guardian, leaving the two young men alone.

"For a moment they spoke not, but maintained a dead silence.

"Charley braced on his sword, which he had carelessly thrown on the grass; but Ned gathered up the flowers that had been plucked by the fair hands of Leoline.

"This action annoyed Charley.

"He bit his lip, and changed colour.

"At length he said, with a forced laugh,

"'I must confess, brother, that you carry out your affection for our fair cousin, Leoline, to a degree that even relationship cannot warrant.'

"'True,' said Ned, calmly, 'I love her with an affection surpassing that of blood.'

"'How?' said Charley, fiercely, with blood mounting to his temples. 'Do you dare to think of Leoline as a bride, then?'

"'Dare?' said Ned, turning pale, and drawing himself up to his greatest height.

"'Yes, I have said the word,' Charley remarked, boldly. 'You must know that I also love Leoline. I, too, claim her as my bride, and never, while I can wield a sword, will I surrender my claim to any living rival. Even,' he added, sinking his voice, 'though that rival be my own brother.'

"Ned answered not.

"His very soul seemed stunned.

"He gazed long and wistfully upon Charley.

"Then turning his face away, left the spot without uttering a word.

"The silence startled Charley.

"Accustomed as he was to give full vent to his own passions and anger, he could not comprehend or solve the forbearance of his brother.

"He knew that Ned's nature was too brave and noble to give way to fear.

"'Might it not be contempt?' he thought.

"As this suspicion crossed his mind, he followed his brother, and placing one hand upon his shoulder, said,

"'Where are you going? Do you consent to surrender Leoline?'

"'Does she love you?' Ned replied.

"His voice quivered with emotion.

"Even the hot-headed Charley felt a pang for his brother's sudden pain, and he did not answer.

"'Does she love you?' said Ned again, calmly, 'and have her own lips confessed it?'

"'I believe that she loves me,' Charley replied; 'but she is too modest a maiden to confess it.'

"'Enough,' said Ned, as he was about to walk away.

"'Stay,' said Charley, fiercely. 'Though she hath not confessed her love, let me tell you this, brother—dare not cross my path in love, if you do, by my soul, and hope of heaven, one of us two must die.'

"'How little canst thou read the heart of one who truly loves,' said Ned, with a smile. 'Think thou I would wed her if she loved thee, brother. Out upon the thought!'

"And Ned walked away, leaving Charley red with rage.

"Pale with thought, Edward, the elder brother, took a lonely walk in a retired part of the castle grounds, and, while musing on what had happened, he encountered Leoline alone, and they began to converse together like brother and sister.

"'Let us rest here for a moment, dear Leoline,' he said; 'I am sick at heart, and have much to say to you.'

"He spoke these words so solemnly, that the fair girl looked up to him in great surprise.

"'Have I ever offended you?' she said, tenderly. 'No, no, you have been too good and kind; forgive me if I have.'

"'No, Leoline, you have not, you could not offend me. But I have a task, a severe task to perform, and, though it pains me, it must be done. Listen, fair Leoline, listen: once on a time,' Edward began, 'there lived among these hills and lakes a certain old lord who had two sons, and an orphan like thyself also dwelt at the castle with them. The eldest son—but no matter, let us not waste words on him. The younger son, then, dearly loved the orphan girl, not for her immense wealth, but for herself alone, and he prayed that his elder brother would urge his suit, for he much feared a refusal. Leoline, my task is done; tell me, tell me truly, dost thou love my brother?'

"Gazing down upon the fair one's drooping eyes

he saw that she trembled violently, and her cheek was suffused with blushes.

"'Say,' continued Edward, mastering his own feelings, 'say, Leoline. Tell me, are not they my brother's flowers you now wear in your breast and hair ?'

"Leoline blushed, as she said—

"'Do not deem me ungrateful because I wear not yours also, but——'

"'Hush!' said Ned Warbeck. 'I am but as thy friend; is not my brother more to thee than simply friend ? He is young, brave, and handsome; Heaven grant that he may deserve thee if thou givest him so rich a gift as thy affections.'

"Leoline spoke not, but tear-drops trickled down her cheeks.

"'Wilt thou be his bride then, Leoline ? Tell me truly.'

"'Yes; and, Edward, I will be thy sister!'

"He hastily kissed her marble forehead, and plunged into an adjacent thicket to hide his own feelings.

"When he had recovered his self-possession, he went in search of his brother.

"He found him alone in the wood leaning, with folded arms, against a tree, and gazing on the ground.

"Edward felt for his brother's dejection.

"'Cheer thee, Charley, cheer thee,' said he; 'I bring thee most excellent tidings. I have seen and spoken to the divine Leoline. Nay, start not, brother, she loves thee ! She is thine !'

"'Generous, brave-hearted brother,' said Charley, with a sudden flash of pride upon his brow, and he threw himself upon his brother's neck, and could have wept, as he said,

"'No, no, brother Edward, this must not be; thou art the elder brother, and hast the best claim to the fair one's hand. I resign her to you with all my heart; but forgive my angry words this morning.'

"'Think of the past no more,' said Edward; 'the love of Leoline is an excuse for greater offences than thine; and now be kind to her; her nature is soft and keen; I know her well, for I have studied her faintest wish. Thou, Charley, art quick and hasty of ire; but remember a word wounds where love is deep. For my sake, as for hers, think more of her happiness than thy own. Now seek her; she waits to hear from thy own lips the tale that sounded cold upon mine.'

"With these words the two brothers parted, and, once more entering the castle, Edward went into the grand old baronial hall.

"The old lord still slept in his easy chair.

"Edward put his hand upon the old man's grey hair, and blessed him.

"Then stealing up to his chamber, he braced on his helmet and armour, and, thrice kissing the hilt of his sword, said, with a flushed cheek,

"'Come, good sword; henceforth be thou my only bride.'

"Then, passing unobserved from the castle he mounted his horse, and galloped away towards London.

"He safely arrived, and offered his services to the king, who was, at that time, engaged in a heavy war with France.

"His behaviour was so noble at court, and so handsome did he appear, that more than one fair maid fell in love with him.

"Temptations were many around him.

"He was courted and feasted on every hand.

"But still he remained true to his purpose, and never forgot his own deep love for Leoline.

"After spending some time at Court among the rich and gay, he started for Dover with a great number of troops.

"They set sail, and safely landed in France, and, ere many weeks, Ned Warbeck's name resounded through all the camps both of friend and foe for deeds of chivalry.

\* \* \* \* \*

"But how fared Leoline at the castle ?

"One night a minstrel sought shelter from the storm in the halls of Warbeck Castle.

"His visit was welcomed by the aged lord, and he repaid the hospitality he had received by the exercise of his art.

"He sung of the chase, and the gaunt hound started from the hearth.

"He sung of love, and Charles, forgetting his restless dreams, approached to Leoline, and laid himself at her feet.

"Louder, then, and louder rose the strain.

"The minstrel sung of her.

"He plunged into the thickest of the battle.

"The steed neighed.

"The trumpet sounded.

"And, in imagination, you might have heard the ringing of the steel.

"But when he came to signalise the names of the boldest knights, high among the loftiest sounded the name of Edward Warbeck.

"Thrice had he saved the king's royal banner.

"Two chargers had been slain beneath him.

"He had covered their bodies with the fiercest of the foe.

"The old lord started from his seat, and clasped the minstrel's hand,

"'Speak—you have seen him, then—he lives—he is honoured ?' said the old lord, excited.

"'I myself am but just from war, brave Warbeck, and, noble maiden, I saw the gallant Edward at the right hand of the king.

"'And he, Lady Leoline, was the only one whom admiration shone upon without the shadow of envy.

"'Who, then, would remain inglorious in the hall ?

"'Shall not the banners of his sires reproach him as they have, and shall not every voice strike shame into his soul ?'

"'Right,' cried Charley, suddenly, and flinging himself at the feet of Lord Warbeck,

"'Thou hearest what my brother has done, and thine aged eyes weep tears of joy. Shall I be the only one to dishonour thy name with a rusted sword ? No! grant me, like my brother, to go forth to France with the heroes of the King's Court.'

"'Noble youth,' cried the harper. 'Therein speaks the voice of a true Warbeck; hear him, my lord, hear the noble youth.'

"'The voice of heaven cries aloud in his voice,' said Charles, solemnly.

"'My son, I cannot chide thine ardour,' said the old lord, raising him with trembling hands. 'But Leoline, thy betrothed, what of her, my son ?'

"Pale as a statue, with ears that doubted their sense as they drank in the cruel words of her lover, stood the orphan girl.

"She did not speak.

"She scarcely breathed.

"She sank into her seat and gazed, till, at the speech of the old lord, her guardian, both maiden pride and tenderness restored her consciousness, and she said,

"'I, my lord, shall I bid him stay when his wishes bid him depart ?'

"'He will return to you, noble lady, covered with glory,' said the minstrel.

"The touching voice of Leoline went to his soul.

"He resumed his seat in silence. Leoline going up to Charles, whispered gently,

"'Act as though I were not.'

"And she left the hall, to commune with her heart, and to weep alone.

"'I can wed her before I go,' said Charles, suddenly, as he sat that night in his chamber conversing with my lord.

"'Why, that is true! and leave thy bride in the first week—— a hard trial.'

"'Better that, than incur the chance of never calling her mine.'

"'Assuredly she deserves all from thee, and, indeed, it is no small sacrifice at thy young age, and with thy gallant mien, to renounce her for a time; but a bridegroom without a bride! Nay, man, much as they want warriors, I am forced to tell thee if thou weddest, stay peacably at home, and forget in the chase the valours of war, from which thou wouldst strip the ambition of love.'

"'I would I knew what were best,' said Charles, irresolutely. 'My brother, ha! shall he for ever outshine me? But poor Leoline, how will she grieve? she who left him for me.'

"'Was that thy fault?' said the old lord, gaily. 'It may many times chance to thee again to be preferred to another. Troth, it is a sin that the conscience may walk lightly under. But sleep on it, Charles, my old eyes grow weary.'

"The next day Charley sought Leoline, and proposed that their wedding should precede his parting, but so embarrassed was he, so divided between two wishes, that Leoline hurt, offended, stung by his coldness, refused the proposal at once. She left him, lest he should see her weep, and then, then she repented of her just pride.

"But Charles, striving to appease his conscience with the belief that her's was now the sole fault, busied himself in preparation for his departure.

"Anxious to outshine his brother, he departed, not as Edward had done, alone and unattended, but levying all the horses, men, and money that the old lord could afford, Charles embarked for France at the head of a glittering troop of horsemen.

"The aged minstrel still remained at the castle, and, affecting sickness, tarried behind, and promised to join Charles in France.

"Meanwhile, he devoted his whole powers of pleasing to console Leoline.

"The force of her simple love was, however, stronger than all his arts.

"In vain he insinuated doubts of Charles's fidelity; she refused to hear them.

"In vain he poured, with the softest accents, into the witchery of flattery and song; she turned heedlessly away, and was pained at the remembrance of how coldly Charles had treated her before departing for the wars.

"She shut herself up in her chamber, and pined in solitude for her absent lover.

"The old minstrel, who was none other than Redgill in disguise, now resolved to attempt darker arts to obtain power over her.

"But from some cause he suddenly left the castle on some secret mission, of so high import, that it could not be resisted by a passion stronger in his breast than love—the passion of ambition and hate.

"Meanwhile, though, ever and anon, the fame of Edward reached their ears, it came unaccompanied with that of Charles.

"Of him they heard no tidings.

"And thus the love of the tender orphan was kept alive by the perpetual restlessness of fear.

"At length the old lord died, and Leoline was left entirely alone.

"One evening, as she sat with her maidens, the ringing of a horse's hoofs were heard in the outer court of the castle.

"A horn sounded.

"The heavy gates were unbarred, and a handsome soldier entered the hall.

"He stopped for one moment at the entrance, as if overpowered by his emotions.

"In the next instant he had clasped Leoline to his breast.

"'Dost thou not recognise me, Leoline?' he said, tenderly.

"He doffed his helmet, and she saw that majestic brow, which, unlike that of Charles, her lover, had never changed or been clouded in its aspect to her.

"'The war is suspended for the present,' said he. 'I learnt my father's death, and I have returned home to hang up my banner in the hall, and spend my days in peace.'

"Time and the life of camps had worked their change upon Edward's face.

"His hair, deepened in its shade, was now worn from the temples, and disclosed a battle-scar which rather heightened the beauty of his countenance.

"He had apparently conquered a love that was so early crossed, but not that fidelity of remembrance which made Leoline dearer to him than all others, and forbade him to replace the image he had graven upon his soul.

"Leoline's lips trembled with the name of her absent lover, Charles.

"But a certain recollection of his coldness stifled even her anxiety.

"Edward hastened to forestall her question.

"'My brother is well,' he said, 'and is now sojourning at Calais; he lingered there so long that the war terminated without his aid. Doubtless he will soon return; a week, nay, a day might restore him to you, fair Leoline.'

"Leoline was much consoled.

"Yet something seemed untold.

"'Why was he so eager for the strife, and to serve the king against the French, if Charles had thus tarried at Calais so long?' she thought.

"She wondered at this, but did not dare to search farther into her heart.

"The generous Edward concealed from her that his brother led a life of the most reckless and indolent dissipation, wasting his wealth in the pleasures of the reckless and gay, and only occupying his ambition with travelling and gambling, and whatever else that was useless and inglorious.

"Edward and Leoline resumed their old friendship, and Leoline believed that it was friendship alone.

"They walked again among the gardens in which their childhood had strayed.

"They looked down on the eternal mirror of the lakes.

"Ah! could it have reflected the same unawakened freshness of their life's early spring!

"The grave and contemplative mind of Lord Edward had not been so contented with the horrors of war but that it had sought also those calmer sources of emotion which were yet found among the sages of the east.

"He therefore had little in common with the ruder lords around him.

"He summoned them not to his board, nor attended their noisy wassails.

"Often late at night, in yon shattered tower, his lonely lamp shone still o'er the mighty stream, and his only relief to loneliness was the presence and song of Leoline.

"He recounted to her his trials and troubles during the war.

"And she listened to him like a child, still thinking of her absent lover, who, at that moment, had entirely forgotten her.

"Paler and paler she grew day by day.

"And the more afflicted she was, the more the gallant young lord comforted her.

"His amusements were varied.

"He did all he possibly could to dispel the terrible gloom which possessed her; but all to no purpose.

"Her heart was gradually becoming petrified.

"From her lonely window she gazed for hours and hours at night.

"The song of nightingale borne upon the breeze, soothed her troubled soul, and tears flowed down her pallid cheek.

"Yet no murmur came from her.

"She believed that Charles—now Sir Charles—would prove faithful to her as she had been to him.

"Her hopes were doomed to be blasted.

"Months rolled by, and still Charles did not return.

"Indeed, no tidings of any kind had been received from him for a long time.

"He seemed to have forgotten poor Leoline, and she pined alone in deep sorrow.

"It was whispered abroad that, with the money which old Lord Warbeck had left him, Charley intended to buy up the estates of a neighbouring castle.

"This rumour proved to be true, and Edward thought that his brother intended it as the future residence of Leoline—his bride.

"The estates which Charles had purchased was in full view of Warbeck Castle, and the whole country around were astonished at the magnificence with which it had been furnished.

"Everything that money could do was done to render this new residence worthy of those who were to occupy it.

"Six months rolled on, and Charles returned not, nor did any one hear a single word of his doings, or whereabouts.

"At the end of a twelvemonth, and when the new castle was fit for habitation, a startling rumour 'reached the ears of Edward (now Lord) Warbeck, and the fair orphan, Leoline.

"Charles had returned, and brought back with him a French bride, of amazing beauty, and fabulous wealth!

"Leoline was the first to disbelieve the rumour, but the only one.

"Bright, in the summer noon, flashed the array of horsemen: for up the steep hill wound the gorgeous cavalcade towards the grand residence of Charles Warbeck.

"The bells rung loudly, and the French bride, with her husband, entered their princely abode.

"That same night there was a grand banquet given by Charles Warbeck to his friends; but Edward and Leoline were forgotten.

"The lights shone from every casement, and music swelled loud and ceaselessly within.

"By the side of her husband sat the fair French bride, glittering in jewels.

"Her dark locks, her flashing eye, the false colour of her complexion dazzled the eyes of all his guests.

"In the banquet hall, among the guests, sat Phillip Redgill.

"Not dressed as a minstrel on this occasion; but in the uniform of an English officer.

"For he had played his part so well that even Charles did not suspect him to be one and the same person, for when Redgill left Warbeck Castle so suddenly, he went to Calais, and then under an assumed name, made the acquaintance of Charles Warbeck, and led him on to ruin.

"As he was such a gay fellow, then, and had become so much linked in with young Warbeck, he was looked upon by all almost as one of the family.

"'By the fates,' said he, as he whispered to the bride and bridegroom, 'we shall scare the owls to-night in the grim towers of Warbeck Castle. Thy grave brother, Sir Charles, will have much to do to comfort thy old flame, Leoline, when she learns what a gallant life you are leading here with your fair French bride.'

"'Poor damsel,' said the bride, with a light laugh of scorn, 'poor damsel; doubtless she will now be reconciled to the pale-faced rejected one; for I understand that my Lord Warbeck, your brother, Sir Charles, is a gentleman, handsome, and of gallant mien.'

"'Peace!' said Sir Charles, sternly, and quaffing a large goblet of wine.

"The bride bit her lip, and glanced meaningly at Redgill, who returned the glance.

"'Nought but a beauty such as thine can win my pardon,' said Sir Charles, turning to his bride, and gazing passionately in her face.

"The bride smiled.

"Well sped the feast, the laugh deepened, the wine circled, when Sir Charles's eye rested on a guest at the bottom of the board, whose figure was mantled from head to foot, and whose face was covered by a dark veil.

"'Beshrew me,' said he, aloud, 'but this is scarce courteous at our revel; will the stranger vouchsafe to unmask?'

"These words turned all eyes to the figure. It rose and walked slowly, but with grace, to the fair bride, and laid beside her a wreath of flowers.

"'It is a simple gift, lady,' said the stranger, in a voice of much sweetness; 'but it is all I can offer, and the bride of Sir Charles should not be without a gift at my hands. May you both be happy!'

"With these words the stranger left the hall like a shadow.

"'Bring her back—bring her back,' said the French bride, hastily.

"'No, no!' said Sir Charles, waving his hand impatiently; 'touch her not, heed her not, at your peril.'

"The bride bent her head over the flowers to conceal her anger, and from amongst them dropped the broken half of a ring.

"Sir Charles recognised it at once.

"It was the half of that ring which he had broken with his betrothed Leoline.

"He required not such a sign to convince him that the figure so full of ineffable grace, that touching voice, that simple action, so tender in its sentiment, that gift, that blessing, came only from the heart-broken and forgiving Leoline.

"But Lord Warbeck, alone in his solitary tower, passed to and fro with agitated steps.

"Deep, undying wrath at his brother's baseness mingled with one burning, delicious hope.

"He confessed now that he had deceived himself when he thought his passion was no more; was there any longer a bar to his union with Leoline?

"In that delicacy which was breathed into him by his love, he had forborne to seek, or to offer her the insult of, consolation.

"He felt that the shock should be borne alone, and yet he pined, he thirsted, to throw himself at her feet.

"Nursing these contending thoughts, he was aroused by a knock at his door.

"He opened it.

"The passage was thronged by Leoline's maidens —pale, anxious, weeping.

"Leoline had left the castle, but with one female attendant, none know whither.

"They knew too soon.

"From the hall of Warbeck Castle she had passed over in the dark and inclement night, to the valley in which the convent offered to the weary of spirit and the broken of heart, a refuge.

"At daybreak, the next morning, Lord Edward Warbeck was at the convent gate.

"He saw Leoline.

"What a change one night of suffering had made in that face, which was the fountain of all loveliness to him.

"He clasped her in his arms.

"He urged all that love could urge.

"He besought her to accept that heart, which had never wronged her memory by a thought.

"In vain Warbeck pleaded ; in vain he urged all that passion and truth could urge.

"The springs of earthly love were for ever dried up in the orphan's heart, and her resolution was immovable.

"She tore herself from his arms, and the gate of the convent creaked harshly on his ear.

"A new and stern emotion now wholly possessed him.

"Naturally mild and gentle, when once aroused to anger, he cherished it with the strength of a calm mind.

"Leoline's tears, her sufferings, her wrongs, her uncomplaining spirit, the change already stamped upon her face, all cried aloud to him for vengeance !

"'She is an orphan,' said he, bitterly ; 'she hath none to protect, to redress her, save me alone.

"'My father's charge over her forlorn youth descends of right to me.

"'What matters it whether her forsaker be my brother ? he is _her_ foe.

"'Hath he not crushed her heart ?

"'Hath he not consigned her to sorrow till the grave ? And with what insult. No warning, no excuse. With lewd wassailers keeping revel for his new bridals in the hearing—before the sight—of his betrothed. Enough ! the time hath come when, to use his own words, "One of us two must fall ! "'

"He half drew his glaive as he spoke, and thrusting it back violently into the sheath, strode home to his solitary castle.

"The sound of steeds and of the hunting horn met him at his portal ; the bridal train of his brother Sir Charles, all mirth and gladness, were panting for the chase.

"That evening, a knight in complete armour entered the banquet-hall, and defied Sir Charles, on the part of Lord Warbeck, to mortal combat.

"Even Redgill was startled by so unnatural a challenge.

"But Sir Charles, reddening, took up the gage, and the day and spot were fixed.

"Discontented, wroth with himself, a savage gladness seized him.

"He longed to wreak his desperate feelings even on his brother.

"Nor had he ever, in his jealous heart, forgiven that brother his virtues and his renown.

"At the appointed hour the brothers met as foes.

"Lord Edward Warbeck's visor was up, and all the settled sternness of his soul was stamped upon his brow.

"But Sir Charles, more willing to brave the arm than to face the front of his brother, kept his visor down.

"Redgill stood by him with folded arms.

"It was a study in human passions to his mocking mind.

"Scarce had the first trumpet sounded to this dread conflict, when a new actor entered on the scene.

"The rumour of so unprecedented an event had not failed to reach the convent wherein Leoline had sought refuge.

"And now, two by two, came the sisters of the holy shrine, and the armed men made way as, with trailing garments and veiled faces, they swept along into the very lists.

"At that moment one from among them left her sisters, and, with a slow, majestic pace, paused not till she stood right between the brother foes.

"'Lord Edward Warbeck,' she said in a hollow voice, that curdled up his dark spirit as she spoke, 'is it thus thou wouldst prove thy love, and maintain thy trust over the fatherless orphan that thy sire bequeathed to thy care ? Shall I have murder on my soul ?'

"At that question she paused, and those who heard it were struck dumb, and shuddered.

"'The murder of one man by the hand of his own brother ! Away, Warbeck !—_I command_ !'

"'Shall I forget thy wrongs, Leoline ?' said Warbeck.

"'Wrongs ! they are forgiven, they are no more. And thou, Sir Charles—(here her voice faltered)—thou, does thy conscience smite thee not—wouldst thou atone for robbing me of hope by barring against me the future ? Wretch that I should be, could I dream of mercy—could I dream of comfort—if thy brother fell by thy sword in my cause ? Sir Charles, I have pardoned thee, and blessed thee and thine. Once, perhaps, thou didst love me ; remember how I loved thee—cast down thine arms.'

"Sir Charles gazed at the veiled form before him.

"Where had the soft Leoline learned to command ?

"He turned to his brother.

"He felt all that he had inflicted upon both ; and casting his sword upon the ground, he knelt at the feet of Leoline, and kissed her garment with a devotion that votary never lavished on a holier saint.

"The spell that lay over the warriors around was broken.

"There was one loud cry of congratulation and joy.

"'And thou, Lord Edward Warbeck !' said Leoline, turning to the spot where, still motionless and haughty, Warbeck stood.

"'Have I ever rebelled against thy will ?' said he, softly, and buried the point of his sword in the earth. 'Yet, Leoline—yet,' added he, looking at his kneeling brother, 'yet art thou already better avenged than by this steel !'

"'Thou art ! thou art !' cried Sir Charles, smiting his breast ; and slowly, and scarce noting the crowd that fell back from his path, Lord Edward Warbeck left the lists.

"Leoline said no more.

"Her divine errand was fulfilled ; she looked long and wistfully after the stately form of Lord Edward, and then, with a slight sigh, she turned to Sir Charles.

"'This is the last time we shall meet on earth. Peace be with us all.'

"She then, with the same majestic and collected bearing, passed on towards the sisterhood.

"And as, in the same solemn procession, they glided back towards the convent, there was not a man present, no, not even the hardened Redgill, who would not, like Sir Charles, have bent his knee to Leoline.

"Once more, Sir Charles plunged into the wild revelry of the age.

"His castle was thronged with guests.

"Night after night the lighted halls shone down athwart the tranquil lake.

"The beauty of his French bride, and the wealth of Sir Charles, attracted all the chivalry from far and near.

"Yet gloom seized him in the midst of gladness, and the revel was welcome only as the escape from remorse.

"The voice of scandal, however, soon began to mingle with that of envy at the pomp of Sir Charles.

"The fair bride, it was said, weary of her lord, lavished her smiles on others.

"The young and the fair were always most acceptable at the castle.

"And above all, her guilty love for Redgill scarcely affected disguise.

"Sir Charles alone appeared unconscious of the rumour; and though he had begun to neglect his bride, he relaxed not in his intimacy with Redgill.

"It was noon, and the bride was sitting in her bower alone with her suspected lover.

"Rich perfumes mingled with the fragrance of flowers, and various luxuries, unknown till then in English climes, gave a soft and effeminate character to the room.

"'I tell thee,' said the bride, petulantly, 'that he begins to suspect; that I have seen him watch thee, and mutter as he watched, and play with the hilt of his dagger. Better let us fly ere it is too late, for his vengeance would be terrible were it once roused against us. Ah! why did I ever forsake my own sweet land for these bleak shores! There, love is not considered eternal, and inconstancy a crime worthy death.'

"'Peace, pretty one,' said Redgill, carelessly; 'thou knowest not the laws of our foolish chivalry. Thinkest thou I could fly from a knight's halls like a thief in the night? Why verily, even the red cross would not cover such dishonour. If thou fearest that thy dull lord suspects, why let us part. The king hath sent to me. Ere evening I might be on my way thither.'

"'And I left to brave the barbarian's rage alone? Is this thy courage?'

"'Nay, prate not so wildly,' answered Redgill. 'Surely, when the object of his suspicion is gone, thy woman's art and thy French wiles can easily allay the jealous fiend. Do I not know thee? Why thou wouldst fool all men—save Redgill.'

"'And thou, cruel, wouldst thou leave me?' said the bride, weeping; 'how shall I live without thee?'

"Redgill laughed slightly.

"'Can such eyes ever weep without a comforter? But farewell; I must not be found with thee. To-morrow I depart for London; we shall meet again.'

"As soon as the door closed on Redgill, the bride rose, and pacing the room, said—

"'Selfish, selfish; how could I ever trust him? Yet I dare not brave Sir Charles alone. Surely it was his step that disturbed us in our yesterday's interview. Nay, I will fly. I can never want a companion.'

"She clapped her hands.

"A young page appeared.

"She threw herself on her seat and wept bitterly.

"The page approached.

"And love was mingled with his compassion.

"'Why weepest thou, dearest lady?' said he; 'is there aught in which Conrade's services—services—ah! thou hast read his heart—his devotion may avail?'

"Sir Charles had wandered out the whole day alone.

"His vassals had observed that his brow was more gloomy than was its wont, for he usually concealed whatever might prey within.

"Some of the most confidential of his servitors he had conferred with, and the conference had deepened the shadow of his countenance.

"He returned at twilight; his young wife did not honour the repast with her presence.

"She was unwell, and not to be disturbed. The gay Redgill was the life of the board.

"'Thou carriest a sad brow to-day, Sir Charles,' said he. 'Good faith! thou hast caught it from the dull air.'

"'I have something troubles me,' answered Sir Charles, forcing a smile, 'which I would fain impart to thy friendly bosom. The night is clear, and the moon is up, let us go forth alone into the garden.'

"Redgill rose.

"And he forgot not to gird on his sword as he followed the knight.

"Sir Charles led the way to one of the most distant terraces that overhung the lakes.

"'Redgill,' said he, pausing. 'answer me one question on thy honour. Was it thy step that left my lady's bower yester eve at vesper?'

"Startled by so sudden a query, the wily Redgill faltered in his reply.

"The red blood mounted to Sir Charles's brow.

"'Nay, lie not. These eyes have not witnessed, but these ears have heard from others of my dishonour.'

"As Sir Charles spoke, Redgill's eye resting on the water, perceived a boat rowing fast over the lake.

"The distance forbade him to see more than the outline of two figures within it.

"'She was right,' thought he; 'perhaps that boat already bears her from the danger'

"Drawing himself up to the full height of his tall stature, Redgill replied, haughtily,

"'Sir Charles, if thou hast deigned to question thy vassals, obtain from them only an answer.'

"'Enough,' cried Sir Charles, losing patience, and striking Redgill with his clenched hand. 'Draw, traitor, draw!'

*       *       *       *       *

"Alone in his lofty tower, Lord Edward Warbeck watched the night deepen over the heavens, and communed mournfully with himself.

"'To what end,' thought he, 'have these strong affections, these capacities of love, this yearning after sympathy, been given me? Unloved and unknown, I walk to my grave, and all the nobler mysteries of my heart are for ever to be untold.'

"Thus musing, he heard not the challenge of the warder on the wall, or the unbarring of the gate below, or the tread of footsteps along the winding stair.

"The door was thrown suddenly open, and Sir Charles stood before him.

"'Come,' he said, in a low voice, trembling with passion, 'come, I will show thee that which shall gladden thy heart. Twofold is Leoline avenged.'

"Lord Edward Warbeck looked in amazement on a brother he had not met since they stood in arms each against the other's life.

"And he now saw that the arm that Sir Charles extended to him dripped with blood, trickling drop by drop upon the floor.

"'Come,' said Sir Charles, 'follow me! It is my last prayer. Come, for Leoline's sake, come.'

"At that name, Lord Edward Warbeck hesitated no longer; he girded on his sword, and followed his brother down the stairs, and through the castle gate.'

"The porter scarcely believed his eyes when he saw the two brothers, so long divided, go forth at that hour alone, and seemingly in friendship.

"Lord Warbeck, arrived at that epoch in the feelings when nothing stuns, followed with silent steps the rapid strides of his brother.

"The two castles, as I have told you, were not far from each other.

"In a few minutes Sir Charles paused at an open space in one of the terraces on which the moon shone bright and steady.

"'Behold!' he said, in a ghastly voice, 'behold!'

"And Lord Warbeck saw on the sward the corpse of Redgill bathed with the blood that even still poured fast and warm from his heart.

"'Hark!' said Sir Charles. 'He it was who first made me waver in my vows to Leoline. He persuaded me to wed yon whited falsehood. Hark! He, who had thus wronged my real love, dishonoured me with my faithless bride, and thus—thus—thus' as, grinding his teeth, he spurned again and again the dead body of Redgill, 'thus Leoline and myself are avenged!'

"'And thy wife?' said Lord Warbeck, pityingly.

"'Fled—fled with a hireling page! It is well! She was not worth the sword that was once belted on—by Leoline!'

"On the very night of his revenge a long delirious illness seized Sir Charles.

"The generous Lord Warbeck forgave, forgot all, save that he had been once consecrated by Leoline's love.

"He tended him through his sickness, and, when he recovered, Sir Charles was an altered man.

"He foreswore the comrades he had once courted, the revels he had once led.

"His halls were desolate.

"The only companion Sir Charles sought was Lord Warbeck; and Lord Warbeck bore with him.

"They had no subject in common, for on one subject Lord Warbeck at least felt too deeply ever to trust himself to speak.

"Yet did a strange and secret sympathy re-unite them.

"They had at least a common sorrow.

"Often they were seen wandering together by the solitary banks of the river, or amidst the woods, without apparently interchanging word or sign.

". "Lord Warbeck was now companionless.

"In vain the king's court wooed him to its pleasures.

"In vain the camp proffered him the oblivion of renown.

"Ah! could he tear himself from a spot where morning and night he could see afar, amidst the valley, the roof that sheltered Leoline, and on which every copse, every turf, reminded him of former days?

"His solitary life, his midnight vigils, strange scrolls about his chamber, obtained him by degrees the repute of cultivating the darker arts; and, shunning, he became shunned by all.

"One night, when Lord Warbeck sat lonely in his chamber, dreaming of the past, the bell at the outer gate began to toll.

"He listened.

"Again and again its solemn sounds struck ominously upon his ear.

"He had never before in all his life heard such a dismal, mournful sound.

"The gate-keeper went out to ascertain the cause, but could see no one about.

"He even went up into the bell-tower.

"But just as he got there the bell ceased tolling; but even then shook to and fro.

"He was about to leave when again it tolled.

"The old porter was struck almost dumb with surprise.

"The bell was not touched by anything that he could see, and yet its harsh grating sound thrilled him.

"'Ghosts!' he cried, and hurried away to inform his master of the strange occurrence.

"'What means this noise at such an unseemly hour of the night?' said Lord Edward, sternly.

"'I know not my lord,' was the answer; 'but all in the castle are in commotion and fear.'

"'Get you gone, knave,' said Warbeck, 'and let's hear no more of such silly nonsense.'

"The porter went his way, and Lord Edward walked about his room in a state of mental excitement.

"'What means this tolling of the bells?' said he, half-aloud.

"'I can explain,' said a voice near to him.

"Lord Edward turned suddenly around, and to his horror, he saw standing before him a ghastly skeleton form.

"'Who art thou?' said Lord Edward, in a firm tone.

"'I am Redgill, whom thy brother slew.'

"'Ha! the spirit of the dead!' said Lord Edward.

"'No, not dead; through the agency of potent spirits, I have been restored to life.'

"'Impossible!'

"'No; I roam the earth with but one sole object.'

"'Name it!'

"'To destroy every one who bears the name of Warbeck.'

"'Be you spirit or mortal, thou liest!' said Lord Edward.

"And at the same moment he drew his sword, and made a pass at the grim visitor.

"In an instant, however, the blade was shivered into halves, and the skeleton laughed loudly and grimly.

"'My life is charmed. Thy steel to me is useless. They hung me on a gibbet, and called me the Red Man from the mass of gore which flowed from the wounds inflicted by thy brother; but, as I have said, my life is renewed through mystic charms and spells, and at certain times of night, during certain seasons of the year, I can go abroad wherever I will.

"'See,' said the intruder, 'I come not alone.'

"He stamped his foot.

"In a moment, Lord Edward was astonished to find that the room was filled with skeleton men.

"'You see I come not alone,' said the intruder again; 'this is my band, the Skeleton Crew; we are the scourge both of the sea and land; fear us, Warbeck, for never, until the last of thy name shall have ceased to live, will I, or my crew, cease to follow, and thwart you in all your designs.'

"'Unholy fiend,' Lord Edward exclaimed; 'if even it be that all of you are endowed with life anew, heaven hath its counter spells for all your charms.'

THE MEETING IN THE WOOD.—(See No. 23.)

"'True,' said the grissly visitor; 'heaven had one on earth who, until to-night, preserved you and yours, but that one has departed, hence our hour of triumph has come.'

"At that same moment Lord Edward's ears were startled by the distant tolling of the convent bell.

"'Listen,' said the grim chief; 'listen to the funeral knell of her you loved.'

"'Leoline?' gasped Lord Edward.

"'Yes, Leoline is no more.'

"'I cannot, I will not believe it.'

"''Tis true, her spirit has left earth, and with it thy only protector, Lord of Warbeck.'

"These words were scarcely uttered, when the Skeleton Band were in turn struck with awe.

"There, in the midst of them stood the spirit form of Leoline, who, in white robes, a slight as air, held her hand aloft, and pronounced a solemn malediction on those who would have injured the gallant knight.

"'Begone, spirits of evil—vanish to the utmost corners of the earth; but never, while heaven hath a protecting arm, can the Red Man of the Gibbet harm or injure the noble race of Warbeck.'

"Such was the potency of the spirit presence that the Skeletons vanished; yet, since that day, and since that solemn hour, have the Skeleton Crew and

the Warbecks been at deadly feud; and never," said the Red Man, "until the last of the race shall have succumbed to my awful power will I rest in peace in my gibbet chains."

The Red Man concluded his narrative, and vanished as he had came—how, or where, none knew whither.

For some time Death-wing and the rest remained as if spellbound.

Never until then had any ever heard how the Skeleton Crew was founded; but now that its origin was unmistakably traced to a deadly hate to the family of the Warbecks, Death-wing, Redgill, and the rest rose in great anger, and swore, in the language of the Red Man, never to rest until the last descendants of the bold Warbecks were numbered with the dead.

With sword upraised, and amid great applause of the Crew, Phillip Redgill swore an awful oath to slay Ned Warbeck the first moment they met, whethe publicly, privately, in night or day.

## CHAPTER XLIII.

THE ATTACK AND COUNTER ATTACK ON THE BLOCK HOUSE—NED WARBECK TO THE RESCUE.

"To action," said Death-wing; "to action then; let

us attack Captain Jack's store-house, and for ever silence the babbling of 'the Dozen;' they are all braggarts."

With an unanimous voice the Skeleton Crew proposed to sally forth, and armed themselves to the teeth.

Led on by Death-wing and Phillip Redgill, who was now recognized as one of their chiefs, they went forth into the darkness bent upon sacking the stronghold where for many years the Dozen had kept their plunder.

"We will serve Captain Jack out once and for all," said Death-wing.

"Yes, if he is there," said Phillip; "but I doubt it. Both he and old Bates are too old birds to be caught with chaff."

"No matter," said Death-wing, "we shall be sure to fall foul of some of the gang, and the beautiful Ellen Harmer shall be the wife of the first one who enters their stronghold."

"Agreed!" shouted all.

With one accord they moved on through the dark streets like phantoms.

In a short time they reached the strong and barricaded store-house of the Dozen.

The sounds of carousing were heard within.

"They do not suspect that anyone is aware of their doings. We can capture the place without trouble of any kind."

"But the place is surrounded by high and thick palisadings of timber," said Phillip; "it has two gates, both of them of amazing strength."

"So much the better," said Death-wing, "when we have massacred all within we will keep the place as our own. Does any of the King's officers know of it?"

"I think not," said Phillip, "for Captain Jack and his men had it built expressly for themselves in such an out-of-the-way place that I doubt much if even Colonel Blood ever heard of it."

"Excellent news," said Death-wing; "if Captain Jack and Bates have thoroughly ransacked the Colonel's house there must be a great deal of treasure inside."

"No doubt of it."

"Then let us surround it quietly. When I give the word let one and all of you scale the walls, and spare no living soul save Ellen Harmer. Have the scouts returned?" asked Death-wing. "We must not commence operations until the coast is clear."

"Here are the two scouts," said Phillip; "they have just returned."

"What news do you bring?" asked Death-wing of them.

"Colonel Blood has been thrown off the scent; he and his soldiers endeavoured to follow Captain Jack and old Bates, but they escaped in the darkness."

"Hang the trick," said Death-wing, "so we shan't have the pleasure of killing those two rascals after all."

"Never mind," said Phillip, "it will only be a pleasure for us to do it at some distant time."

"True," said Death-wing, "but you don't know them so long or so well as I do. If these two notorious rascals find that their men have been all killed or disbanded, they will form another gang, most likely, and cause us more trouble than they are worth. No matter, let us hear what the scouts say. What direction has Colonel Blood and his soldiers taken?"

"They have returned to barracks."

"And the Colonel?"

"I saw him standing at the gate of his own house swearing like a madman at his ill-success."

"So much the better," said Death-wing, laughing hoarsely, "if he has been disappointed we shall not be. Come, follow me."

With this command all the crew followed him silently, like so many shadows.

They approached the outer walls of the timber-built dwelling, and crept out of view.

They could hear the sounds of revelry within, and the tipsy chorus of unsuspecting drunkards.

"Now," said Death-wing.

At the word of command he and his followers scaled the walls with the agility of monkeys.

The next moment they descended into the spacious court-yard.

The huge old building was surrounded by them.

The doors were smashed open.

In a few moments the clanging of arms and the report of pistols were heard on all sides.

But while this was taking place many good citizens were aroused from their slumbers by the noise and tumult, and stood at a respectful distance from the scene of combat, fearful to have anything to do or say in the matter.

For they were horrified to learn that it was none other than the famous Skeleton Crew and Captain Jack's band who were fighting within.

This all could plainly perceive, for the skeleton forms of Death-wing's crew were occasionally seen at the windows and on the roof in deadly struggle with the robbers.

But now a change came over the aspect of the whole scene; Wildfire Ned, with Lieutenant Garnet, Bob Bertram, and Tim, had heard of the atrocious robbery of and abduction of Nelly Harmer from the mansion of Colonel Blood.

On the instant they formed a strong patrol of citizens, and having well armed them, all marched through the streets on the look-out for any of Captain Jack's notorious gang.

They were not aware of what Death-wing and his crew were doing that moment at the "Block House," but the distant hum of voices told them that something more than ordinary was transpiring down by the river bank.

"Come on," said Ned to his patrol; "come on, my merry men. There is something up down by the river; who knows, it may be Captain Jack and his vagabond followers, after all? Come on, don't let us give up our search for nothing. Follow me!"

"Stop! stop! good masters," said several affrighted citizens. "Stay where you are; several of the king's men have been murdered! The Skeleton Crew are out to-night; the demons, led on by Death-wing, are making sad havoc down by the river, and nothing can stop them!"

"The Skeleton Crew!" said Ned. "Hurrah, boys, hurrah! we have met them before, haven't we, Garnet?"

"Yes, my brave lad; and I am willing to meet the scoundrels again, whether on land or sea. Lead on, Ned; lead on."

With a loud shout Wildfire Ned and his followers rushed towards the scene of tumult.

The citizens made way for them, as, led on by Ned Warbeck, Garnet and Bob Bertram, the gallant band of young citizens and London Apprentices, ran towards the Block House.

It was at this moment, and just as Ned Warbeck arrived on the scene of action, that the gate of the Block House was hastily opened and closed again.

A man rushed forth, all bleeding, and with a sword in hand.

"She is mine! she is mine!" said he.

It was Phillip Redgill bearing away the unconscious form of Ellen Harmer from the Block House!

"She is mine! she is mine!" he said, with savage oaths. "Make way there on your lives!"

The good, simple citizens, supposing that Phillip Redgill was a well-disposed and gallant person, who, at the risk of his own life among the terrible crew, had rescued an innocent girl, made way for him to the right and left, and even cheered him.

"Hold, villain, hold!" said Ned Warbeck, dashing towards Phillip Redgill.

Redgill stood stock still as if he had suddenly beheld a spectre.

"Ned Warbeck," he gasped, "again across my path! Make way, fool, or die!"

"Stir but another inch with your precious burden," said Ned Warbeck, with a determined oath. "Stir but an inch farther this way, and my sword to the hilt shall be buried in your craven carcase!"

With wild-looking eyes and dishevelled hair, almost on end with unnatural fright and alarm, Phillip Redgill was about to drop the insensible girl from his arms, when, with a sudden spring, and a gleaming sword, Ned Warbeck plucked her from his grasp.

A terrible hand to hand conflict now took place between these two hereditary enemies.

It seemed as if all the hatred of their forefathers had gathered in the hearts of these two fierce opponents.

Garnet and Bob Bertram would have rushed to Ned's assistance; but said Ned Warbeck, in tones of confidence—

"Away, friends, away! leave the affair to me! Do you and your followers storm the Block House, and let not one of the villains escape. Away, I say! let no one interfere! Make a ring, good citizens, and see fair play; I ask nothing more!"

"Give the poor girl to me, my brave lad," chorused a score of voices; "you cannot fight with her burden in your arms."

"Never fear, good people," said Ned, "whether I live or die, this poor girl shall never leave my embrace while I have power to protect her."

With the ferocity of two tigers Redgill and young Warbeck commenced the duel, surrounded as they were by a numerous company of breathless spectators.

Again and again they cut and thrust at each other with ferocious violence.

Redgill had the advantage of weight, height, and reach, independent of not holding any burden.

But Ned Warbeck was confident and bold.

Again they approached to dangerous nearness, and each moment seemed as if it would decide the combat.

But Ned Warbeck was fully aware of his opponent's cunning, and treated his cowardly thrust with a loud laugh of contempt.

Once or twice it seemed as if Redgill really intended to murder Ellen Harmer as she unconsciously clung to the brave youth her protector.

In looking after her safety, therefore, Ned Warbeck often missed excellent opportunities for wounding Redgill seriously. On the other hand, however, Ned Warbeck was falling weak, and he received several slight cuts in the arms and legs.

Redgill, thinking that he had his antagonist safe, and need not fear his repeated thrusts, stepped still closer.

This was what Ned Warbeck had long wanted him to do, but had so disguised his wish that Redgill could not understand the trick.

"I'll play with you no longer," said Redgill, with a laugh of triumph. "You have ever been a snake in my path; now, Ned Warbeck, die like a dog!"

With a shout of derision, and with eyes glaring in deadly hate and rage, he rushed upon Ned, and a terrible struggle ensued.

With the stroke of Vulcan, young Warbeck struck down Redgill's sword point, and at the same moment Phillip Redgill fell to the earth with a loud groan.

Ned Warbeck's sword had been buried to the hilt in Phillip's body,

A loud shout applauded this unexpected stroke of good-fortune.

"Brave lad!"

"Hurrah for Wildfire Ned!"

"Good luck to you, young Warbeck!" resounded on all sides.

With an elastic stride, and his sword still dripping with Phillip Redgill's blood, Ned Warbeck strode through the applauding crowd, still bearing in his arms the form of Ellen Harmer, and took her to a house near by, that restoratives might be administered to her.

But while this was taking place, let us return to Lieutenant Garnet and his men.

Many of them had wildly rushed at the walls and gates, but were unable to force them.

For Death-wing and his party, finding that they themselves were in turn attacked by the citizens, made superhuman exertions to escape from the trap into which they had unconsciously fallen.

Instead, therefore, of Death-wing slaying all he met with in the huge Block-house, he made friends with all Captain Jack's men that remained unhurt, and they prepared for a terrific resistance to the armed citizen patrol outside, who were making fruitless efforts to break down the heavy, massive wooden stockade which surrounded the immense yard of the Block-House.

They kept up a galling fire upon the citizens with guns, pistols, stones, bricks, and whatever came to hand, from the windows and roof.

Several of the citizens had been killed or wounded long before Ned Warbeck and his friends had arrived on the scene,

When, however, Ned was engaged in the deadly duel with Phillip Redgill, Lieutenant Garnet, like an old and experienced sailor, soon changed the whole aspect of affairs, and cheered on his men.

He took the entire command, re-invigorated their efforts, and completely altered the mode and direction of attack.

He was an able leader, and the consequences of his appearance were soon perceptible in the development of events.

The force immediately beneath the walls, and secure from the shots of the Skeleton Crew, were reinforced, and in so cautious a manner, that the Skeleton Crew were entirely ignorant of their increased strength in that quarter.

Creeping as they did from place to place, now lying prone and silent to the ground, in utter immobility; now rushing, as circumstances prompted, with all rapidity, they put themselves into cover, crossing the intervening space without the loss of a man.

Having thus gathered in force beneath the walls of the Block House, the greater number, while the rest watched, proceeded to gather up in piles, as they had begun to do before, immense quantities of the dry pine trash and the gummy turpentine wood which the neighbourhood readily afforded.

This they clustered in thick masses around the more accessible points of the wooden walls.

The first intimation which the garrison had of this proceeding was a sudden gust of flame, blazing first about the gate of the area, on one side of the Block-house, then rushing from point to point with amazing rapidity, sweeping and curling widely around the building itself.

The gate, and the palings all around it, studiously made as they had been of strong pine, for its great durability, was as ready an ally of the destructive element as the citizens could have chosen, and licked greedily by the fire, were soon ignited.

Blazing impetuously, it soon aroused the Skeleton Crew to a more acute consciousness of the danger now at hand.

A fierce shout of their assailants, as they beheld the rapid progress of the experiment, warned them to greater exertion, if they hoped to escape the dreadful fate which threatened to engulf them.

To remain where they were was to be consumed in the flames.

To rush forth was to encounter the weapons of an enemy four times their number.

It was a moment of gloomy necessity, that which assembled the chief defenders of the fortress to a sort of war-council. They could only deliberate—to fight was out of the question. Their enemy now was one which they could not oppose.

The citizens showed no front for assault or aim. while the flames, rushing from point to point, and seizing upon numerous places at once, continued to advance, with a degree of celerity which left it impossible, in the dry condition of its timber, that the Block-house could possibly, for any length of time, escape.

Upon the building itself the citizens could not fix the fire at first.

But two ends of it were directly accessible to them, and these were without any entrance, had been pierced with holes for musketry, and were well watched by the vigilant eyes within. The two sides were enclosed by the line of strong palings and posts, and had no need of other guardianship.

But while Lieutenant Garnet, Bob Bertram, and others were using their utmost endeavours to storm the strong Block-house, Master Tim, as usual, was skulking out of danger among the crowd or non-fighters, and seemed more inclined to let others share the dangers while he did the talking.

For Master Tim, as we have seen all through this story, could be very eloquent at times, and speak grandly about war and glory, and all such like topics ; but if he could help it, he would not on any account run his own head into danger.

The good citizens, seeing that he wore Ned Warbeck's livery, expected him to distinguish himself after the manner Wildfire Ned had done, before their own eyes ; but, instead of that, Master Tim drank deeply of old ale, and, standing on a door-step, out of danger, began to harangue the idle multitude something in this style :—

"And why, my friends, are we here assembled ?" was his sagacious inquiry, looking round as he spoke upon his inattentive audience.

A forced smile on the faces of several, but not a word, attested their several estimates of the speaker. He proceeded.

"That is the question, my friends—why are we here assembled ? I answer, for the good of the people ; we are here to protect them if we can, and to perish for and with them, if we must. I cannot forget my duties to my country, and to those in whose behalf I stand before the grim Skeleton Crew and the swords of Captain Jack's men.

"These teach me, and I would teach it to you, my friends—to fight—to hold out to the last.

"We may not think of parleying with those in the Block-House, my friends, until other hope is gone. Whatever be the peril, till that moment, be it mine to encounter it.

"Whatever be the privation, till that moment I am the man to endure it.

"Be it for me, at least, though I stand alone in this particular, to do for the people whatever wisdom or valour may do, until the moment comes which shall call on us to pardon the villains.

"The question now, my friends, is simply this—has that moment come or not ? I pause for a reply."

"Who talks of parleying with them ?" growled a smith, as he cast a glance of ferocity at the speaker. "Who talks of parleying at all to these cursed bloodhounds, that hunt for nothing but our blood ? We cannot parley if we would—we must fight, die, do anything but parley with the fiends."

"So say I—I am ready to fight and die for my country. I say it now, as I have said it a hundred times before, but—"

The speech which Tim had thus begun, the smith again interrupted with a greater bull-dog expression than ever—

"Ay, so you have, and so will say a hundred times more—with as little sense in it one time as another. We are all here to die, if there's any need for it ; but that isn't the trouble. It's how we are to die—that's the question. Are we to stay here and be shot like timber-rats, or to volunteer, as I do now, axe in hand, to go and cut down the palings that immediately join the house ? By that we may have a clear dig at the savages inside. I'm for that. If anybody's willing to go along with me, let him up hands—no talk—we have too much of that already."

"I'm ready—here !" cried Ned Warbeck, approaching, and laughing good humouredly, and his hands were thrust up at the instant.

"No, Ned Warbeck," cried the smith, " not you—you must stay and manage here. Your head's the coolest ; and though I'd sooner have your arm alongside of me in the rough time than any other two that I know of, 'twont do to take you from the rest on this risk. Who else is ready ? Let him come to the scratch, and no longer talk about it. What do you say, Master Tim ? That's chance enough for you, if you really want to die for your country."

And as he spoke, he thrust his head forward, while his eyes peered into the very bosom of the little groom, and his axe descended on a door post, near which he stood, with a thundering emphasis that rung through the street.

"I can't use the axe," cried Tim, hurriedly ; "it's not my instrument. Sword or pistol for me, my friends. In their exercise I give way to no man, and in their use I ask for no leader ; but I am neither woodchopper nor blacksmith."

"And this is your way of dying for the good of the people !" said the smith, contemptuously.

"I am willing, even now ; I say it again, as I have before said, and as now I solemnly repeat it," said Tim, pompously ; "but I must die for them after my own fashion, and under proper circumstances.

"With sword in hand, crossing the perilous breach, with weapon befitting the use of a noble gentleman, I am ready.

"But I know not any rule that would require of me to perish for my country with the broad axe of a wood-chopper, the cleaver of a butcher, or the sledge of a blacksmith, in my hand," said Master Tim, in mock dignity.

"Well, I'm no soldier," retorted the smith ; "but I think a man, to be really ready to die for his country, shouldn't be too nice as to which way he does it.

"Now, the sword and the pistol are of monstrous little use here.

"The muskets of our lads will keep off the Crew inside, while a few of us cut down the stakes ; so now, men, as time grows short, let the boys keep a sharp look-out with the ticklers, and I'll for the timber, let him follow who will. There are boys enough, I take it, to go with."

Thus saying, the blacksmith pushed forward.

The blacksmith was one of those blunt burly fellows who take with the populace.

It was not difficult for him to procure men where many were ready.

They had listened with much sympathy to the discussion narrated, and as the pomposity and assumption of Tim had made him an object of vulgar ridicule, a desire to rebuke him, not less than a willingness to go with the smith, contributed readily to persuade them to the adventure.

In a few moments the gate of the Block-house was unbarred, and the party sallied through the entrance, the smith at their head.

In the meanwhile, with sleeves rolled up, jacket off, and face that seemed not often to have been entirely free from the begriming blackness of his profession, the smith commenced his tremendous blows upon the contiguous palings, followed with like zeal, if not with equal power, by the men who had volunteered along with him.

Down went the first post beneath his arm, and as, with resolute spirit, he was about to assail another, a huge skeleton warrior stood in the gap which he had made, and with a powerful blow from the mace which he carried, had our blacksmith been less observant, would have soon finished his career.

But the smith was a man of agility as well as strength and spirit, and leaping aside from the stroke, as his eye rose to the corresponding glance from that of his enemy, he gave due warning to his axe-men, who forebore their strokes under his command.

The aperture was yet too small for any combat of the parties ; and ignorant of the force against him, surprised also at their appearance, he dispatched one of his men to Lieutenant Garnet, and gave directions, which, had they been complied with, had certainly given them the advantage.

The Skeleton Crew rushed upon them, and for a time defeated the aim of Garnet's musketry.

Fighting like a lion as he retreated to the gate of the Block-house, the brave smith continued to keep unharmed, making at the same time some little employment in the shape of ugly wounds to dress, in the persons of his rash assailants.

Once more they gave back before him, and again the musketry of Garnet was enabled to tell upon them.

A discharge from the Block-house in the meantime retorted with good effect the attack of the sailor, and taught a lesson of caution to Ned Warbeck, of which he soon availed himself.

Three of his men bit the dust in that single fire. The brave smith again reached the door with a single unwounded follower, himself unhurt.

His comrades threw open the entrance, but an instant too late. A parting shot from the muskets of the Skeleton Crew was made with a fatal effect.

The smith sank down upon the threshold as the bullet passed through his body.

The axe fell from his hand.

He grasped at it convulsively, and lay extended in part upon the sill of the door, when Garnet drew him in safety away.

"You are not hurt, my old fellow?" exclaimed Garnet, his voice trembling with the apprehensions which he felt.

"Hurt enough, lieutenant—bad enough. No more grist ground at that mill. But hold in—don't be frightened ; you can beat 'em yet. Ah !" he groaned, in a mortal agony.

They composed his limbs, and pouring some spirits down his throat, he recovered in a few moments, and convulsively said,

"When I die——"

"Die, indeed !—don't think of such a thing," said Garnet, sadly.

"Yes," said the brave smith, " it has come to that at last. I feel it. I have done my duty like a man, and am content to die."

After a very brief struggle the gallant fellow breathed his last.

"Avenge him ! Avenge him !" Ned Warbeck cried.

"Follow me," shouted Lieutenant Garnet.

With loud shouts, and amid a storm of shot and other missiles showered down upon them, three separate parties of stormers under the leadership of Ned Warbeck, Garnet, and Bob Bertram, assailed the burning stronghold.

On every side the flames were now burning, and illuminated the darkness of the night.

Past the windows and on the roof could be seen flitting about the forms of Death-wing's and Captain Jack's men, who were nearly roasted alive.

Bravely they fought, but they dared not rush forth to encounter the valour of Ned Warbeck's escaped followers.

Some of the Crew leaped from the roof into the river ; others jumped from windows upon the weapons of those below, until at last a fearful explosion occurred.

Several barrels of powder exploded in the cellars, and in a moment afterwards the old Block-house, which for years and years had been the rendezvous of Captain Jack's men, was a mass of ruins.

While in the river were numerous of the Skeleton Crew and others, who were swimming for their very lives far away from the bright crackling mass of timber.

---

## CHAPTER XLIV.

CAPTAIN JACK AND OLD BATES ARE FUGITIVES— THEY FLY FROM LONDON AND CONCEAL THEMSELVES IN HORNSEY WOOD—THEIR DEPREDATIONS.

WITH the arrest or dispersion of the principals of their gang the greater part of Captain Jack's anxieties and difficulties ceased.

The remainder of the vagabonds pursued through the villages and woods soon fell into the hands of justice.

Beggars, sham hawkers, deserters, came in succession to swell the list of prisoners in the London gaols.

Jack and his friend Bates had withdrawn to the country.

There, in almost inaccessible thicket, they constructed a hut of branches and leaves, very skilfully contrived to deceive the eyes of the passers by.

Only at night did they venture out into the neighbouring commons, and the fears their audacity inspired prevented the peasants from betraying their place of concealment.

Ned Warbeck and others undertook to effect this difficult capture.

Four of them, disguised as wood-cutters, with two others to assist them, and who were well acquainted with every nook and corner of the forest, determined to enter at nightfall under the trees of Hornsey Wood, and bivouacked in silence.

At about four o'clock in the morning they surrounded the retreat of the two outlaws.

Ned Warbeck and one of the wood-cutters, with musket in hand, and finger on trigger, gently drew aside the leafy door, when they perceived the terrible couple lying amid bundles of hay and picked bones.

A gun, loaded and cocked, was lying between them.

Captain Jack opened his eyes, awoke less by the noise than by the vague uneasiness that must ever haunt the guilty.

Seizing his gun he cried,

"Help! Bates, help!"

But Ned covered him with his musket, while one of the wood-cutters seized the gun, and two others rushing in, in another moment both the rascals were safely handcuffed.

"Ned Warbeck," said Captain Jack, "it was not right of you to betray your friends in this manner."

"Thank you," Ned laughingly replied, "but I prefer such friends as you at a distance, anywhere except in our own neighbourhood."

The Captain cast an evil glance at Ned, and followed on to prison.

No sooner did the law show itself stronger than Captain Jack's roguery than the tongues of the people loosened, and singular revelations were made; the former related that several times during the hot days of summer Jack and his friends used to arrive by dozens, and shutting the gates of farms, they opened the doors leading into the cellars, and helped themselves to the farmers' cider.

Then stripping themselves of their clothing, converted thus the yard into a ball-room, where they performed the wild antics of the "beggar's dance," resembling some of the strange scenes described by travellers of what they had witnessed among certain tribes of African and South Sea Islanders.

In other places they would make themselves quite at home, especially Captain Jack, for no sooner was his tall figure recognised, whether he was alone or accompanied by any of his friends, immediately all the servants, ploughmen, and shepherds assembled round their dangerous guest to attend upon his wants for fear of being shot.

The tales told by these oppressed people revealed more than one hidden crime.

To render his authority secure and to prevent desertion and treachery, Captain Jack had established among his regular followers a sort of bond of union secured by an oath of vengeance.

Every member of his new gang convicted of having betrayed their associates, or of refusing an order issued by Captain Jack, was pitilessly massacred, and the executioners selected from among themselves.

It was in this manner that a poor lad suffered for a crime against the association.

He gave, thoughtlessly, no doubt, some wrong information respecting some farm they were going to attack.

He was seized, and carried to the camp of Captain Jack.

His accuser was no less than old Bates, who had stolen the sails of a windmill for some purpose, and the boy had made known this trick to Captain Jack.

Some time afterwards the boy spoke rather freely of the projects of the gang upon the farm of a very poor man near by.

Thereupon it was resolved he should die.

Captain Jack pronounced sentence upon him, and he was beaten to death with sticks.

The terror inspired by Captain Jack had hitherto deterred the peasants from giving information to the magistrates of the murder of this lad.

His bones lay bleaching on the ground where he had fallen, and no one had ventured to inter them.

The remains of the poor boy were collected as evidence against Jack and old Bates.

Another was murdered in the wood for having taken the part of an innkeeper against his comrades, who wanted to cheat him at the reckoning.

A third was also murdered for a similar offence.

They tied him to an oak-tree and burned him alive, first cutting off his ears, and nailing them to a tree, as a terror to others of the gang.

Several would have met with similar fates, and only escaped by a miracle.

"Come here," said Ned to Master Tim. "Have you not often said and boasted that you would take Captain Jack as a deserter from the king's army?"

Poor Tim looked pale, and turned about anxiously for succour, and trembled in every limb.

Several peasants whom Tim had not perceived at first, and several others, formed a circle around him, which gradually grew narrower and narrower, and of which Tim himself formed the centre.

"No, sir, I did not say so," replied Tim, very modestly.

"You lie," said Ned, laughing, at the same time striking a heavy blow on the side of Tim's head with his stick.

The poor groom cast a terrified glance around, and perceived a fellow-servant who had more than once taken his part. But this companion now gave him a very different reception; now, he smote him a blow on the arm with a walking-cane which almost broke the bone.

Then Ned and others rained a shower of blows upon him until he fell to the ground, well punished for all his past boasting.

The energetic and unwearied Ned kept up the pursuit of the gang for one hundred and fifty days, without halting to rest, or scarcely ever putting off his clothes and arms, or quitting his horse's back.

He made captures almost every day.

The terror that had formerly possessed the neighbourhood had now passed away, and two or three mounted men were quite sufficient to send away any of the fugitives, and more than enough to secure many vagabonds.

It was a truly grand affair the trial of those members of Captain Jack's band.

The mass of positive evidence was immense, but scarcely equal to the suspicion that attached to the prisoners for other crimes in which it was supposed they had taken a part.

To let light into this chaos, to collect all the scattered proofs, to separate the facts from surmises, to complete imperfect cases by evidence withdrawn from other cases, and to sift the truth out of constantly varying testimony on the part of witnesses, was a most difficult task.

Continual error and confusion arose from the various aliases assumed by the more notorious members of the gang, while the differences in the calendar between old and new style added to the difficulties that beset the ministers of justice.

Nothing of the kind is more curious than the interminable questions put by the patient counsel, repeated in each new trial month after month with untiring perseverance, and which most frequently elicited the same answers.

But at times the monotony was relieved by

overwhelming proofs by the evidence of some of the culprits themselves, or of others who seemed to grow tired of the suspense of a trial, and convicted themselves to put an end to it.

It was by a very narrow opening that night first entered, but day by day it grew larger.

Confession followed confession.

One appeared to stimulate the other, and they seemed to pride themselves as to who should outvie the other in recitals of the atrocities they had committed.

Much exaggeration was, it is true, mixed up with these communications, and it was only by close comparison and sifting, that the truth could be elicited regarding the atrocious doings of Captain Jack and his famous Baker's Dozen.

But there they were in prison, through the instrumentality and industry of Wildfire Ned and Lieutenant Garnet.

What became of most of them we shall quickly see.

---

## CHAPTER XLV.

### COLONEL BLOOD MEETS WITH DISAPPOINTMENT.

BUT, although Wildfire Ned, as narrated in a previous chapter, made a vow never to rest until he had captured or destroyed all who belonged to Captain Jack's band and the Skeleton Crew, he did not succeed so well with Death-wing's followers as he could have wished.

During the night of the terrible commotion and desperate encounter at the Block-House, that part of the town was thrown into a fearful state of commotion.

Excited citizens rushed to and fro in all directions.

Colonel Blood, himself, was one of the first who was informed of the whole transaction.

For the second time that night he pushed off to the royal palace, and asked for the assistance of the military.

Two companies were entrusted to him, and he marched to the scene of conflict as speedily as possible.

When he got there, however, the Block-House was nought but a blazing mass of ruins.

When informed that it contained most, if not all, of the property and valuables which had been stolen from his own house, he fumed and raved like one half demented.

But what else could be done ?

He stood gazing at the fiery element feeding on his own property, and gnashed his teeth in rage.

" Who led on the citizens to the attack ?" he asked.

" Ned Warbeck, 'Wildfire Ned,' as he is called," the simple citizens replied.

" What, Sir Richard Warbeck's nephew, as he is called ?"

" Yes, Colonel."

" I have heard of him before. He bares no love towards the Skeleton Crew or Captain Jack's followers, I hear."

" If you had seen how fiercely the gallant youth fought, you would have been sure there was no love between them," laughed several shopkeepers triumphantly.

" Who else helped him ?"

Lieutenant Garnet, of the Royal Navy, Colonel, and a strong determined young man from the country ; they call him Bob Bertram, Colonel."

" Were any of the assailants killed ?"

" Yes, a brave and gallant youth, who was the first to break through the barricaded gates."

" Any one else ?"

" Yes, Colonel, several other good citizens were killed or much injured in the fray."

" And where is this Ned Warbeck ?" asked Colonel Blood, biting his lip. " I should like to see him ; I wish to report the full particulars to the king."

" He has saved you that trouble most worthy Colonel," said Tim, who was still in the crowd, " he has gone to the palace himself ; as he did most of the fighting, he thought he had a good right to most of the honor and reward."

" And who are you that speak so boldly ?"

" I, sir, am Mr. Edward Warbeck's groom—a faithful and brave servant, I have ever proved to be ; and, although I say it, no man behaved more gallantly in the encounter than I did."

A general laugh followed this speech, and the crowd around tittered again with merriment.

" And what did you do ?" asked the colonel, with a smile.

" Well, in the first place, most worthy sir, I made a most capital speech to the mob in order to stir them up, and excite them to deeds of valour. The best speech it was as ever I made in my life."

" And what then, my good fellow ?"

" Don't believe him, colonel."

" He is telling a string of lies."

" A perfect coward, sir."

" As timid as a mouse, colonel," said one and another, as they still laughed outright at Tim's account of the affair.

" On my word, most noble colonel, all I say is true."

" Well, go on then, I am listening. What part did you take ?"

" Well, sir, when the fight was at its highest, and when the smith, by not following my advice, got killed, I exhorted all to be more prudent, and to hide their heads well behind the palings and woodwork, for I could see that those devils called the Skeleton Crew were dead shots and knocked over every one they aimed at."

" Well ?"

" Oh, it was beautiful to see how they jumped out of the windows, and off the burning roof into the river," said Master Tim, grinning and chuckling.

" I dare say it was, but I didn't ask for any description of that. I asked and still ask, what did you do, not see ?"

" Well, sir, when my master, Lieutenant Garnet, and Bob Bertram made their fierce attack upon the burning Block-House, and, followed by their gallant fellows, were fighting in the court-yard, in the passages, and other places, I—— Well—I—that is to say, most worthy colonel, because I couldn't get near enough to engage in the combat myself— I——"

" He stood on a door-step and looked on, colonel," said a dozen voices at once.

" Yes, sir," said Tim, meekly bowing, and trembling, as he saw the colonel's blood mounting ; " I stood on the door-step, and acted as commander-in-chief, cheering the lads on."

" I thought so," said Colonel Blood, angrily.

At the same time he rewarded Tim for his great valour by giving him a sound smack in the face, which knocked him right among the applauding crowd.

This was more than Master Tim expected.

But, for fear he'd get any more, Tim sneaked

away among the crowd like a dog who has lost his tail.

"Who is that I saw just now borne away upon a shutter ?" said Colonel Blood.

"That is one of the rascals who were in the Block-House, colonel," said several.

"Is he dead ?"

"Not quite, I think ; but if he isn't he ought to be, for I saw a sword go right through him."

"How did it happen ?"

"The unfortunate young man was making his escape from the Block-House with a female captive whom he claimed as his own, and was making his way off with her, when he was stopped by Wildfire Ned and challenged."

"Carrying off a female ?" said Colonel Blood, in surprise. "Did any of you hear her name ?"

"Yes, colonel. I heard her name was Ellen Harmer."

"Ellen Harmer ?"

"The same."

"You are sure ?"

"Quite sure."

"And did this Ned Warbeck fight a duel with the wounded man ?"

"Yes. His name was Phillip Redgill."

"I have heard of him ; as great a rascal as ever lived. And where was the maiden taken to ?"

"Nobody knows for certain, colonel. She was insensible when he took her away to a cottage near by, but when the fight was over he came with a coach and galloped away, no one knows whither."

"I'd give a hundred pounds to find where he has taken her to," said Blood, with a bitter smile. "I am foiled again, and by a mere boy," said he to himself ; "but I must have her ; yea, I will !" he thought. "Take care, Ned Warbeck, take care ! you are treading on very dangerous ground when you cross my path. I am not to be trifled with. You may be brave, noble and handsome, but if you endeavour to thwart my plans, I will tread you under my heel like a worm !"

There was nothing now to do upon the spot, so, crestfallen and in a rage, he returned with his soldiers, leaving it to the night-watch to keep order among the excited crowd.

"I will go to the palace," he said, "and will be the first to inform the king of this strange affair. It will be good excuse for me, for now I can tell the truth for once in my life, and say that in my absence Ellen Harmer was abducted from my mansion. Yes," he thought, "I will go to the king at once, and be the first to inform him of all that has happened ; he will be sure to believe me."

But Colonel Blood was not the first to see the king, as will quickly be seen ; neither was he believed.

––––––

## CHAPTER XLVI.

### COLONEL BLOOD AND NED WARBECK.

WHEN Wildfire Ned had hurried away with Ellen Harmer from the scene of strife, he was careful that no one should know whither he had taken her.

In order to thwart Colonel Blood, whom he knew would try to ferret her out, he hired a coach, and, with Lieutenant Garnet and himself inside, he trusted the reins to Bob Bertram, who lashed up the animals, and started off at a great pace towards the town residence of Sir Richard Warbeck.

"You have done for Phillip Redgill at last," said Garnet, in a whisper, for fear of disturbing the sleeping girl.

"Yes, I think so," Ned replied ; "but it was in fair fight."

"Oh, no doubt of that. I did not see it, but was told by those who did ; in fact, I was too much engaged in storming the Block-house to observe anything but the skeleton devils jumping out of window into the river.

"How the old building did burn, to be sure ; such a blaze."

"Yes ; it was a grand sight, and lit up that part of the town most beautifully."

"A fit end for such an infamous rendezvous."

"So say I, and a gallant exploit it was, and reflects all honour on those engaged in it."

"I wonder what the king will say to it when he hears it ?"

"Why, reward all who were concerned in it ; at least, he ought to do so, if he's got a spark of generosity in him."

"What do you intend ?" asked Garnet, after a pause.

"I shall leave Ellen in charge of my uncle, and go to the palace at once."

"But how can you gain admission ?"

"Easily enough," said Ned. "Do you see this ring ? I found it near the ale-house."

"What a splendid one it is. Why, it is a signet ring," said Garnet, "and bears the royal coat of arms."

"So it does ; and inside, as you will perceive, it has the royal cipher, with the inscription, 'Whoever presents this is admitted.'"

"How could it have been lost ?" said Garnet, closely examining it. "There is no doubt it belongs to the king."

"I know it does."

"How ?"

"Ellen Harmer explained it all to me. Captain Jack and his men entered Colonel Blood's house, and while there discovered the king, who was bent, during the colonel's absence, to forcibly abduct her. The king was recognised by Captain Jack, and to regain his freedom without discovery by any one of the colonel's household he gave the ring to Captain Jack ; in the hurry, I suppose, he lost it."

"It was a lucky discovery for you," said Garnet.

"Yes ; and I intend to make the best possible use of it, as you will see," said Ned, "and this very night also."

By this time, and while they thus conversed in whispers, the carriage drove up to Sir Richard Warbeck's residence.

The door was soon opened, and, to the old knight's great surprise, Ned explained to him all that had happened.

"What, in another scrape ?" said Sir Richard, "and bring a lady home with you ?"

"Yes, uncle," said Ned, laughing ; "one who is beautiful, and deserving of the temporary protection she asks of you."

"Whether beautiful or not an injured female is always welcome to the shelter and protection of my roof, Ned."

With the greatest gallantry the old knight opened the carriage door, and assisted Ellen Harmer up the stone steps into his princely, hospitable mansion.

"To the palace, Bob," said Ned, jumping into the carriage again.

"Where ?" asked the old knight, in wonder. "Bent on some other mad freak to-night ? Stop ! stop ! Ned ; here, stop !"

But before he could be heard Bob Bertram lashed up the horses, and drove rapidly towards the palace.

# THE SKELETON CREW; OR, WILDFIRE NED.

A DEATH-BED CURSE.—(*See No.* 24.)

On their way they overtook a procession of link-men, who were slowly moving along towards the hospital.

On a shutter they bore the bleeding body of an almost lifeless man.

"Who is that?" asked Ned, as he passed them by.

"A man that young Warbeck fought a duel with."

"He is not dead, you say?"

"No, not quite."

"He must have had as many lives as a cat, then," said Ned. "What does the surgeon say?"

"That, perhaps, by a miracle he may recover."

"The devil!" said Garnet. "Why, you'll have to fight him over again."

"Without the headsman or hangman cheats me," said Ned, laughing; "but there's no telling what may happen. Drive on, Bob; be lively, my lad."

Bob whipped his horses, and soon drove up to the palace yard.

"Halt!" said the hoarse voice of the sentinel, as the carriage approached.

Bob saw the sentinel lower his musket at him, and he pulled up his horses on the instant.

In a moment an officer advanced to the carriage door, and, in rather a sharp, impertinent manner, demanded to know who and what they were, and the business they came upon at such an unreasonable hour.

No. 22.

"Our names you are at liberty to know, sir," said Ned, "but not our business. We are naval officers in his majesty's service; our errand is of the greatest importance, and brooks no delay."

"I don't know that," said the officer. "The king has been disturbed in his slumbers twice to-night; therefore, you had better call at the levée in the morning, if you are officers and do not wish to anger him."

"Leave that to us, good sir. You may rely upon it," said Ned, "if our business were not of the utmost consequence, we are by far too good subjects to annoy the king."

"But what sign have you that warrants me in waking the king?"

"This," said Ned, presenting the ring; "take that to his majesty. When he sees it he will not deny us admission to his presence, whatever the hour may be."

The officer took the royal ring and examined it.

He forthwith went up to the king's chamber, and, it must be acknowledged, that Charles, majesty as he was, was full of wrath at being disturbed in his slumbers.

When, however, the officer in attendance presented to him the ring, he looked amazed.

He rubbed his eyes and yawned.

"The devil take the impudent rogue!" said he.

"But, as I have given my word of honour, why, admit him at once."

In a moment afterwards Ned Warbeck and Garnet were striding up the broad staircase towards the king's bed-chamber.

The king, propped up in bed, was flushed with anger; but when he perceived it was not Captain Jack, to whom he had given the ring, he appeared the more amazed.

The door was closed upon Ned and Garnet, but the half sleepy page, in revenge for being awakened from sleep, listened at the door and heard all he could.

Ned Warbeck, in a few words, explained all that had happened that night, and about his finding the ring.

The king seemed at first very much annoyed, but he laughed off the matter, and said upon his word that the story about his intruding into Ellen Harmer's chamber in Colonel Blood's mansion was all a fiction.

"Call to-morrow at the levée," said he, "and I will see that justice is done both to you and the injured maid ; but to-night I am weary. No, not to-morrow ; I forgot there is no levée until Thursday, so that you will have ample time to arrange everything to your satisfaction. And in token of how much I appreciate your valour in the affair of to-night with the gang of that rascal, Captain Jack, and the terrible Skeleton Crew, I fully pardon from all transgressions whoever aided you in defeating the villains."

"Thanks, your majesty. But what document have we to prove it ?" said Ned.

"Give me pen, ink, and paper."

These were found upon a side table.

With a hurried scrawl, the king wrote down a few words, granting a free pardon for all officers in favour of those who had assisted Ned and Garnet.

Moreover, he signed the paper, and sealed it with his own signet ring and gave it to Ned.

But, while this was going on in the royal chamber, Bob Bertram, in the palace-yard, was very near getting in a serious difficulty.

Ned and Garnet had not left him more than five minutes, when Colonel Blood hastily rode up and dismounted from his horse.

He perceived the carriage, and began to question Bob.

"Whose vehicle is that, sirrah ?" he asked, looking at it attentively. "It looks like a hired one."

"It is my master's, sir," answered Bob.

"And who is your master ?"

"A gentleman, sir."

"If you answer me in that manner again I'll knock you off your seat. Who is your master, sirrah ?"

"Captain Warbeck, of the royal navy."

"Ha ! and is he with the king ?"

"He is."

"The devil ! before me again, eh ?" said Blood, angrily, but in an under tone. "What's his business here at such an unseemly hour ?"

"You had better ask him, sir ; he won't be long."

"Confound the impudence of the rascal. What is your name ?"

"Bob Bertram," was the answer, "and not ashamed to own it," said Bob, with all the innocence in the world, and never dreaming of the consequences.

"Bertram, Bertram ?" said Colonel Blood, thinking. "I have heard that name before."

"Perhaps so, sir ; but what of it ?"

Colonel Blood did not answer at the moment, but referred to a small gold-clasped memorandum book he carried in his breast pocket.

"Robert Bertram," said he, turning over the leaves quickly. "Yes, of course ; I thought I could not be mistaken. You came from Darlington ? Your father was murdered——"

Poor Bob never thought of this.

He shook in every limb, and very nearly fell from his high seat.

His confusion was evident to Colonel Blood, who laughing said,

"And so you are the servant of Ned Warbeck, eh ? If the master is only like the servant, now. Here, guard," said he, "seize this man ; he is a murderer ; seize him, I say, in the king's name."

"In the king's name, hold off your hands," said Ned Warbeck, in a passion, as he and Garnet now advanced into the moonlight.

The soldiers knew not what to do.

"Who are you, sir, that dares interfere in this serious matter ? This fellow is a murderer, or, at least, suspected of being such."

"He is no murderer, sir," said Ned Warbeck, "and, if he was, I have the king's pardon. Read," said he, placing the royal warrant under the astonished colonel's eyes.

"Your name, sir ?" asked Blood, sternly.

"You have no right to demand it," said Ned, proudly.

"But, suppose I insist upon knowing it, and that of your friend ?"

"Insist, sir ?"

"Yes, insist."

"If you wish to meet me on important business in a private manner," Ned haughtily replied, "there i my card," said he, giving it to the colonel.

"And, sir, here is mine," said the colonel, biting his lip in anger.

"I do not need it. I know you too well already, colonel."

"Ah, indeed."

"You understand me ?"

"I do. We shall meet again."

"When you like, and where you like," said Ned, with a light laugh.

"Perhaps we may meet too quickly for your own liking, young sir."

"That cannot be. I fear you not."

"You may learn to do so to your cost, Warbeck."

"It remains with you, then, to name the day and hour. I am always ready to accommodate gentlemen in a small way."

With these words, Ned and Garnet jumped into the coach, and drove homewards.

"I must clip that youngster's wings," said the colonel ; "he is inclined to fly too high."

"Then, colonel, you will have great trouble, I fear," said one of the royal pages, who, in crossing the palace yard, had heard all that had been said.

"Who is that ?" asked the colonel, hastily.

"Your friend Simon, the page."

"Ah, Simon, have you been disturbed again ?"

"Yes, by those two hot-headed fellows who have just left you."

"What news ? Did you happen to ascertain their business at this late hour ?"

"I did."

"Indeed, what was it ?"

"Come this way ; we must not be overheard. It concerns you greatly."

"You speak seriously."

"I do ; come this way. I will tell you all, and put you on your guard with the king."

Blood and the page entered a doorway, and were lost to sight and hearing.

## CHAPTER XLVII.

### THE COLONEL'S PLANS SUCCEED—THE SPY AND MESSENGER.

WHEN Ned Warbeck had left his uncle's house to go and visit the palace, he was not aware that all his actions had been watched.

Yet they had been.

Colonel Blood was a man of too much influence about the king's court not to have a number of spies and informers in his employ.

When, therefore, he was returning from the scene at the Block House, disheartened and annoyed, he met with a person who recognised him.

"Who hails me in the public streets at this time of the morning?" asked Blood, in a surly tone.

"A friend," was the reply.

"Approach, and speak, then," said the colonel, in a haughty tone.

The stranger stepped forward towards Blood, and in an instant he was recognized by the colonel as one of his spies, an old gentlemanly-looking Jew.

"What news to-night, Barnabas?" asked the colonel.

"Good news!" answered the Jew.

"And what is that, pray?"

"I have been watching the doings of Ned Warbeck, his goings and comings, as you told me to do a month ago."

"Well, and with what success? Have you discovered anything?"

"Yes, I think so."

"What?"

"Why, I saw him and a young naval officer not more than half an hour ago, hand as pretty a lady out of a carriage as ever man's eyes rested upon."

"Indeed! are you certain?"

"I am; and, more than that, old Sir Richard conducted her into the mansion with much politeness and ceremony."

"You did not, of course, learn her name?"

"I did. I heard Ned Warbeck and his companion conversing together for a moment after she had gone into the house."

"Where were you then?"

"Hiding in a doorway."

"And what said they?"

"Ned Warbeck swore that the maid should be restored to her father without a moment's delay; that she should start that very night to Darlington."

"Good!" said Blood; "fortune favors me still. I know the rest, and need not ask her name. It was Ellen Harmer."

"The very same," answered Barnabas.

"I thought so."

"But how could you have known that, colonel. I did not see you in the neighbourhood until now?"

"I know it; but, nevertheless, I am perfectly aware of the fair one's name, she has given me a vast amount of anxiety and trouble of late."

"Indeed! then I am fortunate in having made the discovery."

"Yes, Barnabas, you are. But, mark me, that girl must never be restored to her father."

"I do not understand you," said the Jew.

"I mean that she must never be allowed to return to her native village of Darlington. She has escaped from my protection, Barnabas, and I must have her back again, or else many unpleasant things might come to light."

"But how can you prevent it?"

"Easily enough. Have they posted off with the girl already, think you?"

"I know not. I left Sir Richard's mansion but half-an-hour ago, but Ned Warbeck seemed to be in such a hurry and flurry about the pretty wench that I have no doubt they will not lose any time in transporting her to Darlington again."

"Fool that you were! Why did you not stop and watch Sir Richard's mansion? In that case we could have been certain whether the wench had departed or not."

"If I had done so, colonel, I should not have met you."

"True; no matter. I can soon arrange the matter to my satisfaction."

"I am glad to hear it."

"Are you a good horseman, Barnabas?"

"Yes, an excellent rider."

"And can you disguise yourself well?"

"Yes, colonel, with any one in all England."

"Do you know, then, where Darlington is?"

"Yes, well."

"Then, on the instant, disguise yourself as anything you like—say a parson, for that character throws off most suspicion—disguise yourself, I say, and post off to Darlington as fast as horse-flesh can carry you."

"But I have no money."

"You never have. I never knew a Jew in all my life who would ever confess to have more than sixpence if you wanted to borrow any without interest. Take this," said Blood, "that will be sufficient for your purpose. If this wench is really on the road, watch her, and see where she goes to. If you do not find her on the road make your way to Darlington, and try to become friendly with her father, the old miller, and let me know from time to time how you get on and all you hear."

Barnabas left the colonel on the instant, and for a moment Blood appeared to be deeply buried in thought.

"Ned Warbeck is out, eh? And there is no one of the family at home, save old Sir Richard and—— Well, he isn't much to think about, an old man like he is."

In a short time Colonel Blood hit upon a cool manner of proceeding.

He directed his steps to a well-known gaming-house, where a company of genteel thieves and house-breakers were wont to assemble.

His presence did not excite any surprise, for he was often seen in such company.

In a short time, to use his own words, "he gave the wink" to three or four of the better dressed, and left the place as if he had no other object than to lounge away half an hour or so.

Four well-dressed fellows followed him.

"Hello, my lads! are you up to any little game to-night?"

"No, colonel."

"But are you 'game' to join me in a lark?"

"Of course we are. What is it?"

"There is a very pretty girl just gone into Sir Richard Warbeck's mansion, and I want to get her into my possession as cleverly as possible."

"Just so. And how do you intend to proceed?"

"Have you got any masks with you?"

"Yes; we have not long returned from a masqu ball."

"All right, then, we will call a carriage, and when we approach Sir Richard's house, you four get out and hide the carriage round the corner. I will enter the mansion as if on business, and take good care to leave the door ajar. While I am talking to the old knight about his nephew, Ned, and the wild freak he has been playing about town of late, you four enter, put on your masks, and if this pretty wench is not taken from the old knight's abode in less tha ten minutes, without noise, without causing any alarm or hubbub among the servants, I will have every one of you transported."

"So saying, the carriage they had hired drew up round the corner, and Colonel Blood stepped forward toward the house.

He knocked and rang loudly, and it was some time before the door was opened.

At length it was unlocked and opened by no less a person than Tim, the groom.

Directly he saw Colonel Blood, he would have run away, but the colonel seized him by the throat, and gave the unlucky youth such a shake as made his limbs to curl up like shavings.

"Make any noise, and I'll choke you, villain," said the colonel. "Where is your master!"

"Which master?" Tim groaned.

"Old Sir Richard."

"He is in the parlour, talking to a young lady who is sick."

"Take in this card, then, and be quick."

While Tim was gone, Blood opened the door ajar.

His four confederates noiselessly entered, and hid themselves for a moment on the kitchen stairs, until they should have ascertained where Ellen Harmer's apartment was.

"Colonel Blood!" said old Sir Richard, in much surprise, as he walked into the hall. "May I ask your business with me? it must be of some great consequence, or you would not have called at this unreasonable hour?"

"I would not, Sir Richard—my information is of the utmost importance to you, and brooks no delay."

"Come this way then, colonel; I will not ask you into my breakfast parlor, for I have a fair young woman there, who has been lying insensible for the last hour or more."

"Indeed!"

"Yes, it is a painful story, as far as I can understand; but come this way, colonel, into the dining room. Tim, go down to the cellar and bring a bottle of wine for the colonel."

"Yes, Sir Richard," said Tim, and off he went towards the cellar with great glee, for it must be confessed Master Tim was seldom sent to the wine cellar without helping himself to the very best advantages.

He had not got further than the kitchen stairs, however, when an ominous squeak was heard like that of some unlucky rat who has shoved his head into a steel trap.

"Be ye men or devils! Have mercy on a poor unfortunate youth, who was born to be kicked and cuffed like a dog by every one."

"Silence!" said Blood's confederates, "or we will kill you."

They instantly gagged and bound Master Tim, and for fear he should be in the way or give any trouble, they opened a window and pitched the poor groom into a dust-hole beneath, like a bundle of rags.

Quicker than can be described, the four men stealthily entered the breakfast parlour, closed the door again, and perceived Ellen Harmer lying on a couch, attended by two old nurses.

When the four masked men made their sudden and noiseless appearance in the room, one of the nurses frantically clutched her gin bottle, took a hasty drink, and pretended to swoon.

The other, who was an old maid of fifty, seized the poker, and made a brave stand to defend her virtue from the intruders.

But finding that none so much as even attempted

to kiss her, she felt disgusted, disconsolate, and fainted, kicking up her heels high in the air.

In less than three minutes, the four masked men had secured and bore away Ellen Harmer without alarming the household.

Colonel Blood's quick ears could hear the distant rumbling of heavy wheels, and he felt satisfied that his men had done their work cleverly and completely.

"But what is your business with me, colonel?" asked Sir Richard.

"There has been a dreadful commotion to-night. Phillip Redgill, I hear, is killed."

"Killed!—how?—by whom?"

"Yes, killed, I understand, in a brawl or a fight, or a duel, or something of that sort, by young Ned Warbeck."

"Impossible!"

"Nay, 'tis too true, Sir Richard; the information only just reached me, and I thought it was my bounden duty to inform you."

"Thanks, colonel; but how could this have come to pass? I cannot understand it. I know that Phillip Redgill's character of late has been bad, very bad indeed, but I never thought it would have come to this. Killed by Ned Warbeck, too—shocking, sir, shocking. I always thought that something of this sort would happen, for they hated each other since boyhood. But in what manner did all this happen, colonel? Let me hear the particulars."

Colonel Blood was about to tell him all he knew, when a great row took place in the house, which stopped the conversation.

"What is that noise?" asked old Sir Richard.

"I know not," said Blood, coolly.

"Murder, thieves, robbers, burglars, seducers, villains!" screamed the two nurses locked in the room.

They kicked at the door, and made such a terrible hubbub, that it aroused all the servants in the house, who came clamouring to the spot in hot haste.

"Open the door, open the door!" screamed the two nurses, jumping about inside; "thieves, murderers, seducers—help, help!"

The door was quickly opened, and one of the nurses thought proper to enact a little scene on her own account, and therefore fainted right in Blood's arms.

The colonel was disgusted with his burden, and let her fall upon the floor again, rather heavily.

"The girl gone?" said Sir Richard.

"Yes, four men came in upon us—oh, oh, oh!—ho-o-o!"

"All in masks—oh, ho-o-o!"

"Wanted to take liberties with us—ho-o-o!"

"But we wouldn't let 'em."

"They snatched up my lady."

"And drank all the wines and spirits."

"They had all black faces."

"Masks, I suppose," said Blood, coolly.

"Yes, sir; masks, dark lanterns, and daggers. Oh, it was a mercy both on us weren't killed."

"And which way did they go?"

"Can't tell, sir."

"I must see to this at once," said Blood; "this outrage is too great to be endured."

"Do," said Sir Richard; "do, colonel, the girl must not be borne away from my house in this manner."

"You speak and look as if I had had something to do with the affair, Sir Richard."

"Whatever I think is my own business, Colonel Blood; but believe me I shall inform the king of all

I know and suspect, and shall attend the levee next Thursday for that special purpose."

Blood blustered out some angry words, and left the mansion, pretending to be in a great rage with "those villainous rascals" who had stolen the girl away.

Yet when he got into the open air again he could not but laugh heartily at the success of his plans.

He went towards the palace, and there it was that he encountered Ned Warbeck, Lieutenant Garnet, and Bob Bertram, of which we have spoken in another place.

But what became of Barnabas the Jew the next chapter will show.

## CHAPTER XLVIII.

A ROUGH RECEPTION—THE JEW ON HIS TRAVELS—ANDY, THE MANIAC LOVER, MEETS BARNABAS.

In selecting Barnabas as an especial messenger to Darlington, Colonel Blood showed good judgment, for on more than one occasion the Jew had ridden eighty miles in ten hours.

But Ellen's friends had also selected a swift messenger, and a much faster one than the Jew could ever prove to be.

The messenger was nothing else than a carrier pigeon.

In those days, when coaches were slow and letters unsafe for robbers, gentlemen always had by them a number of trained pigeons, who carried messages to and from their country seats.

When, therefore, Sir Richard had found out who Ellen Harmer really was, he wrote a note, sent Tim up to the dormer to catch a pigeon, and, having tied the note to its neck, he threw it off, and away it went with lightning speed to its favourite home—Darlington Hall.

Hence the Jew had not gone far on his journey, when the pigeon, with its important message, arrived at Darlington Hall.

It was speedily caught, and the note, as directed, was immediately delivered to Miller Harmer, and read thus :—

"MY DEAR FRIEND HARMER,—I am happy to inform you that, through the agency of my young scapegrace nephew, Ned Warbeck, we have discovered your daughter Ellen, who was abducted some time ago. Come up to town at once, as speedily as possible, for business of great importance demands it.

"Yours in haste,
"RICHARD WARBECK.

"P.S.—Do not, on any account, whisper a word of your business to any one, but maintain the strictest silence in the village and on the road. R. W."

Miller Harmer, the same hour in which the note arrived, mounted the fleetest horse at Darlington Hall, and set out on his journey to London at a giddy gallop.

He passed the disguised Jew upon the road, who asked the way to Darlington.

"Do you know any one in the village of the name of Harmer?" asked the Jew.

"Yes, I do," answered the miller, with a wicked twinkle in his eye. "Why do you ask?"

"He lost a daughter once?"

"He did."

"Yes, poor man, it was a great affliction, wasn't it?"

"No doubt," said the miller, biting his lips. "Are you journeying to Darlington with any news of her?"

"Yes; that is to say, I thought I'd call and inform her father that she is well, happy and married."

"Very kind of you, certainly," said the miller.

"Which is his house?"

"Down by the mill-dam."

"Do you think he would give me a warm reception?"

"No doubt of it, he couldn't do otherwise to one who has put himself out of the way to oblige him as you have."

"Thank you, good day," said the Jew.

"Good day," said the miller, with a trembling lip.

And the horsemen parted company.

For many weary miles the Jew travelled on through sleet, and wind, and rain.

The storm was very severe, and the clouds were rolling with heavy thunder.

It was towards eleven o'clock at night when Barnabas came near to the village of Darlington.

He had ridden far, and was weak and weary.

The rain poured down in torrents, and the night was so dark he could scarcely see ten yards before him.

Fearful of losing his way, he determined to call and enquire at a cottage close by.

He knocked at the door loudly with his riding whip, and the door was opened by an aged woman.

"What do you want, kind sir?" she asked.

"My way to Darlington."

"The right-hand road, sir, is the nearest."

"Do you know Miller Harmer?"

"I do."

"And his daughter?"

"Yes, sir; why?"

"I came to inform him that his daughter Ellen—"

"That's him! that's him!" roared some one inside the cottage.

In an instant Andy, the maniac, rushed out to the cabin door, a heavy club in hand. (See cut in No. 20.)

"That's him! that's him!" roared Andy, in a frightful passion, at the same time he seized the horse by the reins and dealt the unfortunate Jew three or four such terrible blows as knocked him off his horse into the muddy road.

Barnabas was stunned, and bled freely.

He would have been killed on the spot by the maniac but that several villagers passing by disarmed him, and led the youth, raving, back to the cottage.

When the villagers returned to the spot, Barnabas had mounted his horse again, with great difficulty, and galloped into the village of Darlington, as if ten thousand demons were at his heels.

## CHAPTER XLIX.

THE LEVEE—MILLER HARMER ARRIVES IN TOWN—SIR RICHARD, NED WARBECK, AND THE MILLER ARE GRANTED AN AUDIENCE BY THE KING—THE CUNNING PAGE SIMON—THE CRAFTINESS OF COL. BLOOD—NED WARBECK ALL BUT CHALLENGES BLOOD IN THE KING'S PRESENCE.

THE day agreed on by the king on which Ned Warbeck should again call came round.

In the meantime, Miller Harmer had safely arrived in town, and to his consternation learned every particular of his daughter from the lips of Ned Warbeck, and his uncle, Sir Richard.

The old man's grief was great; but Sir Richard cheered him, and gave such wholesome and encouraging advice that he rested and felt satisfied that ere long justice would fall on all who had had any hand in robbing him of his darling and only daughter.

Sir Richard had not attended Court for many years before, but now he donned his best suit, and even insisted that the miller should accompany him to the levée.

After much persuasion he consented, and went with Sir Richard and Ned Warbeck.

They had not mixed among the great nobles long, when the king suddenly exclaimed,

"Sir Richard Warbeck, as I live! his nephew, and a farmer-looking gentleman also. Welcome, good friend, Warbeck! Why, who were they that told us you were not living?"

"I know not, sire," Sir Richard answered, bowing.

"But they are mistaken considerably, are they not?"

"They are, sire."

"We are glad to hear it, very glad to hear it, indeed, Sir Richard. And who have you with you?"

"An old friend—an injured man, sire; his name is Harmer, the miller of Darlington."

"Ah, indeed! And I am glad to see the worthy miller, who is no doubt deep in market prices, and reeking with floury learning, eh?"

"Not very deep, sire," said the miller, gravely. "I come here as a complainant to the fountain of justice as well as of honour."

"And I too," said old Sir Richard.

"I am sorry to hear it; but you had better go to Lord Bute—you know Bute, our new attorney-general, Sir Richard?—a very clever fellow. Go to him, and say we send you."

"If you will deign to read this, sire," said the miller, presenting a paper to him.

"Yes, oh, yes—at our leisure."

"Now, if it pleases you, sire. There are but four lines upon that paper; but if it possesses you with our great grief it may prevent bloodshed."

"Bloodshed?" said the king, as he opened the note; and then in a low tone, he read,

"Ellen Harmer, my daughter, has been stolen from her father's roof. Colonel Blood is suspected; will you say if you think him guilty or not?"

"Hem!" said the king, "a grave charge this—very, very grave. It is well not to fill all our gossips with such a matter."

"It is, sire, and therefore was it that I wrote these lines for the miller," said Sir Richard, "and took his case in hand."

"You have done well, quite well. Let me think; I hardly know if I ought to do this that you ask of me, but I promise you that I will do all I can to find the lady. I will myself take steps to do so."

"You are ever gracious, sire," said Ned Warbeck, sternly; "but if Colonel Blood shrinks from the pledge required he will have to meet me in arms this day, for I shall else make the atmosphere of honour unfit for him to breathe."

"No, no—no fighting," said the king with a toss of the head. "Simon, where are you?"

"Here, sire," the cunning page replied.

"Search out Colonel Blood, and tell him to meet us in the wainscot chamber in an hour from now. Will that content you?"

"Yes, sire, if you will promise to take steps to avenge my child."

"Yes, oh, yes, we will."

"Do you think of walking, sire?" asked the cunning page?"

"Walking, villain? What do you mean?"

"You talked of taking steps to find Colonel Blood," said Simon, the page, with a broad grin.

"Simon, if you stay here another moment I will sacrifice you to my just resentment. Off with you, rascal!" said the king.

Simon made a rapid retreat, and the king, bowing to Sir Richard Warbeck, Miller Harmer, and Ned Warbeck, added—

"We will put Blood to his word in this matter, and shall expect to see you; and also, I must say, we deeply grieve for you."

There was no resource now for the father of Ellen Harmer and Sir Richard but to make their exit from the chamber.

"This will be one point gained," said Sir Richard, "if we get Blood to convict or clear himself in the presence of the king; it will be either his exculpation or his ruin."

"It will—it must!" said Ned Warbeck, warmly, "and I will take good care that he does not shelter himself under any ambiguity of phrase in the matter. Where is the wainscot chamber the king spoke of?"

"I know not; but here come a royal page, I will ask him," said Sir Richard.

It was Simon who was passing, and to whom Sir Richard said,

"Young man, can you conduct us to the wainscot chamber?"

"Yes, gentlemen," said Simon, with a roguish smile; "I was seeking you for that purpose. Will you please follow me?"

"We will."

Simon led the way to rather a small room that was entirely wainscotted all over the walls as well as the ceiling, and after desiring them to be seated he bowed himself out, and scarcely had he done so when another door was opened, and Simon, appearing again, in a sharp, sudden tone of voice, announced—

"The king!"

"What a mercy," said the king, "that the levée is over at last. But where is Colonel Blood?"

"We have not seen him, sire," said Sir Richard.

"Oh, then he will be here soon."

Simon the page opened the door and announced Colonel Blood.

In another moment Colonel Blood entered the room.

He was most magnificently attired in a semi-official kind of costume.

In his hand he carried a hat, looped with a diamond, and ornamented with a plume of feathers that, as he bowed, swept the floor.

Simon the page had had just time enough to let Colonel Blood know who he had to meet in the wainscot chamber, and why he had to meet them, so that the bold colonel was pretty well prepared to face the affair out with all the nonchalance possible.

"Well, Blood," said the king, "we have sent for you to ask you a favour, for the subject of this interview is not one concerning which we feel justified in impressing a command upon you."

"I am your humble servant ever, sire," said Colonel Blood. "Your requests should be commands to those who are true to your person."

"Well, well, Blood, that is all very well; but here are three gentlemen with grievous complaints."

"Of me?"

"In some degree."

Colonel Blood elevated his eyebrows, and tried to look the picture of candid innocence and surprise.

"I say, only in some degree," said the king ; and then, turning to Sir Richard, he added, "May I show him the note, and that will show him at once what you mean ?"

"If you please," said Sir Richard.

"Well, I think it best. Read that, Colonel Blood, and when you have read it, remember it is my request that you answer clearly and categorically to the questions put to you."

With well-acted surprise Colonel Blood read the note, and then placing his hand upon his heart, he returned it in silence.

Ned Warbeck looked sternly at him as he said—

"Colonel Blood, it is well known to you that it is not without reasons that we point at you the finger of suspicion in this case."

The colonel bowed lowly.

"Therefore," added Ned, warmly, "the circumstances of our coming in this way to the king, and requesting him to exercise an authority that may prevent useless bloodshed, is not altogether so very extraordinary a one as it might appear."

The colonel bowed again.

"I do not wish," added Miller Harmer, "to enter into any dispute with you. What is past I am willing to forget, if it has fallen short of the crime of abduction, which I feel myself in a position to lay at the door of some one."

"And I, too," said Sir Richard ; "I, too, have reason to require an explanation from you, colonel, of rather an extraordinary appearance that you made in my house last night, but am quite willing, for the present, to wave that circumstance in favour of the questions that my friend, the miller here, has put to you."

"Very well, gentlemen," said the colonel, coolly. "You find me peculiarly situated here ; the king, who holds my first duty, can command me to reply to you."

"Nay," said the king, "that I do not. I only stand here as, I hope, the friend of all parties ; and if anything I can say or do will have the effect of preventing honourable gentlemen and good subjects from embroiling themselves in conflict with each other, of course I am only too happy."

"Then," said Ned Warbeck, "do I understand, Colonel Blood, that you will answer what I have to say to you ?"

"You do, sir," said the colonel, with a curling lip.

"On the word of a gentleman ?" said Ned.

"On the word of a gentleman," replied the colonel.

"Which," added Sir Richard, "it is moral suicide to falsify."

"Exactly so," said the colonel, with a smile ; I propose your questions, and here I stand ready to reply to them fully and fairly."

"Then, sir," said the miller, "is my daughter in your keeping as a prisoner ? I say as a prisoner, because such is the only mode by which she could be prevented from seeking her friends."

"She is not, sir," answered Blood.

"Did you or did you not take her from the house of Sir Richard Warbeck last night ?"

"I did not, sir."

"Did you cause her to be taken from thence ?" said Sir Richard.

"Certainly not."

"Do you know where she is ?"

"I do not know where she is."

Colonel Blood in this reply kept his word of honour by a piece of sophistry, rather than by downright candour, for he managed to place a slight emphasis on the word "know," and told him-

self that he could not be said to know anything of what he had been only told by Simon, but of which he knew nothing.

There was now a pause of some few moments' duration, after which the king said—

"Gentlemen, are you satisfied ?"

"We are," said Sir Richard. "I cannot so far malign human nature than to do otherwise than believe that what the colonel has said, on his word of honour, is perfectly true."

"Stop," said Ned, fiercely. "Will you say, Colonel Blood, if you are in possession of any knowledge or information of any kind whatever respecting Ellen Harmer ?"

"Sir," said Blood, coldly, "I have no right to say more than in all honour will clear myself of every imputation. More than that will be to battle about the affairs of others, and to me that is odious."

Thus ended this fruitless interview, which, on the part of Colonel Blood, was naught else than a tissue of lies.

"D——n the rascal!" said Ned to Garnet, as they drove home. "I am certain that the cool, smiling villain knows all about it."

"Then let us make it our business to entrap him," said Garnet. "It is very hard after she has been rescued from their clutches once, that she should again be taken away, and from your own uncle's house, too."

"Never mind," said Ned ; "I'll be even with Colonel Blood yet."

* * * * *

"You played your part admirably, Blood," said the king, when Sir Richard and the others had left the audience chamber.

"Sire," said the colonel, smiling, "I am always your majesty's most faithful subject."

"And when shall I see this pretty wench, colonel ?"

"To-morrow night, your majesty."

"'Tis well. Have you made all the arrangements ?"

"Yes, sire ; but she knows not who you are."

"So much the better. To-morrow night, then ; come early, Blood."

"I will, sire."

---

## CHAPTER L.

### THE ROYAL LOVER.

THE night upon which the king had been promised that the young Ellen, with whom he was so deeply enamoured, would come to his apartments, at length arrived, and set in with squally fierceness.

For the whole day the sun had been obscured by clouds, and although it was not until evening actually arrived that any rain had fallen, yet it had threatened to do so numberless times, and the scud of heavy clouds had been coursing through the air at a terrible rate.

The wind, though, about sunset—when a dashing rain began to fall—had sensibly moderated, and it was only now and then that it whistled about the old towers and chimneys of St. James's Palace.

The two dissolute and unscrupulous men to whom the king had, rather in defiance of the pledge he gave to Sir Richard Warbeck, given an account of his intended adventure—namely, Blood and the page

Simon—were quite ready to play their part in the comedy, which they knew was about to take place.

The ruin of a young girl, who confided in the truth and honesty of one, who, under a false name, affected to love her, was to them a common-place affair.

And without a thought or regret for the evil they were about to do, they joined heart and hand in the infamous plan for the destruction of the fair Ellen.

If we were to say that the king had no terrors upon the subject, we should, perhaps, be, at his age, giving him the discredit of a greater familiarity with vice than he really had.

The career of dissipation which he had fallen into was in consequence of evil councillors surrounding him; and it is certain that, during the day, he had several misgivings with regard to the course he agreed to pursue in this affair.

By appointment, Colonel Blood met the king in his own apartments about one hour before the time appointed for the meeting with young Ellen.

And whatever might have been his own qualms of conscience, they were soon smothered by the reckless manner in which those two dissolute persons, Blood and Simon, spoke of the affair.

In fact, as is ever the case with a young mind that is thrown into vicious company, there was a lack of sufficient courage to assert better principles than were enunciated by that company.

"Well, sire," said Blood, gaily, "you are a lucky fellow, upon my life."

"Think you so?"

"Think I so? I am sure of it. Is he not now, Simon?"

"De-ci-ded-ly," said Simon, "His majesty is always lucky."

"Well, then, I suppose I am," said the king.

"You are," added Blood, "in more ways than one."

"But are all the hindrances got rid of?"

"All, sire."

"Good; and we three alone, then, now occupy this suit of apartments?"

"Precisely so, sire; and I have also said should any inquiry be made for you, you are not here."

"Good again; and the fair one is to be here at the hour of midnight. Is it not so?"

"It is, sire."

"Very well, then, I act the bridegroom, Blood acts the parson, and Simon here acts the clerk. Who is to be the only witnesses of this marriage?"

"By jove, I should like to change places with you, for from the transient glances I have had of the fair girl, she is positively bewitching."

The king was about to make some reply, but such a gust of wind, accompanied by a heavy dash of rain, at that moment came against the windows of the room in which they sat, that they all three sprang to their feet, with the full expectation that the casement was about to be blown in upon them at that moment.

"What a night!" said the king. "Surely she will not come. What think you, gentlemen, shall we indeed see the fair one to night?"

"I say, yes," replied Blood; "I know she will be brought here for a certainty."

"And so do I," said Simon, "for what, after all, will not love adventure?" And that she is desperately enamoured of your majesty, there cannot be a doubt upon any of our minds."

"Not the least," said Blood; "of course not."

"Well," said the king, "there is certainly something in that; but as it is now near the time, I think it but civil that I should be near the door to receive her when she does come."

"Be it so, sire," said Blood; "and while you are gone, we will get ready for the parts we may be about to play. By the bye, which room will you take her into, your majesty?"

"The room next to this."

"Well, perhaps it will be better to do so, sire; and yet the next room that opens to the garden is most private, is it not?"

"Not so; lights can be seen through its windows; but that, to be sure, would not matter much. Hark!"

"It is the old clock."

The old clock chimed the three-quarters past eleven, and the king, waving his hand to his friends, left the room, and took his way through a magnificent suite of chambers.

*        *        *        *        *

A handsome small saloon was already lighted, and into it the king at once made his way.

And, flinging his cap and cloak upon the table, he shook a small silver bell that was at hand.

A female attendant appeared as if by magic.

"Oh, is that you, Lady Gordon?" said the king.

"Yes, sire."

"Well, there is a young lady here, I believe; she has not long arrived."

"She has that honour, sire."

"I hope that she has been treated as belies her rank and honour."

"Her rank and—and——Did you say virtue?"

The king bit his lips to keep himself from laughing outright.

And then, with feigned anger, he said,

"Lady Gordon, do you think it impossible for a virtuous girl to find her way to this house? Do you dare to assert that because a young lady is brought here in rather a mysterious manner, she is henceforth to have a slur cast upon her name? I am really ashamed of you, Lady Gordon."

"I humbly crave your pardon, I really did not know——"

"Pshaw! you ought to know!"

"As you please, sire."

"Tell me at once, has the lady, who was brought here to-night, been treated with respect and consideration or not? Answer me that.

"I can assure you, sire, upon that point, that she has been treated with the greatest possible respect and attention; and I can further say that I have been informed that she is rather impatient under her imprisonment."

"Ah, indeed!"

"Even so, sire."

"Has she made any attempt to escape?"

"I cannot say that, sire; but she has, in terms of indignant remonstrance, demanded her freedom, and proclaimed that she was innocent of all crime."

"Humph! Did she talk of her father?"

"No, sir; but she spoke of Sir Richard Warbeck."

"It is very strange that she should refer less to her father than to old Sir Richard, to whom she is no relative."

"Yes, sire, and if you please, and——"

"Peace, Lady Gordon! I was only communing with myself; you know nothing of all this."

The lady bowed very low and retired a few paces, when the king rather abruptly said,

"Send Lady Connell to me."

"Yes, sir."

Lady Gordon retired, and the king rose and paced the room.

It was evident he was rather at a loss what to do.

In the course of a few minutes Lady Connell made her appearance, and with rather a stately curtsey, saluted the king.

# THE SKELETON CREW; OR, WILDFIRE NED.

THE DEPARTURE.

"Oh, Connell," he said, "how are you?"

"I am quite well. May I ask if you are the same?"

"Oh, yes, thank you. All right. Sit down. Well, how about this girl, eh? What does she say?"

"The child, you mean?"

"The what?"

"The child that was brought here to-night."

"Child, eh?—hem! Excuse me, I don't know anything about a child. I allude to Ellen Harmer. I may as well name her at once, for I hear from Gordon that she has proclaimed who she is."

"It is to that same girl I allude. I call her, I think justly, a child."

"Oh, do you?"

"Yes, I think every female a child under thirty years of age."

"Oh, lord! Well, Connell, we won't quarrel about that at all events. How is the baby?"

"You jest."

"No, on my soul no; but I thought you would like to be met with in your own way, but if you prefer the term "child" better, how is the child?"

"She is well enough."

"Or ill enough—which is it?"

No. 23.

"Ill enough in temper, but well enough in health, I take it," said Lady Connell, tossing up her head. "You'll find her in the next room."

"Many thanks. Go to her and say that a gentleman wishes to speak to her, if she will grant him an audience."

Lady Connell sailed out of the room, and presently returned to say that Ellen had, upon the ground that she was detained against her will like a prisoner, refused to reply to the message in any terms at all.

"You will go to her, I presume," said Lady Connell, "and announce yourself?"

"No!"

"No! Why?"

"That is—I don't know. Ellen Harmer is very virtuous, and is a young lady of surpassing charms. I don't know what course to adopt. She might know me again. Being the daughter of a true old gentleman, I fear I shall have to leave the house as I came into it."

"It's quite a gratification," said Lady Connell, with a toss of her head again, "it's quite a gratification to find you are so scrupulous—much more so than you used to be."

"More scrupulous than I used to be? How do you mean?"

"I mean that you have not shrunk from appealing to the affections of a young lady, despite her rank or birth."

"Have I not? That's all you know about it. I have ever respected rank, and real virtue more so. To whom do you allude, if indeed you allude to any on at all?"

"To Margaret, my daughter."

"To what?"

"To Margaret, the daughter of—"

"Oh! oh! oh!—ha! ha! ha! Good. Oh, that is good!"

"Sire!"

"Excuse my laughing, Lady Connell; but you are talking of the little blue-eyed wench you called your daughter, or your niece, are you not?"

"I mentioned the name, and the descendant of a race of kings!"

"Milesian kings?"

"Yes, Milesian kings; but none the less kings, and I am quite surprised that you should feel any hesitation in regarding the daughter of a mere English miller when you felt none regarding Margaret, a descendant of a long line of kings."

"My good woman, don't make me laugh in this way, that's a dear old soul; now, don't."

"Laugh, sire?"

"Yes, to be sure. Come, say no more, we will go and speak to this ——"

The king dashed out of the room just as Lady Connell, with a preparatory shake of the head, was about to say something further regarding her daughter.

The three rooms adjoining consisted of reception-room, a refreshment-room, and a bed-chamber; and when the king got to the door of the reception room, he found a servant on duty, who had the key of it.

"You are sure the lady is here?" said the king.

"Yes, sire."

"Open the door and lock it after me."

"Yes, sire?"

Without the least change of countenance, the servant opened the door for the king, who at once passed into the reception-room.

The door was shut behind him, and locked; but a glance told him that Ellen was not in that room.

Now there was something of the gentleman about the king, notwithstanding all his libertinism, therefore he thought it would be ungentlemanly to proceed further without Ellen knowing of his presence.

He took an irresolute glance around the room; and while he is debating in his own mind what course to pursue, we may give the reader a slight idea of the appearance of the suite of apartments.

The reception-room the king was in was a very pretty one, and hung with tapestry that was not defaced by any hideous representations of human figures which were ever failures in such material; but had upon it a real flowering pattern that succeeded perfectly well, and had rather a charming effect.

The furniture of this room was of white and gold.

The next room was covered with crimson plush paper.

The furniture was of rosewood, polished up to a great height of brilliancy.

The sleeping chamber was the gem of the whole suite, for it was got up quite regardless of expense in blue and silver, and presented the most enchanting appearance of brightness and elegance.

If the apartments she occupied could have cheered the melancholy of Ellen Harmer, certainly she ought to have been happy enough in them.

The king for one moment knew not what to do.

A certain sense of fear came over him as he noiselessly walked towards the beautiful bed-room.

In a chair beside the glowing fire sat Ellen Harmer, and the soft light of waxen tapers made the maiden to appear even more lovely than she really was.

With an impatient gesture the king advanced towards her and knelt upon one knee.

"Dearest Ellen," he began, in tones of great earnestness; "dearest Ellen, how I have longed for this interview!"

"I was brought here, sire," was the maiden's reply, "by force, and, as a gentleman, as a nobleman, as my king, I demand to know why and wherefore?"

"Dear creature, do not pout so beautifully; do not flash those lovely eyes, I beseech you. It was by my orders you were brought hither."

"Indeed, sire. And was such an action worthy of a king?"

"Nay, do not discuss that point with me, fair one, for you know that Cupid knows no law. Come, fairest of the fair, listen to my tale of love, I beseech thee. We are here alone; no one can hear us, no one can see us; the doors are locked, we are alone!"

"False man!" said Ellen; "would you thus enveigle me to destroy mine honour? Let me go, I say!"

"You cannot."

"But I will."

"Nay, dear Ellen, listen to me. We are alone, I say."

"Nay; not alone," said a voice behind some tapestry.

"Ha!" said the king. "What, rats behind the arras!"

"No rat, sire," said a bold youth, advancing into view.

It was Ned Warbeck.

In his hand he held a sword.

The point was gory, and the brave youth looked flushed and excited.

"What means this," gasped the king, with a hand upon his own sword.

"Mean, sire!" answered Ned, proudly; "it means that Colonel Blood is a villain! It means that he caused the abduction of this fair maid from my uncle's house! It means that he has proved himself a hypocrite and a liar! And, finally, it means that I watched for him, and found my way hither over his vile body!"

"What, dead! Blood dead?"

"That I know not, sire, nor care," said Ned Warbeck, boldly. "He confronted me, sword in hand; I left him gasping on the back stairs."

"And what would you with me?"

"Nothing, sire, but that this injured maid may be restored to her old father's arms."

"Rash youth," said the king, "know you not that I could with one word call around me a whole regiment of soldiers?"

"I know it," Ned replied, with an ironical bow; "you could do so, of course, sire, but you are much too wise to attempt it."

This was uttered with so much emphasis and meaning, that it staggered the king.

And, without saying another word, Ned Warbeck conducted Ellen Harmer from the apartment by the secret back stairway; and before the king could utter a word, the door was locked upon him, and the fair fugitive was safe in the hands of friends.

---

CHAPTER LI.

COLONEL BLOOD HAS HIS REVENGE — STORMY INTERVIEW — MEETING IN THE WOOD — A STARTLING INCIDENT — DISCOVERY OF THE VICTIM—THE DEATH-BED CURSE.

IT WAS a bold thing for Wildfire Ned to do, but he had sworn to accomplish the rescue of Ellen Harmer, and the gallant deed was accomplished.

Outside the palace gardens stood a carriage and four noble horses, ready to convey the fair Ellen to her father's home.

Bob Bertram was the driver, and outside waiting for Ned Warbeck stood Lieutenant Garnet.

"Bravo, Ned!" said Garnet. "You have got the girl safe?"

"Yes," said Ned; "but, as I expected, not without opposition and a sharp fight. I met Colonel Blood, and we crossed swords. He fell in less than a minute. I pushed my way up the back stair-case, and rescued the maiden right under the nose, and in open defiance of the king."

"I fear you will suffer for all this, Ned."

"No matter. I care not for king or any one when virtue and honor are at stake. Drive on, Bob, with all your might."

Bob Bertram did not want bidding twice.

He lashed up his four horses, and away went Ellen Harmer towards Darlington at full speed, whither Sir Edward Warbeck and her father had gone before her.

When she arrived there, Ellen was thoroughly exhausted with the length of the journey, and retired to rest immediately; and in her slumbers did not dream of the cruel fate which awaited her.

In the morning she was much better, and was visited by her foster sister, whom she loved more dearly perhaps than any one on earth.

This foster sister told her all that had transpired in the house since the fatal night of her abduction.

When she heard of Andrew's mishap in being desperately wounded, and thrown from the bridge by some unknown man, Ellen wept bitterly; for in her heart she knew the villain must and could be none other than the cold-hearted, treacherous, Colonel Blood.

But when her foster sister told her also that Andrew, her old and faithful lover, was now a confirmed lunatic, she sank into a chair and sobbed aloud.

"Nay, do not weep, Ellen!" said her father, the old miller, who now entered the apartment, and stood before the two girls with a pale face. "Nay, do not weep for him, Ellen, but weep for me—for your honor and mine is gone for ever."

"Gone!" said Ellen, rising with a flushed face "Nay, father, say not so! Your daughter is as spotless as on the night when she was cruelly carried away by a ruthless villain!"

"The world will not believe it, Ellen; but if I thought for a moment you had disgraced me and mine, I would rather see you dead at my feet."

Nelly wept and sobbed by turns; but the cruel words of her father brought the hot blood to her fair cheeks, and she vindicated herself most eloquently from the foul aspersions of all idle, gossiping village scandal.

What at first, then, had been a stormy meeting between her father and herself (see cut in No. 18), closed as such meetings always should close between parents and children. Ellen threw herself into her father's arms, and, with beating heart, told him all her trials and troubles.

"God bless you, child, God bless you!" said the old miller, as he tenderly kissed her and left the room.

Two days after this meeting of father and daughter, Ellen, accompanied by two female friends, strolled through the woods of Darlington, in order to call upon and console Andrew, who was reported to be dying raving mad.

They had enjoyed their walk, and were much flushed with exercise, when they were startled by a strange sight (see cut in No. 21).

In the distance, and partly concealed by the deep undergrowth of the forest, they perceived two men engaged in a hostile meeting.

So unlooked for was this strange sight, that the timid girls could have fainted; but, seized with horror and fright, they turned somewhat from their own path and ran swiftly away.

Still the clinking of swords sounded in their ears and it was long ere they could breathe freely again.

However, Ellen and her friends pursued their way towards the cottage of Andrew's mother, but were greatly surprised to find that instead of dying, Andrew was not at home, but was well and hearty, except in mind, and had left the cottage rather suddenly a few nights before in pursuit of a strange horseman, whom he appeared to recognise as an enemy.

Since that time nothing had been seen or heard of the poor deranged youth, his old weeping mother said; nevertheless she did all that lay in her power to make her lady visitors as comfortable as possible.

But the good old dame wept very bitterly, for she was a widow, and since her son's fatal accident she had fallen very rapidly in worldly circumstances, and was on the brink of great poverty, if, indeed, not of absolute want.

Ellen and her friends returned to the village, and did not fail to give an account of the duel which had taken place in Darlington Wood.

Miller Harmer and other villagers went forth with their guns and swords, to see what had happened.

They scoured the woods thoroughly in all directions, but did not discover anything noteworthy.

As they were about to give up the search, however, old Harmer came upon a retired spot, and there found a large pool of blood.

The grass all round about had been trodden down as if men had been engaged in deadly combat.

But nobody was found, nor the least vestige of clothing which might have directed any further search or led to the discovery of the unknown persons.

A few days afterwards, however, Ellen Harmer feeling sore at heart, and fretful in mind, went across the fields and through Darlington Woods to visit Andrew's mother, and to ascertain, if possible whether she or her father could do any good for the poor widow and her demented son.

She arrived at the cottage, but no tidings had been heard of poor Andy, and his mother was well nigh broken-hearted.

No one had seen or knew anything of the poor youth, either in or out of the village.

For a second time Ellen Harmer returned home.

The old widow offered to accompany her part of the way through the forest, but Ellen pleasantly declined.

As she journeyed through the wood slowly and thoughtfully, she heard voices near, and suddenly beheld a large encampment of gipsies.

"Perhaps this swarthy tribe might know or have heard something regarding poor Andrew," thought Ellen. "I will question them."

Boldly advancing right into the gipsy encampment, to the no small surprise of both men and women, Ellen walked up to a tall, swarthy-looking man who stood near a covered cart or waggon, and appeared to be the chief man among them.

"Ellen Harmer is your name?" said the tall, swarthy man.

"It is. How know you that?"

"Ask no questions," was the gruff answer, "and I will tell you no lies."

"Perhaps, if I pay you well, it might be different?"

"Perhaps it might," said the man, grinning, as he received a piece of gold offered to him.

"Have you been long encamped in these woods?"

"We have."

"Did you hear or ascertain anything of a duel which was said to have taken place here a few days ago?"

"I did."

"Who and what were the rash gentlemen?"

"They were not gentlemen at all," answered the gipsy chief.

"Who, then, pray?"

"One was a spy in the pay of Colonel Blood."

"Colonel Blood?" said Ellen, with a shudder.

"You know him, then? Ha! ha!" laughed the tall vagabond.

"No—yes, that is, I have heard of him, my good man. And who was the other?"

"A stranger."

"And which fell?"

"The stranger was killed."

"Oh, horrible! horrible!" said Ellen, aghast. "And know you not his name?"

"I do not," said the gaunt, heartless-looking fellow, with a coarse laugh. "It matters naught to me. But, if you want to have a look at the body, here it is," said he, with a grin, as at the same time he uncovered and lifted the lid of a rough coffin which was in the covered cart. (See cut in No. 19.)

From some strange impulse Ellen Harmer darted forward a step or two, and looked.

With a loud scream she fainted and fell.

The dead body was that of poor Andrew, her old and faithful lover, who had been brutally slain out of revenge by Colonel Blood's spy.

She was led away from the spot in a swooning condition by two men.

"Do not go with them—do not trust yourself with those two ruffians," said a haggard-looking old woman who now came upon the scene.

"Hold thy tongue, Hannah," said the gipsy chief, with an oath.

"I will not, I cannot!" said the old woman; "you mean the girl no good; you have evil in your eye. Miss Harmer, Miss Harmer, do not go with them through Darlington Woods. Heed me, hear me, sweet lady, hear me."

But before she could utter another word she was struck to the ground in a brutal manner, and Ellen Harmer, more dead than alive, was borne through the woods towards her native village.

But alas! she never reached it!

The two gipsy men, obeying the secret injunctions of their leader, saw her as far as the little wooden bridge—on which Andrew had met Colonel Blood—and, ere she was aware of any danger, while in the act of rewarding the two gruff villains for escorting her so far, they cast her headlong into the river.

Four days afterwards her body was found lying on the river bank by the same villains, and they were in the act of robbing the body of everything valuable when they were discovered by Wildfire Ned and Garnet, who had been out hunting in the woods.

One of the villains, finding that they were discovered, drew forth his large knife, and looked around to see when and where the threatened danger was. (See cut in No. 16).

At that instant, however, Ned and Garnet, who had been watching the gipsies for several days, felt satisfied of the guilt of both villains.

Without any compunction they took deadly aim and fired at the two rascals, and killed them on the spot.

But the tragedy did not end here.

Several weeks afterwards a terrible storm arose.

Poor old Hannah the gipsy was lying abed, almost dying, from the effects of the brutal treatment she had received at the hands of the gipsy chief.

The wind was howling outside the humble cot in which poor Hannah lay.

Lightning flashed and the thunder rolled.

Rain fell in pitiless torrents, when a horseman, evidently dressed in disguise, and looking pale and weak, alighted from his horse at Hannah's door, and sought shelter from the storm.

A female opened the door for the stranger, who entered.

It was Colonel Blood on his way to Darlington.

For a moment he gazed around him, and then at the swarthy sufferer in bed.

There was something about poor Hannah which attracted his attention.

He stood and gazed at her as she slept and murmured in her dreams.

Opening her eyes rather suddenly she encountered the fixed look of the storm-bound stranger.

With a loud laugh Hannah rose up in bed, looking as wild as the wildest maniac (see cut in No. 22).

With eyes glowing in passion, and with a long, lean arm pointed at him, she hissed out, rather than said—

"Curses befall you, man of blood! Curses before, behind, and on every side attend you; for wherever you are, wherever you go, you despoil the innocent! I have longed to see this hour, Colonel Blood," continued Hannah, in a fierce voice; "your hand robbed me of my husband and my daughters! My children have been dragged into a life of infamy through you, and my husband slain for defending them! I have done with life; my time has come. I die satisfied, knowing that with my last breath I have cursed you and the very ground you tread upon!"

With these words she fell back into bed and expired!

———

## CHAPTER LII.

CAPTAIN JACK AND THE "BAKER'S DOZEN" ARE LODGED IN GAOL, AND AWAIT THE JUDGMENT OF THE LAW.

If, during his whole lifetime, Wildfire Ned had done nothing more, the successful capture of Captain Jack and his noted gang was more than enough to bring his name prominently before the world, with honourable mention for deeds of daring in the cause of the public good.

For a long time the public knew but little of the doings of the "Baker's Dozen," as the gang was called, but after their apprehension so many things came to light to prove their villany that all good people shuddered when they heard of them.

Old Bates and Captain Jack had long been before the world in the character of "thief-takers," but as we have already seen in the pages of this story, they themselves were the greatest rascals left unhung.

And well did Colonel Blood know it.

But Blood, like a wicked, designing man as he really was, never breathed a single syllable of their doings, so long as they payed him well for his silence, or proved of any use to him in his own nefarious practices.

But now that Captain Jack and his companions were in prison, Colonel Blood drew up a report of their doings and mode of proceeding, which, in brief, was as follows :—

"As soon as any considerable robbery was committed, and old Bates received intelligence by whom, he immediately went to the thieves, and inquired how the thing was done, where the person lived who was injured, and what the booty consisted of when taken away.

"Then pretending to chide them for their wickedness and exhorting them to live honest for the future, he gave it them, as his advice, to lodge what they had taken in a proper place, which he appointed, and promised to take some measures for their security, by getting the people to give them a reward to have their things returned to them again.

"Having thus wheedled those who had committed a robbery into compliance with his wishes, his next business was to divide the goods into several parcels, and cause them to be sent to different places, always avoiding them being sent to his own hands.

"Things being in this condition, Bates and Captain Jack went to the persons who had been robbed, and after condoling with them, pretended that they had some acquaintance with a broker to whom certain goods had been brought, some of which they suspected to have been stolen, and hearing that the person to whom they thus applied had been robbed, they thought it their duty to inform them thereof, and to enquire what goods they were which they had lost, in order to discover whether those they spoke of were the same or not.

"People who had had such losses were always ready to listen to anything of that kind, trusting to know something of their goods.

"Therefore, in a day or two, Bates or Captain Jack was sure to come again, with intelligence that they had found part of the things, and that, providing no one was brought into trouble, and the broker had something in consideration of his care, they might be had again.

"This practice of old Bates, if well considered, carried with it a great deal of policy.

"For, first, it seemed a very honest act to prevail on evil persons to restore the goods that they had stolen.

"And then it was a great benefit to those who had been robbed to have their goods again upon a reasonable premium, old Bates all the while apparently taking nothing, his advantages arising out of the gratuity left with the broker, and out of what he had bargained to give the thief, who also found his advantage, the rewards being very nearly as large as the price given by receivers, since receiving became so dangerous, and affording, moreover, a certain security into the bargain.

"With respect to Bates or Jack, this contrivance placed them in safety from all the laws then in being, so that in a short time he and Captain Jack began to give themselves out for persons who made it their business to restore stolen goods to their right owners, and no more.

"When Captain Jack first did this, he acted with so much art that he acquired a very great deal of reputation, not only from those who dealt with him, but even from people of a higher station, who, observing the industry with which he prosecuted malefactors, took him for a friend of justice, and, as such, afforded him countenance.

"He was constantly bringing men to the gallows, and, in order that he might keep up that character which he had attained in all his course of acting, not one man escaped him.

"When this practice of Jack became noted it produced not only much discourse but some inquiries into his behaviour.

"'For do not I,' said Jack, 'do the greatest good when I persuade people who deprived others of their property to restore it to them again for a reasonable consideration, and the villains who I have brought to suffer punishment, do not their deaths show how much use I am to my country ? Why, then, should people asperse me ?'

"Besides these professions of honesty, two great things there were which contributed to his preservation, which were these—

"First, the great readiness government always shows in detecting persons guilty of capital offences, in which cases it is common to offer not only pardon but rewards to persons guilty, provided they make discovery, and this Captain Jack was so sensible of that he did not screen himself behind the lenity of the supreme power, but made use of it also as an authority, taking upon him, as it were, the character of a minister of justice, which, however ill-founded, proved of great advantage to him in the course of his life.

"The other point which contributed to keep him from prosecution, was the great willingness of people who had been robbed to discover their goods, so that, provided for a small sacrifice they regained things very considerable, they were so far from bringing the offender to justice that they thought the premium as a cheap price to get off.

"Thus, by the lenity of the subject and the rigour of the magistrate, Captain Jack claimed employment.

"And, according as the case required it, the poor thieves were either trussed up to satisfy the just vengeance of the one, or protected and encouraged to satisfy the demands of the other.

"If any title can be devised suitable to Jack's character it must be that of director-general of the united forces of highwaymen, housebreakers, pickpockets, and private thieves.

"Now the maxims by which he supported himself in this capacity were these :—

"In the first place, he continually exhorted the plunderers to let him know precisely what goods they at any time took.

"By which means he had it in his power to give a direct answer to those who came to make inquiries of him.

"If they complied faithfully with his injunctions he was a certain protector on all occasions.

"And sometimes he had interest enough to procure them liberty when apprehended.

"But if they pretended to become independent and despise his rules, or throw out any threatening speeches against their companions, or grumbled at the composition made for them, in such cases as these Jack took the first opportunity of informing some of his creatures of the first fresh act they committed.

"He immediately set about to apprehend them, and laboured so indefatigably therein that they never escaped him.

"Thus he not only procured the reward for himself, but also gained an opportunity of pretending that he not only restored goods to their rightful owners, but also apprehended the thief as often as lay in his power.

"In those parts of his business which were not hazardous, Captain Jack made the people themselves take the first steps by publishing advertisements of things lost, and directing them to be brought to him, who was empowered to receive them, and pay such a reward as the person who lost them thought fit to offer.

"Jack in this capacity appeared no otherwise than as a person on whose honour the injured person could rely.

"After he had gone on with this trade for several years with success he began to lay aside much of his former caution, taking a larger house in Lambeth than that in which he formerly lived, giving the woman, whom he called his wife, abundance of fine things, and keeping an open office for the recovery of stolen goods.

"Captain Jack's fame at last came to that height that persons of the highest quality would condescend to make use of his abilities when they had the misfortune to lose their watches or other articles of value.

"But as his method of treating those who applied to him for assistance might be misrepresented, what is given here may be relied on.

"In the first place, when a person was introduced to Jack's office it was hinted to him that a guinea at least must be deposited by way of fee for his advice.

When this was complied with a large book was brought out.

"Then the loser was examined with much formality as to the time, place, and manner wherein the goods were missing, with a promise of careful investigation being made, and of hearing more concerning them in a few days.

"Jack had not the least occasion for questions, but to amuse the persons he asked.

"For he knew beforehand all the circumstances connected with the robbery much better than they did, and perhaps had the very goods in his house at the time.

"When the enquirers came a second time, Captain Jack or Bates took care to amuse them again.

"He then told them that he had made enquiries, but was sorry to communicate the event to them, for that the thief, who was a bold, impudent fellow, rejected the offer that had been made him, pretending that he could sell the goods for double the price, and, indeed, would not hear a word of restitution, unless upon better terms.

"'But,' says Jack, 'if I can but get to speak to him, I do not doubt of bringing him to reason.'

"After two or three more attendances, Jack would say as a definite answer to the enquirer,

"'Provided no questions were asked, and you gave so much money to the party who brought them, you might have the things returned privately at such an hour.'

"This was always done with an outward sign of friendship on his side, and with seeming frankness and generosity ; but when you came to the last part of the agreement, that is to say, what Jack himself expected for his trouble, then an air of coldness was put on, and he answered with indifference, that what he did was purely from a principle of doing good, and as a gratuity for the trouble he had taken, he left it entirely to yourself—you might do as you thought proper.

"When money was presented to him, he received it with the same cold indifference, always putting you in mind that he did not accept your gift as a reward conferred upon himself, but as a favour conferred upon you.

"Thus, by his dexterity in his management, he fenced himself against the rigour of the law, in the midst of these notorious transgressions of it.

"For what could be imputed to him ?

"He neither saw the thief who took away the goods, nor received them after they were taken.

"The method he pursued was neither dishonest or illegal, if you would believe his account of it, and no other account could be obtained of it.

"Had Captain Jack or Bates continued satisfied with this way of dealing, he, in all probability, would have gone down to the grave in peace.

"But he was greedy.

"And instead of keeping constant to this safe method, came at last to take the goods into his own house, giving those that stole them what he thought proper, and then making such a bargain with the loser as he was able to bring him to, sending the porter himself, and taking, without ceremony, whatever was offered to him.

"A gentleman who dealt in silks had a piece of extraordinary rich material bespoke of him on purpose for a birthday suit, and, having bought such trimmings as was proper for it, the gentleman made the whole of it up into a parcel, and placed it at one end of the counter in expectation of it being called for by the purchaser.

"Accordingly the man came for it, but when the tradesman went to get him the goods the parcel was gone, and no account could possibly be had of it.

"As the master had been all day in the shop, there was no pretence of charging his servants either of carelessness or dishonesty.

"After an hour or so he saw no other remedy but communicating with Captain Jack in hopes of receiving some benefit from his assistance ; the loss consisting not so much of the things as in the disappointment of his customer.

"As soon as he called at the house of Captain Jack and acquainted him with his business, the usual deposit of a guinea being made, and the common questions of how, when, and where having been asked, the tradesman, being very impatient, said, with some warmth—

"'Captain Jack, is it in your power to serve me? If it is I have thirty guineas here ready to lay down; but if you expect that I should dance attendance upon you for a week or two, I assure you I shall not be willing to part with half that money.'

"'My dear sir,' replied Jack, 'I am no receiver of stolen goods, nor am I a thief, so that if you do not wish to give me time to inquire you can take what proceedings you may think proper.'

"When the tradesman found he was likely to be left without any hopes he began to talk in a milder strain, and, with abundance of entreaties, begged Jack to help him all he possibly could.

"Captain Jack stepped out a minute or two, and as soon as he came back he told the tradesman,

"'It was not in his power to serve him in such a hurry, if at all; however, in a day or two he might be able to give him some answer.'

"The tradesman insisted that a day or two would lessen the value of the goods one half to him.

"And Jack insisted as peremptorily that it was not in his power to do anything sooner.

"At last a servant came in a great hurry, and told Jack that a gentleman wished to see him instantly.

"Jack bowed, and begged to be excused for a few moments.

"Shortly afterwards he returned with a smiling countenance, and, turning to the tradesman, said—

"'I protest, sir, you are the luckiest man I ever knew; I spoke to one of my people to go to a house where I sometimes resort, and directed him to talk of your robbery, and to say you had been with me and offered thirty pounds for the things again. This story had its effect, and if you go directly home I fancy you will hear more of it than I can tell you. But pray, sir, remember, the thirty pounds was your own offer, and you are free to give it or not, just as you please; but as I have taken an interest in the matter an adequate reward would not be out of place.'

"Away went the tradesman wondering where this affair would end.

"But while walking towards his own shop a fellow overtook him, patted him on the shoulder, delivered him the parcel unopened, and told him the price was twenty guineas.

"The tradesman paid it to him directly, and returning to Captain Jack's house begged of him to accept the other ten pounds for his own trouble.

"Jack told him that he had saved him nothing, but he supposed the people considered twenty guineas, enough considering that they thought themselves safely from prosecution.

"The tradesman still pressed the ten guineas on Jack, who, after taking them out of his hand, returned him five of them, and assured him,

"'That was more than enough,' adding—

"'It is satisfaction sufficient to an honest man that he is able to procure people their goods again.'

"This was a remarkable instance of the moderation Captain Jack sometimes practised, the better to conceal his villanies.

"Another story is no less extraordinary.

"A lady, whose husband was out of the kingdom, and who had sent over draughts for her assistance to the amount of between £700 and £1,000, lost the pocket book in which they were contained near Fleet Street, where the merchant lived upon whom they were drawn.

"She, however, went to the gentleman, and he advised her to go directly to Captain Jack.

"Accordingly she went to Lambeth, deposited the guinea, and answered the questions that he put to her.

"Jack said that in an hour's time some of his people might discover who it was that picked the lady's pocket.

"The lady was vehement in her desire to have it again, and at last went so far as to offer one hundred pounds.

"Jack, upon that, made answer—

"'Though they are of much greater value to you, madam, yet they cannot be anything like it to them; therefore, keep your own council, and I will give you the best direction I am able for the recovery of your notes. In the meantime, if you will adjourn to any hotel at hand, and partake of some refreshment, I will furnish you with an answer as quickly as possible.'

"The lady would not be satisfied unless Captain Jack consented also to partake of some with her.

"He at last complied, and ordered a fowl and other refreshment at the house which he named, and with which he was well acquainted.

"After waiting some time, Captain Jack joined her, and told her he had heard news of her missing pocket-book, desiring her to lay ten pounds on the table in case she should have occasion for them; and, as the waiter came up to acquaint the lady that the fowl was ready, Jack requested that she would just step down and see if there was any woman waiting at the door.

"The lady, without minding the mystery, did as he desired her, and discovered a woman in a grey cloak, who walked two or three times past the door.

"This aroused her curiosity, and prompted her to go nearer; but recollecting she had left the gold on the table upstairs, she went and snatched it up, ran down once more, and went towards the woman in the grey cloak, who still walked before the door.

"It seems she had suspected correctly; for no sooner did the woman see her approach towards her, than she came up directly, and presenting the pocket-book, desired she would open it.

"'Here,' she added, 'is another note.'

"Upon which the unknown woman presented her with a little billet, on the outside of which was written, 'ten pounds.'

"The lady took the money immediately, and presented the woman with a piece for herself.

"This done, she returned to Jack, and told him, with much pleasure, that she had secured her book, and would now eat her dinner most heartily.

"When the table was cleared, she considered it was time to return to the merchant's, who, probably, now had come back from Change, but first considered it necessary to make Captain Jack a handsome present.

"For this purpose she put her hand into her pocket, and, to her surprise, found it was gone, in which was the remainder of fifty pounds which the merchant had lent her in the early part of the day.

"Upon this she looked very much confused, but did not speak a word.

"Jack quickly perceived her confusion, and asked her if she was unwell.

"'I am well in health, sir,' she replied, 'but amazed that the woman took but ten pounds for my lost pocket-book, and at the same time picked my pocket of thirty more !'

"Jack hereupon seemed in as much confusion as the lady, and said he hoped she was not in earnest, but, if she were, requested her not to disturb herself, for she should not lose one farthing.

"Upon this Jack desired her to sit still, while he stepped over to his own house, and issued, as may be supposed, necessary directions, for, in less than half an hour a little boy that Jack kept bolted into the room, and told them the woman was taken, and on the point of going to prison.

"'You shall see, madam,' said Jack to the lady, 'what exemplary punishment I will make of this infamous woman.'

"Then, turning himself to the boy, he said,

"'Was the purse of money taken about her ?'

"'Yes, sir,' replied the lad.

"'Oh,' said the lady, 'I will take the purse.'

"The lady begged of Jack to have no hand in apprehending or punishing the poor wretch,

"'For,' said she, 'I would rather lose all I have than the poor creature should suffer.'

"'Oh, I beg ten thousand pardons, madam,' said Jack, with a very profound bow ; 'I have served your ends, so far, and now this culprit must serve mine ; in less than two weeks you will hear that this pickpocket has suffered the full penalty of the law.'

"True to his word, the poor wretch did suffer, for she was hung at Tyburn in less than the time he had promised.

"Thus acted Captain Jack and Bates towards all the notorious characters with whom they were connected.

"The poor devils in the first place served Jack and Bates by enriching them with systematic roguery, and, after they had 'run their race,' as Jack was wont to say, with a laugh, the gallows was sure to be their reward, and the chief witness against them in all cases was Jack or Bates.

"For a long series of years these two villains and the Baker's Dozen carried on this devilish system of rearing and fostering thieves, and afterwards hanging them ; but now, to use Jack's own words, he and the Dozen had likewise 'run their race,' for within a month after their arrest by Wildfire Ned, Lieutenant Garnet, and the gallant assistance of Bob Bertram, they were condemned to die, and were hung in gibbets on the identical cross roads of which Colonel Blood had spoken in an early chapter of this tale.

They stoutly protested their innocence, of course, and spoke loudly against the knavery of Colonel Blood ; but, before they suffered, Captain Jack and old Bates were seized with remorse, and bewailed their past lives as bitterly as men possibly could do."

———

## CHAPTER LIII.

NED WARBECK AND BOB BERTRAM HAVE AN INTERVIEW WITH CAPTAIN JACK AND OLD BATES IN PRISON—ASTOUNDING REVELATIONS OF DEEDS OF CRIME.

CAPTAIN JACK and Bates wrote long accounts of their career in crime which greatly startled the pious old chaplain who attended them daily.

There was only one request which either Captain Jack or Bates desired, and this was to have a final and a parting interview with Ned Warbeck and Bob Bertram.

This request was, of course, immediately granted, and, at an early hour, Ned and Bob Bertram entered the prison cell wherein Jack and Bates were chained and manacled.

"I have sent for you, Ned Warbeck, to say a few words before I die."

"Then unburden your conscience, Jack," said Ned, "and, in order that what you say may be made public hereafter, I have brought a quick writer with me, who will put down on paper all you say."

"I have no objection in the world," said Jack.

"Nor I," said Bates, in a surly tone.

"Then let me, in the first place ask, why did you arrest young Bolton, old Redgill's travelling collector for ?"

"So as to screen Phillip Redill, who gave me several thousand pounds to shift the guilt from his own shoulders to that of some one else."

"Oh, the villain !" said Bob.

"But why did you still screen him when you knew that he had dealings with Death-wing and his villanous Skeleton Crew ?"

"Because I knew if I arrested him, he might give evidence against me in turn ; for I know, and have long known, that Colonel Blood was only waiting an opportunity to hang me—before my time," said Jack, laughing.

"How can you account for his father's death ?"

"Why, he upset the carriage, and thus drowned him ; but instead of getting any property, the old man was insolvent, and not worth a penny."

"And what became of his wife ?"

"She lived for some time with Mr. Augustus Fumbleton, and kept a house of ill-fame. Her father, old McTurk, however, did not disdain to receive money from her, but ultimately the house was accidentally burnt to the ground, and Fanny, young Redgill's wife, was as the same time consumed in the flames."

"And what became of old McTurk ?"

"He went to the workhouse, and there lingers out a wretched life. His wife is dead, and he himself is like a walking skeleton."

"And do you know how it was that my brother, Charley, got into such disgrace at the Indian house ?"

"Yes. Phillip Regill told me all one night when drunk, and seemed to glory in it."

"What did he say ?"

"Why, that he stole the notes, and lost them that same night in gambling."

"He must have been an unscrupulous, inconceivable villain ! But he is dead, I hear," said Ned.

"No, he is not," said Jack ; "but if he doesn't die, I have written down and sworn to more than enough to gibbet him."

"And are you content to die ?" asked Bob, in great surprise at the coolness of Jack and Bates.

"I must be so," was the reply. "We have had Gibbet in our eye for more than fifteen years, and surely now that the time's come, we are men enough to face it."

"Perhaps 'tis well that society is about to get rid of you ?" said Ned.

———

*THIS TALE WILL CONCLUDE IN No. 24,*

**With which Number will be presented**

NUMBERS 1 & 2 OF A NEW WORK.

"Perhaps it is. We have had a long and success-ful run of it; but if we had lived a little longer, I have no doubt we should have made ourselves more famous than we are."

"Infamous, you should have said," remarked Ned.

"Well, just as you please to word it; it is of little consequence to us now, eh, Bates?"

"Not a particle, as I can see. So they lets us spend all our money in drink and grub, I don't care what they do with us afterwards."

"And cannot this Blood be brought to justice?" asked Ned, in a whisper.

"I think not, Ned Warbeck," said Captain Jack; "he's a bigger villain than any of the 'Dozen' ever were; but, you see, his case is different; he's a great rogue, and tried to steal the crown jewels out of the Tower, and everybody thought he would have suf-fered on the block; but, instead of that, the king not only pardons him, but gives him a handsome pension into the bargain."

"He is a desperate scoundrel," growled Ned.

"Yes; and for that very reason I'd advise you to have as little to do with him as possible, for when one is a king's favourite every one must smile upon him if they wish to live in peace and quietness."

"Good advice," said Bates, "very, and if the young gentleman follows it, he will do well, and enjoy the title and riches, which, as the descendant of the once famous Edward Lawrence, he will be sure to receive from his natural guardian—old Sir Richard Warbeck."

"What mean you?" said Ned, in surprise.

"I mean what I say."

"How know you this?"

"Phillip Redgill once asked us to go down to Dar-lington Hall to rob it."

"No."

"'Tis true every word, my brave lad."

"You surprise me."

"Well, while we were there, I and Jack pulled about the old knight's papers and parchments, while the Skeleton Crew were fighting and hanging the servants, and so drank good wine in the library, and read the family papers."

"And was it Phillip Redgill who planned that attack?"

"Yes, and no other."

"No wonder, then, that I always instinctively hated him," said Ned.

"You two were as different as fire and water. Phillip Redgill planned your murder once or twice."

"I know he did."

"But you had a charmed life, Ned," said Jack, "and no one can harm you; all the gipsies and weird women on the Cornish coast have said so."

"Oh, yes, no doubt about that," said old Bates. "Ned Warbeck must have as many lives as a cat, or he would have been killed long and long enough ago."

"Can you account for the fact that my father was found with his legs cut off," said Bob Bertram.

"Yes. When Phillip Redgill murdered him, he 'limbed' the poor old man to get the bank notes which he heard your father had sewn up in his leather leggings."

"The infamous scoundrel! the barbarian!" swore Bob, in a great rage.

"But he's paid out for that bit of butchery, long ago," said Jack, "for he has confessed it."

"How? In what way?"

"The phantom legs of old Farmer Bertram follows him both night and day."

"Follows him?" said Ned, aghast with horror.

"Yes, follows him; at certain times and on particu-lar occasions they are visible to him, and to others also. I saw them once."

"You?"

"Yes; but I never want to look at them any more," said Captain Jack, shrugging up his shoul-ders, "for it is a most awful sight."

"When did this happen?"

"The very night he, and I, and old Bates were secre'ed in the library at Darlington Hall."

"Aye, true," said old Bates, with chattering teeth, "and when they walked on to the table right afore us, with their gory tops and stumps, an awful voice was heard; but I was too horror-struck to remember what was said."

"But I did though," said Jack.

"And what were the words," said Ned and Bob Bertram, both at once.

"Why, the legs walked across the table, and stood right before Phil Redgill, and some awful voice said,

"'Phillip Redgill, I will follow you for ever!'

"Awful!" said Ned. "It was a judgment of heaven!"

"Whether it was or not, we didn't stop to see any more, but made our exit as quickly as possible."

"And that was the only thing that prevented us destroying all the old gentleman's family papers," said Bates. "If it hadn't been for that, we had all things ready to set fire to the library and the whole mansion."

Much more was revealed to Ned Warbeck and Bob Bertram by Jack and Bates than we have room for in this concluding number of the Skeleton Crew; but what else happened after the gibbeting of the Baker's Dozen, and their two notorious leaders, will appear in the next chapter.

## CHAPTER LIV..

THE RED MAN OF THE GIBBET GIVES WARNING TO THE SKELETON CREW—DEATH-WING LEADS ON THE LAST ATTACK OF HIS CREW—NED WARBECK, BOB BERTRAM, LIEUTENANT GARNET, AND TIM HAVE AMPLE REVENGE—STIRRING SCENES.

BUT although the "Dozen," with Captain Jack, and old Bates, were disposed of by the grim hands of the law, there were other enemies who roamed still at large.

Phillip Redgill lay dying upon his bed in a lunatic asylum, and made night hideous with his awful shouts and oaths.

It almost seemed as if he were haunted by a thou-sand demons, for both night and day he screeched and yelled in the most frightful manner, so that his dismal cries could be heard afar off.

"Take them away! take them away!" he would scream aloud with a foaming mouth, wild, widely distended eyes, his hair standing on end, and gnash-ing his teeth.

"Take them away, take them away! the legs are bleeding—they are walking—they are following me, wherever I go. Away with them—destroy them! Take them away!" he would shout, both day and night, while he kicked and tore the bed-clothes like an incarnate fiend.

The keepers shook their heads, and looked very serious and silent.

Some of the men went so far as to say that they had seen the gory legs.

Others, not so bold, swore that they had heard them walking up and down the maniac's cell, at the hour of midnight.

Certain it is, that after suffering the most terrible tortures of mind and body, Phillip Redgill seemed to become suddenly calmer, and his reason returned.

But on a certain night, just as the tower clocks chimed the hour of twelve, he shouted out—

"Here is the Red Man of the Gibbet, he stands beside me ! on my left hand is the ghost of my father ; and walking over the bed-clothes are the phantom legs !  Mercy—mercy ! pardon—pardon ! A thousand devils haunt my heart and soul. Away, away ! avaunt ! I die—I die !"

He fell prostrate on the stone floor, foaming at the mouth.

Life was not yet quite extinct.

Again he screamed out—

"The legs—the phantom legs are here once more —away, away !"

A voice at that same moment was heard to say in awful sepulchral tones,

"Phillip Redgill, I will follow you for *ever !*"

Phillip Redgill rose to his feet like one again raised to life—uttered a terrible scream, and—*fell dead, foaming blood !*

———

## CHAPTER LV.

### DESTRUCTION OF THE SKELETON CREW BY YOUNG LORD WARBECK.

" Well," said Ned Warbeck, when he had left the condemned cell, in which he had had his interview with Captain Jack and old Bates. " Well," said he, in astonishment, " wonders never cease."

" Just to fancy," said Garnet, " that these scoundrels, with the advice and consent of Phillip Redgill, should for years past have been seeking your disgrace and destruction."

" True," said Ned Warbeck ; " but evil designs and curses, like chickens, come home to roost. What they intended and wished might fall upon myself and Charley have overtaken themselves."

" But Death-wing is not yet captured, Ned," said Garnet ; " it would be an excellent finish to all our adventures to arouse the London Apprentices, at least, a select band of them, and utterly destroy Death-wing and all that remains of his band."

" I intend to do so," said Ned, " and to-night shall see the accomplishment of that design."

During the day, Ned Warbeck, Garnet, Bob Bertram and Tim, were continually on horseback, riding hither and thither, consulting with some of the bravest and choicest spirits among the Apprentices, and towards night all preparations were completed.

Select detachments of the young Apprentices, under the guidance of well-known leaders, assembled at the halls of their several guilds, all armed, and eager for the fray.

The butcher boys with long knives, cleavers, choppers, and ponderous axes, were ready, and

marshalled in fours ready to march at the given time.

The blacksmiths' apprentices, with sledge hammers, crow-bars, and other ponderous weapons, were assembled at another place.

The sword makers, cutlers, and others, with all manner of implements of war, sharp and bright, had gathered together.

Five detachments, from no less than six trades, were under arms ; but none of them, save their chosen leaders, knew on what errand they were bound.

" Who is to lead us ?" some of them whispered.

" Wildfire Ned," was the answer, given in a suppressed tone of voice.

When this fact became known that Ned Warbeck was to be the commander-in-chief on this secret expedition, all rejoiced, for Ned's name acted like a charm on the youth of London, who had long heard his name coupled with deeds of daring.

So secretly had the expedition been organized that but few of the good old tradesmen of the town had any notion of what was on foot.

Hence during the night, that is to say, from eight o'clock until eleven, was unusually quiet in the principal streets, and the night watch went their rounds with staff and lantern, calling the hour in croaking voices, but innocent of the great commotion which was shortly to take place.

Carriers and messengers were galloping hither and thither from Ned Warbeck to the leaders of the valiant Apprentices, giving his final instructions and orders.

Chief of these messengers was Tiny Tim.

He did not like fighting much, but as message carrying was not very dangerous work, and as he was passionately fond of riding good horses, he galloped here and there in great glee, and assuming all the airs of a commander-in-chief, that is to say, where he was not known.

Ned Warbeck, however, had been the busiest of all.

During the day he had sent out trusty scouts to ascertain the precise locality in which Death-wing and his infamous gang were secreted.

All manner of reports were brought back to him, but so contradictory that he knew not which nor what to believe.

At last, when night had fairly set in, he went forth himself, accompanied by Bob Bertram and Garnet, and by superior intelligence and tact he soon discovered where Death-wing and his gang were hiding, and laid his plans accordingly.

Death-wing indeed was not without information of what was intended by Ned Warbeck, for he also had scouts out, who speedily informed him of the intended attack ; but none of them knew when it was to take place, or the number and class of persons who were to take part in it.

Since his defeat and disgrace at the Block-house the leader of the Skeleton Crew had been recruiting his forces.

He sent messengers to different parts calling in scattered parties of the crew who were out on their usual depredations.

So that on the night in question Death-wing had a large number of followers around him, each and all of whom swore to perish rather than allow Ned Warbeck, that hated name, to triumph over them.

One of the skeleton spies had fast returned to Death-wing with the latest information he was able to procure when all the Skeleton Crew sat down to a splendid repast, and drank wine more extravagantly than ever.

"If this is to be our last night let it be a merry one," said Death-wing.

"Bravo!" shouted fifty voices.

"I understand that Captain Jack, old Bates, and all his lot were gibbeted to day," said one,

"No doubt of it ; I heard the bells tolling."

"And I," said a third, "saw crowds of people following the carts."

"It was a tremendous gathering, I hear," said Death-wing ; "such a sight as London never saw before."

"I passed under several of the gibbets to-night," said one of the scouts, "and the night-birds and vultures were very busy with the bodies already. Colonel Blood kept his word with them."

"Serve them right," said Death-wing ; "they were always cunning, tricky knaves, every one of them, and our enemies. Has any one heard of Phillip Redgill?" said Death-wing.

"Yes," one replied ; "he is still in the mad-house."

"I know that ; but is he better ?"

"I did not hear."

"Perhaps he will recover, and, when I am gone," said Death-wing, "he will lead the Crew as I have done."

"Never," said a sepulchral voice near him.

It was the ghost of Phillip Redgill!

All the Crew started to their feet as they saw this ghastly apparition, all gory and horrible.

"Never!" said a voice.

"Dead!" said Death-wing, dropping a goblet of wine from his hand.

"Dead! Yes; for ever dead!" said the apparition, as it stalked through the apartment. "Dead! for ever dead!" it said, and vanished.

Death-wing and his followers had scarcely seated themselves once more when they were again startled out of their propriety by the entrance of a tall stranger, robed in a black cloak from head to foot.

"Who and what art thou?" said Death-wing, with drawn sword.

"The Red Man of the Gibbet!" said the stranger, dropping the disguise from off his shoulders.

Every one rose.

"What wouldst thou with us, worthy chief?" said Death-wing. "You never come without bad tidings. What would you have us do?"

"Prepare for death!" was the solemn answer ; "your hour has come! This is the last time I can ever quit my iron cage and prison house. No more can I walk abroad at certain times, to aid, to guide, and protect you ; the spell is broken. Phillip Redgill has ceased to live, and all is over. Farewell, farewell! Ned Warbeck triumphs."

Thus he spoke, and disappeared.

"Ned Warbeck triumph! never!" said Death-wing. with an oath.

"Never!" shouted all assembled, brandishing swords. daggers, guns, pikes, and all sorts of deadly weapons.

"Let our bones be ground down to powder ere the hated house of Warbeck shall triumph! Victory or death!" said Death-wing. "Comrades, swear!"

Each and all raised a goblet, filled to the brim, and swore, "For victory or death!"

At that moment, however, and as if by magic, all assembled dropped their goblets, and started from their seats.

A loud shout outside rent the air.

"It is Warbeck and his followers ; to arms, men, to arms," said Death-wing ; "spare no living soul ; each of you seek out Ned Warbeck, for if he falls we shall triumph."

*　　*　　*　　*　　*

It must be explained that after making all prepations, Ned Warbeck had issued orders that as the church clocks chimed half-past eleven o'clock all the detachments of London Apprentices should march towards Smithfield, and there join Lieutenant Garnet and Bob Bertram, each of whom had a company of stalwart fellows under his command.

This they did, and in great order, silently marching in military time and step, without disturbing the sleeping inhabitants.

They all arrived before midnight, and were marshalled by Ned Warbeck himself.

When twelve o'clock tolled from old St. Paul's the order to march was given, and by various routes, guided and commanded by Ned, Garnet, and Bob, they took up various positions within a stone's throw of Death-wing's stronghold and rendezvous near the river.

Having done this, and then cut off all hope of retreat for the Skeleton Crew, Ned Warbeck advanced with twenty youths, and examined all the strong points of Death-wing's retreat.

"Who comes there?" asked one of the Skeleton Crew, who was on guard.

"Ned Warbeck and his merry men," said Bob Bertram.

"Three cheers for Ned Warbeck, and death to the Skeleton Crew!" shouted the brave apprentice youths.

The three cheers were given with great heartiness, and these were sounds which startled Death-wing in his banquet-hall.

A moment before all was quietness, and silent as the grave.

But now commenced a scene that baffles all description.

One company, under Garnet, advanced from the river side.

A second, under Bob Bertram, marched towards the north side of the rendezvous.

A third attacked the left side with great fury, led on by the chief of the London Apprentices.

And the fourth and last, commanded by Ned Warbeck in person, assailed the front.

In all directions shouts and cheers and yells were heard.

Sledge hammers, crowbars, guns, pistols, swords, and pikes were making a discordant din.

Dogs barked, people rushed from their beds in terror, and ran affrighted through the streets.

Night watchmen bellowed and bawled, and sprung their rattles.

All the river side was in dire affright and commotion.

"'Tis young Ned Warbeck and the Skeleton Crew," shouted old men and women, in alarm.

"Let us fly—let us fly! we shall all be murdered!"

"Call the night-watch!"

"Go and call out the king's guard!"

"Murder! thieves! Help, help!"

"Rouse up, good citizens, rouse up, the whole river side is running with human blood!"

These and such like were the cries, now heard on every side ; while, on the other hand, nothing but cheers were heard from the bold Apprentices and their leaders, as they gallantly assailed Death-wing and his crew from front, flanks, and rear.

It was a most terrible battle, and lasted long.

For Death-wing had an immense quantity of fire-arms, already loaded and at hand, fit for instant use.

This being the case, he and his followers fired quick and deadly volleys into the ranks of the gallant youths, and knocked over very many.

The sight of their bleeding companions only served to nerve the gallant Apprentices, and instil new courage.

Some of them got ladders, and clambered in through the barricaded windows, axes and hatchets in hand, cutting down all and every obstruction before them.

"The blacksmiths battered in all the doors and bolts and bars.

Once they had got possession of the doors and passages the scene was most fearful.

Some of the crew attempted to jump out of the windows, but in doing so they were caught on the spear and pike-heads of those below.

The Butchers' Apprentices cut all who opposed them limb from limb without mercy.

But still Death-wing and his men fought like demons.

Three times had Ned Warbeck fought with and slain those he supposed to be the Skeleton chief.

But Death-wing was still alive and busy.

More than twenty times he took deliberate aim with guns and pistols at young Ned, and each time had he missed him.

"He is charmed! his life is charmed!" swore the grim chief, as he looked around him, and each instant saw that his men were falling thick and fast.

"Fire the magazine!" said he. "Let us blow up the rendezvous and all in it; better that than defeat and torture at Ned Warbeck's hands."

But this could not be done.

Garnet had fought his way to the magazine, and drowned it with water.

"No, no," thought the gallant sailor, "I know their tricks before to-day; but they are not going to blow up all my brave lads in that way. They must fight; every man-jack of them shall perish with the sword, and their skulls and limbs shall decorate Temple Bar and London Bridge."

Foiled in all his efforts, surrounded on every side, and with the building burning in half a dozen places, the Skeleton chief held a hasty council of war.

Unexpected, they sallied forth, fifty grim Skeletons, led on by Death-wing.

With loud shouts and oaths, they assailed Ned Warbeck's little band.

Ned himself singled out Death-wing, and a terrible battle took place between them.

Thrice did Ned Warbeck stab the grim leader, and his life blood was ebbing fast.

But thrice did he refuse to surrender.

He endeavoured to retreat and shun the combat, and had almost succeeded in doing so, when, with the quickness of thought, Ned Warbeck rushed at him, and, after one moment of exciting cutting and thrusting, Ned Warbeck seized Death-wing's battle flag, and ran the chieftain through and through the heart.

This desperate hand to hand combat was witnessed both by friends and foes, and loud shouts rewarded Ned Warbeck as he waved the banner of the Skeleton Crew high in triumph.

After this episode the battle did not last more than ten minutes.

Every one of the Skeleton Crew were slaughtered, and their bleeding mangled bodies strewed the ground, while the rendezvous itself was committed to the flames amidst the applause and frantic cheering of thousands, who had now run to witness the dreadful conflict, and Ned Warbeck, Garnet, Bob Bertram, and the chief of the London Apprentices, were carried through the streets in triumph, with links and torches, and music, and uproarious applause.

The cheers of assembled thousands greeted him as they carried him to old Sir Richard Warbeck's mansion; and as his brother Charley and his wife, old Dame Worthington, and others, joyfully welcomed his return, old Sir Richard Warbeck took him by the hand before the whole multitude, and said aloud, "Welcome, Ned, to your ancestor's home. I am no longer the owner of the estates; here is the royal warrant, read it. Wildfire Ned is now Lord Edward Warbeck, of Darlington Hall, and I simply the faithful steward of his fortunes.

＊　　＊　　＊　　＊　　＊

Our story is now soon brought to a close.

Wildfire Ned, as Sir Richard had said to the multitude, had been created Lord Warbeck, or rather, though the younger brother, the King had granted him the title when fully informed by Sir Richard of how much Sir Edward Lawrence had done and suffered in the cause of Charles the First; and if history is not at fault, young Wildfire Ned not only greatly distinguished himself in after years, but also married one of the lovliest maidens of great title which England could boast, and was long the pride and the boast of every youth who had read of his daring exploits.

Lieutenant Garnet followed the sea for many years, but afterwards distinguished himself so greatly in many ways, that he became one of the Lords of the Admiralty.

Bob Bertram returned to his native village and was honoured and respected by all who knew him.

He succeeded to several very large farms which his father had rented of Sir Richard Warbeck, for Ned, now Lord Warbeck, insisted upon his accepting them.

Bob, and the old miller Harmer, were great companions, and many a night in the village inn would they recount their strange adventures, and of the various villanies of the famous Colonel Blood.

Colonel Blood, for many years hung around the royal court; but how it was the King could countenance such a rascal, history itself has been unable to explain. Suffice it to say that after a career of roguery, he was seized and cast into prison, charged with plotting against the Duke of Buckingham, and soon afterwards died of a broken heart, or, as some said, from want of sleep caused by terrible remorse for all his crimes.

Old Sir Richard lived to a good old age, as did also good dame Worthington, and Charley Warbeck, who, in the company of Clara, seemed to be the happiest of men; and oftentimes at Christmas, when all were assembled round the festive board, to which Tim and Bob Bertram were always invited, Sir Richard used to shout out merrily, "Fill your goblets high, my boys, let me propose the great toast of the evening."

"Hurrah," shouted Tim in great glee.

"Bravo, Sir Richard," Bob would say.

"And the toast, ladies and gentlemen, which I hope we may all live long to give is this,—

"Success, long life, and all honour to Wildfire Ned who exterminated the Skeleton Crew."